THE GRAND PRAIRIE YEARS

THE GRAND PRAIRIE YEARS

A BIOGRAPHY OF
W.C. PERRY

RON ARNOLD

MERRIL PRESS

Bellevue

SECOND EDITION
Published by Merril Press
First edition published by Dodd, Mead, Inc., New York

LIBRARY OF CONGRESS CATALOGING-IN-PUBLICATION DATA

Arnold, Ron
    The grand prairie years.

    Bibliography: p. 717-722.
    1. Perry, Willie Clayborne, 1910- —Fiction.   2. Texas—History—
1846-1950—Fiction.   I. Title.
PS3551.R552G7   1987   813'.54   87-21996
ISBN 0-936783-01-X

Printed in the United States of America

CONTENTS

DESTINY

ACKNOWLEDGEMENTS

I can never properly thank all the literally hundreds of people who helped put this book together. Let me express first my gratitude to all who gave research assistance no matter how small. You know who you are and you have my thanks.

I am grateful to the Perry family for their encouragement and assistance over the extended period required to complete this book.

Chapter One could not have been written without the immense independent genealogical research on the Perry line done by Max Perry. It was Max who led me to old seventeenth-century Micajah in London. My thanks to Miss K. E. Campbell, honorary archivist of St. Katharine Cree Church, Micajah's parish church, for showing me around the precincts of the early merchant Perrys and for serving as correspondent in completing vital research at Guildhall Library.

My special thanks to Lois Smith Murray, an author in her own right, who generously took on the tedious labor of proofreading the huge manuscript. Professor William H. Marshner's assistance was also invaluable. I am deeply grateful to Professor Robert S. Maxwell, Department of History (emeritus) at Stephen F. Austin State University at Nacogdoches, Texas, for serving as historical consultant. My appreciation to the staffs of the National Archives, the Library of Congress, and London's Chancery Lane office of the British National Register of Archives for yeoman duty in digging out minutiae of history. Whatever historical merit this book may have belongs to all these people, and any errors of either fact or judgment must be laid solely to me.

7

My wife Janet did half the work on this book, researching library materials, transcribing interviews, taking notes during travel, handling correspondence, and keeping my schedule. I also owe my daughters Andrea and Rosalyn a debt of gratitude for understanding why Dad sat at the word processor so much.

And finally, I owe most to Dr. W. C. Perry and his loving wife, Oretta, for their tolerance of my intrusion into their lives and for the time they spent with me answering endless questions. To all Perry family members who gave so generously of their time for interviews, thank you.

FOREWORD

Ron Arnold has a long and distinguished career as a writer in the
environmental field which has included a number of books, scholarly
works and articles beginning from the time when those issues became
prominent in the late 1960's right up to the present.

And although Mr. Arnold's previous endeavors have resulted in a great
deal of Americana work, a look at what has made this country great, I
must say that this latest effort has produced something entirely fresh and
enticing.

With *The Grand Prairie Years*, Arnold has written a book that will
excite even his most devoted readers as it excited me, because he brings
America a new vision of itself, a new awareness of its real past and its
potential future. And he does it in that most ordinary of writer's roles, as
a biographer.

Ron Arnold is no ordinary biographer. He is, without question, an
Americana biographer par excellence.

His writing blends a thorough grasp of basic traditional American
values with breathtaking cultural awareness, scholarship and intellectual
staying power. His readers have come to expect that of him: many of his
essays have been widely reprinted, and he accepted the prestigious
American Business Press Editorial Achievement Award in 1980 for his
magazine series *The Environmental Battle*. But here in *The Grand Prairie
Years*, he reveals a new facet that I am sure will attract wider audiences: a
lyrical, joyous, even passionate writing style that moves us out of
ourselves, that quietly exalts the best within us while powerfully
affirming the simple virtues of the people whose lives he depicts.

9

His portrait of my fellow Texan, Dr. W. C. Perry, does more than bring an era to life: it takes us inside the heart and mind of a remarkable man and lets us walk some miles in his shoes to see his era with our own hearts and minds. Seldom has an American writer shown that wide vistas can be bounded in a nutshell or what plain surfaces can reflect magnificence. The world of *The Grand Prairie Years* beckons us, welcomes us, enfolds us. It bids us stay and learn and return to its pages again and again. This book is a thing of its own: it looks not backward to the twilight of an old literary tradition, but perhaps forward to the dawn of a new one.

Ron Arnold represents a unique blend of the modern writer seasoned with a journalistic integrity of old — the sort of journalism which probes not for the sake of destruction, but rather for the sake of discovery. While he does not spare us the heart-sorrow of sickness and death, basic medical realities, his writing does not radiate the tragic sense of life that sees all as vanity since both the good and the bad come to the same end. He leaves us more convinced than ever that it *does* matter what we do in this life.

He is a son of the Texas soil, born in 1937. He grew up in San Antonio, not two hundred miles away from the man beloved today by many thousands as Baylor's Dean Perry, the subject of this biography. He had the courage to give this book absolute integrity, to draw the unpolished people of rural Texas lovingly but bluntly without shades of quaint. He made no compromise with the facts to satisfy sterile literary conventions; he refused to romanticize the daily grind of farm life; thus his writing represents a blend of the realistic without any of the cynicism of the so-called elitists who neither know nor understand rural America. His very realism is uplifting as it shows a winning struggle against the confining attributes of an uneducated but well-meaning people. In the end he makes us understand perfectly what it cost the struggling farm boy Willie Clayborne Perry to fulfill the dream of striving generations and earn the highest honor education can bestow, the Doctoral Degree.

Because Ron Arnold is in demand as a lecturer and journalist, this book, of necessity, was worked on enroute to and from the major cities of not only the U.S. but the world. That reality was not without benefit, however, as while in London he was able to research the origins of the Perry family in seventeenth century mercantile Leadenhall Street.

In fact, Arnold visited every location about which he wrote from the Tidewater area of Virginia to rural Alabama, to the central Texas towns of Hico, Iredell, Walnut Springs, and Meridian, and to the starving-time flats of Trinchera and Trinidad in Colorado.

Personally, the author is a man who cherishes tradition. He is not wedded to the past. He believes that progress is only possible through men who have changed themselves not by means of an evolutionary societal process. That is what so interested him in the people he encountered in this book.

The people of *The Grand Prairie Years* are faithful to tradition. Their struggles are a dram of antidote to the oceans of cynicism and despair that infuse so much of modern society. Their experience shines like a beacon, dispelling cynicism and despair by a steady inner light. Like the people of *The Grand Prairie Years,* this is a book radiant with hope.

John B. Connally
Governor of Texas
1963–1969

INTRODUCTION

I have always wanted to write this book. Not that I had any idea who its subject would be or the circumstances under which it would be written. But ever since my grandfather first taught me how to push the keys on his venerable Underwood back home when I was ten years old, I have nursed the urge to write about ordinary people achieving extraordinarily.

As I grew, I came to feel that the quintessential American hero is the unremarkable individual struggling against great odds toward ultimate victory and in the process becoming the remarkable individual. Such a person is Dr. W. C. Perry, the principal figure in *The Grand Prairie Years*. His struggle spans seven crucial decades of American history and the interval between his circumscribed origins and his honored victory is filled with everyday epic. He is as perfect an exemplar of the American dream as any automobile tycoon or movie star, for he knew what he wanted and he got what he wanted despite all obstacles and accidents. And of obstacles and accidents there were plenty, which made the telling of his victory all the more gratifying to me.

I was motivated to write this book for another reason. I think every writer sooner or later feels the need to pay homage to his origins. Most first novels pay that debt, and novelists soon get the need out of their system. But a nonfiction writer must go where the assignments, not inclination, dictate. For nearly twenty years my assignments have taken me into the matrix of American enterprise and American politics. There I happily researched the tribulations of industry, the dynamics behind America's contemporary difficulties, and the failures of the alternatives.

When the opportunity finally came to write deeply of the Texas land of my birth, to my surprise I was simultaneously filled with elation and solemnity, an anticipatory elation of sheer fun and a solemnity that rises to become joy rather than fun. The very idea of such a writing task brought to life so many impressions of sun-drenched times from my childhood, of traditional stories my grandmother told me over the dinnertable, of the feeling that this vast territory called Texas was somehow special in the earth! Texas, I said, I've been away from you for twenty-five years. It's time to go back and celebrate you the best way I can.

In my business travels I came to learn, quite by chance, of the subject of this book. As I learned more of this remarkable Texan, I became enthralled. During one of many trips to Texas covering agribusiness assignments, I decided to try to get in touch with him. Dr. Perry proved to be quite cordial and we made the arrangements. In due course I met and subsequently spent several days with him, wandering in his company through the Grand Prairie towns and farmlands of his early days. The flavor of authentic Texana exuded from every word, like pungent barbecued brisket or a plate of okra and catfish. Once I had gotten to know this fine engaging fellow there was no turning back.

The more I probed, the clearer I saw that a study of the life and times of this individual would be a rare adventure. Here before me lay the opportunity to do what few American writers have done before: to trace a detailed whole-life narrative of the unremarkable individual struggling against great odds toward ultimate victory and in the process becoming the remarkable individual. I took the opportunity. For me the book was no longer just a book. It became a cause.

I will leave it to my readers and critics and posterity to say whether it was worth the nearly three years of research and writing to give the world *The Grand Prairie Years*. I have often said that the historian's task is to avoid writing about things that are not worth knowing. I believe it will be obvious where I come down. It was the best investment of my time I could ever imagine, and the reader will soon understand my enthusiasm.

Ron Arnold
Bellevue, Washington
July, 1987

-1-

THE FARM

I T is mid-August 1910. We are somewhere high above North-Central
Texas. The bustling cities of mercantile Dallas and cowtown Fort
Worth lie on the hazy horizon some ninety miles to the northeast, their
electric lights twinkling faintly in the dusk. The state capitol at
Austin, soon to be dominated by Oscar Branch Colquitt, who will win
the governorship this fall with a strong anti-Prohibition vote, is hidden in
evening gloom behind us on the edge of the Hill Country more than a
hundred miles to the south. Directly below spreads a rich blackland
prairie of low rolling hills, its cultivated and productive fields of cotton
and grain clearly visible even in the long shadows of sunset. Small rural
communities dot the flat landscape. Not yet supplied with electric
power, they glow softly in kerosene lamplight. The scattered pools of
light seem to be spider-webbed together by dark lines, traces that are
actually dirt roads, some graded, others little more than wagon tracks.

The prairie below us is rimmed east and west by ramparts of postoak,
blackjack and hickory protruding southward down into Texas from the
Red River like two great thumbs, a forest collectively known for some
obscure reason as the Cross Timbers. The tree peninsula lying to our east,
called for some even more obscure reason the Lower Cross Timbers,
extends southward in a narrow belt past Dallas toward Waco. It is
separated from the much larger hardwood forest to the west, the Upper
Cross Timbers, by the fifty-mile-wide Grand Prairie, our destination.
This prairie is not a pancake-flat expanse typical of the Great Plains but
rather a rolling blend of tree-covered knolls and grassy swales, hills laden

15

with elms and oaks in the midst of prairie benches and terraces sloping to pecan and willow-lined creeks that empty into the cottonwood-bordered Bosque River that empties into the Brazos River that empties into the Gulf of Mexico. North and south the Grand Prairie is fringed by limestone hills with poor, shallow, depleted soils for the most part, harsh hardscrabble country of cedar brakes and postoaks that look down with envious eyes on the darker, richer land below. But these rough surrounding hills open to the east, and the Grand Prairie seems to have been poured into its rocky crucible from the fertile Blackland Prairie Province that stretches up in a narrow strip from San Antonio northward to Dallas.

As we descend toward the spacious Grand Prairie, it takes on the appearance of an ocean top, its gently undulating waves of soil punctuated by occasional breakers of rock. It is no false likeness: geologists tell us this prairie was originally deposited as marine sediments from a vast inland sea during the Cretaceous Period. For eons, earth scientists say, heavy sedimentation went on all over the earth, burying the first flowering plants, burying armored dinosaurs in their heyday and preserving the remains of a new experiment in biology, the primitive mammals. During that era several large dinosaurs left their footprints in mud that is now streambed rock in this Texas prairie, and in a few years men will discover the tracks with amazement. If you are very still during our descent, you can feel the immensity of time crushed into the rocks below.

The prairie is closer now. The grassy surface we see glinting in the nightfall below caps a layer of clay nearly 180 feet deep, called by geologists the Walnut formation. Its top twelve inches or so has moldered over millennia into a teeming topsoil that has borne a tallgrass ecosystem for thousands of years — big bluestem bunchgrass, Indian grass, some of the gramas, even a little prairie three-awn — now a fertile seedbed friendly to the prudent farmer. Where streambanks have cut through this clay — look ahead to the Bosque River draining the Grand Prairie watershed and flowing into the Gulf-bound Brazos — an underlying layer of quartz sand is exposed, the Paluxy formation, packed two hundred feet thick. Below that, the Glen Rose limestone forms a basement. The fraying hills protruding here and there above this clay plain are younger Comanche Peak limestones, and higher hills, like cliff-sided Chalk Mountain there in the far distance, bear caps of still younger Edwards limestone.

We are close enough to see individual buildings now. The farmhouses passing below are part of Hamilton County, and that stream is the Leon River. This land was settled in 1854 by the Robert Carter family, created a county in 1858, and named for General James Hamilton, a former governor of South Carolina who moved to Texas about 1836. He served as a diplomat from the Republic of Texas to France, Holland and England.

The ill-fated general claimed Texas owed him $200,000 in gold for services rendered, but en route to Galveston to collect the debt he was drowned at sea.

Just ahead is the northern boundary of Hamilton County and the booming cotton-shipping community of Hico, pronounced "HIGH-ko" by the Texans in these parts. Hico sits on the banks of the Bosque River now, but the eight pioneer families who founded the town in 1856 had located their log cabins two miles south, near one another on land surrounding Honey Creek about a mile above its confluence with the Bosque. Their town grew and in 1860 John R. Alford opened its first business, a small dry goods store. He was appointed postmaster later that year after residents petitioned the United States for a post office. When given the privilege of naming the office, he chose Hico, the name of his home town in Kentucky.

But when Texas seceded from the Union and joined the Confederacy in 1861, the subsequent withdrawal of federal troops invited the most violent Indian attacks ever suffered in Texas. The Comanche became a scourge again. The Penateka subdivision of the Comanche was a mounted, well-equipped and powerful people organized into bands rather than a single tribe. They had once been the main Comanche power in Texas. All the Comanche had possessed horses for two hundred years, since the Spaniards of Cortez unwittingly released herds of unlovely but desert-hardy mustangs — acquired by the Spaniards from the Moors of North Africa — that eventually roamed wild north from Mexico. When the Comanche found the feral horses in the seventeenth century and learned to ride, they blazed like a terror on the plains, sweeping away gentler peoples, the Tonkawa, the Caddoes, the Wichitas, the Wacos — some of whom had lived as farmers of corn and beans and squash.

These peaceful people got out of the Comanche's new warpath, and in their retreat made first contact with Anglo-American newcomers. The displaced Indians began living near white trading posts, acting as scouts for the armies, and generally steering clear of the Comanche. The Penateka Comanche — the Honey Eaters, as they were known — had formerly used the Grand Prairie as a wintering ground, gathering its plentiful wood for fuel against the searing cold and bitter freezes. The whites had only with great difficulty over time pushed the Comanche aside with guns and sturdy buildings and fierce Anglo determination to take up this land. Now, with federal troops gone, the Comanche wrought bloody vengeance on the intruders who had crowded them from their old wandering grounds. For a while the Grand Prairie was once more the *Comancheria,* the place of the Comanche, as it had been in the great days. Comanche pride flourished again. It had always been reflected in their own name for themselves, which meant simply "The Human Beings." The fear they struck into the hearts of others is reflected in the Ute word for them, *Komantcia,* meaning "enemy," which was corrupted into *Comanche* by the Spanish and adopted by the Texas settlers. But once the Confederacy was destroyed and the Union restored, federal troops returned and the Comanche, as all Indians, were brought under control and nearly obliterated.

Hico began to thrive once more. But its progress was retarded by poor transportation: merchants had to haul goods from Waco, the nearest rail center. Farm families seldom relied on local merchants and made their own annual pilgrimage to Waco where they traded their products for household supplies. Roads from Hico to Waco were so bad that neighbors traveled together to "double team" their way out of one mudhole after another. But in 1880 Hico became the beneficiary of the Texas Central Railway, a line incorporated May 30, 1879, by interests which controlled the Houston and Texas Central. The Texas Central had constructed a track through seven miles of the north corner of Hamilton County by 1880, but no community lay beside their rails. Railroad officials proposed that Hico relocate two miles north, on the right of way, and the townspeople agreed. The present site of Hico was purchased by Texas Central from G. H. Medford, and lots were sold at auction to the highest bidder on November 16, 1880. Old Hico on Honey Creek was quickly moved lock, stock and barrel — except for the J.G. Barbee mill and gin which was made of local limestone. Look down and see the old mill still standing on Honey Creek, but look quickly, for it will be pulled down in 1940, and all trace of the original town will be lost.

We are quite near the end of our journey, passing low over the Hico of 1910. It is a thriving rural center of 1,437 souls, boasting among other features a grain mill and cotton gin, two banks, a livery stable, a cottonseed oil mill and a pool hall, hotel and restaurant facilities, a railroad depot and express office, two dentists, one private nurse, and five physicians. One of these doctors is not at home tonight, for an hour ago he hitched his bay mare to a light topless "Prep" buggy, took his little black bag, and began the eight-mile trek northward to the farm for which we ourselves are bound.

Two miles north out of Hico the graded gravel road passes into Erath County, which was formed in 1856 from Bosque and Coryell counties. Its first permanent settlers were John M. and William F. Stephens, and Stephenville there to the northwest was established in 1854. Between this gravel road and Stephenville begins the belt of trees that is the Western Cross Timbers which extends a hundred miles southward to the Texas Hill Country.

The county is named after George Bernard Erath, an Austrian born in 1813 in Vienna. He came to America in 1832 and fought as a Texan at San Jacinto where the Alamo was avenged. Independence for Texas was assured there with the defeat of Santa Anna's Mexican forces. Erath may

have witnessed the unrestrained pursuit and slaughter of Mexicans after
the battle of San Jacinto. He may have seen the Texas officer who ordered
his men to stop, only to be told at gunpoint by one of his soldiers,
"Colonel, if Jesus Christ were to come down from heaven and order me to
quit shooting Santanistas, I wouldn't do it, sir." George B. Erath served
in the Congress of the Republic of Texas, 1843 to 1845, and in the first
legislature of the State of Texas in 1846. He laid out the city of Waco in
1849, and since his death in 1891 the manuscript of his memoirs has
rested in the archives of the University of Texas. Now we are slowing to
skim the treetops of scattered liveoaks in the county named for this man.

We have crossed Duffau Creek, which the locals pronounce
"DEFF-oh," descending and slowing further to follow its tributary,
Camp Branch. A few feet above the waters of Camp Branch we enter the
farmland owned by the Blackburns and the Perrys, families that have
come to Texas in the past generation or two from Arkansas and Missouri
and Alabama. We are now low over the farm of James W. Perry. That
small house a few hundred feet east from the banks of Camp Branch was
built just last year on the occasion of his son Tom's marriage to the
Blackburn girl, Laura Belle, on April fourth, 1909. Such homes for newly
married children are a commonplace in this landscape, and are known as
"weaning houses." It is here at the home of Tom Perry that our journey
ends, and we come to earth exactly 1,150 feet above sea level. The sun has
been down a quarter of an hour. Hush! Time is ours, and we are
privileged, all unseen, to watch as it unfolds before us.

Summer twilight suffused the blackland prairie. Tom Perry looked
westward from the front door of his spare two-room farmhouse, silently
regarding liveoak silhouettes etched on the orange Texas sky. Peering out
the door to his left he could see down beyond the cow pen and into the
snuffling darkness of the hog pen and beyond to low outcrops of creamy
limestone that still rankled with the day's heat. Then looking straight out
the door, toward the departing day, he watched lightning bugs punctuate
the farther shadows with their cold fire, making a fairy world of hackberry
thickets along the shallows of Camp Branch. His wiry five-foot-seven
frame shifted in the doorway as warm air rich with the aroma of fresh
coffee drifted from the radiating cookstove behind him.

He stepped out to the front porch that ran the length of his simple
board-and-batten home, relishing a sudden evening breeze that finally
came to cut the mid-August stillness here at Dude Flat. Fleetingly, Tom
wondered about that place name: Dude Flat. Who were those
long-forgotten fancy-dress namesakes? Then he remembered why this
ordinary nightfall was an extraordinary event in his life. He felt
suspended somewhere between joy and panic.

Thomas Bunyon Perry, native of Alabama and Texas immigrant, had not in his twenty-six years become accustomed to idly contemplating sunsets, the origin of place names or anything else. No Grand Prairie farmer in the Texas of 1910 was so inclined. Yet Tom Perry stood there on his front porch bemused by the evening star this night because for once he simply did not know what to do. Tonight things were different. His seventeen-year-old wife Belle lay sweltering on their painted iron-frame bed, attended by Tom's mother Lou, by a neighbor lady in her middle sixties known only as Granny Marlow — midwives in those days were commonly called Granny — and by general practitioner Charles Durham, M.D. She labored in the early stages of delivering their first child.

Tom could hear bustling sounds in his front room, footsteps he knew to be Granny Marlow's. "Oh, there y'are out on the gallery, Mister Tom," she called from the door. "I thought I heard ye walkin' through the house."

Granny Marlow clumped quickly across the oaken porch planks, looking up at him with pinched mouth. She studied his farmer's face a moment, scanning its sturdy forehead and prominent nose, the determined chin and arched eyebrows, noting a slight gray film over his left eye, the insidious work of corneal ulcers that had plagued him from childhood, a curse that would in time leave him a one-eyed man.

"Doctor says it's not going to be long," she announced. "But, I swan, I've seen a good many of these first young'uns come when they've a mind to. Doctor says you hadn't ought to go off anywheres, in case you's thinkin' of running over yonder to fetch Miz Belle's Ma."

"She's not home, Mrs. Marlow," Tom said. "My kinfolks are all gone off to Glen Rose. The cotton and the corn's laid by" — final plowing and hoeing were done, in Texas farm lingo — "so they're camping up at the sulfur springs on the Paluxy. Mister and Mrs. Blackburn took little Leona in the covered wagon Sunday and won't be back till Wednesday late."

"Wednesday. Hmph. That's tomorrow," said Granny Marlow, squinting at the fact. "Then they's going to miss seein' their first grandchild come into the world, Mister Tom. Even if that baby of yours takes longer than Doctor thinks, it's coming tonight sure."

Tom gulped.

Granny Marlow pursed her thin lips as she looked at Tom knowingly, seeing dozens of other trying-not-to-be-nervous first-time fathers she had tended in days past. "You'd best come have some coffee, now, Mister Tom," she said, starting back into the house. "Doctor could be wrong. We could be up all night."

A masculine voice called from the doorway, "I'll have some of that coffee, too, if you don't mind, Mrs. Marlow."

Dr. Charles Durham, a tall man forty years of age, stepped out on the front porch, making the simple act of rolling down his shirt sleeves appear dignified. The pungent whiff of carbolic acid came with him.

Tom Perry, careful of his own dignity, asked as calmly as he could, "How is Belle, Dr. Durham?"

The physician smiled reassuringly, "Everything is going as it should, Tom. Your wife is a strong, healthy woman. You'll be a proud father in just a few hours. Probably less."

Tom felt better, but tried not to show his relief. He trusted this physician even more than the Perrys' regular family doctor in Duffau, who lived several miles closer than Dr. Durham in Hico. At a dollar a mile for house calls, Tom's trust had real meaning in the farm economy of this age.

The doctor's mare nickered from just beyond the front porch where she was tied to a fencepost, still hitched to the light Prep buggy. "Does your mare need attending to, Doctor?" Tom asked.

"No, she's just talking to your horses out in the barn, Tom," Durham replied. "She's accustomed to waiting for me. Chores all done?"

"I just come in from finishing up and stepped out again — to catch the breeze."

The doctor sensed Tom's uneasiness about the impending event, clapped him on the shoulder and said in a bluff voice, "Well, sir, I hate to disturb you, but, like Granny Marlow says, it's time to come in now."

Tom had to face it. He had to go into the birthing chamber. He was worried about his young wife, regardless of his efforts at maintaining a stoic exterior. He had never witnessed a human birth. The universal custom in Texas was for all menfolk, brothers, uncles, grandfathers, hired hands — all except the attending physician and the father of the child — to go off by themselves during a lying-in, as the time of childbirth was known. Thus Tom had no idea what to expect. He had been startled, shocked, at the power of Belle's first labor contractions. It was with barely concealed anxiety that he had telephoned first Dr. Durham in Hico and then his mother on the next farm about his wife's labor pains. Plainly, he was scared to death, but he was twenty-six years old, not just some fellow barely out of his teens, and he had certain obligations to stay in control. That Tuesday afternoon in August 1910, Tom Perry was glad he had decided to pay forty cents a month for the hand-cranked contraption a telephone lineman had mounted on his front room wall — at least he could talk to people without their seeing the look on his face.

Now he marched behind Dr. Durham past Granny Marlow waiting at the stove for the boiled coffee grounds to settle, and as he entered the lamplit bedroom, he reflected upon how easily his farm animals delivered their young — except for the cows, that is. And he recalled the line out of Genesis: *in sorrow thou shalt bring forth children.*

A lone kerosene lamp bathed the rustic bedroom in dim yellow light, starkly accentuating its exposed wall studs and dingy open ceiling rafters. The only furnishings were the bed, a dresser, a large trunk, and a small table for the lamp. The window sashes were wide open and the green shades rolled up, one opening on each exterior wall. No hint of the cooling day yet crept in. Belle Perry, her face flushed with heat and exertion, lay still on the bed. She wore a light cotton nightgown, with only a white bedsheet for a cover. A fancy "counterpin," as bedspreads were called, was not ordinarily found among the meager possessions of a young farmer. But the plain white pillowslips covering the feather pillows on which Belle was propped had been decorated with colorful embroidery and edged with crocheted scalloping.

Lou Perry sat by Belle in the carved rocking chair that had been brought in from the front room. Both mother and wife smiled up at Tom as he appeared behind Dr. Durham. Tom made his way to Belle's side, feeling something like an intruder in his own bedroom this night. He bent down over his wife, but did not kiss her. He was not a demonstrative man — no adult male in rural Texas was — and would have thought it highly improper of any man to kiss his wife in public, even though that public was his own mother and a trusted physician. Affection in this time and place was displayed only behind closed doors.

"How are you doing, Belle?" he asked solicitously.

"Doctor says I'm doing fine, Tom" she smiled wanly. "But truth be known it hurts some. And it's so close in here," she complained of the still and humid summer air.

Lou Perry patted her hand, "Now don't take on so, child. Believe me, you'll forget all about the hurt once that little baby comes into the world."

Pointing to a kitchen chair next to the rocker, Lou instructed her son, "Tommy, you sit right down by your wife and keep her company."

Dr. Durham took a seat in a cane-bottomed kitchen chair at the foot of the bed and asked, "Have you had any more pains since I stepped out, Mrs. Perry?"

"No, I haven't, Doctor," Belle frowned. "Is anything wrong?"

"You're coming along just fine, don't worry."

Granny Marlow entered with a brimming white ironstone china cup and saucer in each hand. The steaming black brew sloshed with her steps but did not spill. She announced with a wide grin, "Here's Doctor's coffee, and for you, Mister Tom."

Once the men had been served she disappeared into the front room again, bustled some more at the hot cookstove and poured scalding coffee from the speckled blue porcelain-glazed coffeepot into two more cups. Granny Marlow reappeared in the lying-in chamber, served the grandmother-to-be, and sat herself down on a kitchen chair opposite Tom. And like Tom, she ceremoniously "saucered and blowed" her coffee in time-honored frontier style. Like most rural mothers in labor, Belle had been given only a small glass of cool water to sip.

Now they settled around the childbed: Tom and Lou Perry at Belle's right hand, Dr. Durham at the foot of the bed, and Granny Marlow at Belle's left. A cooling breeze finally began to sift through the room. They drank their coffee and waited for nature to take its course.

The traditional birth ritual in rural Texas was changing in 1910, and this assemblage tonight drew the outlines of its new shape. No longer was the midwife chief manager of childbirth labor. Her original medical role was shrinking to an exclusively social role. No longer were the terms *midwifery* and *obstetrics* synonymous. Trained physicians pointedly distinguished between their medical specialty and the service rendered by their untrained predecessors. A great controversy had erupted over "The Midwife Problem" during the late 1890s, for two central reasons. First, midwives were monopolizing all the childbirths, physicians charged, depriving teaching hospitals of the obstetric classroom cases required to train medical specialists. Second, as early as 1898, a prominent New York obstetrician expressed alarm over the "superabundance of medical men" who needed additional obstetric cases in order to earn an adequate income.

The five physicians we noted in the little Texas town of Hico perfectly illustrate this professional overcrowding. In 1907, only three years ago, a physician writing in a Michigan medical journal warned, "it has been estimated that it requires one thousand of the population to insure a physician a decent living." The five Hico doctors could probably find no more than five hundred patients each, even counting all the nearby farm families. Many doctors came to believe that eliminating the midwife, or at least drastically reducing her numbers, would relieve these two problems. Thus, a campaign was mounted on the Eastern Seaboard to license midwives, restrict their access to medical training, or simply outlaw them.

This campaign had not yet affected Texas, or indeed, much of the United States. In 1910, the vast majority of children were born at home, and more than half of them had been attended by midwives, not physicians. Economics was part of the reason. While doctors charged from $15 to $25 to deliver a baby, plus a dollar a mile in some rural areas for house calls, the midwife commonly charged only $5 to $10, depending on the difficulty of the case. Another reason rural mothers considered midwives the better bargain was that doctors only delivered the baby and returned to their offices, while Grannies helped deliver the baby, cared for the mother and infant, prepared meals, cleaned the house, did the washing, and looked after any other children and the menfolk for from three to ten days after the child was born.

Mothers also favored midwives for reasons of tradition and religion. Women had traditionally held sway over childbirth management in a virtually unbroken line back to the beginnings of recorded history. Female friends and relatives in most cultures have always come to the expectant woman to provide comfort and practical assistance. The role of women as midwives was institutionalized in 1554 by the Church of England when midwife oaths were administered, not only to prevent the use of witchcraft and charms, but also to forbid any man, including the child's father, from entering the lying-in chamber, except in extreme emergency. This "mysterious office of women" was at times raised to bizarre heights: in 1522 a German physician named Wertt dressed as a woman to study a case of labor undetected, but when he was discovered, authorities ordered that he be burned to death. No man is recorded as attending a normal birth until 1663 in France. When eighteenth century advances in medical technology, particularly the development of the obstetric forceps, brought trained man-midwives regularly to the childbed, cartoons ridiculed them and clerics asked whether prurient interest had not prompted them to the work. And when trained male obstetricians began to appear in America in significant numbers after 1860, tradition rebuffed them as well.

While Biblical scholars were virtually unknown in the Grand Prairie of early twentieth-century Texas, most in the ordinary farm family could read well enough to understand the story of the midwives in Exodus 1:15-22 that drew them as heroines for cleverly defying the king of Egypt. Fearing the growing number of Hebrews in Egypt, the king called into council the midwives Shiphrah and Puah, and, little knowing that he was setting into motion the events that would make Moses a prince in his own house, ordered:

When ye do the office of a midwife to the Hebrew women, and see them upon the stools: if it be a son, then ye shall kill him: but if it be a daughter, then she shall live.

But as it turned out, "the midwives feared God, and did not as the king of Egypt commanded them, but saved the men children alive." When the king demanded an explanation, the answer of the midwives was as shrewd as it was brave:

Because the Hebrew women are not as the Egyptian women; for they are lively, and are delivered ere the midwives come unto them.

This biblical reinforcement only added to the respect given by rural Texans to midwives. Yet even public health officials who were not noted for their reliance on scripture, but who were greatly concerned over high mother and infant mortality rates in the United States, felt that training midwives, not eliminating them, would be a sounder approach to reducing the deaths.

Physicians writing in professional journals as well as in popular magazines such as *McClure's* and *Ladies' Home Journal* had convinced many Americans that childbirth, contrary to tradition, was not a "natural" event requiring only minimal intervention by untrained midwives, but rather a process fraught with dangers best left to the medically trained physician. Thus, Tom Perry's hiring of physician and midwife this August day to attend the birth of his first child reflected both a growing belief in medical science and continuing respect for the midwife.

A flannel receiving blanket and a pile of clean rags lay on the foot of Belle Perry's childbed. The sense of family was strong in this simple room, and Lou Perry looked at her Tommy and his Belle with loving eyes. The birth pangs were coming closer together now, and after one particularly strong contraction, Tom's mother broke both the silence and the rhythm of her rocking with an ancient and heartfelt sigh, "Lord, let this one be the one."

No one asked her meaning. Unintentional revelations of inner thoughts were not open to prying questions in the rural Texas ethic. But Lou Perry explained herself:

"None of our line of Perrys ever graduated, not even my Tommy," she said to the air. "I hope this little stranger a 'comin' has the chance to get an education like Dr. Durham here. Law, our family has worked so hard, so long."

The Perry family had indeed worked long and hard. Their line is full of questing, restless souls born into hard circumstances who wanted to better their lot, but few who yearned after education, and none who had achieved it. The origins of Tom Perry's family are lost in time. The origin of their family name itself is shadowed in antiquity: although the first similar name appeared on English records in the Domesday Book of 1086 with the family name Peret, the first likely forebear of a Perry appears in 1176 when Henry de Peri was enlisted on the Pipe Rolls of Staffordshire. The Perry name could have come from a dozen sources: it can be a pet name for the Roman Peter or French Pierre, or even for the uncommon Latin Peregrine, meaning "Wanderer" or "Pilgrim." The Middle English Pirie meant "pear tree" and was the name given to men who lived by pear trees, which may be significant since almost all the Perry coats of arms included a pear. The Welsh name Perry evolved from the elision of two words, Ap Harry, meaning "the son of Harry," to the single Parry or Perry. So veiled in the cobwebs of history is the name that there is no way of knowing from which of these remote forebears Tom Perry and his yet unborn child are descended.

Yet the name Perry is among the first connected to England's colonization of the New World, and it is among the venturesome colonists that we must look for Tom's ancestors. A Captain William Perry sailed up the river of American destiny in the ship *Starr* to Jamestown Colony in 1611, nine years before the *Mayflower* stood off Plymouth Rock

with its burden of oppressed Pilgrims. This Perry knew Captain John
Smith and Pocahontas, and he likely drank of colonial beer at Widow
Lawrence's Ordinary, the first inn to offer spirits in British America. He
settled on the south shore of the James River at a place called Pace's Pains
— named for Richard Pace, its major settler — and there lived through
horrible epidemics of fever, of "scurvie & bloody fluxe" that "did kill us
new Virginians." He survived when 346 of Jamestown's 1,240 colonists
were massacred by warrior chief Opechancanough on March 22, 1622.
That he survived is in large part because an Indian named Chanco in
Richard Pace's employ warned of the planned attack the night before and
allowed Pace's Pains time to prepare a defense.

William Perry lived long enough thereafter to become a respectable
tobacco planter and see a tide of settlements known as "particular
plantations" rise on the banks of the James from upstream Southampton
Hundred to downstream Martin's Hundred — a "hundred" being a tract
big enough to sustain a hundred families, usually more than 20,000
acres. Perry's stature as a planter grew sufficiently that he was chosen to
represent Pace's Pains in the House of Burgesses for the Colony of
Virginia from 1629 to 1632, and was a member of the Council from 1632
to 1634.

Captain Perry then removed some twenty-five boat miles upriver on
the James to Westover, a "particular plantation" of some note. His son
Henry, who also served in the House of Burgesses, married the daughter
of Captain George Menefie, Member of the Virginia Council and owner of
the showplace estate Buckland, which adjoined Westover. Westover and
Buckland are not far from the Berkeley Plantation, site of America's first
Thanksgiving in 1619, two years before the celebrated festival of the
Pilgrims at Plymouth Colony. Henry Perry eventually became possessed
of the whole of Buckland.

While young Henry was coming into manhood, Captain William
Perry died, his burial recorded at old Westover Church and his tomb
bearing the epitaph:

Here lyeth the body of Captaine
William Perry who lived neire
Westover in the Collony
Who departed this life the 6th day of
August, Anno Domini 1637

There are tantalizing indications that this William Perry and his son
Henry are relatives of the child now aborning on the little farm near Hico,
Texas, but the truth will probably never be known. For, in one of
history's gravest ironies, the court records of James City County relating
to all the settlements that grew up around Jamestown were taken to
Richmond during the American Civil War for safekeeping. There these
precious records were burned in the fighting. Had they been left in harm's

way at Williamsburg, the war would have appeared only on May 5, 1862, in a battle that ended as a draw and did not destroy the courthouse. Much colonial history was thus relegated to oblivion and mystery. This quirk of fate means that the story of the American Perrys can be traced more easily from England than from America.

When the mists of time begin to clear in the first half of the seventeenth century, the authentic Perry line can be projected from London in the person of one Richard Perry, merchant. In 1628, during the reign of the Stuart King Charles I, Richard Perry appears in the records as having interests in Virginia affairs, described as the master of John Rishton and responsible to him for a headright of fifty acres in the colony. Perry was beginning commerce as London representative to Virginia colonists. Again in 1635 Richard is said to be responsible to a John Davis for the same amount of land. London records show that by 1660, the firm of Perry and Son had garnered the beginnings of wealth.

While the existence of this London merchant Richard Perry is authenticated beyond reasonable doubt, there are less reliable indications that he may have been related to Westover's Captain William Perry. George Menefie, the squire of Buckland and brother-in-law to Captain Perry, was a lawyer and represented the London Richard Perry firm many times in Virginia. The business relationship was close and persistent and appears to have been kept up in deference to Captain Perry of Westover. The ages of William and Richard Perry overlap by about twenty years: they could have been brothers, or William could have been Richard's father. Or they could have been nothing to each other. It could all be a mere coincidence of name and circumstance. We may never know.

We do know from several documents that London's Richard Perry had a brother Phillip who came to live in America in 1655 at the age of fifty-eight, settling in Isle of Wight Shire near Jamestown. Phillip Perry bought one hundred acres from a Nicholas Aldred on September 10 of that year and soon became a large landowner and prominent citizen. We can see him shivering as he rode a fine horse about the plantation, for this era was cursed with a climatic fluke known as The Little Ice Age, and winters were terrible and severe. What would the Virginia planters have achieved under more seasonable conditions?

It is likely that Phillip from time to time acted as agent in the colonies for his brother Richard back in London. Phillip made his will November 20, 1667, "aged 70 years," which places his birth in 1597, and Richard's near the same time. Phillip probably died soon after 1667.

Our London merchant Richard Perry had at least five sons and two daughters. One of his sons became successor to the family business and became the wealthiest and most influential London merchant to the colonies of his time. One cannot study Virginia history without frequently encountering the recorded exploits of Richard's son Micajah

Perry. The name Micajah is probably a derivative of the Biblical Micah, and, according to the peculiarities of the time, was most likely pronounced "MY-juh" — a lawsuit filed against this Perry by a dissatisfied colonist over a 1673 deal in tobacco records the London defendant as "Mij: Perry." Copyists in those days frequently used phonetic name abbreviations.

We know that Micajah Perry died in 1721, for in his 1720 will he asks to be buried "in Bishope Church in the Middle Isle near the Step into the Chancell, where my dear wife lyes," and an entry appears in the burial registry of St. Botolph Bishopsgate Church in London's busy mercantile Bishopsgate Street thus:

1721   October 10   Micajah Perry

Micajah's birth date, however, is obscure. We have reason to believe he was born not much later than 1640 and perhaps even as early as the 1620s — which would mean he lived nearly a hundred years — for many records say he was in business "more than 50 years." One document even states that Micajah Perry was in business in 1642. If this is so, it was probably as apprentice to his father Richard. Whatever the truth may be, Micajah Perry lived a good long time. Had it not been for his later success as a commission merchant, we should probably know nothing of Tom Perry's forefathers and how they came from England, for history has a way of forgetting its poor and its failures. But of Micajah Perry and his brothers who emigrated to America we know a great deal, and the documents that tell their story illumine a little-known era of American history.

The London of 1670, the London of thriving merchant Micajah Perry, begins with the River Thames, England's commercial and military highway to empire. On the north shore of the Thames, within the old Roman-walled district simply called The City and only six streets east of London Bridge, stands the Custom House. Micajah spent nearly as much time at the Custom House as at his own offices, accepting consignments and authorizing bills of lading to ships destined for Jamaica, for France and Holland, and for Virginia. Through the great Custom House doors and across its grimy docks Micajah dealt in the slabs of lumber and hogsheads of tobacco, the Damask shoes and Congo tea that nursed the early commerce of America.

If Micajah Perry could return to the pathways between the old Custom House and his firm's offices in Leadenhall Street, he would find his business precincts still recognizable in places, despite the turn of three centuries. In 1666, as everyone knows, the Great Fire of London burned most of the old walled City — the heart of the modern metropolis — and Micajah would best remember the reconstructed version from his later years. We still approach from the south, as innumerable seafarers have, coming in from the docks at New Key, in Allhallows Barking, hard by the stone wharfs of the Tower of London.

We cross the paved docks in the shadow of the Tower to enter the brick and stone building with its high bays and rows of offices, and we exit through the Thames Street portal, where Micajah came and went countless times during his long merchant career. From the Custom House front door, Micajah today would still be able to see the familiar corner where Thames Street meets northward-trending Water Lane with its cobble pavement leading off toward his offices. Of Water Lane, he would recognize some half-dozen narrow buildings and warehouse fronts, its leftward dogleg, and its intersection with Great Tower Street. Across Great Tower Street, Water Lane becomes Mark Lane, just as in Micajah's time. At the end of Mark Lane on Fenchurch Street, the Ironmongers Hall once stood, businesslike and staid within its Gothic walls, and Billiter Lane still traverses the last block from Fenchurch Street to where the offices of Perry, Lane and Company once stood. There, on the corner of Billiter Lane and Leadenhall Street — "over against the end of Billiter Lane," as one correspondent addressed it — Micajah Perry plied his trade, situated next to the popular African Coffee House and the great charter house of the African Company, another large mercantile firm. The Virginia Coffee House was not far off. Nor was the coffeehouse run by Edward Lloyd where the idea of commercial insurance was born amongst cups and spoons and gentlemen's agreements.

A few buildings away eastward in Leadenhall Street, St. Katharine Cree Church — "Cree" being a medieval rendering of "Christ" — still stands in its blended Gothic-Renaissance serenity, one of the few structures to escape the Great Fire. Micajah was a parishoner there, even though he was buried some two blocks northwest, just outside the "Bishop's Gate" in the old Roman wall, at St. Botolph's Bishopsgate Church. His name appears several times in the St. Katharine Cree Church Vestry Minutes, where he was excused March 27, 1695, from service in the office of Overseer by paying the customary fine of fourteen pounds. He would rejoice to find that three hundred years later his place of worship continued as a ministry "for finance, commerce and industry."

But he would not find his old office or adjoining buildings — they are long gone. The new edifices are a direct legacy of Edward Lloyd's coffeehouse. For in their street today rises the giant cold steel and icy glass complex of Lloyd's of London, a 1980s office building that looks like an offshore oil rig as much as anything. And over Micajah's very doorstep looms the slab-sided modern Bank Bumiputra Malaysia Berhad. By comparison, the nearby stone churches that survive in the modern financial heart of London — Great St. Helens, St. Andrew Undershaft, St. Katharine Cree — seem warm and inviting. Those who do not understand how Londoners feel about London, who don't know that this area of the old City has always been a financial and commercial capital of the world, may think it a scandalous desecration that these piles of office buildings should so drown ancient holy places. But old Micajah, and all the other merchants who over the centuries have paid for both churches and offices, would be delighted. To London merchants, church and business were not contraries, but complements. Micajah Perry would happily regard the fate of his precincts as altogether fitting and proper.

Micajah Perry operated his commission merchant house first as Perry & Son: Micajah himself was probably the first "Son" under his father Richard, but in 1664 Micajah's *son* Richard was born and about 1690 became Micajah's lifelong partner. Micajah's father and son are frequently mistaken for one another by historians, a confusion compounded by the fact that the younger Richard named his own son Micajah, yielding two sets of fathers and sons with the same respective names: Richard (1599?-1670?) and Micajah (1644?-1721) whom we shall call the Elder and Richard (1664-1720) and Micajah (1695-1753) we will designate the Younger.

Early in the 1670s Thomas Lane entered the business as partner to Micajah the Elder — at least by 1673, for he was party to the tobacco lawsuit of that year. As with many English firms of the time, Perry, Lane and Company was operated as a family enterprise. Thomas Lane had relatives that helped the firm in the colonies, and Micajah Perry's brothers also played an important part in its colonial success, for they emigrated to the New World and there assisted as Virginia agents of the London merchants.

Of Micajah the Elder's four brothers — Peter, Henry, Joseph and Benjamin — only Peter made his whole career as colonial agent for Perry, Lane and Company. The others were more independent and tried their fortunes as plantation owners, with varying success. As farmers they did not enjoy the wealth and repute of their more commercial relatives. But they remained to become the stock from which sprang many sturdy American families.

One of these brothers, Benjamin Perry, a restless soul not closely associated with Micajah's business, is the English link we are looking for. He is the immigrant who brought the Perry name through a maze of history to Texas, and to whom our yet unborn farm boy owes his lineage. Benjamin Perry came from England in hopes of joining the Tidewater aristocracy, but his plan did not come off, for his fortunes were mixed, and he made no money.

All Micajah the Elder's brothers settled around old Jamestown colony in Isle of Wight County, or Shire, as it was called in those days. As the family business flourished in the 1670s, Peter became the primary agent of Perry, Lane and Company and moved to York County in 1679 when he was 28 years of age. At first, Perry & Lane remained merely a traditional merchant company as Perry & Son had been, handling tobacco and furs shipped from Virginia and purchasing for the colonists articles required for their own use or in trade with the Indians. They must have been extraordinary shoppers in London, as they obtained for their colonial clients ironworks for sawmills, scissors, ink, carpenter's augers, "fair Bobb wiggs," white beads for the Indians — "the only kind that will sell" — the *London Magazine,* "White Chapple Needles from No. 6 to No. 12," sets of china, salad oil in pint jars, women's hats, calf skins, linens, books including Burnet's *Theory of the Earth,* and an incredible assortment of stuffs and necessaries that steaded the colonists much.

It was during the 1680s that the family business made its phenomenal rise to wealth and power. By 1684, such prominent Tidewater planters as William Byrd were shipping hundreds of hogsheads of tobacco to London for Perry and Lane to sell on consignment at the best price. Soon Micajah Perry found himself more than a merchant: he was handling the mail that passed between the Mother Country and the colonies, acting as attorney and banker to his clients, executor of wills and administrator of estates, and ultimately serving as fiscal agent to the colonial government itself. He became in effect the financial leader of the entire Virginia colony.

In this capacity he was called upon for many years to recommend councillors for appointment and was frequently summoned to the London Board of Trade to give his opinion on Virginia laws affecting trade. His continued power irked Virginia Lieutenant-Governor Alexander Spotswood, who complained in an official letter of 1714 that "Old Perry really talks impertinently . . . I think it is doing little honor to the Government to have its Council appointed in the Virginia Coffee House" by an advisor "who has no other Rule to judge of a man's merit than by the Number of his Tobacco hogsheads."

The partners of Perry, Lane and Company — Micajah Perry, his son Richard and Thomas Lane — by 1700 were wealthy enough to purchase equal interests in Chester Quay, the best import dock and warehouses on the Thames, next to the Tower of London and right adjacent to the Custom House. Yet Micajah Perry, a man of hard-headed commerce, probably uneducated himself, held education and culture in great esteem, and became one of the founding contributors of William and Mary College in Virginia. For many years he acted as its financial agent in London, and records indicate that Micajah, in a surprising and unexplained episode, helped the government finance the new college through a bizarre scheme. In 1689, Micajah Perry petitioned the Privy Council for the release of accused pirates being held in a Jamestown jail, and for the return to them of 2,316 pounds worth of "plate and other goods" they had obtained in the South Seas by means left discreetly obscure in the petition. The nefarious seamen were released and part of their goods restored, but a portion was retained by the government to be devoted to building a college in Virginia "or to some such charitable objects as the King shall direct." The pirate treasure was in fact used to help found William and Mary College, yet no one has the slightest clue why Micajah Perry took the part of sea bandits before the Privy Council.

The incident appears to have made no blot on the Perry name, for Micajah's brother Peter, agent for Perry, Lane and Company, was elected to the Virginia House of Burgesses from York County and played and important part in the affairs of the colony for many years. Micajah himself was called upon to help Virginia finance the contract work on its first capitol building, and for the rest of his life he played majordomo and factotum to the government and commerce of Virginia. And in London he was certainly regarded with respect, for on July 23, 1701, Micajah the Elder became an armigeral gentleman: a coat of arms was granted him by Sir Thomas St. George, Garter, and Sir Henry St. George, Clarencieux. Thereafter, it was Micajah Perry, Esquire.

His greatest misfortune was the loss of his son Richard, who died in 1720, a year before Micajah himself. Richard's wife Sarah had him buried in St. Katharine Cree Church, where a tablet tells us of his life and death: "He was a man of great integrity and uprightness of life, a good Christian, a loving husband and an indulgent father. He departed this life the 16th of April 1720 in the 56th year of his age."

But in the earlier days as Micajah, Richard and Peter Perry — along with Thomas Lane — gained wealth and power, Benjamin Perry evidently saw his main chance in the colonies slip through his fingers, for his restless spirit drove him and his first wife Elizabeth from Isle of Wight County, seeking more attractive lands to the south. By 1700, Micajah's brothers Henry and Joseph disappear from the records forever, and Benjamin would have vanished as well had it not been for the birth of a son, evidently by his second wife Hannah, in the year England and Scotland united to form Great Britain, 1707. Benjamin's son was born far to the south of Jamestown, in Chowan County in the Carolina Colony.

Benjamin had taken the migration route so many Virginia families followed after 1700, through Nansemond County, Virginia, past the Great Dismal Swamp, westward on Albemarle Sound to its tributary, the Chowan River, in what was then called simply the Southern Colony — not until 1729 was the royal colony of Carolina divided North and South. Benjamin must have been in his late forties or early fifties when his son was born, which was not uncommon. He named the child for himself: there would be another Benjamin Perry to carry on his name. His name seems to be all he had, for no record can be found of any special wealth — only some farmland on the northeast shore of Chowan River — nor has his will been located. And in the way things happen, even his name became obscured, for his descendants followed the paternal pattern and named their own sons Benjamin. With the passage of time, Micajah's brother — the English immigrant — became known as Benjamin the Elder, one of his sons was Benjamin Senior, a grandson became Benjamin II, and a great-grandson Benjamin III. Historians endlessly confuse the obscure Elder with the better-known Senior.

While the American native from Chowan County, Benjamin Perry, was growing up, the colonies found themselves continually in trouble with the Crown. They objected to taxes, disobeyed embargoes, ran blockades, sailed without proper escort and made themselves generally a nuisance to the Admiralty. Young Benjamin, son of Benjamin the Elder, must have had a hard life clearing the hardwoods, draining swamps, tilling the soil and making a farm in this new land. And during his youth hardly a year went by without some community discord to mar the farmer's labor. One serious problem touched the lives of the Perrys for generations: the Church of England's stern and demanding ministers in Carolina ran headlong into conflict with the easygoing Americans. Their stentorian insistence upon strict obedience drove flocks of resentful colonial faithful away into the waiting arms of the Quaker religion. The Perrys appear to have become Quakers themselves, and to have passed the new faith on for several generations. It must have been a hard thing for them to leave the Church of England.

Young Benjamin (soon to be the Senior) married Susan Walton in 1728, and his father Benjamin the Elder appears to have died in the same year, for a deed shows that the son then sold the family lands to Thomas Lane, nephew of old Thomas Lane of Perry, Lane and Company, who had died in 1710. This piece of evidence seems to clinch the poorly documented link between old Micajah and the Benjamin Perrys: even in the colonies, the poor Perrys and poor Lanes stuck together as had their rich forebears in London. Benjamin, now the Senior, and his bride Susan appear to have settled immediately in Perquimans County, North Carolina, not far from his Chowan County ancestral home, and appear to have been householders there more than five decades. Here they lived among relatives long since immigrated from Isle of Wight County, Virginia, the descendants of old Micajah's uncle Phillip Perry: his grandsons John and Phillip provide more evidence confirming this projected lineage. Many branches of the Perrys and Lanes intertwined here in North Carolina. If it was a hard life, at least it appears to have been convivial.

But, as always, times were changing. No trace of mercantile wealth had followed any of the Perrys to their Carolina homes, and the hard working life of modest farmers became their lot. The children were arriving at the Perquimans County farmstead. Benjamin Senior and Susan Perry first had Ezekiel about 1730, from whom the Texas Perrys are descended, then more children to fill out the farmstead: Benjamin II about 1732 and Jacob around 1734. There were probably daughters as well, but records of them do not survive. The farm gave them a living, and close rural community life kept them busy if not happy. They might have been proud to know how well their mercantile relatives were doing on the old sod, and then again, they might have cared not a whit.

While the Perry children were arriving, the Scotch-Irish were arriving, too, immigrating during the 1730s by the thousands to America. Their arrival would, as much as anything, shape the destiny of America and the Perrys. From the wharves at Philadelphia and Charleston these newcomers leapfrogged the settled coast to live on the frontier, and that act contained decisive consequences nobody expected. These Anglo-Celts, as historians have called them, had many reasons for marching past the big plantations and the growing cities. The land below the fall line of the Atlantic seaboard was already taken up, and the dour Puritan ethic handed from Calvin through Knox to these Scotch-Irish also gave them a distaste for the Tidewater aristocracy, and all who would put on airs. Neither would they submit to being servile tenant farmers: thrift, self-reliance, and industry, their great public virtues, would not let them. And so they went through no civilized filter of settled American land. They went directly from war-embroiled Europe — the British Isles — to the only place they could take up land as free farmers: to Indian country, to the West, to the Wilderness, to the frontier. They neither asked nor received permission. No one helped or hindered them. Few even noticed. Yet within a few decades their growing numbers and restless spirits were to suck America behind them willy-nilly, government and all, into a century of expansion.

Back in London, September 29, 1738, the younger Micajah Perry, grandson of the old merchant now dead seventeen years, took the family to its zenith of gentility: he was elected Lord Mayor of London by The Livery Companies of the City of London — an elegant name for the businessmen who over time have chosen more than 640 lords mayor from among their own. Every lord mayor needs the cash to pay his own expenses, which can be enormous during his year in office, and also needs a companionly wife with feet sturdy enough to stand in endless reception lines. Micajah the Younger had the cash, but didn't need it much: he had no mansion house to keep up with its many servants and other daily expenses — it was being refurbished during his term. And, tragically, his wife died eighteen days before he became lord mayor. Nevertheless, this worthy fulfilled his office dutifully, leading the Lord Mayor's Show Day on the Thames as the aldermen, sheriffs and guilds accompanied him in their own dazzling barges, rowed upstream in pageantry from Three Cranes Wharf to Westminster. It must have been a pretty sight. Micajah processed in state with his medieval entourage, resplendent in magnificent robes and chains and in the evening hosted dinner at Guildhall. He was no stranger to public life: he also served a long stint as Alderman of Aldgate Ward, Sheriff of London and Middlesex in 1734, and as Member of Parliament from 1727 until 1741. The Perry glory was not to last: after 1741 failing health took the business gradually out of the second Micajah's hands, and the fortunes of Perry, Lane and Company everafter drooped. By 1746, Micajah the Younger had retired as alderman, and he died in 1753, leaving no children to carry on the Virginia trade. Thereafter, we hear of the firm no more. The commercial dynasty had ended.

It was as well. Things were not going aright in the colonies. In 1754 the French and Indian War took men and money from the colonists for military use for the first time. Two years later this fight merged into the Seven Years War, concluded by the 1763 Treaty of Paris which left Great Britain in control of eastern North America. The British victory over France should have increased the Mother Country's solidarity with its colonies, but it did not. Yes, the colonies had helped achieve victory with troops and supplies. They had fought and suffered and died alongside their overseas brethren. But they resented being regarded by the British high and mighty as mere provincial bumpkins, an affront felt particularly keenly by a young soldier-planter named George Washington. Americans realized they could raise a pretty good fighting force — by themselves, if they had to. Americans felt more self-reliant than ever. They discovered their own strength and power. With that discovery the fate of British America was sealed.

Ezekiel Perry, Benjamin Senior's firstborn son, had come of age in the relatively peaceful days before the French and Indian Wars. He married a local Perquimans County girl, Sarah Eason, daughter of Abner Eason and Rachel Docton, in about 1749. By 1760 when the French conflict was in full sway, Ezekiel and his Sarah had moved away from the Perquimans County farmstead to the piney woods of Hertford County, North Carolina, near Old St. John's Chapel. There they farmed and had five of at least seven children. Ezekiel's sons, six of them, were born into the new American mood of self-reliance. They all became successful farmers but not rich, and their loyalties were to home and family and community.

Like most Americans, these Perrys resented British efforts to exert more control over their lives from distant London. They disliked the ban that forbade them to settle in former French areas to the West — although they would never have thought of moving to the wilds of Alabama or even to such a place as Georgia, which had been founded in 1733 as the thirteenth colony of British America to prevent Spanish expansion out of Florida. Georgia had gained a nasty reputation, for it had been settled mostly by unsavory Englishmen who emigrated rather than face debtors' prison at home. The Perrys hated the Stamp Act and other measures enacted by Parliament to make the colonies pay for stationing British troops in America. Most of all, they despised British restrictions on American trade. The situation could not last.

By the time of the American Revolution, Ezekiel and his eldest son

Abner had lost all family ties to Great Britain. The Perrys were American now, and only American, and they were ready to fight for independence. Ezekiel and Abner both rose to the rank of captain in the Continental Army, and Abner's gallant service at the Battle of Guilford Courthouse stood him in good stead in later life: he was a favorite of the people and was elected to Congress in 1801, serving nine years. Even Ezekiel's father Benjamin the Senior, advancing in years during the Revolution, served by supplying a horse, for which the United States, through the Militia, paid him 90 pounds in 1781. Ezekiel had no military ambitions and returned from the Army to a new homestead in Bertie County, North Carolina, about 1780. Here another ancestor of the Texas Perrys was born: Ezekiel's sixth son Docton, named for his maternal grandmother Rachel Docton Perry.

Docton Perry was born into a time of great ferment and social change. The Revolution left in its wake a devastating depression and a weak central government formed in 1781 by the Articles of Confederation. The new independent America was not shaping up as expected. Farm prices fell and the populace was impoverished. Farmers and laborers clamored for the new American Congress to issue large amounts of paper money. The central United States government had no power to levy taxes, or to regulate interstate commerce. Each state could impose tariffs on the goods of sister states. Congress was authorized to borrow money from the states, but was powerless to compel the states to honor its requests for funds. The United States were united in name only. Businessmen and landowners especially felt the need of a stronger central government to deal with foreign trade problems, particularly British interference with American shipping. The new nation had serious problems.

Docton Perry's early life and young manhood were spent in rural poverty and seething political unrest. By the time he reached maturity, the new nation made a decisive change: Congress adopted a new Constitution in 1789, providing for a strong central government and simultaneously guaranteeing liberties unprecedented in human history, yet the standard of living Docton found on the farm with his father Ezekiel was lower than his grandfather Benjamin had enjoyed, humble as that had been. And what of Ezekiel, himself now advancing in years? He realized that the family farmstead could no longer support his many children. He made a firm decision in 1792, the year George Washington was elected to his second term as president: he would migrate with his family westward to South Carolina where he had heard there were new farms to be had and a new life to be forged. Ezekiel and Sarah took their youngest children Docton, Simeon and Susannah and pulled up stakes. They settled in undeveloped Edgefield County, not far from the Savannah River that formed the border between South Carolina and the state of Georgia.

Thomas Jefferson was elected president in the year 1800 when Docton Perry married Martha Wimberly, a local Edgefield girl about whom little is known. Docton took her to live on the family farm. In that same year Docton's father Ezekiel died after eight years on the new farm. By 1803 Docton's own first son William was born, who would carry the Perry name a generation further to the Texas Perrys. Docton's second son Ezekiel was born 1804, his third son Simeon in 1806 and his fourth, Abner, in 1811.

There is no telling what made Docton the restless man he was. Living in hard times may have forced him into some of the migrations of his long life. Although his children were born at Edgefield, South Carolina, we find him voting in 1813 in Orange Parish, some 70 miles by bad roads from his original farm, yet the 1820 U.S. census finds him back at Edgefield as a head of household. As his children grew up and married, Docton appears to have followed his eldest son William westward with the growth of the new nation.

Docton's first son William W. Perry is the earliest of this family line that can be traced reliably in U.S. census records throughout his life. The evidence is frustratingly partial for the earlier Perrys. Too many links must be made by projection and piecing together incredibly complex shreds of documentary evidence. What records there are bear out the line from Micajah's immigrant brother Benjamin the Elder to his son Benjamin the Senior to his son Ezekiel, and thence to Docton and to William. But now we find the first member of this line whose life is documented from one end to the other: William W. Perry. Even so, it is hard to know what influenced his character.

We know that William was a farmer and poor. We know that a great religious revival swept America while he was a young man, and idealistic cooperative communities arose such as Robert Owen's New Harmony, Indiana. We know that the first public high school opened in America. Of these forces, only religion ever likely reached him, and it appears certain that he had abandoned his ancestral Quaker faith. Young William grew up in sparsely settled, almost wilderness communities that succeeded in teaching him to read and write, but formal education had little place in his life. He seems to have wandered widely in South Carolina, particularly near the Atlantic coast, for he married Sarah Joanna Williams from Charleston, South Carolina — yet their marriage took place November 19, 1829, in Franklin County, Georgia, far inland on the Tugaloo River that forms the boundary between the extreme northern parts of South Carolina and Georgia.

William W. Perry's marriage was fruitful, producing five sons, the first two born in Georgia, probably in Franklin County. William's first son, John Bunyon Perry, who is the grandfather of our Texas farmer Tom Perry, was born September 15, 1831, and another son William "Billie" was born in 1836. The family may have lived near the only well-known local settlement of the time, Toccoa. Georgia had lost its penal colony reputation and moved into an age of general prosperity as William's children were born. Prosperity followed after the United States of America had flexed its first muscles as an international power. The War of 1812 had ended in victory for the Americans, proving independence once and for all. Andrew Jackson had decisively defeated Britain's allies, the Creek Indians, at the Battle of Horseshoe Bend in 1814. Peace settled on the land and diplomatic relations had been established with the British Crown. During the 1830s the hostile Indians were removed from Alabama by the federal government to Indian Territory, now Oklahoma. British demand for cotton increased substantially, and small inefficient cotton gins dating from 1802 were being replaced by large cotton mills. The hopes of the young nation for commercial success were being realized.

But the piedmont plateau of Georgia where William Perry had settled was not productive. His difficulties were compounded by the tariff act passed by Congress in 1832. Like most Southern cotton farmers, William sold his small output in the export market, and received the world-market price while having to pay for Northern manufactured goods at relatively high domestic prices artificially maintained by high tariffs. While William and his family struggled brutally with their thin soil to survive, Robert Y. Hayne passionately debated Daniel Webster, charging that a U.S. high-tariff policy would be "utterly destructive" of the South's interests, and would "spread ruin and desolation through the land." William Perry probably never knew of it, but the tariffs he lived with had caused the Southern States to first talk of secession in 1827, when South Carolina's Dr. Thomas Cooper said the time had come to "calculate the value of the Union." It may have been privation and it may have been the pioneer urge that seemed to run in these Perrys to pull up stakes and move on, but by 1839, William had removed his family to Alabama, which had been a state only twenty years. His father Docton, now in his sixties, moved with him.

William W. Perry's last three sons were born here in northeastern Alabama's ridge and valley region near the tiny community of Heflin. Francis Marion was born in 1839, James J. in 1842, and Docton Cornelius in 1844. It was nearby in the middle 1850s that their grandfather Docton Perry died. The children grew up in a state rapidly developing its economic, social and political structures based on the plantation system and slavery. But they did not share in the riches of the cotton kingdom. They soon fell into the hands of the furnishing merchant, a businessman who gave them supplies and clothing for a year on credit, a businessman who, to make sure the Perrys "paid out" their debt, took a crop lien on their cotton. For a few years the Perrys and their neighbor farmers thought they could work their way to eventual financial security, but the ridge and valley soil got the best of them — it was too thin to make much cotton, and as time went on the land gullied and eroded and lost its nutrients. No one then understood the value of cover crops or of planting alternate seasons in legumes to restore depleted nitrogen. It did not take many years for the Perrys to realize that they would never pay out their debts. And there was the increasing tension in the air, tension about war.

Influential citizens in the South strongly favored the expansion of slavery, and supported the war with Mexico that raged from 1846 to 1848 in hopes that more slave territory would be gained, as indeed it was in Texas. Mexico's defeat would further complicate things by forcing California's cession to the United States as a free territory, along with the area called New Mexico, which would later be divided into the states of New Mexico, Arizona, Utah, and Nevada. The Perrys on their thin-soil farms were unconcerned with these national developments if they even heard about them. They had no grasp of geopolitics and no stake in slavery or the plantation system. Few of their neighbors did, either. For certainly no more than 30 percent of the white population ever became slaveholders, including even farmers who only hired one occasional slave from his owner.

Raising cotton in competition with slave labor and planter capital would have been a highly unprofitable occupation for the majority of Southern whites even if some benevolent dictator had given them the rich soil of lowland farms. But being relegated to the dregs and leavings of the Plantation South and having no capital or hope of raising capital, the Perrys and thousands of other hardscrabble farmers never had a chance. They, like most pioneer farmers of the day, were themselves virtual slaves to their own stingy land and meager crops. Many remarked that they were worse off than the black slaves. One observer noted that "our poor white people are wholly neglected, and are suffered to while away an existence in a state but one step in advance of the Indian in the forest."

As William's five young sons were growing up, the slave issue came to the fore. When Docton Cornelius, the youngest, was only six years old, Congress in the far-away District of Columbia adopted the Compromise of 1850 by which California was admitted to the Union as a free state to balance the slave state of Texas. Utah and New Mexico territories were permitted to choose their status. But Congress also passed the Fugitive Slave Act, making it a federal crime to aid an escaping slave. A large band of strangers in the North formed the Free Soil party, and anti-slavery sentiment grew from a simmer to a boil. Even farmers in the remote hills of Alabama could not miss the mounting sentiment for secession in the South.

By 1857 the condition of poor farmers in the South like William Perry had attracted serious attention. A passage from M. Tarver's *Domestic Manufacturers in the South and West* was included in Helper's *Impending Crisis in the South:*

> The non-slaveholders possess, generally, but very small means, and the land which they possess is almost universally poor, and so sterile that a scanty subsistence is all that can be derived from its cultivation; and the more fertile soil, being in possession of the slaveholders, must ever remain out of the power of those who have none. This state of things is a great drawback, and bears heavily upon and depresses the moral energy of the poorer classes. The acquisition of a respectable position in the scale of wealth appears so difficult, that they decline the hopeless pursuit, and many of them settle down into habits of idleness, and become the almost passive subjects of all its consequences. And I lament to say that I have observed of late years that an evident deterioration is taking place in this part of the population, the younger portion being less educated, less industrious, and in every point of view less respectable than their ancestors.

The Perrys could hardly avoid this demoralizing influence, and maintained their fiber by dogged persistence bolstered with strong religious faith. All around them people were pulling up stakes, escaping futile toil in the wornout soil, fleeing from the furnishing merchant, running from the law in some cases. The Perrys saw emigrants all around them perform the new ritual: before they left, they smeared their cabin doors in axle grease with the letters GTT — Gone To Texas. Poor farmers from Kentucky and Tennessee and Alabama, from everywhere, had heard that Texas land was free for the taking, that Texas had passed the first homestead law in America, a law stating that a family's homestead could never be seized for debt. Thousands felt their destiny in that vast and faraway land, felt they could find what they were looking for: a chance, a chance to work hard and keep some of the fruits of their labor, a chance maybe even to get a little ahead. And those thousands wrote GTT on their doors. The Perrys thought about it, thought hard, for it might mean the chance to get a little ahead and send one of their children to school one day, *all* of school, not just the fourth or fifth grades they themselves had finished. But moving to *Texas* . . . It was too far, too unreal. They did not write GTT on their door. They stayed put. Their hopes for education and prosperity yielded no better results than those of the bulk of poor farmers who remained in Alabama.

For all the general poverty and misery, these years saw the invention of the electric motor, the reaper, the steel plow, and the first practical telegraph. Stephen Foster was writing his immortal songs and the sewing machine came into use. An unrelated Perry, Commodore Matthew C., opened Japan to trade. All the Perry boys who heard of these interesting things had reached manhood by the end of the 1850s — Docton at sixteen would find himself old enough to enlist in the military. Alabama may have taken little note of its poor whites, but by 1860 it had grown tired of government interference with its slave economy and moved toward secession. The tension of war reached the snapping point. Before news of Lincoln's inauguration reached the Alabama Perrys, their state had seceded from the Union and joined the Confederate States of America. The Perry boys all realized that the storm clouds of a great Civil War were rapidly gathering around them.

The next four years were a time of testing for the Alabama Perrys and for the sundered nation. All five Perry boys joined the Confederate Army. James served in Company C of the 22nd Alabama Regiment and Docton in the 30th Alabama Volunteers. The others served in various detachments, and all saw action. Docton, the youngest, was the only one to see a great historic battle. The Confederates had trapped Union General W. S. Rosecrans after badly defeating him at Chickamauga and laid siege to his position in Chattanooga. The Union was determined to raise that siege. November 24, 1863, General W. T. Sherman, commanding the Army of the Tennessee, attacked the Confederate left flank, while General Joseph Hooker, with a corps from the Army of the Potomac, attacked the right in a sweep over Lookout Mountain where the 30th Alabama Volunteers were entrenched, successfully pinning down Rosecrans. Their savage encounter became known as the Battle Above the Clouds. There Docton was wounded in the mouth by Union fire and was carried in the retreat to safety. He recovered and served the Confederacy until the bitter end in 1865. Then he and all his brothers went home to Heflin. By some miracle they had each survived the terrible conflagration. The Civil War was over.

It is again an August night in 1910. We are once more in the weaning house on the Perry farm near Hico, Texas. The childbirth progresses. Powerful forces of family survival, of generations of toil, are at work in this room. The young Texas farmer whose lineage we trace is caught up in the moment where his forebears are about to meet their future. See him by the bedside.

Tom Perry realized why they called it labor as he watched his young wife bear down in a strong transition-stage contraction. He was glad to have Dr. Durham managing the birth and Granny Marlow assisting. His mother gave him comfort and example in helping to comfort Belle, who was now heavily perspiring and panting with exertion. Perhaps there were ghosts in the room, or perhaps it was only reminiscences of a grandfather he could not remember, but for some reason Tom thought in this moment of his grandfather John Bunyon Perry, who never came to Texas.

John Bunyon Perry was the oldest of William W. Perry's five sons. When he married September 29, 1857, in Heflin, Alabama, his bride was a South Carolina girl, Elizabeth F. Glasgow. She was pretty and whimsical, and she insisted that her maiden name had come from the founders of Glasgow, the largest city in Scotland, but there is little evidence to back her conviction. The first of their ten children, Thomas, had been born in 1860 just months before the Civil War broke out at Fort Sumter, April 12, 1861. The second son, James W. Perry, was born during the war in 1862 — and was to become the father of our Texas farmer, Thomas Bunyon Perry.

Except for a few disorganized foraging raids by scattered Union soldiers, the Civil War did not reach Heflin, Alabama, and young James Perry until it was over. True, Heflin's young men went away to become soldiers, and many never came marching home again. But the closest real battles were fought more than sixty miles away at Chattanooga and Atlanta. Not until the South had surrendered did the full impact of Sherman's scorched earth policy during the March to the Sea become evident. Not until peace returned did the shattering of supply centers such as smoldering Atlanta hit home. Basic commodities such as sugar and coffee and grain that had been scarce and expensive during the war now were completely unavailable for weeks at a time. Markets for farm produce languished. Reconstruction carpetbaggers and scalawags bred extravagant government, bankruptcy, and undying bitterness. For decades the immediate scars of defeat would linger in the South. For more than a century to come the hateful war now ended would still be fought daily in the hearts and minds of Southerners by the million.

It was in an atmosphere of defeat and privation that John and Elizabeth Perry's second son Jim grew up, but he never realized it. The piney woods of Northeastern Alabama was not prime farmland, and that meant a life of grueling hard labor for a farm boy. From the time he could do a chore Jim Perry knew all the work it took to make the reluctant soil yield a scanty harvest of food and fiber. But it was the same for everybody, and he did not grow into a bitter man.

In early 1864 Jim's younger sister Mary was born, followed late the same year by Joanna, then at two-year intervals came Suzie and Emma. Four more brothers and sisters would come later. New mouths to feed would grow into new workers in the fields, and of such full tight bind was the knot of family in this rural community that it would have been sacrilege to begrudge a child existence. More pines would simply be cleared and the stumps grubbed out with a mattock or "grubbing hoe," more food would be grown, and that would be that.

Young Jim Perry enjoyed living close by his grandfather William and grandmother Sarah. Grandmother Sarah always set great stock by schooling, although she herself had little, and often told her grandchildren the story of how their uncle Docton married the educated Abercrombie girl Isabella on December 28, 1865. Isabella had been reared on a rich plantation in Cleburne County near Heflin and had been provided with an Englishman for a tutor. That made her an *educated* woman, by local estimates. That made her a *high-toned* woman deserving of respect. But Emancipation had freed all her father's slaves, and the War Between the States had impoverished her family. When Docton came back after the fighting was over, he saved her from starvation: he married her. She was only fifteen. And that was the end of her education.

But someday, Grandmother Sarah insisted, education would come to the Perrys. Her boys had missed it, but now her grandchildren might have the chance. Might grow up to be a doctor or a lawyer. Might make enough money never to go hungry and maybe even have a fine possession or two. She had no memory of the great mercantile wealth of old Micajah, for the Perrys had lost the old family Bibles, had lost all record of its past during generations of westward migration. Grandmother Sarah could hope all she wanted, but it was not to be. Not for her grandchildren. And not for her great-grandchildren.

After that bloody war the only comfort anyone could take was in religion. Somewhere in the generations, the Quaker faith of the colonial Perrys became the Baptist faith of the Alabama Perrys. The Baptists originated in 1609 when a group of separatist refugees who had withdrawn from the Church of England was brought together by John Smythe and Thomas Helwys in Amsterdam. Since 1644 the name Baptist has been applied to those who believe that baptism should be administered to none but believers and that immersion is the only mode of baptism indicated in the New Testament. American Baptists founded a church at Providence, Rhode Island, in 1638 or 1639. When Roger Williams and his companions there rejected infant baptism, they were persecuted in New England, and one group emigrated from Maine to Charleston, South Carolina, around 1684. Back in England, the Baptists prospered as part of the general congregational movement: a London Association was formed in 1689 — during the lives of old Micajah and his brothers — and consisted of more than a hundred Baptist churches scattered over England and Wales. This London Association reflected the principle of organization "That whatever is determined by us in any case shall not be binding upon any church till the consent of that church be first had." The first such association in America was the Philadelphia, organized in 1701 and regarded as the mother of all American associations. In 1749, Benjamin Griffith wrote for the Philadelphia Association a statement of congregational government, saying, "Each particular church hath a complete power and authority from Jesus Christ to administer all gospel ordinances . . . as baptism and the Lord's supper, and to receive and cast out, and also to try and ordain her own officers, and to exercise every part of gospel discipline and church government independent of any other church or assembly whatever." Baptist associations were formed in 1751 in Charleston, South Carolina, and in 1784 in Georgia. William, now the Southern patriarch of the Perry clan, could have become a Baptist in either of these associations.

The social life of the nineteenth century rural Southern community centered around its churches. There was no other focus, no secular institutions, no diversions. All-day visits with church brethren were special events, weekly for those towns lucky enough to have a resident preacher, monthly where the circuit rider had many scattered flocks to keep. Jim, his parents and grandparents, as well as his uncles and cousins, would foregather with other local church members on these special days. The children would play together and the grown ups would separate into groups of women and knots of menfolk. On these days, it was not "Mister Perry," it would be "Brother Perry." It was fellowship in more than name.

The Methodists and Missionary Baptists held Sunday School but the Primitive Baptist Church did not believe in it. Heflin, Alabama, had all three churches. Some of the Alabama Perrys belonged to this "Hardshell Baptist" faith, but most, including John Bunyon's family, were Missionary Baptists. The Primitive Baptists tended to be looked upon by outsiders without understanding, branded with epithets and thought of as ignorant hillbillies who practiced footwashing and opposed both Sunday School and foreign missions. But few were illiterate, and they were as much pillars of their community as their detractors. And the Missionary Baptists with their Sunday Schools promoted literacy through Bible reading. All the sons of Grandfather William and Grandmother Sarah could read and write, and their Church was as responsible for it as the common schools, where attendance by farm children was sporadic at best.

One day early in 1870 before Jim Perry was eight years old, his grandfather and grandmother paid a visit to his parents with sorrowful faces, and left a gift of two small tintype photographs, one of white-bearded Grandfather William and one of Granny Sarah — she had become a midwife — taken at a small Heflin studio that used an angular geometric design as a backdrop. Copies are still owned by modern Perrys. It was a final memento, for they were GTT — bound for Texas — to live near their three youngest sons and their families, who had already journeyed westward. Only the two oldest sons John and Willie were to remain in Alabama. William and Sarah knew they would never see them again.

In 1882, when he was twenty years old, John Bunyon Perry's son Jim married a local girl whose name was Lou Pendergrass — she that would take up the hope for education and carry it a generation further. She was two years older than Jim, knew that she wanted to be a farm wife, and did well as a Perry. Things in general were getting better in Alabama. The inflation and corruption of Reconstruction had brought the state to bankruptcy in the early 1870s, but by 1874 home rule had been restored, local Democrats came to power, and Alabama began to prosper once more. The road up had not been without its problems. The Ku Klux Klan arose to terrorize freed Negro slaves and whites who catered to the black vote. The use of federal troops to suppress the Klan helped drive it to virtual extinction by 1877. But in some ways, things in 1882 looked very good. Governor Edward A. Neal touted the new steel mills being planned for industrial areas around Birmingham, citing a new era of jobs and well being. But Alabama remained overwhelmingly agricultural. One-crop cotton farming remained the major economic staple for many years, perpetuating the plight of the poor farmer.

James and Lou Perry had their first child, a son, December 16, 1883. They named him after his uncle and after his grandfather: Thomas Bunyon Perry. Tom was born at home on the little forty-acre farm near Heflin his parents had bought. Five more children followed at intervals until 1900. When Tom was only three years old, his grandfather John Bunyon Perry died, and shortly thereafter his great-uncle Willie Perry followed. Both were buried in New Harmony Baptist Cemetery near Heflin. The older generation of Alabama Perrys was dying out.

As young Tom grew to teenage, farm life around Heflin, Alabama, grew more impossible with every passing year. The soil that once grew two bales of cotton on ten acres now grew only one, and one bale of cotton each year could not provide the cash they needed. Even though everyone helped run the farm, picking the cotton by hand, ginning it by hand, spinning it into thread by hand, things were getting worse. They had to find other sources of income, and when Tom turned fifteen, his father was obliged to walk to the little shingle mill three miles west of the farm and asked for a job. He got it. It was heavy work: walk three miles to work, carry your lunch, use an iron tool called a froh to split shingles from heavy cedar bolts for ten hours, walk three miles home. But the pay was good: fifty cents a day.

Tom and his brothers were left to work the farm all day. A year of supplemental income from the shingle mill proved that even an extra job was not enough. Although the turn of the century had come — it was now 1900 — growing industrialization in the South could not save the poor farmer. The Perrys simply couldn't make a go of farming the Alabama piney woods any more. They would obviously starve to death if something wasn't done. There was nothing to do but go west. Correspondence from the Perrys who had done well in Texas promised Jim and Lou and their children help if they should choose to emigrate.

So Jim sold the little farm near Heflin for something more than $400, boxed all their tools and their plows and all their other family possessions, packed them on a freight car, and paid $40 for their tickets to Texas. They chalked GTT on their cabin door and left it forever. Jim and Lou had just become parents again for the last time, and the infant had fallen seriously ill. They were afraid the baby would die on the train. They took along a little hickory split basket to the train station, and told their problem to the train conductor. He said that if the child died during the trip, he would let them put it in the hickory basket in the baggage car for burial when they arrived in Texas. The worried family rode the train for two days and two nights. When they arrived at the railway station at Iredell in Bosque County, Texas, uncles and cousins who had prospered in this new land met Jim and Lou and the children with a wagon and shuttled them a few miles westward to their new home.

The vast open spaces of Texas were strange to them. The closeness of the Alabama piney woods filled their memory. The sky was so huge here, the distances so intimidating. Meadows of bunchy big bluestem and tall Indian grass and short Muhly opened into endless grain fields rippling with golden wealth. Clumps of gnarled liveoak and limby hackberry and Texas hickory gave way to enormous cotton rows glistening in the pounding sun like white fuzzy diamonds. Huge expanses of wildflowers added to the strangeness: the splashy buttercups, the startling red and mottled gold Indian paintbrushes, the black-eyed susans, the evening primroses. Yes, the place was strange to the immigrants. But their people were here, and that was all that mattered. The strangeness would pass, and the town of their future, Hico, lay ten miles farther over low rolling hills to the west in Hamilton County.

They had arrived in Texas with only their few possessions, some $180 in cash and a sick baby. The infant died a month later. They gave their dead to the remorseless soil of Texas. It was a somber time.

Jim and Lou Perry and their surviving offspring nursed their grief privately. Neighbors could only see a family "working on the halves" on the farms of relatives, raising cotton and grain and paying "toll" of half their crop. The new Texas Perrys worked a year with one family, a year with another, and two years with a third, a system commonly employed by family groups to spread the burden of new immigrants. Established relatives provided new arrivals with the necessary seed, tools, and mules. It was a good plan.

Jim and Lou Perry had thought they could do better in Texas, and they could. By 1905 they had saved some money, looked around, and found the 211-acre farmstead in Erath County eight miles north of Hico. They bought the farm on contract from James and Mary Ann Blackburn for $2,500, $600 in cash and $1,900 in notes at ten percent interest, with fear and trembling: it was more money than they had ever seen or could imagine.

The new farm was covered with Johnson grass, a pernicious weed to Texas farmers although tolerable grazing for ranchers. Some of the Perrys' new neighbors maintained that nothing would ever grow there since the Johnson grass would return and choke it out. Perhaps they did not know how thorough an Alabama piney woods farmer had to be to stay alive, for Jim and Lou and the children cleaned out the weeds and kept them out. On the fertile blackland Texas soil they grew cotton and corn and grain and a family kitchen garden. They did well. The new farm was paid for in two years. Now Jim and Lou Perry were landowners. And they were gradually becoming Texans.

James and Mary Ann Blackburn had come from Missouri and settled this farm in 1870, buying 2,500 acres for fifty cents an acre. James hauled the lumber to build their house all the way from Waco, more than sixty miles east over wretched wagon roads. But a flaw in the farm's title was discovered in 1890, and they lost the north half of their land in a dispute, leaving the Blackburns 1,250 acres, which was still a respectable spread.

Their son Charley — one of nine children — eventually bought part of the farm as his own. He married Susan Laura Johnson in the courthouse at Stephenville, Texas, June 29, 1882. They worked their part of the Blackburn farm diligently and were reasonably well off as Texas farmers went in those days. Laura Belle was the sixth of their nine children, and was twelve years old when the Perrys bought the eastern part of the Blackburn farm in 1905. Four years later she married Tom Perry and went to live in a weaning house not a mile from the farmhouse where she herself had been born.

Now the circle is complete. We began in this weaning house in 1910, and we have returned to it. We have traced the family of this child aborning to its English origins. We have followed its line across the fateful landscape of American history.

And here, on August 16, late in the evening, the first child of Tom and Belle Perry is born. Dr. Charles Durham delivers the healthy baby boy, sees to the needs of the young mother, and just before first light returns to his home in Hico. Granny Marlow cares for the new mother and infant and then prepares a normal country breakfast of biscuits, country gravy, eggs, bacon, and heavy dark sorghum molasses.

Later that morning it is decided to name the new arrival Willie Clayborne Perry. The name Clayborne has come from a great uncle, the first son of Docton Perry who survived the Battle Above the Clouds. In

Texas country style, the newborn's given name is not William, but Willie. He will grow up not liking all that long name, and go by the initials W.C. And he will be the first of this particular Perry line to make the generations-old dream of education come true.

-2-

THE WEANING HOUSE

"DINNERTIME!" called Belle.

Tom peered over a mass of white bolls, looking back over humid cotton rows streaming toward the Dude Flat weaning house. He took the bulging cotton sack from around his neck, glad to be rid of its clinging heat, and got up off his knees, still bent over and stiff. Little clots of Texas soil fell from the leather knee pads tied around his legs, bits of dirt bouncing on his shoes and dusting the heavy canvas bag he had filled and emptied twice since dawn. The earth-stained cotton sack lay quietly distended, nearly full again.

He stood up straight, feeling the ache of noon in his back, and wiped the sweat from his brow with a red kerchief as Belle approached. The brash September sun sparkled in her hair, stirring in Tom feelings of love and pride he would never be able to express in words.

Cotton twigs scratched at the food basket Belle carried as she made her way in the swelter up the row where Tom stood waiting. She extended a full gourd of water to her husband. "How's little Clayborne?" she wanted to know.

Tom took the gourd and drank deeply, then looked down at a small form he had carried most of the morning on top of his bulging cotton sack. Snug in a baby nest of coarse fabric, his two-year-old son lay curled up sound asleep, shielded from the sun by a hat several sizes too large.

"He's dead to the world," Tom smiled.

"You never get tired of hauling him up and down the rows, do you, Tom?"

49

"No. I don't."

They stood looking down at their sleeping child for a long moment. The wide and ancient Texas horizon framed them in a tableau that could have been painted by Millet or Van Gogh or Winslow Homer, whose brushstrokes whisper shapes hinting why farm families might stand thus in a cotton field, at peace, satisfied, bound to each other by love, bound to the earth by the benediction of sun and rain and harvest. It was a time of innocence in America, and although it would soon end in tumult and clamor and disenchantment and industrialization, the Grand Prairie was yet firmly anchored in sleepy agrarian serenity. The pace here was slow but productive, the living hard but honest, the people simple but good.

"We'd best have dinner in the shade of the wagon, Tom," said Belle. The noon meal was called dinner, not lunch, the day's three meals always called breakfast, dinner and supper. The name and idea of "luncheon" would have seemed effete and faintly ridiculous to these farmers.

Belle scooped up little Willie Clayborne Perry. The two-year-old blinked sleepily at his mother as she weighed him in one arm and balanced the family's food basket in the other.

"Mama wake me up," yawned the lad. His mother agreed, "I sure did wake you up, didn't I, Clayborne?" Face close to his, she bragged as all mothers brag, "You're getting to be such a big boy, so heavy and all."

Tom strapped the cotton sack over his shoulder again. It was the emblem of struggle and hope: determined rent farmers could become landowners carrying one long enough. The sack was too long to walk with. It would drag the ground and hinder his normal stride. He bent down, grasped the brass ring on the bottom seam and pulled it up, bending the bag double in the process. He stood a moment to make sure he had his balance, then hugged the doubled-up cotton sack to his bib overalls, flattening its mouth shut so none of the precious fiber could escape. Whenever he looked down at such a load, Tom always thought privately that the sack's flattened top looked like nothing so much as a frog's wide mouth and imagined the stray cotton bolls hanging on its edges as insects about to be consumed.

Tom and Belle wordlessly carried their burdens to the high-sided wagon standing exactly in the middle of the field, straddling the cotton rows, where it made the shortest haul for a heavy-laden picker from any point in the cottonpatch. The wagon hovered on its spindly wood-spoke wheels above a veritable sea of wispy lint bolls, the scene harshly outlined half light, half dark in the sharp glint of noon.

Belle deposited her lunch basket in the pool of shade beneath the wagon and gently sat her little boy down on the dirt. They would dine between cool cotton rows. In a mother's lilting sing-song, Belle discussed with her child the same weighty questions of elimination and general well being that have been so discussed since there have been mothers and little boys. Clayborne babbled happily.

While Belle tended to the boy, Tom went to take care of his cotton sack. The wagon's tongue had been propped up to a forty-five degree angle by a wooden breast yoke. Protruding from the end of the wagon tongue was the usual steel eye-fitting from which hung the family's cotton scale. Tom slipped his full collecting bag onto the scale's weighing hook. Forty-eight pounds. The four bags he and Belle would pick during the afternoon, he calculated, would finish off this load at more than 1,500 pounds — a good bale.

Tom heaved his weighed bag up over the wagon side, grasping the sack's brass ring and shaking forty-eight more pounds of fluffy bolls from its frog mouth into the brimming wagon. Tom turned his head away as the lint flew, favoring his good eye. He was a small man and had trouble throwing a full cotton bag over these high sides: Two extra sideboards had been added after grain harvest for height — the normally two-foot-deep wagon bed was now four feet deep to contain the extra bulk of cotton. Within a few seconds of shaking the bag, an hour and a half's work tumbled into the nearly full wagon.

"Well," said Tom, sitting with a thump in the shade beside his wife and boy, "looks like the three of us are going into Hico tomorrow morning and sell our first cotton of the year."

Belle smiled. "I'll be ready on time. I expect we'll sell some cream and eggs too." She busied herself laying out their ample meal on a floursack tablecloth: steaming cornbread wrapped in a cloth, a still-bubbling pot of red beans and onions, baked sweet potatoes — a favorite from the garden this time of year — several thick hot slices of ham, and a jar of pickles. She had stooped over the massive iron cookstove in their kitchen for more than an hour to prepare this meal, feeding its firebox batches of chopped and split stovewood at frequent intervals to maintain an even baking temperature for the cornbread, pausing once to empty the overflowing ash box. She had been lucky today: while she was emptying the ashes no stray gust of wind chanced by to scatter them all over her little house. At least it was not canning time this week or washday today. Still, dinner was as much a respite from drudgery for Belle as for Tom.

"Wa-wa," Clayborne demanded. Tom leaned back into the shade of the wagon and crooked his finger into the handle of a big cool crockery water jug wrapped in wetted burlap sacks — "towsacks" to a Texas farmer. Tom pulled the corncob stopper from the jug's mouth while Belle held three cups to be filled with gurgling water fresh that morning from the well.

They spooned up the red beans and onions, ate the sweet potatoes and ham, devoured their squares of cornbread and drank their sweet water. No dinner conversation filled their time together, only a laconic and taciturn bond that said as much as needed to be said. After the simple farmer's meal, Belle pulled Tom's left hand to her in a simple gesture of ownership.

"How's that infection?" she inquired. Tom shrugged and chewed a pickle.

Belle examined the canvas bandage. "I'm going to take off this finger stall, Tom. It doesn't look like your finger's any better." A "finger stall" was a homemade protector, much like the single finger of a glove, worn over an injury and held in place by string thongs tied around the wearer's wrist. When Belle pulled the finger stall off, an angry red hangnail glowed in the shadows.

"I'll fetch up the peroxide after dinner," said Belle. "It's still bad."

Clayborne looked on with rapt attention, reaching out to help. "Papa hurt," he consoled. "Ouch, ouch," rubbing his own finger in sympathy.

"It's all right, son," said Tom.

Belle retied the finger stall to Tom's wrist. "You know it's the wet cotton in the mornings that does this, Tom," she complained. "Wet leaves are rougher, they'll tear you up. You ought to wait 'til the morning dew is off before you start picking. It's that wet cotton give you this finger for sure."

"Now, Belle," he replied patiently, "you know I'd never get the cotton picked if I did that." He knew how lucky he was to have married this tough, solicitous, demanding and helpful woman. "The finger ain't my problem," he said, hiding a grin, "The real trouble's my picking bag."

He unfolded the long canvas bag and spread it on the grass near his son. The boy recognized his riding toy and patted his small hands on his knees in delight. Tom pointed to the wear marks on the lower end of the bag where it had been dragged along cottonpatch rows. "This end of the bag's just about wore out," said Tom. "Time to change ends."

She flipped the bag, looking at both well-scraped sides in exasperation. "Sakes alive, Tom, I sewed this bag just two weeks ago! There's only a week's work on either side of this bag. This ain't lastin' half as long as last year's bags."

"What do you think could've done it, Belle?" Tom asked with a straight face.

She examined the bag closely, searching for clues. "Could be the ducking we bought from Marshall's is bad . . . Now, wait. You're hoo-rawin' me, Tom, I can tell. What have you been doing with it?" Belle demanded. "You haven't been pickin' seventy-pound loads again, have you?"

Tom said nothing, only smiled and looked with a twinkle toward his son who stroked the bag's worn ducking.

Belle now realized why the bag was so worn and said, "It's all the hauling you been giving Clayborne, that's what it is." She tried to look stern. "Just look at how you two drug it near to pieces!" She sat with arms akimbo. "Tonight I'll have to take this bottom seam out and make it into a new top." She fussed with the seam, muttering about the amount of work she'd been sentenced to.

Homemade cotton-picking sacks were fashioned from duck, or "ducking" as Texans called it, a durable closely woven cotton fabric similar to canvas. To make a cotton sack, farmers would fold four yards of duck double, sewing two of the open sides together with heavy thread, leaving one end open to form a rectangular bag. The bag would be turned inside out to hide the seam and a brass ring would be sewn on the bottom for ease of lifting and to provide a means for hanging the bag on a cotton scale. Finally, a four-ply strap of duck would be sewn to opposite sides of the mouth, and the bag was ready to use.

A picker normally pulled the sack so that only the lower, cotton-filled half was exposed to dragging up and down cotton rows, the upper half remaining untouched and wear-free. Most pickers pulled their bags with one side facing the ground for two weeks, then turned the bag over to even out the wear for another two weeks. With normal fifty-pound loads, the bag's lower end would be well worn on both sides after about four weeks in the field. It would then have to be reversed end for end: the worn bottom-end seam would be taken out to form a new mouth, and the wear-free collecting mouth would be sewn shut to make a new bottom, with the brass lifting ring sewn on the new bottom seam and the strap sewn onto the new top.

Belle mock-complained to Tom: "Look at all this work! I'll have to use the sewing machine, sew up this here top and take the brass ring off, sew it on t'other end by hand. You know how hard it is to push a needle through this ducking by hand, don't you, Tom?"

"We're just going to work you right to death, Clayborne and me, aren't we?" smiled Tom, giving Belle a hand up from the grass. They stood together for a brief moment, joying in each other, not needing the words they could not find. Peace shone from their faces.

"I'll take the boy indoors while I warsh the dishes," said Belle, gathering up the utensils from their dinner. "It won't be long afore I'll be back to help you pick. And I'll take the peroxide to that finger again." As she strolled toward the weaning house with little Clayborne by her side, Belle called back over her shoulder, "I'll have my cream and eggs ready by ten tomorrow morning. I know how you like to get going good and early."

Simple life, simple pleasures, simple times.

The mules stood ungratefully hitched to the cotton wagon, not eager to work. The eggs and cream snuggled under the cotton, burrowed into soft lint and covered against the spoiling sun. Nine dozen eggs rested safely in their crate beside the cool cream mellowing in its three-gallon shiny metal bucket. A tarpaulin covered the wagonbox tailgate, ready to be unfurled over the billowing cotton in case wind or rain blew up on the way into town. A brief thin September shower still lay puddling on the Grand Prairie clay this Saturday morning, but not enough to make the roads muddy. The clouds were clearing off and the rest of the day promised enough sun to temper the chill.

Breezes riffled through the oak trees around the weaning house, rousing old tannin and the smell of acorns ripening. Hackberry trees added their sharp and pungent note. The dirt gave off its sweetly musty bouquet, rich and savory like wild mustang grapes, the maturing green smells of approaching autumn.

At exactly ten o'clock, Tom had finished the chores and helped Belle up to the high spring-mounted wagon seat. He handed little Clayborne to her, then walked around his mule team checking their doubletrees, as customary, and climbed into the driver's seat. The boy babbled happily, "Ride! Ride!" as Belle wrapped a canvas wagon sheet around him so that only his nose and eyes were exposed. The boy bit the fabric's edge with satisfaction.

As Tom snapped the reins and got his mules moving, he choked, his breath suddenly labored and coming in wheezes. He gasped heavily and struggled to keep control of the wagon as they pulled out of the farmyard and onto the old ruts leading to the road.

"Your lungs congested again, Tom?" sympathized Belle. "Ought to see Doctor Durham about it."

"It's just the asthma come again, Belle," Tom said in an alarmingly liquid voice. "It does that sometimes just from lifting things. Doctor Durham gives me things for it" — wheeze — "when it's real bad."

Clayborne watched his father wide-eyed, too young to realize what was happening or to be concerned. His father was breathing funny, that's all, and it made an interesting show.

With Tom fighting for breath, they drove stubbornly northward past their cottonpatch and made a U-turn southward through the farm gate shared by Tom and his father, James Perry, and onto Chalk Mountain Road. "This spell ain't too bad" Tom reassured Belle. "I can feel it lettin' up already." Despite the distress he had the presence of mind to cast a glance at the line of mailboxes near the gate, but no mail waited in the metal box on which was painted:.

Tom B. Perry

Route 2, Box 66

Hico, Texas

Perhaps it was the rain that had kept the road dust down, but his chest gradually heaved less fitfully as they drove southward to Hico. Belle still frowned in concern, even though her husband's breathing gradually settled to normal. Minutes later, when Tom seemed more relaxed, Belle asked, "How did you ever catch the asthma, Tom?"

"You don't catch it," Tom explained. "Most folks that have it" — wheeze — "are born with it. But it happened to me when I was about twenty-three, I guess, or maybe twenty-four, I'd have to think."

In counterpoint to his words, the wagon jolted and clattered on its leisurely way to market eight and a half miles away. Clayborne sat back to watch the mules and the road passing under their hooves.

"It was across the way on Papa's farmstead, down in the rootcellar, you know, by the front gallery. You can" — wheeze — "just barely see where it is right now, see there?" He pointed back to the Jim Perry farmhouse which lay farther off the road than his own place. Clayborne looked where his father pointed, but saw only his Grandad's familiar farmhouse and paid no further attention.

"Well, we had rats down there that summer, getting into the potatoes and onions and things. So I took some sulfur and wrapped it in a wool cloth and tied it around a stick. I took it down in the cellar and set it on fire to kill the rats — or drive them off, anyways. While I was getting out, I got a good whiff of sulfur fumes and it like to knocked me out. After that I always had the asthma."

Tom turned his mules half-right where Chalk Mountain Road made its bend into Prairie Springs Road. His breathing was steady now. He stuck his chest out, testing his lungs. "It's done. That wasn't a bad spell at all. Doctor Durham can't do much with the asthma 'til it gets real bad. I remember one time I just about died from it. Papa had to call him in the middle of the night and he came out and gave me some morphine. It's a pain killer, but it fixes the asthma so you can breathe better. But if you're born with it, Doctor Durham says, you can go live in Colorado. I guess the air's better for you there."

The conversation stopped and the wagon went on, bearing nearly a ton of cotton slowly westward, past Camp Branch School. A half-mile further, they passed Prairie Springs Baptist Church on Little Duffau Creek. By then little Clayborne had fallen asleep leaning against his mother. Two and a half hours after pulling out of their farmyard, the Perry family was in town.

Saturday in Hico was always a big day for local farm people. Many wagons white with cotton streamed into town from all directions on this market afternoon. Tom and Belle Perry drove into the town's north entry on the Hico-Duffau road that became Cedar Street in the little city's grid. They turned right at Second Street, past the gasoline pumps of the new filling station, past the Porter Drug Store and into the crowded center of town. One- and two-story business buildings dominated the small downtown area, which boasted two hotels, four restaurants, five boarding houses, a bank, two barber shops, a lumber yard, Driscoll's furniture store, an ice plant, three butchers, a baker, a soft drink bottling works, a harness shop, a life insurance agent, two jewelers, a laundry, a livery stable, a furniture store; three grocery merchants — Petty's, Carlton's and Randall's — two hardware merchants, a milliner, two photographers, a shoestore, two cotton gins and a cottonseed oil mill, a newspaper — the *Hico News Review* — two feed stores, a saloon, two clothing stores, a pool hall, two print shops, an auto stable, a Texas oil company salesman, an implement store, two dry goods stores, a variety store, a tailor shop, a tombstone marble cutter and a candy kitchen. Six blacksmiths and a tinner also plied their trade at various locations in town, along with two well drillers. In sum, it was a thriving little rural community.

Several automobiles made their way through the bustling streets of Hico today — the Perrys saw Vincent F. Wieser's new 1912 Olds touring car on its way out of town down Walnut Street. Years ago Wieser had immigrated from Germany and now owned Wieser Flour Mills, the biggest business in town. Everyone envied his car. But the few automobiles in evidence today, mostly Ford Model Ts, were lost in the throng of farm wagons. Mule-drawn cotton wagons jammed Hico's main drag, Second Street, the in-town stretch of an east-west road that would one day become Texas State Highway 6. Most of the traffic seemed to flow to the two cotton gins between Avenue A and Avenue B on Pecan Street, just south of the Texas Central railroad track.

Tom maneuvered his wagon through the traffic directly to Hansen's Produce Company on First Street. Clayborne woke up when the rhythm of the wagon wheels changed. He looked around with sleepy eyes. The ritual first stop on a Saturday trip to town was always the produce store where the cream and eggs were sold — no farmer could risk carrying them any longer than necessary. They might go bad, and that would be a domestic tragedy, since the cash they provided made up a substantial portion of the week's grocery money. And besides, the townfolk liked their eggs and cream fresh, the fresher the better.

As the Perrys pulled up to the hitching rail of the produce market, a neighbor farm family from a mile north of the weaning house drove by in their wagon. "Yoo-hoo, Mrs. Perry," called a fine-featured woman. "How do, Mrs. Tate," answered Belle. Everett Tate called to Tom, "We were followin' behind you maybe half a mile! I'll see you at the gin." Little Clayborne took it all in with a wide stare. The families waved to each other, and the Tates drove on to Driscoll's furniture and grocery store.

Tom helped Belle down from the wagon, retrieved the farm goods from their cotton nest and carried them into the market. Today, across the busy produce counter, Belle's eggs brought 15 cents a dozen: nine dozen yielded $1.35. Her two and some-odd gallons of cream brought $1.50. She left the produce market $2.85 richer and felt wealthy indeed. She could buy the coffee and baking soda on her shopping list and have money left over. Their customary grocery store, Petty's, stood a few doors away from the produce market down Second Street. They clumped along on the wooden sidewalk, trying to dodge the crowd of busy Saturday shoppers. Clayborne saw a stray dog in the street, head low and tail wagging, trying to sidle up to the family. The boy cried, "Pup, Papa, Pup!"

"That's somebody else's pup, son," said Tom. "Don't you try and pet him any, you hear?" Turning to the dog, Tom sternly commanded, "Get out, suh!" in the typical Texas manner of addressing unknown dogs. The dog understood the instructions only too perfectly and scampered away tail between legs. Tom leaned close to Belle and told her quietly, "Notice he calls every dog Pup? I've a good mind to call his new dog Pup when we get it tomorrow."

The staples were purchased and it was time for dinner. Of course, there was only one place in Hico to go for dinner as far as Tom and Belle were concerned, Lynch's Cafe. And for a good reason: it was owned and operated by Belle's sister Sallie and her husband Wiley Lynch.

It was only a few hundred feet down First Street from the grocery store to the eatery. In the middle of the block, in the middle of the town, wedged into a solid string of attached business buildings on the south side of the street, stood the store-front cafe. When Tom pulled up in front, he peered through the big windows and saw Sallie scurrying among busy dinnertime tables. He hitched his mules to a post and helped Belle and Clayborne down from the wagon. Sallie Josephine Lynch looked up from serving customers and broke into a pretty smile that lighted the cafe interior. She ran out the door and stood waiting for them on the wooden sidewalk. "How's that young 'un?" she grinned.

Willie Clayborne Perry was not a shy two-year-old, and returned his aunt's smile with compound interest, laughing and saying "Auntie! Auntie!" He pronounced the word "Aint-ee" in the time-honored Texas habit of making As say their name. Belle coaxed her son: "Can you say 'Sallie', 'Hello, Auntie Sallie?' Are you going to say hello like a little man one of these days?" The child responded with the closest he could come to "Auntie Sallie," but his young soft palate and tongue could not yet manage *l*'s. "Aintee Sawee!" was good enough. Everybody laughed and gave him credit for trying.

"Howdy do to you, Sallie," said Tom, appearing from behind the wagon where he had been securing his load of cotton. "Do you have some chili for us today?"

"Do we have chili? Today we have the best chili this side of where ever it first come from. You all come right on in," enthused Sallie. "Linchie and me, we'll fix you up something good." Wiley Lynch was universally known to his fellow Grand Prairie denizens by the nickname "Linchie." Sallie hugged her sister and beamed at Tom. "We figured you'd be a'comin' into town today with your first cotton," she said. "Law, the wagons, they just been pouring in."

The four of them entered the small cafe amidst much talking and joking and looked for an empty table among the crowd of Saturday customers. Sallie remarked, "You'd think we were the railroad cafe the way we're filled up for dinner today. It must be the first cotton. But I expect some of these folks will be gone directly." The Lynch's hired waitress carried platters of chicken-fried steak to a table of laborers having their weekly splurge. The girl worked competently but unsmilingly in the noon rush. Sallie pointed across the thronged cafe and said to her sister Belle, "You all go take that place over yonder by the window and I'll bring you up some good dinner. Tom, you're going to want a big fifteen-cent bowl of chili today, I can just see it from the hungry look on your face. And I saved some roastin' ears for you that come in fresh this morning. I think my little Clayborne will like that." Sallie swooshed away, expertly dodging tables and customers on her way to the kitchen.

As the Perrys finished their meal, Sallie Lynch pulled up a chair from a vacant table and sat down to chat. The noon rush customers had gone and the cafe was nearly empty: neat oilcloth-spread tabletops shone in the dull light. Two travelling salesmen remained, trading business anecdotes. Both had ordered Kansas City steak dinners.

Sallie asked Belle, "Would you like to come over to the house with me while Tom takes the cotton to the gin? The hired girl can take care of customers this afternoon."

Belle looked hopefully at Tom, who nodded and said, "Sallie, I'd be obliged if you would take Belle and Clayborne up to the house. What with all these wagons comin' in today I'm like to be a long while at the gin." He peered out the window briefly, seeing ragged rows of clouds scudding across the autumnal afternoon sky. "Might even rain. Anyways, Belle, no point you and the boy sittin' out there in the chill."

Belle beamed and said, "I'll be glad to keep you company, Sallie."

Sallie added, "And you can pick up some sweets at the candy kitchen before Mr. Rainwater closes up tonight. I know how you like to get some of that peanut candy before you go home."

"I always figured you and Linchie picked that house just because it was right next door to the candy kitchen," joked Tom.

"Now, Tom, do you think me and Linchie's getting fat?" In the kitchen Wiley Lynch overheard their banter, and patted his belly at them from behind the order counter. In reality, both Wiley and Sallie retained the spare build common among farm people in this era.

"Well, I got to hoo-raw you about something, don't I?" smiled Tom. "It wouldn't be a Saturday in Hico without teasing you town folks a little."

Sallie smiled and sighed and said, "Town folks? I swaney, Tom, town

folks is what we are now. But Belle, you know how much I miss the farm.
It's so noisy here in Hico during cotton season. The gin runs all the time,
day and night, until the cotton's all in. I can hear it all the way up to the
house on Second Street. Then there's dogs a 'barkin' and cars backfiring.
You can't hardly hear the bugs humming in the trees around here. The
farm's a good life," Sallie concluded. "Don't you think about moving this
little fellow into town," she said, grasping Clayborne's arm.

The boy paused in his gnawing on a nearly stripped corncob and said
"Aintee Sa-wee" again, to everyone's delight.

"No need to worry about us movin' into town," said Tom, rising to
depart. "We're going to bring up this little fellow right, and that's on a
farm." He stood up and tousled his son's hair, eliciting a giggle. "Belle,
here's the money for the dinner." He laid several coins on the small table.
"Give it to Linchie when you two leave. I've got to be gettin' on down to
the cotton gin now. It has been good visiting with you, Sallie. Tell
Linchie it was a good dinner — he makes a proper bowl of chili. I'll bet it
is the best this side of where ever it first come from. And them roasting
ears was as good as what we grow. You tell him that."

As Tom walked by the kitchen on his way out, he swung behind the
counter for a short moment, and called to his brother-in-law, "I just told
your wife to tell you the food's good. Don't let it go to your head none,
you hear?" Wiley Lynch grinned his reply. Tom said, "If I don't see you
after I'm done at the gin, I'll say goodbye now. Take care of yourself and
don't work too hard."

When Tom drove his wagon across the Texas Central railroad tracks
toward the gin near the Bosque River, he found nearly forty wagons in
line in the street before him. He patiently reined in at the rear. Two dingy
metal-roofed gins served Hico, opposite each other across Avenue A — an
elegant name for a muddy dirt street — and both usually sprouted lines of
cotton wagons in the fall, like long seasonal tails in the streets. Each
wagon took twenty minutes while the gin removed the dirt and twigs,
separated the cottonseed, cleaned the lint, and condensed and wrapped
the single bale that was the yield of a wagonload of cotton. Most gins
handled three loads at a time, which meant processing nine wagons an
hour. Tom faced a wait of more than four hours. During heavy cotton crop
years, it was not uncommon for farmers to stay in line all night waiting to
be "ginned off," as they called it. The womenfolk did not accompany
their men into town during such times.

As he walked toward the sign-up shed, Tom thought he saw the wagon
of his father far ahead in the line. Making his way forward, Tom ran a
regular gauntlet of obligatory neighborly greetings:

Everett Tate, who had passed Tom at the produce market, waved and
called, "Told you I'd see you here. You must of stopped in at Linchie's,
huh, Tom?"

"Yessir, that's just what we did. Have you seen my Papa, Mr. Tate?"

"No, I haven't, Tom. But I haven't been looking for him. Did you expect him?"

"Just thought I saw him, that's all. I'll find him. So long."

More wagons brimming with cotton and another neighbor.

"See you got here early, Mr. Arnold." Brooks Arnold and his large family lived some two miles north of the weaning house. He had come alone today.

Arnold replied, "Started out right after chores, Mr. Perry, about nine o'clock. You know your Pa was here before any of the rest of us from Dude Flat."

"He is here then? I thought I saw his wagon, Mr. Arnold. I'm going up the line to find him right now."

Tom's footsteps crunched on the gravelly dirt street as he passed the massed cotton-laden wagons of farmers he did not know, people from south and west of Hico. He soon saw another neighbor.

"Hello, Tom Moore!"

"Hello, Tom Perry! You seen any cotton lately?"

"Haven't seen any all day," Tom deadpanned.

"Are you coming over after Sunday School to pick up that pup for your boy?"

"I'll be over in the buggy tomorrow soon as I get Belle home from Sunday School. How's the pup?"

"He's all weaned, but he ain't housebroke yet. He's a cute pup. Your boy'll really take to him."

"Clayborne takes to any dog. Had to keep him from petting a stray in the street today. Tom, I'm looking for my Papa up here somewheres. Have you seen him?"

"He was palavering with Mr. Robinson just a few minutes ago. Must have been talking politics because their arms was waving real big. Looks like they must of started out early this morning because both their wagons are about ten places up the way there. I think the cotton-yard man chalked number forty-seven on the side of his wagon. You'll find him easy. See you tomorrow."

The next wagon.

"Hello, there, Mr. Blair."

"Howdy, young Mr. Perry," replied the elderly farmer. "Your Pa's up the line a bit, you know."

"I was just looking for him, sir. You know where he is?"

"Right yonder."

"Thank you, sir."

Standing among the wooden wheels and side planks of the queued farm wagons, the elder Perry was absorbed in conversation. Jim Perry was a taller, patriarchal prototype of Tom, with heavy eyebrows that tended to the shape of a steep gable-end roof, giving him a perpetual slightly astonished look. His prominent nose shadowed a bushy walrus mustache that hid a gentle mouth frequently tipped with a smile. His gray hair was parted on the right, far to the right of his head, and combed up and over the dome of his finely shaped cranium, giving him somehow a slightly regal appearance.

Tom spotted his father. "Papa!"

Jim Perry looked over his shoulder and squinted. "There you are, son. I wondered if you were going to make it into town today."

"Yes, sir, we had a load to get in. Belle and me stopped in at Linchie's to get some dinner. She and Clayborne are gone over to Sallie's and I'm tied up back at the end of the line."

"Say hello, to Mr. Robinson, son."

"Hello, there, Mr. Robinson."

"'Afternoon, Tom."

"We were just talking about President Taft running for reelection. I read not too long ago in the *St. Louis Republic*" — this semiweekly Missouri newspaper had attracted subscribers among Texas farmers for many years — "about this Woodrow Wilson fellow the Democrats have nominated. He's a college professor, did you know that? How would you like to have a Democrat for president, Tom?"

"I saw it in the *Republic*, too, sir, but I don't follow politics much, like you know. It just seems t'me that we have better cotton prices when a Republican's in, that's all. But don't let me interrupt. You and Mr. Robinson go right on."

"Oh, no, son, we're all done. We've already decided that the Bull Moose party won't split the ticket. Teddy Roosevelt's going to win for president in 1912, so we'll have the Rough Rider back with us. All we have to do now is wait and see if the voters agree with us. Mr. Robinson's wagon's ahead of mine, and his turn is coming up to get ginned off right quick anyway. You stay here a minute."

Jim Perry turned to his neighbor and said, "It's been good talking to you, Ed. I can always count on you for a lively bout of politics."

Ed Robinson walked away and father turned to son, holding up a gin ticket, Number 47. "Forty-six folks beat me to it this morning. First cotton's always like this. I've been in line about four hours now. I expect you'll do the same."

"Yes, sir, I expect so," replied Tom. He shifted position uneasily. "Papa," he said. "I'd like to ask you about my rent this year."

"What's on your mind, son? You look troubled. Is something wrong?"

"Oh, no, sir," Tom protested, looking to see if any bystander might overhear. He spoke softly, confidentially. "It's just that our cotton is pretty good this year — better than last — and we've kept it clean and all."

"Well, then?" asked Jim Perry.

"Sir, I've figured out about how much cotton we're going to have, and it looks like we're going to have ten bales, two more than we did last year. I don't know what kind of pay — "

"Same rent as we agreed, son. One-quarter toll on your cotton, one third on your feed. You already gave me a third of your oats, and the corn's starting to come in now, and it'll be one-third of your cottonseed to feed the cows like it was last year."

"Yes, sir. I know that, sir."

"Well, what is it, son?"

"It's not the rent part I'm worried about. It's the cottonseed prices, Papa. I know that cotton is up a little, but I haven't heard what cottonseed's paying this year. With those extra bales of cotton I've raised, after they're ginned I'll have two extra bales of cottonseed. The way I've figured it, after I pay you one-third toll, and bring home enough cottonseed to feed my own animals for the year I'll still have enough left to sell some for cash. If cottonseed's bringing at least thirteen dollars a ton I'll have enough money to save something this year, Papa. I heard what cotton's going for, but I don't know how cottonseed prices are." Tom smiled tentatively, hoping for some good news.

"I see," said Jim Perry. "You're thinking like a good farmer, Tom. And you know that cotton's bringing about 11 cents a pound this year. That's better than the 10-cent cotton we had last year, but we'll probably not see 13.83-cent cotton like 1910 for many a season. And I don't think we'll see $22.88-a-ton cottonseed like 1910 for many a season, either."

The father paused for effect. "But you're in luck, son. If you need $13 dollar cottonseed, by Gaddies, you're going to get more than what you need to tuck away some cash: it's going for $16.74 a ton today!"

Farmers prided themselves on such precision with decimal places when it came to cotton prices.

"Well, I'll be switched!" cried Tom, overjoyed. Then he paused and asked, "What are they asking to gin a bale this year?"

"Both gins are charging eight dollars a bale, worse than the six dollars they wanted last year. Cotton prices go up, gin prices go up."

"That's all right," said Tom, grinning. "I'll still do better than I figured. Now here's something else." He looked earnestly into his father's eyes. "How are you doing for cottonseed feed? Do you have enough left so I can sell today's bale of seed for cash? It would sure help to pay off my ginning costs for the rest of the crop."

"We've got enough left," replied his father. "You go ahead and cash this bale out. We'll start taking toll on your next load."

"Thank you, Papa. That will help a lot. I've got to go sign up and get my number. Belle and me will see you and Mama in Sunday School."

"Now wait just a minute, son. I wanted to talk to you about tomorrow.

Don't forget that your mother and me are coming over to the weaning house for Sunday dinner, too, young man. And we expect a right proper chicken dinner."

"Oh, yes, sir," Tom said, embarrassed. "I'm sure that Belle didn't forget. We'll put on a good feed, don't you worry, sir. But I might be a little late because I have to go over to Tom Miller's after Sunday School to pick up Clayborne's pup."

Tom went to the foreman's shed and received card Number 85, which meant that 84 farmers had arrived before him since sunup this Saturday in 1912.

"Where's your wagon, suh?" demanded the cottonyard foreman.

"It's back down the street there nearly two blocks," replied Tom.

"Take this here chalk and write number eighty-five on the side," ordered the foreman. "And bring the chalk right back. I need it. And bring your wagon up to the window next time so's I can write the number on it myself."

"Yes, sir."

Tom returned to his rig, chalked a big 85 on its side, returned the chalk to the foreman, went back to his wagon and began the long wait. He decided against bringing his wagon up in line next to Tom Moore's because he wanted to do some private thinking. The wagon line was really not in any rational sequence, since everyone did what Tom had decided against, bunched up with their friends and waited until their number was called. Helter-skelter, all around Tom the Saturday life of the town buzzed and thrummed like a busy hive.

Tom used the hours of waiting to perform fresh calculations of his farm income this year. At about $56 per bale, he would bring in at least $565 gross with his ten bales, less $80 for ginning. He would pay his father $141 — one-quarter toll for rent on the land and weaning house, which would leave him $344 or more in cash for the year. As it came out, that was some $20 more than he got for his 8 bales of cotton last year. And if he could sell 2 bales of seed — about one ton — at more than $16 a ton to the cottonseed oil mill, which offered better prices than the gin, he would have nearly $40 more than last year, and he could put all of that and perhaps more in savings. He had recently bought a sorrel mare colt — and named her "Pet" — but even with that expense he could cover 1912 with $320 cash. It wasn't much, but it was enough to live on, albeit frugally, and he would have a little something to put in savings.

Half a block away a mid-afternoon freight train came clanking and screaming into the Hico station. It stayed only long enough to switch a string of boxcars and cattle cars onto the town siding and then left westbound for Cisco, Texas. People were beginning to move west out of Hico. West to Lubbock and Dalhart. They could have that restless life, Tom told himself. He was now on the way to being a real Texas farmer right here near Hico, saving money so he could put the weaning house behind him and one day buy his own land. The idea of owning his own land was becoming an obsession with him, but one he never spoke about with anyone, not his friend Tom Moore, not his father, not even Belle.

When Tom's turn came at the gin, he drove his wagon next to two others under the high corrugated metal tower with its big dark bays, and then into the deep shadows of the vacuum lift, pulling under one of three large snakelike suction pipes. A gin laborer took Tom's ticket and then wrestled the nearest suction pipe into the wagonload of billowing white bolls that had only hours ago been growing in the Perry cottonpatch. The ravenous suction device quickly devoured nearly a ton of fiber and seed, emptying the wagon, and the twenty-minute ginning process began. The cotton had been sucked up into the tower where a series of extractors, feeders and cleaners — actually nothing but specially constructed rollers and toothed wheels — removed stems and other trash. A conveyor took the clean lint to the gin stand, a device to remove lint from seed.

In the gin stand, ganged fine-tooth circular saw blades mounted on a revolving shaft performed two functions: the saw teeth took the seed cotton up to a series of bars between the ganged saw blades where the lint stuck to the teeth and passed through the bars, while the seeds — too large to pass through — were separated from the lint and fell out, nearly a thousand pounds of them, into a collector bin. Revolving brushes removed the lint from the saw teeth. The lint then went through a cleaner and condenser and finally into a hydraulic press that formed the wagonload of cotton into a bale. The 1,500-pound load of picked cotton yielded a bale of marketable medium-grade lint weighing about 500 pounds, and a thousand-pound bale of cottonseed.

When his bale of cotton was ready, all burlapped and strapped, it was loaded back in his wagon, along with the heavy bale of cottonseed. Tom drove to the cotton yard where his bale was weighed. His first bale of 1912 came in at 537 pounds and had been graded, so Tom was told, at "high middlin'" — as opposed to "fine," or "strict middlin'" or "fair middlin'" or "poor," the informal farm-town designations used instead of the alien language of official cotton-grade standards.

Tom also received a one-pound sample cut from his bale, which he took first to one buyer and then another, seeking the best price. The first buyer offered him 11.31 cents a pound, the second offered 11.32 cents a pound and the third only 11.29 cents per pound. There were usually three or four buyers in Hico during cotton season, and Tom suspected they spoke to each other frequently, because their prices tended to stay in a close range with each other. Tom felt that the second offer was as good as he could get, and sold his bale for a total of $60.78. The cotton buyer wrote Tom a check in that amount and the deal was made. Tom's bale would be batched with the others from this area, compressed, loaded in a boxcar on the Texas Central Railroad and shipped to Galveston, where it would be sold on the export market. Virtually all Texas cotton during this era was destined for international trade.

By the time Tom pulled up at Wiley Lynch's home, it was nearly six o'clock and he had to hurry to take Belle next door to the Rainwater Candy Kitchen before it closed. He strode briskly up the walk to the Lynch home, an unpainted but solid and adequate house set back from the street. Tom knocked on the door urgently. Belle appeared immediately with little Clayborne and said, "I wasn't sure you'd make it in time." She swung the door shut behind her, calling, "We'll be back directly, Sallie," and took off toward the street with Tom and Clayborne in tow.

The final ritual of a Saturday in town was no more to be missed than the first one of selling the eggs and cream. The Rainwater Candy Kitchen was a typical small-town business with its wooden walk and shed-roof porch right on the street front. Its glazed door and twin windows could have guarded any kind of store, a cobbler's shop or a millinery salon, but once the customer got past its spring-hinged screen door — to keep the bigger flies out — there was no question what kind of store this was. The air was redolent of peanut candy, purveyed in two types: soft white and brown brittle. "Eat! Eat!," cried Clayborne.

Tom and Belle found themselves forced to wait in line. A last-minute crush of little boys with their Saturday pennies had arrived before them and clamored for their weekly sweets, pressing freshly washed after-dinner faces against Mr. Rainwater's glass display case and ogling the candy pans that came from his wood stove. Clayborne looked uncertain what to make of this crowd of little boys that were so much bigger than he. One young fellow dressed better than the others — which immediately identified him as a visitor, an outlander — had patiently awaited his turn at the counter and eagerly held out a single penny to the candy store proprietor. He asked in East-coast accents, "Please, sir, could I have a penny's worth of mixed sweets?" Without batting an eyelash, Lee Rainwater took the boy's penny, picked out one piece of white candy and one piece of brown candy, handed them to his young customer and said: "Here you have two sweets. You can do the mixing yourself." The boy's companions were hugely amused, but gave him no time for humiliation, tugging him by the sleeve and urging him, "C'mon, we still got time to watch the 6:15 freight train go by." Clayborne grabbed his mother's hand and warily looked after the little mob as they all crammed through the door at the same time and then vanished into the street.

Then the proprietor turned to his last customers of the day and said, "Ah, Mr. and Mrs. Perry, will it be the usual?"

Belle produced a dime and smiled, "The usual."

A dime in these times would buy a half-pound of peanut candy, and it had become a Perry tradition to take a quarter-pound of soft white and a quarter-pound of brown brittle. Lee Rainwater, a tall bald man of florid complexion and jolly countenance, commented, "It won't be too long before that youngster of yours starts coming in here by himself of a Saturday with his own penny in hand."

Tom smiled boyishly. "No sir, I expect it won't be too long now. Couldn't let him grow up without some good Rainwater candy, now could we?"

"Well, I hope not!" cried Mr. Rainwater. "Miz Perry, I hope you find the candy to your liking tonight."

Tom and Belle — feeling like two kids themselves — left the candy shop with Clayborne. The half-pound of Rainwater's candy would last the whole two-and-a-half-hour trip home and well into the next week.

A little before eleven o'clock Sunday morning, the Perrys arrived at Prairie Springs Baptist Church along with some forty other souls who came variously in buggies, hacks, wagons and surreys. Tom had hitched the new mare Pet to his Emerson buggy — at $115, a better vehicle than the cheaper Moon brand owned by most young farmers. He was proud to drive his family to church in this rig, but was not one to show off or make a spectacle of himself.

"Good morning, brother Perry," called a familiar face as Tom helped Belle and Clayborne down from the buggy.

"Good morning to you, brother Miller. Do you have that special item all ready to go after church?"

"Yes, indeed, brother Perry," smiled Tom Miller. He winked at Tom and glanced furtively at the two-year-old Clayborne. "You come on over then and we'll give you something somebody will not soon forget. And I don't think your cat will forget it soon, either."

In the crowd outside the church this morning were Tom's parents, Jim — age 50 — and Lou Perry — now 52 — with their youngest son, 15-year-old Pitchford. Their older son James Leonard, 22, a large, gawky, carefree young man full of spirit and adventure, was attending church this morning in Iredell with his sweetheart Verna Morgan. Jim and Lou's daughter Julia, 17, was attending church in Hico with her gentleman friend Frank Cramfill. Also present in the crowd were Belle's parents Charley W. — 55 this year — and Laura Susan Blackburn — 49 in 1912 — with 12 year old Leona LaRue Blackburn, their youngest daughter and only child living at home.

The congregation slowly made its way into the white-painted frame church, ascending the four steps up to the large double front doors. This house of worship could boast no steeple and no bell, but possessed a steep gable roof which set it off unmistakably as a rural church, as did its rows of high plain windows on each sidewall. The churchliness of the structure was enhanced by its high foundations: they made the building appear taller and more imposing than it really was. The church stood on stilts against the three-foot floodwaters that occasionally overflowed from Duffau Creek and Little Duffau Creek — perhaps less than Biblical wisdom had been used to select the site of this church between two streams and near their confluence.

The worshippers — see them as they saw themselves — slipped quietly through the front double doors and across the bare plank floor into rows of long wooden benches fashioned from 1x4 lumber — the men generally sat on one side of the middle aisle and the women on the other. Church members would every so often have to take a hammer to these benches and pound in nails that had worked loose to snag clothing. Bare wall studs and bare rafters had been left exposed, a sign of the humble circumstances of the church's farm congregation. At the head of the aisle stood the pulpit and the minister's platform — the preacher would face north while the congregation looked south to him, the long axis of the church building having been oriented as close to north/south as rough carpenter's calculation would allow. At the south end of the church near the pulpit, two benches on each side of the aisle were turned inward, facing east and west — the "amen corner," as it was known, where members would come sit and testify, and where visiting dignitaries would sometimes sit in rural pomp and splendor, such as it was. In the southeast corner of the church sat a primitive organ that served its purpose, which was to accompany vigorous hymn singing that found its merit in inspiration rather than art. A dozen feet in front of the pulpit, in the center of the middle aisle stood a cast-iron wood stove, the only source of heat for the large building. A sheet-metal stovepipe towered above the stove and vanished into the roof planks at the high center ridge peak. In the harsh Texas winter when blue northers swept the desolate flats — fierce blasts of Canadian cold streaking down from the Arctic — the congregation would select benches prudently huddled close to the woodstove, and one of the faithful would always adjust its damper so the wood fuel wouldn't burn too fast.

Today was the third Sunday in the month, and there would be no preacher. No single small community in the rural Texas of this era could support a full-time minister of the gospel. Thus, church leaders worked out a circuit system in which one ordained preacher served four scattered flocks, holding worship services in a different community each weekend. The circuit rider came to Prairie Springs Baptist Church on the fourth Sunday of the month, leaving the local congregation leaders responsible for conducting Sunday School on first, second and third Sundays. The forty- or fifty-member attendance on Sunday School days would swell to eighty or more when the preacher was there.

Brother Frank Dickson had been elected Sunday School Superintendent, and it fell to him this day to lead the worshippers, who were now settled and waiting in their rustic wooden pews. He stood before the congregation and asked them to rise. "Brothers and sisters, today my sister Alma Dickson is not able to be with us as she is tending the sick. Would Sister Belle Perry come forward to be our organist today."

Belle left little Clayborne in the care of Tom and went forward to take her position at the organ. She had learned to play by ear — using a chord method popular in these days — on the piano in her parental home. Brother Dickson instructed, "We'll first sing Number 32 in your Hymnal, *Amazing Grace*." The gathered farm families raised a joyful noise unto the Lord.

After this perennial favorite and a homely rendition of *The Old Rugged Cross*, Brother Dickson issued a call for prayer: "I would like to ask Deacon Charlie Blackburn" — Belle's father — "to lead us in prayer this beautiful September morning." Charlie Blackburn, a steady and imposing figure, knelt down, and waiting for the congregation to do likewise, bowed his head. He raised a prayer in tones that could be heard throughout the church, not reciting from a creed or a prayer book, but speaking from the heart. He thanked his maker for the blessings of the earth, and for the health and plenty they enjoyed, parsing out his thoughts in measured phrases perfected from long devotion. Deacon Blackburn remembered the sick and afflicted and asked divine guidance for lost souls who had not been converted to the fellowship of Christ. The prayer lasted about three minutes, and when it was done, the congregation answered with him with a great "Amen!"

Brother Dickson then read announcements of a forthcoming church supper and board meeting, and reminded members to always bring their lesson books from home study for Sunday School since Prairie Springs Baptist Church could not afford to purchase extras. Then Brother W. D. Partain was called upon to read from the Scriptures. He selected four verses from the synoptic Gospel of Luke, the parable of God's gifts:

> Consider the ravens: for they neither sow nor reap; which neither have storehouse nor barn; and God feedeth them: how much more are ye better than the fowls?
> And which of you with taking thought can add to his stature one cubit? If ye then be not able to do that thing which is least, why take ye thought for the rest?
> Consider the lilies how they grow: they toil not, they spin not; and yet I say unto you, that Solomon in all his glory was not arrayed like one of these.
> If God so clothe the grass, which is to day in the field, and to morrow is cast into the oven; how much more *will he clothe* you, O ye of little faith? (Luke 12:24-28)

These were verses a farmer could grasp, filled with homely images of barns and grain, familiar creatures and the humility of mind which recognizes that flights of fancy cannot make a body taller by the magic of thought. And these were verses that had been fleshed out in rolling pentameter, the King James version translated by scholars who had learned much from Shakespeare about lifting the hearts of men everywhere by setting lofty thoughts in lofty language.

After the Bible verses had been read, Brother Dickson announced, "At this time we will dismiss here and go into our classes. Our lesson for today, as you will find in your lesson book is Giving." Whereupon the congregation broke up into eight groups, evenly divided across the middle aisle between men and women and further divided into four age groups, adults on the two front rows of benches, then an empty row where the instructor could walk back and forth observing classwork, then young adults on the next two rows, an empty row, then younger teens the next two rows, another empty row, and finally two rows of children 12 and younger. Sunday School class this morning consisted of Bible readings in which a class member would read a verse and another would be asked to comment on it, to give its meaning, or to explain its application to Christian life. The youngest class had Bible cards with illustrations of some particular event on one side and written verse and explanation or questions on the other. The church hummed with activity during these simultaneous classes. During class time, a collection plate was passed and a report prepared by the church secretary. When the alloted class time was up, Brother Dickson stepped in front of the pulpit and announced, "Let us all gather once more up here in front for assembly." When the congregation had reorganized itself, the church secretary was called upon to read the report: attendance today was 42, and the collection was $4.13 — you didn't give more than a few pennies at church in this place and time. Another hymn was sung, another prayer offered — a benediction — and the Sunday School gathering was dismissed. Total elapsed time: one hour and ten minutes. This short period of foregathering and fellowship was a powerful dollop of social glue that held the community together.

No one rushed to leave the churchyard after Sunday School. It was a time of chatter and gossip, of informal farm reports and general keeping up on the rural news. On this September day the chill had gone from the air by noon, and the families spilled out to enjoy the autumn warmth among the standing buggies and wagons.

While the menfolk talked politics and cotton prices, Belle Perry spoke to Mr. and Mrs. Tom Miller. Clayborne sat on the gravel playing with pebbles. Belle thanked Mr. Miller profusely for his offer of "that special item," and then took Mrs. Miller aside — keeping an eye on Clayborne — to regale her with tales of the 1912 Perry kitchen garden:

"I heard all about *your* garden last Sunday, Mrs. Miller, so now you get to hear about mine. Now, our garden is off up in the field toward the gate from the weaning house," Belle began.

Mrs. Miller asked, "You mean up by the cotton patch?"

"It's practically right in the cotton patch, but over toward Camp Branch more. We planted in a low wet place over there where dirt kind of washes in and water stands sometimes in winter. This year we put out cabbage and tomatoes and onions and it's all come up real good."

"Oh, you know, Mrs. Perry"' said Mrs. Miller, "my grandmother used to call tomatoes 'love apples' and she wouldn't let us eat them because she thought they were poison."

"Well I declare," said Belle. "I never heard of that. I declare. They can't be too poison, because we've had tomatoes for years at my house and nobody ever got sick. I declare." Nothing daunted, Belle went on: "Well, we put out Irish potatoes" — as spuds were called — "and sweet potatoes this year, too. And radishes and beets and turnips and okra. And the squash comes in just about by itself any more. And of course we got the corn. And watermelons. And pie melons and crenshaws" — Crenshaw melons. "Oh, and this year we put out some mushmelons" — a melon somewhat similar to cantaloupe. "Tom just loves them mushmelons."

"We put out mushmelons this year too, Mrs. Perry. My Tom loves 'em like yours."

Tom Perry broke in and said, "Belle, I'd best take you and Clayborne home if I'm going to go get that special item right quick before dinner."

"Oh, yes, Mrs. Perry," interjected Mrs. Miller, "we'd all best get a move on. Clayborne will be so thrilled. Me and my Tom will be off now, Mrs. Perry."

As they climbed into the Emerson buggy, Tom reminded Belle, "Don't forget that Pitchford is coming to dinner with Mama and Papa, but Julia and Leonard are off somewhere else." They pulled out of the churchyard and drove away toward home.

"I know who's coming and who's not, Tom," Belle retorted. "I'd a'had you kill more than two chickens this morning if Leonard was coming — that big ole' brother of yours eats like a mule."

"Acts like a mule, sometimes," Tom chuckled. "He's still set on marrying that Morgan girl, you know. Us Perrys can be stubborn when we know what's right. I talked you into marrying me, didn't I?"

Belle laughed. "You don't need to tell me about that, Mr. Stubborn Tom Perry Mule!"

"Mule!" said Clayborne, practicing a new word. "Mule! Mule!"

Tom and Belle lost themselves in simple rustic hilarity.

"Don't let on, Papa," said Tom. "Clayborne's just woke up. I've got the pooch for him out here on the gallery. He's right in this pasteboard box."

Tom had watched through a porch window and saw Clayborne awaken from his nap in the weaning house bedroom. The boy was ready to face the world, and toddled into the kitchen where the women were preparing Sunday dinner. "Hello, Clayborne, did you wake up?" inquired his Grandmother Perry solicitously.

"Wake up, G'anma. Wake up, Mama," agreed the little boy, not quite making the "r" in Grandma but making his meaning plain.

"You're such a darling boy," cooed Lou Perry.

"Oh, Mother Perry," fretted Belle, "you're going to spoil that child rotten giving him all that attention."

"Well, I ain't never had me a grandchild before, and I like it right proper," asserted Lou. "And what do you think Grandma's are for, anyhow?"

The object of her affections leaned yawning against a leg of the kitchen table, staring blearily out the kitchen door to the front porch. There he saw his Grandpa Perry.

The boy's face lit up and he hurried onto the porch, calling "G'anpa!" As he trotted to the waiting arms of Jim Perry, he saw his father standing farther off and stopped in mid-step, nearly taking a tump. "Papa! G'anpa!" He paused for a second as if trying to make up his mind which way to go, but the cardboard box in Tom's hands caught his eye, and curiosity overwhelmed him.

Tom bent down to little boy level. Mysterious whines emanated from the box. Clayborne approached the cardboard container almost cautiously, with nearly theatrical slowness, and cocked his ear to listen intently. The child put his face close to the source of the whines, his diminutive hands prying aside the flaps that hid the little dog. Then the box was open. There it was! Two dark eyes in a black mongrel puppy face looked up pitifully from the box. Two bright eyes in a child's wonder-filled face looked down into the box. Magic! It was love at first sight.

The boy tentatively reached down to pat the puppy on the head. Thump, thump. The puppy responded with vigorous posterior wiggles, thrusting his two front feet on the side of the box. Grandpa Perry came and stood over them. The boy gave no shouts of glee as if he had won some prize. He seemed to understand that this was a living creature. "Pup, Papa. Pup, G'anpa. Pup," said Clayborne factually.

Tom indicated that it was all right to pick up the puppy, and said, "He's yours, son. You can hold him, but take care not to drop him. He's just a pup."

Clayborne picked up the dog gingerly and lifted it to his face, then hugged it close. "Pup," he said to the little dog. "Pup."

"Well, I'll be, Tom," said Jim Perry. "The boy seems to have a way with animals. He ain't rough and he ain't scared. And the dog likes him."

"I think they'll do fine together, Papa," said Tom. "Clayborne, you go show Pup to Mama, now, you hear? Go show Pup to Mama."

"You know that'll get your mother's goat, Tom, letting a dog in the house," smiled Jim Perry.

"I know, Papa."

As the boy disappeared into the kitchen with his new friend, Tom turned to his father, "We can wash our face and hands out here on the gallery bench soon as I fill up the wash bucket. Dinner ought to be ready right soon. The comb is inside on the dresser to comb your hair." It was understood that all men went out on the gallery and washed their hands before meals in Texas custom. Tom excused himself to go fetch some water for the wash bucket.

At the well — some fifteen feet around the back of the house — Tom tugged a rope looped over a high pulley hanging from a wooden wellhead box and hoisted a four-foot long, six-inch-diameter, bullet-shaped container up from the well. The dripping vessel hung suspended from the pulley while Tom secured its rope. He placed the family's cedar water bucket beneath the dangling metal container. At the trip of a valve in the container's bottom, cool well water splashed into the cedar bucket. When the bucket was full, Tom shut the valve and lowered the water vessel back into its sheet-metal well casing. Most local farmers owned this particular and peculiar type of domestic water apparatus.

Tom hauled the water bucket around the weaning house to the long front porch. The cedar bucket had its own special space on a shelf nailed between two porch posts, and Tom automatically set it in its proper place.

Lou Perry appeared in the kitchen door and demanded, "Which one of you two hillbillies told this little tyke to bring that varmint in the house?"

"Now, Mother," cajoled her husband, "we just thought you and Belle would like to see Clayborne's new friend. And don't forget, we let the cats in every now and then."

"That's right, Mama," agreed Tom. "Besides, Pup there ain't no varmint. I got the pick of the litter from Tom Miller."

"Must have been some litter," grumped Lou Perry. "Well, come on in, grub's ready. And call Pitchford in from the branch."

Jim winked slyly at his son and said, "I think she likes the critter — but don't try and get her to admit it."

"I'll run down and get Pitchford, Papa," called Tom, already ten strides toward Camp Branch. "He's probably catching frogs."

The kitchen table was set for a regular farm Sunday dinner, with bowls of crisp Southern fried chicken, Irish potatoes, baked sweet potatoes, boiled turnip greens, steaming biscuits, canned pears, dark sorghum syrup, and plenty of fresh churned butter. A peach cobbler bubbled in the oven. The table was set for five, which was almost as many as the Tom Perry family had chairs for — six cane-bottom, slat-back chairs was what they had for proper sitting at a dinner table. All the sturdy white china had been brought out of the safe, a peculiar type of kitchen cabinet common in 1912 Texas, with perforated metal doors to keep out insects and marauding rodents — the perforations were to permit ventilation for certain foods that were also customarily kept inside, such as bread. This item of Texas kitchen furniture is in 1912 becoming obsolete: the Sears catalogue for 1910 offered only two models of safe. By 1928, the word *safe* will be only a cross-filing for *cabinet*, and by the 1930s the article itself will fall victim to rural electrification and refrigeration.

Everyone sat down at the table — when large crowds came to most farm homes for Sunday dinner, it was necessary to eat in shifts, with the children coming last. But today, all sat together, Tom Perry at the head of the table with Belle opposite him, Jim and Lou Perry on one side, their son Pitchford and grandson Clayborne on the other, the two-year-old in his highchair next to his mother. Tom asked, "Papa, will you return thanks?" Tom Perry himself never said grace before meals. Nor did a living soul ever hear him offer a prayer of any kind in public. Perhaps it was the stubborn Perry streak in him, for he had once decided that Scripture called upon the faithful to pray only alone "in your closet," never in public like the Pharisees and hypocrites, and he stuck to it all his life.

Grandfather Jim Perry, however, was strong on returning thanks, and offered a heartfelt blessing at which everyone pronounced, "Amen!" Grandpa immediately gave the starting signal: "Everyone take out and help yourself, now." The savory food began its swift passage from party to party, following no particular system, and they busied themselves with "stoking up on vittles," as Jim and Lou would say.

Amid scattered conversations about the new puppy — who was lapping up milk from a saucer on the kitchen floor — and the price of cotton, Tom Perry asked his father, "Papa, why is it that this place is called Dude Flat? I've been meaning to ask you that ever since Clayborne came — I thought of it the night he was born."

Everyone at the table looked to the patriarch for the answer. Jim Perry buttered a biscuit and slathered it with sorghum syrup. In measured tones he said, "Well, now, then, I don't rightly know, son." The disappointment around the table was palpable — everyone relished his dinnertime stories, and there would evidently be none about Dude Flat. "You know how these names are," Grandpa Perry led them on. "Like Camp Branch: we don't remember any famous camp on this here creek. And east of here at Rocky, why do they call it Rocky? Lots of places have just as many rocks. And over southwest there's Prairie Springs — ain't hardly no springs on either Duffau Creek or Little Duffau around there. Maybe there was once."

Even when Jim Perry didn't know the answer, he could still weave a tale around it. "And we never have found out what they're talking about when they say Black Stump Valley. I've heard tell that up northeast in Black Stump Valley there used to be a big old liveoak tree, so well known all the travellers used to camp beside it in the old-timey days. People say it got burned down, maybe hit by lightning. Supposed to be a big old black stump over there somewheres, but I never saw it. Never knew anybody that saw it. I expect somebody just makes up these names to suit their fancy. And what about Sugar Hill? Anybody ever grow sugar up there? Might have been some cane grow there once a long time ago, but not since I been here."

Young James Pitchford Perry spoke up: "Papa, tell us again when it was that we came here."

The patriarch of the Perry clan straightened up. He knew the answer to this one. So did everybody else, but they loved to hear the story repeated, almost as if the words were solid treasures to be hefted and clutched and held up to the light. Jim W. Perry recited their migration as if it were a tale out of Scripture:

"The year was 1900. Hard times had come to Alabama. Terrible hard times. There was suffering and there was tribulation. You were only two or three, Pitchford, and I don't expect you remember it any. But, Mother, you remember. And Tom remembers. We were about starved out. The farm at Heflin wasn't enough to make a living for the eight of us. My job at the shingle mill wasn't enough to make a living. There we were trying to scratch a living out of that poor piney woods soil. And we'd just had a new baby. Law, we were sore afflicted."

"Then come a letter, a letter from our people in Texas, telling us to come work with them 'on the halves.' And we took up and went to town in Heflin, Alabama. There we sold our three mules. We sold all our plows. We sold all our tools. The hardware man at Heflin, he gave us $400. Just a few pieces of paper for all the years we'd worked that Alabama land. That was all we were worth, a few pieces of paper. So it was goodbye to suffering. I bought us all tickets for the train to Texas. We wrote 'Gone To Texas' on the cabin door. But the suffering wasn't over. The baby fell sick. It was so sick we brought a basket in the train in case he died on the way. We travelled on that train for two days and two nights, going west, going west, always west. West to Texas. West to a new life. When we got off the train, all we had was $180 and hope in the Lord. In about a month, the Lord called our baby home. It was a pitiful and a sorrowful thing to bury that poor little baby in this cold Texas ground. It was a terrible grieving time. But we tarried on, we did, working the new land 'on the halves.' It was good land, it made good crops. The hard times, the times of sorrow passed, and we did good. Bought our own land, we did. Paid for it in two years, we did. The Lord's been good to us.

Right good. Some of our Perrys have kept on going west, out to Lubbock. Going west. Doing good. It was going west that saved us. And that's how we come to Texas, son."

Lou Perry said, "Oh, Jim, you tell that so good. It makes me cry but it makes me proud. I can't hardly listen to that story without remembering back to Alabama where I was born. It wasn't all hard times, and young ones dyin', you know. I'll never forget that poor baby, but, then, we had some real good times, too. We had folks live a long time. We had folks live to be a hundred. Why my own Grandma Elder, she lived to be 107. We still have a picture of her over at the farm. That picture was took when she was 103. That was the year she decided to get baptized. I remember it well. Grandma Elder was born a Methodist and baptized as a baby, you know how the Methodists do. But she decided to join the Baptist church and be baptized again when she was 103. Now don't that beat all? Well, sir, the Baptists made a big to-do about it. It even got into the newspapers. She was all crippled up with the rheumatism, you know, and she had to have a wheelchair. And she couldn't get out of it so the preacher could baptize her. Well, they figured and they figured, and the preacher took up with a farmer who had a deep tank to water his stock. And the whole town turned out on that farm to see it when they took Grandma Elder, 103 years old, and they raised her up in the air with a block and tackle, wheelchair and all. Well they shooed away the cows, lowered her down, and the preacher baptized her right there in that farmer's stock tank. Now that was really something. I swaney, we had some good times."

"Oh, yes," agreed Jim Perry, "we had some good times. Back in Alabama my mother used to tell me about the first time she saw a heating stove. She said it was about 1852. Of course, she had never seen anything before then to heat with except a fireplace. One fierce cold day she went to town with her father and he took her in a store. She was just a young girl, and it was a strange experience for her. She was shy and hung back, just stayed near the front door. She noticed people in the back of the store standing by some big iron thing with a pipe running into the ceiling. It was a very cold day and it appeared to her that the people were getting warm by this big iron thing. She moved closer to it and realized that this funny looking iron contraption did the same thing as a fireplace."

Belle smiled and said, "Hard to imagine in these modern times how someone could never have seen a stove. What did they cook on?"

"Oh," answered Lou Perry, "they cooked right in the fireplace. Hung their pots on iron hooks over the fire."

"Must have been dirty work, and hard bending over that way," said Belle, looking toward her four-burner wood-fired pride and joy. "We ain't even *got* a fireplace here. I'd druther have my good iron cookstove."

Lou Perry said, "Well, I remember something my mother saw for the first time, Jim Perry, and it's more peculiar than what your mother saw. My mother had just gotten married, must of been right around 1860 when the War Between the States started up. Her folks had bought a slop-jar and she'd never seen one before. There it was, all nice and shiny porcelain with a pail and lid. She thought it was a cook pot for vegetables or stews. She piped up and told the folks, "Oh, this is so nice and big. It'll hold enough vittles so we can cook enough for dinner and supper both!" When they told her it was a chamber pot, she like to died of mortification. She'd tell me that story and say, 'Confound it to thunderation, daughter, don't you never make a fool of yourself like that.' Oh, I miss my old Ma in Alabama."

As 1912 had been, 1913 was a good year on the farm. Woodrow Wilson had won the election, and now slogans of "the New Freedom" were heard from Washington. It was supposed to mean Wilson's program to create conditions of greater economic opportunity for labor, farmers and small business. But under Wilson's vigorous prodding, Congress for the first time in years substantially reduced tariffs. And that would have an effect on cotton farmers in the next year. The Sixteenth and Seventeenth Amendments to the U.S. Constitution were passed in 1913, the former providing for taxation of incomes by the federal government, the latter providing for popular election of senators instead of by the state legislatures.

Tom's happy-go-lucky brother James Leonard Perry married the Morgan girl in 1913 just as he had set out to do, and at the wedding young Clayborne registered his first permanent memory: the bride Verna's white wedding dress. In that year Clayborne also got his first cherished toy, a new red metal wagon, which would be a prized possession for more than fifteen years. He spent many an hour in spring and summer lying on his belly under the shade of that wagon, his dog Pup beside him, watching his father and mother work in the cotton patch. The sun came shining and jackrabbits hunkered and Clayborne watched them, learning. He spent joyous hours playing with his little black mongrel friend, walking and running, chasing shadows and exploring the secrets of the barn with the cats that seemed to pay no attention to Pup.

The weaning house was the center of a simple but rich and earthy life. When work was done, day after day, Tom pulled his son in the little red wagon all around the farm, mile after happy mile. In summer, the rain some days fell so hard it felt like stinging wasps. Then Clayborne ran under the farm wagon where he and Pup sat listening to the water hammering the wooden wagon bed above their heads and staring out through the spoked wheels, watching the thirsty ground drink greedily. That fall Tom pulled Clayborne on his cotton sack during picking time, even though he knew the boy was getting too big. While the evenings of 1912 were still warm, they would stay out until the stars seemed bright enough to cast shadows. They would lie on the grass, scratching chigger bites and looking for the Big Dipper. Sometimes it was fun to pretend that the black sky was down, and that you could fall into it and fly away to the moon. Cotton prices went up again in 1913, and that made Tom Perry happy. He felt that progress was coming, slowly, painfully, but surely. While his boy grew and his wife became more lovely, Tom went on working hard, saving money to buy better tools, putting something away to buy his own land.

By 1914, Clayborne was old enough to ride the sorrel mare Pet. And that year Otis Perry was born, Clayborne's oldest cousin, son of the tall, rawboned Leonard Perry. The Perry clan was growing. In the summer, since the weaning house did not have an inside tub, the family often took their baths in Camp Branch, but Tom would not let his son play there alone because it was a favored habitat of venomous snakes — copperheads, water moccasins, and an occasional rattlesnake. And in a distant land, the rumblings of war in Europe fell ever so faintly on American ears.

Some argue that it was the loosening of tariffs, some that it was not, but in late 1914, cotton prices fell to 7.22 cents a pound from their 1913 high of 12.09. By early 1915, Texas farmers realized they had suffered a disaster. Their savings were all but wiped out. Tom Perry did not escape. His frugal life now became hard indeed. He had managed to scrimp together four hundred dollars, but it was safe in Hico National Bank, and would stay there until he had enough to buy his own land. His obsession to own his own land now grew into stinging frustration. And now he talked about it, to his brother Leonard and Belle's brother Fred Blackburn. Something had to be done. And there were other tragedies. Life had just dealt young Fred Blackburn a harsh blow: his infant son had fallen ill and died. At the funeral in the Blackburn home, four-year-old W. Clayborne Perry saw a dead person for the first time, a lasting image. Tom held the hand of his own son tighter looking at the pathetic little corpse. The evil times had come again. Indeed, something had to be done.

To the Perrys, it was obvious what the answer was: go west. Their father had gone west from Alabama and had done well in Texas. His father before him had gone west from Georgia and improved his lot. Their uncles and cousins had been going west within the past few years to Lubbock and other parts of West Texas, and they too were doing well. It had to be done.

In August, 1915, just as Clayborne was turning five, a land agent in Hico told Tom and Leonard Perry, Fred Blackburn, and now a fourth determined emigrant, neighbor Robert Dozier, about free government land. It was good land to be had for homesteaders under the Homestead Act of 1864, they were told. For a mere $50 dollar registration fee, they could sign up, get 320 acres of prime Colorado farmland, and if they proved it up in three years, it was theirs, legally theirs. The four young men decided they would go to Colorado to see the land before they signed on the dotted line. They took the train and spent two days in Colorado looking at free government land. What they saw was rolling expanses of grassland, rich short- and midgrass prairie. A real river, the Purgatoire — French for purgatory, how aptly named the young farmers would discover — a tributary of the mighty Arkansas, ran right next to the four half-sections that were being offered them, and pure springs came up in Trinchera Creek right next to the northeast 320-acre half-section. The land agent told glowing stories of successful farmers right here in Las Animas County, Colorado.

What he didn't tell was that these successful farms were all on riversides and all were irrigated. What the young Texans didn't see was the scant rainfall that made farming impossible on the benchlands they had been offered in this sere place. And they didn't see that twenty acres of this country could not provide grazing for even one head of livestock. They were young and eager. They were not experts in geography, soils, or meteorology. It looked good. They would learn otherwise. There were four 320-acre plots, a half section each, blocked up together, just waiting for the four of them. They signed on the dotted line.

-3-

COLORADO, HO!

TOM and Leonard Perry got much cotton in by early October. Fred Blackburn and Robert Dozier, too, had harvested good crops. At the gin they were relieved when the foreman told them prices had returned to some semblance of normalcy. Eleven cents a pound was better than seven. But the return of King Cotton to economic normalcy was not enough to keep them in Texas. It only meant they would each have a more reasonable amount of cash for their new beginning. Nothing could dissuade them from their visionary plans. They were taking up land in Colorado! Images of the new land burned in their minds. They had seen the future, and they thought it worked.

All efforts to talk the young men out of their dream failed. Jim Perry tried measured reasoning, pointing out that Colorado offered no supportive family to work with 'on the halves' during startup, it had no community of helpful neighbors close by, no Baptist church to nurture their souls, no telephone, not even a good farm market town, and that it was wrong to uproot their wives and children from security. They would not listen. Lou Perry tried emotional pleas, imploring them not to take away her precious children and cherished grandchildren, not to go off somewhere in the raw and dangerous West to this Colorado place. They would not listen.

In their hearts Jim and Lou had known that their sons would not listen, but they felt obliged to make the effort. Years ago, they too had felt the primal call of the West when they came from Alabama; it was not dire necessity alone that drove them to Texas, strong as that had been. Now it was that same call, of possibility and promise hiding in the prairie grass, that would lure their children to Colorado. But Colorado was so *far* west. It made them grieve, but in the end they were both resigned to the inevitable — four families would leave Texas, perhaps never to return. And so, in the way of their own ancestors, they said their tearless goodbyes.

"If things don't work out there in Colorado," said Jim Perry, shaking hands with his sons, "you come on back. I got more land than I can work and you're always welcome here."

Tom Perry told his father, "You're the best Papa a fellow could have, but you said it yourself, sir: it's you that's got more land than you can work." Leonard added, "We got to work our own land, sir. This is our chance, Papa."

Jim Perry brushed a hand across his wooly mustache and looked long upon his departing sons. "Do good, both of you, you hear?" he said. "And take care of your families."

The four young men took their family possessions to Hico, a wagonload at a time. Tom and Leonard Perry, Fred Blackburn and Robert Dozier together had reserved two cattle cars — not boxcars, but slatted, open cattle cars, normally used for hauling livestock. Half a car, they had decided, would be enough to carry the belongings and animals of each family. The four had laughed and joked when they placed the order with the railroad, but when they drove their loaded wagons into Hico and first saw the cattle cars hulking by the depot, the reality shocked them a little. Even high-spirited Leonard was taken aback. This was it. There were the cars, stark symbols of the perennial American questions: Where to? What next?

In the growing chill of October 1915 the farmers gathered on a siding of the Katy Railroad — the old Texas Central had been bought out by the Missouri Kansas & Texas line, the "Katy", and leased to Katy of Texas May 1, 1914. There, in view of the dingy tin-sided cotton gin and not far from Lynch's Cafe, the men wordlessly dismantled their wagons and their buggies and handed the pieces into the open-framed cattle cars. They loaded their cultivators and their turning plows, their walking plows and their planters. They loaded their cookstoves and dinner tables and a few chairs. They loaded their beds and lamps. Tom Perry loaded his son's highchair. When their hard goods were secured they drove their horses and mules on board. They took their chickens in crates. They brought feed for the animals, and hay and seed for their crops. Tom tossed in the dog Pup, now three years old and full grown. Then tall, rawboned Leonard Perry slid the slat doors shut and said aloud, "Fellows, that door just latched closed on everything the four of us own."

"Except the land in Colorado," grinned Robert Dozier.

Fred Blackburn clapped Dozier on the shoulder and said wryly, "Bob, Uncle Sam owns it until we prove it up."

At least, Tom Perry mused ruefully, they weren't leaving Texas with only a few pieces of paper money, as their parents had left Alabama. And he had nearly four hundred dollars still in Hico National Bank.

Now they stood waiting for hours beside the track for their train to come. The travel arrangements had been settled: the four men would go ahead of the women and children. The men would ride in the cattle cars with their goods and animals. The women and children had tickets for passenger accommodations on two different trains a few days later: first, Verna Perry and Mary Ann Dozier would go, then the sisters-in-law Myrtle Blackburn and Belle Perry. The men had said their goodbyes to friends and relatives, had seen to their wives and children back at their farms. The west-bound freight finally hissed into the station. They climbed into the cattle cars, two men to each car, and endured the jolts and bangs as their car was coupled into the Katy train. Now it was done. They were ready. The train began to move. As the steam locomotive chuffed and clattered out of Hico, each of the travellers fought back memories of what they were leaving. Think only of what is to come! All this — the homes and harvests, the strong weeds and hot summer days — all of Texas, was now the past. Merely prologue to what's to come. They would venture forth into the great world. They would be immigrants building tomorrow. Texas, goodbye! Colorado, ho!

The reality of their great adventure bit hard when the rumbling train got up to speed: the searching wind in their open cattle car erased the warmth from all it abraded. The train would not stop again until it reached Morgan, some thirty miles and nearly an hour away. Tom and Leonard in the first car unpacked canvas wagon sheets, shouting to Bob and Fred in the car behind them, "You folks got something to wrap up in?" The blasting wind fought their voices.

"We got wagon sheets and bed blankets," hollered Fred over the staccato music of the rails.

The four wrapped themselves tightly, each in the hay huddling alone against the miserable chill.

At Morgan their two freight cars were uncoupled from the Katy's string of cars and transferred — with a four-hour wait — to the Ft. Worth and Denver City Railway, the line that would take them through Ft. Worth, Amarillo, and on to Trinchera. Other Texans also heading west in cattle cars lined up here on the same siding. Night fell as the train consist was made up, and with the vanishing sun the temperature dipped below freezing. A friendly brakeman on the Ft. Worth and Denver told the men from Hico, "You go up and talk to the brains" — an uncomplimentary term for the freight conductor — "and he might let

you spell each other off in the clown wagon, the mail car up thataway."
They asked, and the conductor was agreeable. They could alternate, two
in the cattle cars to tend the animals and two in the mail car behind the
locomotive: the mail car was not only sealed from the wind but also
boasted a pot-bellied stove for real comfort. It was an unexpected
privilege — none relished the idea of spending three unbroken days and
nights in the freezing cattle cars.

Finally the lurch of couplings pulling taut crashed back through the
train a car at a time. They were going, going, going away, going west.
All through the night and morning the gentle rolling hills of central
Texas deflated, giving way little by little to austere horizon-held terrain
as they drew westward beyond Abilene — flat as the proverbial pancake.
At every little town on the interminable track, at every stop it seemed
that cars of new emigrants coupled into the train and immigrants
separated out. The state, the nation, were tilting, sheering west. On the
second day out from Hico they ascended the escarpment of the Cap Rock,
a gigantic table-topped plateau stretching well into New Mexico, and
began their long journey across the Llano Estacado, the Staked Plain.
There the old truism had originated, "Texas has miles and miles of
nothing but miles and miles." Slowly upward, slowly climbing the
imperceptibly leaning land, they headed into thinner, rarified air. When
the train descended the far side of the Cap Rock early the third day, out of
Texas and into the northeast corner of New Mexico, the immigrants had
gained nearly a mile in elevation. They had risen league by league in giant
iron-railed strides up the gradual slope of the Great Plains and into the
geological province of the Rocky Mountains. By twilight of their last day,
the highest peaks of Colorado's Front Range sawed the distant western
horizon.

All trace of the day had vanished. Each of the four men had elected to
ride with the animals on this final leg of their momentous journey.
Beyond the rattling slats the velvet winter sky soon took on the
disquieting dark of absolute space: there would be no moon tonight. For a
while it seemed to make no difference whether their eyes were open or
shut. But gradually out of the shivering gloom emerged silhouettes of the
patient mules and horses, swaying with the train's motion, outlined by
the distant Milky Way. The ragged path of light across the night sky now
seemed to blaze forth in galactic fire among the hard and splendid stars.
Towns went by on the midnight land, measured off from each other in
thirty-three-foot sections of iron rail, and the train stopped briefly at
every burg with a ramshackle station. Men got off and men got on.
America, the country itself seemed to be falling, leaping, galloping
westward.

The long starry night swung 'round, but the four men in the cattle car
did not sleep. They sat huddled quietly in wagon sheets, each sensing

dark mysterious shapes in the flying land out beyond the train. In the ridges and the mesas they felt the future stirring. Was it asking questions they could not answer? Overhead the Colorado sky was bigger, deeper even than in Texas. The land too seemed somehow bigger, the horizon farther off. Each of the men knew their journey would soon be over and they would be left to dwell with their families in this empty wind-swept place. They could feel the vastness draining their confidence away. Even the clatter and shake of the train seemed small now, swallowed up in the desert immensity outside, where there was only timeless silence and ancient grass and solitude and space. Deep, cold, eternal space, just a bubble in the glass of God.

Inside the cattle car, the heap of their dismantled possessions seemed pitiful, their immigrant ambitions pathetic. Though they said nothing, each man saw doubt growing within himself as the hours passed. Misgivings whispered in the metallic whir of wheels drawing them ever westward. The land would prevail. Fear. They might own the land for a while, but it would defeat them. Plain fear. The wilderness was like a horse nobody could break. It would dash their brains out, smash them to pieces. It was not panic they faced, but a staring, solid, unmoving fear. And although none said a word, each man finally made a pact with his fear. Each admitted to himself, yes, old sod, you can defeat me. Do your worst. I will live. Or die. Each man found his own cold resolve, and wrapped himself inside. Each would grapple with the imperial earth. No guarantees. How we face uncertainty is after all more important than how we deal with our convictions. At last, endless hours later, Tom Perry felt the train swing into the great leftward half-circle and gradual downhill run he and his friends remembered from their August journey. The lights of Trinchera, Colorado, glimmered only a mile ahead in the crystal night. Behind them, faint hints of yellow-mantled dawn washed the eastern rim of the Great Plains.

Willie Clayborne Perry was a bright five-year-old when his parents decided to move to Colorado. He was not concerned about leaving his home, because home to his mind was not a place, it was his people. Where his Mama and Papa went, he was pleased to go, too. And so he looked upon the move with unconcern.

In fact, Clayborne actually noticed the move only when all the furniture disappeared from the weaning house one October day. He paid more attention when Grandpa Perry drove him and his mother to Hico in the buggy and said goodbye in a way he had never said goodbye before. That evening Clayborne liked staying overnight with Auntie Sallie — she lived right next door to Mr. Rainwater's wonderful candy kitchen. Next day, the move became an adventure when his mother told him they were going for a long ride on the train. Clayborne had seen the trains of the Texas Central and later the Katy go by many times on Saturday trips into

Hico with his parents, but actually to ride on one was only a remote dream. When he and his mother went to the depot that morning and the locomotive moaned and squealed to a stop, Clayborne was ecstatic. Stepping up into the coach car was like entering a new world, a moving world going off into some unknown land. To sit on the shaped wooden seat with its cushion stuffing was to sit on the throne of a travelling kingdom. To the child's quick imagination, the grimy passenger coach was at least as fascinating as any fabled treasure cave. It was so fabulous, in fact, he didn't mind travelling with Mrs. Blackburn, his Uncle Fred's wife — Uncle Fred called her Myrtle — and her two-year-old boy Lawton.

Clayborne didn't even mind sharing his throne with the Blackburns' other child, his cousin Claytia — she was a month older than he, and she was a girl, but that was all right, because she tagged along quietly and was good at rummaging up interesting things from depot grounds during station layovers. At the Morgan, Texas, layover she and Clayborne shunned the crowded and dirty depot building with its dingy windows and bad smells. Instead they combed the dirt and grass outside, looking for tobacco cans, sacks and tags. Cans were the easiest to find, and several came immediately to hand. And, look! There's a good sack, there! Dump the remaining tobacco dust out. Why did grownups put that awful stuff in there in the first place? Now, it's better empty, it makes a fine treasure sack, with long drawstrings and a label marked with those mysterious symbols: HORSESHOE BRAND.

But the most valued object they sought was the tobacco tag, a circular metal seal attached to turn-of-the-century sacks of roll-your-own cigarette tobacco. They were pretty little things, and some had a colorful ribbon tail to enhance the bright reds and yellows of the button-sized metal tag. Say! What's that? There, just under the steps in the wooden sidewalk of the depot! It's one of those nice red ones with the long, *long* ribbon! Clayborne and Claytia *ooh*ed and *ah*ed at the ribbon on this tobacco tag, wondering what the lettering meant: "W & D. T. Co's Grainger. We have changed our tag to tin and added this piece because our paper tag is being imitated." The boy and girl surmised it must be an important message instructing children to find as many tags as possible. They looked further, but found no more. Too soon it was time to go, and their mothers instructed Clayborne and Claytia to get in the passenger coach of the new train and be quiet. Their total swag: two tobacco cans, a Horseshoe Brand and a Star Brand tobacco sack, and one Grainger tobacco tag. They spent hours admiring their loot.

The three days and nights riding to Colorado were a blend of tedium and excitement. Many people were joining the great movement west. Two burly men in the seat across the aisle talked about vast herds of buffalo that used to roam here and how hundreds of thousands of the huge animals supported bands of wild Indians. One of the talkers, a wiry muscled man with a bristling mustache, claimed to have lain awake at night on bivouac with the cavalry in his youth, listening to the eerie rumble of stampeding buffalo fifty miles off, and even at that distance feeling the ground tremble with millions of hoofs. The two five-year-olds listened transported — for a while. When the stories paled, the young boy and girl decided to fidget. They were intent upon fidgeting. They went to the toilet. They went for water in paper cups. They asked when they would be in Trinchera. Then they did it all over again. And again.

On the second day out from Hico, more people got on and got off at every stop, going west. Going west. The inexorable movement west. The third day it was the same, but shortly after noon, several passengers pointed out a distant range fire near Amarillo, and everyone strained to see out the dirty windows. A mile-high billow of smoke towered in a mushroom cloud over the landscape. Clayborne was disappointed that he could see no flames at the base of the faraway smoke. What kind of range fire has no flames? Then back to boredom and nightfall. Late that night, while many travellers slept, the train made another of its endless stops. Then the Blackburns and the Perrys got off.

They were in Trinchera, Colorado. They stepped into the depot to get their bearings and find accommodations for the night: their menfolk would not arrive to take them to the new homesites until morning. The little station was typical of thousands that dotted America's booming rail network five and ten miles apart: a long, gable roof with projecting eaves over a clapboard frame box of a building perforated with tall dirty windows. Passengers going into such stations stepped off their trains onto the usual wooden platform where a four-wheeled baggage wagon stood at the wait, attended by a man known in railroad argot as the baggage smasher. At this particular station, the educated and alert among the Ft. Worth & Denver City's customers might wonder why the name on its depot sign did not match their tickets or contemporary maps: a lackadaisical sign painter had misspelled the place name as TRINCHERE on both ends of the station, and railroad officials were loath to expend funds or effort to correct such a trivial mistake. How many homesteaders could read that well anyway?

Inside the grimy building they found a stuffy little waiting room with a cast-iron coal stove and wooden seats with iron arm "rests." The floors squatted in disarray, littered with sawdust and discarded scraps of paper. The walls hung papered with a disorderly spectacle of tacked-up handbills advertising excursions, announcing a local church "sociable," and inviting one and all to a cattle auction down the tracks at Coloflats — last summer. Painted on the south wall of the freight room stood an inscription in black paint: J. J. Primrose and Co., Wool Broker, Trinidad, Colorado, 6-11-'95.

Although it was nearly midnight, the little depot crawled with people. A boom in homesteaders fed the railroad, and three crews were required to keep the station open twenty-four hours a day. In addition to the ticket agent, a freight agent stayed on duty selling passage for sheep, wool, cattle, hogs, grain, goats, buffalo bones, building supplies, lumber, groceries and household goods. An operator-telegraph agent also remained on duty, his services required to insure safe operation of the trains. The operator-telegraph agent's quarters contained the usual assortment of railroadly paraphernalia: a table with telegraph instruments, jars of battery acid, a wall clock, a chair with each leg set into the socket of a glass telegraph insulator to guard against lightning storms, another chair not so protected for callers who qualified for entry into the inner sanctum, a small safe, lanterns with red and clear glass globes, red and white signal flags, handled hoops for passing orders up to locomotive engineers and conductors of moving trains, rate books, ticket stamps, a brass seal, a stick of sealing wax, a torch for melting the sealing wax, Bullinger's Postal and Shipper's Guide (out of date), broom, duster, typewriter and a large cuspidor in the far corner.

Belle discovered from the ticket agent that Trinchera was graced with exactly one hotel and one cafe. The cafe lay but a block away on the main street of Trinchera, but was closed now after midnight. But Mrs. MacKenzie's Hotel could be found up the street, several blocks away from the depot in the gloom. With some trepidation, the two women and three children made their way along Trinchera's single southbound thoroughfare, past a dark and spooky general store and post office, thence onto a rutted wagon path and so to the hotel. It was a low-slung, one-story, gable-roofed adobe structure not twenty feet wide and sixty feet long, with a shed-roof porch over a rickety wooden platform — the grand foyer for the single front door with tattered screen. The proprietress of the hotel, Mrs. MacKenzie, had remained awake to receive them at this late hour. She had been expecting them, it seems, for Tom Perry had left word with her. The hotel could boast only six small sleeping rooms, five of which were already occupied, so the families fared the best they could in a single room. They were glad to have a motionless bed at last, and they all slept the sleep of the exhausted.

Next morning in downtown Trinchera, the Kane Cafe breakfast, as usual, was a frantic affair in the kitchen but a somewhat leisurely experience for the waiting mob of boom town customers. Mrs. Kane, as usual, waited table as best she could and did some of the cooking while her husband, as usual, served as busboy, dishwasher and overworked fry cook. Belle and Myrtle peeked timidly in the door first, unsure about these roisterers, then quietly took their children inside and slid into a vacant booth. Mrs. Kane, the beanery queen, as the railroaders called her, noticed the women and children and hastened to introduce herself loudly and cordially.

"How-do, ladies! You folks new around here?" she bawled.

"Yes'm," replied Belle. "Came in on the train last night. Our men folk's comin' to get us in a little while, take us out to the new place."

"Goin' to settle here?"

"Yes'm, we sure are."

"Well, you just make yourselves to home here and have some breakfast. This here's a friendly place and these galoots won't hurt ye none." She shouted to her customers: "Will ye, boys?"

Murmurs of "No, Miz Kane, Nope, Unh-uh" came gurgling through sips of coffee and bites of scrambled eggs.

The Texas women relaxed a little, put at ease by Mrs. Kane's friendly attention. After ordering a light breakfast they found the food to be rushed in the cooking and slow in the serving, but it was fresh, including the butter which Mr. and Mrs. Kane churned each morning right in the kitchen. They poured heavy cream into a steel cylinder suspended in mid-air between two springs, one under, one over. They gave the bizarre device a good slap in passing every minute or two, and its springy up-and-down dance did the rest — the butter was ready in little more time than in a regular churn.

When their order was delivered, Belle remarked, "Trinchera seems to be growing up in a big way, Mrs. Kane," pointing to a dozen construction wagons plying the main street.

"It surely is, honey," the stout and sturdy Mrs. Kane replied. "We're getting a new school and a service garage for automobiles, and we got a new church and a gasoline pump right across the street there. This main drag is growin' right up." There may have been twenty buildings in all of Trinchera.

"A school . . ." mused Belle, reminded of the future education of her boy. "Will they have a first grade, do you think?"

"Oh, I'm sure they will," assured Mrs. Kane. "And I'm sure they'll have class at least five months of the year."

Frontier education was taken seriously in a sometime sort of way.

By nine o'clock, Tom Perry and Fred Blackburn appeared in their buggies at the Kane Cafe of Trinchera to retrieve their families. The women and children saw them approaching, and swarmed out of the eatery into the cold air, dressed in their warmest clothing for the wagon ride, Clayborne wrapped in a heavy coat and swathed in a muffler. They all looked at each other for a moment, the men at their families, the women and children at their menfolk, trying to see themselves in this new setting. Tom jumped down from the buggy with a broad grin on his face. He had brought along a special treat for his son:

"Pup!" cried the five-year-old. The black dog leaped for joy, bounding out of the buggy and dancing around his master. "How are you, my Pup?" asked Clayborne, bending to hold the wiggly little creature to his face. Pup could barely reach the boy's hugging arms — he had not grown into a large dog in his four years and seemed to have had some Boston terrier in his mixed ancestry. "I sure missed, you, Pup, I sure did. And Pet! Papa, you brought Pet to pull the buggy!" He patted the sorrel mare, the old family friend. "Papa, Pup and Pet look just fine, huh, Papa?"

"They're just fine, and you're just fine," said Tom Perry, scooping up his son and giving him the hug he could not give his wife in this public place.

Fred Blackburn helped Myrtle and Claytia and Lawton into their buggy and signalled that they were going to the general store, a place that was to become a rock and harbor for the Texans in this community where they knew no one and had no roots. They had found the general store of Trinchera, Doherty Mercantile Company, to be run by two bachelor brothers, Joe and Eddie Doherty, kindly and helpful men in their forties. But Tom concerned himself just at present not with supplies. He stood aside and said to Belle, "Mrs. Perry, how might you be this fine day?"

She stood discreetly away, but the love on her face was plain to read. "I might be fine, Mr. Perry. And I expect you're going to take me and Clayborne to this wonderful new land of ours?"

"Yes, Ma'am," said Tom, hoisting her cardboard travelling bag into the rear buggy boot, "I certainly am."

And off they went, with Pup sitting happily in Clayborne's lap. They first followed the railroad tracks westward past the station where shaggy red grass grew along the ditch. This was the first clear look Belle actually had of Colorado. It shone flat and bare and sun-baked, red soil with a tinge of yellow brittle grass, last season's prairie three-awn, and little bluestem rattling in the wind. Far off there lodged cliff-sided mesas, desert top hats fringed with grey-green sagebrush trying to make a living on the rockfall bottom slopes. To the south lay the long spine of Raton Mesa culminating thirty miles to the west in Fisher Peak near Trinidad, Colorado. It all had the clean feel of arid places, but she missed the temperate hills of Texas already. This was not a proper land, this vacant place, she thought, but merely the raw material out of which a proper land might be made.

The tiny town of Trinchera sat atop the earth's crust like an afterthought. The train depot had been there for twenty-five years, since 1888 when the Ft. Worth and Denver City Railway finished its track near Folsom, New Mexico — 528 miles from Ft. Worth and 280 miles from Denver. But miscellaneous piles of oak ties, some old iron rails, and leftover cradles and pins still lay here and there in the station yard. Ghosts of that 1888 boom time seemed to linger about, the echoes of construction gangs, tent cities, little houses on wheels and the wagons of the camp followers — gamblers, business sharks and their women of dubious virtue that plucked the pay envelopes of free-spending railroad laborers who had nowhere else to go. But they were only ghosts. Across Trinchera Creek bridge and over the flat railroad grade, the Perrys headed north into the sea of grass that was Southern Colorado.

They rode past nameless low hills, past shallow arroyos filled with juniper and leafless shining cottonwood trees. An occasional mesquite tree, still heavy with bean pods, crowned above the scattered junipers that broke the monotony of the plain with their unearthly shapes. The reunited Perrys were bound for a spot ten miles due north from Trinchera, and thirty miles east from Trinidad, the only town of any size for nearly a hundred miles in any direction. To the northwest, on this clear sunny day, the Front Range of the Rocky Mountains stood out sharply, clad in new snow.

"That's Pike's Peak, over yonder," said Tom. "Mr. Newcombe showed me when he brought us out here last week."

Clayborne seemed unimpressed.

But Belle tried to absorb everything about her new home. "Well, I do declare," she said. "I've heard so much about it. Grandpa used to tell me about Zebulon Pike and the gold rush at Pike's Peak. 'Pike's Peak or Bust,' he used to say. That's what they all used to say. I never saw mountains like that before. Pike's Peak looks so small."

"That's because it's far away," said Tom. "Distance makes it look small. It's really very big, very big. Over 14,000 feet high."

"My lands," said Belle, not knowing quite how much that was, "so tall."

As they approached their new homesite, Belle noticed they had gone beyond even the faintest cowpaths. There were no roads and there were no telephone poles to decorate them and give them dimension as back home in Texas. Their absence made her feel hollow somehow. Scattered junipers that most immigrants called cedars spread withered branches to the cold sapphire blue sky. Most stood dead or dying: there was little green to soften the tawny grass. Tom pointed to the distant outline of a reassembled wagon and buggy where the form of a man was barely discernible, working with a shovel at some kind of low structure on the grassy soil. Belle stared at the mound and finally recognized the shape as a dugout home, a pit house with floor dug a few feet into the earth, board sides above ground and posts holding up a beam and plank ceiling high enough to stand up in. As they came nearer she could make out Robert Dozier throwing dirt from the floor excavation pile onto the outside wall, forming a berm for insulation and support.

Tears welled up in Belle's eyes. "Are we going to live in one of those dirt houses, Tom?" she asked plaintively.

"No, Ma'am," Tom responded. "I know what a fuss you put up about it back in Texas. I went into Trinchera here a day or so ago and got us a good sturdy Army tent, must be sixteen by twenty feet, as big as the kitchen in the weaning house back home. If you look sharp, you'll see it clear over yonder." He indicated a pyramidal white shape a quarter of a mile off over the shortgrass prairie.

Belle was unsure whether living in a tent was better than living in a pit house, but as they drew up to the new Dozier home under construction, she looked down from the buggy into the cavernous hole. It was five feet deep, and its above-ground sidewalls of raggedy planks added another two feet of height. The pit was lined with more planks, and it was dark and smelled faintly. Snug, but not homey. Belle decided a tent would be preferable. Robert called down inside the house to his wife Mary Ann, who came running out from the small structure and cried, "Well, hello, Belle, honey. You and Myrtle made it safe on the train, did you?"

"Oh, yes, Mary Ann. It was an awful long ride and the children were so fussy, but we're all here. Say hello to Mr. and Mrs. Dozier, Clayborne."

"Hello, Mrs. Dozier, hello, Mr. Dozier," came the dutiful reply.

Mary Ann Dozier said, "Robert Junior and Alma are inside helping to fix things up. Would Clayborne like to come in and play with them?" The two Dozier children peered out from the rough doorway. Clayborne waved a tentative little wave at them.

"We aren't going to be able to stay long," responded Tom for his wife. "I'm sure Belle wants to get some rest from the train trip, but thank you anyways."

"My brother and Myrtle are right behind us a few minutes," said Belle. "They stopped in at the store to pick up some groceries. Did you and Verna come through the trip all right?"

"We did fair to middlin', I expect. Leonard and Verna are getting set up in their dugout over yonder by that little flat hill. See there, it's some off up that way," Mary Ann Dozier said pointing the way.

"Oh, yes, I see it up by the wagons and animals. But I don't see Leonard or Verna," answered Belle.

"I think they've moseyed on off getting water at the spring," said Robert Dozier. "I saw them driving off that way in the wagon with little Otis an hour or so ago, going east across your place."

"You have to drive off for water?" asked Belle. She realized with a shock how primitive this life would be.

"You'll get used to it," reassured Robert Dozier. "We'll get up a system soon so the men will take care of that. We would go up to the Picketwire River, if we could" — early trappers in the area had mispronounced the French word *Purgatoire* and the tradition stuck — "because it's close, runs right through the tip of Leonard's land. But the canyon's too deep, can't get down to the water. We got plenty water in the other direction, off by your land about a mile, don't you worry."

"But this place is so bare and cold. Does the wind blow this way all the time?"

"No," Robert deadpanned. "Sometimes it blows the other way."

Mary Ann Dozier grumped, "Bob, don't you hoo-raw her like that. She's had a hard trip."

"I'm sorry, Miz Perry. What did you mean to say?"

"Oh, don't apologize for bein' full of fun. I ain't that tired. But will anything grow here?" she asked uncertainly.

"Oh, it's good black soil, Mrs. Perry," said Robert Dozier, filling a shovel for her to examine from her seat in the buggy. "We've all took a plow to it a little, just to see how it'll work come spring. You can plow it pretty as you like. It's nice and easy to work. It feels good and fertile. The land agent showed us the farm records from Las Animas County — that's the county here — and there's plenty of good farms, more comin' all the time. The Mexicans have gotten along here hundreds of years. Good corn crops, even some wheat. Good soil for a garden."

"Oh, I hope so," said Belle, trying to take it all in stride. "Well," she said, looking around, "I see our tent and I see Leonard and Verna's things, and here's yours, but where is the Blackburn place?"

"It's right straight east. Look there, Belle" said Mary Ann to her friend.

Tom pointed to a low mound nearly a quarter mile away, and explained to his wife, "The way our land is laid out the four of us have plots right together." He pulled a paper from his jumper pocket and spread it out for Belle to see. It was a map of their property.

"Now this here," Tom said, pointing to two squares on the map that had been heavily outlined in pencil, "is the whole thing, two sections of land split up into four half-sections, one for each family. A half-section is 320 acres, that's what each of us has got. See this, it says Township 33 South in Range 59 West of the 6th Principal Meridian — that's just to show the land agent where we are on a bigger map. But this part in here that we've marked in pencil, that's Section 5 and Section 6, our sections."

Tom took a worn pencil from his shirt pocket, and using it as a pointer, explained, "This big stripe that slants up to the right is the Picketwire River" — the Purgatoire — "and it comes from 'way up in the Rockies and flows down into the Arkansas. It's just north of our claims, up that way. Up here in the northwest corner Leonard and Verna have the north half of Section 6, and straight east we have the north half of Section 5. Right below Leonard and Verna is the Doziers in the south half of Section 6, that's right here where we are now. And straight east, right below our place, Fred and Myrtle have the south half of Section 5."

Robert Dozier leaned on his shovel and said, "You see, Mrs. Perry,

we've decided to build our places near the middle corner where all four
pieces of land meet. That way we're not too far off from one another, about
a quarter-mile apart, each one of us. Three hundred and twenty acres is a
lot of land — it's a whole mile long and half a mile wide. If all of us had
built right smack in the middle of our half-sections, we'd be a mile off
from each other and wouldn't hardly be able to even see one another."

Tom Perry, sensing Belle's uneasiness, said, "Bob, we got to be going.
We just stopped by to say hello on our way to get Belle and Clayborne
settled in. We'll come back for a proper visit tonight, okay?"

"You all come on over for supper, you hear? Isn't that right, Mary
Ann?" said Robert.

"Sure fire," enthused Mary Ann. "Me and Verna's been here two days,
now. We got most of our furniture set up and we'd all like a good visit.
You bring something and I'll talk to Verna and we'll all eat here."

"See you tonight," agreed Tom. They drove the quarter-mile through
dry air and the brushy winter grass to their Army tent, the kind with four
vertical sidewall flaps and a pyramidal roof. A spidery array of ropes held
the frail canvas shelter taut. The heavy pegs mooring their home seemed
insubstantial, mere pinpricks in the earth's tough skin. Belle was not at
all sure she liked it here.

They climbed down from the Emerson buggy, and Tom remained
silent. He knew the shock Belle was suffering. Without speaking, he
took her travelling bag into the tent.

Clayborne put Pup down and ran into his new home, the dog following
happily behind. "Oh, boy! It's a real tent!" he hollered. "Can we live here,
Papa? I like this." The boy scampered from corner to corner. "And looky
here, here's my high chair! And there's the bed and our dinner table and
the safe and everything. Look, Mama, even the cookstove is here, and it
has a pipe that goes right through the tent."

Belle noticed first the dirt floor, and then the small pile of firewood
Tom had gathered during his first days here. "Where do we get firewood,
Tom?" she asked blankly.

"There's plenty of dead cedars around the place, especially around the
canyons," Tom said, watching Belle's reaction out of the corner of his eye.
"Makes a good hot fire, but it burns a little fast. We can take a wagon
around, collect wood for the four families. There'll be plenty. And with
Clayborne to help we can keep a good store," he said winking at his son.

Belle walked around inside the tent, sizing it up, inspecting her
familiar belongings in this unfamiliar setting. She said nothing for a long
time. Then she sat down at the dinner table on one of the cane-bottom,
slat-back kitchen chairs. She made up her mind.

"All right. It's home," she said. "I'll just have to watch out to keep
from tripping over the tent ropes. Where have you put the groceries?"

Tom looked at her, silently acknowledging her final decision. "The flour's in the safe," he said, "and there's some ham and pork shoulder left."

In the waning days of 1915, Tom purchased some knotty scrap juniper boards and laid them on edge all around the bottom of the tent, shoveling dirt over them to make the tent wind-tight. When the tent had its protective earth buttress, the work began on a shelter for the animals. The days became a succession of short cloudy episodes of hard work: two juniper posts, side by side, were set into the ground at intervals in an ample rectangle, and brush was piled between the posts to form a sort of wall; then several of the sorry cull-grade planks were piled sideways on top of that; then alternately more brush and more boards until a three-sided windbreak-shed some seven feet high was formed, leaving one end open. Tom nailed the same rough lumber into place with wide gaps for a roof, and piled native brush on top of that, making a sort of brush arbor. The animals had their shelter.

Cooping the chickens proved to be another matter. Tom had seen coyotes prowling and sneaking through the grass, lying in wait, conspiring with one another how to obtain a free chicken dinner. On several occasions Tom had fired his shotgun at the wily animals, but only succeeded in frightening them off temporarily — his shotgun was ineffective beyond thirty or forty yards. Keeping the coyotes out of his chickens was going to be a problem. While scouting the northern boundary of his claim, Tom found a dead twenty-foot high juniper with many sturdy branches and a butt diameter of about a foot. He cut it down and hauled it to the place he had decided upon for a chicken coop. He then dug a hole and planted the dead tree for a chicken roost. He fashioned a circular chicken wire fence some twenty feet in diameter with the tree at its center. The fence was supported by a few raw juniper posts cut from scrawny trees found here and there, and a crude gate was formed by fastening two loose fence posts together with twisted baling wire. Most of the chickens — birds not known for their cunning — got the idea and roosted in the high branches of the enclosed tree. On several nights, independent birds that had decided to roost on the ground outside the coop were carried away by eager coyotes amid much squawking and turmoil of feathers.

They worked out a rotating firewood circuit in which the men took turns going collecting in their wagons. This meant spending the better part of a day scouting up and gathering firewood on the four half-sections of land. It was a simple matter of driving around until the searcher found enough firewood, then gathering and taking it to a central point more or less equidistant from each of the four family shelters and dumping it in a large pile. Members of each family would supply themselves from the pile until it was exhausted, when the next man on the list did firewood duty.

Christmas week the snowfall was so heavy that drifts threatened to crush the Perry's tent. While Clayborne and Belle slept in the family bed, Tom kept an all-night vigil, hoe in hand, raking the tent roof when it began to sag. Christmas day for the four families was one of happy greetings and little else. There was no money for gifts, and little for holiday treats — no turkey and trimmings, none of Lee Rainwater's delicious peanut candy, half soft white, half brittle brown, only a little hard candy from Trinchera's general store. But at least everyone had an apple brought from Doherty's. The Texans were effectively exiled from their friends and parental families to a foreign land where even their religion was distant. Trinchera had only one church, a Catholic parish church just completed in the fall of 1915, its faith a legacy of the early Spanish explorer Ulibarri who claimed southern Colorado for Spain in 1706. But these Texans were Baptists who did not attend Catholic services. The nearest Baptist preacher was thirty miles away — a two-day wagon ride — in Trinidad's First Baptist Church, so they heard. Even the territorial Baptist "Spanish Mission Schools" from the late 1800s had closed down.

They might as well have lived on another planet except for the weekly mail. The immigrants had worked out another rotating system for trips into Trinchera: every four or five days a different family would ride into town, buy groceries and supplies for the four families, coffee, sugar, baking soda, salt, pepper, perhaps some flour, deliver and pick up the mail — and talk. They talked to the Doherty brothers and whoever happened to be in the store. They talked about the weather, about all the new automobiles on the roads, about the Kaiser in Germany, about President Wilson, anything. When Tom needed cash, he gave the Doherty's a check drawn on the Hico National Bank, and they honored it without question. The Doherty's were the sheet-anchor that tied the transplanted Texans to the outside world.

About once a week, one or another of the families would hear from home, from Texas. How far away and strange even the names now seemed! Hico! Duffau! How often they dreamed themselves back into home's cradling arms and, awaking to the cresting snows of Colorado, wept to dream again. But they would not admit it when they wrote to family back home. They would "take pen in hand in hopes of finding you in good health. Everyone here is well. We have finished building our new homes. When we get our first crop in, we will build regular houses for all." The immigrants provided glowing descriptions of the new land. They wrote of their progress in sheltering their animals. They wrote of collecting firewood and how fast the cedar burned. They wrote of the children's antics. But they kept their own counsel when it came to the isolation and poverty and primitive living conditions. Only the Doziers let slip in one letter the laconic statement: "It is pretty slim out in the country."

The new year — 1916 — came to the new Coloradans on the back of a Rocky Mountain snowstorm, bucking and howling. But the rowdy air did them a service as well: it rearranged the impassible snowbanks, clearing many paths into Trinchera. Winter was unpredictable. Some days they had to mush through drifts just to get firewood. On occasion, the winter sky would clear and a glittering, dazzling sunny day would appear over ground free and open to travel. On such a day in January, with an icy sundog to decorate the blinding sky, Tom went to Trinchera in the wagon and led home behind him nine donkeys for the four families.

A resident of Trinchera had grown tired of the hardy creatures and volunteered them as a donation to the transplanted Texans. They would provide entertainment for the children and perhaps prove useful mounts when rounding up the horses — even hobbled, the horses might wander off in search of open grass in the snow for a mile or two. Donkeys could be tied up and needed little or no supplemental feed as did horses and mules. Tom kept two donkeys for Clayborne, but the boy took the rope off one and it walked back to Trinchera, thank you — as did three more left similarly unfettered by the other families. When the men later gathered to talk of many things, the humor of the four donkeys' commentary about their living conditions was not lost on them. So, young Clayborne had only one donkey to ride, as did the other families — except for the Doziers who kept two, one for Robert Junior and one for Alma. But Clayborne's intelligent little beast became a new friend, quickly accepted into the fold with the mule Jack, the mare Pet and the dog Pup.

By February 1916 the snows were tapering off and the ceaseless wind had blustered the grass clear in large areas: no longer could the settlers rely on snowmelt for drinking water. Getting water became another rotating ritual. The nearest accessible water for the four families lay just beyond the northeast boundary of Tom Perry's half-section in Rail-O Canyon, a side canyon of Trinchera Canyon, which itself was a side-canyon of the Purgatoire River Canyon. Trinchera Canyon had been cut by the same Trinchera Creek the Perrys had driven across as a small stream ten miles south in the town of Trinchera. By the time it ran seven miles due north the creek had chiseled a stepped waterfall with turquoise churning basin, and by ten miles had carved itself a respectable two-hundred-fifty foot deep canyon. Rail-O Canyon met Trinchera Canyon on the west, and near the head of Rail-O Canyon a nameless subcanyon split off trending northwest. In the bed of this subcanyon stream rose a series of five substantial springs, bubbling up cool and pure from the rocks, strung on the creek like big blue beads. They lay sixty to eighty feet below the bench land, and the trail down was nothing more than a wash that had been eroding the soil for some thousands of years.

The men, usually all four of them, would take two wagons, each loaded with two or three empty barrels and bailing buckets, and park them at the head of Rail-O Canyon. Clayborne often tagged behind on his donkey. They took their large buckets down the steep trail past sheer rockwalls to the clear springs where clustering cottonwoods and willows grew, and Clayborne would oftimes carry a syrup bucket to help the menfolk. Hauling a gallon of water back up that trail was a reasonable accomplishment for a lad of five and a half. The procession down to the springs, up to the barrels, back down to the springs, filling the barrels one bucket at a time, went on for two or three hours. Only big, lanky Leonard Perry seemed to relish the water ritual. He was a happy- go-lucky man who seemed to thrive on adventure and hard work. Whenever one of the others made the inevitable complaint "This would be fine country if only the water was closer," Leonard cheerfully snorted, "Yes, so would hell."

On one occasion after a rain, the men were making their final ascent of an arduous day's work, slogging through mudpuddles in the trail, when Robert Dozier shouted to his companions: "Watch out! There's a rattlesnake in that puddle there." They had no idea how many times they might have marched up and down past the reptile without seeing it — or it molesting them.

As the routine went, when the barrels were full enough — not too full so that water would be lost through excessive splash and spill — a square of canvas would be drawn over each open barrel mouth and a barrel hoop seated snugly over it, forming a lid against sloshing. The mule teams would strain against the heavy load on the return trip, and the wagon boards groan under the pressure. At each homesite all four men would be required to wrestle the massive weight of a full water barrel safely off the back end of the wagon, slipping and sliding it where possible, and finally dropping it with a thud that made the ground tremble beneath their feet. A barrel would last three or four days of drinking and washing and cooking.

It was at the spring that Leonard Perry discovered Trinchera Canyon to be inhabited. There one day in early March while fetching water alone he met four Mexican-Americans who had come to get water in wooden buckets. Leonard smiled readily, unlike most Anglo settlers, and quickly shook hands with the startled Hispanos, jabbering in fractured Spanish, "Buenos dias, todos el hombres! Mucho gusto, you all, mucho gusto! Yo soy en esta rio para el agua! Mi llama, el es Leonard Perry! Como se llama, todos?" *Good day, gentlemen. Glad to meet you. I'm here for water. My name is Leonard Perry. What are your names?* He had learned a little Spanish in Texas — not enough to speak grammatically — and the Hispanos spoke a little English. As soon as they realized this friendly Anglo was speaking Spanish — almost unrecognizable in his thick Texas accent and impossible word combinations — they returned his smile and tried out their English on him: "Welcome to our home, Senor Perry. I am Servando de la Garza , and this is mi hermano" — my brother — "Refugio. This is Jesus Nanez. And this is Miguel Fuente."

Amidst smiles and arm waving they made themselves understood to each other well enough. With much gesturing, Leonard managed to convey the idea that he and his family were new arrivals now living in dugouts up on the bench land. *Yo vive con mi esposa*, that's 'wife', isn't it? *y mi nino en el* — whatayacallit — *el llano. No tengo una casa grande.* I only got una casa en el. . . el. . . *el cerros. En el* dirt. Down *en el* ground, get it?"

The Hispanos got it. They expressed astonishment that Anglos would try to live up there on the exposed plain, but they were polite about it and displayed their welcome by inviting him to visit their homes, perhaps to trade with them for their goat meat.

Leonard delighted in his discovery and was game for anything. He followed them a quarter mile to the confluence of Rail-O Creek and Trinchera Creek. There he was surprised to find that just down stream Trinchera Canyon broadened out into a more valley-like trough. Horse paths straggled down from the high bench lands to the riverbottom. Nestled among the cottonwoods were several dozen pale little adobe houses with curls of blue smoke drifting from their tile chimneys. Their flat roofs and straight walls seemed somehow to fit the eternal earth line, the horizontal rock strata of the canyon wall. The adobes were like cave dwellings that might be found in other canyons in other times, and smelled of tortillas and history. On the hillsides above, scattered flocks of goats peacefully grazed. The air was several degrees warmer here in the canyon bottom, and the steep walls gave off a sense of protection rather than claustrophobia.

This community was listed on no map; it was unconcerned about maps. The farms of these people must have been productive, Leonard thought as he walked the sandy path to the village, for hanging outside their doors were many ears of squaw corn — a variety favored by the local Indians and Hispanics, actually a type of flint corn with large, hard kernels growing on long, slender ears, the kernels on the same ear often of several different colors. Two varieties of chili pepper hung drying from porch poles: dark smoky pasilla and mild pungent ancho. After discussing possible barter items for goat meat and goat milk, and drawing pictures in the creek sand for objects beyond their respective vocabularies, the Hispanos agreed with Leonard to accept iron nails, chicken wire, corn, white flour, and other useful items, the amounts to be decided upon at each purchase.

Young goat, *cabrito*, as the dish is known in Mexico, is excellent eating — particularly when rubbed with garlic, chili and spices, marinated in vinegar overnight, then roasted and basted in the vinegar sauce which cooks to a rich savory crust on the meat. Only an unreasoning prejudice prevented its wide enjoyment north of the border. Many Anglos, especially city folks, thought that young goats were "too cute to eat" — but had no compunctions about devouring cute little cows and sheep. Farm people such as Leonard Perry and his fellow immigrants were not afflicted with such overactive — and selective — sensitivities. Leonard was certainly glad of any fresh meat his family could come by, as were the other families.

The Hispanics arranged with Leonard a signal when they wanted to make a market. On days when they butchered their goats and meat was available, they would fly a red flag from their porch. When they had extra goat milk, a white flag would indicate which house had some for sale. No flag meant nothing for sale. That way the Anglo settlers could see from the canyon rim whether it was worth a walk down to the community and which house had what to offer. The system worked excellently, and the neighbors carried on the trade to their mutual satisfaction — but only outgoing Leonard Perry ended up making the deals, for the rest kept their reticence and reserve.

The last few days before spring brought a respite from dreary labor: they had fixed up their homes about as much as could be done and it was too early for plowing. At times during these days the women would gather and do nothing in particular for hours — just talk, drink coffee and hope for the future. But the idleness was short lived: washday saw to that. On Monday washdays, they gathered outside before sunup to get a good fire roaring under the huge brimming iron wash pots — each family brought their own. Small children would be placed on pallets in the shade of nearby junipers to be near their mothers. In the age-old weekly ritual, three tubs for each family were set up next to the boiling wash pot, two filled with hot water. The men hauled water from the centrally placed barrels, each carrying two zinc buckets containing thirty pounds of water each, sixty pounds total per trip, a task that ordinarily fell to the farm woman during plowing and planting and harvest.

The family's bedsheets came first, dumped into waiting twelve-gallon Number Three zinc washtubs — empty tubs, not yet filled with water. Then each woman, glad of the men's help and the other women's company, scooped boiling water in a wooden bucket from her bubbling wash pot and poured it over the waiting sheets, leaving them to soak a while. After a few minutes of soaking came the backbreaking work: the rub board was stuck into the wash tub, the lye soap the women themselves had made was taken out, and the scrubbing began. Poor farmers could not afford store-bought soap, and homemade lye soap was not a very effective cleaning agent. The secret was in the scrubbing, up and down, up and down, endlessly, bent over the scrub board. It was miserable hard work, the worst of drudgery.

After the sheets had been scrubbed on the board with lye soap, the women wrung them out to remove dirty water as best they could, then tossed them into the big boiling wash pot. Here stubborn dirt had to be punched out with a broomstick or a tree branch with its bark stripped off, more up and down, up and down, hard on the arms, hard on the back. Well-to-do farm wives threw away their tree branches and boasted of their store-bought wash paddles, sticks with metal cones on the end specially designed to "blubber up" the wash pot and get the bad dirt out, but even these still required the up and down, up and down, hard on the arms, hard on the back.

The women lifted their sheets from the boiling pot by broomstick and transferred them to the rinse tub, letting the dirty water drip off first, no easy task itself. Then more bending, now over the rinse tub — "rinch tub," they pronounced it, you "rinched out the warsh" — and sloshed each separate item through the rinse water. Then they wrung out each sheet, twisting to get rid of as much dirty water as possible, and tossed it into the third tub, the bluing tub. Each sheet was stirred through this bleach water to get bluing on every part, making it as bright as possible. Then it would be wrung out once more and hung up on the clothes line — here in Colorado, strung from a makeshift arrangement of juniper branches and cull lumber.

On it went, tub after tub: first the sheets, then the light clothes, then the colored clothes, dresses, red handkerchiefs, jeans, jumpers, overalls — overalls were the worst, big and heavy and coarse — and the process repeated for dish towels and "warsh rags" and baby diapers. After each type of wash the water was dumped out and everything done again for the next batch — from lighter things to darker things. More water hauled, more wood hauled to heat the water, more scrubbing and punching and wringing and stirring and rinsing and bluing. At the tag end, a dishpan of starch was added for Sunday-go-to-meeting shirts. Four loads, one for sheets, one for white clothes, one for colored clothes, one for "linens," would not be uncommon in any farm family — families with many children might have to repeat the whole process, *eight* loads instead of four. The water barrel would be emptied on washday.

In Colorado, as it had been in Texas, washday was a succession of hours with nothing but misery and brutish labor, human muscle power performing basic tasks, wringing, scrubbing, punching, stirring, over and over and over, grunting, aching labor — and the women did most of it. They did it every week, fifty-two times a year, sick or well, young or old. If they were lucky, they had children who would not shirk and whine away from hard work. If not, they worked alone. No wonder the bloom of youth faded so quickly from rural wives, no wonder the stooped shoulders came so soon, no wonder the skin leathered prematurely in the sun and wind and sweat, no wonder the joints hurt and the mind dulled.

But these Texas emigrants took what pleasure they could from each other's company these spring washdays, even though they could not foregather on Tuesdays — ironing day. Ironing required a cookstove, and cookstoves were not portable, could not be hauled outside like the wash pots and tubs and dishpans. Ironing day began before sunup, too, starting up the wood stove, opening the damper that hardly drew a useful draft even on windy days. It took a real expert to keep these contrary beasts going, for the fire would smoke out at the slightest excuse. These women, Belle and Verna and Mary Ann and Myrtle, however, had mastered their woodstoves and routinely had them roasting the kitchen — such as it was — within less than an hour. On cold days, it might take all of an hour for the stove to heat up properly for ironing. And ironing was harder than washing. An iron in those days was exactly what its name said, iron, seven pounds of iron — and it took three or four of them to do a day's ironing. Irons had no internal heating coils powered by electricity. Irons were heated by sitting them atop the woodstove and letting the fire within soak into the dead iron. Once heated, an iron would stay hot for perhaps two useable minutes at the most. A work shirt took two irons, coveralls three or four, and a short-sleeved shirt might occasionally be done with one.

Keeping the irons clean was a frustrating chore. The iron bottoms were sanded and scraped and scrubbed with salt and even coated with whatever nonstick material seemed useful — beeswax and pine resin were tried with varying degrees of failure. The tiniest fleck of soot or dirt on an iron bottom spelled disaster, transferring without fail to a nice starched white shirt or a pretty calico dress which would have to be washed all over again.

Then there was the sheer labor, often stretching into the night, the labor of lifting seven pound irons all day, wilting in the raving heat, suffering with burns and blisters from inevitable accidents with the irons, screaming inwardly when soot-stained clothes slid out from under the irons, suppressing the pain between the shoulders, keeping on long beyond the time you were ready to drop. The four women begged silently for Wednesday, a day of ordinary labor, conjured it to come early. And then, after preparing six meals during this two-day ordeal, it was done. Monday and Tuesday were done. Washday and ironing day. The Good Old Days.

Sometimes the men would ride around the property, Leonard telling jokes about country matters, the others laughing, and all loafing around. Leonard talked the others into a favorite pastime: riding to the canyon of the Purgatoire River and pushing big old rocks over the cliff. Young Clayborne accompanied them to this spot on numerous occasions, and it always frightened him when his big daredevil uncle stood right next to the edge of the cliff and pushed a rock over. It seemed to the boy that the chasm must be thousands of feet deep — actually about three hundred feet at this point — and he was afraid to get too close to the edge. There was always that unbelievable urge to jump, that figment of desperation that you might lose control and *really* jump. But he enjoyed the heady excitement anyway, and his Uncle Leonard never jumped. No one lived in the bottom of this gorge, and the falling stones made a splendid sound as they smashed into splinters on the rocks below.

On such a day of loafing about, the men discovered they had other unknown neighbors, this time to the north. From their first inspection visit to the homestead claims, they had known that a primitive wagon road meandered from the southwest corner of Leonard Perry's half-section in a northeasterly direction, crossing out of his northern property line somewhere near its middle and heading for parts unknown. They had never inquired as to where it might lead and had never seen anyone travelling it, nor had they themselves followed it to where ever it went. During a leisurely wagon ride in early March 1916 the four men decided to do a little exploring. They followed the trail downhill, as it happened, downhill toward a stretch of the Purgatoire River beyond Leonard Perry's land. Halfway to the river they were stunned speechless to find an eerie adobe chapel and a cemetery full of white wooden crosses, grave markers. The place was forlorn and surprising, yet obviously *still in use*. They had stumbled onto a *morada* of the Brothers of Our Father Jesus of Nazareth, a controversial lay religious society of the Roman Catholic Church commonly known as the Penitentes — the Brothers of Light, the Brothers of Blood.

The *Hermanos Penitentes* — Brotherhood of Penitents — is probably the most misunderstood organization in Southwest U.S. history. The Brotherhood, headquartered in Santa Fe, New Mexico, requires of its members sincere faith and unstinting commitment to Christian charity through mutual aid and unobtrusive good deeds for all neighbors and fellow citizens. They sponsor wakes for the dead and wakes for saints. But the Brotherhood also preserves the medieval practice of public penance, particularly during Lent, culminating in Holy Week observances. It is this public penance that gave the Brothers of Light their sinister public reputation, for theirs is not simply a penance of fasting and self-abnegation. Individuals among the Brothers of Blood strip half naked, go barefoot, and carry massive wooden crosses in long outdoor processions of atonement for sin. Others braid yucca stems into sharp whips and follow behind the cross-bearers, lashing themselves with the yucca whips first over one shoulder and then over the other in bloody self-flagellation. One man in each procession usually pulls a painfully heavy wheeled cart bearing a carved figure of death, the *Carreta del Muerto*, the cart of death — but the wheels do not turn; they are fixed, so the heavy burden must be dragged along the ground by main force. And on occasion in times past, a Brother has been known to be tied to a large cross in a short simulation of the Crucifixion on Good Friday.

These and other practices appeared to the eyes of early Anglo settlers as masking a dark fanaticism which threatened to subvert decency and extinguish the true Gospel. Despite the fact that such public penance was once carried out under the spiritual guidance of the Franciscan friars — an instance was recorded as early as 1598 by Don Juan de Onate in Spain — the Catholic Church itself discouraged and then banned the lay American Brotherhood. Secret societies were anathema to the Catholic clergy which viewed them as merely disobedient organizations likely to be involved in political intrigue. In the face of persecution, the Brotherhood went underground, but efforts to extinguish it were futile. For what the church and the American settlers did not understand was why the Brotherhood had arisen in the first place.

Two hundred years ago New Mexico was still a province of New Spain. Its capitol had been the Villa of Santa Fe since 1610. The Hispanics who followed as settlers in this semiarid world numbered fewer than 19,000 in 1799, and they lived among the Pueblo Indians, who numbered at that time fewer than 10,000. This core population found itself remote and isolated from New World cultural centers. It was repeatedly exposed to the depredations of hostile nomadic Indians. It is hardly surprising that they evolved an insular mentality and formed a tight-knit enclave in a harsh land. It is less surprising to find that in this isolation the churchly discipline of the Franciscans should be gradually exaggerated into a lay order of penitents.

In 1821, Mexico became a nation independent of Spain with the signing of the Treaty of Cordoba, and in the fall of that year, Missouri trader William Becknell brought the first Anglo pack caravan to Santa Fe along the Purgatoire River, walking over what would become the 1915 claim of Leonard Perry. The Santa Fe Trail brought Anglo settlers in its wake and pushed the Hispanics northward from the trading centers of Taos, Abiquiu, Santa Fe and Las Vegas, hardening their insular mentality. By 1833, the *Hermandad de Penitentes*, Brotherhood of Penitents, is recorded as having kept its paraphernalia of crosses, whips and carts of death in a *piesa*, or room, of the church at Santa Cruz in New Mexico. In time, such rooms came to be called *moradas*, "a dwelling place" or "residence" in the Spanish of the times. When ecclesiastical intolerance and pressure from Anglo immigrants forced the Brotherhood to build separate meeting houses, the word *morada* came to mean a Penitente meeting place, and still later, a local chapter of the organization. The Brotherhood came to be predominantly a mutual aid society, much like an Anglo lodge, helping its members, burying its dead, caring for widows and orphans, protecting its own. But this aspect of the Brothers of Light went unnoticed.

The end of the American Civil War brought hordes of immigrants west, and many settled in the New Mexico Territory. Anglo newspapers soon found that accounts of the spectacular devotions of the Brotherhood made good copy. For decades, hardly a Holy Week went by without a sensational story of men walking on their knees with cactus stems for kneepads or orgies of flagellation in some *morada* where the floor splashed with pools of blood. But the religious suspicion of the Anglo settlers gradually grew into political suspicion. Politically ambitious Anglos and Hispanos were rumored to have undergone ritual initiation in the Brotherhood, not out of religious zeal, but to secure an entire *morada*'s vote in a single bloc. The Brotherhood was supposed to have been dominated by Republicans. In 1901, J. R. Killian, an attorney in Walsenburg — some 60 miles northwest of the Texas immigrants' claims — accused one Juan Dios Montez of "keeping a harem like the Sultan of Turkey" and heading "a strange religious sect" with men and women flagellants, which only served to put an edge on his real accusation: "several hundred votes are cast each year just as Montez directs, which is generally for the Republican candidate" — an ironic charge against a party that would one day be accused by certain benighted souls as being aloof and unfeeling toward minorities. The *Denver Post* printed the story, and a few days later the *Denver Times* answered it by calling Killian's accusations "a base libel." Whatever the truth of the situation, the Penitente Brotherhood seemed destined to attract unwelcome attention.

The Penitentes were implicated by newspapers in murders and political intrigue, but somehow no evidence was ever cited and no charges were ever brought. Yet when New Mexico became a state in 1912, its non-Hispanic population tended to look upon the Brotherhood with a tinge of fear, as did many residents of Southeastern Colorado. It was suspected that every male of Hispanic heritage was a member, along with an unknown number of Anglos. In 1910, one scholar in New Mexico Territorial University claimed that "only a few years ago, nearly every native in the Territory belonged to the order including the highest or controlling political class," which was probably an exaggeration. The immigrants from Hico, Texas, had heard only vague rumors about the Penitentes, but they recognized the *morada* with its stacks of large wooden crosses against the chapel wall and its cemetery. Even Leonard Perry's devil-may-care brashness faded at the sight of the *morada*. The Hispanos living over in Trinchera Canyon may have liked him and even called him by the nickname "Texas Longhorn," but why tempt fate? The settlers wanted nothing to do with the Penitentes. They paid the *morada* no further visits. And they never mentioned it to anyone.

In mid-April the plowing began. There would likely be more snowstorms, they knew, but that would not harm the hardy wheat they would plant. In fact, more snowstorms would be essential to supply the necessary moisture for a good crop in this region of scant rainfall. And so they went ahead with gusto and hope. Breaking new ground was arduous work, but it went quickly. The shortgrass turf yielded easily to the turning plow. Clayborne often rode his donkey beside his father as Tom worked the turning plow and in later days the planting sulky. Tom began to complain of pains in his joints, particularly in his hips and legs, but he carried on and finished the work.

By the first of May each of the four families had a wheat crop in the ground. On May 4th, a sleety barrage mopped the Rocky Mountains from the skyline, dumping six inches of sticky snow on their fields. The four farm families rejoiced: it was the water they needed. It would make their crops. The family gardens were well seeded with corn and onions and other good things. By the 8th of May the weather turned warm and the green shoots of a wheat crop began to show. It was a time of unbounded joy. They would celebrate by going into town, into a real town, not miniscule Trinchera, but cosmopolitan Trinidad!

Planning for the trip into Trinidad became almost an event in itself: Tom made sure he inquired of the Doherty's for proper directions when he went to draw some cash for the journey. The thirty miles or so, Tom knew, would take two days each way in the family wagons. That would mean a stay in Trinidad of two or three days just to make the journey worthwhile. A six- or seven-day venture away from the animals, particularly the chickens — the horses, most of the mules and Pup would go with them, of course — meant they had to get someone to feed them, most likely a family from the next claim south, two miles away. Getting to Trinidad itself was no mean trick, especially during snowmelt when the creeks were running out of their banks. They would have to begin on wagon trails that more or less paralleled the south rim of the Purgatoire for three miles to a place just across from the tiny town of Alfalfa on the river's north bank. Then they would have to cut southwest across the open prairie along San Francisco Creek to the nearest bridge, which was just west of the two small Hispanic communities of Barela and Marguerite. They would have to camp overnight in their wagons somewhere near here. Once to this point, however, it was a clear shot to Trinidad, for there was a good road alongside the Ft. Worth & Denver City railroad tracks for some five miles. The wagon track continued southwestward through the communities of Garcia and Cordova in the giant shadow of Raton Mesa's Fisher's Peak, and so into Trinidad's Main Street.

The new Coloradans drove into Trinidad just as they planned, except that summer had suddenly arrived. Day after day of full sun and high temperature oppressed them. They all got sunburns, even sitting under the canvas tops of their covered wagons. The cold climate had aggravated Tom's rheumatism, and this sudden heat seemed to make it even worse, but he said nothing about it. This was to be a great adventure, like driving into another world. Never had these humble Texas emigrants seen streets paved in red brick before, and certainly never a *whole town* paved in red brick. "Look at this," gasped Verna Perry: a sign pointing east to Dodge City, Kansas — practically the edge of the world — and west to Santa Fe and the California Trail. This was their intersection with the Santa Fe Trail, the famous cattlemans' highway. "Just think," Verna said, "this very road goes all the way to Dodge City. And probably to New York!"

And the houses! Why, there were veritable mansions right on Main Street: the Bloom house had *three* stories and ornate Victorian Rococo gingerbread all over it. It even had a towering cupola *four* stories high. Its red brick trimmed with native sandstone may have been fashionable, but it looked extravagant to the poor immigrants. And the decorative wrought iron railings around the second story balcony and the roof must themselves have cost ten years of a farmer's income. Mr. Frank G. Bloom must have been a very wealthy merchant when he built this house in 1882 — in fact, he was a banker and a cattleman as well as a merchant. To a Texas ingenue, his home was just plain unbelievable. There was sure nothing like it in Hico! And the Baca house! It too was three stories high — or at least two stories with a big pyramidal roof — and even though its Greek Revival style was more restrained than the Bloom house, and its adobe construction more appropriate to a frontier town, it certainly must belong to a prosperous Hispano family, as indeed it did: the Bacas were successful sheep ranching entrepreneurs.

The rest of the town was similarly astonishing. While driving with their wagon brakes poised in readiness on the steep brick streets that reflected the heat at their faces, the Texan tourists gawked at the First National Bank building with its Romanesque Revival style. Clayborne shouted, "Papa, it's got faces on the front door!" In fact it did: numerous carved faces decorated the bank's doorway arch and upper facade. Close by was the Trinidad Opera House that seated eight hundred people. Belle read the name of the building to Clayborne and tried to explain that an opera was a play in which people sang the words instead of talking, but since no one among them had ever seen an opera to give a firsthand account of the artistry involved, the boy was baffled by such a peculiar idea. And who would go for that old-timey music anyway? Two wagons to the rear of the Perrys, Claytia Blackburn pointed to the people in front of a corner cafe, "Look at the funny hat that man has on." It was a turban. Strange looking people walked the streets of Trinidad, people such as the Texans had never seen before: Turkish, Chinese, Russians, Poles, Finns, Greeks, Portugese and more. Now they believed the saying they had heard in Trinchera: "In Trinidad you can hear sixteen languages on one street corner."

And on this street corner there was something else they had never seen: an electric streetcar. The Trinidad Electric Transmission Railway and Gas Company ran streetcars from the center of town to the outlying districts of

Starkville, Piedmont and Cokedale, according to the signs on the front of the strange looking contraptions. The humming and snapping of sparks on the overhead power wires fascinated young Clayborne.

They drove by the Columbian Hotel where presidents had stayed, then they turned north on Commercial Street, past the Victorian Sherman Building and the First Presbyterian Church. They knew that a First Baptist Church was somewhere in town and meant to ask around as to its whereabouts. They crossed the Commercial Street bridge over the Purgatoire River, built in 1905 by Marsh Bridge Company, Des Moines, Iowa. Tom led the four families up a hill toward Kit Carson Park where they would camp in their wagons. At the entrance they swung their vehicles into the wooded park among other wagons and buggies and paid a nominal fee for three days of camping.

Kit Carson Park occupied a large city block on San Pedro Street in a residential area of substantial but not pretentious homes. A few examples of Carpenter Gothic style and poor man's gingerbread decoration could be seen surrounding the park, but most houses here were simple, solid, plain homes. The park was a regional gathering place full of tall oak trees towering over greening lawns and shrubs, children's swings, picnic tables, a bandstand and a bronze equestrian statue of the heroic trapper, guide, Indian agent and soldier, Christopher "Kit" Carson.

Tom Perry winced as he helped Belle down from the wagon, and she asked, "Are you okay, Tom?"

"Oh, it's nothing," he said stoically, fighting down the pain in his joints. "Must have sat wrong driving the wagon." She did not believe him. It was getting worse, she had noticed in the past weeks. But she said nothing. The families dispersed through the park to enjoy themselves, taking food baskets to picnic tables. Clayborne and Claytia and Pup immediately made for the swings, where they occupied themselves for hours. Around the sidewalk border of the park, lines of apple trees bore lush green apples still some weeks from ripeness. "I sure wish those apples were red, Claytia," said Clayborne as they drifted back and forth in the lazy rhythm of the swings. "Me too, Clayborne," she sighed, inwardly tasting the crunch of the crisp fruit. They had not had an apple since Christmas.

Their Trinidad visit had brought them to Kit Carson Park over a weekend, showing them the ordinary social life of a thriving frontier town at first hand. On Saturday, an early season company picnic of brickyard employees from the refractory north of town occupied half a dozen park tables. A touring band with fancy orange and white uniforms and glittering euphoniums and trombones serenaded the neighborhood with popular favorites of the day such as *Neptune's Court* and the cornet trio *Three Aces*. Mobs of people crowded around the raised bandstand for a rousing rendition of the classical war horse, *Poet and Peasant Overture* by von Suppe. Strange as it was, Clayborne took it all in stride: this was just what people did in towns.

Tom and Leonard Perry fell into conversation with some of the locals, miners from the nearby coal fields at Jerryville. The economy of Trinidad was booming, they said. The brick works was doing well. The five stage lines were dying out, but seven railroads served Las Animas County. The sheep and cattle business was thriving. Up at Thatcher, northeast of Trinidad by Hole-in-the-Rock stage station there was a new helium well, and helium was destined to take the place of explosive hydrogen in the dirigible industry, which was well established in 1916 — the Zeppelin *Deutschland* was flying passengers between Dusseldorf and Friedrichshafen in Germany right now. In short, there was work to be had, the Texans were told — just in case the farming didn't work out. Plenty of coal mines around here, and the coal business would never go bad, the miners said, not as long as there were trains, and that would be forever. There were almost fifty coal mines in Las Animas County alone, but the best pay was north in Pueblo, where there was a steel mill to go with its coal mines.

Only one problem with working the coal mines, the locals said, and that was the unions. Just last year they'd called a seven-month strike. Meant going without work and without money. A strange way to get the better wages and working conditions they were supposed to be out for. So what if miners worked twelve hours a day and seven days a week? It beat not working at all, and, besides, that was better hours and wages than a farmer got. But some corporation managers were not about to grant any concessions to workmen; one had said, "If a workman sticks up his head, hit it." They had hit heads pretty good here in Colorado last year, the locals said. There were about 9,000 men on strike during that seven months last year, and at one coal mine not too far from here, company guards decided to attack a workers' encampment with firearms, pinning them down for hours. Twenty-one coal miners had been killed in the barrage and more than a hundred wounded. But other than strikes, the locals swore up and down, coal mines were the best thing that ever happened to the state.

Fred Blackburn and Robert Dozier joined the conversation, and Robert in particular wanted to hear what the miners had to say. He did not like the dry weather that had set in, and he had been talking to other farmers at the Doherty store in Trinchera. He had told his fellow settlers all about it. The regulars at Doherty's had said that you couldn't make a wheat crop on the bench land one year in seven because there was not enough rain. That all the successful farmers they had been told about were successful because they irrigated. That the Texans were doomed to certain failure. The Trinchera old-timers seemed very certain about what they said. Robert Dozier could not face the idea of going back to Texas whipped like a cur. If the farm didn't come off, then he would stay here in Colorado until he made good at something. Even if it was coal mining. Even if there were strikes.

The men discovered that the First Baptist Church was practically next door to Kit Carson Park and determined that their families would attend services on Sunday morning before the trip back to their Trinchera farms. All felt the need of a close conversation with their maker.

It was completely dry in Southeastern Colorado after the May 4th snowstorm. When the four families returned to their claims from the Trinidad holiday, the wheat crop was scarcely any higher than when they had left it seven days earlier. Their jubilation now turned to cautious concern. The hot weather continued with no sign of rain. By the end of May, their concern turned to alarm. The sun rose every day to a cloudless sky and set the same way. The crops were not growing. The wheat turned brown. The kitchen garden had not even come up. The farmers at Doherty's had been right: they would fail.

In mid-June, Belle told Tom she was in "the family way" again, as the polite circumlocution of the day went, due in early September. By that time, Tom could no longer hide his rheumatism: it had worsened to the point that he could hardly walk. He was badly bent over and he finally had to make a pair of crutches for himself from dead juniper limbs. Things were coming to a crisis. The families called a joint meeting to say openly what they had known privately for weeks. There was no hope left. Only when hope is abandoned can action be taken. They met in the tent of Tom Perry.

Tom was the oldest among them, and they all looked up to him. He hobbled to his kitchen table and sat down slowly, resting his homemade crutches on the cane-bottom chair. Then he plainly told them, "It's no use. The crops are not going to grow. We're not going to make it here, and I guess we better face the facts."

Robert Dozier said, "We all know that, Tom. I been tellin' you."

"You're right, Bob. You told us, and we should have listened. I think we all did listen, though. We just wouldn't come out and say it when we were all together."

Fred Blackburn spoke up, "The question is, what are we going to do now?"

Belle Perry insisted, "Well, Tom's not going to work in any coal mine, that's a fact. I've heard you all talking about it. I know about those strikes and those men getting killed. Tom's not afraid of that. But he's too stove up with the rheumatism to walk. He can't work in any coal mine."

"And Fred is not going to work in any coal mine, either, sick or well," asserted Myrtle forcefully. "We're farmers. We don't need any of those strikes and all that killing. We're going back to Texas, and we're going to farm, and that's that."

"Now, Myrtle," said Fred gently. "You never can tell. We might go home to Texas and then come back just to prove up this claim. It could be worth something some day. We might have to work in a coal mine. They don't always have strikes. Could be a good thing. Don't count it out too soon."

Leonard Perry spoke carefully now, his fun-loving spirit subdued: "Tom, I know you're in no shape to come work in the mines. And I know you're going to need help getting back to Texas. I can tell that you've decided to go back. I just want you to know that *I* can't go back. I came here to make my own way, and I'm going to stay here until I do it. Then maybe I'll come home to Texas. Tell Papa. Maybe then. But not before. I'm sorry."

"You don't need to apologize, Leonard," said Tom. "You're my brother." Verna Perry said, "But, Tom, Leonard's right about you needing help to get back to Texas, loading the cattle car and such. We'll help."

"There's no money for a cattle car, Verna. I appreciate your offer, but I think we'll manage in the wagon."

Fred Blackburn said, "There'll be no problem, Tom. I'm going home to Texas, too, just like Myrtle said. I think we'll end up coming back and proving up the claim here, but I'm going home first. We've got no money for any cattle car either. You and me, we'll take the wagons back, Tom, follow the Ft. Worth & Denver tracks. Tie the buggies on behind 'em. We'll go together. We can double-team across rivers and up canyons if we have to. We'll make it."

Robert Dozier said, "I'm sorry, Tom, but I'm staying along with Leonard. I can't go back and face my Pa with nothing. We've put everything into this place. If we leave now, we'll only get a couple hundred dollars for the claim from some big rancher around here, if we're that lucky. They're like vultures, just waiting for us to keel over. That's how some of them got so big already, skinning the homesteaders."

"I understand, Bob," said Tom. "You do what you have to. We all got families, we all got responsibilities, and we have to do what we think is right."

"Oh, you're so right about them vultures," said Belle bitterly. "That land agent was the worst of them. He knew what farming was like out here when he sold us this claim. He knew we'd starve out. And, by cracky, I'll bet you he comes up here with an offer to buy us out for just what it cost us!"

Leonard Perry went on, "Tom, if Bob and me can stick it out and prove up our claims, we'll get the land for just our registration fee of fifty dollars. We don't have to live on it the full year, only three months out of twelve. If we can work in the mines up in Pueblo nine months of the year, we can make enough to spend the summer down here and make our obligation. After three years it's ours, and then we can sell it for a thousand dollars or more for livestock range. The real estate agents are getting three dollars an acre now. Think of the farm you could buy in Texas for a thousand dollars! Isn't that worth staying for?"

"I hope you do that, Leonard," said Tom gently. "I'd like to stay with you just to see it happen because you're my brother, but I can't. You're still young and plucky. You need to prove yourself. I don't seem to need that anymore. Got it out of my system. I've gone west, and owned my own land, and my profit on it is to see what it's like to starve out. Papa was right, I should have stayed home and worked his land, and when I get home I'll look him in the eye and tell him so. I'll rent a while on his land and one day I'll have my own place, close by family and friends in a land I know." Tom heard himself speaking this speech and wondered if he would be able to live up to his brave words.

They sat quietly for a time, pondering their ruined hopes. A meadowlark outside somewhere sang at the gold sky. Flies crooned in the tent. There was pain and grief in the air. But the cold resolve was again taken out from the cabinets of their souls, and it drowned all tender feelings in waves of necessity. They could be destroyed. They could fail. But they could not be defeated. Not really defeated.

"Then it's settled?" asked Myrtle Blackburn. "Leonard and Verna and Bob and Mary Ann are staying? And Belle and Tom and Fred and me are going back to Hico?"

"It's settled," said Tom Perry.

Fred Blackburn and Tom Perry had all the help they needed getting ready to go home. Leonard and Robert helped build jets out the side of the returning wagons, widening them to accommodate a sleeping bed: Tom's and Fred's families would be living in these vehicles for many weeks. The four men did the heavy work in the cool of the June evenings, with Tom mostly crippling around on his crutches carrying small objects. Tom did manage to get into Trinchera to write a check for the funds his family would need on the way back — leaving barely a hundred fifty dollars in his account. They finished loading late one hot June afternoon. The food for Tom's family was stashed in the Emerson buggy, which was then tied behind his wagon. The Blackburns, likewise. When all the movable goods were ready to go, it was dark and time for their last night together on the plains of Trinchera. No one said much.

In the russet dawn of June 22, 1916, they brought their draft animals out to the wagons. Tom hitched the mule Jack to the right of the doubletree and the mare Pet to the left. Pet always worked best on the left. Clayborne climbed into the covered wagon with his dog Pup and waved goodbye to Robert Junior and Alma and Otis. The women hugged each other and the men shook hands. Tom tied Clayborne's donkey to the back of the wagon. The Blackburns lifted Claytia and Lawton into their wagon and climbed up behind their children.

Then Tom and Belle and their unborn child took their places on the spring-mounted seat. This was it. Time to go. Tom looked around wordlessly for a long minute before pushing off. It was a sere alien land he saw. It had never been, would never be home. Home. They were going home now. Home to Texas. Migrating again. Moving on. Moving . . .

"East," Tom thought astonished as he flicked the wagon traces. "Dear God, we're moving east."

Colorado, goodbye.

-4-

RETREAT

THE first few miles out from their homesteads on that sad Thursday, June 22, 1916, they said nothing, not the Perrys, not the Blackburns in the wagon behind. They only attended to their slow progress toward the first day's goal, Trinchera. The horse Pet and the harnessed mules strained in the heat, heavy laden. Frequent stops would be needed to rest the animals: the travelers would be lucky to make ten miles a day, twelve maximum.

The families looked on impassively as the scenery went lazily by. It was the last time they would behold the nameless low hills and the shallow arroyos with their green junipers and shimmering cottonwoods in full leaf. This scoured and pure land where the wind blew forever had never been theirs. Its implacable beauty had not burned into their souls. The sorrow Tom felt as his covered wagon rumbled away from this crucible of testing was not for the place, it was for a future that would never happen. He could feel his illusions withering back there, forsaken in the abandoned Colorado soil. Going west! Taking up land! On his own! What vanity it had been. The land, the wind, the sun did not even laugh at him, only ignored him in sublime indifference. All he could do was bear his lot stoically. If failure can be graced with a somber majesty, Tom wore its mantle.

In his own way, Tom Perry had discovered a hard historical fact in Colorado: the frontier was closed. Settlers in droves had taken up nearly all the workable homesteads already. Like Tom, dozens of settlers in Southeastern Colorado had realized that the grassy slopes of the Rocky

Mountains were unfit for proper farming — low volume grazing, surely, but not farming. America had conquered as much of this wilderness as it ever would. No one would ever break this land to the plow. Ever. The settlers were leaving, leaving for towns. It made no difference whether they went west anymore, as long as they went toward towns.

West! What did that mean now? The West was no longer a giant mythos of national expansion and wilderness living and prospecting for gold and frontier justice, it was just a place on a map. West beyond the Rockies in the parched Great Basin, dryland farmers would never thrive. Even the romantic Western badman had become just another thug; the image of Pinkertons and Butch Cassidys was fading into mere cops and robbers. West in golden California there were too many settlers already. It was positively citified. Nowadays, California meant Hollywood, the sleepy little palm-studded suburb that had become home to the new magic of the movies. There was no farther west to go. Tom realized in his rough-hewn way that this had something very important to do with the spirit of America.

A professor from Wisconsin named Frederick Jackson Turner had know it clearly and dispassionately since 1893. One evening in July of that year at a program of the Columbian Exposition in Chicago he had read his paper, "The Significance of the Frontier in American History." He told his audience that America's most cherished institutions had arisen because of the "transforming effects of the American wilderness." Turner wrote of the American pioneer: "out of his wilderness experience, out of the freedom of his opportunities, he fashioned a formula for social regeneration — the freedom of the individual to seek his own." In short, the pioneer life fostered individualism, independence and qualities in the common man that strengthened self-government. But as thousands of farmers had discovered and Will Rogers was about to observe, there is a lot of difference between pioneering for gold and pioneering for spinach. Fed up with failed crops, they opted for the towns.

Tom sensed that the days of American wilderness life had vanished with his own fortunes. Big things were changing. Farm families everywhere were drifting to the cities. World war was brewing on the near horizon. A droll little man named Einstein was saying strange things about matter and energy and c^2. The Armory Show of 1913 in New York had swept away America's artistic innocence in a wave of Pablo Picasso and Marcel Duchamp modernism. A new music called jazz was creeping out of New Orleans' notorious Storyville bordellos into Chicago night-clubs with Tom Brown's Dixieland Jass Band. Because of men like Henry Ford, industry was replacing agriculture as the largest employer. The solid and coherent past was preparing to crack like a jolted windowpane: all the glass of society would remain in place, but it would be fragmented, each fragment a different shape, and isolated from the rest by thin fractures, the geologic faultlines of society. Tom Perry had read of these changes in the *St. Louis Republic* back in Texas, but now he could sense them in his bones: he felt he was not only driving east, he was driving into a different America.

Pup impertinently stuck his nose into the wind behind the driver's seat, tasting the warm air. Tom smiled at his son's dog, and took comfort: at least the family was together, Pup and all, even if they had to live in a wagon that held all their earthly possessions. Their possessions, how few! The bed, placed sideways so its head and foot extended out beyond the wagon sides, where they were supported by wooden jets constructed for the purpose; the iron cookstove; the safe and its burden of dishes; their tools and plows; a little medicine chest; the kitchen table and chairs. Everything they had brought to Colorado they were taking back to Texas.

Above their scanty possessions, large wooden hoops had been attached by brackets on the wagon sides. Over the hoops a large canvas wagon sheet had been lashed in the semblance of a Conestoga or prairie schooner. At the rear, this wagon sheet could be pulled shut by a drawstring, leaving only a little circular opening that Clayborne liked to peek through. The front also had a drawstring, but couldn't close as tightly. The buggy trailing behind had been tied securely to the wagon, its twin shafts tucked under the wagon bed and its shallow body stuffed with goods and food from its front dash rail to its rear boot. Walking along behind the Perry's wagon trudged the little donkey Clayborne had come to love. Clayborne! The boy was Tom's delight, and the father looked forward with both dread and anticipation to the child that would come in September — another precious soul, but how would he support it?

They reached the tracks of the Ft. Worth & Denver Railway late that afternoon and one last time the misspelled TRINCHERE station sign hove into view. Beyond the railroad station, the way would be easier to follow: graded wagon roads paralleled the tracks from here all the way to Hico. As the sun vanished behind Raton Mesa, the families made their farewell passage through tiny Trinchera and began searching for a place to spend the night. Several other wagons seemed to be doing the same. A quarter mile east of town, Tom knew, there was a little draw that would offer shelter from the night wind. There the Perrys and Blackburns turned aside, rolling a few yards into a grassy swale between the wagon road and the railroad track to make their first camp. While the men unhitched the teams, Belle and Myrtle got out the cooking utensils and the children scouted the area for firewood.

"Here's some old railroad ties, Papa," shouted Clayborne from the roadbed, Pup prancing around his feet. "Claytia, come look at all these crossties!"

The just-turned-six-year-old girl came running, her calico skirt flapping. She stopped by Clayborne's side and frowned, looking skeptically at the dirty and mostly smashed ties discarded in the sweet summer grass. "Will crossties burn?" she yelled to her father.

"They'll burn fine," called Fred to his daughter as he filled the feedbags for his two mules. "We'll just have to take an axe to them, that's all."

Fred Blackburn approached the site of Clayborne's discovery, Tom limping behind. Fred looked at the strew ties and said, "If it's like this all the way home, we'll never lack for firewood." Twenty-five years worth of replaced and discarded crossties seemed to lay scattered along the railbed as far as the eye could see in the gathering gloom, the gift of many maintenance section men over the years.

"Clayborne and Claytia, see if the two of you can grab that end of the tie so Mister Perry won't have to lift this heavy weight," said Fred Blackburn. "And kick the tie first to make sure there's no snakes under it."

The children were only too happy to oblige. Somehow, they felt very grown up helping to carry an important object like a crosstie. Tom hobbled ahead of them and took his axe out of the wagon. When the tie was trundled in, Tom had finished sharpening the axe on a worn whetstone from his toolbox. Now everyone stood back for Tom's short, deft strokes. Even with this hounding inflammation in his joints, Tom was still an expert axeman. He needed no long swing to take apart the splintered old tie: some gandy dancer years ago had made a good start on it. Two or three short axe blows split the tie into long sticks and a few well-placed wedge cuts reduced them to firewood length. One stick was reserved for slivering into kindling; for this the axe was not swung, but rather pushed down the woodgrain, layer by layer, shearing off thin strips. When the pile of kindling was big enough, Tom laid aside his axe and looked for the softest piece of wood in the pile. He turned the stick he had selected in the air, judging its grain. He laid the end of the stick on a rock and with his pocketknife made dozens of quick short cuts that peeled back little curls of wood from the stick's shaft, but did not sever them. He worked the piece into a whifflestick that looked like a Christmas tree with small, bushy, easily ignitable curls of wood curving like limbs from a long trunk.

When Tom was through making the firewood, Belle and Myrtle carried it to a fire ring they had cleared in the bare gravel a few yards from the railroad bed. Myrtle arranged the sticks and kindling, and touched a match to the whifflestick, a perfect firestarter. They had no other firestarter, no coal oil, no paper — paper was a precious commodity not to be found along railroad tracks. Before long a respectable cookfire tapered into the darkening sky.

Clayborne and Claytia and three-year-old Lawton played at catching grasshoppers while the women cooked supper. Myrtle and Belle had spread the glowing coals with a stick into an area large enough to accommodate four cooking utensils. A pot of beans had been bubbling for half an hour on one edge of the fire, supported by three flat rocks. Two skillets got the rest of the fire: one open and sizzling with bacon, the other covered, with biscuits steaming inside, protected from sticking to the pan by a thin coat of lard. In a few minutes, the biscuits would have to be turned over to keep their bottoms from burning. The ubiquitous enamelled coffeepot boiled away at the edge of the coals. A gallon sorghum bucket heavy with dark syrup had been set out on a large rock along with the dishes and knives and forks. There was no butter, no milk, no eggs. The usual crockery jugs of water wrapped in wetted burlap lay on the ground with the usual carved and shaped corncob for a stopper. Four kitchen chairs had been brought out of the wagons and now made a half-ring around the campfire where the two women sat watching supper cook.

The two men went apart from the rest, talking so they could not be overheard.

"I don't want to scare the womenfolks, but I'm worried about the water," said Tom.

"For the animals," agreed Fred. "I've been worried about it too. This has been a terrible dry year, no rain since the fourth of May."

Tom said, "There's precious little water here in the draw, and we'll be hitting some dry country up ahead. Beyond Coloflats it's a long way I hear, two days, to Folsom. We don't have barrels or anything to carry water for them."

"I don't know what we can do, Tom," said Fred.

"Just keep going, I guess. And hope. But I wanted to make sure you knew."

Supper was quiet that night.

They bedded down in their wagons and soon found that sleeping next to a railroad track was going to be noisy business. The midnight westbound passenger train was the first to waken them, then a 1:36 a.m. eastbound fast freight, then a 3:10 a.m. local way freight that left a short string of cars on the Trinchera siding amidst extended huffing and banging. They quickly accustomed themselves to the racket, but not enough to sleep through the 6:00 a.m. westbound freight that told them it was time to arise.

Another cloudless day. Another meal to prepare. Another stretch of miles to drive. After breakfast and hitching up the teams, the two families reloaded their food and supplies and set off. As the two covered wagons pulled onto the graded gravel road, Fred Blackburn studied Tom for a moment, then called from his driver's seat, "How far to Hico, Tom?"

"Five hundred miles, Fred, give or take."

"I'll race you!"

Tom smiled and Clayborne perked up: "Let's race, Papa!" Pup barked his approval.

When no sign of a real race appeared, Claytia in the other wagon yelled a challenge, "I'll bet we can beat you! Come on, Papa, let's race!" Lawton piped up, "Race! Papa, let's race!"

Squinting ahead into the yellow morning, Clayborne had second thoughts: "I can't see Hico, Papa! How far is five hundred miles?"

The heavy mood of the first day out was broken, and the wagons rolled eastward into the morning light. The women had donned their poke bonnets as a ward against sunburn, the road was good, the going easy, the track downhill with few grades to pull. Perhaps all was not right with the world; neither was it all wrong.

There seemed to be a great deal of traffic this Friday. Two or three farm wagons appeared every mile or so, a chugging automobile went by, and a few solitary horsemen had decided to use the main road as a traverse from one ranch to the next. It soon became evident that the railroad's discarded crossties constituted a staple resource for the wagon traffic: cookfires dotted the roadbed by encamped wagons and old ties crackled while sidemeat fried.

At Chaney Arroyo the wagons slacked down a steep pitch and hauled back up, slowly passing the thrusted bulk of Alps Mesa on their right and then joining the long straightaway that pointed toward the little boom-town of Coloflats. Out here they were beyond the ranches. They were in the exact geographic center of nowhere. As they passed the spire of Watervale Butte, which separated them temporarily from the Ft. Worth & Denver's tracks, the landscape glinted empty tawny green in every direction, grass, grass, nothing but grass. And rocks and mesas and buttes and spires and heat. There were no sideroads, no houses, no homesteaders, not even travellers, no sign of humanity at all. Just a mirage of straight dirt road vanishing into infinity in front and a mirage of straight dirt road vanishing into another infinity behind. For all they could tell, the road might go clear around the world like this and come back under their rear wheels. Where the gravel road finally curved to skirt Doss Arroyo they could look north for miles and see no sign whatever of civilization. And the men noted silently that Doss Creek had no water in it.

Several hours after dinner, as the arc of the afternoon sun drew to the amber West, they began the sweltering trudge up Trementina Hill to Coloflats. Here, just west of the rawhide town, within a mile of each other, three headwater forks of Trementina Creek gullied under the road. None sheltered a drop of water. Tom and Fred exchanged looks as their wagons came abreast in the new town of Coloflats. Would there be water here? They found tent buildings and falsefront stores only a year old, created to milk the boom of homesteaders. They passed a post office that advertised locking mail boxes and a hotel where the new arrival could find a larruping good meal and a soft bed for fifty cents — if he had fifty cents. Set in the surrounding hills were the spreads of a few old-timers, ranchers who looked with amusement and contempt upon the jimmy-come-late-lies who thought they could farm this country. Just ahead, not far from the Coloflats unloading platform of the Ft. Worth & Denver, the men's question was answered. There lay a dusty public watering trough. The animals would drink their fill this afternoon.

But Tom complained to Belle, "I'm right reluctant to water the animals here, Belle. I don't like these public watering troughs. Might have been animals drinking here that have the distemper. I'd sure hate to have ole' Pet or Jack come down with the distemper."

Belle looked at him squarely. "There's nothing for it. You'll just have to get down and water them here, Tom. You haven't seen any more water in the creeks than I have. And I don't expect it's going to get any better up ahead for a long ways."

Tom looked at her a long moment, realizing he could not shield her from problems she could plainly see.

At the eastern edge of Coloflats, an hour or two before sunset, Belle pointed to an unpainted ranch house beside a large eyesore of a barn off the road on the left and said, "Oh, Tom, let's see if we can buy some milk for the boy. He hasn't had any for a couple of days now. And maybe some eggs, too."

Tom pulled the wagon up the long trail to the decrepit house while the Blackburns waited on the road at the gate. A prematurely aging and painfully thin ranch wife wearing a flour sack calico dress came out to see what they wanted and agreed that they might buy some milk and eggs.

"You folks come far?" she said with a friendly smile.

"From just up north of Trinchera, Ma'am," answered Tom. "We weren't too happy with the farming up there. Going back home to Texas now." Tom reached back into the wagon, pulling up the milk jar, a one-quart metal container much like an oversized Army canteen with screw-on top, and handed it to the woman. Her husband appeared around the back of the tumbledown barn and said peevishly, "A quart will cost ye a dime."

The woman added, "And eggs are seventeen cents a dozen."

"We got the money all right," said Belle, shaking a tattered black silk change purse. "We want our Clayborne here to have a little milk."

"All right," said the irritable rancher, who took the canteen from his wife and disappeared around the back of the weathered house.

The woman said, "Don't pay him no mind. He's just a bit tetchy on account of the heat. He's going after the milk in the ice box. We got ourselves an ice box, we do. Get the ice in Coloflats. Train leaves it. Milk keeps longer that way in this heat. And you're going back to Texas, are ye? Well, by Grannies, there's lots of folks come by here looking for milk and eggs going back to somewheres. And a chicken or two."

"What's that, Ma'am?" asked Tom.

"Chickens," the thin woman smiled. "We got chickens. Lots of folks come looking to buy chickens. What do you hear from Trinchera about the drought? And what about this here war in Germany? We get Germans come by every now and then, come to America to get away from the war."

"Haven't heard anything about the war, Ma'am. I just hope we stay out of it. I do know about the drought. Drought's what drove us out. The Dohertys up at the Trinchera store say it's a bad one. Only the irrigated farms are going to make any crops this year. Starved out lots of folks."

"Oh, you're telling me!" exclaimed the farm lady. "Why, folks coming by lately tell us the most miserable tales of misfortune you can imagine. It's just terrible what's happening all over this land here. I never drempt we'd have such a dad blamed drought as this. We've got cattle ourselves, you know, so we won't be hurtin', but we aren't going to make no corn or wheat this year. No extra cash. Won't be able to fix the barn this year. And if it warn't for me and my water bucket, there wouldn't be no garden this year, either, by gum."

The ranch woman turned to Belle and said, "I see you're in a family way, Missus. What kind would ye like?"

Belle blushed. Not accustomed to open comments on pregnancy, she wished she could have plugged Clayborne's ears. "Well, we got our fine boy here. I expect I'd like a girl. But we'll take what the good Lord provides."

The crotchety man reappeared, canteen in hand. He carried a basket containing a dozen white eggs. "You got an egg basket, Missus? Better keep 'em in a cool spot in this heat."

"Right here," said Belle, extending her own basket.

As he transferred the eggs, the farmer asked Tom, "Which way you going?"

"East," said Tom, reminding himself.

"Well, you better pick all the places you can to water your animals. Ain't a whole lot of water between here and Folsom. The hot spell done dried it all up."

"And how far is Folsom?" asked Tom.

"See that cut where the railroad tracks go through the rocks?"

"Yep."

"Well, that's Emery's Gap. And see right next to it where the mesa comes down to the flat and the wagon road goes out of sight?"

"Yep."

"That's Tollgate Pass. Ain't no tollgate there anymore, it's just a name. Well, Emery's Gap and Tollgate Pass is both right on the state line. Colorado here, New Mexico there. Folsom's a good sixteen mile off from there. And you got Seven Mile Canyon to go through on the Cimarron. Take you two days to Folsom with that load. You and your friend down on the road."

"What about water in Seven Mile Canyon? In the Cimarron River?"

"They don't call it the Dry Cimarron for nothing."

The Perrys and Blackburns looked for a campsite with water while the light held. When darkness finally overtook them they were perhaps two miles into New Mexico. Next to the railroad tracks they found a parched streambed with scattered pools of water in the scooped rock. Several other wagons had already set up camp there. The two newcomer families were waved in amid calls of welcome. "This is about the only water around here, mister," said a burly man standing in the evening shadows by a heavy-duty freight wagon. He ate from a tin cup of beans. "It's here or nowhere, so y'all come on in."

"You come camp over here," called a sturdy woman of Teutonic extraction. Two covered wagons of German immigrants had made an L in the gravel by the railroad track. "We got a good flat place for the both of you, huh, Papa?" Next to their campfire a small wiry man sporting a bushy mustache looked up from sharpening his axe and agreed with his wife. Two blonde boys looked over the axehandle at the new arrivals, particularly eyeing Clayborne's donkey walking behind the wagon. Pup barked at the campers. "Hush, Pup," quieted Clayborne.

The mother of the two blonde boys talked up to Belle, walking alongside the wagons as Tom and Fred threaded them through the campsite. "We coming to America to get away from the Kaiser. You know a big war he's making in Europe. Papa got a job in Colorado, America. He's a streetcar mechanic back in Germany, and they got streetcars in Colorado, America. In a place called Trinidad we got work. You know how far is that?"

Tom spoke down from his wagon as he pulled into place, "You ought to be there in four days, Ma'am."

"Four days!" cried the woman. "You hear that, Papa? Four more days, and we be there!"

The Blackburns and Perrys made the most of their welcome to this fortunate campsite and began the ritual of unloading and cooking. The two German wives made introductions all around and insisted on helping Belle and Myrtle with everything. "We going to have a fine time tonight," Helga Bauer said in unison with Marta Kohl. Their husbands were of a similarly congenial frame of mind.

"You going east," said Albert Kohl to Tom and Fred as he helped unhitch their teams. "Not much water back there. We just come from New Braunfels in Texas. We have brothers there. Help us get jobs in Colorado, America."

Fred Blackburn said, "I'm from Hico, Texas, myself. Never been to New Braunfels. Hear it's a right nice place."

Heinz Bauer smiled ironically and said, "Nice place. No work. Only farming. We don't know how to be a farmer. We both been mechanics in Germany."

Tom remarked wryly while putting hobbles on Pet, "We been farming all our lives, and it doesn't look like we know how to be a farmer either. We starved out on our homesteads in Colorado."

"Yes, I hear you have no rain this year in Colorado, America," said Kohl. "You go back to Texas, they have enough rain there."

Just then Belle called to her husband "Consarn it, Tom those folks in Coloflats didn't fill this jug up full. Look at here, it's a ways down to the milk. For a dime they ought to fill it plumb full."

Tom sniffed into the canteen and grunted in disgust. "You're right. It smells fresh enough, but it's not full. They seemed like fine people, too."

The headlight of an eastbound fast freight pierced the blue gloaming on the roadbed above them and the train's roar ended their conversation.

The third day dawned hot and cloudless. The Perrys and the Blackburns awoke to the aroma of meaty German sausage and convivial memories of the previous evening's camaraderie. The Kohls and Bauers had long bestirred themselves and were nearly ready to depart. "You get plenty water now, Mister Perry," said Heinz Bauer. "It be hot and dry today, you'll see."

Tom and Fred made sure the animals drank their fill, and took care to see that the families' own water jugs were full. The Perrys possessed only a single gallon jug and a spare half gallon jug, the Blackburns, two one-gallon jugs. That might not be enough today unless they found water along the way.

The temperature by noon would soar to over 100 degrees, and that was an important biological fact. Normal human skin temperature is 92 degrees F., which is several degrees less than internal body temperature. If the air is cooler than the skin, any excess body core heat flows to the skin where it can be harmlessly conducted away by the air itself. But when the air temperature is higher than skin temperature, there is only one way the body knows how to keep cool: by sweating. On a hundred degree day, even at rest in the shade, a normal human being will perspire away a quart of water in two hours. If that water is not replaced by drinking, the body will lose control of its temperature. A water loss equal to ten percent of body weight will render even the toughest person critically ill. Much more will result in quick death. On this Saturday, the margin of survival of the Perrys and Blackburns hung on simple arithmetic: with only half a gallon of water per person, how many hours of hundred-degree-plus temperature would they face?

There was little traffic this Saturday, but they pulled out first thing behind another eastbound wagon and Belle said to Tom, "Look at the sign on that wagon. Isn't that perfectly terrible!" Scrawled in what looked like axle grease on the backboards was the defiant message: "In God we trusted, in Colorado we busted." The blasphemous wagon soon pulled off the road, probably to let one of its occupants answer the call of nature, and the Perrys and Blackburns eyed the driver disapprovingly as they rumbled by. Belle remarked, "I hope you don't feel angry at the Lord, Tom." Tom patted her arm and said, "Of course not. He gave me you and Clayborne."

Several hours down the gravel road to Folsom the Blackburns and Perrys entered Seven Mile Canyon. An approaching passenger train voiced its steam-throated whistle from within the chasm, complaining of its long haul up out of the river channel and belching a revenge of pungent black smoke into the white summer air. The wagon grade was steep and jolting, and the drivers had to apply their brakes for long stretches. Down, down. The canyon walls gradually rose above to enclose them, stifling the roasted breezes: it was as if they were entering the maw of a great bake-oven. Tom and Fred stopped frequently to give the animals a breather, even on this downhill leg — they knew that the uphill grade on the far side of the Cimarron would be murderous. Hot winds ran blistering down the rocks, stirring miniature avalanches of pebbles and dust. Sweat blurred the men's vision. Down, down. The air temperature was 110 degrees F. The ground temperature was 140 degrees F. Even deep shadows under rimrock itched in the stone furnace. Only the hardy little donkey tagging behind the Perry's wagon seemed to be enjoying himself.

Young Clayborne shivered with heat, even though protected in diffused light under the covered wagon's hooped canopy. He stood up behind the driver's seat to catch the breeze, hot though it was, and looked out at the dust-laden rocks and the sweltering dirt. Without warning he shouted in his father's ear, "Papa! Look! Two big rattlesnakes!"

Tom looked around, quickly spotting the two reptiles some yards off the road to the right, and stopped the wagon to watch. The snakes, two healthy three-foot-long specimens of *Crotalus atrox*, the Western Diamondback rattlesnake, were oblivious to their human observers, intent upon raiding a prairie dog town. Tom called to the Blackburn family to pull up, rest their animals and enjoy the show. The prairie dogs had not yet spotted the snakes, but stood wary of their human visitors. The snakes continued to ease their way unseen among tufts of dry bluestem grass, seeking out the burrow entrances that would lead them to a meal of tasty young prairie dog pup.

Furry heads bobbed on the mounds of earth that protected each burrow entrance. The invaders had been spotted! With a shrill bark, a male prairie dog announced to the colony Snake! Snake! and immediately more than half the bobbing heads vanished into their burrows. But not all. A prairie dog "police force", coarse reddish-gray fur bristling, ran headlong for the rattlers. The reptiles both decided to quickly pop into the nearest burrow. The stocky little prairie dogs immediately posted themselves over the snake-infested burrows and several other openings as well — possibly linked to each other by inner chambers — and set frantically to work throwing dirt into the holes. They would bury the snakes alive. A solitary male, seeming to act as supervisor, stood upright on a burrow entrance mound, showing his pale buff underside and flipping his short, flat tail. The snake holes were soon filled and the entrances packed firmly with dirt. When all was finished and the four or five holes sealed, the supervisor prairie dog leaped into the air, throwing his forelimbs up and his head back. While in the midst of this jump he gave what can only be described as a wheezing, whistling yelp. Soon the entire population of the town joined in the jump-yelp. All clear! All clear! As suddenly as it had started, the display stopped. Having presumably entombed two live rattlesnakes permanently, the prairie dog town went back to eyeing its human visitors. The whole exercise had taken less than five minutes.

The pull up the south wall of Seven Mile Canyon grew into exquisite agony. The animals — except for Clayborne's donkey — were hurting. There had been no water in the Dry Cimarron, as expected. The two families had consumed their entire water ration. It would be at least three hours more before sunset. The temperature hovered above a hundred degrees. Their progress was fitful: short haul, breather; short haul, breather, for more than two hours. The animals suffered. The women and children began to feel nauseous. As they gradually emerged from the canyon, the heat seemed to dissipate slightly, and prairie winds taunted them with promises of cooler air.

Up, slowly, maddeningly, up, stop, up, stop. Pet lolled her brave head at every stop now, flecks of foam at her mouth. Jack stood miserably still. Tom feared for the lives of his animals. Only a few more short pitches. Only a few hundred more blistering yards. Up. Up, you poor creatures! Here it comes. Here's the burning top. Now. Here. Out. Out. Out at last.

The sun hung low and red over the desert dust above the canyon. The air was cooler now, but no water in sight. It would be impossible to reach Folsom's public watering trough even if they drove 'til midnight: it still lay eight miles off. The animals could not stand another eight miles today. The Blackburns suffered and the Perrys suffered. They pulled on slowly, slowly. The sun set and no water. At every little gully they stopped and inspected and came up dry. Ten o'clock and still no water. Eleven o'clock. Dry. In desperation they pulled off at a promising arroyo near the railroad tracks but were again disappointed: no trace of water, not even in the hollow rocks. They had seen no one else encamped anywhere nearby.

"We've got to stop here, Tom," said Fred. "The animals can't go on."

"You're right. I'm going to hobble Pet and let Jack go. Together they may find some water. But I hate to do it. I'm afraid somebody might steal them."

"I'll let my mules go, too, Tom. I feel the same way about horse thieves, but we can't keep the animals here without giving them the chance to find water. They'll die for sure."

"I'll tie up the donkey to a mesquite here," said Tom. "He's the only one of us not thirsty. Then at least I'll have a ride to look for them in the morning."

They could only hope the animals would find water or recuperate in the cool of the high plains night. The trail-weary band ate cold leftovers. Clayborne tried to explain to his long-eared friend tied to the tree why there was nothing to drink, noting sadly that he himself had nothing. There was no water to cook with, none to drink. Pup whined a little, but seemed to understand. The families went to bed miserable and exhausted and thirsty, and Lawton cried. The trains that went by that night did not awaken them.

When Tom awoke the fourth morning, he heard no animals. Only the donkey stood tied to the tree. Tom awakened Fred and together they went in search of Pet and their mules. They scanned the arroyo with no luck. They called and called, but heard no answering whinny. Tom said, "I'm going to ride ole' donkey down the gully to see if I can find them. Wish me luck."

Tom bounced with ole' donkey as he clopped his way down the arroyo, swaying between white-stained boulders. The camp vanished behind. Tom called and called. For half an hour he called. Then, at a scarred rock face where the dry streambed veered southward, he heard a faint answering neigh. The donkey's ears pricked up. Tom and ole' donkey took off in the general direction of the sound, scrambling over cobbles and riverstone. The bleached streambed widened and there the mules and Pet grazed beside a deep pool fringed with a mesquite copse. A canyon spring at the pool's head gushed clear. As Tom and Fred had hoped, the horse and mules had smelled water during the night and simply followed their noses.

Back at the camp, their thirsts well slaked, the animals had a good time putting on the feedbag. With full jugs and plenty of water to cook with, the people had a happy breakfast that morning, too.

The evening of the tenth day found the migrants in the New Mexico town of Clayton, not a dozen miles from the Texas border. Clayton was the biggest town they had encountered in a string running from Trinchera and Coloflats and Folsom to Des Moines and Grenville and Mt. Dora. Clayton's adobe houses and frame stores blended into the great grassy sweep of old Kiowa hunting grounds, still home to herds of pronghorn antelope. The grass hid prosperous ranches and even a few successful farms. The sky was no longer desert white, but plains cobalt, almost sapphire, and the land had less of the look of raw wilderness about it and more the feel of conquered territory, a sense of human permanence, though still on the outskirts of civilization.

Clayton, New Mexico, had a wagon yard, a public convenience for travellers somewhat equivalent to the modern motel. Within a fenced compound the wagon voyager could find water and feed, a place to brake the wagon and cook on the ground beside it, most places for a dollar a night — fifty cents, here on the edge of existence. When the Blackburns and Perrys had settled in for the night, Tom took Clayborne aside and had a talk with him. Heat lightning flickered silently on the western horizon.

"Son, your donkey's limping and not keeping up."

"Yes, Papa. I've seen him holding back. Is he sick?"

"No, son, he's not sick. His feet are just getting tender. It's too much walking on these gravel roads. It hurts him. He can't keep it up."

"Can't we get him shoes like Pet?"

"We don't have the money, Clayborne. And Pet needs the shoes. She pulls the wagon for us."

"But, Papa, I think the world and all of ole' donkey. He's my friend, like Pup or Jack."

Tom looked at the pain on his boy's face. "What's the right thing to do, son? Should we keep on making ole' donkey hurt his feet?"

Clayborne squelched the tears he knew to be unmanly and he gave the right answer. "No, Papa. We shouldn't make him hurt his feet anymore."

"Son, you're almost six years old now. You think about what we ought to do, and you tell me tomorrow. Most likely ole' donkey can only keep up with us a couple more days."

Sundown the eleventh day. They pulled into the wagon yard of Texline, Texas. It was even more elegant than the wagon yard in Clayton: in addition to the usual water and feed and outdoor accommodations it offered private sleeping rooms and a good bed for those who could afford the extra dollar. The Blackburns and Perrys slept in their wagons.

The next morning after breakfast, leaning on the Texline wagon yard rail fence, a great big tomboy of a girl stared at ole' donkey. She was probably twelve or thirteen frecklefaced years old, and she contemplated the little beast with covetous brown eyes, her lithe arms splayed on the top fence rail and her chin driven into the tops of her flattened hands. Three boys, all smaller than she, swung from the fence rail beside her like house apes. They watched as the Perrys washed their dishes and began to load their wagons. The girl could stand it no more.

"Hey, mister, you wanna sell that donkey?"

Tom and Clayborne turned in startlement. Cold dread grabbed Clayborne's throat.

"Do you live around here?" asked Tom, sauntering to the fence. Belle and Myrtle looked up from their loading chores to watch the haggling begin.

"Yeah. Me and my brothers live over yonder in the yellow house. 'Cept Jimmy, he ain't my brother, he's just a kid. His Daddy works for the railroad."

"Have you got enough money to buy a donkey?" asked Tom, cocking his head.

How much will you sell him for?"

"I don't know, he's a pretty fine animal. Do we want to sell this donkey, Clayborne?"

"It's up to you, Papa," Clayborne mumbled, biting his lip.

"You see my boy's not too keen on it," said Tom. "You'd have to pay a right good price before we could let him go. Say about three dollars."

The tomboy squinted. "We can't pay no three dollars. Mr. Guthrie over at the livery stable sold a donkey once, dollar and a half. We could get up a dollar and a half. What do you say, mister?"

"Oh, no, that's not enough. We couldn't sell our friend here for any dollar and a half. Maybe two and a half," said Tom, leaning casually on the fence.

"Two and a half?" The tomboy brought the heads of her two brothers together in a secret conference. Jimmy the railroad kid listened through the cracks in the huddle. After much buzzing and whispers, the girl faced Tom Perry, a little uncertain, and said as firmly as she could: "Two dollars is what we got at home, and two dollars is all we got. Final offer."

"Two dollars, hmm?" mused Tom. He waited a few seconds, deliberately drawing out the tension. He turned slightly as if to go, muttering, "Well . . ."

"Please, mister," cried the tomboy, losing all reserve. "I'll take real good care of him. I've always wanted a donkey. Your boy's had good times with him. Let me buy him now! Please, mister. Please?"

Tom pushed his face close to the girl's and said softly but sternly, "You show me the color of your money and you got a deal. Two dollars. Now we have to be getting on the road, so you go get the money and you got yourself a donkey."

Calling "We'll be back, don't go off!" the youngsters beat feet home in jig time. They begged and borrowed and got as much money as they could and ran back to the wagon yard as fast as they could. They only had a dollar forty, Tom explained after counting out their dimes and nickels and pennies. Back home they ran, begging and borrowing more. Then back to the wagon yard.

"Here's the money, mister!" yelled the big girl breathlessly. "We got it all, two dollars, just like you said." Tom examined their funds once more, and Clayborne watched the transaction forlornly.

Tom counted the small change out carefully. The youngsters were two cents shy, but Tom made no comment. He looked back at Clayborne, who stayed in the wagon, not saying anything, and not trusting himself to say anything. Tom felt for his son, but it must be done. The donkey was duly untied from behind the wagon and delivered to the big-boned girl. "You can have the rope, too," said Tom.

When the girl took the donkey her smile lighted up the wagon yard. "Oh, boy, mister! Oh, boy! Thanks! Oh, boy!" She led the little gray beast to the street amid sounds of joy from her brothers and the railroad kid. Then she ceremoniously mounted her new prize. From behind the driver's seat in the wagon on Sunday, July 2, 1916, Clayborne watched his friend disappear forever. Ole' donkey gave his former master a good final performance, though. The instant the girl took a seat on his back, he tore off bucking and pitching with a coterie of screaming boys following in the dust. The creature ran and jumped and the girl yelled in delight as she rode him out of sight beyond her yellow house. And that was the last of ole' donkey. Clayborne never forgot him.

Their fourteenth day on the road was July 4, Independence Day. They rolled in the vast middle of a three-day stretch of Panhandle road between Texline and the next town, Dalhart, forty miles away. Red dawn came up on a land that spread away table flat, horizon-to-horizon grass, not a tree visible in any direction. This, they knew, was the last empty quarter they would traverse: east of Dalhart the towns lay no more than 20 miles apart and water would be easily available. Even in this desolate part of Texas the wagon road got better maintenance than roads in New Mexico or Colorado. A horse-drawn grader had recently smoothed the gravel. The grader blade had not only sliced off the humps and filled in the chugholes but had also thrown up a neat foot-high curb of gravel along the edge of the roadway, lending it a tidy geometrical perfection as far as the eye could see.

Mid-morning they saw a house not far off the road and stopped to see about buying a chicken or two, something festive for the Fourth. When they drew near, it became obvious that the house, no more than a sturdy cabin, really, was abandoned, and evidently had been for many years. Something caught their eye about it, though, and they stopped to inspect the front door. Painted across the strap-hinged planks stood a neatly lettered message that had been weathering there exactly thirty years. A rush of fellow-feeling swept the Perrys and the Blackburns as they read it:

250 miles to the nearest post office

100 miles to wood

20 miles to water

6 inches to hell

God bless our home!

Gone to live with wife's folks

1886

"Poor soul," said Tom as he climbed up to the driver's seat after reading the message, "This is worse than Trinchera. What would you do if you got the rheumatism out here?" He felt his left elbow, then his hip, and remarked, "Say, I haven't been hurting as much from the rheumatism lately."

Myrtle Blackburn said, "I was telling Belle yesterday, you don't look so bent over as you did back on the homestead."

"I think it's the climate," said Fred. "Must have been the altitude or something."

"I just hope it goes away and stays away," said Belle.

At four o'clock that afternoon they still had nine miles to go before reaching Dalhart. The Perrys trailed behind the Blackburns on a long shallow uphill pull when Fred called back, "Tom, it's clouding up real bad up ahead. Looks like the father of all thunderstorms. Gonna be a gully washer for sure."

Within minutes the sky darkened around the two covered wagons. They suddenly seemed like tiny frail specks isolated in this vast Texas Panhandle. A stiff easterly breeze began to blow straight into the front of their canopies, billowing each wagon sheet like a paper sack blown up and ready for popping. Long curling breakers of blue dust rose like solid walls from the plain. Tumbleweed skeletons bounced crazily over grass-stalk tops. The wind rose steadily and the sky was transmogrified into an eerie yellow smear. Tom shouted into the torrent of air: "Fred, you better turn around so you don't get hit straight on. Put your back to the wind!"

The fresh gale blowing up threw his words back in his teeth, and he realized that Fred would know what to do without his advice. Tom then turned his own team to the right, up and over the road grader's gravel curb. As he turned out into the roadless prairie, a rough gust grabbed the wooden vehicle broadside and shook it mercilessly; had the wagon not been so heavily laden it would have overturned. Tom maneuvered the wagon skillfully on the rough prairie turf, fighting the shaking wind, and turned in a large circle. Lightning struck nearby, frightening the animals momentarily. The air smelled of ozone and dusty rain not yet fallen. When the animals calmed down, Tom completed their turn to the west. With the wind at his tail, he reined the team back over the gravel curb and into the roadway. The wagon seemed reluctant to come back from rough turf to smooth road: the team and the front wheels had managed to bounce over the gravel jump-up, but the rear wheels struck it wrong and mired there. Jack and Pet rose to the occasion heaving their shoulders into the load when a mighty crack split Tom's ears. The front wheels jerked nearly out from under them and the wagon lurched to a painful stop. Tom immediately slacked the reins and the animals stopped their futile straining against the doubletree.

"What's happened, Tom?" asked Belle in alarm.

"What was that, Papa?" yelled Clayborne.

His mouth set in disgust, Tom snorted, "The last time I heard a noise like that we'd broke a coupling pole." He jumped down to the gravel roadway and bent over to look under the wagon's front axle. The main 2x4 plank that held the front and rear axles properly spaced had sheared off a few inches behind the front axle. As a result, the front axle hung askew, suspended from the wagon bed only by the rocking bolster. The vehicle required a major repair.

"Yep," said Tom when he saw the problem, "it's the coupling pole." As he stood up the lowering clouds let loose a clatter of rain that immediately drenched him. Fred Blackburn had successfully turned his rig around and pulled alongside the disabled wagon as the rain grew to a cloudburst. He yelled, "Is that what it looks like, Tom?"

"It sure is, Fred. We're stuck."

"Then you folks get in here with us and we'll go look for a place to ride this thing out. Move over Myrtle. Claytia and Lawton, you make room for Clayborne and Pup."

Belle grabbed some blankets and shoved one into Clayborne's hands. She shouted to her brother as she dismounted the tilted wagon, "Fred, there was a place not far from that crossroad back there." The rain plastered her hair to her head within seconds and soaked Clayborne to the skin as he jumped from the wagon. Pup jumped out and became instantly bedraggled. "Look there, Fred," Belle said, "you see it?"

"I see it, Belle. Looks about half a mile away. We'll make for it."

They unhitched Jack and Pet, tied them to the back of the Blackburn's wagon and made for it. There was nothing to do but take what bedding they could, leave their wagon and buggy and all their possessions here just off the roadway and run to seek help.

The road melted into a mess of gumbo in the pelting rain, but they slogged to the ranch house in less than fifteen minutes. It was a fine home, with trees planted around it for a windbreak. Behind it, a big solid barn stoutly resisted the tempest, and a sturdy, madly spinning windmill whined like a banshee in the gale. The big one-story house itself had a long gallery around two sides, forming a sheltering L. The home gleamed with white paint even in the dull gloom of a stormy sunset. The front screen door flapped on its hinges, and a slatted wooden porch swing hanging from chains bucked in the wind, and . . .

They all saw it at once. "Land sakes, Myrtle," shouted Belle, "their doors and windows are wide open!"

Myrtle involuntarily put her hands to her face. "Look at the curtains blowing out the windows! They'll be ruined." Obviously expensive drapes did a fancy fandango out every window.

Fred pulled his wagon into the rancher's front yard and they all dashed to the front door yelling, "Anybody home?" Half expecting to find the ranch family tied up by outlaws, they cautiously entered the living room, still shouting, "Hello, there! Anybody here?" The children joined in the chorus an octave higher: "Hello, anybody! Are you here?"

"There's nobody here, sure enough," decided Tom. "Let's get these windows down and the doors closed." They ran through the house, dragging the flapping drapes back inside, pulling the counterbalance sashes shut and latching the doors.

When the last window was closed a magical calm descended on the house. The thundersquall seemed quiet outside, and they felt suddenly snug and safe, in a real house for the first time in many months. They had forgotten what it was like. Myrtle looked around the living room and said, "Look at that. These folks are right lucky. The curtains are only damp on the bottoms. And this rug, my it's a fine rug, and it's hardly wet at all. Think how the water stains would a' ruined it sure if we hadn't showed up."

"What could these folks have in mind," wondered Belle, "going off and leaving the house wide open like this? And with all this fine furniture!"

"They prob'ly went off this morning to the big Fourth of July doings in town and never gave a thought to any storm coming up," said Fred. "Been clear for days until the storm blew up. And hot. That's why they left the house open. It was hot."

"Well, it's not hot anymore," said Tom. "Belle, we'd best find a sheltered spot on the front porch where we can stay while we wait for these folks to come home. I'm sure their Fourth of July shindig in Dalhart is rained plumb out."

Supper was leftovers that evening. They waited for the ranch house owners to appear, but no one came. The high winds calmed and a steady warm rain settled in. After a long wait, the Blackburns bedded down in their wagon and the Perrys found what protection they could on the L shaped gallery. The front porch was least swept by the wind, and near the front door Belle curled up in a blanket with Clayborne. Tom wrapped up in a wagon sheet and occupied the swing, waiting for the rancher's return. By midnight Tom decided that no one was going to show up. A chill nipped at the air now, and Tom told Belle to take Clayborne in the living room and sleep there out of the weather. With his wife and children safe in the house, Tom huddled in his wagon sheet and spent the watchful night on the porch swing — just in case.

The storm had passed by morning. Gray clouds loitered in the sky, reflected in brown puddles. Still no sign of the ranch's owner. Tom began to have a bad feeling about this situation. He had a disabled wagon unattended on a public road, he had ensconced his wife and child in a stranger's home for the night and the owner was nowhere to be found. He kept an uneasy watch on the cloudy horizon where the road vanished while they went about the usual morning cook chores.

A morning freight train had gone by, they had finished breakfast and stowed everything in the wagon when about nine o'clock a large open-topped Overland car turned off the gravel road and into the muddy ranch house driveway. The two families closed ranks by the Blackburns' wagon, men standing protectively in front of the women and children. They waited nervously. Clayborne was scared stiff, but kept as brave a front as he could.

The car pulled up alongside them and stopped, its engine chugging at idle. A grizzled man in his fifties sat at the wheel eyeing them, his rugged face expressionless beneath the bent-up brim of a flat-top ranch hat. Beside him in the front seat, a strapping young man with the same large features gave them a cold going-over. Two rough-looking men in the back seat, probably hired hands, glared at the migrants. The driver said in a voice as full of gravel as the roadbed: "And what might you folks be doing here?"

Tom looked at his feet and then stepped forward. "Well, sir, we got caught when the storm come up last night after my wagon broke down . . .'"

"That was your rig we passed then," the driver butted in. "And I suppose you came here looking for help."

"Yes, sir, we did. But we found the house wide open and nobody home and all, so we just closed it up. Figured you didn't want the rain to blow in, you know."

The driver and his front seat companion looked in astonishment at the house. "Well bless my soul," said the driver. "Did you folks do that? You did, I see you did! You closed it right up."

"Rain hadn't hardly got to it at all, sir," Tom ventured.

"You saved my home, mister," said the rancher, virtually leaping out of the car door. "My wife like to had a fit last night when the storm come up," he bellowed, walking around the long engine hood and over to Tom Perry. "She was worried sick that her curtains and her rugs would be ruined, and there we were in Dalhart for the big Fourth picnic and no way to get home but this open car."

The rancher's son and his two hired hands got out of the big Overland and gathered amiably around the two families. The children huddled close to their parents.

"Mister, I'd like to shake your hand," beamed the rancher. "I'm so proud of you folks. That was a right neighborly thing you did. I don't know what to say. If there's anything I can do to help you people, just name it."

"Don't thank us any, sir," said Tom. "It was the Christian thing to do. But . . ."

"I know," said the rancher. "You don't need to say it. Your wagon's broke down and you'll need some help. My two wranglers here will give you all the help you need."

"Well, sir," said Tom, "I'm obliged for your kindness. But all we got is a busted coupling pole, and if I can find a big jack somewhere, Fred here and me can fix it by ourselves."

"No sooner said than done," said the rancher. "I'll call up Sam Kimura up on the Ft. Worth & Denver. He's the section foreman in these parts and he's got jacks of all sizes in the shed up yonder. I'll tell him you'll be there, what, about noon? Oh, and tell me your name, if you please."

"I'm Tom Perry and this is my wife. That's Fred Blackburn and his wife. And all our children."

"Well, I'm pleased to meet you good folks. I'm J.R. Conlen, and this here's my boy Charley, and this is the cowpokes on the place, Nick and Bill. I'd like my wife to meet you, but she didn't come with us this morning. Martha stayed there in Dalhart at the hotel where we put up last night. She just worried herself to death about the rugs and the window curtains and everything being ruined. She'll be so thankful. Your womenfolk can stay in the house while you fix your wagon. They'll be proper safe. I'll see to that. Now, I'll go right in and telephone Sam. Come on in, everybody."

Tom had saddled up Pet and appeared at the section station at noon. The section station was really only a large toolshed beside the track. It had no office space, but instead held pry bars, sledge hammers, stores of spikes and plates, coal oil, hand cars, everything needed to change ties, clear switches, fill and clean switch lamps and generally perform the ordinary day-to-day repairs that keep a rail system tuned up and running.

A short rail spur ran from inside the shed to the mainline's roadbed, a runway for the section's hand cars. This was where the maintenance crew showed up every morning at 8:00 a.m. to begin work on their twenty-mile section of track.

Section crewmen were the lowest paid workers on the railroads: the only qualifications were good health and strength and ability to stand outdoor work. But they enjoyed an advantage their better paid brothers did not: they worked regular hours in one place. Whilst their nomadic counterparts frequently found their family life destroyed by constant reassignment, humble section laborers could acquire homes, marry local girls, enter a lodge or church, and expect to be buried in the local cemetery. As a place of employment, though, they could only point to the endless track and a shed called the section station.

There Tom met Sam Kimura — Japanese Americans made up a large percentage of Western railroad foremen, just as Hispanos made up a large fraction of the crews. Kimura had the qualifications listed by the U.S. Department of Labor for section foremen: "Ability to handle men. Must know how to replace ties, remove and install frogs, switches, and track crossings. Must know all the rules for signalling trains and all rules for running hand or gasoline cars on main track and switches."

"You must be Mr. Perry," said Kimura.

"And you must be Sam Kimura," said Tom. "Mr. Conlen said you were the section foreman."

"Yes, and he said you need a jack big enough to lift a loaded wagon for repairs. I think I saw your rig when I took my crew up the line this morning. We're weeding the right of way this month. You were broken down not far from where the new state road meets the Clayton-Dalhart road."

"That was us, all right."

"Well, let's see what we have in here," said Kimura, unlocking the shed. The sun played peek-a-boo this July 5th noon and the maintenance station lay in a pool of cloud shadow, making the shed interior darker than usual. "Don't trip over the rails, Mr. Perry. Ah, here we have several jackscrews. This one should do your job. And we'll need a handle that fits." Kimura pulled a heavy metal object to the center of the shed. "It's heavy, about 60 pounds. I'll help you tie it to your saddle."

Fred had brought his rig to the Perry's disabled wagon, trusting the women and children to Conlen's hospitality. The two men got to work silently, each knowing exactly what to do. They first squared the jack on a flat rock under the wagon, then inserted its crankhandle and turned it slowly. Within a few minutes they had jacked the front end of the wagon six feet off the ground. They dismounted the front axle assembly from the wagon bed, and pulled the wheels out from under. With the front wheel assembly rolled aside in the clear, the damage was immediately evident: the shattered stump of the coupling pole hung sadly from the front axle's central king pin.

The front axle assembly of a wagon is a complex affair consisting of several vital parts. First is the sturdy 4x4 beam on which the wheels themselves are mounted. Second, mounted midway between the wheels on top of the axle proper, is the fifth wheel: two circular iron plates, well greased — the bottom one rotates with the axle during turns, the top one provides support for the non-rotating wagon bed above. Third, attached to the fifth wheel by a vertical 14-inch king pin, is the horizontal rocking bolster — a heavy oak beam tapering from a thick center to thinner arms left and right, the arm ends capped by metal fittings that attach directly to the wagon bed and give it support. On more expensive wagons, the rocking bolster might ride the axle on leaf springs to pamper the traveller's aching posterior, but Tom's wagon had none. The king pin spiking the center of this assembly also passes through the coupling pole, a 12-foot long 2x4 which rigidly holds the front axle a precise distance from the rear axle.

Fred and Tom disassembled all these parts, first removing the king pin, then unstacking the rocking bolster, the smashed connecting pole stub, and the top plate of the fifth wheel. Wagon makers knew that broken coupling poles were a common problem, and generally left enough excess length protruding behind the rear axle to allow for several repairs. Tom and Fred removed the broken coupling pole from where it hung uselessly by the rear axle mount. Tom sawed off the splintered front end of the coupling pole and squared it in a workmanlike manner, then took a brace and bit and drilled a new 3/4-inch diameter hole for the king pin and another for the rear axle pin. The repaired pole — some 8 inches shorter than before — was reattached to the rear axle. Then the front axle assembly was rolled back under the wagon, and one by one its pieces were reassembled: axle beam and fifth wheel lower plate on which all else rested, fifth wheel upper plate, the new coupling pole, and the rocking bolster, all held together by the king pin. While Tom lowered the jackscrew a little at a time, Fred carefully eased the axle assembly into a perfect match with the wagon body mounts. The rocking bolster's mounting bolts were reattached; the jackscrew was removed from the wagon bed bottom; and the repair was finished. Within an hour they had retrieved their families, said goodbye to Mr. Conlen, returned the jackscrew to Sam Kimura and set off for Dalhart.

July 28, 1916, thirty-six days out from the Colorado homesteads, Tom Perry, Fred Blackburn and their families reached Wichita Falls, Texas.

There they found a wagon yard and hauled in with dozens of other wagons and teams. Tom and his family would rest here two days, but Fred and his family would leave the second day. It was to be their parting of the ways. They had travelled the far country together: from Colorado to Dalhart, then a longer way through Amarillo and Clarendon, through Childress and Vernon, and when they reached Wichita Falls they had made some major decisions.

Tom Perry had struggled with himself, but decided that he could not go home to Hico in total defeat, not yet. Feelings of failure still stung him, try as he would to tamp them down. The shame would not go away. He had an uncle and aunt — the Herrins — in Ringling, Oklahoma. He had been close to them as a young man. They would most likely help him find work, help him gain something to show for all this trouble. Aunt Mary and Uncle Will would surely be a comfort when the new baby came. Tom sent a penny post card to let them know of his plans and approximate date of arrival. In Oklahoma there might be oil field work. He might be able to hire out with his wagon for road work. He didn't know. Besides, back in Hico the weaning house had been taken by cash renters, and Jim Perry's other rent house would be occupied until November — Tom had gotten the letter telling him there was temporarily no place for him months ago. There was no cash to rent from somebody else. He *had* to go somewhere besides home.

Fred had made up his mind in another direction: he was going home right now, right here from Wichita Falls, straight down to Hico. He ought to arrive in a little over two weeks. His father Charley would make room for them, although they would need it for only a month or two at most. He had decided to go back to Colorado and prove up his claim, to work in the mines and the steel mill at Pueblo part of the year, live on the homestead the other part with Tom's brother Leonard and Robert Dozier. It wouldn't be a failure that way. The Blackburns hated to leave the Perrys, but Wichita Falls would be their last stop together.

The farewells were reserved but heartfelt. Fred put his arm discreetly around his sister and told her, "Take care of yourself, Belle. Write to us. I'll tell Papa you're well."

"Take care of your family, Fred," said Belle, hiding her grief.

"Goodbye, Tom," said Fred, shaking his hand solemnly. "You sure you won't come with us?"

"You go on, Fred. We'll come home when we can. Tell my Dad. Take care of yourself."

"Myrtle, you write to us. I'm going to be so lonesome," implored Belle.

"We'll write, Belle. You take care of yourself now."

"Goodbye, Clayborne."

"Goodbye, Claytia. Goodbye Lawton."

Then the Blackburns rumbled out of sight down a Wichita Falls street. They were gone. The sense of isolation in a strange city closed around Tom and Belle, but Clayborne didn't seem to mind. He had his Mama and Papa and Pup and that was enough for him.

It was just the three of them now. Tom felt restless and Belle remained stoic. They decided to take a Saturday walk after supper, strolling from the wagon yard in the summer evening to the trees and benches and great pavilion of the Wichita Falls city park. It seemed pleasant enough. But when a crowd gathered and dance music started, a regular hoedown, Tom looked alarmed and urged Belle and Clayborne rapidly away to the edge of the park, some fifty yards from the dancers, and sat them on a bench.

"We don't want to look like we're any part of that dancing," Tom said firmly. "Dancing is against the Lord's Word. We Baptists don't do such things." A few years earlier Tom and Belle would likely have been in the thick middle of the dance floor themselves, but they had got religion at a revival meeting one summer and were now staunch rocks of faith. Half of Wichita Falls seems to have turned out for this night of round dancing, and music filled the air, twinkling like the electric lights. Was it perhaps a wistful comment that Tom did not simply return his family to the wagon yard, but remained on a discreet park bench to watch the dancers' flashing feet and witness their stomping good time? Clayborne watched from the prescribed distance and wondered vaguely why they couldn't go closer, but he sensed his father's strong will, and as a respectful child he gave it no further thought.

Suddenly in the middle of the music an alarm bell went off and everybody looked past the pavilion to a row of private homes just beyond the park square. One of them was totally engulfed in flames, and a horse-drawn fire engine came clattering and clanging around a corner to the scene. The crowd of dancers stopped in their tracks, mesmerized by the conflagration. The Perrys too were petrified by the horrifying spectacle. Despite everything the firemen did the fire raged on. Clayborne stared wide-eyed, watching the huge column of flame and sparks rise fast, too fast, terrifyingly fast, into the night sky. The lurid scene frightened him, people running, the home owners wailing and crying, the firemen unable to stop the blaze, to do anything about it. A stark reality hit the boy: the inferno was viciously destroying a home, a haven, a place where people *lived*. It seemed impossibly evil to Clayborne; he could not fathom it. The home burned to the ground. The fright stayed with him for days. It was the first house fire he had ever seen. But it would not be the last.

In the first week of August the three Perrys bumped down the gravel roads alone. Their covered wagon passed solitary through the little

Texas towns of Henrietta and Gainesville, and then veered off north across the Red River into Oklahoma. Belle was eight months gone with child. On the 12th of August, 1916, at the home of William and Mary Herrin in Ringling, Oklahoma, 52 days out from the abandoned Trinchera homestead, their long road ended for a while.

-5-

OKLAHOMA SOJOURN

OM and Belle gazed at the comfortable farmhouse of William and Mary Herrin. How inviting it was, a real house, not rich, but a nice painted house, resting contentedly back from the little country road and embedded in a field of freshly opened cotton bolls, bordered with rows of peanuts and festooned with scattered oaks circling the animal yard. A nurturing orchard of peach trees fostered yellow clusters of ripening fruit. These symbols of the Herrins' sweat and persistence intimidated Tom: he sat deadlocked in his own failure in the August afternoon heat, dreading to get down from the covered wagon and walk through the barred gate. He was embarrassed to impose his poverty like this upon his relations, no matter how close he felt to them. He earnestly hoped they had received his penny post card . . .

The screen door burst open and the smiling face of Mary Herrin appeared, solid and agreeable and radiating the resemblance to her brother Jim Perry, Tom's father. "There you are! I was beginning to worry that something had happened to you. Come on in, come on in, you must be just tuckered out."

Mary hurried to the gate like a young girl, yet somehow maintained the dignity of her fifty-two years. She swung the gate open, hastened to the right side of the wagon, and gazed up at Tom's wife. "Belle, Belle, you've grow into such a pretty woman. It's been so many years."

"I'm twenty-three now, Auntie Mary," said Belle shyly, "and I have children of my own — well, I have a child . . ."

". . . and it won't be long 'till it's 'children', all right," Mary Herrin smiled, glancing at Belle's burgeoning figure. She noticed Tom staring at Belle's face, pride and love shining from his countenance. "Tommy!" Mary commanded, "Wake up. Don't you just sit up there like a lump on a log. You drive that wagon off this road and pull up in front of the house. Why, the very idea of letting Belle sit up there when she could be in the nice cool house!"

Tom obeyed with a grin. Auntie Mary was still the businesslike lady he remembered. When he had pulled the wagon into the front yard and set the brake, Mary Herrin gave Belle a hand down, but saw something out of the corner of her eye up under the canvas canopy. She gasped, "Oh, and who is this?"

Clayborne peeked out from behind the wagon sheet, Pup under his arm. "Are you my Auntie Mary?"

Mary Herrin was transfixed with delight. "Oh, Willie Clayborne, honey, I sure am your Auntie Mary. Come let me look at you." The boy stood up and followed his mother down from the wagon.

"Oh, you sure favor your father," Mary said hugging the boy tightly.

William Herrin, a wiry square-faced man in his middle fifties, heard the commotion from the barn and strode briskly to join the greetings, calling back to his sixteen-year-old daughter in the garden: "Lucia! Tom and Belle have got here from Colorado! Go get Henry and Addie and the children from the weaning house."

Will sized up Tom for a short moment — they were of similar stature, Will at five-foot-seven and Tom at five-foot-eight, both a hundred thirty pounds — then heartily shook his hand. "Tom and Belle! It's so good to see the two of you again. You don't know how we've missed you. We still remember the summer you were newlyweds and came to pick cotton with us on the farm down in Hood County."

Belle said, "We think about those Texas days so much, Uncle Will," hugging him with the semi-formal public embrace appropriate for close relatives.

"So this is the boy," said Will Herrin, reaching down to pick up Clayborne and raising him high in the air.

"Woop," said Will, "if you'd waited another year to come see us I wouldn't be able to do *that*! You're quite the man, young Willie Clayborne Perry."

"I'm going to be six next Wednesday!" announced the lad. "And my Mama and Papa just call me Clayborne, Uncle Will."

"Do they now," said Will Herrin, lowering the boy to the ground. "Well, that's still a lot of name. Maybe I'll have to give you a real short name for a birthday present. Let's see. Hmm. . . Willie Clayborne. How about W.C.? I like the sound of it. W.C."

"Papa," asked Clayborne, "can you give somebody a *name* for a birthday present?"

Tom smiled at his youngster said, "You be thankful for whatever you get, son."

Lucia herded the Herrins' twenty-seven-year-old son Henry and his wife Addie — and their children Ernest, Cecil, and Henry, Jr. — to the happy group, saying, "They were fixin' up the cotton sacks, Papa, but I told 'em to come see cousin Tom and Belle." The eleven of them made a leisurely promenade to the refuge of the Herrins' farm house, chattering, remembering, redoubling strong family bonds.

At supper that evening they sat down to a traditional country groaning board, heavy with hand-raised beef and ham, biscuits, sorghum syrup and gravy, beans and squash, peach cobbler and poke salad — cooked pokeweed. Pokeweed, a tall coarse native herb, was favored by old-timers for its succulent shoots and smooth leaves. Herbalists extracted from its poisonous seeds an emetic and purgative medication, and the crimson juice of its berries was used in making an ink. Occasionally an incautious cook discovered the hard way that the thick fleshy roots of *Phytolacca americana* — pokeweed — were poisonous. But Mary Herrin knew how to prepare the perennial delicacy safely, and she carefully pampered the wild pokeweed that grew around her barnyard.

Suppertime conversation revolved around the Perrys' adventures in Colorado and their arduous road back. But as the dishes were cleared away, present matters came to the fore. "We don't want to be any trouble to you, Uncle Will," said Tom. "We're mighty obliged to you for letting us keep our wagon out front and our animals with yours. And we've got the bed in the wagon to sleep in."

"You're no trouble to us, Tom," reassured Will Herrin. "You've always been special to us. Why, I can remember the day you were born, just three days after Mary and me were married back in Heflin, Alabama. December 16, 1883, you were born, I remember it like my own birthday. We went over to see you and your Ma and Pa just the day after. You're like our own, like our Lucia and Henry and his Addie and the children here, ain't that so?" All agreed.

Mary Herrin said, "Tommy, we always think of you, especially at every wedding anniversary because of your birthday being so close. Thirty-three years it'll be this December. You've always been our special nephew. It does our hearts good to be able to help you out."

"You know I want us to find a place of our own as soon as I can," said Tom, still anxious not to impose.

"Why sure you do," said Mary. "We know how it is. We can help. Will, don't we know somebody over at Cornish who could find Tom a place that wasn't too dear? Cornish is only three or four miles off, Tommy. There ought to be some places there without too high a rent."

Will said, "I think we can call on ole' Jack Cook to help Tom find a place. He's a friend of ours over at Cornish, Tom. When the railroad came west from Ardmore, they missed Cornish by a couple of miles. So Cornish is moving north to be on the tracks. That's what Ringling is, just Cornish moved north. Ringling's only had a post office a couple of years. And, you know, Jack Cook says they named the town after John Ringling of the Ringling Brothers Circus, can you beat that? Some folks will probably live there at Cornish a few more years, but since everybody started moving away up to Ringling, the rents have got pretty low. We can talk to our friend Jack about it."

"That's real nice of you to offer, Uncle Will," said Belle.

"It sure is," seconded Tom. "And I want to find work as soon as I can."

Henry Herrin spoke: "Tom, is your eye going to keep you from finding work? I noticed it's much worse than when we saw you last time."

"I hope not. It is a problem sometimes. I can't hardly see out of it any more at all. But my right eye's good. Can't think of too many jobs where you have to have two good eyes, maybe railroad engineer. We'll have to wait and see."

Mary broke in: "Belle, these menfolks are going to talk work and I want them out of my kitchen. Lucia, you come help clean up and Belle, we'll let the mother-to-be just sit and watch."

"Oh, Auntie Mary, there's nothing wrong with me," Belle protested.

They all stood up around the supper table and Henry Herrin said, "Papa, me and Addie have to get those cotton sacks finished, so we're going on back to the house. Good to see you again, Tom and Belle."

"I've been so pleased to see you folks again after all this time," said Addie. "Don't think we're rude, but we also have to get things ready for church in the morning. Good night to you all."

Belle told Clayborne he could go out and play with the Herrin children until it got dark. The boy pleaded, "Can't we stay out and catch lightning bugs, Mama? Ernest says they have lightning bugs here."

The three Herrin boys nodded their heads vigorously.

"We'll see, young man. You listen for when I call you, you hear?"

Mary said, "You men go sit in the front room. I'm going to take Belle out to see the garden once we're through with the cleaning up. We'll join you after 'while."

Tom and Will ambled into the big front room. Will said, "Would your family like to go with us to church in the morning, Tom?"

"We don't have any Sunday best to wear, Uncle Will."

"Don't worry about that. We don't stand on ceremony too much at this Baptist Church. We have a lot of farmers, a lot of poor rent farmers. Just put on something clean and feel easy."

They sat in the spare but homey living room and fell to considering what to do. "Like I said, I want to find work as soon as I can, Uncle Will."

"Oh, I know you're eager to work. And I can see you don't particularly want to go home to your Pa in Hico after the way things went in

Colorado. But you have to think about the right kind of work. You're a farm boy, and you're probably thinking about taking up some ground somewhere and giving it a try. But let me tell you, you won't find anything around here in farming, Tom, not rent farming. Rents are too high and cotton prices too low. If Mary and me had a bigger place than just this hundred and twenty acres, we'd offer you work with us on the halves. As it is, we've got Henry and Addie and their boys in the weaning house, and they're working all the land I can't handle. And we're doing good just to keep even with the world ourselves. It's a good thing we have this place paid for, too. Why, two years ago cotton prices got down to six cents a pound, and last year they were still only about ten."

"I know," said Tom. "We had seven-cent cotton in Hico two years ago and eleven-cent last year, not much better than yours. But farming's not what I had in mind, Uncle Will, not yet. I thought maybe some work hiring out with my wagon, like on roads, something to earn a little cash for when the baby comes."

"We don't get a whole lot of work done on our roads here in Oklahoma, Tom, not out here in the country," said Will. "Oklahoma's only been a state, remember, since 1907, only nine years now, not like Texas. I don't think those fellows in Oklahoma City know where we are yet. Wait 'till the first rain. You'll see how big a road crew shows up. Here in Jefferson County we usually get up a volunteer road crew of our own when it gets too bad."

"Well, what about the oil fields?"

Will straightened up and frowned. "Might be something there, maybe you could find work selling to the oil field crowd. But I wouldn't advise working roughneck or roustabout in an oil town."

"Why not?"

"It's pretty bad work, Tom. Too many people coming in too fast. Some are good farmboys that just want to go earn the big wages, others are a bad sort. Right over at Healdton there's a big oil field, can't be eight miles away. Big oil field. There's little boomtowns pop up around it when they drill new wells. Like Ragtown up the road, mostly just tents, that's why they call it Ragtown. They got a little bitty row of stores and a bunch of shotgun shacks, you know, the kind if you fired a shot in the front door, it would go straight out the back door without hitting nary a thing. Little ole' hovels that run straight from front to back, about twelve by twenty feet, no more'n the size of this living room. It don't attract a good type, Tom.

"And you can't go through a boomtown without seeing half a dozen knife fights on the street, all day long and all night long. Fightin' and brawlin' all the time. Up at Drumright they're always fishing out dead bodies from the creeks — the creeks are covered with crude from leaky storage tanks, so the bodies don't show. And there's more. Now I wouldn't repeat this in front of the womenfolks, but there's the worst trash you could think of in all these boomtowns, gambling dens, houses with fancy women, and saloons everywhere."

"Saloons?" asked Tom. "I thought Oklahoma was a dry state."

"It is," said Will. "Prohibition is written right in Article One of the state Constitution. I read it when we moved here from Texas in 1912. But it don't matter what some piece of paper says if people can't do anything about it. Every oil town is like Healdton, and they have fifteen law officers for twenty thousand oil boomers. There's a hundred bootleggers to every policeman. And oil field supply salesmen, they just look at liquor as part of doing business. They have to get chummy with the oilman, throw him a party with a lot of whiskey and you can imagine what else, and then they get a swell order for their supply house. You wouldn't want your family anywhere near there."

"I certainly wouldn't, Uncle Will. I see what you mean by the right kind of work. But then what is there left?"

Will Herrin thought a minute. "Well, if you found Belle and the boy a good safe place to live in Cornish, you know, I've got a friend name of Lew Wheeler runs a little ice cream factory there. His outfit bottles sody pop, too. There's honest workers up at Ragtown I'm sure wouldn't mind buying ice cream and sody pop from an honest man. It's not like sellin' whiskey or chiselin' their money out of them. You got a wagon, you could get some ice and straw, cover up the ice cream to keep it cool, haul it up the six or seven miles to Ragtown, and I'd say you could make two dollars a day, maybe three."

"That sounds just fine, Uncle Will. I'm ready to do anything for Belle and the boy."

Cornish, Oklahoma, was settled in eastern Jefferson County in the late 1880s and named after a local rancher, John H. Cornish. It had been granted a post office July 10, 1891, and remained home to some three hundred Sooners until the St. Louis and San Francisco Rail Road Company drove its rails west from Ardmore in 1912. The right of way passed some two miles north of Cornish, and the town of Ringling grew up beside the new track, its post office designated June 9, 1914. Many citizens of Cornish in 1916 were removing to Ringling — on rollers, one house at a time. They saw the hand of destiny. Some Cornish residents secretly laughed up their sleeves at neighbors who, fired with railroad mania, moved up to Ringling: already several Oklahoma railroads had begun to abandon unprofitable lines and they believed Ringling would wither on the vine — but the ridiculous migrants would have the last laugh. Ringling would survive. Cornish was fated to lose its post office March 5, 1918.

But now, on Monday, August 14, 1916, Cornish may have been a town in decline, but it was a town nevertheless. It had electric lights, a general store and a mercantile, a bank, a four-room stone school house, an ice cream factory, a blacksmith, a hotel and restaurant, a Baptist Church, and a sizeable residential district. The little town had an ironic aura of permanence that belied its decline: most of its businesses and public buildings had been constructed of hard local sandstone. They shed a sense of everlasting natural rock formations rather than of man-made structures. The whole town exuded protective benevolence: Cornish had no oil wells and it had few oiltown boomers, and it was a peaceful place to live.

It was the first time Tom and Belle had driven the buggy in two months, and they enjoyed its feeling of lightness as they turned down the narrow streets of Cornish. Uncle Will had come with them that morning and carried on a long conversation with his friend Jack Cook, who had been as good as his word in finding them a place to rent early that afternoon. It was a good-sized two-bedroom house, on a south corner, facing east, only a block from the business district. Perhaps it stood inelegantly on two-foot stilts, and perhaps the house was unpainted, but it had six rooms laid out in a T-shaped plan, a small front porch, a screened-in back porch, and they could connect their own cookstove to the gaping chimney flue and fill the empty house with their own furniture. Behind the house was space for their wagon and buggy and at the back lay a fifty-foot by seventy-foot horse lot with a modest shed and feed crib — plenty of room for Pet and Jack. It would be their home as long as they wanted it — and could pay the monthly rent of five dollars.

Uncle Will had returned to his farm at noon, but not without first accompanying Tom and Belle on a round of introductions. They met just about everyone who ran a store in town, and they met Lew Wheeler, a slim, amiable man in his early forties who enjoyed making soft drinks and ice cream. His factory was little more than a glorified shack twenty feet wide by fifty feet long next to a blacksmith shop, but it was sanitary enough to pass state inspections. Tom made an agreement in principle with Lew: Tom would act as Wheeler's agent selling soda pop and ice cream from Tom's own wagon. For each bottle of "sody water," as Wheeler called it, Tom would pay three and one-third cents. Tom was authorized to sell the six-ounce bottles of refreshment for five cents and pocket the cent and two-thirds profit. On a case of twenty-four bottles, Tom would pay 79 cents and make a profit of 38 cents: the sale of ten cases — 240 bottles — would net Tom $3.84. The deal on the ice cream was similar: Tom would realize about a fourth of the selling price as profit. Tom and Belle rode back to Uncle Will's farm that afternoon with a house key in their pockets and high hopes in their hearts. That night Tom dreamed he had become a well-to-do ice cream merchant with dozens of wagons in his crew.

Wednesday dawned warm and dry. Belle had fixed breakfast on their own cookstove in the new house, and Tom was preparing to venture forth on his first day as a boomer, selling to the oil town folks. Over a cup of coffee Tom confided to Belle, "I don't know how this work is going to go. But I got a feeling it's going to come up good. It's the boy's birthday today, and I'm going to bring him back some ice cream."

"I'll keep it a surprise. I got a feeling you're going to do good, too, Tom, the good Lord willing."

Tom rose to go out and hitch up the team. "You take care of yourself, Belle. It's getting right close to your time. When the boy gets up, you have him do the carrying for you. And if anything starts to happen, you send Clayborne to run over and get the doctor."

"Don't you worry about me, Tom Perry. You just go out there and sell as much ice cream and sody pop as you can."

He drove down the dirt streets of Cornish in his open wagon, Jack the mule pulling right-hand gee position and Pet in the haw spot. The wagon sheet canopy and hoops had been removed. The wagon bed contained only a pile of hay and a large toolbox waiting for its first commercial cargo of soft drinks and ice cream. Tom regretted losing a day's work yesterday while moving the wagonload of their possessions into the rent house. He was anxious to get to work because their money was running out — there was now less than a hundred dollars in his Hico bank account.

Tom had been able to wrestle everything into place by himself except the iron cookstove — a kindly neighbor, Etrius White, a grocery worker, had given him a boost up the back stairs and helped in attaching the stove's sheet-metal ductwork to the brick chimney. The heavy lifting had aggravated Tom's rheumatism and he had lain awake how long? hours? during the night, wondering how much of his insomnia was pain and how much the uneasy anticipation of a new career. His Uncle Will had given him all the help that could be expected. Now it was up to him.

It was seven o'clock when Tom pulled the wagon up to the freight dock of Lew Wheeler's plant. After signing for twenty cases of soda pop — twenty-four stubby thick glass bottles of six ounces in each case — and six five-gallon wooden kegs of ice cream, Tom began hefting his cash crop of goods into the wagon.

"Ten cases of red strawberry sody water!" called youthful plant foreman Archie McDonald as Tom took each item from the rough loading dock planks. "Five cases of orange sody water! Five cases of cream of sody!" — creme soda. The redheaded young crew-leader sang his invoice list as if it were a sort of obligatory commercial catechism.

"You come from one of the farms around here?" asked Tom as he loaded the last of his soda pop cases.

"No, I ain't no hick. Born right here in town. My Pa runs the blacksmith shop next door. Blacksmithin' is a dyin' art. What with the automobile comin' on there'll be nothin' but mechanics any more. Besides, it's too much like work. Runnin' a factory is more to my likin'. Three kegs of vaniller ice cream! Three kegs of chocklit ice cream! There y'are Mr. Perry."

Tom had laid the products neatly in the large wooden tool chest near the tailgate of his wagon. "Mr. McDonald, I'd like to buy some ice and rock salt from you, enough to keep the ice cream from melting all day. And maybe you could show me how to keep it cool the best."

"We got block ice and crushed ice over yonder in our ice making machine and rock salt in bags right beside it. You'll need crushed ice. Ice for a day will cost you a dime, and a bag of rock salt enough for a couple weeks will cost you another dime. You put the ice all around the kegs, and put the rock salt and straw over it — I see you brought some straw with you."

"Mr. Wheeler told me I'd need it."

"Well, you put the ice around the kegs, and you keep a few cases of your sody water right next of the ice cream kegs — you got plenty room in your tool box — and put ice over them too, 'cause you're going to run into folks what want to buy sody water for drinking cold right on the spot. Keep the sody water and ice cream real close together 'cause they'll stay cool longer that way. Cover the ice over with rock salt and straw, and close the box lid. Then wet down your wagon sheet real good and lay it over the whole thing."

Tom shifted on his feet uneasily and rubbed his face. "Um, one thing. How do you sell ice cream?"

"Don't worry about that none. You don't have to sell it, people buy it. You haul this up to Ragtown, stop in at the grocery, and that little supply store, maybe the hotel, and make sure you stop special at the pool hall — it's kind of a wicked place, but I know the owner. Joe Franklin in there won't hurt ye none, he's gruff, but he's kindly at heart. You ought to sell more 'n half this load right there in that row of stores. Then you go around to the shotgun shacks and the house tents. That ought to get rid of a quarter of it. Then you go around some more to the drill rigs and the work tents. And be sure to stop at the Denison Oil camp, if they're still drillin'. That ought to get rid of all but a little. Then when you see anybody walkin' along on the road back, holler out 'sody water, get yer ice cream and sody water here', and it'll all be gone afore you come home. And don't forget to take your ice cream scooper and a church key. You know what a church key is, don't you?"

"Church key?"

"A beer bottle opener. You know, for the sody water."

"Why do you say church key?"

"Well, you know how them real religious folks is, always harpin' on the evils of drink and demon rum, and all that, while they's prob'ly sneakin' nips from the bottle all day long and partyin' all night like hypocrites. Callin' a beer bottle opener the church key kind of takes some of the wind out of their sails."

"It's no key to my church," said Tom, in startlement more than outrage.

McDonald said with a twinkle in his eye, "No offense, Mr. Perry. It's just an expression."

As Tom busied himself with packing the ice around his commodities, he realized for the first time in his thirty-two years that people really aren't all alike — certainly people in commerce were not like farmers. The nerve of that young man! To insinuate that honest church-going people were furtive drunkards! How could he think that? But he *did* think that. And he tossed it off so lightly, as if it really didn't matter much anyway. Yes, these people were different.

Ragtown lay nine miles north by northeast of Cornish. Tom drove nearly three hours over rutted dirt roads before the forest of wooden derricks loomed all around him. The maze was incredible. It was the heyday of the legendary Healdton oil field. The Healdton pool was to go down in history as a giant oil field, one with an ultimate recovery of more than 100 million barrels. Healdton produced oil at such a shallow depth, from 800 to 1,200 feet, that drilling costs were almost negligible, seldom in excess of four thousand dollars. It became a "poor man's oil field." The lease size, the low cost of drilling, the short time from drilling to payout, all made it possible for small independent operators with minimal financial resources to compete with the big money. And compete they did. In mid-August, 1916, the Healdton field had some 1,200 wells in operation producing more than 75,000 barrels of Oklahoma crude daily.

The rapid influx of money, manpower and supplies needed to sustain this teeming madhouse had tremendous impact on local society. In the few years since the first big finds of 1912, the tranquil and obscure farm town of Healdton had grown into a zoo of outsiders, 20,000 people overwhelming an indigenous population of less than 500. Dozens of small temporary boomtowns sprouted around Healdton like toadstools after the rain, Ragtown one of the toadiest. The frantic tempo of drilling, the optimistic bluster of the wildcatter, the grim determination of those intent on getting theirs from the riches of the oil find were separated by no more than a "bob-wire" fence from the picturesque, regular, quiet life of local farmers who tried to ignore it all and go about their rural business. One commentator noted that "Millionaires, laborers, hoboes, gamblers and prostitutes, as well as lawyers, hucksters, speculators and men of modest means flocked to the boomtowns of Oklahoma with the hope of sharing in the proverbial pot of (black) gold."

Men who had once been regular guests at Boston Brahmins' chamber music evenings mingled with closemouthed prospectors who could not sign their own names. Ingenuous farm boys mixed with professional oil tramps that followed the booms across America from one field to the next, carrying their rootless nomadic culture with them. The astounding cross-section of humanity thus thrown together at the Healdton field yielded not a society so much as a flamboyant yeasty stew of excitement, grinding toil, adventure, violence, vast riches and sudden death. The Oklahoma oil boom ranks with the California gold rush and the later silver stampede to Colorado as one of the most colorful, romantic and dangerous eras in American history. Tom Perry drove his mare Pet and his mule Jack into it for the first time on his boy's sixth birthday to sell ice cream and soda pop.

"No, we don't want any goddam ice cream! Or sody water! What are ye tryin' to do, ruin my reputation? This is Joe's Pool Hall! Joe Franklin's Pool Hall! This here's a right tough place!" Big brawny Joe Franklin towered over Tom Perry like a thunderhead about to let loose a cloudburst.

Tom stood his ground. "Mr. Franklin, I know what kind of establishment you run. I came here because Archie McDonald at Cornish said I should. And I'd appreciate it if you wouldn't take the Lord's name in vain."

"You'd appreciate it if I wouldn't take the Lord's name in . . . Why, you one-eyed pipsqueak of a tinhorn! I ought to . . . Wait a minute. Did I hear you right? Archie McDonald? Did you say Archie McDonald?"

"Yes, I did," said Tom, ready to defend himself if necessary.

"Why didn't you say so when you came in? That's my son-in-law! Married my Etta, he did. I used to work blacksmith with his daddy down in Cornish before the oil came. How is the rascal doing?"

"He looked okay this morning." Tom definitely did not understand these people.

One of Joe's clients peered up from prowling a bad six-ball lay and barked, "Cut the guff, Joe, and buy a couple cases of strawberry. It beats that rotgut you sell for whiskey."

"Hush up, Clyde, I'll get to the business in a minute. Now, Mr . . . What's your name?"

"Perry. Tom Perry."

"Well, Mr. Perry, you seem like a proper religious person. Did that redheaded honyock hooraw you about the church key?"

Tom didn't know if he liked being tagged "a proper religious person" in such a manner, but he answered straightforwardly, "As a matter of fact he did."

"Don't pay him no never mind. He does that with every new route driver what's got religion. He don't mean no harm by it. He's still young and high spirited. He's a good boy. He takes good care of my Etta."

Clyde's partner at the near pool table growled, "Buy the strawberry, Joe."

"I'm gettin' to it, I'm gettin' to it, Enoch. Now, Mr. Perry, we haven't had a reg'lar route man here since spring. Do they still make that good cream of sody?"

"I've got four cases left."

"Now don't you tell anybody, but that's my favorite. Here's what you do: you can bring me two cases of cream of sody and two cases of strawberry, and one case of orange every time you make a run. But bring 'em in the back way, will you? Some folks here might not understand me buyin' sody water. How often you going to come by Ragtown?"

"Mr. Wheeler said every other day would be best."

"I don't see eye to eye with that Wheeler. He's too straitlaced. But he's right. You come by every other day in the week and leave what I said. You go on and bring it on in for today. In the back way."

As Tom walked out to get Joe Franklin's order, Clyde said, "Don't let this big galoot fool you, Mr. Perry. He's a regular softie. In the winter he even lets newcomers sleep in the Pool Hall when the hotel's full."

"You got too big a mouth, Clyde," grunted Joe Franklin.

"Who are you? Hey, Mack, are you the labor agitator?" Entrepreneur Robert Denison stomped past stacks of rotary drill pipe through the mud to Tom Perry, jaw jutting and anger stamped on his face. "Are you?"

"I don't think so, sir," said Tom, not exactly sure what a labor agitator might be. "I'm selling ice cream and sody pop."

"Ice cream? Then where in blazes is that blasted agitator supposed to be? My chief engineer Johanson told me there was some blamed socialist out here trying to organize my men."

"I don't know, sir. I haven't seen anybody except workers between here and Ragtown. Maybe he was spoofing you. Would your men like some ice cream or sody pop?"

"The socialists are thick as ticks on a hound's ear down here in the Red River counties," muttered Denison. "Even the farmers are turning socialist. And they brought labor agitators down from up north. But I won't have them coming up here and causing trouble. I run a good camp. Tents for the men. Feed them even, not like most of these operations. I pay them good money and I expect a day's work for a day's pay. And no union!"

"No, sir," said Tom, by now accustomed to fretful customers with bizarre worries. He had decided that letting them talk themselves out was the best policy, and that his job was only to sell his wares. "Do you think your men might like to buy some ice cream or sody pop?"

"If you see any agitators, would you do me a favor and tell me quick?"

"I'd be happy to. What do they look like, sir?"

"You've never seen a labor agitator? Or a socialist?"

"Not that I can think of. I've read in the *St. Louis Republic* about socialists. Don't know about agitators."

"Well, agitators are . . . They're . . . They stand around trying to get workers to join their union. They wait 'till end of shift, go-home time. They stand just off of your property, mostly, so's you can't arrest them. There's usually two or three agitators together. They have leaflets and sign-up sheets. Tell the men how bad working conditions are, how lousy the pay is. Claim the union will make 'em all rich. I think they're in cahoots with the socialists. Might be socialists themselves. And the socialists, they stand by the road and make speeches to anybody who'll listen, sound almost like a preacher. All fired up. You'd know 'em if you saw 'em. But you're not one of them?"

"No, sir."

"Anyway, so you're selling sody water and ice cream?"

"Yes, sir. Got strawberry and orange. The cream of sody's all gone. And the chocolate ice cream's mostly gone."

"You have a case of strawberry and a case of orange?"

"Got two cases."

"You take a case of each into the commissary tent there. The head cook'll pay you out. You going to come around regular?"

"Every other day."

"Friday you ask the head cook what kind of sody water the men take to the most, and see if he wants any ice cream. His name's Hoffman. German. You better go talk to him before you take the sody water in. Tell him Denison ordered it. And what's your name?

"Perry. Tom Perry."

"Okay, Perry. I got to get back to work. And don't forget, you see any agitators or socialists, you let me know, you hear? I'm countin' on yuh!"

Tom watched the bulldog of a man stomp off as he had stomped up, and heard him yell into the machine noise: "Johanson, you crazy old goat, you're pulling my leg again. I almost cold-cocked that guy you said was a labor agitator! He's just selling sody water!"

While Tom went through his initiation into the mysteries of oil field booming, Clayborne watched Cornish go by. Today, on his sixth birthday, he studiously observed as strange men came to the house across the street and moved it away. Clayborne first noticed that something was up when the professional house mover drove his buggy up across the street shortly after eight o'clock. The mover met the owners, the Hamiltons, Ezra and Matilda, on their front porch. He spoke in a stentorian voice that carried throughout the neighborhood like a circus barker's. Clayborne heard him boasting that his moving job was so smooth they would be able to sleep in their own house at night while it was being moved up to Ringling.

The burly man said, "You go ahead and stay in the house every night. The only thing we'll have to take out is the brick chimney flue up in the attic. You can't tell about brick chimneys, they might fall down while we're moving. Everything else can stay. You keep all your furniture inside, your bed, your cookstove, everything. Nothing will be damaged. Nothing at all." Everyone in the block could hear him.

The Hamiltons then handed the mover some papers, which he took, announcing to the world: "That's fine, that's fine. You're all taken care of now. You can take whatever personal belongings you'll need today. It'll be a few minutes before my crew gets here. You can go spend the day with your friends and we'll be three or four hundred yards closer to Ringling when you come back at sundown. You'll be able to sleep in your own bed tonight! Ain't that grand!"

Within minutes the work crew arrived with the mule team, supply wagon and a massive long square beam slung under a big-wheeled carriage. Clayborne asked his mother if he could sit out on the porch with Pup and watch them move the Hamiltons' house away. "If you don't get in the way of the workmen, Clayborne," she said. The boy took his place and was immediately enthralled when the mover barked a series of terse orders: "Jameson and Noonan, down with the chimney. Dorsey and Sharp, you get the main beam pushed under. Blum and Craig, you get to the jack points. When that chimney's down, Jameson and Noonan, you set the dollies with Dorsey and Sharp."

The men attacked their work with deliberate haste. The huge beam's snub nose was maneuvered into position by the mule team, leaving it pointed under the center of the house. Dorsey, the rigging slinger, looped his cable around the head of the long beam, and scampered under the house to the far side, which presented no difficulties because the structure's underpinning was completely open: the house sat on two-foot high wood stilts. Dorsey and Sharp harnessed the cable to the mule team; then Dorsey spraddled on all-fours to check on the progress of the main beam under the house. Mule-skinner Sharp bellowed "Cope!" and the mules lunged forward against the load on the cable, dragging the great beam into place within seconds. When the main beam had been thus positioned, three smaller extension beams were laid on top of it, spaced evenly under the house, using the same method.

By the time the carrier beams were in place the masonry men had dismantled the chimney, saving as much intact as possible, and loaded it into the supply wagon for later reassembly. Six large jackscrews, two on each end of the extension beams, were set in place, some on rocks, some on heavy planks for firm footing. Long crank-handles were inserted into the jacks, and the men began the arduous and touchy job of lifting the house off its foundations. A miscalculation or an uneven raise could literally tear the house apart as if it were made of tissue paper. The lifting process took longest.

It was after dinner before Clayborne came back to his porch roost to be rewarded with the sight of a house suspended nearly six feet off the ground. Nine large foot-and-a-half diameter dolly wheels were then placed in crucial support points under the center and perimeter of the house, and the undercarriage of beams were lowered slowly and carefully on top of them.

Finally the house was ready to be moved. The old foundation pilings were removed and a runway cleared to make way for the Hamilton house's descent to the street. Enormous blocks and tackle were attached to the pull points on the beam undercarriage, and the first heave by the mule team began. The house complained, and only shuddered at first, resisting this importune motion after so long at rest. Then slowly, ponderously, with much plaintive groaning, the trussed-up house slid on heavy dolly wheels from its old familiar berth. Its slow glide into the street seemed dreamlike and unreal. If houses have memories, this must have been a time of reminiscence and anguish.

Clayborne watched wide-eyed as the building loomed slowly closer and closer to his place on the rent-house porch. In the end, his curiosity overwhelmed his fear and he stayed put. Finally the travelling house moved no more. There it was, Clayborne thought, the Hamiltons' home, squatting in the middle of the street. Somehow, it reminded him of the Wichita Falls house on fire, but it didn't frighten him. Watching houses move was fun. What novel entertainment for a six-year-old on a fine August day!

The house formed a bulky and unlovely parade by itself, occupying the entire width of the street and forcing traffic into alternate thoroughfares. Each pull of the mules at the block and tackle yielded some fifty feet of progress. By the time Tom returned home, the house was two blocks down the street.

"Clayborne! Oh, Clayborne! Time to come in off the porch!" the familiar call of his mother's voice rang out. "Coming!" he answered. He swung open the screen door and dashed into the kitchen. "Is Papa home?" he asked, "is he home yet, Mama?"

"Yes, your Papa sure is. He's out back unhitching the team. But I want you to stay here in the kitchen and welcome him home from his first day at the new job. He's probably tired out, so don't you go hanging on him, you hear? And you let him know what a good father you think he is, going off and doing this new kind of work for us."

"Yes, Mama," said Clayborne, eager to tell his father all about the Hamiltons' house.

Clayborne could hear his father coming up the rear steps through the little screened-in porch and in through the back corridor. The boy wiggled in anticipation. Then his father appeared, framed in the kitchen door. Clayborne didn't notice that when Tom stooped over to hug his boy one of his father's arms was hiding something behind his back.

"Papa! Papa! Thank you for going to work for us!" he yelled, hugging his father tightly. "And you should have seen what me and Pup saw today! While you were gone off to work some men with a mule team came and took the Hamiltons' house plumb away! Look! Look! It's gone, see?" The boy pointed out an east-facing window to the empty lot where only that morning had stood the home of Ezra and Matilda Hamilton.

"Well, how about that!" said Tom, sharing his boy's excitement. "It *is* gone. Where do you think they're going with it?"

"I know where they're taking it," announced the boy proudly. "I heard them say so. They're going up yonder to Ringling by the railroad tracks. Papa, why do people want to live by railroad tracks?"

"Oh," said Tom, "because they want to be close to everything that's happening, and the railroad goes everywhere, all over the forty-eight states. But haven't you forgotten what day this is?"

"It's Wednesday!" smiled Clayborne. Then he realized which Wednesday it was. "It's my birthday! You knew it was my birthday!" Tom revealed what he had been hiding behind his back: three bottles of red strawberry soda pop.

"Sody water, Papa! Wow, that's swell!"

"And there's something else," said Tom, reaching into the kitchen corridor and pulling out a wooden keg.

"Ice cream!" yelled Clayborne. "Sody water and ice cream! Wow, what a swell birthday present!" Then Clayborne was quiet for a second, and said, "Papa, I know we don't have much money for birthdays. We're glad you worked hard so I could have some sody water and ice cream, aren't we Mama?"

"Oh, yes, we certainly are. We're proud of your father," said Belle.

Tom said, "You'll be more proud when you find out how much I made today. I sold everything, Belle, everything except what I held back for the birthday. Belle, that's over five dollars! In one day!"

"Land sakes, Tom!" Belle was almost speechless. Five dollars a day was dream money.

"Even when you figure only making a run every other day, that's still fifteen dollars a week," said Tom. "We're going to do all right."

"This is a real happy birthday, Papa."

"Clayborne, son, it sure is. Happy birthday!" said Tom.

"Happy birthday!" said Belle, kissing her beaming six-year-old.

The next day, Auntie Mary came to visit them. Clayborne was sitting on the porch, as usual, playing with Pup, as usual, when he saw her buggy turn the corner from Cornish's main street toward their house. "Mama, Auntie Mary is coming to see us," he shouted into the open front door. "I'll go meet her out back, son," she replied.

Mary Herrin had a habit of sitting bolt upright, smack in the middle of the buggy seat, looking all prim and proper in her long-skirted, brown shirtwaist taffeta dress. Its slightly Gibson-girl look gave her an all-American woman air that had been passe in the big city for a decade but was still very much in vogue in the rural hinterlands, thanks to the Sears, Roebuck & Company catalogue. Clayborne waved to his Auntie Mary as she reined in her horse and pulled around back to the horse lot. Pup and the boy raced around the house to meet her. Belle walked slowly down the back hall of the house to the rear door and called, "Hello, Auntie Mary! I'd come down these stairs, but I'd better stay up here."

"Don't you put yourself out, Belle, not in a delicate condition like that. I'll be right up." Mary Herrin stowed her buggy whip in its mount and tied her horse to the feed crib. "I came into Cornish this morning to sell my butter and eggs and thought I'd drop by to see how you're doing in your new rent house." She took Clayborne by the hand and walked him to the back door and up the steps. Belle led them along the back corridor to the roomy yellow kitchen.

"You look like you're getting along just fine, young man, you and your dog Pup."

"Yes, Ma'am, Auntie Mary. I sure am doing just fine. I had sody water and ice cream for my birthday yesterday, and some men came and took the Hamiltons' house away."

"My, my, such a lot of going on for one day."

"I'll get us some coffee, Auntie Mary."

"Don't do it on my account, Belle. Where's Tom? I thought he was only going to work every other day."

"Oh, he's over to the ice cream plant," Belle sighed as she filled the blue enameled coffee pot. "He wanted to see how they make ice cream and the sody pop. You know men, can't resist machinery. He'll be back by dinnertime."

"Auntie Mary," asked Clayborne, "where's Uncle Will?"

"Well, Clayborne, I left him back at the farm to pick the cotton."

"You mean he can't come with you when you sell butter and eggs?"

"Certainly not! I wouldn't think of it. He'd just be in the way."

"Papa used to go when my Mama sold eggs back in Texas, and she didn't mind. And my Mama used to sell cream and eggs. Why do you sell butter and eggs?"

"You're just full of why? why? why? aren't you? Well, sir, it's this way. I've got a churn, and I've got the time, and if I churn my cream into butter, they pay me more for it at the grocery than if I just left it cream. I make more money for myself that way."

"For yourself? Isn't it Uncle Will's money, too?"

"Nosiree, young man. The egg and butter money is all mine. I work for it, just like your Uncle Will works for the rest of it."

"Mama, is that what Papa means when he says Auntie Mary is a right sharp business lady?"

"Now, Clayborne!" said Belle sternly as Mary Herrin laughed out loud. "You mustn't repeat things you've heard around."

Mary said between giggles, "No, no, Belle, let him go on. What else does your father say about me?"

Clayborne cast a fearful eye at his mother, but then leaned close to his great aunt in a conspiratorial manner and whispered: "He says you're as good a cook as Mama is, but you like poke salad more than he does." Then aloud to his mother, "Mama, is it okay to tell about the poke salad part?"

"You already told it, Clayborne. What ever am I going to do with you?"

"You could let me go out and play in the horse lot! Please, Mama?"

"Go on and play, my little scamp. But you watch out for rusty nails and snakes with those bare feet." Clayborne was out the door in a flash, Pup galloping behind.

"That's a bright boy, Belle. You make sure he gets good schooling."

"I plan to take him over to the Cornish school as soon as it opens. The baby ought to be here by then."

"How are you coming along?"

"Oh, about usual, I expect. My back hurts and I get tired easy, but it was the same with Clayborne. I guess that's just part of having babies."

"Yes, I was that way with ours. How much longer, do you think?"

"Two more weeks, I figure. Two more weeks."

Clayborne was surprised on the morning of September 2, 1916, with the news that he had a little brother whose name was Clyde Hoyt Perry. A country doctor had come to their house in the night, he was told, and delivered the new baby. Clayborne asked "Oh boy, Papa, can I play with him?"

"In time son, in time."

The new baby seemed to make everyone happier. Belle felt better than she had in a long time; her back quit hurting and her energy returned. She could maneuver around the house better and she loved babies. Tom left the house for work in the mornings feeling less apprehensive. He had come to terms with the raucous milieu of the oil fields, found he actually liked some of the strange people, and had met his first socialists. He was making at least fifteen dollars each week, and that alone gave him a great boost in morale. Clayborne was fascinated with his little brother, watching over him for hours, helping his mother with dirty diapers and learning how to treat babies ever so gently. He particularly enjoyed going for walks in the town with his mother and new brother.

One of the walks ended at Cornish school, an enduring stone structure like the town's business buildings. As they strolled by the school ground, Clayborne carefully examined what was going on: lots of boys and girls playing with a ball, running, playing tag, hanging onto each other, shouting, general joy. The boy wondered why grownups talked about education so seriously. School looked like it was going to be fun. He was certain he could master that ball game, whatever it was.

"This is the school, Clayborne. Do you like it?" asked his mother.

"Oh, yes, ma'am. That school work looks easy!"

But he was not so sure when his mother, holding the infant Hoyt nestled in her left arm, opened the big high door and ushered him into the dark school interior with its long drab hallway illumined only by dim transom windows. This cast an entirely different light on things. Those lucky school children outside might have to come in here, might have to sit at those little wooden desks on a beautiful September day. Maybe the grownups were right. The inside of the school looked like serious business.

He did not quite grasp what his mother was talking about so long to the woman behind the big counter near the front door, but he gathered that it had something to do with his going to school here. Well, why not? He rather liked that loud bell. When the talk was over and they began the stroll home, Clayborne saw that his guess had been right: there were no children on the playground.

One evening at suppertime, as Belle nursed Hoyt — they had decided to call the new arrival Hoyt rather than Clyde — Tom read a letter from home, from his father in Hico. "Belle, did you read this part about Grandma coming from Alabama to live with my Papa?"

"No, I didn't see that, Tom," said Belle. "Seems to me we got a letter out in Trinchera said your Grandma was plannin' on coming to live with them."

"Well, she did. Been there for couple of months. I haven't seen her since I was, what? twenty-two, I guess. Before we moved to Texas. She must be getting up in years. And look at this, Fred and Myrtle are going to stay with your Papa until November and then go up to Pueblo. Says Leonard and Bob have got jobs in Pueblo already. They say Fred can get one easy. I sure hope they're right."

Belle commented, "You haven't said anything about the first part of the letter. The part I read. You see that about your Papa's rent house going to be empty come November?"

"I saw."

"Does it make you think, Tom?"

No answer.

"Think, Tom," urged Belle gently. "It's the middle of September. It's getting chilly of a night. How long can you keep selling ice cream and sody water?"

Stiff silence, then Tom said, "I didn't sell my whole stock today, Belle. Had to take a couple kegs of ice cream back to Wheeler's cold room."

"See, it's come already. I took Clayborne over to the Cornish school today. We have to make up our minds if we're going to send him there or not. Pretty quick."

"Uncle Will and Auntie Mary's coming over Sunday. I'll talk to them about it."

Clayborne said, "It's a swell school, Papa. They have ball games. Can I go there?"

"We'll see, son."

"Papa, have you seen Pup since you came home from work?"

"No, son, I haven't. I'm sure your friend is out running around having a good time. He needs time to just be a dog, you know."

"I hope so, Papa, but he always comes in at suppertime for his table scraps."

"Come to think of it, I can't recall Pup ever being late for anything to eat. Maybe you better go look for him after supper."

"There he is!" said Clayborne, "I hear him at the back door now. Can I be excused to go let him in, Papa?"

Tom nodded.

Clayborne ran down the back corridor and opened the rear screen door. Pup came in unsteadily. Clayborne didn't notice at first. Pup stumbled, then walked into a wall.

"What's the matter with you, you silly Pup?" asked Clayborne playfully. Then a cold chill froze his blood. Pup fell over, his eyes rolling, his belly convulsing. "Papa! Papa! Something's real wrong with Pup! He can't stand up!"

Tom rushed to the back corridor where the little dog lay jerking and trembling. "Dear God," he gasped. Quickly he turned the animal over several times, inspecting the skin for signs of injury. There were none. He looked in the dog's eyes. They were glazed and his tongue hung out. "Poison!" he muttered, picking up Clayborne's pet and running with him to the kitchen.

"Quick, Belle, hand Hoyt to Clayborne and get the grease gravy. It looks like Pup has run into some rat poison."

Belle sat dumbstruck. She had just watched Hoyt peacefully fall asleep, and it took her a moment to gather her wits. She said slowly and clearly to Clayborne: "Son, you come take Hoyt very gently and hold him without waking him up if you can. We're going to give your Pup something for the poison."

Clayborne took the sleeping infant Hoyt from his mother as he had learned to do during the past two weeks. But he could not keep the big tears from rolling down his cheeks. Belle quickly but calmly placed the skillet of pan grease on the woodstove and told Clayborne, "You're going to have to be a man for a little while, Clayborne, so we can save Pup. You just hold Hoyt and comfort him if he needs it."

Clayborne watched in disbelief as Pup's glazed eyes fell half shut. Only the quivers in the dog's back legs showed any sign of life. The grease gravy in the skillet quickly softened on the warm woodstove. Tom roughly held Pup's jaws open while Belle dipped her finger in the skillet. "It's ready," she said.

"Better get it down him. He don't have much time."

"You hold him tight. He's going to kick."

Belle poured the warm grease into Pup's mouth. The dog gagged and choked, but Tom held his jaws apart by main strength. "Pour some more, Belle. He's just spitting it back up."

More grease gravy fell into the miserable dog's mouth, but this time the gag reflex did not push it out. Great gulping swallows went down, coating the animal's gut. The glaze vanished from Pup's eyes and helpless terror showed there instead. The grease kept flowing into his mouth and glugging into his stomach. It was like filling a bottle, Tom thought. "That's good," Tom said. "You can quit now."

"I'll get a blanket for him to lay on," said Belle, clanking the gravy skillet on the drain board.

"Is he going to live?" asked Clayborne in a quavering voice. Belle took Hoyt from his arms.

Tom said, "Can't tell yet, son. But it's the only thing to do if you got a poisoned animal, cow or a horse, anything. Grease seems to coat their innards, helps them throw off the poison. It's all you can do."

"But is Pup going to live?" asked Clayborne through the tears, standing alone.

That weekend the Herrins, Will and Mary, came to Cornish for Sunday dinner after church. Clayborne sat on the porch, but without Pup. He saw them coming in their fine Emerson buggy, and waved to them as they reined in their horse and pulled around the back to the horse lot. Clayborne raced around the house to greet them. "Pup got poisoned, Uncle Will, Auntie Mary."

"Yes, your mother told me when I was in to sell my butter and eggs," said Mary Herrin. "Poor old Pup."

"Yes," consoled Uncle Will. "Poor old Pup."

Tom greeted them from the back door, holding a baby-sized bundle in his arms. "Poor old Pup, my eye," he said, pulling the blanket away to reveal a panting little black dog face. "This dog has been babied more since he took sick than a regular person. Now that we're sure he's going to live, I wish he'd get well real quick."

"Aw, Papa," said Clayborne, "it won't hurt none to baby him a little bit more, will it?"

"I don't expect so, son. Come on in, Auntie Mary, Uncle Will."

After a Sunday dinner of chicken bought at the Cornish grocery, the women shooed the men out of the kitchen. Clayborne took Pup out into the sunshine, and the men retired into the rent house's front room, wanly furnished only with two cane-bottom chairs brought in from the kitchen. Tom and Will did not complain about spare surroundings, and discussed more important things.

Uncle Will said, "Tom, you and the family has got to come out to the farm this week and pick some goober peas. Drat, I mean 'peanuts,' Tom. You say 'goobers' to these Oklahoma folks and they don't know what you're talking about. Never learned to speak proper Alabama talk around here. The peanuts are ready for picking."

"We'd be pleased to come, Uncle Will."

"How do like your new work, Tom?"

"Well, I been at it a month, and I've got to know most of the people in Ragtown, I think. It's a right peculiar place, but the people are nice once you get to know them. Most of the people that is."

"You've run into some of those bad sorts I was telling you about."

"Oh, yes. I've seen the fist fights and the knife fights, and the fancy women and the gamblers. Those are the drifters, they come and they go. They don't have any home, they got nothing. I talk to a few of them, not many. It almost makes you sick."

"Really rotten, eh?"

"No, Uncle Will. I don't know how to explain it. They're not bad through and through like you'd expect. That's what makes me feel funny about 'em. When I see 'em, the fancy women, they're nice, buying ice cream. Some of those dance hall girls have children, can you fathom that? Living right with 'em there in their houses. The women'll come out every now and then, buy a sody water for their little boy or little girl. They're nice to their children, call them pet names, hug 'em tight. You can see those women aren't bad all the time. There's some good in them. You can't just condemn them completely. It would be easier if you could. That's what makes you sick."

"Oh, Tom, you've seen the sorrow of the world. Good people gone bad."

"And some of them aren't really bad at all, like Joe Franklin who runs the Pool Hall. He's got a terrible bark on him, but he wouldn't bite a good person. There he is in that awful place with those fallen people all around him, and truth be known, he kind of protects folks. Young farm kids come in and he won't sell liquor to them. Sells them my sody water. But a card shark can come in and try to scalp some newcomer. I've seen him throw a rotter right out the door with his own hands. Beats 'em up real good, too, if they need it. Yep, it's a strange place. I wouldn't want my family to even drive through Ragtown in the buggy. But there's something about it, Uncle Will. I can't help *likin'* some of those people, Lord forgive me. I don't know." Tom was troubled by emotions he had only read about in Sunday School: going among publicans and sinners, hate the sin and love the sinner. He was seeing a world of new and disturbing complexity.

Tom sighed and said, "It's those socialists that worry me most."

Uncle Will agreed: "Yes, they seem to be getting strong around here. It's worried me too."

"Over in Marshall County, so Mr. Denison tells me . . ."

"Bob Denison?" asked Uncle Will.

"Yes, Bob is his name."

"You mean you know Bob Denison?"

"Yes, I sell him ice cream and sody water and tell him where the socialists are when I see them giving speeches by the roadside. Or in the towns. Why?"

"He's a millionaire, Tom. Owns his own oil company."

"He is? He don't act like one."

"Oh, yes, big oil money."

"I knew he was a little strange, in such a hurry all the time, but he wears work clothes like everybody else. He's not a fancy kind of millionaire, and he's right smart. Understands that socialism. That's what he was telling me about."

"Yes, go on, I didn't mean to butt in. I was just surprised."

"Surprises me, too. Well, Mr. Denison says over in Marshall County, just the other side of Ardmore, the Socialist Party got 21 percent of the vote in the 1914 election. And when that Eugene Debs ran on the Socialist ticket for president in 1912, the rest of the country only gave him 6 percent of the vote and Oklahoma gave him 16 percent. There must be a great bunch of socialists in this state."

"They're all just atheists, Tom, trying to seduce Christian souls into foul practices," said Uncle Will.

"It's hard to figure them out, Uncle Will. I've listened to some of their speeches. This one fellow O.E. Enfeld used to be an elder in the Presbyterian church up in Shattuck. He became a socialist, and now he says capitalism means a very few men owning the means of production and distribution. I remember him saying that, very few men owning the means of production and distribution. He says it's class warfare, capitalist class against the working class. He talks like a school book. Says we got to pick sides in the coming struggle. He says that today one man has millions and does nothing, but millions do everything and have nothing. I don't guess he ever saw Mr. Denison. But this Enfeld says working men ought to support the socialists. You can be a proper Christian and be a socialist, he says. He's a socialist but he's still a Christian preacher. I heard him talk to a crowd in Ringling. He blames the capitalists for taking four-fifths of the poor farmers' wealth so they can't dress themselves fit to go to church with fine people. That's what he said, four-fifths of the poor farmers' wealth. What do you make of that?"

Uncle Will was perplexed. "He's a Christian and a socialist? Doesn't make sense. Maybe the Presbyterians are different from the Baptists."

"I think the Presbyterians tossed him out, Uncle Will. He's just a preacher on his own, doesn't have a regular church. I heard another socialist talk to the rent farmers just north of Ringling. He was out on the road when I drove by, had a little gathering around him. I just stopped to listen. He didn't talk about Christians at all, just asked these rent farmers about what their plans were when they first came to Oklahoma, their plans to work hard and buy a little farm house. He asked how their dreams had panned out. Then he said the fact that you're still renting was answer enough."

"Well, who's to blame if you can't make it as a farmer? Is a farmer with his own land bad because he's a good farmer? Am I wrong to charge Henry rent on the land I worked and sweated to earn? That sounds like what they're saying." This talk about socialists made Uncle Will very uneasy.

"I don't know, Uncle Will. Another fellow just Friday was talking at the railroad station in Ringling. He said that school had begun in the towns, but the children of tenant farmers are still in the cotton fields. Says their children will be there two more months. The children of the bankers and landlords are in school now, though, getting a good education. He says the workers pay for the schools with their taxes, but high rent and bank interest keeps them so poor their children have to work so they can't get an education. I couldn't help but think of my Clayborne."

"Tommy, you're not getting to be a socialist, now, are you?"

"Law, no, Uncle Will. I'm just telling you what they say. I don't know what to think of them, except they're strange. Those socialists say that if they take over the government, the small farmer and laborer will get immediate aid. That's what they keep saying, 'immediate aid.' They talk about the revolution coming. The socialist revolution. That's not for me. I got enough troubles without a revolution. Far as I'm concerned, we already had our American revolution once, and I'm partial to the Constitution the way it's writ. And the socialists don't say what will happen to all those capitalists they don't like if their revolution does come. Would it be good for America to get rid of Henry Ford, Uncle Will? Mr. Denison says Ford's a capitalist."

"Course it wouldn't, Tom," said Uncle Will. "Socialism is all just foolishness."

"I don't understand socialists very much. They're all riled up about the poor rent farmer. Well, the rent farmer sometimes does have it bad. But that 'immediate aid' the socialists talk about — who's going to pay for it? It sounds just like pie in the sky. Did I tell you, Uncle Will, that's what some of the oil field workers called me at first for having religion, old pie-in-the-sky Perry. They hoo-rawed me about Christians believing in Heaven, that when you die you'll eat pie in the sky. They're a blasphemous bunch, but somehow they seem goodhearted about it. They quit raggin' me after they got to know me. But the fact is, it's the socialists that sound like pie in the sky, now that I've listened to them a while. 'Immediate aid.' Revolution. I'll just keep on working for my pie right here on the ground, and let them socialists have their revolution somewhere else. But it still worries me, Uncle Will. They're serious about it. It worries me."

"There's something else on your mind, Tom. I can tell."

"You're right, Uncle Will. Papa wrote and said I should come back to the rent house. Work the land on his farm."

"Are you going to go?"

"I don't know. I like being on my own, earning my own way. The ice cream job has done all right. Been making fifteen dollars a week, Uncle Will. That's not bad. But who'll buy ice cream and sody water in the winter? I see it coming already. My Friday sales were down, and it's only getting a little chilly."

"What will you do during the winter?"

"There's nothing, Uncle Will. I know every job they got up at Ragtown now. Nothing I could do. They need roustabouts and roughnecks and mechanics. The rheumatism wouldn't let me be a roustabout and I don't know anything about being a mechanic. Anyhow, I don't think I'd like to work with some boss standing over me all the time."

"There's not a lot of choice, then, is there, Tom?"

"Not a lot."

The wagon rumbled into the town of Bowie, Texas, in late October. Hoyt had been crying for more than an hour. A blue norther had roared down from Canada that morning and the temperature was headed for freezing. Clayborne sat with his mother and father wrapped in a wagon sheet and blankets on the spring-cushioned wagon seat. He held a bag of peanuts from the Herrins' farm, now ten days behind them. Tom was saying to Belle, "You and Hoyt can't spend another night in the wagon. We've got to put you and the children on the train."

"But what about the money, Tom?"

"The train from Bowie isn't too much, not for one adult ticket. Clayborne's still not seven and they don't charge you for babies. It'll take a few dollars. But I'd rather that than have Hoyt come down sick in the freezing weather. Or worse. There's no two ways about it. We're going to stop and put you on the train."

Belle stewed on the idea for a moment, then seemed reconciled to it and instructed Clayborne, "Son, when we get on that train, don't you sit up too high. You're big for your age and we don't want the conductor to think you're overage and trying to cheat on fare."

"Okay, Mom," the boy cheerfully agreed. "Are you coming on the train, too, Papa?"

"No, son, I've got to stay with the wagon and the animals." Hoyt's lusty howling made conversation difficult.

"Won't you freeze out here in the cold, Papa?"

"I'm a grown man, son."

"Don't grown men get cold?"

"Yes, son, we get cold. But a man has to protect his family and bear up with things he wouldn't want his family to suffer."

"Will I have to do that when I grow up?"

"I expect so, son."

"Want some peanuts, Mama?" the boy offered.

"How can you think of eating at a time like this?" said Belle. "We're going to be separated from your father . . . Oh, Clayborne, honey, I'm sorry. I'm just upset. Of course I'll have some peanuts."

She rattled the paper sack and reached far down, only to come up with. . "A ring! Look at this, Tom, here's a little old baby gold ring!"

Tom and Clayborne looked intently at the prize. The boy asked, "Do you think we can keep it, Mama?"

"No, son," said Belle. "I'm sure this is one of the children's rings, Ernest or Cecil or Henry, Jr. We'll have to send it back to them. I'll bet this came from the granary bin where we were picking out peanuts. That would be the likely place for a child to lose his ring. Henry and Addie have probably been looking high and low for it. Land sakes."

"Here's the railroad station, coming up," said Tom. The grubby little station hulked grey by the rutted dirt street like a thousand others on the Ft. Worth & Denver line. The day had grown dark at noon with roiling black clouds. Tom drew the wagon with its buggy in tow up to the hitching rail near the ticket window. Hoyt still rent the air with his wailing. Tom said, "We'll get our tickets inside, Belle. You all just go right straight on in out of this weather."

Tom tied the team to the rail, then followed his wife and sons into the stuffy, dirty waiting room. Belle told him firmly, "I'm going to stay with my own folks, Tom, with my Papa and Mama. We should let them know we're coming on the train. Nobody expects us for another week or ten days in the wagon."

"We can send a penny postcard from here," suggested Tom.

"It won't get there any faster than us. They carry the mail on the passenger trains, like you used to tell me, Tom."

"That's right. I'm not thinkin'. I guess the only thing to do is call them long distance. Maybe when you get to Morgan so the call won't cost so much."

"I can just wait 'til I get to Hico. Only cost a dime that way. We won't have to wait too long before my Papa comes in the buggy. You better see about our tickets home, now, Tom."

He stepped up to the inside ticket counter, his mind echoing Belle's words, Home. Tickets home.

"Where to, mister?" asked the agent.

"Hico, one adult."

"Ticket to Hico, Texas. That'll be three dollars fifty-five cents. Train will be on time at three-fifteen. That's about two hours ten minutes now."

Tom looked on the wall. "Is that calendar on the right day?" he asked.

The railway agent glanced at the calendar, then at Tom. "Yessir, it's near the end of October."

"Thank you."

It had been a year, just a year, since he had gotten off a train in Colorado and left Texas behind. What had it all added up to? He had no answer. Tomorrow his wife and children would be back in Hico. He looked at the strips of heavy paper in his hand. Railroad tickets. Tickets home. But *was* it home, the home his restless soul yearned for, *his* home? Again, he had no answer. Only emotions as stormy as the norther outside. Home. He wanted home.

-6-

GRAND PRAIRIE REDUX

WHY are you digging holes by the creek Grandpa?" asked Clayborne over the crunch of shovel against dirt. The boy peered into a four-foot-deep pit, trying to see past the fringes of the bulky muffler and cloth coat that bundled him against the eager November air. Pup sniffed the fresh earth.

Jim Perry kept on digging, intent on gouging and punching the rocky soil. "I'm building a bridge, Clayborne, my boy," he answered. His shovel clanged on a chunk of blunt limestone. "Building a bridge over Camp Branch so we won't have to drive clear around the school to get to your Grandpa Blackburn's."

"But there's no road here."

"Don't need a road. The ground's hard enough for a full wagon."

"Is it shorter to Grandpa Blackburn's this way?"

"Sure is, boy." Jim Perry stopped his shovel in mid-thrust and used it as a pointer. "Look yonder, down southwest of here. If it wasn't for the post oaks you could see your Grandpa Blackburn's house just about three-quarter of a mile straight across. I figure going the regular way," — he pointed the shovel east — "out the gate, south past the mailbox, west around Camp Branch School and then back up north, it's about two and a half mile, it is, two and a half mile to the Blackburn place."

"Papa, are you building a bridge, too?"

Tom Perry looked up briefly at his boy while prying a stubborn stone fragment from the unyielding Texas soil and said, "Yes, son, I am."

"What are the holes for?"

"They're to put the bridge piers in, those big cedar posts stacked over yonder. Pup, you get away from there! Go find someplace else."

"I see 'em, Papa. You and Grandpa are going to put them in these holes and cover them up? Come on, Pup!"

"We'll put 'em down in the ground and leave the tops stickin' out. Then we'll put some ole' rocks and gravel around the posts and tamp 'em in real tight so they'll stay put. Then we'll lay the bridge beams across the creek and nail 'em to the posts. Then we'll nail those deck planks from the other pile on top of the beams. The piers hold the beams and the beams hold the deck. That's about all there is to a bridge, son."

The boy studied the pieces of unbuilt bridge lying at the ready all around him. "Are those long boards the bridge beams?"

"That's right, son." Tom scraped his shovel on a rock with a sound that made his skin crawl, then picked a dirty white slab of limestone out of the ground and tossed it into a growing rockpile.

"Grandpa, will floods wash your bridge away?"

"You mean the way they lose bridges on the Bosque or the Brazos? Not a chance. Camp Branch isn't big enough. Up here by the rent house Camp Branch isn't even as big as it is down by the weaning house where you used to live. That must be half a mile downstream. Camp Branch picks up a good deal of water 'twixt here and there, and even down there it's not big enough to wash away a good bridge."

Grandad Jim pulled out a clean red handkerchief and blew his nose loudly. He went on, "This here bridge is only going to be eight foot wide and fourteen foot long, maybe a little longer. Why, high water right on this spot, even in a bad winter, won't get more'n one, two foot above this here bridge we're buildin'. But there's a secret to keeping your bridge from washing away, young feller, and I'll tell you what it is if you want to know."

"What is it, Grandpa?"

"It's all in knowin' how to tilt your bridge, boy."

"Bridges are flat, Grandpa."

"Oh, I know. And this one will be flat too. All that rough cedar one-by-six in the pile right there is going to end up being the bridge deck, flat as a flapjack. But flat don't mean it ain't tilted." Jim Perry stopped a minute to lean on his shovel. Clayborne watched his graying walrus mustache as he talked.

"A bridge is sure flat enough to drive across without your wagon sliding off. But it's usually tilted sideways a little so the rain will run off'n it." He held out a flat hand, slanting it to make his point. Pup looked closely to make sure he wasn't being scolded.

"And that's where the secret comes in. If you're dumb, you tilt your bridge so the high side is upstream and the low side is downstream. Then when the creek rises the water comes under that high front side just like a pry bar. It gets under the bridge and pushes it up. And once the water gets a bite on a bridge like that, it's goodbye bridge." Jim Perry's hand gestures dramatically followed his narrative. Pup removed himself a few feet just to be sure.

"But if you're smart, you tilt that front edge down. Then when the creek rises the water rolls over the top and pushes down on the bridge instead of up. The flood helps your bridge to stay put, holds it right down on its piers." The old man resumed digging, and asked, "Now what do you think about that, Clayborne?"

"You're a smart bridge builder, Grandpa. You should build all the bridges and they wouldn't wash away so much."

"It's a bright youngster that knows his Grandpa is smart, boy. But they couldn't pay me enough to stop farming and build bridges. No sir, farming is the life for me. I'll stick to building bridges on my own farm."

"Are we going to stay here on the farm, Grandpa?"

"You're just full of questions this morning, aren't you, young man? I'll let your Pa answer that one."

Tom Perry faced his son, not quite knowing what to say. The shame of failure still stung him, had made him closemouthed, even sullen, since his return to Texas. But the boy's face offered no rebuke, only waited for the truth. Tom saw it, and responded. Before he could think, he heard himself saying the words he'd been choking back for two miserable weeks: "We're going to stay here, son. No more takin' up land out West. No more sellin' ice cream and sody water. We tried it and it didn't work out. That's that. We're just going to be Texas farmers and stay put like Grandpa's bridge."

"That's good, Papa," said the boy. "I like it here."

There. He'd said it. It hadn't been so hard.

Tom went back to his digging. Then, in a sudden dizzying rush, the pain and grief of months seemed to lift away. It was as if Tom's heartfelt words to his son had released some great power to dissolve his bitterness, to work an unexpected catharsis on his soul. It took his breath quite away. Then the strange experience ended as suddenly as it had begun.

Jim Perry asked "Are you all right, son?"

"I'm fine, Papa. I just . . . I'm fine. And Papa, I keep meaning to tell you: I appreciate your having us back."

"I know, son. No need to say nothin'." The two men stood with eyes locked like a physical bond. Jim seemed to sense what had happened to his son. "Sometimes the Lord tests you hard, Tom. It makes a man feel small to starve out, terrible small. I found it in Alabama. You found it in Colorado. But when times get better you let it go. Maybe it's your time to let it go and be here with us. Let's just say we like your company and we're partial to having family in the rent house."

Tom Perry smiled, then grinned. He felt good, really good, even though he didn't understand why. "Thanks, Papa. Thanks. We like your company, too, don't we Clayborne?"

"Of course we do. Papa, can I go up to the rent house now? Old Grandma said she'd teach me how to quilt."

"I see how well you like my company, young feller," snorted Jim Perry.

"Aw, you know what I mean, Grandpa. I've been out here a long time. Old Grandma's waiting. Is it okay, Papa?"

With two grandmothers and a great grandmother living close at hand, the family had taken to addressing Elizabeth Glasgow Perry as Old Grandma.

"If your Old Grandma's expectin' you, you shouldn't keep her waitin'," Tom said. "You go right on up to the rent house."

The boy dashed off, Pup at his heels, the two bounding over the low winter hummocks in unison.

"That's a bright boy you got there, son. You ought to see he gets proper schooling," said Jim Perry.

"That's what Aunt Mary said up at Ringling."

Clayborne ran up to the two-room rent house yelling, "Hello, Kitty!" to their orange tiger-striped cat sitting on the tiny stoop. The wary cat ducked under the house as Clayborne burst through the back door and scrambled into the kitchen like a one-boy mob with Pup galloping after. "Mama! Mama! Is Old Grandma here yet?" he shrieked.

"Don't slam the door when you come in, young man," admonished his mother from the cookstove. "And learn to act like a gentleman. You like to broke my eardrum with that hollerin'. And I expect you scared Hoyt."

"Yes, Ma'am," he said sheepishly. Pup tucked his tail between his legs and slunk to his box in the kitchen corner.

"Hello, Hoyt, are you scared?" Clayborne said to the baby in the highchair. Hoyt continued his goo-goo-ga-ga monologue with no apparent fright and Clayborne turned to leave the room. "But is Old Grandma here?

"Not yet, Clayborne. You can go look for her. She'll be comin' up from Grandpa Perry's house directly."

The boy unwrapped his muffler and unbuttoned his coat as he walked from the little shedlike kitchen through the passway door into the big front room. The warmth of its banked woodstove soothed him as he hung his wraps on the proper wall hook and turned to gaze out the front window. Beyond the wide front porch he could see southeastward across the two-hundred yards of grass to Grandpa Perry's house. There was no one on the path. He went to the front door and opened it a crack to widen his view. Straight out the door to the east, he saw only the animal sheds and idle farm equipment. He stuck his head out in the winter breeze and craned his neck. To the north, only the copse of postoak and liveoak and a few mesquites they used as a woodlot. To the south, only the withered grass stretching away toward Camp Branch where his Papa and Grandpa were building a bridge. No Old Grandma.

"Shut the front door, honey," called his mother through the kitchen door. "It's making a draft on Hoyt."

"Yes, Ma'am." Clayborne sat impatiently on his bed in the big front room. The open rafters and exposed wall studs here were much like those of the weaning house. He was almost used to his new home. Still, he kept noticing that this all-purpose room where everyone slept was much bigger than the weaning house bedroom, and the kitchen where his mother now stood brewing up coffee much smaller.

With no warning, Old Grandma's footsteps clomped on the oak porch deck. The front door unlatched and swung open. "There ye be, sonny," said Elizabeth Glasgow Perry, her seventy-eight-year-old eyes twinkling mischievously.

The boy popped up and hugged his wizened and cheery great grandmother. "Where were you, Old Grandma? I looked and looked and I didn't see you coming."

"I was out in the one-holer, young 'un, doin' what comes natcherly." She took off her coat and chuckled at the boy's consternation over her remark. "Don't be so prissy about me talking on goin' to the outhouse, sonny. Everybody does it. I don't know what this younger generation's comin' to, gettin' to where you can't say a natural word without raisin' a fluster of blushes. Well, come on, come on, if you're goin' to learn how to sew a quilt."

She took the boy by the hand and led him to the kitchen table. "Howdy, grandaughter," she said to Belle who returned a bright hello. "And howdy, to you, too, little tyke. Oh, you're about to drowse off, there, child." She whispered, "Hoyt's your name, isn't it, newcomer? You see, Belle, I remembered this time. Clayborne, you go fetch the quiltin' bag."

"I've got some coffee boiling for you, Grandma," said Belle.

"Why bless your heart, it'll do my old bones good. Your Texas winters are too wet and cold, you know that.

"This one surely is," said Belle. "This is the worst one I can recollect since I was just a girl."

"There ye are so quick, sonny! You got the scraps and everything," said Old Grandma to Clayborne. "Put it right there on the kitchen table."

Belle wrapped herself in a shawl and said, "Clayborne, look after Hoyt for me, I'm going out in the smokehouse and get some meat for supper. I won't be a minute."

"Yes, Ma'am." Clayborne glanced at the sleepy Hoyt and settled down at the kitchen table with his Old Grandma. Together they emptied the quilting bag's contents and examined them intently. After silent minutes separating the scraps from the working quilt from the sewing necessaries, Clayborne asked, "Old Grandma, are you really Grandpa Perry's Mama?"

She pushed a pile of scraps toward the boy and said, "Here, sort these out. Why, I shore am his Mama. He's my baby just like you're Belle's baby."

The boy thought about that for a minute. "Grandpa's gettin' to be an old baby, Old Grandma."

She cackled and patted the boy on the shoulder. "And he's still right spry for somebody all of fifty-four years old."

Belle returned, placed a large ham on the sideboard and said, "Clayborne, you let Hoyt fall asleep in his high chair."

"Sorry, Mama. He wasn't cryin' for anything. Did it hurt him any?"

"No, son," she said, lifting the baby gently and taking him to sleep on a front room bed. "Just make sure he don't slip down and fall out of the high chair when he's sleeping."

"I will, Mama, promise. How old are you, Old Grandma?" the boy asked, sorting scraps.

"I'm sixteen, sonny, goin' on seventeen," she tittered, laying out the quilt.

"You are not, Old Grandma. Lucia in Ringling was sixteen. I bet you're real old."

Belle called from the front room, "Don't contradict your elders, young man."

Old Grandma grinned and winked at Clayborne and said, "You listen to your Mama, young' un."

"I won't contradict her again, Mama. Where's Grandpa Perry's Papa, Old Grandma?"

"Oh, young 'un, my John, he's dead and gone. Gone to his reward. Years before you were born." She gathered the sewing needles and thread. "Died in eighteen and eighty-six. Buried him in the New Harmony Baptist cemetery back in Heflin, Alabamy."

"Are you sad, Old Grandma?"

"Me? Not nohow. My John lived a good life. Worked hard. Earned his rest. That was a long time ago. I miss my John sometimes, but here I got Jimmy and his young' uns and you 'uns. And we're about to piece a quilt. All I need now is my pipe."

She produced a venerable clay pipe with a cane stem from her apron pocket and took out a five-inch long twist of tobacco she had rolled herself.

Belle stepped to the cookstove and poured two mugs of coffee.

"Old Grandma, I've seen you makin' those tobacco twists from big leaves you get out of that little wooden crate that came in the mail. Why don't you get store-bought tobacco so I can have the tag?"

"The tag? What you talkin' about, boy?"

"The tobacco tag. It's a red thing to play with; the good ones have a long ribbon."

Belle said, "Don't pester your Old Grandma, Clayborne."

"Well, boy," said Old Grandma Perry, "ain't no more sense than use gettin' store-bought'n tobaccy. It ain't worth burning up, much less smokin'. I gets my tobaccy right from South Carolina, back where I come from. Good air-cured Burley leaf."

"How come you have to sprinkle it with water when I see you taking it out of the box and spreading it on the table?"

"Got to make it supple, boy, that's what my ol' Pap used to call it, supple, so it'll bend into a twist. You try to twist it straight out'n the box, it's too dry, it'll just break on ye. I just dampens it, gets it supple, and works it up into a nice good twist."

"Here's your coffee, Grandma," said Belle.

"Oh, thank you, girl. You're a good heart. I been meanin' to ask you, Belle, how's your sister bearing up?"

"Bethel's pining away since Charley died. I'm terrible sorry we hadn't got back yet from Oklahoma so I could be with her. If we'd only got here just three days earlier! Poor Charley Slaughter. The TB got him. He was only thirty-six years old, Grandma."

"The good die young, I heard tell back in Alabamy. How long were they married? I haven't been here but a few months, never got to know Charley much, what with him havin' the TB and all."

"Fifteen years, Grandma. That may not seem long to you, but they were so close. They never were able to have children, and I think that made the two of them closer. I'm afraid she's got the TB, too."

"Lord a' mercy, Belle. Poor Bethel, poor child. I hope she gets over losin' her husband. We have to keep goin', you know. But, law, I sure hope she don't have the TB." As she commiserated with Belle, Old Grandma twiddled the tobacco twist absently and then broke off a piece large enough to fill the clay pipe.

"Why do you smoke a pipe, Old Grandma?" asked Clayborne, who had been listening long enough to grown-up talk. "Papa and Grandpa don't smoke."

"Been smokin' a pipe since I was three, four years old, young 'un." She rolled the little wad of tobacco in the palms of her hands until it was ground into fine particles, which she let fall into her pipe bowl and tamped down firmly as she spoke. "My old Pap was a shoe cobbler back in South Carolina where I was born. We lived in the north end of the cabin and he cobbled in the south end. He loved his pipe, and he done give me the job of keeping it burning for him."

Elizabeth Glasgow Perry got up and marched to the kitchen stove, opened up the burner box, and with a stick of kindling wood scooped a glowing coal into the clay pipe. "I was just a little snip then, but I'd take his pipe over to the fire just like this, get a coal out and stick it on top of the tobaccy. Then I'd give it back to my Pap." She lighted her pipe with the hot coal in five or six deep draws.

"But the onliest way I could keep the consarned thing lit was to suck on that pipe stem. That was my job in the cobbler shop for years. After 'while, it just got me into the smokin' habit, young 'un." She marched back to her chair and sat with great country dignity. "Now, you take those two scraps and lay 'em by this pattern here."

The boy watched raptly as the old-timer puffed her pipe and shared her quilt-making craft. He cut scraps to pattern and asked, "Where's South Carolina?"

"Oh, it's way back east, t'other side of Georgia. Long ways, long ways."

"Did your Papa always live there?"

"No, he come from Scotland, he did." She drew contentedly on her pipe. "He used to tell me that us Glasgows was old Scottish blood. That's what my maiden name was, boy, it was Elizabeth Glasgow."

"Is that what you were called before you got married?"

"Yep. And that Glasgow name goes back a long ways. There's a famous city in Scotland, named after our family, Glasgow, Scotland. Big city there. Named right after us Glasgows. You're doin' good with that piece. Now you got the stuffing in there, you sew it up like this. Watch how the needle goes, sonny."

"Did you ever do anything famous, Old Grandma?"

"Me? Oh, no. Never even seen anything famous. Well, except maybe the War Between the States."

"Are the states fightin' one another?"

"No, sonny. Not any more. The War Between the States happened a long time ago. North against South, Yankees against Confederates. We was Confederates. My John and his four brothers all joined the Confederate Army. Fought in that long war. The part of it I saw wasn't no regular battle or anything, not like the Battle Above the Clouds where your Great Uncle Docton got shot in the mouth. It was eighteen and sixty-three, and the Confederates were losin.' There was dad-blamed Yankee soldiers swarmin' all over, right round our farm at Heflin. Back in Alabamy. Those Yankee curs come down takin' everything they could get, stealin' horses, takin' meat out of the smokehouse, pickin' all the corn out of the crib. Low-down varmints. They took everything we had, we couldn't make crops to amount to anythin'. We like to starved to death.

"My John was off to the war, like I say, fighting for the Confederates, and one day he come home, right in the middle of all these reprobate Yankees. They didn't see him, and he didn't see them. He'd wore his shoes out and the Colonel had let him come home to get some more shoes. When he realized that them Yankee cullions was all over the place, he knew he couldn't make it back to the Army without gettin' killed. So he hid under the bed. We had one of them raised beds with a trundle bed underneath that you could pull out for the children. My John hid behind that trundle bed all day long, wouldn't come out 'cause he knew the confounded Yankees would kill him sure. He hid for days on end, hid 'til all the Yankees moved on, must of been a week or more. Then he came out. He got the shoes he needed, and he went back to the Confederate Army.

"But the South fell. Oh, child, that was a terrible day! It was just awful, those good-for-nothing Yankees. And you know, when it was all over it was the freed slaves took care of us. Those no-account Reconstruction scalawags didn't care if us poor farmers lived or died, them and their carpetbagger friends. They'd just as soon rob us as look at us. But the poor old darkies, bless their hearts, they let us come pick cotton with them. Gave us food. If it wasn't for those old darkies we'd a' starved for sure. When times got better, we helped them out too, hired 'em to come pick cotton when the crop was big. Worked with 'em, side by side in the field. Law, they were near the onliest friends we had. Now you hear all this fightin' and killin' between whites and niggers. Why just a few months ago over in Waco some ugly mob killed a nigger name of Jesse Washington, stabbed him, hung him, finally burned him, even. That's just hateful. My heart is so grateful to our niggers back in Alabamy. Don't know why these Texans can't get along like we did. Are you paying attention, young 'un?"

"Oh, yes, Ma'am. My Papa and Grandpa Jim are building a bridge down on Camp Branch, Old Grandma. Me an' Pup went down and watched 'em all morning. They're digging holes for the bridge right now. Did I tell you?"

"You sure were payin' attention, boy. Well, the War Between the States was a long time ago. Don't reckon you youngsters ought to be interested."

"He's still young, Grandma," said Belle. "He doesn't realize how important it is. He'll be in school once he turns seven, and he'll learn."

"Yep, it's in all the school books now. He'll read it. Oh, Belle, talkin' about readin', Jimmy told me he was plannin' on comin' over here after supper to bring Tommy the newspapers he's through with."

November night rain clattered on the shingle roof overhead. Clayborne hitched his feet on the base of the little reading table and leaned forward on the cane-bottom chair. A book lay open in the yellow glow of the coal oil lamp. Tatted frills of a doily crept out from under the book like a geometric spiderweb, lending civility to the plain tabletop. The boy soaked in the warmth of the woodburning heater next to the reading table as he examined the first page of his reader, imitating the hand signs he found there — the letters of the alphabet and their corresponding signs in the standard one-hand alphabet for the deaf. After playing at sign-making for a moment he turned the pages to his place. He fleetingly wondered why there were hand-signs in this book since he never used them for anything.

"Mama, Papa, can I read to you?"

"Why, certainly, son," replied Belle, setting her sewing down. Tom lowered his newspaper and attended. Clayborne held M.W. Halliburton's *Playmates Primer* to catch the light best, and read aloud:

"Page seventy-eight. Father is going to the store. Father is going to town. Will, don't you and Tom wish to go? Rate and I do."

The youngster lurched haltingly through the text word by word, struggling to make out the meaning, his voice a monotone heavy with effort. "Ask father to let us go. I will ask mother. Mother, where are you? Father is going to town. May Kate and I go, too? May Tom and Will go too? Oh, thank you, Mother."

Clayborne's face glowed with determination, conquering each word as if it were a stubborn obstacle. "Kate's Mother says that we may go with your father. What did father say? Come on, girls. Father says that all of us may go."

The boy paused for breath a moment but did not look up: the intensity of his concentration was not diminished. "Good, Good! Run, Kate, run! Jump the rope, Kate. And now, father, all of us are in the wagon. Where will you sit, Kate? Father says Kate may sit with him. Now you can see the big horse. Here we go to the store! Goodbye, Mother."

Although Belle had heard that page and all the others a dozen times or more, she told him, "That's good, Clayborne. It's a hard page and you didn't miss any words at all."

"You're doing fine, son," said Tom.

The boy beamed in unconcealed triumph and laid his *Playmates Primer* aside.

Rural tradition throughout much of the United States kept farm children from entering public school until age seven, although their city counterparts began at age six. The practice was widespread in the South and almost universal in rural Texas. Many country parents, including Tom and Belle, believed the extra year at home should provide some kind of education, and an over-the-counter textbook market developed in rural America to fill the need. Halliburton's little 96-page text became one of the more popular primers, available at most drug stores for eighteen cents a copy. Children liked it for its homely treatment of the familiar: wagon rides into town, Will and his dog Fly, Kate and Tom and Kitty the cat.

Schools adopted the *Playmates Primer* for its easy teaching method: its four-lines-per-page format with only two new words on each page guaranteed that few children would fail to master its opening lessons.

Clayborne had received his primer at age five: he had taken it to Colorado and back, studied it faithfully, and could now read all of its words. It was his prized possession. When he first got the primer, the bright five-year-old quickly realized that letters conveyed meaning. But because he could not yet decipher that meaning himself, Clayborne became keenly attentive and curious about the lettering on everyday objects. He tended to suspect people of reading simply because there was lettering in their vicinity.

Clayborne nursed a long misunderstanding because of this suspicion. It came about one Sunday when preacher Will Green joined the family at dinner. The table had been set in country fashion with the plates upside down, to be turned upright only after grace had been said. When Brother Green bowed his head to return thanks that day, the boy was convinced that the preacher was reading a prayer someone had printed in green ink on the back of his family's dinner plates. He could see the writing plainly on the back of everyone's dishes. Three years later, Clayborne discovered the truth while removing a new floral-pattern dinner plate that had been included as a premium in a box of Quaker Mother's Oats. This breakfast cereal premium was just like the old dishes, and he happened to notice what Brother Green's "prayer" actually said. With a red face he made out the words:

Homer Laughlin China Company
Made in USA
Virginia Rose

Amen. Tom and Belle had nurtured their son's urge to learn, even though they themselves had no more than a fifth and sixth grade education respectively. Tom still retained his Blueback Speller from Alabama school days and taught Clayborne from it the best he knew how. Word recognition was strictly see-and-say with no hint of phonetics or structural understanding, but this rough-and-ready reading had sufficed for generations of aspiring Americans. Such rote learning meant that the boy would struggle for comprehension, unable to read silently until years later, having to read aloud to grasp the words and their meanings. These difficulties left him undaunted: by the winter of his sixth year, Clayborne had surpassed the abilities of most of his peers who had less careful tutors that found more hours for vainer pastimes. From time to time, Belle would take a volume from her father's small library and read a chapter a night to the family from DeFoe's *Robinson Crusoe*, or *Black Beauty*, or *The Swiss Family Robinson*. And so the young mind discovered reading and literature before entering school.

"That must be Papa," said Tom, getting up and going to the door.

When Tom pulled the from door open, the splash of rain on the porch roof nearly drowned his father's words: "Let me drip off out here on the gallery for a minute, son."

Tom Perry watched his father's black slicker and hat fairly pour clinging water onto the oak porch slats. "I brung you over some newspapers I'm through with," he said as he unbuttoned his rain garment. "Here, take 'em in while I get this wet thing off."

Tom took the stack of dry newspapers, laid them beside his chair and then carried his father's raincoat to a wall hook near the heater.

"Don't put it too close to the stove, Tom. Might melt the rubber," said Belle. "Come on in, set a spell, Papa Perry," she added.

"Don't mind if I do. See you got a chair from the kitchen waitin' for me."

They made themselves comfortable in a half-circle around the heater.

Clayborne said, "Old Grandma told us you were coming, Grandpa."

"I wasn't sure she'd tell you. When I asked her to this morning, she said to me, 'Carry your own mail, sonny.' She's a right independent lady, you know. Once we got to buildin' on the bridge it plumb slipped my mind. Well, son, how's the plowing comin' along? I kept you from it today all day."

"Just about done, Papa. I took the Sanders disk to the field last week. Got the forty acres of cotton turned under, and the fifteen acres of corn. I should have the fifteen acres for grain turned under next week."

"How's your new mule workin' out?"

"Rhody? Oh, he works with Pet and Jack pretty good. Maybe wants to lead a little too much. I got him in the far gee harness so he don't take his head too strong and I got Pet hitched as near horse. But ridin' that three-wheeled sulky disc I can feel Rhody wantin' to lead."

"Stubborn mules, stubborn creatures. Which calls to mind, did you see that Jim Ferguson got reelected governor?"

Belle chimed in, "We heard about Farmer Jim. He's a good-for-nothing, that man is."

"You know how Belle and I feel about him," said Tom.

Belle volunteered, "We were for Tom Ball and the other prohibition candidates all down the line. I saw your Farmer Jim shy away from prohibition in 1914 and he did it again this year from what the papers say."

"He just didn't think prohibition was the most pressin' issue, that's all, Belle. He figured the plight of the rent farmer was so terrible he had to do something about that first. Did you see the new rent farmer law he got passed?"

Tom replied, "We been away for a year, Papa. But Farmer Jim's law couldn't be any worse than what the socialists wanted in Oklahoma. They were goin' to abolish rent and private property along with it."

Belle asked, "That Farmer Jim didn't abolish rent, did he, Papa Perry?"

"No, daughter, nothin' like that. You know how proper rent goes, one-fourth of cotton and one-third of other crops. And how some farmers been charging their tenants a cash rent on top of the share-crop."

"I remember Farmer Jim makin' a fuss over it when he was running for governor back in 1914," said Tom.

"Well, Ferguson got the legislature to outlaw cash bonuses, or anything over proper rent. It'll help poor rent farmers. Don't you think that's good? I think Farmer Jim is a great man, a great man. But I will tell you a story I heard during the reelection campaign. Want to hear it?"

"Sure, Papa," said Tom.

"Well, seems as if some assistant came rushin' up to Farmer Jim while they was swingin' across the state makin' speeches. 'Governor, Governor,' the fellow says, 'you got to get up to Dallas. They're tellin' lies about you.' Farmer Jim says to him, 'No, young feller, I got to get to Galveston. They're tellin' the truth about me down there.'"

They all laughed.

"But that Farmer Jim did help the rent farmer," repeated Jim Perry.

Belle didn't like the idea of Governor Jim Ferguson doing something good, and only said, "I just wish he'd turn prohibition, Papa Perry, I sure do."

"You'll likely get your prohibition from Congress right soon, if President Wilson don't veto it," Jim Perry said.

Tom said, "I see President Wilson got reelected too. But while I was drivin' down from Bowie, I saw a newspaper in one of the towns that said Hughes and Fairbanks got elected. What was that all about?"

"A downright muddle," chuckled Jim Perry. "Some chump on a big newspaper back east decided to write the story before it was done. All the votes had been counted in the eastern states, but it took three days to get word back that Wilson carried California. That was enough to do it. Not by much. Wilson got less than half the votes, I forget, something over 49 percent. But it was more than poor ole' Charles Evans Hughes got. So we have another four years of Wilson."

"I don't like the sound of that war in Europe," said Tom.

"Me neither," said Jim Perry. "I hope Wilson keeps us out of it."

"Old Grandma told me about the war today," said Clayborne.

His grandfather looked surprised. "Ma's never said a thing about it to me. She doesn't seem too interested in current events."

"She told me about states fighting one another, Texas and Colorado, maybe. Your Papa fought in it and had to get new shoes, Grandpa."

"Oh," smiled Jim Perry. "The War Between the States. Oh, yes, I've heard that story many a time. Ma used to tell that story on Pa back before he died. He never said much about the war himself."

The boy said, "Your Mama told me how the niggers gave you food when the war was over. There's none around here to help us if we have a war."

Tom said, "Your Old Grandma was tellin' you true, son. Why, I recall when I was just your age back in Alabama, six years old, we lived among a lot of old darkies. Papa, you remember, too. When I was too little to get through the brush on the way to the pickin' fields, there was one old nigger named Nassau, he'd give me a ride on his back. He was big and strong and he always looked sad. I'd hug my arms right around his neck and he'd carry me through the tall grass and the rough spots. He didn't have to do it, just wanted to. After all that white folks had done to them, you'd think they'd hate us. Not dear old Nassau, I thought the world and all of him. Maybe it was because we'd never owned slaves and was always poor."

Jim Perry said, "You can't call 'em niggers any more. There's a piece in the *St. Louis Republic* about some outfit says its impolite to call 'em niggers. Wants to be called colored folks."

Belle frowned and said, "Colored folks, well, sir. Ain't we puttin' on airs. Next we'll say we don't want to be called farmers, and have everybody call us like the preacher does, 'tillers of the soil.' I never meant anything impolite by callin' a nigger a nigger."

Tom said, "You never lived with niggers, Belle, bein' brought up here in Texas all your life. Closest niggers lives in Waco. I called 'em niggers in Alabama and they never corrected me. I always thought nigger was the polite word. I've heard 'em called things I couldn't repeat in this house."

Clayborne asked, "Is nigger a bad word, Papa? What does it mean?"

"Just means a black man, far as I know. You ever hear anything contrary, Papa?"

"Nope. But, you know, the way some folks say it, with the hate in their voice, right un-Christian-like, makes it sound like a bad word. I recall old Ollie Dobson in Hico told me about the time the railroad was comin' into this part of the country, oh, 1889 I guess it was. The work gang had twelve niggers in it, workin' side by side with white men. Three riders wearin' masks ran their horses right up to the roadbed and hollered, 'Count these niggers with the white men. There's twelve niggers here. It'll take twelve ropes to take care of 'em.' They like to spit out the word 'nigger' full of hate. And they rode off. The niggers just sort of disappeared after that. They knew they'd get killed if they stayed. Soon after, somebody put up a big sign at the edge of town, said, 'Nigger, don't let the sun set on you here.' Ollie says that sign must of been there 'til, oh, 1905, about the time we come from Alabama. Never saw it, though."

Such warning signs were common in Texas towns during the 1890s and early 1900s, and such conversations over race relations were common during the 'teens. Racial tensions were growing in November, 1916. Patriotic nationalism was already beginning a crescendo that would culminate within months in America's entrance into the Great War in Europe. Rising like a bitter froth on the tide of that nationalism were the specters of national, religious and racial intolerance. The second incarnation of the Ku Klux Klan had already appeared in 1915, inaugurated at the Atlanta, Georgia, premiere of David Wark Griffith's motion picture, *The Birth of a Nation*, which glorified the first Klan. Federal troops had been authorized by Congress to suppress the first Klan in 1871, but it never entirely died out. The sentiment of white supremacy remained rigidly powerful in the South, and Texas was its bulwark.

Although blacks had much worse to worry about, wiping out prejudicial words became a major concern of organizations such as the National Association for the Advancement of Colored People, founded in New York in 1909. Their campaign to eradicate "nigger" from the American vocabulary stumbled for many decades on the rock of Southern rural semi-literacy — as late as 1960, sociologists could find that when rural Texans were asked whether "nigger" was 1) polite, 2) neutral, or 3) derogatory, most respondents felt it to be polite rather than neutral. Their pronunciation of the more acceptable "Negro" tended to come out "Nigrah", which sounded to them like a mere variant of "nigguh", the dominant Texas rendering of "nigger". Hispanos were similarly upset by the Texas rendering of "Mexican" as "Meskin". Most rural Texans simply didn't understand why black people were offended by "nigguh" — although some true bigots who fully understood black revulsion to the word feigned innocence in order to get in another dig.

A perfect April sky hung over the Grand Prairie. Tom rode the seed drill up and down the forty-acre field, getting the cotton in the ground. With Pet, Jack and Rhody in harness, the three-wheeled disk opened furrows while mechanical feeders dropped cottonseed into the soil and a chain loop dragging behind closed the furrows over. Tom surveyed his work as he rode the planter. The cotton rows were even and the spring grass in the middles had been turned under. In the next field his oats were coming along nicely, and beyond that the corn showed a good start. The hog pen wallowed with two good Poland Chinas and the cow suckled her calf unconcerned in the barnyard. The cold wet winter was over and cobalt blue splendor graced the top of the warm days. But America was at war.

"Dinnertime," called Belle.

Clayborne carried the dinner basket while Belle carried Hoyt and the water jug. Tom halted his team and dismounted the planter, asking, "Any word in the mail from Leonard?"

"Yes, there was," said Belle, depositing Hoyt and the water jug beside the dinner basket which Clayborne was unloading. "He's still working in the coal mine at Pueblo. He says Verna writes to him every day about Otis and the new baby."

Tom said, "We have to take a Sunday to go see Verna and the children over at Tolar. I'm glad Leonard sent her back to have Lucille at her folks' place. Those mining camps are no proper place for a family, as bad as the oil camps. But what about the war?"

"They haven't heard anything about the draft in Colorado, either. Oh, Tom, what's going to happen if they call you up?"

"I'll go, Belle. It's the proper American thing. Your Papa and mine can take care of you and the boys if I'm drafted. But it's all still just talk, they haven't started any draft yet."

"Tom, I'm scared. Boys from Hico have already volunteered. People we know. Dale Elkins, John Higgins, Marsh Bennett . . . "

"Why, that Bennett kid's not old enough."

"He fibbed about his age." Belle would not use the words, "He lied about his age," out of old Texas custom: to say that anyone had lied was a mortal offense and the word 'liar' carried as stinging an emotional burden as any curse word. No one in polite society would dare say that another had lied.

"I heard it on the telephone, Tom. A lot of boys are doing it. His mother's just sick. She'd a' told the draft board, but she was worried it would be unpatriotic. He's gone already. It's not even two weeks and he's already gone!"

"So soon. It was just the sixth they declared war, this is only the, what, the seventeenth, isn't it?"

"Seventeenth of April."

Germany had announced in January, 1917, that unrestricted submarine warfare would be conducted against all ships destined for European Allied ports and by the end of March had made good on its threat. United States ships were sunk and hundreds of American lives lost. Woodrow Wilson, who had unsuccessfully urged both sides in the conflict to accept peace "without victory," knew that his 1916 campaign slogan "He kept us out of war" was now ironically hollow. The isolationism of the quiet past was about to crumble in the catastrophe of the stormy present.

When the President and the American people realized that the point of no return had been reached, their manner of entry into the war revealed a profound lack of international experience. America had not fought a major war in fifty years. The Army could boast all of 208,034 men. The air service counted 130 pilots and 55 rickety airplanes held together with adhesive tape and baling wire. Wilson's war message did not refer to practical necessity or implacable determination to forward America's strategic interests. Instead, the nation was to launch an idealistic crusade "for the right of those who submit to authority to have a voice in their own Governments, for the rights and liberties of small nations, for a universal dominion of right." Wilson assured the world that "We have no selfish ends to serve. We desire no conquest, no dominion. We seek no indemnities . . . no material compensation." The goal, said the president, was simple: "The world must be made safe for Democracy." Ardent citizens across the land took these selfless goals to heart. Naive America thus set itself up for crushing postwar disillusionment, but as philosophers have said, wisdom comes by disillusionment. Philosophers remain silent on how long wisdom stays.

And on this glorious April day as Belle Perry worried about the draft, across the world in Petrograd an intellect cold and vast and by no means naive took advantage of the European war, and set a task that in October would shake Russia and ever after shake the world. Vladimir Ilyich Ulyanov, a small, intense man with a faint oriental cast, now refreshed after his long journey from Switzerland in a sealed railway car with thirty-one other political emigrants, recommended that the provisional Russian government be abolished. In its place would stand "not a parliamentary republic . . . a bourgeois republic cannot solve the problem of the war, because it can be solved only on an international scale." His international goals had been made abundantly clear the year before: "Only after we have overthrown, finally vanquished and expropriated the capitalists of the whole world, and not merely of one country, will wars become impossible." For Russia now, "No government except the Soviet of Workers and Agricultural Laborers' Deputies." He also recommended that his party change its name from Social-Democratic to something the people would understand: the Communist Party. He signed his recommendations with the alias by which the world would soon come to know him: Lenin.

While Lenin wrote his "April Theses" in Petrograd, Tom and Belle Perry and their two children ate a simple farm dinner on the Texas grass beside their cotton field.

"Clayborne, you be sure to put the calf in the pen outside the barn tonight," Tom instructed his boy. "You forgot last night and the calf got the milk from the cow's other teats." It was common farm practice to take milk for human use from three of a cow's teats, leaving one for the calf.

"Sorry, Papa. But I did put the corn and oats and the cottonseed in the cribs. And I took down some hay from the loft over the stock door like you said."

"You're a good hand, son. Don't get me wrong. Just don't forget to put the calf out."

"Papa, I hope you don't have to go to the war."

"Hush up, young 'un," said Old Grandma Perry as she skirted a line of river rocks beneath the stream bank. "If you're goin' fishin' with me, you got to keep your mouth shut. You'll scare the fish away. No talkin'."

"Yes, Old Grandma," said Clayborne, looking miserable, but following her away stone by stone to the next fishing hole.

The June sun glistened and sheened on ripening dewberries along the limestone and clay banks of Camp Branch. The boy was beginning to recognize the flowers and the trees of the Grand Prairie, to be at home with them and to expect their flowering and fading in the course of time. He consoled himself in his enforced silence by seeing how many trees he could name. Overhead, dappling the sky with luminous foliage, he knew the old cottonwoods that fanned the air while trying to keep their feet wet in the creek. He looked into the glassy rippling current but reflected suns tickled his eyes, making him squint. He looked up and could identify the pecan tree by its oblong seed pods, now beginning to swell within their fleshy green coat that would one day turn brown and split open to reveal the prized thin-shelled savory nut.

Clayborne's foot slipped on a slick rock, and he nearly dropped the fishing pole and can of worms he carried. Old Grandma glanced back over her shoulder but did not stop her steady tromp forward. The boy quickly regained his stride and resumed his botany study. Over there, by the shadowy limestone outcrops where it was easier to look, a black walnut tree was just beginning to form its edible seeds. The mysterious rhythm of the seasons was slowing becoming intelligible to the boy.

As Clayborne ambled along behind Old Grandma, he heard a sharp "Ptui!" and saw a streak of brown juice the old lady had aimed at a scaled lizard basking on a stream cobble. "Almost got ye," snickered the old-time snuff-dipper as the lizard vanished into a crevice.

Two dozen steps later Old Grandma stopped and said, "I guess ye can talk here, long as ye don't holler. Just around this bend there's my favorite perch hole. Once we get there you'll have to hush up, but right now I'm goin' to have myself a drink of creek water. It's good runnin' water here between fishin' holes. And I'm a' goin' to cut myself a new fishing pole."

Elizabeth Glasgow Perry took from her skirt pocket a folded piece of paper and reworked it with gnarled hands into a paper cup. "You want some creek water, young 'un?" she asked.

The boy winced, but he was thirsty. "It's not good like the well water, Old Grandma."

"Oh, don't be so persnickety, boy. It's just water. Nice and clear here where it's runnin' fast. Not like still water. Won't hurt ye none. Here, dip some up for yourself with the cup." He obeyed, closely eyeing the swirling debris that spun in the little paper cup. There were no identifiable living creatures in it so he glugged the drink down, shivering involuntarily as it slid down his throat. Then he dutifully scooped another cupful for Old Grandma. She swigged it down with gusto, smacking her thin lips and winking at the boy. "Afraid you might get a little meat with your water, boy?" she asked, guffawing at her own joke. "Nothin' to fear, nothin' to fear. I been drinkin' creek water all my life and I'm gonna live to be a hundred." As it turned out, she was not far wrong.

Now she got to making a new fishing pole. She tested several lithe willow stems and rejected them. "Too consarned limber. You don't have proper cane brakes in Texas. Oh, what I'd give for a good cane fishing pole." She spied a ten-foot tree that stood straight with a thin central stem and spidery branches covered with smooth silver-green leaves. "Young 'un, what sort of tree is that there?"

"That's a cottonwood shoot, Old Grandma. Papa uses 'em for fishing poles. You want me to cut it off?"

"Here's my pocket knife. Go cut it off."

Old Grandma Perry always carried a man-sized pocket knife with three blades. She cherished it and would sharpen it with nothing but a special whetstone brought from Alabama. It was a rare trust to place her precious pocket knife in the hands of another, and Clayborne understood. He clambered halfway up the bank to the cottonwood shoot and opened the knife's big blade. With swift downstrokes he girdled the little tree, then whittled it to a point and broke it off without effort. The cottonwood was more than twice the boy's height but not heavy. Clayborne closed the knife blade, carefully letting Old Grandma see that he had shut it, then carried both knife and tree to her.

"You're right good at that, young 'un."

She took the knife, opened it and began trimming the light branches. "Take these branches and go scatter 'em around on top of the bank, boy. They say the Creek Indians back in Alabama used to leave no sign of where they'd been so nobody could track 'em. You do the same."

The youngster thought she was merely trying to get rid of him so he couldn't see how she tied the tightline to her new fishing pole — he'd never actually seen her do it. He trailed a leafy branch at a time in a random walk and wondered what difference it would make if she left the cut branches in the creek bed? There were no Indians around here to track or be tracked. And who would want to track an old woman and a six-and-a-half-year-old boy anyway? Besides, the high water next winter would clean out Camp Branch, scour it good. When Clayborne returned to the creekbed, Old Grandma was biting the heavy lead weight into place on the line just above her fishhook.

Old Grandma said to the boy, "Bitin' that sinker reminds me. I'm about to get hungry, boy. You know what I ain't seen since I come to Texas? A plum! Is there any plum trees in Texas? I'd properly favor a good plum right now."

"There's plum thickets up toward Chalk Mountain, Old Grandma.

But they're just ol' hog plums, no good to eat. They're just good to cook and make jelly."

"Well, that's too bad."

"Grandpa Blackburn has an orchard. He's got peaches, but I don't remember any plums."

"I'll just have to get me a store-bought'n plum, I reckon. But tonight we're gonna have fish gravy for sure."

Half a dozen of the perch they stalked would provide hardly enough flesh to make a meal for one, but fried in a skillet until it became brown "fish meal" and then added to white gravy, a day's catch would become "fish gravy," a savory treat served over the ubiquitous country biscuit.

"Fish gravy stinks up the house, Old Grandma."

"Do ye like to eat it?"

"Yeah."

"Come on, then, let's get to fishin'."

They rounded the bend in Camp Branch where a wide, still pool lay fortified within the stone banks, fringed by oaks and pecans and cottonwoods. The old lady recalled her discovery of this markless place one autumn day as the year died and the short grass yellowed. She had not expected its round perfection and stood alone and very still to simply admire her find. It was several minutes before she saw the fish. Resting near the surface, tail weaving slow patterns in the sky-streaked water, gills filtering old oxygen, wallowed the father of all perches, bigger than any she had ever seen. It had not seen her. In stealth she could have killed it with a rock. She bent gradually on her ancient haunches into a squat, looking in wonder a long time upon the lunker, the angler's dream. Then she stood straight up and walked to the brink of the pool, casting her shadow in the water. She watched in satisfaction as the great fish slowly descended, not hurried, sliding backward into deep murky invisibility, into the abyss of time.

"Nobody is going to kill you, you Grandpap fish," she said. "I'm the only one knows you're here. Nobody but me is old enough or smart enough to catch you. When I come fishing, I'll give you a sign. You'll know it's me. You stay away from my hook. You live, you hear? You live."

Old Grandma stood today with Clayborne, remembering. She walked around the pool, picked her fishing site, laid a finger across her lips to command absolute silence, and baited her hook from the worm can. When the wriggling bait was suitably impaled, Old Grandma spit on the worm and cast her line into the pool. Clayborne had always intended to ask her why she did that, but Old Grandma demanded silence at the fishing hole, and by the time they were on their way home he had forgotten all about it. He never knew it was her sign. That June day in 1917 they went home before noon, Old Grandma carrying four small forgotten all about it. He never knew it was her sign. That June day in 1917 they went home before noon, Old Grandma carrying four small perch on her line, and Clayborne carrying one. That night, they had fish gravy, just like Old Grandma said.

"Let's get a move on, Tom," shouted Jim Perry from outside the barn. "I want to get to revival meeting before sundown."

"I'll have the sorghum cane all set for the cows in here right quick, Papa," he replied, laying heavy armfuls in the feed crib. "Belle's got Hoyt and Clayborne all ready to go. They just have to get into the buggy. We can leave as soon as I wash up. Is Old Grandma going?"

"Wouldn't miss it. Brother Green's going to give us religion tonight sure, she says."

"Are you taking your new Model T Ford, Papa?"

"Nope. Don't want to spend the money on gasoline. We'll be goin' to revival meeting every day for two weeks. Can't afford the gasoline, not after spendin' $295 on the ol' Tin Lizzie. And $2.50 for the license plate!"

Tom dropped the last of the canes into the crib and asked, "Think what Papa Blackburn paid for that Grand Overland he just bought. I know he traded eight mules, but he ain't sayin' how much cash went into the deal. I think the whole thing come to around eleven hundred dollars. And I don't see him drivin' it a whole lot. Leona says the battery keeps goin' dead. Just a big white elephant."

"That's a powerful lot of money for a white elephant."

The orange cat caught a mouse in the shadows at the far end of the barn.

"I've been meaning to ask, Papa, when is Brother Green coming to dinner with us?"

"We've got him for dinner at my place Tuesday, and you have him Wednesday. He'll stay at our place Tuesday night and go home with the Strepys Wednesday night."

"I wish we had the room to put him up during revival," said Tom as he stepped out of the barn and latched the stock door.

Jim Perry stood outside waiting for him, dressed in a freshly washed and ironed shirt and clean work pants. "Don't you bother yourself about it, son," he said. "The Lord understands. Besides, it looks like in a year or so you'll be able to get a bigger rent house and after that get your own place. By Gaddies, the war's going to bring good cotton prices this year. Not that we want to be war profiteers, God forbid. But you're a good farmer. You don't let any grass grow under your feet. You're on your way up, son." A mockingbird on the barn roof told its melodious lay.

"I'm learning to be patient, Papa. Can't really plan anything with the war on. Since I went down to the school house and registered for the draft, I've just been waiting for my call-up, just going day by day."

"That's been over a month — June fifth, wasn't it? — and they haven't called you yet. Besides, with that blind eye they're not likely to take you, son."

"I can see just fine, Papa. I'm no shirker."

"Course not, boy. Didn't mean to say it. I'm no shirker, either, but I know they won't take an ol' stove-up farmer like me. They need young men, son. They're just not likely to take you, that's all."

Clayborne ran up with Pup at his heels. "Papa, Grandpa! Are we about ready to go to revival meeting?"

Grandpa Perry grinned and said, "You're mighty anxious to get a dose of hellfire and brimstone, young man."

"What's brimstone, Grandpa?"

"Why, brimstone's sulphur, child, comin' from the sulphurous pit where sinners go. Brother Green is sure to tell you all about it this next week of revival."

"Can we go soon? I want to see revival meeting."

Tom said, "You've seen lots of them, son. We've taken you every year, well, except last year when we were in Trinchera."

"There's revival every year? I don't remember."

"Sure is, son. Every July after the crops are laid by. We all get together from the farms and go to Prairie Springs Church."

"It's hot in there in summer, Papa."

Grandpa Perry interjected, "Look at you. You got knee pants to wear, boy. Wait 'til you grow up and see how hot long pants are!"

Tom said, "We'll be out in the brush arbor, son. It'll be cool out there once the sun goes down."

Grandpa Perry said, "Young man, I understand you got a ride in your Grandpa Blackburn's new Overland the other day. How'd you like it?"

"Wow, it was swell, Grandpa! It's the first time I ever rode in a car! We went . . ."

"You went forty-five miles an hour, boy."

"I wasn't supposed to tell. Dad, did you or Mama tell Grandpa?"

Grandpa Perry said, "I have my ways of finding things out."

"Well," confided the boy, "Auntie Leona was driving Mama and Papa and me to Duffau, and she wanted to show us how fast the car would go. So on the way back she speeded up to forty-five miles an hour! We must have gone half a mile that fast before she slowed dow again!"

"That's a seventeen-year-old for you," said Grandpa Jim. "What's this world comin' to, speed crazy, that's all. You'd think she'd know better. When I give you a ride in my new Model T Ford, we aren't going any forty-five miles an hour, you can bet your boots. But was it fun?"

"Oh, boy, Grandpa, it sure was!"

Belle walked up in a pretty pink calico dress, a supper basket in one arm and Hoyt in the other. "Go wash up, Tom. Chores are all done and we're ready to get to revival meeting."

The dusty road was alive with wagons and buggies, streaming in from the farms after chores, as if some invisible organizing hand had started them in a prearranged sequence. At every crossroads new buggies joined the procession, and drivers tipped their hats to the ladies passing ahead. Some men wore their bib overalls and some wore their Sunday-go-to-meeting best. Some women came in calico, the better-off in taffeta. The pilgrims each looked forward to the evening's events with a spirit only to be found during the annual two weeks of revival time. It was a feeling that began with washing up and getting dressed, a feeling almost like Sunday, although it was really the middle of the week. It was a feeling of childlike expectancy but not frivolity. It was a feeling of reverence, but not solemnity. It was a country feeling, full of animal smells and hard work and toughness, the toughness you feel when you're ready to do battle with the devil. City folks would never understand. If you looked, you could see the feeling on their country faces as they made their rumbling way through the gritty dry air over the dirt roads.

The midsummer sun was still high off the far horizon when the two buggies of the families Perry turned into the wagon lot of Prairie Springs Baptist Church. A great gathering of wagons and buggies from six and eight miles around overflowed the lot and sprawled over the grounds all around the whitewashed church. The Perrys had to find a hitching place down the bank almost to Little Duffau Creek, several hundred feet from the night's revival meeting.

Already more than a hundred farm folk from all around had assembled, the women congregating around outdoor tables where a pot-luck supper began to appear, the men carrying in early watermelons which they dunked in a big zinc washtub full of cool water. Tall glasses of iced tea marched in phalanx down half a table. Dozens of fresh biscuits peeped out from under red-and-white checkered cloths covering brimming white porcelain bowls. The rows of tables were jammed with convivial farm families and buzzed with country conversation.

"You sit here, Old Grandma," said Tom to Elizabeth Perry. "Next to Clayborne. He so loves your company."

"He's goin' to get religion tonight, aren't you, boy?" she grinned.

"Yes, Ma'am, Old Grandma," agreed Clayborne, not quite sure what getting religion meant.

Lou Perry said, "Tommy, you come sit by me. I haven't had hardly a minute with you since you started planting cotton. Come sit by your Ma."

"Yes, Mama. Belle, sit here with Hoyt."

Jim Perry spoke to his son from across the crowded supper table, "Tom, did you hear on the telephone that Governor Ferguson vetoed the money to run the university?"

Belle answered first, "I told you he was a good-for-nothing. Now, why would he do a thing like that, keep money from the University of Texas? Why, the very idea!"

"Don't know, daughter," said Jim Perry. "Didn't see the paper, just heard it while I was talking to Everett Tate on the phone. I reckon ol' Farmer Jim's mad that the board didn't ask his approval before they appointed that new Vernon fellow president of the university."

Tom said, "You always said Ferguson was in favor of education, Papa."

"Well, he is, son," said Jim Perry. "He just got the legislature to pass a rural education bill. Gives country kids school for nine months instead of five, just like city kids, and gives them the money, state money, to do it. Now, that's good for schools."

"Your Farmer Jim's a hard one to figure, Papa. Gives more money to country schools and takes all the money away from the university. It just don't make sense. I'll believe that nine months of school for farm kids when I see it. And the money, too. I've a good mind to run for school board myself. I don't trust these politicians."

"Oh, Tommy," said his mother. "You do that. You run for school board. I'll vote for you. All your friends will. I'll be so proud of you."

The evening had its own rhythm. When supper was finished and the last stragglers had hitched up their teams and come to revival, the red sun had touched the hills of the Western Cross Timbers. Without a word, men who knew it was their task began the rounds of lighting oil lamps in the brush arbor, talking quietly among themselves in the purple evening. The arbor lay nearly a hundred feet behind the little church, an open air chapel constructed among the oaks and cottonwoods. Just above the banks of Little Duffau Creek, men had strung three strands of sturdy fence wire, low, middle and high, around nine sturdy trees to form a three-sided thirty- by forty-foot open room with only branches and sky for a roof. Willow brush had been cut and hung over the wires to form a wall against the chill night breeze. Rough benches had been set in rows to accommodate the one hundred fifty or so worshippers expected. The pulpit had been brought from the church and stood in proper aspect to the congregation, with the few customary benches behind it for the "amen corner." Now it was ready. It was a temple in the woods, a church out where God lives, silently preaching its own sermon to the farmers' hearts.

Six oil lamps had been hung from the big spreading liveoak branches overhead, lamps of the type that glowed from a rosette burner of perforated metal beneath their tanks of coal oil. The men lighted them and the emerald gloom was dispelled with lambent golden flame. The women busied themselves spreading pallets and quilts at the edge of the brush arbor, baby-nests for their children. The congregation now gathered to their places, quiet, happy, expectant. Some carried lanterns that sputtered softly among the murmurs of the people.

The brush arbor was now filled to capacity. It had an ancient feel to it, an archetypal band responding to a primal worship urge as old as humanity, glowing with the inner light of coal oil lanterns and believing souls. Tom and his family found a place next to the arbor wall near the back. Belle laid a quilt on the ground for Hoyt, half in and half out of the arbor, sheltered over by willow boughs. Brother Will Green ascended the step of the pulpit and greeted his flock.

The service began with three or four rousing hymns, as usual, and continued with the first rousing sermon, as usual. It was an exhortation to patriotism, echoing war posters that had sprouted in Hico and everywhere else in America. "Feed a fighter, Brothers and Sisters, eat only what you need. Waste nothing, that our valiant fighting men and their families may have enough. Take heed of what our great leaders, what President Wilson and his cabinet have asked, tighten your belts, ration your food. Let us have wheatless Mondays and Wednesdays, meatless Tuesdays and porkless Thursdays, as our Food Administrator Brother Herbert Hoover has asked. And save the grain that goes into ardent spirits, cease the manufacture of intoxicating liquor and bring sobriety and prohibition to our fair land during this time of trial." The Amens and Hallelujahs were deafening. Brother Green knew full well that his congregation had nothing to waste, and were already teetotalers for the most part, but in this era it would have been folly to begin revival on any other note.

More hymns followed, and the second sermon came. It was a preachment against the racy fashions of the day — skirts were shorter, but high-buttoned shoes covered every well-turned ankle. Although transparent skirts had appeared in the big city, they revealed only a heavily patterned and quite opaque lining — not that a single farm woman present could have afforded such finery. But Brother Green admonished in his most exalted revival style, "Never in history were the modes so abhorrently indecent as they are today. They are revealing the flower of womanhood to wanton eyes. They are bringing us to a state of decadence that shows all around us, in drunken revelry, in divorce, in breaking up of the home, conditions found chiefly in primitive society.

"And need I remind the congregation that another threat to the family is being bandied about? Of course, I mean women's suffrage. The suffrage movement cannot help but distract the mother's attention away from her husband and children, cannot help but lead her to a world of political turmoil and confusion, cannot help but lead her into the workplace and diminish her femininity. As our church matrons have confided to me, in their own words, I am suffering enough now and am really too busy to bother with the suffrage movement at all. And as far as women's rights, remember that even May Irwin, a veritable star of the scandalous stage, has said, "I wish all women felt as I do; I have more rights now than I can properly attend to." Brothers and Sisters, we must resist these temptations and find refuge in the Word of the Lord."

Through the evening it went, hymn singing and preaching, at an increasing pitch of devotion. The faithful were reminded that erring mortals had once been punished by Noah's flood and that next time God had plans to finish the job with fire. Clayborne listened intently, trying to visualize the fiery pit. It had a festival air to it the way he imagined it, and he knew he was getting it wrong somehow. But he had promised God to be good in the future, and he had worn himself out with singing. He left such apocalyptic matters in the hands of the Creator and nodded off.

Then came the call for testimony. Many volunteered and gave inspired accounts of sin vanquished and temptation overcome. Brother Green, his revival spirit burning bright, then called specifically on Tom Perry to testify. Tom had been returned to Texas for nine months now, and had solidly reaffirmed his place in the community, regained the good will and high regard of his neighbors. His testimony had never before been heard. It would be respected and influential. But most in the arbor knew of his strict personal faith that forbade him to pray in public. The sudden tension was electric. Tom was on the spot and Brother Will Green realized it as soon as he had asked Tom to testify. Tom did not rise or move from his seat for a long moment. Then he slowly and deliberately stood and straightened himself as tall as his modest stature would allow. He pointed his right finger aloft to the trees and the stars, he gazed up, then with his one good eye looked Brother Green straight in the face, finger still pointing above, and said:

"I'm a' goin' to heaven."

And he sat down without another sound. The congregation was dumbstruck at the simplicity and faith of Tom's few words, stunned speechless until Old Grandma, proudly ensconced as a matriarch in the amen corner behind Brother Green shouted, "Hallelujah, Brother Tom! I'm a' going to heaven, sure enough! Amen!" It was contagious. The cry went up. "I'm a' goin' to heaven." "I'm a' goin' to heaven!" They had got religion. They were a' goin' to heaven, every one. Brother Green's call for a hymn could hardly be heard above the tumult. "Onward, Christian Soldiers" sounded out but the heavenward cry continued.

Tom had not realized how his neighbors and friends cared for him, how they sympathized with his hardship in Colorado, how they respected his stubborn integrity, how they considered themselves his larger family. Now he saw the scene anew, as if he were out of himself, above this little brush arbor that shone like a beacon in God's great night. His spirit was surrounded by the benevolent trees, the many farms spread all across the Grand Prairie, vastly embraced by the vaulted stars and the warm vestiges of amethyst Texas sunset and the searing beauty of . . . home. Home! Could it be? No, not after all his struggle and striving far away. Was that the emotion overwhelming him now? Home? Oh, home, this soul-shattering peace in time of war, these friends and loved ones passing with him through time! How could it be? Home, not so much a place as a state of mind. It was so strong. It must be home. How it filled his chest too much, this radiant sense of home, how it deeply hurt him, this too big sense of love. Home! His family looked at him with glowing smiles. Home! His neighbors, faces lined with dignity and admiration, nodded their approval. Home! The music of religion filled the night, the souls. Yes, he finally realized, this is it, this is what he had sought in Colorado. He surrendered himself utterly to the event. In failure he had found success that few achieve. He was home!

Revival was over and the cookstove glowed with the heat of canning time. From May to August in the Grand Prairie the scorching summer sun outside could not compete with the inferno of canning inside. The little shed kitchen of the new rent house made the air around it shimmer even on the hottest days as summer marched in and one vegetable after another came ripe.

"Clayborne," called Belle, "run get me some more water will you please?"

"Yes, Ma'am," came the obedient reply.

With Pup tagging along, the boy popped out of the sweltering house, bucket in hand, and made for the well behind the house. The new rent house had the same kind of metal-cased well and bullet-shaped water vessel as the weaning house. Clayborne untied the well rope he had already fastened and unfastened dozens of times this morning and heaved his body against the burden — his arms alone had not yet grown the strength necessary to haul some thirty-two pounds of water up twenty-seven feet of well shaft, even with the mechanical advantage of a head pulley six feet above ground. The brass water vessel emerged slowly from its casing and Clayborne walked to it, hand over hand on the rope, holding his prize of water still as it dangled from the pulley. He secured the rope around a wooden well head post, placed his bucket beneath the vessel and tripped its release valve. Four gallons of water fell out the water-bullet's bottom and into the waiting zinc bucket. The boy closed the valve and once again lowered the empty bullet back into its casing and down to the water table, hitching the rope not for the last time today.

He hauled the water bucket first in one hand and then the other. Within a few years he would be able to manage two buckets at once and have an easier time balancing his load, but now he lurched and swayed with his single bucket as he traded hands.

"Git out of the way, Kitty," Clayborne muttered as he walked up the steps into the steaming kitchen.

"How many more you need, Mama?" asked the boy as he handed her his burden.

"Two more will do it for now," she replied, dashing the water into a large black pot atop the cookstove. "But don't you go away. I'll need you to pack more water so's I can boil more tomatoes before long, and I'll need more firewood, too." She watched over the tomatoes in the cookpot, a long wooden spoon at the ready."

"Your face is all red, Mama," the boy said.

"I think I got a fever on top of all this heat, son. I've been feelin' right puny the last few days."

Sick or not, she would trudge on today and tomorrow and next week and next month. Canning was not optional for the Texas farm wife. As it had been with the peaches and plums last week and the cucumbers from the kitchen garden the week before, and the green beans and English peas before that and the blackberries before that, so it was now with the tomatoes: can now or starve next winter and spring. And before summer was over there would be apricots and beets and black-eyed peas and Crowder peas. No Grand Prairie farmer except perhaps for Fouts over by Rocky was rich enough to buy more than a little of his food at the grocer's. In the wet and frigid months ahead they would live on fruits and vegetables preserved in Mason jars sealed during the ranting heat of summer. And the food set the pace — you canned when it was ripe, not before, not after, certainly not after, for to can rotten vegetables was to ask for ptomaine. To can carelessly anytime was to invite deadly salmonella or the unspeakable horror of botulism. Nobody canned carelessly: illness from poor canning practices was virtually unknown here, and none of the Perrys ever suffered its effects.

When Clayborne had just stepped out to get his next bucket of water, Belle staggered backward from the scalding stove, overpowered by a wave of nausea. She could stand it no more. She lurched to the wide-open kitchen door and leaned on the jamb for support, leaving the boiling pots and incandescent wood burner glowing behing her — and Hoyt asleep in the sweltering front room. She gasped and felt faint, perspiration beading on her flushed face. She hung there a long moment, looking down at the cat serenely grooming himself by the steps and Pup sleeping in a cool dirt wallow in the shade of the house.

Clayborne walked up to the back door and saw his mother. "Are you all right, Mama?" he asked in alarm.

"It's nothing, son. Just the heat," she choked. "I'll be fine in just a minute. I'm feeling better already." She stood straighter, the nausea subsiding.

"You shouldn't work so hard, Mama," the boy advised sagely.

Belle smiled in irony. "You're right son," she said. "I'll take me a good rest come January."

Buster Brown and his dog Tige came to Hico in late October of 1917, just after cotton-ginning tapered off. The Brown Shoe Company of St. Louis, makers of Buster Brown brand shoes, sponsored a series of midgets, each dressed as Buster and accompanied by a trained dog to put on promotional touring shows throughout America. The rural shows were timed for the weeks just before schools started in November, after the farmers had gathered their cotton and had a little money. This year the seven-year-old Clayborne was to get some real Buster Brown shoes — and a whopping sidewalk show.

The Buster Brown character had originated in 1902 with R. F. Outcault's New York Herald newspaper comic strip featuring a bright-eyed rascal in a blonde pageboy haircut and Little Lord Fauntleroy suit. Outcault had studied art in Paris under the sponsorship of the Wizard of Menlo Park himself, Thomas A. Edison. His new Buster Brown character lived with Ma and Pa, sister Mary Jane and his constant companion was an outsize bulldog named Tige who inserted asides as acerbic as a Greek chorus. The strip idealized pure mischief thinly veiled by a frame at the end of each episode sermonizing over what every young boy in America easily recognized as their own love of sheer deviltry.

In one Sunday comic strip, Buster falls for the tale of woe of Willie, a street bum. Buster takes him home, cleans him up in the family bathroom, provides a shave and a haircut, and even his father's clothes, including a fine diamond stickpin. When Willie the bum stands thus bedecked, Buster admires his handiwork, saying, "You're the *candy*, Willie." The dog Tige all the while laments "Let me see, how can I get him out of this. I'll go mad," and "I believe in astrology now. By what law of nature is this coming to that bum?" However, when Mother comes up and hugs the tramp from behind, Buster yells, "Let go, Ma, that isn't Pa!" Pa, however, walks in at this inopportune moment, sees the scene, and asks the bum, "Who are you?" As Willie replies "Search me," Ma faints in horror.

Thousands of boys yclept Buster, along with their dogs dubbed Tige, lay on the parlor floor and turned chuckling to the next strip without so much as glancing at the last frame, which delivered this homiletic harangue:

Resolved: That a tramp is not a victim of hard luck nor ill fortune. He is just the effect of a *cause*. Selfishness, and ignorance, and laziness are the *cause*. Filth, disease and poverty, the *result*. A bad effect never came from a good cause. If you *do* right, you'll *be* right. If you do wrong, you'll get the worst of it. No man ever got wheat who planted weeds. Laziness is a *mental* disease. All action must first be a thought. If you are 2 lazy to think, you can't *act*. If you don't exercise your brain, it will grow useless. Don't let the doctor, the orator, the lawyer, the newspaper do your thinking for you. You smile at the child who believes in Santa Claus, while you believe *worse* piffle. God gave you your brains to think with.

Cashing in on the phenomenal success of the comic strip, the enterprising Brown Shoe Company bought the rights to the Buster Brown name in 1904. The firm had been founded in 1878 by a young man named George Warren Brown who believed St. Louis could become a manufacturing center for the shoe industry. His company gave America a superior pair of shoes and a whiz-bang free show on those October Saturdays like the one that found Clayborne Perry in front of Connally's Dry Goods, the local dealer in Buster Brown shoes, with his mother and father and Hoyt, along with perhaps two hundred locals who had stopped to watch the antics of a personified Buster Brown and his dog Tige.

The midget, togged out in a Little Lord Fauntleroy outfit, complete with comic strip hat, gave his show in the dirt street, allowing the audience to spread out and turn the wooden sidewalk into a amphitheatre. Traffic was no problem, since the wagon drivers who happened by fully understood what was going on and poked along slowly to catch some of the show. The Tige of the moment was a little brown Boston terrier — not a large bulldog as in the comic strip — that jumped a rope, rolled over, fetched a stick, and danced on his hind legs, all at the command of the day's Buster Brown. Each new dog trick brought peals of applause from the adults and squeals of delight from the kids.

When the dog tricks were through, Buster passed out little gifts for the youngsters, today a metal "cricket," two pieces of thin sheet metal, the hollow painted top resembling a bug and the bottom strip a noisemaker that produced a sharp click! when pressed. With this largesse distributed, Buster regaled his audience with hoary humor that probably originated in the hinterlands of the Roman Empire, the product of some distant unnamed jokesmith properly relegated to oblivion. But the people ate it up.

"Did you hear the one about the farmer who complains to his neighbor, 'Your cow just got into my garden and ate up all my vegetables.' T'other farmer says, 'All right, I'll send you over a quart of milk.'"

Roars of laughter.

"The farmer says to the tourist, 'This here's a dogwood tree.' The tourist asks the farmer, 'How can you tell?' The farmer says to the tourist, 'By its bark.' "

Snorts and cackles.

"'Your house is on fire,' says Rube to Lem. 'Ah knows it,' says Lem to Rube. 'Then why ain't you doing nothin' about it?' says Rube to Lem. 'Ah am," says Lem to Rube, 'Ever since th' fire started I been prayin' fer rain.'"

Shrieks and giggles.

"This farmer whose pig just got killed by a Model T is hoppin' mad. 'Don't worry,' said the driver, tryin' to calm down the farmer. 'I'll replace your pig.' The farmer says, 'You can't replace my pig, mister.' 'Why not?' asks the driver. The farmer says, 'You ain't fat enough.'"

Cheers and huzzahs.

And so it went for half a hour. When the show was over, the crowd broke up, but dozens crammed into the dry goods store to buy shoes. Clayborne came out proud as punch in a brand new pair of $3.98 Buster Brown shoes.

"Son," said Tom as the family walked to the buggy, "today we're going to buy something else for you. Can you guess what it is?"

The boy's eyes lighted up. "Is is something I can use when I go to school?"

"I can see you've guessed it," grinned Tom.

"It's a donkey like we talked about!"

"Right you are, son. Let's all get in the buggy and we'll go get him."

Their route took them by the Lynch Cafe, where Wiley Lynch stood on the board sidewalk with a deliveryman, accepting a shipment of meat from a heavy duty wagon. "Hey, bo!" called Wiley to Tom. "How you all doin'?"

"We're all fine, Linchie," said Tom, slowing Pet's gait to a walk. "Just goin' to get Clayborne a donkey to ride to school."

"Speakin' of donkeys, did you see where Governor Ferguson got impeached? They done kicked him out and passed a law sayin' he could never hold office again! Will Hobby's governor now!"

Belle called across the street, "I told everybody he was a good-for-nothing!"

"I saw that, Linchie," said Tom. "Caught him with a hundred fifty-six thousand dollars in campaign money they can't find out where it came from! Caught him good!"

"You all come see us soon, you hear?"

"Next week, Linchie. Say hello to Sallie for us."

The donkey was for sale by a private individual at the eastern edge of Hico, a Charles Walker whose brother attended Prairie Springs Baptist Church, where Tom had heard of the animal's availability. The home was on the run-down side, unlike most Hico residences. Tom halted Pet in the street and went alone to make the transaction, leaving Belle and the boys to wait in the buggy.

"Mister Perry?" said Charles Walker as he walked out of his back door. His bib overalls were patched and a little shabby. Tom felt wary of the man.

"Yes, sir, Mister Walker. Your brother Bill said you had a donkey you'd let go for three dollars."

"Yes, siree, by God, got me a donkey for sale. Bill says you want him for your boy to ride to school. He's a gentle critter, he is. Real gentle. Won't hurt your boy none. Come on back and take a look."

Tom examined the donkey and quickly completed the transaction. As they led the donkey to the street from the large unkempt field where the beast had been pastured, Walker plied Tom with distinctly unpleasant conversation. "I was just readin' in the paper about them goddam niggers in Houston that killed all them people this August. They gonna hang thirteen of 'em, give forty-one life in prison. They oughta kill the whole bunch of 'em."

"Those were soldiers in the U.S. Army, Mr. Walker," asserted Tom. "The Houston police roughed up some nigger soldiers and their unit fought back. It was a terrible thing happened, but they was provoked right badly. And I'll thank you not to take the Lord's name in vain."

Walker stopped in his tracks seething with anger and Tom went on his way with no further leave taking. Tom disliked the man intensely and he could not comprehend the racial violence Walker seemed to relish. He had no quarrel with the 1909 Texas law that had mandated racial segregation in most public facilities — "separate but equal" — and had devoted little thought to the issue. He had read that no Red Cross services were available for black soldiers in many Texas military installations. He had read that some twenty-five percent of the troops called up from Texas — 31,000 men — were black although they formed only sixteen percent of the population. He had read that black troops at Camp Bowie had been stationed in separate quarters surrounded by a high barbed-wire fence. He regarded these events with a certain resignation. But the violence of whites against blacks and blacks against whites appeared to him most unchristian. It was a disturbing undertone of the war years he could never fathom.

His upset was quelled when he saw Clayborne's face glowing with the thrill of a new donkey. They tied the animal to the buggy and drove home.

"Come on down from the buggy, Clayborne," said Tom. "You don't want to be late for your first day of school. Belle, make sure he brings his dinner bucket."

The boy looked at the little one-room schoolhouse — really looked at it — for the first time. He had passed it hundreds of times with no more than casual glances and simple acceptance. Now he was keenly aware of everything about it, the three-cornered crossroads where it stood, one road going northwest to his Grandpa Blackburn's house, one going northeast back to Grandpa Perry's and the rent house, one going southwest to Prairie Springs Baptist Church and Hico. The little eighteen by thirty-six foot wood frame building with its many-paned windows and board shutters, the shingled gable roof with its chimney flue sticking up, the little front porch, the outhouse behind the school just above the banks of Camp Branch — a mile and a half downstream from the rent house — all took on a new solidity. Today he had to go *in* there. Today he had to walk with his parents and his brother Hoyt up the stepped bridge over the school fence and down the other side — there was no other way to pass the barrier of the barbed-wire fence. As they went up and down the rough steps, as they crossed the bare dirt playground, as they climbed the wide flat rock that was the first step of the schoolhouse porch, Clayborne felt a little — just a little — intimidated.

"Mister and Miz Perry, come on in, we're just about ready to get started," said Miss Belle McCallister, the spinster school teacher. Clayborne stepped into the classroom just in front of his parents and looked around wide-eyed. Children of every age seemed to be penned up in here, he thought. In fact, there were thirty of them, in grades one through seven. They ranged in age from seven to fifteen years. Clayborne quickly saw that he knew many of them: Eddie Yoakum and Clifford Mackey from adjoining farms, Minnie Rucker and Burton Tate from over by Rocky, Grady Arnold just up the road from Grandpa Perry's farm, Irma Jamison from Prairie Springs, Randy McCarty from over by Grandpa Blackburn's farm and Ira Robinson just beyond the McCartys, and even Mary Wilson from over toward Chalk Mountain. They sat at desks lined up in military order, rank and file, facing the teacher's large and formidable desk at the front of the class. Between stood the long recitation bench, long enough to seat as many as eight scholars at a time. The wall boards had been painted black to serve as a chalkboard, and a cast iron box heater radiated the warmth of burning wood into the room. School trustees in the community had brought in pole wood and stacked it by the school building for the larger boys to cut into sections that would fit the heating stove. Clayborne decided that even though school was strange, it was not at all a bad place.

"Do we need to sign anything, Miss McCallister?" asked Tom.

"No, sir, not a thing. You just leave Clayborne and his dinner pail with us and we'll send him home when school's out. Clayborne, you sit at that empty desk in the second row. We'll be taking first roll call shortly and everyone will tell us their names. Then we'll assign the permanent seating plan."

"We won't need to come by and pick him up before noon or anything, will we?" asked Belle. "We have to go into Hico for Tom's Army examination and it's like to take most of the day."

"Oh, you got your call-up, Mister Perry! It would be a shame for our community to lose a fine man like you to the Army, but we must do our patriotic duty. School isn't out until four o'clock and I'm sure that Clayborne knows his way home if you happen to miss him."

The buggy ride into Hico was silent. Belle held the year-old Hoyt forlornly, fully expecting her husband to vanish on the next train to fight in those terrible trenches in France. Tom simply drove the buggy, not planning, not hoping, not fearing.

The draft board had taken months to get itself organized. The United States had declared war on Germany in April, yet it was June before draft registration began and November before Tom and the other local farmers in North Central Texas received their notices to report for physical examination. The boys' locker room at Hico High School had been requisitioned for the purpose. Tom pulled up and stopped the buggy under a large oak tree in front of the school.

"You bring Hoyt on in and wait inside, Belle. Don't sit out here in the chill."

"Tom, I'm scared."

"I know. It'll be all right."

They entered the big front doors of Hico High School and inquired at the principal's office. They were told to follow the hand-lettered arrows taped to the walls, signs that announced simply "Draftees." In addition to the directional arrows, the hallway was decorated with a variety of war posters. On one poster, yellow letters blared "Enlist," over the silhouette of a civilian looking out a window at rows of marching soldiers, and asked, "On which Side of the Window are YOU?" On another poster, an illustration of a mother in supplication was accompanied by the query, "Must children die and mothers plead in vain? Buy more Liberty Bonds." On yet another, an American Red Cross symbol loomed behind a yarn basket, below which stood the large message: "Our Boys Need SOX. Knit Your Bit."

At the end of a hall they found themselves in the school's physical education office, now labelled "Induction Center — Physical Examination." Inside they were confronted by a uniformed U.S. Army registrar wearing sergeant's stripes. He said tonelessly to Tom, "Sign your name here, leave your draft notice in that box and go into that room. The attendant there will tell you what to do. Missus, you'll have to wait out here."

Belle looked around the small office where half a dozen anxious women seemed to line the walls, sitting at school desks that had been pressed into service for the purpose. Belle watched Tom lay his draft notice on the table and sign the register, then disappear through a side door into the dimly lit corridor leading to the boys' locker room. She stared blankly at the empty door for several minutes, holding Hoyt, fighting back her fear.

"You'd best take a seat, Missus, advised the sergeant. This is going to take a while. We've only got one doctor and there's a dozen men ahead of your husband."

Belle sat. And sat. And sat. She dared not enter into the chit-chat the other women shared. She could not trust herself to keep from bursting into tears. The tension gripped her throat. Hoyt became fussy and she walked him down the halls, which gave her some relief, but made her more aware of the stone and plaster walls that separated her from her husband. As she walked the long halls with her little son she wondered: What would they decide? Would Tom be shipped to a training camp? Would he be forced to drill with a broomstick for a rifle like she had heard other men were doing because the Army was so poorly prepared for war? Would he have to study French and eat terrible Army food? She walked. She trembled. She prayed. She cooed to Hoyt. She hid the tears in her handkerchief, pretending to have a head cold. She went back in the little office and sat some more. And some more.

Three hours after walking in, Tom came out the door from the dimly lit corridor and into the waiting room where most of the women had now left. He was downcast, lost in a brown study. He absently took Belle aside, out into the hallway. He stood there a minute and said, "It's going to be a painful thing, Belle."

"Oh, Tom, no!" She grimaced in anguish, tears streaming.

"Not for you, Belle. For me. The doctor says it's my teeth."

"What?"

"My teeth. That's what's been causing the rheumatism. You know how my gums have been bleeding bad."

"What are you talking about, Tom?"

"The bad teeth's been poisoning my system. Gives me the rheumatism. Got to have them all pulled out, the doctor says. It ought to cure the rheumatism. But it's going to be a painful thing."

"But what about your draft notice? What about the Army?"

"Oh, that. Papa was right. Once I got in there the doctor looked at my eye and wasn't even going to examine me. Said I was unfit for service, couldn't shoot a rifle with just one eye. I told him I aim with my good eye, and I'd take on the best shot he could find. I told him I wasn't no shirker, and I wanted a physical examination fair and square, just like the other men. That's when he saw my teeth and asked about my rheumatism. Wasn't no use. The asthma, the teeth, the rheumatism, the eye. He said I'm a walking collection of medical symptoms, what he said."

"You mean you don't have to go to the Army?"

"They wouldn't have me, Belle. It makes me ashamed."

She hugged him desperately, sandwiching Hoyt between them, not caring whether they were in public or not. "Tom Perry, I'll have you. And Hoyt and Clayborne will have you. We'll all have you."

"I know. But a man's got to help with the war."

"You stay home, Tom," said Belle, taking his hand firmly. "You stay home and grow cotton and raise your boys and run for the school board. That'll help with the war. You just stay home."

-7-

TAKING ROOT

ORNING. A gentle mist laced with snowflakes washed the dark expanse of winter sky like a wedding veil thrown across a slate chalkboard. Trudging through the wet lace with dinner bucket and books in hand, the raincoated boy could see his donkey waiting in the barnyard gloom, ready for another school day. Pup frisked behind, biting snowflakes on the wind.

"It never snows enough to make snowballs, Pup," said Clayborne as he walked under the sheltering roof of the barn's back shed. "Me and donkey are just gonna get cold and wet today."

After depositing his dinner pail and books safely on the dry hay under the shed, the boy pulled his donkey cart from the shadows into the open rain. Clayborne's little vehicle was scarcely more than an applebox on wheels, tinkered together by his father from a 2-by-4 axle with two metal-rimmed wheels, a rough plank platform on top of the axle and an applebox from the Hico mercantile store for a seat — just big enough to contain boy, books and bucket.

Clayborne maneuvered his cart from behind the donkey so the beast was flanked on both sides by its two forward-pointing shafts, or "shavs," as these Texans called them. The boy ran stiff leather traces through a little singletree near the apple box seat and back to a collar hung around the donkey's neck. When the beast was properly hitched, Clayborne retrieved his school books and dinner bucket from the shed and led the donkey and cart through the barnyard gate. "Come on out, Pup," said the boy.

Once firmly seated in his apple box, Clayborne began the daily ritual of coaxing the donkey into motion. The animal obdurately resisted all snapping of traces and shouted encouragements. He flicked his ears temperamentally. He did not go. The boy was determined to out-stubborn his donkey this Friday and kept up the harangue for minutes on end. Without warning, on a complete freak, the furry critter suddenly decided to obey. He obeyed with a vengeance, lunging like a bull out of a rodeo chute with his rural scholar hanging onto the apple box for dear life. The runaway beast careered at a gallop around the barnyard fence, making tracks on his customary route to Grandpa Perry's bridge with Pup barking and snapping at his heels. Now to make a sharp right turn at the fence corner. . . Too short! The cart came up hard on the fence with a bone-rattling jolt. The donkey stopped dead in his tracks and Clayborne looked down in disgust. The right wheel was solidly hung up on a shaggy cedar post.

Clayborne indignantly unseated himself and lifted the little vehicle, straining to extract his jammed cart wheel from the rough wet fencepost. Exasperating! "Pup," he said, "this animal just ain't the sweet type like Ol' Donkey in Colorado." Clayborne had been taught that certain words were never to be spoken, regardless of the circumstances, but he felt them welling up in his throat this morning. He resisted the urge and called up other imprecations, words that only teetered on the brink of the forbidden. After looking around first to make sure that only he and his maker could hear his wrath, the youngster said, "Don't you listen, Pup," and heaped a regular dose of "consarn it" and "by gaddies" upon the donkey's head before resuming his seat. Then they were on their way again across the soggy Grand Prairie ground at a more reasonable pace.

"Look at the high water around the bridge, donkey," yelled Clayborne, already forgetting the animal's misbehavior. "If it keeps on raining like this, Camp Branch is gonna come out of its banks for sure!" Pup stopped at the wooden bridge as was his daily habit now. "So long Pup see you this evening!"

Over the bridge and across the open fields Clayborne and the donkey jounced, soon passing through Grandpa and Grandma Blackburn's leafless orchard, up by their barn and to the main gate that opened onto the dirt road. Grandpa and Grandma Blackburn saw the boy from their kitchen window this morning and waved to him. He waved back as he heaved open the big swinging board gate, then led the donkey and cart out into the road to school and shut the gate behind him.

In the farm kitchen, Charley Blackburn remarked to his wife Laura, "Havin' that donkey pull him to school is goin' to make that boy mean to animals. I keep tellin' Tom and Belle, but they won't listen. Donkies are lazy animals, you gotta whip 'em to make 'em mind. Clayborne'll turn out plumb mean, you'll see."

Laura Blackburn replied, "The boy don't have a whip, Charley. He just hollers at the donkey. He don't use curse words, neither. And if Belle caught him bein' mean, she'd clean his plow but good. That lad'll turn out just fine, just fine."

Charley Blackburn knew better than to argue with his wife. He only shook his head in a characteristic gesture and took another sip of his "saucered and blowed" coffee. Their tubercular daughter Bethel coughed on the sleeping porch built just for her along the back of the house. The cough seemed better this morning.

Clayborne drove his donkey and cart alongside the Camp Branch school fence at exactly 8:55 a.m. that March morning, five minutes before class time. On the woodpile protected by overhanging schoolhouse eaves sat Eddie Yoakum and Clifford Mackey, boys from farms adjoining the Perry property. They casually waved Clayborne into his usual hitching place under a big liveoak tree just outside the fence, saying nothing and pretending not to be cold. They wore that studied nonchalance elementary school boys put on when trying to look like grown men.

A trickle of students coming in from Camp Branch road walked up and down the stepped bridge over the school fence. Standing in the chill on the school's little front porch, Minnie Rucker eyed Clayborne steadily. She liked him, but he had given her heavy competition for best grades since mid-November, and she could not afford to become too good a friend. She desperately wanted to beat him for the spelling prize when school was out two months hence in mid-April.

Clayborne tied his donkey to its customary fencepost under its customary tree, where the hapless creature would stand all day, unsheltered from the mizzling, drizzling rain. At least the showers had chased away the late-season blue norther of the past few days; after this morning there would be no more snowflakes until next winter. As soon as Clayborne had scooped his books and dinner pail from the cart's applebox seat, he strode up and down the school fence's step-bridge and his two woodpile friends wordlessly dismounted their high throne and ambled with him into class.

Inside, the sound of rain beat a muffled tattoo on the shingle roof, students toasted frozen appendages at the wood burner and the smell of wet wool pervaded the room. The heating stove stood free in the middle of the room atop a layer of bricks resting on sand curbed by two-by-fours nailed in a rectangle to the wood floor. Coals inadvertently knocked out of the firebox would thus fall harmlessly to the bricks and sand.

A few students stood looking in the locked glass-front cabinet at the school library — a collection of some forty volumes of classics such as Dickens, bestsellers such as Zane Grey and Booth Tarkington, and a few tattered issues of *National Geographic*. No one was allowed to handle these precious books except on overnight loan to read at home under parental supervision. The school owned no maps or other teaching aids, and was allowed only two wooden boxes of chalk each year, purchased by the school board at fifty-five cents each. The teacher in such a rural school earned sixty dollars a month for five months each year.

A few seconds before class was to begin, with no prompting from the teacher, each student quietly and automatically assumed the proper seat — boys sat with boys and girls with girls in the old fashioned double-desk school seats. A few of the older boys immediately fell to gazing abstractedly at the rivulets of water patterning the windowpanes, daydreaming of dark oaken woods and favorite fishing holes. Promptly at 9:00 a.m. Miss Belle McCallister brought the class to order. "Good morning, pupils."

"Good morning, Miss McCallister," came the music of their reply in voices ranging the scale from squeaky soprano to crack-throated baritone.

Miss McCallister told them, "Today is Friday, March 1, 1918. We will begin the day with the Pledge of Allegiance. Clayborne Perry, will you lead the pledge today, please?"

The youngster self-consciously rose with the class and stepped beside his desk. He and the rest saluted in the military hand-over-eyebrow manner and began:

"I pledge allegiance to my flag, and to the Republic for which it stands, one Nation, indivisible, with liberty and justice for all."

This early flag pledge has changed with time. Not until the Flag Conference held in 1923 was the original 1892 pledge by Francis Bellamy of *Youth's Companion* magazine revised to replace the phrase "my flag" with "the Flag of the United States." In 1924 the phrase "of America" was added. In 1954 a Congressional resolution approved by the president inserted the words "under God." With the original simple but stirring patriotic devotion Clayborne Perry's school day began.

Miss McCallister sat still for a long moment. As usual, she had walked to school that morning from her modest rented dwelling a mile and a half away. Normally she would have been cheery and glowing, but today, as during the past week or so, she looked wan and pale, what her fellow Texans would have called "peaked." Normally, she would have called for the singing of a rousing song, "America," or "Onward Christian Soldiers," but today she seemed not to have the energy. She called the roll in a wavering voice and then gamely began the day's scholastics.

"First grade Number class, rise . . ." she called out in military fashion. Three students out of thirty stood up and awaited her next instruction.

"Turn!" The two little boys and a girl made a crisp right-face at their desks.

"Pass!" They marched from their desks to the recitation bench facing Miss McCallister's desk and stood in line.

"Be seated." They sat. "Grady Mackey, will you come forward and give the first grade Number class this work, please?"

The twelve-year-old scurried obediently to the teacher's desk, took the arithmetic work sheet and sat down with the three first graders to tell them their assignment. Grady had been born with a malformed left arm, extending only to a place slightly above where his elbow should have been. He was not the type to feel sorry for himself and had not been babied because of his handicap. His classmates had long outgrown their morbid curiosity about his misfortune. Grady and his brother Clifford — Clayborne's age — had uncles who were professional baseball players. The relationship had stood the two boys in good stead: they had grown to be playground favorites at recess time, Grady turning out to be a mean dead-eye right-hand pitcher, wearing his glove on the stump of his left arm. Batters never felt sorry for him and were even heard at times to mutter oaths at him under their breath after being struck out.

In his newly acquired basso profundo voice, Grady prepared his young charges for their arithmetic lesson and took them to the chalkboard at the front of the room behind the teacher's desk. This chalkboard was in actuality a rough and ready wall, an entire wall of shiplap lumber joined none too snugly and painted black for the purpose. Sounding like a frog with laryngitis, the Mackey lad read aloud the first grade problems to be written on the board. Students quickly acquired the skill of writing across the cracks between boards to avoid breaking their precious chalk. While the first grade labored, Miss McCallister barked her "Rise! Turn! Pass! Be seated!" orders to the second grade. Clayborne Perry strode to the recitation bench with four other classmates, including Minnie Rucker. Miss McCallister had advanced Minnie and Clayborne to second grade level shortly after Christmas, 1917. Home schooling had paid both of them dividends.

Grade after grade thus passed to the chalkboard, each with a tutor from a higher grade, until Miss McCallister read the seventh grade its arithmetic problems herself, to be solved at their desks, with a busy-bee line of pupils and tutors cramming the wall-long chalkboard in the background.

The one-room school buzzed with activity. No one was idle. No one was disruptive. Half an hour of high intensity math had gone by when the teacher announced, "Pupils, take your seats for spelling lesson," and the entire class quickly and silently resumed its places.

"Take out your spellers, pupils," intoned Miss McCallister. "I'll have John Word and Irma Jamison and Mary Wilson come up to give out spelling words. Pupils, form your spelling lines."

The spelling ritual consisted of standing in line and spelling the day's words as they were pronounced by a tutor. The words, four of them, usually, were selected by the helper from the top of the appropriate page in their graded spelling text. If the student missed a word, it was back to the foot of the line to try once more in turn. When Clayborne Perry came to the head of the line, spelling helper John Fred Word intoned: "Went."

Clayborne responded "W-e-n-t, went."

"Again."

"A-g-a-i-n, again."

"Horse."

"H-o-r-s-e, horse."

"Barn."

"B-a-r-n, barn."

Each student that successfully spelled all the words was given a "head mark" for staying at the head of the line. Clayborne had another head mark. At the end of each school year, the speller with the most head marks would receive the prize that Minnie Rucker so coveted: a fifteen-cent reader. That day Minnie Rucker also got another head mark.

By dinner time the rain had become a steady pounding down pour. Clayborne stayed inside today, but the older boys ventured into the soaking noon with their food pails before realizing what they were in for. Clambering up the woodpile, each acted as if he had adequate shelter. They ate their biscuits and ham and fried peach pies with as much enthusiasm as they could muster, none wanting to be the sissy who went inside first. A soggy dinner was had by all.

For the rest of the day, the second grade class went a few steps further in learning the names of the states and their capitals while the other six grades pursued their own tasks. Clayborne would occasionally listen to the classwork of higher grades, pondering the Byzantine romance of Texas state history and the secrets of diagramming sentences, wondering if he would ever be able to master such arcane mysteries.

At the end of the school day, instead of the formal dismissal the students had learned to expect, Miss McCallister stood before the class and gave a brief speech:

"Boys and girls, today is the last day of school for this year. I won't be able to continue teaching and no substitute teacher can be found. Your parents have been notified. You have completed three months of the five you should have received this year. I'm sorry that you will miss the last two months of school, especially you first and second graders. But you are bright children and you will have another chance next year. I have enjoyed teaching you and I wish you all the best in the years to come. Please remember to take all your books and your personal belongings home with you because school will not be open after today. And please do not stay after dismissal. Class, dismissed."

Shock ruled the room. Miss McCallister sat behind her great teacher's desk and the students rose from their seats like zombies. They milled around, gathering their things, wanting to talk to this teacher they had grown to love, but dreading to pry into her personal affairs. Clayborne gathered the books his parents had bought him — the state did not provide texts in 1918, and all books were student property. He walked out of the school room with the rest of the class into the misting rain, not knowing whether to be happy or sad. School was out for the year, and that did not necessarily make him unhappy, but he had seen the tears welling up in Miss McCallister's eyes. He liked her and felt sorry for her, whatever her problem might be. Most of all, he wondered why she would bring about such an abrupt end to his first year in school. As he buttoned his raincoat, he decided it certainly couldn't have been anything he had done, because there were so many other farm youngsters in school and he had behaved as well as any — well, almost any. His father had told him that if he got a whipping in school he could expect another when he got home, and that provided a certain incentive to good behavior. Nobody had been really bad. Then why was Miss McCallister quitting? He had no answer and shrugged off the question. He crossed the fence-bridge, untied his donkey, got in his soaking wet cart and drove home.

Past Grandpa Blackburn's orchard and approaching Camp Branch, Clayborne looked for Grandpa Perry's bridge. Where was it? A flood of swift brown water sluiced down the creek and rushed upward where the bridge ought to be. The boy watched intently for a few seconds and then made out the tilted bridge deck hidden under turbulent eddies. The watery surge held down the bridge, just as Grandpa Perry had said it would.

"The bridge is still there! And didn't I tell you, donkey, didn't I?" Clayborne cried. "I knew the branch would come out of its banks."

Clayborne saw a figure moving in the distance. His father approached from the barn, strode purposefully to the bridge and then stopped to size up the down flow. Pup ran down from the rent house and drew up well short of the muddy torrent. Tom waded across the bridge carefully, fighting the knee-deep current with every step. "You stay over there, son," he shouted. "I'll walk you back." Pup barked his loudest.

"Do you want me to drive back to school and come around the other way?"

"No, it's not that bad. Water's not even two feet over the bridge. Just stay put a minute." Tom Perry advanced cautiously at mid-bridge, the swift water raising bow waves around his wiry legs at every footfall and threatening to knock him down. A few more perilous steps and he made it across. He slogged up to the high ground where Clayborne and the donkey waited and said, "You stay in the cart, son. Hold up your books and your dinner pail so they don't get washed away."

Tom gathered the donkey's traces in one hand and began gingerly retracing his steps across the flooded bridge.

"The teacher says we're all done with school, Papa," shouted Clayborne.

Tom yelled his answer without turning to look at the boy. "I know. She's real sick, son. The school board says they can't find another teacher until school starts up again in November. Don't worry about it. There's plenty for you to do here at home."

That night at his accustomed place by the heating stove, by the light of the coal oil lamp, Clayborne skimmed the latest issue of the twice weekly *Dallas Farm News*. His mother and father and little brother were occupied in their own quiet pursuits in the living room-bedroom. In the sea of print, Clayborne found the black-lined box he sought. He scanned it, realizing that his reading skills had increased considerably in his first three months of school. There, in a long list of names and places in boldface print, he found a town he knew, along with the name of an unfamiliar person: Marshall Bennett, Hico, Texas.

"Who's Marshall Bennett, Papa?"

"He's that young Bennett kid what fibbed about his age so he could enlist in the Army last year. Why do you ask, son?"

"His name's in the paper. In the box for War Dead. He was killed in France."

"Dear Lord" gasped Belle, dropping her knitting.

"He was only a boy," whispered Tom.

"I see they got you farmers out workin' roads, Tom Perry," called Tom Strepey from his heavy duty wagon.

"Well, they got you carpenters out here, too, don't they?" grinned Tom at his neighbor. They both waited in line at a gravel pit where their wagons would be loaded out for delivery to the community volunteer crew working nearby.

"Think they got any gravel in this pit?" asked Strepey, eyeing gigantic mounds of the stuff.

"Nope, no gravel here," replied Tom Perry with a straight face.

Strepey said, "My rig couldn't stand driving over many more chugholes, so I figured I'd come out and show them county engineers how to fix roads right."

"You just show 'em how to fix roads so they stay fixed. You do that and you'll be a right rich man, Tom Strepey." They both laughed.

There was nothing terribly voluntary about the Texas community volunteer road crews of 1918. All able-bodied rural men over 21 and under 45 worked one week each year on public roads as labor-in-lieu-of-taxes unless they had an official medical excuse. The sheriff would have come and encouraged shirkers to donate their time, but in the superheated mood of national solidarity brought on by the Great War, no one needed to be encouraged.

"Oh-Tom!" called Strepey as he helped the pit crew shovel gravel into his wagon.

"Yay-bo?" answered Tom Perry, likewise busy shoveling.

"You hear the special session done passed a loyalty law?"

"Loyalty law? What's that?"

"Ol' Sullivan, the lawyer in Hico that writes my carpenter contracts with the county, he told me about it. You hadn't ought to say nothin' about the war, cause they'll put your bohunkus right in jail if you do."

Jack Tanner sitting in the wagon behind them called out, "What did you say, Tom Strepey? Did you say the legislature's passed a law against free speech? You can't speak your mind proper?"

"You heard me right, Jack. But it ain't against free speech, just anything about the war. I think it's to hush up them pacifists and Kaiser-lovers in the big city. The new law says you speak against the flag or the soldiers or the government, you done committed a crime. Oh, and you better keep quiet about us gettin' into the war, too."

"I don't have nothin' against us gettin' in the war," Tanner said. "And I don't love the Kaiser. But I mean, can they do that? You know, what with the First Amendment and all?" Tanner asked.

"They done it. It's wartime, my friend. And just be glad you ain't no German. Folks are gettin' mighty ugly against Germans over at Waco and down at Austin."

Tanner asked, "You mean like ol' Fouts over by Rocky?"

"No," snorted Strepey. "He ain't German like I mean. His folks must of come over in 1890 or earlier. I mean like Germans got here the last two or three years. Fouts! Why the very idea! He's so strong American I wouldn't even have thought of him. He'd never say anything against America!"

"That must be why they changed the name of German measles to Liberty measles," remarked Tanner.

"What?" asked Tom Strepey.

"I heard on the phone listenin' to Doc Russell that German measles is called Liberty measles now. And hamburger is Liberty steak. And sauerkraut is Liberty cabbage. I wondered what that was all about. Must be that new law."

Tom Perry chuckled, "If there's a law against criticizin' America, I bet there's goin' to be a lot of socialists in jail up in Oklahoma."

Strepey replied, "It's a Texas law, Tom."

"They need one like it up there more than we need it here. Nobody in these parts is anything but one-hundred-percent patriots. But you should hear what those pigheaded socialists were sayin' about the United States when I was there in 'sixteen. It was shameful."

"Well, nobody better say anything around here or the Texas Rangers'll be after 'em," remarked Strepey as he mounted to the seat of his loaded wagon. "Hey, you going to work all day, Tom, what with Easter bein' tomorrow?"

"No, going to take the family into Hico after this next load. Goin' to the store and to see my wife's sister. Belle says to say hello to your wife. See you in church tomorrow."

"Florence says to say hello to your wife, too. So long, Tom."

"See you Tom, see you Jack."

With one-quarter of a road crew workday credit under his belt, that noon in Hico Tom hitched the buggy in front of Lynch's Cafe and helped Belle down to the board sidewalk. Clayborne jumped off the vehicle, grabbed Hoyt under the arms and swooshed him from the buggy seat to the dirt street. "Come on, Hoyt," he said, bending down to the two-year-old's level, "we're going to get some chili and see Auntie Sallie. Can you say Auntie Sallie? Auntie Sallie?"

"Aintee Sa-wee!" said the boy.

"Hey, Mama, did you hear that?" yelled Clayborne. "Hoyt said 'Aintee Sa-wee!'"

Belle turned and beamed at her youngest boy. "I sure did hear it, Clayborne. And it wasn't too many years ago you first said it right here this very same place. This very same place."

It was a busy dinner hour inside, and Sallie Lynch hustled them to the only vacant table in the cafe. They all had their customary bowl of good Wiley Lynch chili and snatches of conversation with Sallie as she dashed to and fro taking customers' orders and delivering meals. When Tom paid the check, Sallie told Belle, "Sister, you all go on up to the house when you're done at the mercantile. I'll come up soon as the hired girl can handle the business by herself."

An hour later Sallie joined them at her modest home up the street from Lynch's Cafe, the home where the Perrys and Lynchs had spent so many Saturday afternoons together. Sallie bounced in the front door calling, "Yoo-hoo, you folks back from grocery shopping?"

"We're in here, Sally," said Belle, popping her head into the hallway. "Come on in to your own front room, why don't you?"

"I believe I will. You know, Belle, today another customer said you and me must be twins after you left the cafe." They both enjoyed a burst of girlish giggles. Even though Belle was younger by two years, many took her for Sallie's twin. In their earlier days they had sometimes played the part out of sheer mischief.

"Linchie's going to be here in a minute," Sallie said to Tom, who had settled into a comfortable rocking chair and was reading a magazine to Hoyt and Clayborne. "Looks like a slow afternoon after that busy dinnertime, and Linchie's just going to close up. Must be it's Easter comin' tomorrow, everybody's gonna be eatin' supper at home. Linchie'll be here directly. Give you somebody to talk to instead of listenin' to girl talk, Tom."

"It don't make me no never mind, Sallie. The boys and me always enjoy bein' here."

"Oh, Tom, you got such good manners. I wish some of our city-folk customers knew how to say the right thing like you. Some of them is low-down cusses, use the worst language you can imagine."

"Must be Linchie a' stomping up the steps now," said Belle.

Wiley Lynch marched into the house, greeting all with his good-natured smile. "Let me put this in the icebox," he said indicating a package of meat wrapped in butcher paper. "I'll be right back."

"You going to church in the morning, Sallie?" asked Belle.

"Easter? We surely are. We go a lot, even with the cafe. Not like the Christmas and Easter Christians the preacher talks about, just goes to church twiced a year. We go a lot."

"Well, Tom," said Wiley Lynch as he sauntered into the living room and rolled up his sleeves. "You been reading about the big German push on the Western Front?"

"Not much, Linchie. Been busy planting. Just read enough to see about Big Bertha lobbing shells 70 miles into Paris. Can you imagine that? A cannon that shoots 70 miles? Why, that's more'n here to Waco."

"Hard to imagine," agreed Wiley, taking a seat in his overstuffed chair. "That howitzer is some weapon. Won't be long now, though, there'll be enough Doughboys in France to give the Kaiser something to worry about. I saw somewhere we're sending enough in March alone to end the war. Sure hope it ends quick."

The Western Front had been characterized by British poet and soldier, Robert Graves, author of *I, Claudius*, as "the Sausage Machine, because it was fed with live men, churned out corpses, and remained firmly screwed in place." Now, in late March, 1918, the Sausage Machine had come unscrewed: the Bolsheviks under Lenin's orders had signed the Treaty of Brest-Litovsk and Russia dropped out of the war, which allowed Germany to move its men and equipment from the Eastern Front to the Western. The reinforced Germans immediately began a push on the Western Front from Arras to Reims in an obvious effort to split the French forces from the British, drive the British into the Channel and win the war. All the Europeans could do was hang on until the Americans arrived. In all the excitement, no one paid any attention to news reports during March that in Detroit more than a thousand workers had to be sent home with a new kind of influenza.

The pleasant Saturday afternoon at the Lynch's turned toward evening. Goodbyes and Easter wishes were shared all around. Before departing, the Perrys bought their traditional half-pound bag of peanut sweets at

Rainwater's Candy Kitchen and enjoyed their ride back to the farm. The night and Easter dawn, March 31, 1918, passed clear and peaceful. Morning services at the Prairie Springs Baptist Church retold the nearly two-thousand-year-old story, explaining once more the meaning of the Empty Cross, renewing once more the firm and steady faith. It was a little after noon, a little after Easter Sunday dinner, that the telephone rang in the rent house of Tom and Belle Perry. One long and two short rings came from the local operator in Duffau.

"That's our ring, Tom," said Belle as she cleared the dishes from the table.

"I'll get it," said Tom, going to the front room. Hoyt remained sound asleep in his high chair and Clayborne looked out the kitchen window at crows beating southward in the spring air on their crooked wings.

Tom lifted the earpiece from the wooden-cased instrument on his living room wall and heard the usual click, click, click, click as interested neighbors picked up their party-line receivers to keep informed on community affairs — the telephone rang in the homes of all twenty-two customers on the little rural system.

In the kitchen Belle could hear Tom over her clatter of dishes, even though he spoke softly. Clayborne only half listened and watched Pup curled up asleep in the far kitchen corner by the woodstove.

"What? Say that again, Linchie. Are you sure? Are you sure? Oh, Lord, are you sure? She's not just real sound asleep? Oh, Dear Lord. Oh, Dear Lord. Yes, we'll come right away. Yes, Linchie. Yes, Linchie, I'll tell her. No, don't you try to. Not on the telephone. I'll tell her."

Belle was petrified with dread as Tom walked into the kitchen. Tears streamed down his face. Clayborne looked up and was stunned. He had never seen his father cry, not his father who tended toward the taciturn and regarded any expression of tender feelings as unmanly. The absolute Texas precept echoed in his young mind: Grown men don't cry. Grown men don't cry. But this grown man with the quizzically arched eyebrows was crying.

"Belle, sit down," said Tom.

"Oh, Tom, what is it? That was Linchie, wasn't it? I heard you. Is it Sallie?"

"Sit down, now." Tom said softly, holding her by both shoulders and gently pushing her into a cane-bottom kitchen chair.

"Is it Sallie, Tom? What is it? What is it!"

"It's Sallie, Belle. Brace yourself for some hard news. Linchie says she passed away half an hour ago. A little before noon."

"No, Tom. That can't be. It must be a mistake. She's only twenty-six years old. We saw her just yesterday. She was fine. It's a mistake."

"It's no mistake, Belle. It's true. It happened all of a sudden. She was fine one minute, and . . ." His voice broke. "She was gone the next. Just like that."

Silence, stupefied silence.

"She's gone then?"

"Gone."

The wail seemed to grow slowly and organically from the air rather than from her throat, seemed to be a nature-sound more than the agony of a human soul. Hoyt was startled awake by his mother's shriek, breathless with fear, then mingled the din of his fright with her grief. Tom hugged Belle while patting Hoyt, sobbing his own grief as quietly as he could. Pup had jumped up and stared around to see what was wrong. Clayborne looked upon the scene from his seat at the table, peering over the bowl of leftover mashed potatoes and the sorghum pail and the salt and pepper shaker to the safe next to the wall beyond. The ordinariness of the kitchen table, the room, the house seemed an affront to the devastating grief he felt. He could not contain the pain. Auntie Sallie! Not Auntie Sallie!

Tom hitched Pet to the buggy and the family made their way toward Hico. On the road not too far from Camp Branch School, Belle gibbered softly "How could He do this? How could He take her like this, Tom? On Easter Sunday!" The cry grew to a caterwaul: "On the day of Resurrection! How could the Lord do this? Take my sister away, my Sallie!" Frenzy possessed her brain. "He can't be a God of Love, Tom! No loving God would do this! Not today! Not any day!"

Tom put his hand on her shoulder in gentle reproof but tried to make his words as stern and commanding as he knew how: "Don't you carry on that way, woman! Get ahold of yourself. Think of the boys. The Lord has his reasons. It's not for us to question Him. I don't understand it any more than you do, but you're not going to lose faith. You hear that, Belle Perry? The Lord giveth and the Lord taketh away. You're not going to lose faith!"

They arrived at the Lynch home about 3 p.m. A crowd of friends and neighbors had gathered, quiet knots of people in the sunshine on the front lawn and in the shade of the little front porch and throughout the house. Some neighbors had brought food for Wiley and the growing congregation of mourners. Several ladies of the community had dressed Sallie in her best church clothes and laid her out on a cooling board. It was the custom of the day, before undertakers dominated the time of death, for neighbor women to prepare women, men to prepare men, and to arrange the body on a homemade slab known as a cooling board. This rough-and-ready funeral bier was normally arranged from two side-by-side six-foot long, twelve-inch wide boxing planks, the boards wrapped in a bedsheet and laid between two straight-back chairs facing each other. The dressed body was laid out on this arrangement and left in a cool place, mindful of the lack of embalming, usually in the best room of the house before a bank of open sheltered north-facing windows. Today, Sallie's cooling board stood in the parlor before the front windows.

When Tom and Belle and the boys made their way up the steps and into the hall where Wiley stood receiving guests and trying not to cry, the crowd opened before them like grass waving before the wind. Murmurs followed in their wake: "She looks so much like Sallie." "They were so close." "Nobody knows why Sallie died." "She was happy and healthy right to the end." "Look how her sister's suffering." "Poor Belle." "Look, Tom's been grieving, too." "The boys don't seem to understand." "Lord have mercy."

Belle stood before Wiley. They looked silently into each others' faces, engraving the day's unspeakable pain on their souls. Then Wiley hugged Belle, and guided her, arm around shoulder, into the parlor to see Sallie. Tom followed, with Clayborne holding Hoyt's hand.

There lay the earthly remains of Sallie Lynch on the low cooling board. Eternal silence closed her voice. Night upon her eyes. Belle gazed at her beautiful sister long and long. There was no horror left, no room for more pain. Belle lovingly scanned Sallie's still face, searching for traces of vanished smiles, joying in the flood of precious memories that bathed her, staring, trying to see where death had left its fatal wound. The only wound Belle found was on her own heart. She leaned over and kissed her sister's forehead. It was cold, the spirit flown, the blood quiet. "Bury me with her," said Belle softly. "Bury my heart with her."

Sallie's funeral was the next day. Embalming was not practiced in these times in rural Texas and the speedy lying in of corpses was a matter of practical haste. On Monday morning Sallie was borne in a wood coffin on a horse-drawn wagon up the long hill to the east of Hico where the cemetery overlooked the town. A procession of buggies and farm wagons and horseback riders, slow and solemn and sweet, trailed up the road for more than a mile behind her casket. The fair Grand Prairie day warmed a lonely hawk quartering the empty sky and the benevolent sun brooked no gloom. The funeral service was a dot in time, a simple period, a punctuation mark ending the life story of Sallie Blackburn Lynch. Dirt filled the grave. The burial party broke up their watch in shining grief and ancient hope of salvation. After some days, Wiley Lynch sold the cafe, bought another building in Hico and some new equipment, and remained a widower shoe repairman for many years. There were no more Saturday bowls of steaming chili and good talk. There was no more Lynch's Cafe. For young Clayborne Perry life was never the same again.

"Ooo-ee! That thing makes a racket!" shouted Belle against the growling propeller roar.

The biplane taxied toward the crowd across the bumpy field, its twin wings dipping left and right like a pair of vast circling buzzards jolted by a rowdy wind. Clayborne watched the tall lanky host of the Glen Rose Chamber of Commerce as he stepped between the aircraft and his fascinated guests and yelled through a megaphone, "Stay back, folks, stay back for just a minute. You'll have plenty of chance to get right close to the plane once he's come up and turned his engine off."

The pilot turn the airplane about, barely missing the pressing crowd, and shut off the motor. He stepped out of the open cockpit and onto the lower wing as the propeller wound to its characteristic flapping stop and rebound.

"Captain Eddie Paul, ladies and gentlemen," megaphoned the hawker. "A real flying ace of the Great War!" Applause riffled through the crowd, the sound absorbed by the vast clear Texas sky. The uniformed pilot took the megaphone and addressed his admirers.

"Thank you, Mr. Bates. From all that clappin' I'd 'a thought you said Captain Eddie Rickenbacker. I'm real proud to be here on behalf of the United States Army, even though I'll have to beg off on that part about bein' a flying ace. I got to France too late for Max Immelman and too early for Baron von Richtofen, and I can only lay claim to three of the enemy's aircraft before being shot down myself just a couple of months ago." Patriotic applause spontaneously erupted from the farmers and small-town Texans gathered in the field.

"I'm a Texas boy myself and I've been asked to cooperate with our fine citizens here in Glen Rose to show you something about aerial warfare as it's being carried out by the American Expeditionary Force. This here's a French-made aircraft called the Spad, converted for the United States military." Captain Paul gestured with obvious affection toward the double-winged vehicle with its big solid landing wheels forward of the wing and its rounded rudder above the miniscule tail skid.

"You can see the American insignia on the side of this plane in the shape of a shooting star. This is one of our more serviceable types of fighter plane. A Spad is what I was shot down in. The fact that I could walk away from the wreckage is a tribute to the workmanship of our French allies. This particular aircraft is in use training American pilots and that's why it's here in Texas so you folks can see it this weekend instead of bein' over in France fighting the Kaiser."

The captain went on: "The AEF is using aircraft built by France including the Nieuport and the Spad and we're also using the British-built DeHavilland. The United States presently has over 40 squadrons in action and they've shot down over 600 enemy aircraft." More applause.

"I'm going to let you fine folks take a close look at this aircraft before I give you a demonstration of flying tactics. But first I'd ask that when you get near the airplane you don't touch the wings because they're covered with ducking just like your cotton sacks — I know a little about picking cotton from workin' my Daddy's farm down by Kileen. The ducking's just been stretched over spruce ribs and coated with dope, so don't go punchin' no holes in it. And this here long metal tube on the sidebody, don't touch it because it's the engine exhaust and it's hot as a fifty-cent pistol. And finally, don't forget to buy more War Bonds. Our boys Over There need your support. Thank you, folks."

The Perry family walked slowly through the milling crowd around the little biplane, peering intently at its strange wires between upper and lower wings, its wooden propeller, its oddly rickety construction.

"Wow!" said Clayborne, "have you ever seen such a big airplane, Hoyt?"

The three-year-old merely gawked at the looming contrivance and held tightly to Clayborne's hand.

"Look at that machine gun up on top," said Tom.

"Ugh," said Belle with a shudder. "Just think, Tom, the Germans got guns like that on their airplanes to shoot our boys too. Look how flimsy this contraption is. It's just sticks and ducking. And looky here, that's baling wire holding the wings together. You could knock this thing down out'f the air just chunkin' rocks at it."

"Well, it may look big to Clayborne, but it's brave men that goes up in little things like this," said Tom.

Belle whispered so no one in the crowd could hear her: "Brave or blame fools."

Captain Paul topped the afternoon's excitement by performing dogfight maneuvers against the hazy early summer sky and then diving to skim low over the exhibition field, harrowing the dust in his propwash. Clayborne watched quietly, soaking it all in, imprinting on his memory the shape of an airplane in the distance so he could later distinguish it from errant birds.

In the days and weeks after this first encounter with flying machines, Clayborne from time to time would rest leaning on his hoe or standing with the cotton sack dangling from his neck, scanning the horizon for an airship's outline and straining to discern engine drone. On rare occasions such vigils were rewarded.

The soap kettle bubbled with rendered hog fat in the August sun. Flames beneath the pot glowed smokelessly, but the outdoor soap-making workspace with its racks and pans between the rent house and the oak woods seemed suffocating. For no particular reason, the little area had always been used to make soap, even though it trapped the heat and compounded the soap maker's toil. Yet no one thought to move the arduous job to another cooler spot. Belle perspired as she stirred in the lye with a practiced hand, watching for subtle changes in color and consistency that would tell her when to stop.

"Belle, I'm going off to Partain's cane mill with a load," said Tom Perry, walking around the back of the rent house. "Clayborne's coming with me. Hoyt's going to stay with you."

Belle looked up from the soap pot. "Tell Miz Partain hello for me. And take a watermelon for them."

"A watermelon?" asked Tom.

"Now, Tom, be neighborly. I know how partial you are to watermelon, but we've got more than we can eat this year. More than we can preserve, too."

"But . . ."

"No 'buts' about it, Tom Perry. Take Miz Partain a watermelon."

Tom and Clayborne bumped westward along the dirt road toward the Partains separated by a fat green watermelon bulking between them on the wagon seat. Man and boy, Tom and Clayborne stoically prepared themselves to relinquish the prize. Their sunburned faces remained stolidly expressionless. Clayborne's freckles had tanned well in the Texas sun. He eyed the melon wistfully, hiding his regret behind a vivid polkadot mask of resignation.

"Do you think we did the right thing, son?" asked Tom.

For a moment the boy looked away from the watermelon, pondering the flat green countryside speckled with opening cotton bolls.

"How come you took such a big one, Papa?" asked the freckleface.

Tom Perry smiled.

A roadrunner flashed across in front of old Pet, its brown and white feathers catching iridescent colors in the sun.

"How's it feel to be seven years old, son?"

"Just fine."

"Not much different than bein' six?"

"Nope. Papa, what's it mean that you're running for school board?"

"Did your Grandpa Perry tell you about that?"

"Yes, sir. But I haven't seen you running around anywheres."

"Well, it doesn't mean running with your legs, it means that you're up for election against somebody else to see who gets the most votes. It's kind of like a race, so I guess that's why they call it running, like you run a race. Whoever gets the most votes gets elected. If I get the most votes, I'll be on the school board. I'll help decide how the school runs, help pick new teachers, put my signature on their paychecks, things like that."

"Is that an important job?"

"Well, I think it's important to be interested in your school, don't you?"

"Sure, Papa."

At Partain's cane mill on the long slope above Duffau Creek, the watermelon was delivered to Mr. Willie Partain with all neighborly ceremony, and the Perry's wagonload of cane was transferred to the mill.

"That's a right fine watermelon, Tom Perry," said Willie Partain. "Not even a mark on it. How'd you keep the crows from pecking it?"

"We had a lot of watermelons this year and not many crows. Guess there was just too many watermelons for the crows to get around to."

While the revolving mill ground out the juice that would cook up into "good ol' sorghum syrup," Willie Partain and Tom Perry traded news.

"You see where the legislature's going to lock up all the books in the state library about Germany?" asked Tom.

"Heard it on the telephone, forget who told me," said Willie. "Don't know who'd want to read how great the Hun is in the first place. Around here, wouldn't be any need of locking up such books, nobody'd ever ask to see them. Not with our noble boys dyin' by the thousands Over There. And did you hear about the legislature requiring ten minutes a day in every school to teach about patriotism? You'll need to know that in case you get elected to the school board."

"Hadn't heard that, Willie. I'll sure look for it in my Papa's newspapers, though. Sounds like a real good idea to me."

"And what about those Bolsheviks in Russia?" asked Willie Partain. "Threatening to bring their revolution all over the world! We ought to send the Army in there and clean them out!"

"If they're anything like the socialists in Oklahoma, they may seem like crackpots, but they're dead serious. You couldn't be more right about cleaning them out. They're worse than the Hun."

"Not likely we'll send troops to Russia with all the fighting in France, though, I guess. Anyways, how's the rheumatism since you had your teeth out?"

"You know, Willie, I think that Army doctor must of been right. Haven't had a spell at all since I come back from the dentist that last time. I still ain't used to these store-bought'n teeth, though. Makes me whistle when I try to say 's.' And they don't stay in proper. I'll have to talk to the dentist about it when I go into Hico next."

Clayborne wandered around the cane mill trying to see the working parts. He noticed that a pretty four-year-old girl — nearly five — seemed to be following him around. He thought it was probably Oretta, Maxie Partain's younger sister — Maxie was about six years older than Clayborne, and he had occasionally struck up conversations with her in church. The little girl kept staring at him. Clayborne was big for his age, and he fleetingly suspected she might be admiring his athletic physique.

Little Oretta soon walked away and out of sight. She found her mother in their house next to the cane mill. "Mama," she said, "I just saw the ugliest little boy with freckles all over him. He's out at the cane mill with his Papa."

"I hope you didn't tell him that."

"Oh, no, Mama," said Oretta. "I didn't say anything."

The girl had no idea she was talking about her future husband.

"Students at the board, turn," said Mr. Hillary Hay. "Pass to your places, be seated."

The four second grade students of Camp Branch school obeyed the orders automatically, long accustomed to the deep voice of this year's man teacher. He was a short man with dark hair, and finely molded, almost aquiline features. The children had come to like him, not so much for his flat and stuffy manner as for his wife with the flaming red hair who occasionally walked to school with him. The class had also come to like his two daughters, redheaded Blanche in first grade and raven-haired Opal in fourth grade — after watching Mr. Hay like hawks for several weeks to sniff out any sign of favoritism toward them. Mr. Hay turned out to be an evenhanded taskmaster.

Clayborne and Minnie Rucker, it seemed, were fated to compete once more for the fifteen-cent reader to be awarded at the end of this school year. No one got it the year before because of Miss McCallister's illness. But Mr. Hay didn't look like the type to get sick, and the edge of competition sharpened their grades.

There were not so many pupils in the one-room schoolhouse this November. Many stayed home for fear of the pandemic of Spanish influenza that now raced across the world sweeping millions upon millions into the arms of death. It was no ordinary influenza. It was the most horrendous disease in history, something vastly more dangerous than medical men had ever seen: at first they guessed it was not flu at all, but pneumonic plague, the medieval Black Death transmitted by breath. The first wave had hit central Texas between September twenty-eighth and October fifth. Thousands became ill and hundreds died quickly, coughing up bloody gouts of destroyed lung tissue, sometimes only forty-eight hours after the first sniffles appeared. Perversely, like the Great War that raged alongside the epidemic, Spanish influenza seemed to prefer men in the prime of life, young, strong, and healthy: they died like flies while women, children and older people tended to recover.

No one realized it then, but nothing, no war, no famine, no plague, has killed so many people in so short a time as the Spanish influenza pandemic of 1918-19 — official statistics state that 21 million died in the world during the year of the flu, but historians know that was too conservative a guess: 40 million is more like it. A staggering 510,000 American civilians died of Spanish influenza and the pneumonia it brought, and 38,000 American soldiers were felled by the diseases.

Physicians and research scientists failed to accurately identify the micro-organism responsible for the disease — medical experts to this day doubt the final diagnosis that swine flu was the actual microbe of the great epidemic — and nothing could be done about it but hope: avoid contact with the infected and stay away from crowds. Surgical masks became standard wearing apparel in the larger cities. At the first sneeze, students were sent home from schools.

General insanity became the rule of the day as war-inspired anti-German sentiment combined with influenza hysteria. The United States Public Health Service in the fall of 1918 found itself obliged to test Bayer Aspirin tablets to put down the war rumor that Bayer, producing aspirin under an originally German patent, was poisoning Americans with flu germs hidden in their tablets. As one writer remarked about the test results, "The tablets proved to be uninhabited."

Others, feeling themselves to be ultrapatriotic rather than crazy, demanded that the infection no longer be called "Spanish influenza": "Let the curse be called the German plague!" How could any disease that diabolically sought out the strongest and best be anything but a German plot? Wasn't influenza sapping the uncanny strength of the American Expeditionary Force — universally called simply the AEF — our soldiers in France? Even German commander Erich von Ludendorff called the Americans pitifully inexperienced but gallant in the face of gunfire and disease. A chaplain with the French Army noted their courage but complained that "they don't take sufficient care: they're too apt to get themselves wounded." Nor could their cocky valor bluff influenza: in one month of 1918, September, over 9,000 American soldiers in France died of the disease.

And when the United States decided to attack the new Soviet "Dictatorship of the Proletariat" and clean out the Communists, the AEF contingent sent there was ravaged by influenza on shipboard in transit. When the Americans arrived in Archangel aboard the three British troopships *Tydeus*, *Somali* and *Negoya* September 4, 1918, 175 of the 339th Infantry's 4,500 men were flat on their backs with influenza. The dreary and relentless winter of Russia and the typhus epidemic flourishing there were more daunting to the British and Americans than were the followers of Lenin.

President Wilson ultimately decided that "America would be fighting against the current of the times if we tried to prevent Russia from finding her own path in freedom. Part of the strength of the Bolshevik leaders is doubtless the threat of foreign intervention." It would have been more realistic had he admitted that 4,500 American Doughboys had little chance of controlling a Communist revolution, the worst influenza pandemic in history and the worst typhus epidemic in modern times all happening at once in one of the most amorphous and inhospitable inhabited countries of the world. By the time Wilson decided to pull the

Americans out of Russia in February, 1919, 192 Americans had died there, 112 killed in action and 72 dead of influenza.

But on this November day in 1918, at Camp Branch School, the students sat at their twin desks as far from each other as possible, believing that a few inches could make a difference to the dread infection. Mr. Hay stood and addressed the entire seven grades.

"Pupils, now that you are all seated, I wish to announce that if it is not too cold this Friday, we shall spread dinner again, so come prepared."

To spread dinner was to have the equivalent of a school picnic during noon hour. Several recitation benches would be brought from the classroom onto the playground, lined side by side to make a low table, and pupils would bring goodies such as cake and extra sausage from home. Mr. Hay had his class spread dinner often, nearly once a week, and his love for other people's boiled eggs had become a byword among his students. There was little doubt that his personal poverty had something to do with this obsession with vittles. Clayborne and his friends were also beginning to suspect that Mr. Hay's interest in grub extended beyond frequently spreading dinner: the teacher would daily send his entire seven grades outside for recess and order the wooden shutters latched over the windows. The whisper went about that Mr. Hay stayed invisibly within not to grade papers but to rifle his students' dinner pails for tidbits. Despite these private feelings about him, every pupil unquestioningly accepted Mr. Hillary Hay's authority.

Mr. Hay went on, "We shall next take our ten minutes of patriotic instruction. Who can tell me why the date November 11, 1918, is important to Americans?"

A dozen hands went up. Mr. Hay asked John Word, whose hand was not up. The embarrassed boy stood up to recite, but mumbled, "Well, that was Monday two weeks ago today. Cotton was just about picked?"

Mr. Hay was not pleased. "Minnie Rucker," he said, "perhaps you can tell John why November 11 is important."

Minnie Rucker stood and smiled and looked smug — she was a grade lower than John and she knew the answer: "That's the day the Great War was over," she said and sat down.

"Indeed it was," said Mr. Hay. "Can any of you recall what thoughts you had when you first heard about it? Mary Wilson?"

Mary stood beside her desk and said, "I remember it because I was helping my mother with the baby and the telephone rang. We listened in and it was old Mr. Blair telling everybody the war was over. What I thought was about all our soldiers in France and how glad they'd be to come home."

"Very good. Clayborne Perry?"

He stood and said, "I was out in the field with my Papa picking cotton when my Grandpa ran out and told us about it. He'd heard it over the phone, just like Mary. I thought about how there won't be any more wars, like President Wilson said that this would be the last war."

Mr. Hay said, "Very good. Do all of you recall President Wilson's saying that? He said the Great War would be the war to end all wars. Very good. Eddie Yoakum?"

And so it went. Clayborne liked this new man teacher, even though he made the students work harder than Miss McCallister had. But Clayborne liked the harder work: it seldom gave him time to think about the approaching end of the school day and the homework kept him busy evenings. Frequently, as today, he was caught by surprise when he heard Mr. Hay snap, "Class dismissed."

The lives of millions were regulated these days by fear of influenza, and Clayborne did not linger even though he wanted to play ball with his friends. The boy strapped his books on the donkey's saddle — his cart had been discarded as unnecessary for a big second grader — and quickly urged the contrary beast homeward.

As Clayborne and the donkey approached Grandpa and Grandma Blackburn's gate, the animal's temper turned sour. He bucked and pitched for no reason, but from the attitude that some donkeys have in abundance: plain meanness. Clayborne had been tossed off this critter several times since school started, always without injury, and he had learned to handle the varmint's bad spells. He thought he was going to ride this one out when the donkey twisted in midair like a main event bronco and Clayborne sailed off once more. He hit the gravel hard on all fours and gashed his right leg. The paroxysm of pain left the boy hugging his knee and wishing he could scream. When the flashing lights in his head stopped and his breath came unpenned, he gasped a few times and looked up to see the donkey contentedly munching yellow grass by the roadside ditch. "You dumb dondey," he panted, "you don't even know what you did."

Limping after the creature, Clayborne muttered, "Oh, boy, is Papa going to be mad at you. You're lucky he doesn't believe in mistreating animals or you'd get beat a good one."

The donkey made no effort to escape and Clayborne made no effort to remount. He lamely led the balky long-ear through the Blackburn's orchard, over Grandpa Perry's bridge and all the way home.

His mother saw him leading the donkey past the rent house on his way to the barn. She was alarmed and ran out on the front porch.

"What's wrong, Clayborne?" she called out.

"Oh, this donkey threw me off. It's nothin'."

"You're limping, Clayborne. That's something."

"It's just a scratch."

Pup heard his young master's voice and came out from under the house. The cat on the back stoop looked on in sublime indifference.

Tom heard the fuss from the barnyard where he was opening a sack of cottonseed feed. "What's going on?" he hollered from the barn door.

"It's nothin', Papa," replied Clayborne, limping toward the barn. His mother ran down the front porch steps and caught up with her son.

Tom walked out to meet Clayborne and told him, "Your knee's all bloody, boy. Look at that. You got yourself a deep cut there. Belle, take this boy in and peroxide that cut real good."

Pup walked around Clayborne trying to lick his wound.

"Tom, what are we going to do about that donkey? This is the fourth time he's thrown Clayborne, and I'm tired of puttin' up with it."

"We're going to sell him, that's what we're going to do about it," said Tom grimly.

"But, Papa . . ." pleaded C'ayborne.

"Don't you 'but Papa' me, son. That's a mean critter you got there. He ain't like Ol' Donkey back in Trinchera. It was a mistake I ever bought this animal from that Walker fellow. Donkey's as mean as he is. It ain't so far to school you can't walk. I'm going to take this donkey back into Hico soon as the influenza's over and sell him. And that's that."

At supper that evening the question of the donkey was forgotten as a church bell began to toll mournfully some two miles in the distance.

"Listen," said Belle. "It's the Hardshell Baptist's bell. Somebody else has died of the flu."

Tom halted his biscuit in mid-sop. It dripped gravy in his plate as he listened, as everyone, as Belle, as Clayborne and three-year-old Hoyt listened. "Law, how they ring it," Tom said quietly. "Listen how sad it is."

The sonorous tones carried on the wind, modulating and taking on the vastness of the Texas sky.

"Listen," said Tom. "Listen how they ring it. It's like that bell's talking. You can hear it say 'Dead . . . and Gone . . . Dead . . . and Gone . . . Dead . . . and Gone . . .' You can just hear it."

Clayborne listened intently, hearing the eerie words in his mind. He shivered.

Belle wept softly.

"Come on, now, Belle," said Tom. "There's nothing will bring him back."

It's just that bell ringing. It reminds me so of poor Frank. And your sister Julia, what's she going to do with those three little ol' kids now that the flu's taken Frank? I'm cryin' for them as much as for Frank."

"I know," said Tom. "I worry about her, too. Papa's helping out some and Frank's folks, the Cramfills, are helping, too. Just be glad Julia didn't get the flu, or the kids — what if Ben, or Olin or Vinita had got it? There's whole families around here have caught it and can't wait on themselves, can't even get food for themselves."

"We should have gone to the funeral, Tom."

"You know what Doc Russell over at Duffau said. Keep away from crowds. We'd a' had to go through Hico and Clairette both to get to the cemetery. Why, we don't even go next door to see my Mama and Papa, or yours, either. We don't even have them bring the mail to us. We prob'ly hadn't ought to let Clayborne go to school. There wasn't no shame in staying away. Julia understands. We talked to her a long time on the phone long distance."

"Oh, Tom, I just hate this influenza. I'll praise the Lord when it's over."

"Papa," interjected Clayborne, "can I say something?"

"Certainly, son. What is it?"

"I forgot to tell you when I came home because donkey threw me. I brought Mr. Hay's voucher home. He asked me if you would sign it and send it back. Do you have to do that because you won the school board election?"

"Yes, son. It will be a regular duty. You just make sure you don't lose those vouchers. That's Mr. Hay's money, you know. A voucher is just like money."

"I'll be careful, Papa."

The new barn was going to be a beauty. Jim Perry was tired of having only the one old barn, having to split the space half for his stock, half for the rent house — not that he begrudged the room to his son, but he'd wanted a new barn for a long time. Cotton prices had been good and he could afford it. Tom Strepey was a good carpenter and the barn was going up quickly.

"This is more fun than watching you build the bridge, Grandpa," said Clayborne as he patted Pup's head.

"You've watched just about every board go up, young feller," smiled Jim Perry, standing back and admiring the finished west gable end. "What do you think of it?"

"Best barn in Erath County, Grandpa."

"So you know about Erath County, do you?"

"Yep. Mr. Hay promoted me all the way up to fourth grade. I went from second grade to fourth in just four months. Been in fourth grade since last month, since January. We're learning the names of the state capitals and county seats and all that government stuff."

"Not bad for an eight-year-old. You keep right on learnin', grandson. Maybe you'll get to be that educated Perry your Old Grandma keeps prayin' for."

"How come you put the new barn out here, Grandpa?"

"Closer to the road, closer to my cotton patch. I'll be able to look out my front door and see the sun shinin' on it of a morning."

The boy looked out to the road and saw three trucks raising dust in the February afternoon.

"Hey, look, Grandpa. Trucks!"

"Right on time," grinned Jim Perry. "Can you beat that."

"What is it, more wood for the barn?"

"No, young 'un, that's something you've never seen before. That's oil pipe. Didn't your Pa tell you? Magnolia Oil Company's building a pipeline right across the farm. They're bringing the pipe out startin' today, just like Edwards said they would."

The three trucks chugged and rumbled up the dirt driveway to the unfinished barn and stopped in military order. The driver of the first truck jumped out with a handful of papers and walked briskly up to Jim and Clayborne Perry. Pup growled low in his throat, and Clayborne corrected him sharply, "Quiet, you Pup!"

"You Mr. Perry?" the driver asked the farmer.

"That I am."

"We're from Magnolia Petroleum Company. Got the first batch of pipe to lay out. Map here says it goes just south of your house off that way." He pointed south.

Clayborne stared at the trucks heavy laden with twenty-foot sections of 10-inch diameter steel pipe, wondering how the ends would be attached to each other to make a pipeline. Jim Perry told the driver "The survey stakes are a couple hundred feet beyond the windmill behind my blacksmith shop there. You'll see 'em. We'll walk over there on the hard ground, you follow us. Come on, Clayborne."

The driver yelled to his crew, "Follow me. And watch out for mud. We don't want to got these crates stuck again."

Like a parade of elephants the lumbering trucks circled around singlefile, following in the footsteps of the farmer and his grandson and Pup. When the truck train reached the staked-out path of the pipeline, Jim Perry waved them by and stood ready to watch the unloading process.

"Grandpa, when did they put these stakes in the ground? And that string between them?" asked Clayborne, looking westward into the setting sun.

"While you were at school last Friday."

"You mean they've been here three days?"

"Yep, strung up all the way from the west side of the farm to the east."

The boy looked eastward down the long row of stakes and gasped, "Grandpa, it's going right through our cotton fields! How are we going to make a crop this year?"

"Well, we're not, young feller, not where the pipeline's going. It'll cut a path about seventy-five feet wide all through here. It'll be torn up good. But we got other cotton patches. This farm's a big place. We'll make enough cotton, don't you worry. And Magnolia Oil is going to pay us for all the cotton we can't make, can you beat that? They're going to pay us for not growing cotton. Now, shush up, I want to watch how they do this."

The three trucks spread apart down the stake row. As they crawled slowly down the stringline, a two-man crew atop each truckbed maneuvered single steel sections of pipe onto the ground, one at a time, spacing them with practiced precision. Within a few minutes the trucks were empty and the ground was lined with a snaggletoothed picture of the continuous pipeline that would materialize as the months went by.

"Well, now, wasn't that something, boy?" asked Jim Perry.

"The whole mess of pipe laid out next to the trench just like that."

"What trench?" asked Clayborne.

"It ain't there yet. It's going to be where the string runs between the stakes. It'll be about twenty inches wide and two feet deep, just far enough down so the plows don't hit it. That's what we're going to work on, helping 'em with the pick and shovel work on that trench. You remember how we did on the bridge over yonder on Camp Branch, how we took a pick to those rocks and then dug it out with a sharpshooter" — a shovel with a long narrow blade much like a post-hole digger. "Well, we'll dig the trench while they put the pipe together. Prob'ly won't start digging 'til April, won't get finished until October. It's what, the seventeenth of February? That's eight more months."

"Where's it going to, Grandpa?"

"Well, all they told me is that it's going to Valley Mills over by Waco. I don't know if it'll hook into some other pipeline there or what. But I do know that your Pa and me is going to be hired to do a lot of their work. This ought to be a good year for us. Come on, I got to get back to the house. And you got chores to do over at the rent house."

"Is that Papa running this way?" asked the boy.

"Looks like it. Now why'd he be running like that?"

Tom Perry called from the distance. "Papa! Clayborne! Come right away!"

They ran the hundred yards that separated them, Pup dashing ahead to meet Tom, and where they met Tom breathlessly told his son, "Clayborne, it's hard news again. Your Aunt Bethel passed away an hour ago. We've got to get on over to the Blackburn's. Papa, you tell Mama and Grandma, will you?"

"Of course, son. I'll tell them. I'm powerful sorry to hear it. It's mighty hard news, it is."

"Clayborne, come on, son," Tom said. "We have to go with your mother over to see her sister this last time."

The little family of four walked together in the failing light, Clayborne holding Hoyt by the hand, their footfalls crunching the stalks of last year's grass. The eight-year-old watched his parents as they trudged to another wake, another sister's doom. Belle wept, and said to her husband, "So much dyin'. First Sallie and then Frank. And now Bethel. Oh, Tom, it's so much dyin'!"

Tom comforted her. "Well, we've felt it coming for Bethel. That TB she got from the Slaughters. So many of them Slaughter folks has died from it. And then Bethel's never got over losin' Charley. You've said so yourself. After her Charley died back in 'sixteen she's just wasted away to nothing, and it hasn't all been the TB."

"Oh, I know. But it's so sad. She's the oldest girl, my oldest sister, and I looked up to her. Always counted on her. Made me feel good just to know she was there, even after she and Charley got married. Law, how I'll miss her."

"What worries me is how your sister Cora has kept comin' over, helping Bethel, washing for her. She's like to catch the TB too, you know. And if she does, Belle, I'm not going to have you goin' to help her any more than I let you get real close to Bethel while she was sick. I won't have you comin' down with no TB."

When they knocked on the Blackburns' door, a neighbor lady let the four of them in.

"Hello, Mrs. Robinson," said Tom. "We appreciate you comin' to help our folks at a time like this."

"Aw, don't thank me none," said the wizened woman. "The Lord expects us to be of help in time of need. Your people are in the front room here. Better go console them. They're pretty broken up. You want me to take the boys out on the sleeping porch?"

"No," said Belle. "We'll take them with us. They've been through it before. They were with us at Sallie's."

The front room of the Blackburn house was crowded with neighbors come to help the bereaved family, putting away their fear of tuberculosis. Laura Blackburn wept for her dead daughter, sitting in her rocking chair with her husband Charley sitting by. Farm women from close around had taken care of all the details. They had dressed Bethel in her best church clothes and laid her out on a cooling board, much as the Hico women had prepared Sallie. The bonds of community filled the room. No stigma of the dread disease marked their sorrows. Belle's brother Clyde, the oldest of the Blackburn children, came forward and hugged his weeping sister.

"It's all right, Belle," Clyde said. "She went peacefully. There was no pain at the last, just slipped away. She's in the arms of the Lord now."

They stepped to the rocking chair where Belle's mother sat shrouded in grief. "Mama," Belle said. "I'm so sorry. We all loved her so much."

"Oh, child!" Laura Blackburn cried. "Two of you gone. Sallie first, then Bethel. Sallie was only twenty-six and Bethel only thirty-two. I'm so afraid for the rest of you girls, for Cora and Leona and you. Especially Cora since she's been taking care of Bethel."

"Now, Mama, don't you be afraid for me. I'm like Old Grandma Perry, I'm going to live to be a hundred. Don't fear for me."

"You're a good child, Belle, a good child," sobbed the mother.

"Papa," said Clyde. "We'd best make arrangements for the casket."

Laura dissolved into bitter tears.

Charley Blackburn held his arm around her shoulder and said to his oldest child, "I'll go into Hico first thing in the morning and pick one up at Driscoll's."

"Now, Papa'" said Clyde, "don't you go payin' any more than fifty dollars. I can get the same casket where I work at the Elkins' store in Duffau for forty dollars."

"I'll see to it, son."

Now Tom and Belle and Clayborne and Hoyt went to the cooling board to view Auntie Bethel. The pitiful body of the woman looked drawn and old beyond her years. The release of death had not erased the ravages of tuberculosis or the heartache etched on her features, the years of pain and longing for her dead mate. Belle looked into her face.

"Poor Bethel. She looks so tired, so old. Tom, she wanted so to join Charley Slaughter. She loved him so fierce. Now she's with him."

Charley Blackburn went into Hico the next morning and hauled the fifty-dollar casket eight miles home in his wagon. The undertaker came that afternoon with a glass-enclosed, rubber-tired hearse drawn by two great white horses. He charged five dollars for the team and ten dollars for the hearse to make the trip to Hico cemetery where Sallie had been brought only months before. The procession this time included automobiles interspersed among the wagons and buggies and horseback riders. The horses were too slow for the cars and overheated radiators popped off as they went eastward up the long troublesome hill overlooking the town. The ceremony at graveside was mercifully brief. The second Blackburn daughter was laid to everlasting rest. At the edge of the cemetery a solitary scissor-tailed flycatcher hovered over a clump of dark cedars, its salmon pink underwings flashing and its plaintive cry *ka-quee* filling the endless space of the Grand Prairie. Goodbye, Bethel.

Spring came to Texas late that year, alternating warm sunny days with pale overcasts and sounding showers. Life at the rent house settled into a routine of plowing and planting part of the day and working on the Magnolia Oil pipeline the rest. Local farmers had the choice of working at piece rates, a dollar per twenty-foot section — a good man could dig six or seven sections a day in cultivated ground — or on day rates, $4.50 a day in hardpan or rock. That was big money to a poor Texas farmer. Skilled workers from Magnolia Oil were sent out to join the pipe, wrap it in tar paper, and tar it on blocks next to the progressing trench. When a two- or three-hundred-foot section of completed pipe was ready to bury, a large crane was assigned to lift the line and lay it in the trench. The hired locals then covered it over. Clayborne enjoyed watching the crane most of all. And so spring came and went.

There were no crises to deal with and only one major change: Belle's discovery that she was once again "in the family way," due in December. Clayborne was growing into a good field hand at home, but found himself struggling at school near the end of the term. "Papa," he would say to Tom, "there's lots of words I can't pronounce in the fourth grade reader." He showed his father arithmetic problems Mr. Hay had assigned from sixth and seventh grade level materials. And with a certain sense of youthful irony, the boy realized that he actually missed competing with Minnie Rucker. He didn't care about winning the prize book this year. His attention was riveted on simply learning the textbook's unfamiliar polysyllables and compound words.

Tom became concerned and met with Hillary Hay. "Fourth grade is too hard for my boy," he told the teacher. "The work you're giving him is too hard."

"That's the only way to get kids to work hard, Mr. Perry. You have to make the work challenging, push them. It's the only way." Clayborne stayed in fourth grade. When school was out in April, the boy did not win the fifteen-cent reader. He didn't even notice that Minnie Rucker had not won it either. A few weeks after school was out Clayborne was not unhappy to hear that Mr. Hay had taken a position at another school for the next academic year.

The great event of the summer was a rat killing at Grandpa Blackburn's barn. Cats have always been the farmer's first line of defense against rodent infestation, and they make a fairly efficient rodent patrol. But every few years on Texas farms they needed reinforcements. In the Grand Prairie, those reinforcements came in the form of a rat killing.

At Grandpa Blackburn's, the rat killing began as a simple gathering of all the grown men in the neighborhood, Tom and Jim Perry, Jim Cooper and Charley Blackburn himself — all armed with .22 caliber rifles and accompanied by their dogs — and as many youngsters as cared to participate, which was normally all of the older boys, but today was only Clayborne. Once they were assembled at Charley's farmhouse and lubricated with steaming cups of Laura Blackburn's coffee, the men advanced to the barn and opened every door possible. Then they lined up in front of the corn crib.

In most Texas barns, the corn crib usually took the form not so much of a structure into which corn stalks might be placed for the cattle, but of an open pile up against a barn wall, and so it was with Charley Blackburn's corn crib. He had brought corn stalks in from the field — after harvest, of course, for the people got the roasting ears and the livestock got the stalks — and laid them against the middle wall of his barn. The cows and calves rummaged around among the stalks at their leisure, and as the pile grew year to year, the local rat population found it a perfect site for their nests. Thus, every few years the corn crib had to be cleaned out and the rats along with it.

When the line of armed men with dogs at their side had taken their places — remorselessly calculating the likely escape routes of alarmed rats and making sure no human stood in the line of fire — the top layer of corn stalks was shoveled off, usually by the youngsters in attendance. Clayborne, of course, was assigned to shovel duty.

The first shovel strikes left the corn crib as quiet as a church — no stirring, no scurrying. But when the top foot or two had been sorted into a new pile near the big open west-facing doors, the rustle of little feet became distinctly audible down among the stalks. The dogs wiggled in place beside their masters, antsy to see some action. Clayborne tossed another shovel full of old stalks to the new pile and — panic — the first rats broke and ran.

Clayborne quickly stepped back among the men.

Crack! Crack! The high pitched report of .22 long rifle cartridges blasted through the barn. Two rats bounced high in the dust, skewered by the deadeye shots of waiting farmers.

"That's two," said Charley Blackburn. "Clayborne, let's dig us up some more varmints."

Clayborne dug. Mouldering corn stalks flew. Half a dozen rats scampered from their invaded nests, heading out the big west doors.

Crack! Crack! Crack!

"Only got one," yelled Charley Blackburn. "Get the dogs on 'em."

Pup and Jim Cooper's two mongrels broke from the line, chasing the retreating rats out the door in a flurry of flying dirt and scrambling paws digging into the earthy barn floor. With deep throaty growls each dog intercepted his fleeing quarry within seconds, savaging the rodents in quick and bloody death. It was all over in less than a minute.

The three dogs stood in the settling dust, heads low over their vanquished prey, awaiting further instructions.

Clayborne shoveled the last of the corn stalks into the new pile. A final rat, guardian of the nest, stood exposed on the bare floor. He raised up on his hind feet like a kangaroo, backing into the wall and baring his teeth in defiance. The dogs ran toward him.

"No!" shouted Charley Blackburn, sidling warily between the rat and the dogs. "Hold 'em off!"

Clayborne and Jim Cooper barked orders to their dogs. "Down! Back, Pup!"

"This is your king rat," whispered Charley Blackburn hoarsely. "Don't want him biting your animals. No tellin' what he's got. Might have the hydrophobia. Shoot him, Tom."

Tom reloaded his single shot rifle, pushed the bolt shut and took aim. Crack! The rat turned a flip in the air and lay kicking on the floor, pure hatred shining out of his dying eyes.

Charley Blackburn surveyed his cleaned out corn crib. "Well, sir, looks like a good job. A real good job. Thank ye kindly, gentlemen."

He looked dispassionately at the expiring rat at the wall. "You know," he said, "a rat's got as much meanness in him as the Devil himself. Good riddance."

When the first sweet potatoes came ripe in September, the annual ritual began.

"Dig farther off, Clayborne," said Tom Perry. "This hole's got to be ten feet square, big enough for a wagon-load of sweet potatoes."

"And don't forget about the turnips," added Belle, who sat in the shade of the barn doing nothing in one of her rare moments of true relaxation.

"Now am I digging right, Papa?" asked the boy, peering at his father for approval.

"That's about right, son. You remember last year over t'other side of the barn how we dug our potato hole."

"Yessir, I remember. It was about knee deep. And we put oat straw on the bottom and laid all the sweet potatoes and turnips on it."

"Yep," said Tom, "and covered the whole mess with corn stalks and cane and buried it with the dirt we dug out. Well, that's what we're makin' here, another sweet potato hole."

This crude method of preserving root foods was sufficiently effective to keep sweet potatoes from September to February or March.

"What's wrong with the sweet potato hole on the other side of the barn?" the boy asked.

"Gonna change the animal lots around, son. Now that your Grandpa Perry's finished his new barn and we don't both have to work out of this one, we got it all to ourselves. We can run a couple more cattle and hogs, and the new cow lot'll cover up the old sweet potato hole."

"Papa, did you see Hoyt tryin' to milk the cow this morning?"

"No, son," said Tom. "He's only four years old. He can't milk a cow."

"I know, but he kept pestering me to milk the cow, so I let him try. At first he couldn't get anything out at all, and I thought he'd hurt the cow. But he finally squoze out a little bit and decided he'd try to shoot it in the cat's mouth like you do sometimes." It was common farm practice to feed the cats a little dish of fresh milk and occasionally to squirt it directly from the udder into a happy cat's mouth.

Belle sat up, smiling. "Did the cat get any milk, son?" she asked.

"Everywhere except in his mouth," Clayborne laughed. "Pretty soon old Kitty just got up and walked away. She got more from lickin' her fur afterwards than she got from Hoyt."

The Great War had passed into history, but its turbulence had not. Governor Will P. Hobby in 1919 vetoed the appropriation for the German department of the University of Texas. His only comment was that it would promote purer Americanism. A state historian noted another symptom of war aftermath: "Influential and esteemed" citizens of a central Texas town flogged six of their neighbors who declined to join the American Red Cross. A newspaper editor in a nearby community endorsed the action, remarking that "whipping may convert some, while others are beyond conversion and should be shot." The devouring grace of superpatriotism tended to get out of hand.

The defeat of Germany, however, had turned a new page in history. The triumph of democracy swept away the old order and ushered in a new era. Soldiers coming home found themselves absorbed easily into American industry. A decade of boom was on the horizon and the first rays of its dawn streaked the Grand Prairie when the early season cotton prices of 1919 were posted.

"Tom! Tom!" hollered Jim Perry as he stomped into the cotton patch. "Have you seen what cotton's going for in Hico?"

"No, Papa," yelled Tom across the snowy white bolls that crammed his field. "This is my first load I'm picking right now."

"You won't believe it! It's forty cents a pound!"

Tom got up from his knees and took the cotton sack strap from around his neck. "Forty cents!" He looked in his picking bag and then at his father. Before he could think he jumped in the air with a joyous "Ya-hoo!" He danced around his father between the rows and then stopped abruptly, slightly embarrassed at his display. "Forty cents?" he asked with a grin.

"That's two hundred fifty dollars for a good solid bale, son. And look at all this cotton you got this year. I figured from my first load that you and me are going to make a third to a half bale per acre. That's more'n double what we usually make. You know what that means, don't you?"

Tom knew. He had carefully husbanded his resources for three years now. A good crop this year would enable him to buy some land of his own. This was the best crop he had seen in his life and the highest prices. His dream was about to come true. It was in his grasp.

Tom and Jim Perry stood looking at each other and smiling for some time. Tom bowed his head a little and finally said quietly, "Thank the Lord."

Jim clapped him on the shoulder and grinned at him. "First time I ever heard you pray in front of anybody, son."

"Well, I guess it is, Papa."

September blended into October. The Grand Prairie made a tremendous cotton crop and the three gins of Hico couldn't handle it all fast enough. They found themselves faced with a welcome problem: they had to hire three shifts of workmen, laboring night and day against the press of wagon after wagon streaming in from the surrounding farms. The gins never stopped. Outside their gates farmers lined up for half a mile and more, considering themselves lucky to bring in a load one afternoon and have it ginned off by the same time next day.

Tom had hauled load after load into Hico by mid-October and his fields were not yet half-picked. He was feeling particularly good that Friday afternoon when Pet pulled the wagon into line at Barber's gin, got number 172 chalked on the side of his wagon and pulled up beside a neighbor from Dude Flat.

"'Afternoon, Tom," called Jesse Arnold from his wagon seat.

"Hello, there, Jesse," Tom responded. "Say, this is twice so far this season I've got here right behind you. Have you been checkin' up on my loads just so's you could beat me to the gin?"

"Aw, Tom, I been so busy this year I ain't had time to check up on my own loads."

"It is a bodacious good season. And looks like we're going to be here all night again."

"Yep, might just as well relax. We ain't goin' anywheres for a spell." Arnold dismounted his wagon and strode over to Tom's, rubbing Pet's flank as he passed by. He stood waiting for Tom to come down from his wagon and asked, "And how is the good wife these days, Mister Perry?"

"She's comin' along just fine," said Tom, stepping to the ground and leaning against his wagon's sideboards. "She still picks a little cotton."

"When's that new youngster supposed to be here?"

"Right after hog killing time, prob'ly early December, Doc says. Yep. Really looking forward to it. Say, Jesse, you bring your tarp along? Looks like a norther blowing up. Think I'll put my jacket on."

Both men peered into the darkening north sky behind them. An immense wall of blue cloud high above the prairie slowly and majestically swallowed the light.

"Dad rat it, Tom, that's just what I was afraid of. But I come prepared. Got myself a wagon sheet and my wool jacket to put over my coveralls. Got my supper for tonight and my breakfast and dinner for tomorrow, too."

"Me too. Didn't bring a newspaper this time, though. I guess I'm just goin' to have to talk to you, Jesse."

The two men stood shifting their weight from one foot to the other, dressed in jumper and jacket. It was scant protection against the wintry bluster that began to raise the dust around them.

"What you want to talk about, Jesse?" asked Tom.

"How about religion? That's always good for a long talk."

"No, we talked that one out last time. Wouldn't be nothin' left to argue about."

"Let's talk about Democrats and Republicans again, Tom," said Jesse Arnold. "I want to hear that part about higher cotton prices when there's a Republican in office. Wilson's still president, you know, and I ain't ever seen cotton prices like this year."

"But the Republicans control the Senate, Jesse, don't forget that."

"I can see this is going to be a good one."

Indeed it was. Their conversation carried on in waves, drifting away from politics to the cotton market, lapsing into moments of good-natured silence, then surging again into the details of their families, their farm animals, and their implements. They both complained that hired cotton picking was going for four dollars a hundred — four times normal — when they could get anyone to pick at all this busy season. All the while the great blue cloud moved overhead. Aching cold fell upon them at sundown. They rigged a wagon sheet as a windbreak under Tom's wagon and sat in its shelter on the chill ground. At supper time Tom and Jesse ate quietly from their cold syrup buckets and later retired to their separate wagons: they had talked themselves out and decided to turn in early.

"It's a bad one tonight," said Jesse Arnold from his wagon bed. "Better dig down under the cotton, Tom."

Tom took the advice and burrowed into the linty mass of cotton in his wagon bed. No matter where he turned or how he wrapped the canvas wagon sheet around him, he still felt shivering cold. He hoped that Pet would be safe against this frigid arctic air come down from Canada. He had given her plenty of feed. Before he dozed off to fitful sleep that night, he once more mulled over the plan he had settled on for becoming a land owner. Even though he would be able to afford to buy property after a few more loads, he would not move immediately to a farm of his own. Perhaps he would move to another rent house for his growing family next year, but he would take the money from this year's crop and buy a forty or fifty acre spread nearby. Instead of living on it, he would rent it out for a year or two, supplementing his own farm income with the rent. Then he would be able to afford another fifty acre spread — if luck was with him, adjoining his first property. A few years' rent from both these holdings would give him enough to fall back on no matter what might happen. Then it would be time to move the family to their own land and farm it themselves. Satisfaction oozed from his pores, a solid, gratifying sensation. He relished it. He deliberately called back the harsh memories of Colorado and Oklahoma, his return home in failure and shame.

Vindicated, he was vindicated. The failure was now all wiped out. He was about to achieve his ambition, he thought as he drifted off. It was sweet, he dreamed, so sweet.

By the time his cotton was ginned off the next afternoon and he had been paid handsomely for the bale it made, Tom had begun to sniffle. No warming sun had come to the Texas sky that Saturday morning and the shuddering norther still stung the open land. Tom was coughing and sneezing by the time he passed Camp Branch School on his way home.

Sunday morning Clayborne sat on his bed wondering why the family had not gone to church. His mother had made breakfast and brought it to his father who lay wheezing in the bed by the far wall of the large front room. Tom had not eaten anything or spoken all morning and it was nearly noon. The boy was worried, and he carefully listened to his mother as she picked up the telephone to make a call.

"Clara, is that you on the line?" she said into the mouthpiece. "Clara, this is Belle Perry. Are you on an important call right now? Oh, it's you Clara's talking to, Miz Malone. You don't say? Land sakes! You had to pay forty dollars for a pair of high top shoes? I knew prices was sky high, but that beats all. No, Miz Malone, I hate to disturb the two of you on your social call, but my Tom has taken sick with a bad chest cold, and I need to call Doctor Durham in Hico. Would you please? It won't take a minute, then you can get right back on the line."

Belle cranked the telephone handle one long ring to summon the Duffau operator. "Hello, Miz Jenkins, this is Belle Perry. Would you ring up Dr. Durham in Hico for me please? No, it's Tom. He's got a bad cold and I think the Doctor should come see him. Thank you, Miz Jenkins. I'll wait. Hello, is this Doctor Durham's home? Oh, hello, Miz Durham, this is Belle Perry, Tom's wife. Is the doctor back from church yet? Can I talk to him?

"Doctor, yes, it's Belle Perry. I'm feeling fine. It's Tom. He slept out overnight waiting at the gin in Hico and he's come down with a terrible cold. He's burning up with fever and he's been coughing something awful. I'm afraid he might have the influenza. No, I know it's been over for months, but I'd feel better if you come took a look at him anyhow. No, he's flat on his back. He couldn't even get up to go to church or pick today and we still have a lot of cotton in the fields. No, we don't have a thermometer. Yes, he's sweating a lot. No, he hasn't been eating. All right, we'll look for you this afternoon. Goodbye, Doctor. Clara? You and Miz Malone can go right on, now, I'm all through. Yes, I'm worried about Tom. And that's awful about those forty dollar shoes. Say hello to the family for me. Bye-bye."

Dr. Charles Durham arrived late that afternoon in his light trap buggy pulled by the bay mare.

"Hello, there, Mrs. Perry," said the doctor as he was let in the front door. "And hello to you Master Clayborne and young Hoyt. I understand your father is a bit under the weather today."

"Yes, sir," answered Clayborne, uncertain how to address a physician. He stood in awe of the man.

The doctor took a seat in the cane-bottom chair beside Tom's sickbed, and went through his usual procedure of taking temperature, examining mouth, eyes, nose and ears, then listened to his chest and back for rales in the lung. In a few minutes he spoke quietly to Tom and Belle, so that Clayborne could barely hear.

"This is a very sick men, Mrs. Perry. He has a very bad chest cold and I want you to give him two tablespoons of this medicine every two hours, even through the night. Give him plenty of fluids, water, soup. Feed him as much as he'll eat and keep him in bed. I don't like that high temperature he has. I think I should come back tomorrow to see if it's come down any. And whatever you do, don't let him get up and try to work. I know there's cotton in the fields. But we don't want this to turn into pneumonia."

Dr. Durham returned on Monday afternoon and again on Tuesday. Belle had been up with Tom all night for three nights now. She was exhausted. Tom's fever had not ebbed by Tuesday afternoon. It was a bad sign. Belle and the children were asked to leave the doctor alone with his patient on that dreary Tuesday. When Charles Durham, M.D., departed he seemed grave and preoccupied.

That night Clayborne lay awake, worrying about his father, unable to sleep. He could hear his Papa's congested breathing on the other side of the dark room. He could hear Hoyt breathing quietly in the bed next to him. Then he heard voices.

"Belle," said Tom in a rasping whisper, "I've got to talk to you now that the boys are asleep."

A sense of dread caught at Clayborne's gut. *They don't know I'm awake,* he thought.

"Dr. Durham says the pneumonia is in both of my lungs, Belle." Silence and darkness.

"You know what double pneumonia means, don't you, Belle?"

"I think so, Tom," came the tremulous answer.

"It means that once you got double pneumonia you can't get well."

"Dear God, Tom, what are you saying?"

"Dr. Durham says I'm not going to get well."

"Not going to get well? You'll stay sick?"

"You don't stay sick with double pneumonia for long, Belle. Do I have to spell it out for you?"

Muffled racking sobs. Clayborne realized, *He's trying to tell Mom he's going to die.*

"Belle, you need to know some things, so pay close attention. You can

cry later. I haven't got much time.   With the cotton from this year and
our savings we've got about nine hundred dollars in the Hico National
Bank. Make it last as long as you can. I'm sure your folks and mine will
help raise the boys. You hear?"

"I hear, Tom," came the anguished whisper.

"Bury me in my blue serge suit. Have Brother Green speak over me.
Tell him to keep it short, because he gets a little windy. Get a wood coffin
and not one of them fancy caskets. Put me in Hico cemetery and don't
have one of them glass-window hearses carry me up there like your Papa
did with Bethel. That cost five dollars. Have Papa take me up in the
wagon. You're going to need all the money you can get. Don't spend it on
no funeral. I'm sorry to leave you like this with the new baby a'comin' in
December. I know it'll be hard. You'll manage, Belle. You're a strong
woman."

After a brief silence, Tom said to the ceiling, "There goes all my plans.
I'm losing it all. And I was so close. So close."

If there was more, Clayborne did not hear it. His heart broke and the
hot tears would not stay back. He buried his face in his pillow, laboring to
keep his sobs from being heard.

I can't let them know I'm awake.

He had turned nine years old only two months ago. Soon he would have
to be the man of the house. How could he do it?

*I'll have to pick the rest of the cotton by myself. I'll have to drive the wagon into
Hico. How will I know if they're paying me enough?*

His Papa, his dear father was dying. How he loved his father, how he
hated the idea of losing him forever.

*There's too much dying. Auntie Sallie, Uncle Frank, Auntie Bethel. Not
Papa, too. Please, God. I'll work hard, I'll be good, I'll do anything. Please,
God. Don't let my father die. Please.*

When the yellow Grand Prairie dawn touched the high streaked
eastern clouds, Clayborne's pillow was still drenched with grief.

-8-

RIPENING SEASON

H E worked the rows in the warm afternoon, scarcely able to see over the highest cotton bolls. The cotton sack dragged behind him in the crunchy rich black dirt, its rough canvas tube bigger than his husky young frame. He could see back across the two hundred yards north to the rent house where his father lay fading abed and his mother stood hovering by. The unpainted gray frame house seemed little and distant and inconsequential. Pup wagged along slowly behind the boy, now wallowing in the hot dirt, now dreaming under cotton stems, tongue hanging out.

Rehearsing his plight to himself, Clayborne picked the linty bolls and drilled a new reality into his own mind. He heard his boy voice say: *I'm nine years old. I'm the man of the house now, Mama. I'll take care of you and Hoyt and the new baby when it gets here. Don't you worry, you hear?*

No good. The sobs would not stay down. Once again, for the hundredth time today, he found himself groping blindly into the rough stalks for his next handful of cotton fiber. Pup sat beside him, understanding only the passions and hurt and anger and joy that drive the human heart, not grasping the complexity, the thought, the awareness of mortality that curse and bless our lives, but cocking his head in sympathy anyway. Chagrin in his heart, Clayborne straightened up stiffly, determined not to surrender to his pain, not to wipe his eyes lest any casual observer spy his softness. By sheer force of will alone he would see through, pierce these unworthy tears, view the bleary world sharply. In a pig's eye. New salt grief gushed mockingly, blinding him more and layering atop the crust of hours.

241

Papa's going to die. Help me, God.

And so he went a progress down the rows, picking and crying, picking and crying, with only Pup to hear his snuffling sorrow.

I love you, Papa. Don't die.

He had picked ninety pounds a day for two days now, two days since he had heard the fateful secret night whispers of his father's destiny. This wasn't real. Oh, the cotton and the sheltering oaks and the nurturing farm, even the mind-absorbing sky, were real enough. But not death, not heavenly death. There had to be a way out of it.

From habit he stopped for a moment and looked from horizon to horizon for the tiny black dot of an airplane, any airplane, straining to hear the helical whir of propellers. No magic craft appeared to rescue him or his father. And no God came to enwrap and comfort and heal. Just a little breeze to make miniature dust devils in the rows.

I'm alone. All alone.

Weariness and misery sapped his body. He stumbled. He felt light-headed and tenuous, almost as if he were nothing but baseless space. For a second he could feel the wild prairie wind running vagabond through the desolate canyons of his spirit. He moved his right hand slowly over his chest, feeling the frightened breathing through rough overalls, sliding his hand up his shoulder and down his left arm, gripping his own wrist to make sure it was still there. He looked around uncertainly. The empty plains offered no solace: Chalk Mountain to the north and the hilly Cross Timbers to the west had exhausted millennia watching the comings and goings of mere living creatures down here on Dude Flat. Implacable time shone from the rocks, from the dirt, from the sky, capacious, unconcerned with another human death. He was a tiny boy in immensity. He felt, but could not have said, what men and women before him had confronted in extremity: We each die alone, and that itself is a bond between us.

God, don't take my Papa away. Please.

It was Old Grandma who finally broke his ordeal that languid October afternoon.

"They got you out working all by yourself again, do they, child?"

Surprise and relief colored his voice. "Oh, it's you, Old Grandma. I didn't hear you comin'. Yesterday I saw you steppin' off of Grandpa's porch."

Pup sniffed Old Grandma's feet.

"You was just too busy pickin today, that's all," said Elizabeth Glasgow Perry, pretending not to see the tears on Clayborne's cheeks, the anguish in his eyes.

"Mama couldn't find any hired hands to help. That's why I'm pickin' alone. Did you come to help me pick again?"

"Brought you some grub, young 'un. Here, you take that cotton sack off a minute. Stop workin' and eat some."

"What did you bring me, Old Grandma?"

"It's cake I got in here," she said, opening the dinner basket. "Had some blinky milk in the house. It was on the turn, would 'a been clabber by tomorrow. Still makes good cake, though. So I made you some yellow cake here, young fellow. You eat it. It's larrupin' good. Brought you some cool water, too. Nope, nothin' for you, Pup. Go catch a rabbit."

"Thank you, Old Grandma," said Clayborne, unwrapping the cloth cover. "I'm ready for some cake. I was gettin' plumb wore out."

Old Grandma had brought enough for both of them and they ate their cake in congenial silence. After feeding and watering her great-grandson, Old Grandma helped him on with the cotton sack and remained in the field with him, picking cotton and helping fill his sack.

"I sure like havin' you with me, Old Grandma," said the boy.

"You just like my yellow cake, young man. You don't fool me none."

That evening at the supper table Tom was absent once more. He had grown too weak to get out of bed.

"Old Grandma helped me pick again today, Mama," the boy said over his ham and potatoes.

"I'm glad for you, son," said Belle.

"I saw Dr. Durham come again today, too" ventured the boy, looking away to hide the knowledge in his eyes.

"Oh, he'll be comin' every day 'til your Papa gets well, son," Belle said gripping the seat of her chair unseen, as if her effort could hold back the truth. "He's a good doctor."

"Yes, Ma'am," is all Clayborne could muster.

The telephone rang for the third time in less than half an hour. It was Grandpa Perry's ring, two short, two long. Belle said, "Clayborne, that's your Grandpa's ring. There's been an awful lot of calling tonight. You're about done with supper, you go take a listen while I make sure Hoyt finishes up, see if anything's going on we hadn't ought to know about."

The boy obediently got up, tiptoeing out of the kitchen and through the living room-bedroom where his father lay motionless. Clayborne saw that his Papa's eyes were open. The face was pasty, daubed with a deathly pallor. Tom smiled feebly at his boy. Clayborne smiled back, then expressionlessly picked up the earpiece and held it to his ear, trying to listen and not to feel.

In an exaggerated stage whisper that he hoped would not disturb his father, Clayborne called, "Mama, I can't hear any talking or anything."

Tom said in a weak voice, "The ground wire's prob'ly not makin' contact, son. It's been dry lately. You go pour a dipper of water on the ground wire outside and you'll be able to hear. You go on now."

Clayborne dreaded to see his father make such a fearful effort speaking a few simple words, but he went quickly and did as he was instructed. With the task accomplished and the empty dipper still dripping in his hands, he came back through the front door and listened again to the telephone.

"It worked, Papa," he whispered, covering the mouthpiece with his hand. Clayborne listened in utter concentration now, absorbing the eavesdropped conversation as half a dozen other locals were doing. Belle came in holding a well-fed Hoyt by the hand — the expectant mother could no longer pick him up easily — and sat to wait for the recounting. After a few minutes of intent listening, Clayborne replaced the earpiece and began the traditional rural ritual of announcing the telephone's word:

"Well, it was Mr. Ford down by Brittain's Chapel. He was calling Grandpa Perry to talk about a pair of mules he bought. Then in a while he started talking about Papa bein' so sick and all, and not bein' able to get the cotton in. Said he's called all the neighbors and asked each family to send one person over here next Saturday for a free day's picking. Wanted to know if Grandpa would drive our wagon to the gin once it's full. Said he figured there was about twenty people going to show up Saturday and prob'ly pick two wagon loads or so. Then he talked about cotton prices being so high this year, just like you told me about, Papa."

Belle said in a wavering voice, "Why that's a fine neighborly thing for Mr. Ford to do, askin' folks to help us. Just a fine neighborly thing." A tear escaped her control.

Tom spoke with great effort. "It'll sure help, son. They'll have most of our field picked before I'm well enough to get in the last of it."

They maintained their pretense. No one spoke the fatal words.

Saturday the hands came from all directions. They showed up early in the morning and picked all day, two wagon loads amounting to about three thousand pounds. Belle fed and watered the volunteers as best she could, but many had brought their own necessaries. The cotton picked this Saturday would add nearly five hundred dollars to Tom and Belle's bank account. It would be sorely needed.

Sunday morning Dr. Durham came to examine Tom. Clayborne sat in the kitchen near the door, cocking his ear to glean every word, fearing the worst, breathing shallower and shallower, as if his breath could capture hope and hold it.

"Tom, this may not mean anything, but one of your lungs is cleared up some," said the doctor. "Your fever's still high, but you're a little better now. If things keep going this way. . . Well, I don't mean to give you any false hope. Let's just wait and see. Mrs. Perry, you keep Tom dosed up on this medication and I'll see you again tomorrow."

The boy leaned against the kitchen wall, wild with hope, striving with himself to keep from demanding that the Almighty keep his father alive.

God, are you answering my prayers? Are you, God?

Monday morning Clayborne went out to the green and brown field. He marvelled at the cotton that had been picked by twenty sweating men in a day. Whole rows had been cleaned, only leaf-trash left in the dirt and spiders barricading the withered stems with their tiny cables. But then he saw the remainder, nearly eight acres left unpicked, four or five bales, a thousand dollars worth of cotton.

I'll never be able to pick all that.

He wasn't. Early in November, gentle autumn rains came murmuring to quench the summer's drought. The unpicked cotton rotted in the field. A thousand precious dollars mouldered in the splashing mud. Clayborne did not despair for it: his father was alive. The doctor had come out every day for more than two weeks now. There was little more for him to do. Tom was now under Belle's care.

Within another few days Tom Perry was up and around. He recuperated slowly, slowly. But he recuperated. He was able to do light chores when Clayborne began school in mid-month.

One Saturday in late November Tom told his family at the breakfast table: "I'm going into town today, and Clayborne, I want you to help hitch the buggy and come with me. It's time to pay the doctor for pullin' me through the pneumonia."

At 10:30 they drove down the rutted dirt road, watching the tangled branches of newly bare trees fringe their way, enjoying the brisk air and bright sunshine. An hour later, when they pulled up in front of Conner's Drug Store in Hico, Clayborne jumped down from the buggy and hitched Pet to the rail. He followed his father up the long flight of stairs to Dr. Durham's office. The boy opened the frosted glass door and stepped in after his father. Dr. Durham stood in the far corner at an old-fashioned clerk's high desk, sorting papers. He looked around and smiled. "Tom Perry," he said warmly. "I'm just so pleased to see you."

"We made a pretty good cotton crop this year, Dr. Durham," said Tom. He stood awkwardly still for a time. "I figured that since you kept me around to put it in the bank the least I could do was come pay your bill. I got a check here for fifteen trips out to my place at five dollars a trip, all comes to seventy-five dollars." Tom looked down at the check, then placed it on the reception desk in front of him. "We'd be honored, too, if you'd come out to take care of the birthing when my wife's time comes."

Tom looked up again at the aging doctor for a moment, reaching for words beyond his power, a faint lip-lift token to his effort. Then he said simply, "And thank you besides."

"Tommy, you're a tough customer and a good man," said the doctor. "To be quite honest, I did not expect you ever to climb the stairs up to my office again. But you've made it, sir. You've made it. You're going to live."

Thank you, God.

Even tears could not express the fulness of his joy.

Thank you.

"I'm sorry, Clayborne, but you'll just have to stay home from school for a week," said Mrs. Manda Hollon. "If you went into the Cooper's house, you've been exposed to rosiola and we simply can't risk a outbreak at school."

"But Mrs. Hollon, I was just in there a few minutes. I didn't even go close to little Jay," pleaded Clayborne Perry, nervously twisting his coverall strap, feeling like disease had polluted his garments.

"It doesn't matter," the teacher said. "The germs were all around when you went in. Even a few seconds could have exposed you. Now you go on home and don't get near the rest of the class. If you haven't come down with rosiola by next Monday you can come back to school." She turned to her class. "Pupils, if anyone else has been exposed to rosiola over the weekend, put your hand up."

Clayborne stood by the teacher's desk looking forlornly out at his schoolmates, all of whom studiously kept their hands out of sight. He felt betrayed.

"Third grade, if any of you have been close to Clayborne Perry this morning, put your hand up."

The whole third grade, Otis Ship, Clifford Mackey, Nancy Campbell and Minnie Rucker, didn't stir a finger. The Rucker girl's hands were firmly planted in her lap, prim and prissy. Clayborne gave her an especially plaintive look. He had finally managed to pass her in spelling headmarks just a few days ago. But now, if he had to stay out of school a whole week and she got to stay in . . . He wished disgustedly that he had held a close conference with her on some matter of importance this morning.

It's just not fair, he thought as he crept out the big door and down the school's wooden front steps. He dawdled on the large flat rock that formed the lowest step, slowly buttoning his coat against the raw December chill, squirming to hold his books secure under one arm at the same time.

Glancing back at the schoolhouse and feeling shunned, the lad trudged up the fence-bridge and down to the road homeward.

Stupid ol' rosiola. Mrs. Hollon's just not fair.

Yet he knew she had his interests at heart, even though his feelings might have been hurt by her curt dismissal. She had realized that fourth grade work was simply too hard and put him back in third grade, hadn't she? Now he was doing well in all his subjects, wasn't he? And he was back in the same grade as Minnie Rucker and fired up with competitive zeal, wasn't he? And Mrs. Hollon really was concerned for his health, wasn't she? Oh, well.

The outcast found a discarded tin can in the road and kicked it in ten foot relays for nearly half a mile before losing interest in it.

After stomping over Grandpa Perry's Camp Branch bridge just to hear his footsteps rattle the boards, he decided to visit Old Grandma before going home with the news of his week's exile from school. Then he saw his Grandpa out by a large liveoak behind the little blacksmith shed where he routinely performed small mechanical miracles.

"I thought you'd sold all your cotton, Grandpa," the boy called.

Jim Perry looked up from tucking a wagon sheet around several large bales of cotton. "What are you doin' out of school? Are you playin' hookey, young son?"

"Mrs. Hollon sent me home 'cause I might have the rosiola."

"From visiting the Cooper's t'other night?"

"Yep. Got to stay home for a week."

"You don't look none too happy about it."

Clayborne didn't want to explain about Minnie Rucker and the headmarks. "Nothin' to do in the winter," he hedged. "But why's this cotton here? Couldn't you sell all of yours?"

"Oh, I sold it all, my boy. These are some extra bales I bought me at the gin."

"I don't get it. We grow cotton to *sell*. How come you *bought* cotton?"

"Prices, grandson, prices!" the old farmer grinned through his big walrus mustache. "When I saw cotton going for forty cents a pound, I just knew that prices was going to keep goin' up. I bought these three bales at forty cents a pound. Give it a few weeks and we'll see fifty-cent, sixty-cent cotton for sure. Then I'll cart this stuff back into Hico and unload it for a handsome profit. How about that, young man?"

"What if the price goes down?"

"That's your Pa talking. He's extra careful after you folks starved out up in Colorado. No disrespect meant, boy. But I've watched the cotton market real close this year. Cotton and everything else is goin' sky high since the war was over. Prices been goin' up so steady they can't come down. You'll see."

"I hope so, Grandpa. Is Old Grandma in the house?"

"Nope, up at your place helping your Ma take care of the new baby. How do you like your sister by now?"

"Just fine," Clayborne smiled. "Nadine cries a lot like Hoyt did, but I like her just the same. Hoyt thinks she's a toy and wants to play with her. But I help Mama keep him entertained so she can take care of the baby. I'm a big help."

"Oh, I'll bet you are."

Up at the rent house Clayborne found the living room-bedroom a veritable hubbub. Nadine and Hoyt both filled the air with seamless howls and wailing while Old Grandma indomitably shouted over the racket in her piping voice, comforting Hoyt in her arms and reciting an old family recipe designed to cure infant colic. Belle paced back and forth with the new baby, trying to convince Old Grandma that any colic cure

involving a teaspoon of whiskey and molasses would not go a generation
further in this Perry family.

The boy stood astonished in the front doorway, uncertain whether he
should simply go back out and reenter through the kitchen, but his father
spotted him from the reading chair by the heater.

"How come you're out of school, son?" he mouthed, not seriously
attempting to be heard. He motioned his son toward the kitchen.

Clayborne came in and shut the door behind him. "I had to come home
because I might have the rosiola," he ventured in the absolute noise.

His mother and Old Grandma nodded at him as if they were not
terribly concerned and kept up their animated conversation within the
pandemonium. Clayborne followed his Dad to the kitchen table.

When they were seated as far from the din as space afforded, Tom
asked, "Did you say you might have the rosiola?"

"Yes, sir."

"From visiting the Coopers the other night?"

"Yes, sir. Mrs. Hollon says I have to stay home a week. Do I, Papa?"

"Well, of course, son, if Mrs. Hollon says so. She's the teacher."

"Oh."

"Well, don't get too down in the mouth. If you're going to be home a
week, you can help with the chores. I still don't have my strength back.
And you can look over our accounts with me. We've got some important
decisions to make."

"We do?"

"Sure do. Look here." Tom spread out the papers he had been trying to
read. "You know we made a good crop this year, even with my
pneumonia. See here in the ledger book, we have over fourteen hundred
dollars in the bank, including savings, and that's after paying toll on our
cotton to your Grandpa. Son, that's enough we can live the year and buy
some land of our own." Tom sat back to watch the reaction.

"We're going to have our own farm?" the boy asked wide-eyed.

"That we are."

"Oh, boy, Papa! Are we going to have our own house and everything?"

"Hold your horses, son. We have to go a step at a time."

"What do you mean?" A fresh burst of squalling from the front room
nearly obliterated his question.

"The money we have — that thousand dollars savings — isn't enough
to buy even a fifty acre farm outright, it's only about half enough. But the
bank will lend us the other half. So we can start out with fifty acres."

"But that's not enough to farm on, Papa. We farm almost two hundred
acres here on Grandpa Perry's."

"You're thinkin' like a farmer, son. Even though we're going to buy
our own land right away, we'll stay here in my Papa's rent house prob'ly
another year. We'll have to get a renter onto our own land for a few years

to pay us toll. We can stay that few years in a rent house, maybe a bigger one somewheres, and save up to buy another fifty acres right next to the first. Then we'll keep it up 'til we got a big enough place of our own to move onto, farm it ourselves."

"I get it. Then what's the decision?"

"Now, your mother and me, we've found a couple places for sale we could buy right now. One's up toward Duffau, beyond the Coopers, the other's over by Rocky, nearly to the Fouts place, and another one's about three, four miles out of Hico the other side of the church. What do you think?"

The boy pondered. "There's no gin at Duffau, and Rocky's farther off than Grandpa Perry's. The place by Hico sounds best. You wouldn't have to drive so far to the gin, or to the store, or anything."

"That's what your mother and me thought, too."

"This is more fun than bein' in school, Papa. I don't think I'll mind stayin' home for a week because of the rosiola."

And so, in the course of time just after the new year came in, Tom and Belle took the earnings from their big crop and bought the fifty-acre farm four miles out of Hico. They paid a thousand dollars cash and borrowed a thousand from Hico National Bank. Mr. John Honea, his wife and two children, rented the little spread and some adjacent land to meet their farming needs. The Tom Perry family were now landowners in the Texas soil. They were inching their way upward.

As it turned out, Clayborne stayed home for a week, did not catch rosiola and went back to school the next Monday mad as a wet hen. The world simply wasn't fair.

The year 1920 was a harbinger of great change in America, yet the Texas Grand Prairie was remarkably insulated against it. In early January the Red Menace flamed across newspaper headlines. The Denver *Post* shouted, "Soviet Revolution in U.S. Shattered as Federal Agents Jail Plot Leaders: 5,483 Radicals Are Captured in Net." Simultaneous raids were made in fifty-one cities throughout the United States to put down a planned Communist revolution. The U.S. Justice Department found completely equipped military organizations ready to establish "a soviet America." Many alien undesirables were summarily deported without trial, in full accord with the Constitutional provision in Article I, Section 9, suspending the privilege of habeas corpus in cases of rebellion when the public safety may require it. The Communists had asked for it with their Marxist revolution. Only a few intellectuals even batted an eyelash, men such as "socialist highbrow" Walter Lippmann and Max Eastman, publisher of the radical magazine *The Masses*. Tom Perry read the accounts of socialist revolution and swift federal retribution with no warmth for

Communists or their sympathizers: he agreed with many Texas newspaper editors who said hanging would have been too good for the revolutionaries.

Mid-January brought the boozeless regime of Prohibition with the implementation of the Volstead Act. The new law stated: "No person shall, on or after the date when the 18th Amendment to the Constitution of the United States goes into effect, manufacture, sell, barter, transport, import, export, deliver, furnish or possess any intoxicating liquor except as authorized in this act." Getting around the law became a national pastime. As each old-time saloon vanished, a half-dozen underground gin mills sprang up — the speakeasies — and the bootlegger and gangster became king in America.

Moonshiners installed their stills in the limestone crevices of Chalk Mountain. Glen Rose became a famous supply point for the young in search of rotgut. Treasury agents raided the area with pale caution, scouting the carved horizon for tell-tale wisps of blue smoke from the stills: the hillbillies of hooch were pretty rough old boys who supported their wives and children with the illicit joy juice. They vigorously requested privacy with shotgun and rifle, and did in a number of revenuers. The shaggy outlaws put their white lightning in syrup buckets, hid it under the back seats of their Model T Fords, and drove up and down the Grand Prairie roads with their families astride the product, peddling fifteen gallons at a time. But Prohibition didn't make much difference to Dude Flat. Erath County had always been dry. Hamilton County, including Hico, had likewise never voted for beer, despite long clamor in the towns. Almost nobody in these country parts drank in the first place, so almost nobody missed it.

Then came the vote for women with the Nineteenth Amendment. It too made few waves among the farm families of North Central Texas. The Perry women, in their own words, were "not real strong on it." They felt like maybe politics belonged to the menfolk. They didn't approve of women getting jobs. Belle Perry voted in all the elections thenceforth, but never became much of a political activist. She did, however, continue to voice her opinion firmly and with little provocation on many issues, particularly the subject of liquor.

And the new year also brought with it a strong, albeit brief, depression. The Grand Prairie, alas, was not insulated against the ebb of the dollar. Prices that had gone through the stratosphere during the Great War fell through the basement. Wages were down, merchandise was down, money was short, cotton prices plummeted. Everything changed, as if the chemical composition of living had been altered. By mid-March, Jim Perry realized that he would never live to see sixty-cent cotton, and maybe not thirty-cent cotton. Maybe not fifteen-cent cotton. Maybe not seven-cent cotton. With a sigh in the unechoing fields, he hauled his forty-cent speculative bales back to town in his lurching and banging wagon and sold them for six cents a pound.

The summer, though — ah, the Texas summer. It ignored depressions. Amid cotton-fluffy clouds and color-happy sunrises, Texas became a summer fruit filling the rind of heaven. School was out and Clayborne had gotten over the disappointment of losing the headmark contest. As he had expected, the no-rosiola episode delivered the laurels and a fifteen-cent Horatio Alger book to Minnie Rucker. But now, with the gritty black dirt baking his bare feet and the high sun radiant above, all that mattered nothing. There were baths to be taken in Camp Branch again and stars to be watched in the warm fragrant nights.

This year Clayborne started plowing with a pair of mules and really made a hand in the field. Walking behind Jack and Rhody, sometimes behind Pet and Jack, plow in tow, harness chain clanking, made him feel very grown up. He had not yet mastered the immemorial art of plowing straight lines, and his father retained the duty of planting. But the youngster could haul well enough to plow under the grass that since spring had grown up between rows "in the middles." And he was adjusting the invisible compass in his head that would one day navigate straight lines in the field. He didn't know it, but he was teaching himself to be a better than fair field hand.

Work occupied his weekdays, and the regular round of Saturdays in Hico and Sunday mornings in church took most of his weekends. But Sunday afternoons were free, free as only a Texas countryboy can know. With Eddie Yoakum from the next farm, Clayborne wandered the hackberry-canopied gullies and green dappled flats watching for stickerburrs and pursuing bumblebees. Bumblebee burrows were dug in the soft yielding dirt. The boys worried the bumblebee nests with pointed sticks and learned just how long they could torment the creatures without paying a penalty of stings.

Down the clattering stony creek beds they scrambled and ambled, stepping in the low water when scorching rocks hurt their feet, listening to woodpeckers knock on nearby oaks, and staying on the lookout for basking water moccasins. Occasionally they found a wasp nest in a bush or under a stone ledge, which always signalled war. It was much more fun than fighting bumblebees, for the skill needed to chunk rocks at nest-sized targets was more demanding, the wasps quicker to anger and gifted with a keener sense of battle. It was altogether a better game.

Some Sunday afternoons the Partain boys, Forris and Odell, would come over from Duffau Creek after church and roam the brilliant land with him. They were both of an age with Clayborne, not older like their sister Maxie or younger like their sister Oretta. In time the Partain brothers became his close friends even though they lived some five miles away, halfway between little Duffau and Hico.

Together the three boys would set out in search of after-church adventure, daring each other to eat the astringent mustang grapes that grew abundantly along roadside ditches, dreading the mouth burns they left behind, but taking the dare anyway. Once they came upon a group of six town boys, kids in their teens from Hico, out hunting quail with their fathers' shotguns. Odell, Forris and Clayborne followed in awe for hours as the young men bagged nearly a hundred birds among them. The countryboys sauntered back to the Perry place at sundown, marveling at the slaughter, wondering why anyone would deign to hunt such small quarry. Might as well shoot bluejays or whipporwills.

As often as possible, Clayborne and his friends went swimming in Duffau Creek or Camp Branch, sometimes even Little Duffau Creek near Prairie Springs, anywhere they could find a hole big enough. Here they reverted to the quenchless clarity of boyhood, needing no law laid down, as much a part of the living earth as the water they swam in. They did not go back to the dawn of man but to the dawn of boy. What they reverted to was nature, not wildness, for wildness was not in them and nature was. They fished local streams for little Texas perch and when they tired of fishing they lollygagged about the landscape annoying jackrabbits and capturing june bugs bare-handed, sticking the stratchy insects down each others' shirts.

More frequently now, Tom went into Hico Saturdays while Belle stayed home with Hoyt and Nadine. At these times, it was just Clayborne and his father, the two of them bonded together in the buggy. After selling Belle's cream and eggs, they went to Bradford's meat market for dinner. Fifteen cents bought enough barbecue for two and they ate among the common customers on wooden tables outside. Mr. Bradford gave them bread and crackers free. It was not Wiley Lynch's cafe, but the food was good and it did not remind them of anything.

Some Saturdays Clayborne saw black men coming through Hico with the drummers — travelling salesmen — in a car. They helped unload the merchandise, but wouldn't go into the stores. The black men wouldn't dare go in a cafe to eat or into a hotel to spend the night. Their fathers and grandfathers had been manumitted from one kind of slavery and they had been born into another. Vengeance would never be theirs and justice was a long time off. They stayed in the drummers' automobiles, scared to death.

On the way out of Hico one day, Tom stopped by a roadside fruit stand to buy some apples — he avoided Mr. Rainwater's candy kitchen on Second Street these days because it stood beside a sad and vacant unpainted house. The fruit merchant was a man of at least eighty summers whose harrowed old brows shaded young eyes that had taken in good times and bad. He offered apples two for a nickel, and in these lean economic times kept a supply of blemished fruit on the side at six for a nickel. "Here," he said, "are some with little old rotten spots on them, about the size of your finger." Tom took a bag of spotted apples while Clayborne looked on, grasping the nature of the bargain. It was another day in late summer that Clayborne walked there alone while his father was occupied at the mercantile and confronted the ancient fruit man. Without prologue, confident of being recognized, the boy said , "I only have a penny. I want some of those apples with rotten spots in them." The old man smiled knowingly and replied, "I'll tell you what, sonny, I'll just cut them out and give you the rotten spots for free."

"You better move up, Clayborne," Belle said to the boy dawdling over his oatmeal. "You're going to be late for school."

"Aw, Mama, I'm almost done."

"Your Papa has been out working in the barn for hours already. You're going to be a good-for-nothing today."

"It's Friday, Mama. I'm just sleepy."

"You prob'ly won't even be able to tell the teacher who's President of the United States now."

"Oh, Mama, I will too. We had that in patriotism last week. It's President Harding. I'm just sleepy, I said. Can't a fella get plumb wore out from a week in school?"

"Don't you talk back to me, young man. Just get a' goin'. I don't want you to be tardy."

"Yes, Ma'am."

"And give these scraps to Pup and the cat on your way out. And be sure to button your coat all the way up, it's real cold out today."

"Yes, Ma'am." He always had to button up when his mother was cold.

Clayborne left the food for Pup and patted the wiggly creature, his friend who shared lucid memories. The cat was nowhere in sight. Then the boy bathed his face with a frigid lick and promise at the wash bucket where a few ice crystals fringed the water's edge. He trudged out to the bridge over Camp Branch and on to Grandpa Blackburn's bleak skeleton-fingered orchard. He waved to his Grandma Blackburn as he passed her kitchen window, realizing that the January chill was colder than he had expected, just as his Mama had warned. He hunched down into his coat and kicked a few rocks in the road, just to keep warm. As he drew near the schoolhouse, he could see that the playground was empty. His mother had been right again: he was late. Was he was going to catch it for sure. This was not starting out to be a good day. Up the fence bridge, down the fence bridge. Something on the schoolhouse roof glinted against the overcast winter sky.

Flames coursed around the sheet-metal chimney boot, eating a black circle in the shingle roof. Someone inside had fed the heater too

generously against the freezing cold. Clayborne was paralysed with
fright. Vivid images of a night many years ago in Wichita Falls lived
again in his memory. The house, the one beyond the festive city park, had
been reduced to cinders in mere seconds, the images disclosed. What to
do? He stopped himself from shaking, went in the school's only door,
ignored the looks of *tardy boy, are you going to get it!* from his fellow
students, and marched straight to the teacher's desk. Mrs. Leah Arnold
— sister to last year's teacher Manda Hollon — looked up as if waiting for
some feeble excuse. Clayborne leaned over and whispered, "The school
roof is on fire, Miz Arnold. I just saw it."

Mrs. Arnold scrutinized his face. "Really?" she asked skeptically.

"Really." Clayborne answered, anxiety in his aspect.

The teacher stiffened, then quickly arose and dashed outside to see for
herself. It was true: flames shot skyward in spreading waves. "Good
heavens!" she cried, and ran back to the door. "Pupils," she called, "File
out as quickly as you can. There is a small fire on the roof and we must get
you to safety."

Children poured through the door, older ones gripping the younger by
the hand. The class gathered in an orderly group well away from the
building as Mrs. Arnold counted noses. "Is everyone here?" she asked. No
one was missing.

Now she began barking out orders like a drill sergeant: "Willie
Matson, go around back and bring the ladder up here. Farley Moore and
Russell Johnson, you go to the well and fill the bucket. Bring it here
quick. Recess monitors, line up your pupils and keep them from going
back into the schoolhouse."

Willie Matson scampered up the ladder with the jerky speed of a silent
movie, and the two bucket boys passed the water brigade-style to him on
the roof. Roof-captain Willie clambered up to the ridge, splashed water
over the flames and tossed the empty bucket to the ground for a refill.
Three bucketloads doused the exterior fire, but the Matson boy called
down, "There's still some fire in the attic, Miz Arnold."

"Russell, you're tallest." the teacher said. "Have Farley give you a
boost into the attic. If there's no smoke, you can throw water on it from
inside."

The two sixteen-year-olds cautiously entered the school building and,
seeing no smoke, stood on a desk and pushed aside the attic access panel.
"I can get it from here," said Russell Johnson. "Give me a boost up and
tell Willie to get the water."

"He's got it already," replied Farley Moore. "Here."

Three more buckets and the fire was dead out. The excitement was
over.

It had not been too bad a blaze. The boys said that gaps in an aging
chimney flue had been responsible, and most of the damage had been

confined to the underside of the shingle roof. The acrid rancor of smoke would linger for weeks, but repairs would be relatively simple and inexpensive, thanks to the fact that Clayborne Perry had been late to school this Friday in January, 1921.

After sizing up the immediate damage, Mrs. Arnold relaxed visibly, and called from the school porch, "Clayborne Perry, you come here, sir."

All his classmates were watching him, still standing in their fire-drill recess monitor lines. He did not expect a hero medal. A brief ceremony would do fine.

Mrs. Arnold leaned over and smiled, "Clayborne, do you have a written excuse for being late this morning?"

"You need enough stretching boards!" insisted Clifford Mackey.

"I've got four of them right here in the barn," said Clayborne. "All different sizes. I'm ready."

"Let's go, you guys," demanded Eddie Yoakum. "Sun's gonna come up and the 'possums will go back in their holes." They slogged out of the barn and into the starry Sunday morning before light and without breakfast. A sickle moon hung in the dark above the indistinct prairie horizon where streaked clouds harbored, faintly sun-smudged.

Dude Flat families did not attend church regularly in winter: the dirt roads became impassible quagmires under January rains and sleets. This Sunday morning the intrepid company of Mackey, Yoakum and Perry trooped not to the hard benches of religion but to seek their fortunes in opossum hides.

"That was quite a sight last Friday, you and Miz Arnold on the porch," joshed Eddie Yoakum as the three clomped through a hackberry thicket near the creek.

"Yeah," agreed Clifford Mackey. "You could jist see it on your face. You thought you was going' to get some kind of prize for spottin' the roof fire and the teacher asks you for a tardy excuse! Aw-haw!"

"Well, well, I *did* save the school!" snapped Clayborne, pushing a hackberry branch out of the way.

"Aw, come on, Clayborne, we know it. We're just hoo-rawin' ya," said the Mackey boy.

"Well, just hush up so you don't warn the 'possums," Clayborne muttered.

They were keen woodsmen already and getting steadily better and better. They knew their way in undergrowth, could tell where the fallen leaves hid slithering snakes, could find game most of the time. Stalking the little marsupial *Didelphis virginiana* was no great problem, even in broad daylight, for it was abundant in the Grand Prairie of 1921 and little given to hiding. Its chief defense in time of danger was the skilled feigning of death, so universally familiar that the popular phrase "playing 'possum," was tacked to everything from battlefield cowardice to political chicanery.

The three wood sprites sneaked loudly in the pre-dawn along the channel of Camp Branch toward their favorite 'possum pasture, a forest of persimmon trees among the shadowy blackjack and liveoaks.

"Here, Clayborne, stuff your coat pockets with good creek rocks for your nigger shooter," instructed Clifford Mackey.

So deeply had racial prejudice infused Texas vocabulary that the slingshot made from a Y-crotch stick and strips of rubber from an old inner tube had been ignominiously dubbed "nigger shooter." Yet so insidious was this racial slur that virtually none of the young men who pronounced it daily had the faintest awareness that the name implied a weapon for projecting stones at black people. To them, it was just another meaningless nickname like "Tin Lizzie" for the Model T Ford. It was an invisible festering linguistic splinter blinding the mind's eye.

"Don't pick those flat ones, Clayborne," grouched Eddie Yoakum. "Ain't you never killed a 'possum before?"

"No," he admitted. "But I went 'possum hunting with my Papa before."

"Your Papa's got a .22 rifle an' we got nigger shooters. You gotta have the right kind of rocks. Them flat ones are for skippin'. They ain't no good in a nigger shooter, they'll sail off all directions. Pick these round ones. This here's a good 'possum rock, right about this size here" — as big as a large shooter marble.

Armed with stones, the little platoon crept stealthily into the persimmon patch to ambush a 'possum. Fruits still clung to many stems, the bait that waited in fatal attraction. The dissolution of winter lay scattered everywhere under the leafless trees, branches broken in storms, trees fallen with crumbling age. The hunters stepped now between the dead and down stems on the noiseless humus where old life relinquished its nutrients for rotting and rebirth. The boys peered upward, scouting bare branches for the fat outline of a prowling 'possum against the breaking day. There it was!

"Okay, Clayborne, shoot it. We'll give you first dibs today," whispered Eddie Yoakum.

Clayborne slipped a smooth spherical stone into the leather seat joining the twin rubber thongs of his slingshot. He gripped the leather with a practiced hand, long accustomed to target shooting, moving the stone to the best "shooting spot" with his right thumb and forefinger, all the while slowly lifting the crude weapon to eye level. With the crotch-shaped stick in his left hand pulling the rubber strips taut, he held the rock near his right eye, judging distance and position, judging, judging. . . . The 'possum stirred and Clayborne let go. The missile was a blur through the branches.

"Missed!" complained Clifford Mackey. "Shoot again, quick, before he gets away."

"Possums can't run fast," reminded Eddie Yoakum.

Clayborne reloaded and shot again. Another miss. Another shot, another miss.

"Confound it, Clayborne, what's the matter with you?"

"Nothin'," he hissed defensively. "It's cold out here and I'm a little off, that's all. Heck with this nigger shooter," he said slipping the weapon into his rear overall pocket. "Ol' 'possum's still up the 'simmon tree. He's scared. I'm going to twist him out with a stick."

The boys followed as he looked around at the litter on the woods floor. Several long sticks presented themselves, some still hard and sound against the decomposing bacteria, but none with the requisite forked end.

"There's a good one," said the Mackey boy.

The long forked stick was made to order. Clayborne dragged it directly beneath the persimmon branch that the little marsupial grasped in terror. He pushed his stick up between the limbs, upward, upward, closer to the frightened animal. Now! He pressed the forked stick under the forearms of his prey. With a quick twist he twirled the opossum out of the tree and dashed him to the ground where the beast lay feigning death.

"Kill him quick," said the Mackey boy.

"Don't you hit him with a stick," warned Clayborne. "I want a good hide." He picked a hand size rock from the ground and delivered one hard blow to the opossum's skull, dispatching the beast instantly. He felt no sorrow at the death. He knew it had been a creature like him of blood, muscle, bowels, memory, but he had respected the primordial rules and rituals of hunter and hunted. It was his rightful game.

"That's a big one, and he ain't a mother 'possum with a pouch," said Clayborne, holding his quarry by the prehensile tail. "I'll get fifteen cents for that hide, betcha."

"Where you gonna get any fifteen cents a hide?" said Eddie. "Ten cents is what they pay."

"I'm gonna get it same place as you, at the poultry house in Hico," said Clayborne. "My Papa said he got fifty cents for a good hide once after the war. Fifteen cents is what they're goin' for now. You just wait. You'll see."

A little before noon they returned to Tom Perry's barn with five dead opossums. It took about two hours to properly skin and stretch a 'possum hide. The stretching boards had to be the right size and shape, about 8 to 10 inches wide and 18 inches long. In shape, a stretching board looked something like a snowshoe, with the critter's head fastened over the small pointed end and the rest of the hide stretched fur inward — toward the board — and nailed every few inches along its rounded sides and end.

"Hey, you ain't got enough stretching boards, Clayborne!" groused Clifford Mackey. "I told you."

"I said we had four," retorted Clayborne. "I didn't know we'd get five 'possums. Here, here's an old boxing plank, take the ax to it, shape it up. It don't take but a few minutes."

While the grumbling Mackey boy hacked out a new stretching board, Eddie Yoakum picked an unidentified object from his coat pocket and popped it in his mouth.

"What's that you got?" asked Clayborne.

"Stretchberries. Found 'em by the creek."

"Stretchberries? You eat those things? Ugh!" said Clifford Mackey. "They got hardly any meat on 'em."

"Got lots of juice. And I like that gum around the seeds."

"You know what my Old Grandma does with stretchberries?" said Clayborne.

"What?" the other two asked in unison.

"She boils the juice out of 'em in a pot and makes ink. The seeds got a good ink in 'em."

"Ugh!" said Clifford.

"I don't care. I like 'em," said Eddie, munching another one. "You think they call 'em stretchberries because they get ripe in the winter when you hunt 'possums and stretch their hides?"

"Naw, couldn't be," said Clayborne. "My Papa hunts 'possums all year round, stretches hides all year round. Couldn't be."

The stretched opossum hides would hang up to dry in the barn — on a wire so the rats couldn't get to them — for three weeks to a month. As the hide dried out, Clayborne would pull off the remaining fat. Just prior to shipping, the skin would be turned fur side out, removed from the stretch board and rolled up in a little package for the hide dealer.

Clayborne had been right. They got fifteen cents each for their 'possum hides at the Hico poultry house.

In January, 1921, Tom began to complain about his digestion and soreness in his mouth. The condition persisted for several weeks before he hied himself into Hico to see Dr. Durham about it. The good doctor found redness and scaling of Tom's skin, especially around the neck, white sores in his mouth, and asked whether he'd been irritable and suffering with diarrhea. Tom said he had.

"There's no doubt about it, Tom," said Dr. Durham. "It's the pellagra."

Pellagra. The shock was automatic. Pellagra. Tom recoiled from the word as from a blow. It was a disease of poverty, a disease endemic to the Southern poor especially. Its cause was unknown, but its outcome was certain: slow wasting away, progressive bodily disfigurement, mental collapse, eventual death. By some ironic twist of fate, the disease seemed to affect poor whites and blacks unequally — pellagra was virtually nonexistent among poor blacks, but seemed to seek out their white sharecropper neighbors with a vengeance.

"Can you do anything for it?" asked Tom.

"I'm going to put you on a medication, Tom. It works in many cases, but medical science has not discovered the cause of the pellagra. There are some quacks who'll tell you they can cure the pellagra, but this medication I'm prescribing for you is the best thing we know about, and it's actually only a helper. Your strength never properly returned after that bout with the pneumonia. The main thing you need is rest."

"I'm a farmer, Dr. Durham."

"I know, Tom."

The condition did not improve. Tom grew weaker by the day. Belle became alarmed by his deteriorating health and asked around about what could be done. Medical science of the official school had been tried and found wanting, and things were beginning to look desperate. Nobody could offer any help. Then one day a neighbor came by as Tom struggled to get in his early spring plowing and told him about a naturopath up at Glen Rose that had cured several people from around here of the pellagra.

Tom checked around, confirmed the story, and took a buggy trip up into the hill country of the Paluxy River to Glen Rose. Dr. Millings of the Millings Naturopathic Sanatorium confirmed Tom's pellagra and told him a two-week course of therapy and a closely supervised diet thereafter would cure him. And all for only a hundred dollars.

A hundred dollars was a small fortune to Tom Perry. But what is the price of a life? Belle did not even hesitate when he came back with the news. He would go to Dr. Millings' sanatorium right away. Jim Perry would help keep the farm going for the two weeks he'd be gone. And so he went.

The Millings Naturopathic Sanatorium at Glen Rose was a strictly room and board affair. The medical fraternity, always close to the hearts and pocketbooks of the pragmatic Texas legislature, had seen to it that State law forbade naturopaths from charging for their diagnosis and treatment. Doctors didn't want to *outlaw* naturopaths, no, no, that would be uncivilized. Doctors didn't need to — simply forbidding naturopaths from charging for their services would do the job nicely. However, naturopaths were just as full of American ingenuity and indirection as their medical adversaries, and got around the law by setting up sanatoria and charging room and board — at somewhat higher rates than Grandma Logan's up the street.

Fifty bucks a week was pretty stiff for a hospital bed and a diet of rabbit food. But Tom Perry got his rest, plenty of it. Dr. Millings' sanatorium was a wooden frame building, not unlike the regular resort hotels that studded Glen Rose, except for the large porch that completely surrounded the building. The gallery was festooned with deck chairs, where inmates sat all day and got plenty of fresh air — in early March the chill of winter had vanished except during the late evenings. The Dr. Millings diet tended heavily to whole grain cereals and green leafy vegetables, which did not particularly thrill Tom Perry. He missed his corn bread and ham, but unknown to anybody in that era — including Dr. Millings — Dr. Millings had prescribed exactly what Tom needed: the perfect pellagra cure.

As would be discovered in 1926, pellagra is caused by a deficiency of niacin and other B vitamins — a few dollars worth of 1940s vitamin pills would have alleviated the problem promptly. Corn, one of the basic grains in the Texas farmer's diet, contains almost no niacin. Unbleached wheat flour and green leafy vegetables, on the other hand, are rich in B vitamins. A perfectly healthy person can survive on the traditional poor Texas farmer's diet without contracting pellagra, but anything that disturbs the body's ability to absorb food — shock, alcoholism, digestive problems, *pneumonia* — can cancel out the diet's marginal supply of B vitamins and bring on pellagra's horror of wastage and death. Poor blacks never got pellagra because they drank "pot licker," the liquid left over after boiling their collards and mustard greens, and therefore recovered all the B vitamins that leached out into the cooking water. Poor white farmers, scorning this black habit out of racial prejudice, tossed out the pot licker — and life-saving B vitamins along with it — thus bringing down on their weary backs the scourge of pellagra.

Tom had been in Dr. Millings' sanatorium exactly a week when he had an unexpected visitor.

"There's somebody here to see you, Mr. Perry." said the attendant.

"Well, tell 'em to come on in."

"He said he wouldn't come in. He wants you to come out to the gate at the street."

"What? Consarn it. Oh, all right." Tom ambled out to the gate in the Sunday afternoon sunshine.

"Good evening," came the cheery greeting — any time after noon was commonly referred to as "evening" in rural Texas.

"Dr. Durham!" said Tom. "What are you doin' here?"

"I heard you'd come up here to this naturopath and I wanted to check up on you. Professional duty."

"Well, come on in and check up all you want."

"I can't do that, Tom. Naturopathy is not scientific. I can't lend the dignity of medical science to it by coming on their premises. But I feel it's my obligation to make sure they're not just making things worse with whatever treatment they're giving you. Now, you come let me look in your mouth, if you will."

"Why, sure, Dr. Durham," said Tom, somewhat embarrassed at being found out by the physician from whose care he had slipped away.

Dr. Charles Durham carefully scrutinized the gum tissue under Tom's dentures, "umm"ing and "uh-hmm"ing to himself. He put his tongue depressor back in his little black bag.

"Well?" asked Tom.

"You stay here, Tommy," said the doctor. "Whatever they're doing, it's working. You're getting well."

A week later Tom went home cured, took Dr. Millings' advice about his diet, and never suffered pellagra symptoms again.

The seasons turned, April brought the end of the Camp Branch school year, and Clayborne finally won the headmark contest in the fourth grade. His Horatio Alger book seemed anti-climactic, but it was the victory, the fierce pride in having won it, that counted. And now, July, 1921.

The air of summer pressed heavy on the creek bottom, redolent of hackberry and sumac. The four boys lay on rocks in the shady afternoon, fauns drowsing in the heat, trying to think of something to do.

John Fred Word, Clayborne's school seatmate, said, "We could play town ball."

"No," said Eddie Yoakum. "We played that yesterday."

Eddie's older brother Lloyd suggested, "We could hunt 'possums."

"No," said Clayborne. "'Possums are poor this time of year, too many sores under their skin. Besides, it's too hot."

Eddie Yoakum volunteered, "We could go swimming."

"No," said John Fred Word. "Water's too low. Camp Branch has nearly stopped running. Duffau Creek's got water in it but it's too far off."

"John's right," put in Lloyd Yoakum. "Even the *fishing* holes on Camp Branch are getting low."

"My Old Grandma's all upset about it, too," said Clayborne. "Her favorite spot's too low to fish."

"Is that the Grandma you were tellin' us about that wanted store-bought'n plums?" asked Eddie.

"Yeah," said Clayborne. "She's real strong on plums. She loves plums the way my Papa loves watermelon. Watermelon! That's it! Let's go up to my place and get a watermelon out of the patch!"

"Yeah, yeah!" the bunch yelled. "Watermelon! Ya-hoo!" The rebel yell had not died.

Heat or no, they ran swoopstake across the clay soil, leaping over limestone rocks, skirting thickets of grass burrs, craving watermelon, watermelon.

"We can only take one," Clayborne shouted at full gallop. "My Papa's real partial to watermelon."

When they arrived at the Perry garden there was no hesitation. Down the rows they ran, straight to the tangling vines of the watermelon patch. They panted and puffed.

"Wow, look at the size of 'em!" shouted Lloyd.

"Look at this beauty!" yelled John Word, pointing to a monster melon under the glossy green leaves, twenty pounds if it was an ounce.

"Here's the one," beamed Clayborne. "Look how dark it is. It's ripe for sure! Let's take it!"

John Word was the oldest and had his own pocket knife. He pulled out the implement and opened its business blade. Snip! The long melon rested free of its stem and lay temptingly in Clayborne's hands.

"Open it! Open it, John!"

Around the girth of the luscious green bulk slid the blade, around and back to its starting point. Snap! Clayborne broke the big watermelon open in two nearly equal halves. Disappointment wrinkled each face.

"Hey, it's only half ripe," said Eddie.

"Look, it's still got a big green rind," said John.

"There's only enough ripe in there for a couple of bites each," said Lloyd.

"Let's open another one!" arose the general clamor.

As Clayborne looked frowning at the small ripe heart of the first melon, John Word cut off another and opened it.

"It's the same! Cut another one! Come on, let's take 'em back down to the creek!"

Huggermugger, they made for Camp Branch at a dead run each with a watermelon in tow. Like stags hounded by demons they leaped the creek bank into its dry gravel streambed and set upon the fruit with gluttonous haste.

"Hey, I'll bet I can get you with this rind, Skinny," shouted chewing Eddie at his big brother.

Chomping Lloyd ducked the flying fruit and shouted "Aw-haw, you missed. Gimme a chunk of that other rind, John. I'm gonna show this little squirt how to throw watermelon!"

It degenerated into an instant food fight. Broken bits of green rind sailed through the air, plastering the rocks, while four greedy boys stuffed their faces with the scant ripe melon heart. Two whole melons were pulverized and a third started amid howls of laughter and tossing of green fruit. Into their merriment stepped Tom Perry, face aghast.

The boys stopped dead in their tracks as if hit all at once by a baseball bat.

Tom Perry stood very quietly surveying the littered pieces of his prized watermelon. When he spoke, he only said, "I think you boys ought to go on home now."

They backed off slowly and cautiously until well out of fist swinging range, then broke and scattered for home.

Tom was left standing in silent confrontation with Clayborne. "Son," he said slowly and with perfect control. "That's a right sorry waste you fellows done here. Another two or three weeks the family could've had some fine melon here, some fine melon. I think you and me have to go have a talk in the barn."

Clayborne had suffered few "talks in the barn" during his life, and this time he knew he'd asked for it. The walk back to the barn was a marching agony of anticipation. When they were inside where no prying eyes could see, Tom slipped the leather belt from his jeans and instructed, "Son, take your britches down and lean over the bale of hay there."

Clayborne did as he was told, heart fluttering and pulse ragged, fear and humiliation turning his guts to jelly.

"You're going to get three whacks for this, boy. One for each melon you wasted. You ready now?"

He gritted his teeth, hating to speak the words. "Yes, Papa."

Whack! Whack! *Whack!*

Each blow was worse than stinging bees, squirting tears between his tightly shut eyelids. Yet the moral pain was far worse, the scar on his conscience much deeper. The welts would go down and vanish in a day. The lesson would last a lifetime. Tom left his son to cry himself out in the barn and never said another word about the incident. Clayborne never had another talk in the barn with his Papa.

Come October the Perry family — Tom and Belle, Clayborne, and Hoyt and Nadine — moved to a new rent house just over half a mile south and west of their old one. It was practically a straight line from the familiar rent house on Jim Perry's farm to his Camp Branch bridge to the new rent house on Grandpa Blackburn's land. The house was bigger and there was more land to work and it was not out of the neighborhood. The Honeas paid their cotton toll to the Perrys, and Tom felt like a regular landowner, magisterial and rich, even though he had paid a larger sum in toll to his father. Cotton prices had been weak, but most farmers managed to scrape through.

Clayborne returned to Camp Branch school in November, entering fifth grade, instructed by a young girl serving her first year out in the teaching world, Miss Rilla Loden. Eddie Yoakum and Clifford Mackey returned, along with Grace Rich and Minnie Rucker, making five with Clayborne for the fifth grade. Clayborne was once again assigned John Fred Word as seatmate, even through Word was a grade ahead.

They were salad days, the winter and spring, succulent with learning's sweet green growth. Clayborne came to terms with Minnie Rucker, for the headmark contest did not involve fifth graders, who were expected to thirst for knowledge of their own accord. In Clifford and Eddie and John, Clayborne had baseball teammates and companions for fishing and 'possum hunting expeditions.

By March of 1922, the postwar economic slump was over and a decade of boom started in earnest. Clayborne entered the spirit of the thing by saving fifty cents — no mean achievement — and buying a long-coveted baseball glove from a school friend who no longer wanted it. He regarded his purchase as a milestone in his young life: he owned a real gen-you-wine baseball glove. Owned it.

It was about that time when Clayborne's happy-go-lucky Uncle Leonard returned from Colorado with his wife Verna and their three children, eight-year-old Otis, Lucille, age six, and Grace — Grace had been born at Trinidad during May, 1919 and was now nearly three years old. They took up residence in Jim Perry's rent house, the same rent house vacated the previous fall by Tom Perry's family. Leonard had proven up their Colorado land claim, had even received a regular U.S. land patent number on it, 754684, registered all proper in Book 207, Page 470, in the Patent Deed Records of Las Animas County, Colorado. The grant is still in the court house at Trinidad. The Leonard Perry family came home in triumph — well, almost triumph: it was still impossible to farm the Colorado claim, patented or not, and they had not yet found a buyer willing to invest three or four thousand dollars in marginal range land. So they had only the cash Leonard had earned in the stygian coal mines of Pueblo and a hankering after a willing buyer for their land. Hail-fellow-well-met Leonard figured he could find one for sure somewhere around Hico, and he turned out to be right. He sold the homestead a few months later for $4,000.00, which was a great deal of money — one of Old Grandma's people, W. L. Glasgow of Hamilton County, Texas, had bought it, registered on a Warranty Deed filed at 1:30 P.M., July 31, 1922, by Las Animas County Recorder J. B. Romero. At any rate, Leonard's return with his family was welcomed with festivity and joy, and the community of Dude Flat was richer by a few more strong backs and strong wills.

In April school was out again and there was spring planting to do. Clayborne was eleven years old and made a regular hand in the fields, learning to plow straight rows and once more turning over the grass in the middles. The larger cotton patches by the new rent house were more fun, even if more work: the novelty of it, no doubt.

With his boy through another year of school and the family fortunes rising despite the short depression, Tom made a serious decision: he would buy their first automobile. He took his money into town, a hundred sixty-five dollars of it, and came back with a 1920 Chevrolet Four-Ninety. One wag said the numbers were a code meaning the car spent four days on the road and ninety in the repair shop, but the two-seat touring car held up nicely. Now the Perrys went to church in comfort, weather and roads permitting, as five in the Moon buggy had come to crowd it to the limit.

"Where have you been? I've called and called," fretted Belle.

"I was over to the Partains to see Forris and Odell," said Clayborne sheepishly, rubbing his toes along the edge of the front-room braided rug.

"Why, that's five miles away. What were you doin' there?"

"Nothin'."

"That's a long ways to go to do nothin'. Gadding around, layin' out with those Partain boys, just wastin' time. Sometimes I don't know what I'm going to do with you, Clayborne Perry."

"Yes, Ma'am," the boy said, wondering why his mother was so upset. "Did I miss supper?"

"No, you didn't miss supper. We need to tell you something very important. We need you to be a big help."

"Sure, Mama. But what? Crops are all laid by," said Clayborne. "Nothin' left to plow, nothin' left to hoe."

"It's not that kind of help. Your father and me and Hoyt and Nadine are going off with your Grandpa Blackburn to visit your Auntie Cora over at Miles by San Angelo. She's come down with the TB from takin' care of Bethel so long. She's terrible sick and we feel like we have to go out and see her. It might be the last time, God forbid." She choked back the tears.

Tom walked in from the barn and saw Belle talking with the boy. "You tellin' him about goin' to see Cora?" he asked.

"Yes, Tom. You come tell him the chores he's got to do."

"Son, we're going to be gone a week or so in your Grandpa Blackburn's Model T. We want you to come feed the hogs and horses and cows every day, milk the cows regular and help out your Grandma Blackburn."

"She's not going to see Auntie Cora?" Clayborne asked.

"No, she says she just couldn't stand it, seein' another one of her babies dyin'. She's right broke up about it. Now you help her feed her stock and milk her cows. She's got eight of 'em, so it's going to take a while. And you help her separate the cream . . ."

"Oh, boy, do I get to crank the cream separator?"

"I'm sure you do, son. And you keep Grandma company at night. She needs a man to protect her."

Clayborne stood a little straighter, smiling inwardly to be considered a man. "When should I go over there?"

"We'll be leaving tomorrow morning bright and early. You go over now and tell Grandma that she can count on you. They've got a cot put up for you out on the sleeping porch."

Belle interjected, "And you wave to Miz Cooper when you go by their place. It's right impolite to just walk by like a lump."

"Yes, Ma'am."

Three days later he had settled into the new routine. The animals were all taken care of and supper was done. Summer twilight gently faded and the supper dishes were drying on the drain board when Laura Blackburn brought the coal oil lamp into the large front room.

"That was a fine supper, Grandma. You cook real good," said Clayborne, patting his stomach in satisfaction. "Just like Mama."

"Why, thank you, young man," said the old lady, carefully placing the lamp on her reading table. "You talk just like a gentleman. I told your Grandpa you'd come out fine. He's fussed for years about me and your Grandma Perry and Old Grandma spoiling you, giving you too much attention. But you're turning into a regular gentleman, just like I thought you would." She sat in her rocker and put on her glasses, then leaned over to the boy saying, "And I'll let you in on a little secret."

"What's that?"

"Grandma cooks just like Mama because Grandma taught Mama everything she knows about cooking."

"I never thought of it that way," the youngster said. "I guess it's the other way around, huh?"

"Guess so," smiled Grandma Blackburn.

"Can I go catch lightning bugs a while?"

It must have been three in the morning when Clayborne was awakened by the sounds of shoveling. He lay propped on one elbow in his cot for a moment, trying to decide whether he was dreaming. Then, restless stamping about of horse hooves, skulking low whispers, more sounds of shoveling. It was no dream. Clayborne jumped out of bed, clad only in his summer short pants, and crept through the living room to the big front door with the glass pane and curtain. He opened it a crack, taking care to make no sound. He cautiously stepped out. It was a moonless night with only the stars and airglow to illumine the scene. He peered into thick gloom, slowly making out the form of the big barn where the shoveling sounds seemed to come from.

A horse stamped the ground and Clayborne looked leftward toward the road with a start. Three horses were tied to the gate, one of them pure white.

I've seen that white before.

Bulging cotton picking sacks had been slung across the backs of the two sorrels. The outline of Grandpa Blackburn's empty car garage across the road stood out behind the horses.

It can't be cotton in those sacks. Cotton's not even starting to open yet.
Muffled conversation came from the barn, rasping and hateful.

"You carry this one out, you lazy brat."

"Carry it yourself, you jackleg trash. I took the first one! You ain't no real kin to me. You can't push me around."

"By God, your Pappy'll slap your sassy mouth when I tell him!"

"Shush up, the both of you. You'll wake up the Coopers down the road. This is the last sack. I'll carry it. Now shut up, and let's git goin'."

Three vague forms moved from the barn door to the open yard.

It's the Foster brothers and their cousin Mike! They're stealing Grandpa's corn right out of his barn! They must have seen the garage empty and thought nobody was here.

The large burly leader heaved a full cotton sack over the back of his white mount. Several ears of corn tumbled to the ground.

"Pick 'em up, little brat," he snarled, kicking out at the young man beside him.

"You ain't gonna tell my Pap anything, I'm gonna tell him about you, that's what!" came the heated reply.

What should I do? Grandpa's shotgun is up on the wall. I've shot Papa's shotgun once or twice. But there's only two shells and three men. And I don't want to wake up Grandma and scare her. I'm supposed to protect her. I wish I knew what to do!

The thieves solved his problem for him: they rode off into the starry night with four big sacks of Grandpa's corn, leaving Clayborne standing on the front porch feeling utterly helpless. When he told the night's events to his Grandma Blackburn next morning, he did not feel like much of a protector. The Foster brothers and their cousin got away clean and were never held to answer for stealing the Blackburns' corn.

"Do you think he'll come today?" asked Eddie Yoakum.

"Yeah," said Clayborne. "He'll come. He's like Brother Green at the Baptist Church. He comes on the third Saturday of the month. Sometimes more often."

"Are you sure?" asked Clifford Mackey.

"I'm sure."

The three of them promenaded as usual through the streets of Hico this Saturday afternoon, a bottle of red "sody water" in one hand and an ice cream cone in the other — ten cents worth of weekly treat. Their parents were busy with marketing and welcomed the opportunity to get the kids out of their hair. The boys' conversation rambled as aimlessly as their bare footsteps, bubbled as effervescently as their soft drinks.

"My Papa used to sell sody water up in Ringling, Oklahoma," said Clayborne proudly, holding up his red pop bottle.

"Bet he didn't," said Clifford.

"Bet he did," said Clayborne. "Took the wagon every other day, went out to the oil fields, sold sody water and ice cream to the workers."

"My Dad sold magazines for a while," said Eddie.

"My Dad's always been a rent farmer, and I mean a good rent farmer, too. So there," said Clifford.

"My sister's got poison ivy," said Eddie.

"Wow, really?" asked Clifford.

"Yeah, and boy, does it itch!" said Eddie. "I have to keep away from her or I'll get it, too. Lannie got it under the trees in back of our barn. Mama's put soda on it, all kinds of stuff, it just keeps itchin'. Dad says she'll have a dickens of a time getting rid of it."

They turned another corner in their rounds of the city.

"The Strepeys came to church in a car last week, did you see?" said Clifford.

"I saw," said Eddie. "My Dad's going to get a car after we make the cotton crop and move to the new place."

"What new place?" Clayborne and Clifford demanded.

"We're movin' out to McCamey, over by Odessa in West Texas, didn't I tell you?"

"No, you didn't tell us," said Clayborne. "That means you won't be in school next November."

"Sure I will," said Eddie. "Over at McCamey."

"I mean at Camp Branch."

"Clayborne," said Clifford, hesitatingly. "I guess I didn't tell you either. Me and my family is movin' too, over here by Hico, after the cotton's ginned off, I think. Maybe over to Cranfills Gap."

"Both of you movin'?" said Clayborne, abashed.

"'Fraid so. My Dad needs a bigger place to rent."

"Mine too."

"Well, mine does too," said Clayborne. "But we're movin' to the rent house on my Grandpa Blackburn's place, not off somewheres like a bunch of gypsies. I'll still be at Camp Branch school. What'll I do without you guys? Who'll I play town ball with?"

"We'll come visit," offered Clifford.

"Sure," said Clayborne sourly. "That's what Nancy Campbell said when she moved away last year. She didn't show up once."

"It's not our fault, Clayborne."

"Oh, I know. Hey, look at the clock on the jeweler's store. It's almost time for the 3:15 from Waco! He's going to be here soon! Last one to the station's a rotten egg."

They ran ragtag-bobtailed through the streets, countryboys having their big day in the city. At the Katy railroad depot they looked up to the stationmaster's black chalkboard to see if their train was on time. It was.

They scrambled up the street alongside the tracks for nearly two blocks, then sat beneath a lone tree, a big old oak that had survived the citification of Hico.

"Watch out for the bull nettles down there, Eddie," Clayborne warned of slender treacherous stalks growing by the gnarled oak roots. "You'll be as bad off as your sister."

"I'm going to listen to the track to see if the train's coming," said Clifford.

"Me, too," said Eddie.

Instantly they all had their heads flat to the warm steel rail, ears glued to the smooth crown.

"Quit movin' around, Clayborne," complained Clifford. "You're making the rails click and I can't hear nothin'."

"I am not," said Clayborne.

"Shush up, you two," said Eddie.

They shushed.

"Nothing," said Clifford. "It's not comin' yet. Semaphore's yellow, though."

"I hear it! I hear it!" whispered Clayborne. "Listen."

Very faintly, very faintly down the rails came the regular beat of a fast train, the impact of wheels on every rail-joint transmitted as a vibrant hum through the metal body of the tracks.

"Must be just about to the near bridge over the Bosque," said Eddie.

"It'll come around the curve in thirty seconds, watch," said Clayborne. "I'm gonna put a penny on the track before the engineer can see me. I'm gonna get me a long skwushed penny."

"It'll make the train go off the tracks, my Mama says," cautioned Eddie.

"That's silly," said Clifford. "Otis Ship has a skwushed penny he put on the tracks right here, and it didn't make the train jump the tracks. How could a teensy little penny do that?"

"I'm warnin' you," bristled Eddie.

Clayborne put his penny dead center on the near rail.

Waiting. Looking. Listening.

"There is it! The 3:15 from Waco!" shouted Clifford.

The black locomotive rounded the Bosque curve into Hico like a Texas typhoon, shaking the trees, rattling the dishes in the houses, oiling the sky with gray smoke, screaming steel wheels against steel rails, old steam whistle mourning the vast land it had tamed, calling good people to their timetables, calling honest misfits to go back on the bum. Rural Eden was ravished once more, the hulking machine clattered into Hico's garden, and those who noticed at all smiled in approval.

Clayborne retrieved his long thin flat penny, devoid of any remaining imprint, lying in the rock ballast several yards from its starting point on the rail. It was hot to the touch. The boys quickly ran across the street and took their places around the edge of a stone building opposite the train's two passenger cars, peeking out at disembarking riders from Waco.

"I don't see him," said Eddie Yoakum.

"He'll come," said Clayborne.

"He's not on this train," said Clifford Mackey.

"He gets off last," said Clayborne. "There he is!"

He carried a little black bag much like a physician's, he walked tall and slim on the far side of the street, wearing a black derby hat, a turned-around Roman collar and a long black frock robe. The Catholic priest walked directly uphill north from the railway station, pressing on to the tiny solitary Catholic church serving Hico. To the three boys hiding in espionage, he might as well have been from Mars.

"What do you think he is?" whispered Eddie.

"I don't know," said Clayborne in a muted voice. "He goes into that little church four blocks up. I've watched him."

"Maybe he's a Church of Christ," suggested Clifford. "My Pa says there's Church of Christs live around here."

"No, I've seen Church of Christs. They're just people," said Clayborne.

"Maybe he's a Methodist king, or something," offered Eddie.

"No, I've seen Methodists, too," said Clayborne. "We go to the Methodist church lots of times when the Baptist preacher don't come. The Methodist preacher don't look like that."

"Is he a person? Maybe he's God," said the Mackey boy.

"That's dumb, Clifford. Why would God ride the train? He can be anywhere He wants," said Eddie.

"If God can be anywhere He wants, He can be on the train, too," rebutted Clifford.

"That's still dumb. God don't need no suitcase," snorted Eddie.

Eddie's logic seemed irrefutable, and the three spies looked on in puzzlement as the priest drew away up the low hill, gradually lost in the car and wagon traffic.

The conductor's singsong call from the station rang in their ears: "Waco, Hico, Cisco. 'Board."

"Hey, it's a Mother Goose rhyme," said Clifford Mackey.

"WAY-ko, HIGH-ko, SIS-ko," imitated Clayborne Perry.

"I've never been to Cisco," said Eddie Yoakum.

"Me neither."

"Me neither."

"Are you guys really moving away?"

"Yep."

"Yep."

It was Miss Rilla Loden again. Sixth grade for Clayborne would have the same old teacher as fifth. But now the class within many classes had been struck a terrible blow: Eddie and Clifford were gone. Only Minnie Rucker and Grace Rich stood up with him when Miss Loden called the sixth grade to the board. Other grades seemed to be suffering, too. The one-room, seven-grade schoolhouse was losing students to the irregular movements of the rent farmers it served. At least John Fred Word still sat beside him. But this day was getting too long.

"And last, what did *you* do while school was out, Clayborne Perry?" purred Miss Loden in teacherly manner.

Like all the others had done before him, he stood up in the afternoon to recite, wondering how to answer such a strange question. Like most of the boys, he said, "I just did regular stuff, Ma'am. Helped with the plowin', picked cotton, you know."

"Now, Clayborne," cajoled Miss Loden, "something unusual must have happened during all those months. You heard how Mary Wilson took a trip to Galveston. Didn't anything different happen to you over the summer recess?"

"Well," he drawled, thinking hard. "We went into Hico a lot. Is that something?"

"Go on . . ."

"Well, we went in my Papa's new car. That's different. It used to take us a couple of hours with Pet pullin' the buggy, but it only takes half an hour to go eight miles in the car. We don't have to leave the farm at ten in the morning any more. We can leave at one in the afternoon and stay until four. The cream and egg money is enough to buy five gallons of gasoline, and that lasts a whole week. And we buy some candy at Mr. Rainwater's kitchen when we come home, too. Oh, and I saw a picture show! I saw two of them!"

"Oh, that's wonderful, Clayborne. What shows did you see?"

"You mean the names of the pictures? I forgot. But one of them was a cowboy show about train robbers and William S. Hart finally caught the bad guys. It was real good, lots of fistfights. The other one was spooky, about this man that's good most of the time, but he drinks this awful stuff and turns into an ugly bad man that kills lots of women. I think his name was Mister Hide and Seek."

"That was *Dr. Jekyll and Mister Hyde*, Clayborne, and John Barrymore played both parts, the good man and the bad man. It was an excellent dramatization, and you older children should see it if you can," gushed Miss Loden.

Clayborne tossed a shrug at her evaluation and went on: "The part I liked best was the Keystone Kops. They do everything wrong, especially the fat guy that drives the police car on the train tracks. They're funny! But I saw city kids in Hico that get a dime to see the show every Saturday, not just once in a while like us country kids."

Miss Loden chose to ignore his resentment of small town affluence.

"You see, Clayborne," she said, "you did do some unusual things over the summer recess. Can you think of one last thing before school's out today? Some trip you made? Perhaps a short trip?"

"Well, we did go camping over to Glen Rose just after my birthday. We stayed in one of those little cabins by the Paluxy River for a week, sat in the mineral springs and drank five kinds of mineral water from a rock fountain by the Court House. My Mama and Papa liked it, but I think it stinks like rotten eggs."

"Did you do anything different while you were there?"

Clayborne's eyes lit up as he remembered. "Oh, yeah! I know a good one! It's the part about how my Papa treats me like a regular partner in the farm now that I'm almost growed up," he bragged.

"We went off to Glen Rose on a Saturday, and I didn't have a good shirt for Sunday School next morning. When I turned twelve — that was just before we went to Glen Rose — my Papa told the bank to take checks on me, so while we were over at the mineral springs, Papa sent me to buy a new shirt at the store all by myself. I wrote them a check on Hico National Bank for that shirt. They took it and didn't even ask any questions, and we were twenty-five miles from home. So I can write my own checks now and my Papa tells me everything about the family's money."

He sat down, noticing the envy on the faces of other farm boys whose fathers had not extended them the same trust.

"Thank you, Clayborne. Now you have your homework assignments, pupils, and I expect you to get in the homework habit again this year. Every night there will be work to do, and I expect it back first thing in the morning. This year there will be no more stories about your dogs eating the homework."

There were no stories that year about dogfood homework, only the daily routine of those ordinary things that went up together to make living in rural Texas. In mid-December the school once more put on its traditional Christmas pageant, attended almost exclusively by mothers and siblings — fathers avoided the poetic recitations and choral extravaganzas whenever possible — and April, 1923, brought Clayborne through the sixth grade with flying colors.

The big long-eared jackrabbit sat motionless in the August dust, hiding behind a tall hummock of fading Johnson grass. Clayborne held the heavy double-barrelled twelve-gauge shotgun propped on the cornerpost of the yard fence. He judged the distance. *Twenty-five yards. In range.* He peered with both eyes open down the barrel to the sights, aiming carefully. He slowly squeezed the trigger . . .

Blam! The jackrabbit turned a final flip in the air and lay dead as a doornail in the dirt. Clayborne went to inspect his handiwork and saw not a quiver. He immediately set to work with his prized pocketknife gutting and skinning the jackrabbit.

"What're you shootin', son?" called Tom Perry from inside the barn.

"Big old jackrabbit, Papa! First critter I ever got with your shotgun. Got him with one shot. Killed him right out!"

"That's good, son. You remember everything I told you about huntin'? Not to shoot when there's somebody in front of you. And what I told you about not lettin' your game suffer. And you put the shotgun on safety before you laid it against the fencepost?"

"Yes, sir. I know what you said about people gettin' killed pickin' up guns that weren't on safety."

"That's fine." Tom looked out of the barn. "What're you doin' with that jackrabbit?"

"Skinnin' 'im. Gonna stretch his hide and sell it."

"Save your strength, boy. Ain't nobody buys jackrabbit hides."

"Nobody?" the boy asked disappointed.

"Nobody. 'Possum hides bring you a dime, fifteen cent these days. But nobody'll give you a penny for a jackrabbit."

Nothing daunted, Clayborne skinned the animal anyway, and later marched across Camp Branch past his old rent house and knocked on the Jim Perry's front door. Old Grandma answered, as he had hoped.

"Well, come on in, young 'un," she grinned. "Don't see you as often as before you moved to the Blackburn place. It's a fur piece to walk next door, ain't it?"

"It's not far, Old Grandma. I've just been busy plowin' and hoein'."

"Well, if you come over to tell me President Harding's died and that Coolidge feller is president, I already know. Jimmy heard it on that newfangled Crosby radio of his. Just heard about it along about dinnertime this morning. I sure don't like that radio thing, got to put those little round pieces on your ears. Gives you a headache. And Jimmy spent thirty-two dollars on it and that battery thing what makes it run. Sure don't like it."

"I hadn't heard about President Harding. That's too bad. But that's not why I'm here. I come over to tell you about my great accomplishment."

"Did you learn to drive your Pap's car again?" she cackled.

"No," he said scornfully. "You can't forget how to drive a car. And besides, I learned to drive when school was out back in April. I drive the family to church when Papa has to stay home and work."

"Oh, my, what a big man you've become," mocked Old Grandma.

"Well, I have," the boy insisted. "Today I killed my first jackrabbit with Papa's twelve-gauge. What do you think about that?"

"Well, now, I do declare!" said the old lady with genuine admiration. "Kilt your first varmint with a shotgun, did ye? Now that *is* getting growed up. Law, I recollect back in Alabamy, my John would go out and kill a brace of swamp rabbits jist about every day. Good eatin'."

"Swamp rabbit? What's a swamp rabbit?"

"It's a big old rabbit about the size and shape of the jackrabbits runnin' around these parts. Oh, my, they's powerful good eatin'. Tell you what, young Clayborne, you go kill me one and bring it back here so I can cook it up. Oh, just thinkin' about them swamp rabbits makes my lips smack."

"Are you sure you don't want a cottontail, Old Grandma? Lots of folks eat cottontails."

"Those little bitty things that go hoppin' around the garden? Not enough meat on one of them to feed a bird. Nope, I mean for you to go out and shoot me a great big dad-gummed jackrabbit."

"I'll do it, Old Grandma."

The next day he was as good as his word. Into the Jim Perry kitchen he trod, the mighty hunter, holding a huge dead jackrabbit by the ears.

"Well, now, ain't that somethin'!" said Old Grandma, her eyes wide with anticipation. "Let's go dress it out. I'll let you keep the entrails for Pup. Oh, gracious, larruping good swamp rabbit stew! Gracious sakes alive!"

They stood over the cutting board in the kitchen when Lou Perry walked in.

"Hello, Grandma," said Clayborne. "Did you hear that my Elam cousins are comin' to live with Grandma and Grandpa Blackburn?"

"You mean those two boys and that girl, what's their names?"

"J. C.'s the one older than me, Foncyne is the same age as me, but she's not comin', and Charley's the one younger. Their Mama is Auntie Cora. She's real sick with the TB. Papa says she's going to die."

"Lord have mercy," said Old Grandma. "They usually dies what gets the consumption. Poor boys, gonna be motherless."

"When they comin'?" asked Grandma Perry.

"Next month. Grandpa Blackburn's gonna drive out to Miles to get 'em."

Grandma Lou Perry looked at the dead animal on the cutting board. "You gonna eat a jackrabbit?" she asked her mother.

"Shore am," giggled Old Grandma, deftly separating meat from bones. "Clayborne, you screw the sausage grinder to the table while I finish up here. Ooo-eee, does this ever look good!"

Grandma Perry remarked, "That's what you said about the 'possum Clayborne brought you. You remember how you worked at it, burnt all the hair off'n it, roasted it up with good sweet potatoes and all in with the nice fat 'possum, and the boy wouldn't eat nary a bite?"

"I recollect. This ain't for him. He's too squeamish. I heard him talkin' about summer 'possums, sick-poor ones with sores all under they skins.

Winter 'possum's good eatin', good eatin'. Swamp rabbit, it's so good, it'll like to make you slobber all over yourself."

"Old Grandma, that's not nice," chided Clayborne.

She only giggled in response.

Clayborne stayed while she ground the jackrabbit and began cooking it into a stew, but had to return home for his own supper before he was missed.

"Thank you, boy," Old Grandma called. "Thank you for the swamp rabbit."

"You're welcome, Old Grandma," the lad called in departing.

"It ain't swamp rabbit, Ma," said Lou Perry.

"We'll soon see," the grinning old lady replied.

Clayborne was not sure of the final culinary judgment on jackrabbit as swamp rabbit. But Old Grandma never asked him to shoot another one.

It had been another Miss Loden for seventh grade at Camp Branch school, Helena Loden. She was Rilla's sister, another young single girl entering her first year out of college as a real, live teacher. Such young and inexperienced greenhorns expected no nonsense from their class, and no nonsense was offered; discipline was built into the community and order was still a virtue. Thus Miss Helena Loden's maiden year in the educational field went forward without incident.

The seventh grade was as the sixth, made up of Grace Rich, Minnie Rucker and Clayborne Perry. J. C. and Charley Elam had come to live with the Blackburns and attended Camp Branch school that year, arriving in September of 1923. In the early spring of 1924, Miss Loden sent the lower grades home early one day and walked the older students three and a half miles to Duffau. There at Duffau school, which offered ten grades of instruction, they saw their first basketball game. They were enthralled. When Clayborne got home that day he jumped on his newly acquired bicycle — an eight-dollar investment and significant step forward for a thirteen-year-old countryboy — and rode over to tell Old Grandma all about basketball.

March 7, 1924, Belle's younger sister Cora Blackburn Elam died of tuberculosis in Miles, Texas. The Perry family did not attend the funeral. Belle cried for weeks. Another sister gone. That year a solitary painted bunting was sighted near Hico, some miles above its normal range out of Mexico and South Texas.

The rough winds of May brought rain to the Grand Prairie. Rain meant no work in the fields; early grain harvest would have to wait. Teenaged field hands liked to play baseball on rainy days, or failing that, to walk over to Duffau and watch the community teams give each other a good chase around the bases.

John Fred Word came by the new rent house and knocked on the door.

Belle called out, "See who's at the door, Clayborne. I'm feeding Nadine."

Clayborne opened the door. "Hi, John."

"Hi, Clayborne. Wanna go to Duffau and watch the ball games?"

"Hey, Mama, can I go to Duffau and watch the ball games with John?"

"I expect so, son. No work in the fields today. Take your coat. It's drizzling and it might turn cold."

"Okay, Mama."

They took the shortcuts, anxious to get to the games, mud or no mud. They arrived at Duffau in mid-afternoon just when the better teams and the sunshine came. The teams were informal affairs, mostly older teenagers and a few college boys from Tarleton over at Stephenville, with a few young employed men from nearby towns. Some of the businessmen in the little commercial district of Duffau could usually be counted on to pitch in enough change to buy three or four baseballs at sixty-five cents each.

John and Clayborne shunned the low bleachers and ambled out to the right field fence. That was where most of the action was anyhow.

The first game was dull; neither side had a good pitcher or talented hitters and there were as many walks as runs. The second game was just the opposite: plenty of action, lots of hits and good base play. In the fifth inning one of the better hitters fouled into deep right field.

"Hey, look at this!" said John Word. "It's comin' right this way!"

"Yeah, must be a brand new ball it's so white!"

"That fielder's never gonna catch it!"

"Wow, 'way over his head!"

"Boy, look at that! It's way past us. It's clear out in the sumac bushes! If he'd hit it fair it would have been a homer!"

"That fielder's looking in the wrong place," remarked Clayborne. "It went a lot farther out, clear to the bushes." He could visualize exactly where the ball had come to rest.

"Oh, well," said John. "They lose a ball every now and then."

The fielder bumbled about, some hundred yards away from the two boys, coming up empty handed in one clump of grass after another. Clayborne waved for him to go farther out, but the harried fielder just waved back.

"What a dumb-bunny," muttered Clayborne.

A fresh ball was broken out and play resumed.

In the eighth inning, it became evident that the team with the volunteer firemen from Hico was going to trounce the farm boys.

"Let's go home, Clayborne," said John. "This game's already over."

"Yeah, okay."

It was nearly six, and the sun dipped low to the Western Cross Timbers. They started back toward Dude Flat across the deep backfield, far beyond the play area, and nobody on the teams or in the spectator crowd paid any attention to them. Clayborne recalled the fouled baseball and wandered toward the thicket of sumac bushes where he had seen it land. He kept his eye exactly on the spot he remembered. He knew where it was. He just knew it.

What a prize it would be. Every boy wanted a new baseball. But who had sixty-five cents to buy one? Certainly not Clayborne Perry.

When they were still a dozen steps away, Clayborne saw it. The new baseball lay propped in a clump of Johnson grass matted and shaped like a worn catcher's mitt. The ball gleamed irresistably in the fading light. It seemed to beckon like gold, to radiate a mythic attraction. What a prize! But to take it would be wrong. He knew that.

I ought to go give it to the owner.

He walked closer, straight toward the ball. Closer. He stooped over and nimbly plucked the ball from its grass mitt. The temptation was too great. He stuck it in his overall pocket and just kept walking toward home as if nothing had happened.

He glanced furtively at John Word. John was nonchalant, said nothing, just walked. Without conversation, they took the Hico road home, then turned east and walked past Duffau Cemetery with its stately oaks and mowed lawn punctuated by headstones of all sizes. They walked a little faster past the cemetery.

Over the low hill, Clayborne began to think about his new toy. He was thrilled to his toes that he would have a baseball to play with, a *new* baseball! It was fully an hour after they had left Duffau, as they turned southward toward Dude Flat, that he finally took the purloined ball out of his pocket and looked it over.

Then it hit him. How would he explain to his Papa where he got a new baseball? How could he have paid for it? His Papa knew as much about Clayborne's finances as Clayborne knew about his Papa's — and that was everything.

"John," Clayborne stuttered uncertainly. "I just thought, you know. This ball and all . . ."

"What, Clayborne?"

"Well uh . . . Well my Papa knows I don't have any money. He'd wonder where I got a new baseball. And this one is *so* new!"

"Yeah?"

"Yeah, well, uh, I . . . You know, there's no way I could hide it at home. My Papa would know it didn't belong to me. If he found out that I'd picked it up and not given it back, he'd blister me good."

"Yeah?"

"I can't take the ball home."

"I see."

They walked along the last stretch of road before the new rent house. The sun was down by a quarter of an hour.

John Fred Word said, "I'll give you a quarter for the ball. You can hide a quarter real easy."

"A quarter!" Clayborne said. He pondered the offer and decided quickly it was the thing to do. "Okay, John, I'll give you the ball for a quarter. Right now. You got it on you? Can I see it?"

"Yep. Right here." He reached in his coverall pocket and produced the coin. "Here you go. Here's the quarter."

"And here's the ball. John, you're a real pal."

"Of course I am. And don't you forget."

Clayborne said goodbye to John at the long driveway that curved from the road to the rent house, clutching the quarter deep in his pocket. That evening he helped milk the cows and feed the animals feeling everything was in order. He'd gotten away with it.

The next day he went down to Grandpa Blackburn's place to visit his cousins J. C. and Charley Elam. They fell to playing marbles in the dirt next to an ornamental juniper in the front yard. After a dozen or so turns, lying flat to get the right sight on his cousins' aggies, Clayborne felt in his pocket to finger the coin for good luck.

It was gone.

"My quarter!" Clayborne said in a sudden sweat. "Have you seen my quarter here?"

His cousins both allowed as how they hadn't seen a quarter in weeks.

"I've got to find that quarter. Oh, boy! I've got to find it."

J. C. remarked, "Boy, Clayborne, you're as nervous as a long-tailed cat in a room full of rocking chairs. That must be some important quarter."

"It is! It's . . . I . . . I've got to find it, that's all."

They looked and looked. The cousins lost interest after a while and went back to their game. Clayborne continued the search, on and on, hunched over to the ground until he finally realized his illicit coin was gone forever. All that trouble. All for nothing.

He stood up. He peered beyond the front yard, to Grandpa Blackburn's orchards. He turned slowly, looking around, all around him, at this sullen, solemn land that had taught him to be honest and four-square. He could feel its silent reproach. It spoke to him. It was not hallucination, it was just there, the land saying things to him. It was, as a poet once said, as real as a soul, not entirely as mystical as hands. "You have to choose," the land said to him wordlessly. What had he done to himself? He hated the way he felt. He vowed never to feel that way again.

-9-

CHILDHOOD ENDING

THE first of June, 1924, Clayborne hired out to work at harvest. His employer was W. C. Fouts, a respected well-to-do farmer some four miles east of Dude Flat in Black Stump Valley. Fouts, whose family had immigrated from Germany before the turn of the century, had operated a contract grain harvesting crew in the Grand Prairie for many years. His twenty-five or so regular grain-farming customers enabled him to employ a good-sized crew — twenty to thirty men, according to the yield — for six weeks each summer. The reliable reappearance of these jobs year after year became a legend among field hands all over Central Texas.

When the redoubtable Fouts let it be known to Tom Perry that Clayborne could sign on as a wagon driver, there were no misgivings, no hesitation. Clayborne was exuberant. It was a golden opportunity for a boy not quite fourteen, as grain harvest paid three dollars a day. He could work away from home and make nearly a hundred dollars in a summer. In 1924, that was a man's wage.

The young man showed up with his heavy bedroll on a Monday morning and drove the mule team provided to him into shorn wheat fields cut the previous week by a crew operating Fouts' Deering reaper-binder. When Clayborne pulled up where he had been directed, he saw shock after shock of grain standing at attention in tidy formation as far as the eye could see.

"You the new driver, young fellow?" asked a husky man with a pitchfork.

"Yes, sir. It's my first day."

"My name's Bill Guinn. I'll be your pitcher."

Clayborne reached down to shake hands. "I'm Clayborne Perry. What do I do?"

"You just go from one shock to the next, while I walk along and pitch the bundles onto the wagon. When you're loaded full, you drive the mules back to Fouts's thresher. That's where they gave you the wagon, ain't it?"

"Yes, sir, it is."

"Well, when you get back there, you pitch the load off into the thresher. The ground men will show you where. You'll heave the bundles in that old JI Case machine and the baggers will catch the threshed wheat in big tow sacks. When you've emptied the wagon, you drive on back and we'll do it again."

"Mr. Guinn, this Fouts place looks awful big."

"You'll find out *how* big. This ain't really the Fouts place, though. It's just one of about twenty-four places we'll work, and we just harvest their grain for wages. We'll work Fouts's place, too. It's up north a bit, three, four miles. He's got about 4,000 acres all of his own. But the whole thing we're goin' to harvest is about three miles wide and twelve miles long. When we get done in August, you'll know how long a mile can be."

"How much do they expect me to haul?"

"Depends. On a regular day we'll make about eight loads. On easy ground maybe nine, on broken ground maybe seven. But let me tell you this, boy: Mr. Fouts pays us a little better than he has to, and we all work for him a little harder than we have to. You do that and you'll fit in just fine. You won't never find a better man to work for. So let's see how much money we can make for him today."

With that they got to work. Clayborne quickly caught Guinn's stride, and paced his mules with expertise beyond his years. When the wagon was full to the sideboards, Clayborne began to turn his team aside for the trip to the thresher.

"Hey, where you goin', Clayborne?" yelled Guinn.

"Back to the thresher. Got a load, don't we?"

"You call that a load?" snickered the pitcher. "That ain't *half* a load. I'll signal you when you're loaded. Just get back on the row here now."

Clayborne got.

When Guinn finally signalled him quarter of an hour later, the bundles of wheat towered six feet above the wagon bed.

In the hot late morning, on the fourth load back to the thresher, Guinn jumped up on the wagon with Clayborne. "I'll help you pitch this one out so's we can get to the cook shack in time," he explained.

"Where's the cook shack?"

"Where ever Tom Roach drives it. Him and his wife Lillie is the cooks.

They usually move the cook shack along with the thresher, 'cause that's where most of the hands are."

"Roach," smiled Clayborne. "That's some name for a cook."

"Wait'll you taste the grub, boy. Name won't mean a thing. He lays the best table in Texas, and I've et at a few of 'em."

When they pulled up beside the thresher, it was strangely silent and a crowd of workmen had gathered around its business end. In the midst of the huddle stood two men in confrontation, one in work jeans, the other in a business suit.

"What's goin' on?" Clayborne whispered to Bill Guinn.

"Thresher's broke down again. Looks like one of the new men's complainin' to Mr. Fouts. Watch this, boy. It'll teach you somethin'."

They looked quietly on as the new man made a display of himself.

"This damn thresher is a piece of junk!" shouted the new operator angrily. "I sent the bagger to your place for that part you got there over an hour ago. You took your sweet time gettin' it back to us! An hour for one crummy little clevis fitting!"

"Yes, Mister McAden, you're absolutely right," replied W. C. Fouts. "We expect a lot from the JI Case here and it usually delivers, so we keep giving it clevis fittings and whatever else it needs. I'm sorry it took so long this morning, but I was on my way back from taking a neighbor to the doctor's in Iredell, and your bagger had to wait on me. It's entirely my fault."

This did not soothe the irate operator. "Look here, Mr. Fouts, I don't mind repairin' old rattletraps like this, but I didn't hire on to sit on my butt waitin' for parts and havin' my pay docked." The experienced men around McAden silently exchanged smiles.

"I'm sure you didn't Mr. McAden. And I know you're as good a repairman as you are a fine operator. Mr. Nelson said you're the best, and that's why I hired you. But you don't need to worry about your pay being docked. We don't do things that way around here. I know you'll have the thresher up and running in a jiffy. You're an honest workman and you'll get a honest day's pay without being docked for breakdowns."

Genuine shock registered on McAden's face. He looked to the hands gathered around: "Is that true? It's not a crock?"

They nodded affirmation, giving him their best *Oh, you dummy!* expression.

"I, uh . . . Damn . . . Gee, Mr. Fouts, I didn't know. Uh . . . Well . . . Oh, hell, give me the clevis fitting and I'll get this hunk of junk goin' again."

He gruffly took the new replacement part from Fouts's hand and slunk sheepishly away to the innards of the thresher.

"Thank you, Mr. McAden," called Fouts. "I'll try to be more prompt next time."

The crew grinned at W. C. Fouts, who smiled back at them and turned toward the loaded wagon and Clayborne.

"Oh, hello, there, Mr. Perry, Mr. Guinn. We've had another little breakdown, sorry to say. We should be back up shortly. Mr. McAden is an excellent mechanic." The venerable boss got back in his Model T and chugged off.

Clayborne said to Guinn in openmouthed astonishment, "He called me Mr. Perry. Nobody ever did that before. I'm just a kid."

"Not to Fouts you ain't," said Guinn. "To him, you're one of his workers, and if you can cut the mustard, you're as good as any man. Besides, you're just about as big as any man here, kid or not."

The cook shack was a horse-drawn chuckwagon some twenty feet long and seven feet wide. Noon dinner enticed their nostrils even before Clayborne and Bill Guinn finished pitching down the wheat shocks. When they finally walked over to the mobile open-air dining hall, Clayborne saw that it had hinged sides folded down into high tables where the crew stood eating a formidable meal. The workaday food dished out to them by Tom Roach and Lillie surpassed many Sunday dinners the boy had known.

Dinner conversation was sparse and cryptic. One hand was heard to mumble around a mouthful of savory ham, "Got another rattler."

Chewing, thirty seconds or more of it, then another mumble from another man, muffled in a huge glass of milk, "Ollie, too."

More chewing, and another man mushed, "Lee, too."

Appetites sated and thirsts slaked, Clayborne and Guinn mounted the wagon to return to their field. The youngster asked his partner, "What were they talkin' about back there?"

"The rattlers? Oh, that's the rattlesnakes they killed so far today. Dan Culver said he got one, and the other fellows said that Ollie Lawson and Lee Gamble killed one, too."

"There's that many rattlesnakes over here?"

"Well, that's unusual. You mostly kill one a day, sometimes one every other day."

"And we have to sleep out here on the ground? With all those snakes around?"

"Ain't never bothered anybody yet."

"It bothers me."

Later that day it bothered Bill Guinn, too. He ran across a bullsnake among the grain shocks and automatically lashed out with his pitchfork thinking it was a rattler, skewering the reptile amidships. The mortally wounded snake whipped and struck in its death throes, giving Guinn fits of sudden terror.

"Snake! *Snake!*" he hollered.

Clayborne looked down startled. "Kill it, Bill! Kill it quick!"

After some fancy dancing to escape the harmless fangs, Guinn saw his mistake: "It ain't no rattler." He booted the creature a good one in the head anyway. In these times most rural folk had not learned the usefulness of venomless reptiles in running efficient mouse patrols and had been taught from lack of ecological understanding to fear snakes. Snakes in general. As time went on, the more enlightened farmers and field hands encountering a blue racer or a corn snake or a bullsnake just let it go by.

But today Bill Guinn kilt him a bullsnake.

"Whew!" he said.

"Whew!" Clayborne agreed.

The new wagon driver made his eight loads that first day of harvest, and after an outrageously good supper settled into his bedroll uneasily in the dark, waiting for sleep. The crew had assembled in a recumbent circle around the glowing guttering campfire. But it was not the gathering of cowboy legend. There were no tall tales, no garrulous conversations. It was a convocation of politic field hands worn out with the day's labor. The voices were low, private, quiet and weighty, reflecting, recollecting distant places and things. Wives and children loved, homes lost, farms worked, places to go back to on weekends or when harvest was over. Two or three of the men confided in dark tones to a work partner personal tales that did not echo or carry across the fitful crackle of the fire: whiskey guzzled, women chased, machinery fixed or given up for dead, bosses cussed and fistfights fought. The men who talked such things were the drifters. Most of their listeners were locals who kept such events in their own lives, if they ever happened, to themselves.

There's twenty other guys sleepin' on the ground around the thresher. They don't seem to be scared. I hope no old rattlesnake comes and bites me tonight.

He stayed awake a long time after the others, listening to every little sound, every hoot of distant owls, every barking dog by the far houses, thinking of Pup, every crunch of grass as the mice held their own grain harvest. No heat-seeking snake slithered to his warm and vulnerable body. No reptilian disaster overtook him. No poisoned fangs pumped iron death into his veins. The hum and chirruping of amorous insects lulled him. The circling majesty of the chanting stars reassured him. The age-old landscape glowing under the crescent moon cradled him. The Texas nocturne of warm sights and sounds and the sheltering sense of *place* comforted him at last. He was not just lost out here on the rim of some little planet chasing around the edge of the galaxy. This was Earth, Texas Earth, his Texas Earth. Maybe not *the* center, but *his* center. He awoke after long and restful sleep to a sunrise he might have seen when the world itself was young.

In mid-July, while Clayborne was spending the weekend at home from harvest, the telephone rang at 4 a.m. The young man knew something was wrong. Nobody called on the telephone at that hour. He could hear his father and mother stirring, sitting up on the edge of their bed in the next room. He could hear his father shuffle into the kitchen and pick up the telephone earpiece to listen in. Tom only listened for a moment before abruptly hanging up, then rushed out the front door and stood looking to the northwest.

The sky glowed an evil orange.

"Good Lord," Tom gasped. "It is. It is. Duffau's burning!"

Within seconds Belle and Clayborne and Hoyt joined him outside, slackjawed at the sight.

"Oh, dear Lord," said Belle. "It must be the whole town!"

"It is," said Tom. "That was Miz Jenkins calling Dr. Russell to come in case the people in the apartments got hurt. She said it looked like the whole thing was goin' up. They got no fire department."

After breakfast, the Perrys took the Chevrolet and toured the smouldering remains of Duffau. The town's commercial district was flat, burned to the ground. A ruin. A few stone wall sections stood amid the rubble. The post office, general store, barber shop, bank, three mercantile stores — including an undertaker's establishment — and apartments above all the buildings were gone. Simply gone. Miraculously, none of the dozens of apartment dwellers had been injured. But the commercial heart of the town was gone. It was never rebuilt.

Revival came to Prairie Springs Baptist Church as usual in July of 1924. The faithful at harvest usually found a way to church of an evening, and Clayborne managed to get a ride almost every day. He was nearly fourteen now, and beginning to think seriously about the larger questions in his life. His father's brush with pneumonia and pellagra, his three aunts gathered to eternity, his flirtation with theft and the baseball, his observation of a kindly boss who had the power to hurt and would do none, the fiery destruction of Duffau, all moved him and prodded him in private places. His spirit was turning, slowly, in its own time, working in dreams, irresistibly growing.

One evening at Revival he made his decision: he stepped forward at the close of the service and dedicated his life to Christ. The following Sunday Brother R. H. Gibson took him and a dozen others who had made their confession of faith, took them into Little Duffau Creek and there baptized them. It was a new Clayborne that emerged. Now his spirit stood indomitable, absolved of mortality, personally covenanted with God. Outwardly, he may have seemed to some still a child. He was inly a man grown.

As a full member of Prairie Springs Baptist Church that summer, Clayborne participated in the life of the congregation, even playing piano at church services. Tom that year had bought a piano, and the sounds of old hymns rang out in the warm evening shadows around the new rent house. Belle, now expecting her fourth child in January, taught her oldest son to play by chords and by ear, the way she had learned in her youth. Learning to read music was not part of the course. Clayborne had to select the hymns he played at church carefully to make sure they were ones he knew.

By August his young body was toughened and sinewy, his mind honed and buttressed. He had shown his mettle alongside grown men. He had a hundred dollars to prove it. He had also a new sense of self, proud but not puffed up, important but not imperious, superior but not supercilious. These new feelings were still wrapped in the homely virtues of humility. When his last pay envelope was handed over to him, and he walked home again as he had for so many weekends, he thought not of himself, but of Mr. W. C. Fouts.

Watching him this summer has taught me something I didn't get even from my Papa or either of my Grandpas. Mr. Fouts was always doing something nice for his hands, things he didn't need to do, like bringing 'em newspapers and magazines, or giving them seed corn or grain to take home and plant. He taught me that if you be nice to your neighbor, he'll do something, nice for you. If someone gets mad at you, reply in a nice friendly manner and your enemy feels ashamed and becomes your friend. If you give somebody something it always comes back to you two-fold. Always be fair. Never make excuses or tell lies. Work hard for your friends and they'll work hard for you.

The young man was shaping a personal code of honor.

In 1924, politics turned ugly. Felix Robertson declared as a candidate for governor. He was the candidate of the Ku Klux Klan. Since its revival in 1915, the Klan had become ever more deeply involved in politics and now grasped for control of the state. The Klan had wide support, much of it drawn from the Great War's tide of resentment against all "foreigners," which were taken among the lower classes to include Catholics, Jews, and blacks. But the Klan also drew much of its power from the hardshell conservatism of the ordinary Texas farmer, wary as he might be of Klan violence. Farmers had a strong desire for law and order and were against government corruption — and government corruption had become a way of life in Austin. For a while, it looked like the Klan candidate would triumph. But then a ghost from the murky past came to haunt the Texas hustings: James E. Ferguson, good ol' Farmer Jim, impeached in 1917, besmirched, dishonored, barred by law from ever again holding elective office, threw his hat in the ring by the ingenious expedient of entering his wife's name in the Democratic primary.

Everyone realized that Miriam Ferguson was a mere catspaw for Farmer Jim: she herself admitted he would make all the decisions as governor. But Texans loved fun and games in politics, and they were a little afraid of what the Ku Klux Klan might do if it got control of the governor's mansion — which Farmer Jim had accurately sensed. Miriam, "Ma" to her fellow Texans, espoused that version of democracy which glorifies the ordinary man, makes a public virtue of being common as an old shoe, and there were a lot of old shoes in Texas. The Fergusons mounted a bitter anti-Klan campaign and beat Felix Robertson in the primary by 100,000 votes. Ma was a shoo-in at the general election and became Texas' first woman governor. And Farmer Jim got his third term as governor in everything except name.

Ma Ferguson appointed Farmer Jim to the mighty Texas Highway Commission — it wasn't an *elective* office, you see — which enabled him to influence letting of the juiciest state contracts; he already influenced the executive office from his bedroom. The city folks shouted in dismay, but most of the farm community, which still retained a majority at the polls, thought this was great good fun. Ma Ferguson quietly reinstated the policy Farmer Jim had inaugurated back in 1914 of pardoning off convicts — for a discreet consideration, everybody said — which emptied the prisons and substantially lowered the cost of government, and was therefore not really as unpopular as it might seem. Farmer Jim had a nice little ranch in the Grand Prairie, up above Meridian, and when parents or spouses of convicted felons came pleading for him to release their loved ones — so Jim Perry told Tom — Farmer Jim sold them a calf from his ranch for five hundred to a thousand dollars, sometimes more, if the traffic would bear it. Miraculously, Ma Ferguson's executive clemency would soon be granted, and a full pardon would release the next of kin of these well-heeled livestock connoiseurs. Some people were outraged, but many Texans — including Tom Perry, who had not voted for Ma Ferguson — felt it was the best circus they'd seen in Austin in a long time. Ah, bread and circuses! Texans would provide their own bread, thank you, but a few circuses — well, what could you expect from even the *best* government, eh? Ma and Pa Ferguson took the ordinary man's mind off his troubles, and that was worth a little graft at the very least.

In October Clayborne went back to school, but not to Camp Branch school. The school of his childhood taught only seven grades, and he was now off to Duffau for instruction from the eighth through tenth grade. Somehow the two-story stone and brick school building felt alien and not right, not yet. It was particularly eerie since the business district of Duffau had been destroyed: there was really not much Duffau left and the school had been unofficially demoted from a town school to a slightly glorified country school. It made Clayborne uneasy. The only thing he enjoyed without qualification was basketball. He stayed two weeks.

"Clayborne," said Tom one night as he returned to the new rent house. "We just had our school board meeting and I want you to quit Duffau school."

"What's happened, Papa?"

"You know how we've been losing pupils when the rent farmers move on . . ."

Clayborne recalled his friends Eddie and Clifford. "I know . . ."

"We thought of a way to get more pupils and keep the school open. We're going to have an eighth grade. That'll keep the students we have another year and attract others to our school. I want you to finish eighth grade at Camp Branch."

Two weeks later Mr. Oswald Freeman was hired to teach grades five through eight, and Miss Rhoda Criss retained to teach the lower four at Camp Branch. And so the one-room, one-teacher schoolhouse became a one-room, two-teacher schoolhouse. The school board selected the simple expedient of a curtain drawn across the middle of the long room to separate upper from lower grades. As expected, more students came in and the future of Camp Branch school was assured.

But the basketball bug had bitten Clayborne. There *had* to be a way to get up a basketball team at Camp Branch. A useable basketball cost at least five dollars, an impossibly astronomical sum to add to the school budget. So Clayborne and a few friends took up a collection among the older students, trying to eke out fifty cents each. They reached their goal.

With the new basketball in hand, the boys cleared a court out of the playground, tearing up some unwanted grass here and an intruding bush there, and set up two makeshift backboards — built by many hands — at approximately the right distance from each other and approximately the right height from the ground. Clayborne went home one day and appropriated two discarded iron buggy tires, took them to Grandpa Perry's blacksmith shop, bent them up, beat them up, and converted them to hoops to be bolted to the backboards. Tom hauled them to school for his son.

Success! Word spread quickly about the Camp Branch basketball court. Black Stump Valley school some three and a quarter miles east as the crow flies brought their seven-man team to test the new facility. The first thing every visiting team said was: "Hey, one hoop is larger than the other. You guys take the little hoop. We want the big one for our goal." It had never occurred to Clayborne to measure the diameter or circumference of his ironmongery project.

It was a busy autumn, 1924 was. Tom's brother Leonard was getting ready to move out of the rent house. He and Verna found something to do with all the money from their claim at Trinchera they had sold to the Glasgows. Happy-go-lucky Leonard had grown prudent, and had squirreled away the money from the claim with his earnings from the Pueblo mines and from two reasonably good cotton crops at the rent house. He now had enough for a large, respectable farm up in the Texas Panhandle. He was always looking for that greener grass, and now he thought he had found it. So in November of 1924, Leonard Perry moved to Kirkland, Texas, near Childress in the Panhandle, not a dozen miles from the Oklahoma border. He invited Tom and family to visit in the summer.

Leonard moved away about the same time the old Chevy 4-90 began to spend four days on the road and ninety in the repair shop. Tom dumped the lemon and bought a brand new 1925 model T Ford. It cost $445.00, and had demountable rims — which meant you had a spare tire — and an automatic starter. The Perrys felt they had the finest transportation available. Gasoline was still fifteen cents a gallon and seventy-five cents worth — the cream and egg money — was still enough to run around for a week. Now the family used their fine Model T when they went into Hico on Saturdays, or to church on Sundays and church meetings other days.

And about the same time Belle's brother Fred and his wife Myrtle decided they had had enough of Colorado, too. They came back home with a passell of kids, Claytia, the same age as Clayborne, Lawton, now eleven years old, and two youngsters the Perrys had never seen: Carl Wendell Blackburn, born in Hastings, Colorado, and now four, and Grace Evelyn, born in Trinchera and now two. They came to live not half a mile from Tom Perry and his family. Grandpa Charley Blackburn moved the weaning house where Clayborne had been born, had it moved right across the road from the Coopers on the northwest corner of his land. The two rooms were expanded in country style with additions tacked to the sides, and the Fred Blackburn family had themselves a decent place to live that wasn't a dugout and wasn't in a mining town — for the first time in a decade. It was a grand reunion. Belle hugged her brother, and Tom gabbed for hours with Fred about how things had been in Colorado. The kids all got to know each other. The Blackburns were sorry they had missed seeing Leonard Perry's family by a few weeks. The prodigals returned gave the community another close hand, another strong back in time of need, another friend and active church family. Hardly a Saturday night went by in the warm weather that the Blackburns and the Perrys weren't together at one house or the other cranking up ice cream and having a good time. And so the summer turned to fall, the cotton crop was made, and the first chill of winter came to the Grand Prairie.

Early winter meant hog killing time. On the coldest clear day of late November or early December — rain would cancel all meat processing activities — Grand Prairie farmers got up very early in the morning, did their chores and by eight o'clock had a big fire going under two or three eighteen-gallon wash pots. This was Tom Perry's third hog killing at the new rent house on Grandpa Blackburn's land, and the local farm tradition of assisting each other during butchering went on: Jim Perry and Jim Cooper and Fred Blackburn came over to help wrestle the 250- to 325-pound carcasses step by step through the process, a favor Tom would pay back in the next few days.

This chill December morning, everything was set up out between the barn and the hog pen: the water barrel had been dug into the ground at a forty-five degree angle, the block and tackle hung from a liveoak tree, the butcher knife sharpened, the pulling knife at the ready, tow sacks on the ground — and the .22 caliber rifle leaned against the barn. The four men and fourteen-year-old Clayborne hovered around the wash-pot fire.

Jim Perry spoke hoarsely in the morning light: "Tom, why don't ye let the boy shoot the hogs this year? He's jist itching to do it."

Tom looked at Clayborne's eager face and thought a moment. "Do you know how to do it right, son?" he asked.

"I've watched you do it every year," the boy answered.

Tom said, "There's a trick to it that you can't see." He walked to the barn and picked up the .22 rifle. He aimed it at an imaginary hog, peering down the gunbarrel. "You have to draw an imaginary cross on the hog's head, son," he explained. "Draw a line between the right ear and the left eye, and another one between the left ear and the right eye. Get it so you can see that cross firm in your mind. Where those two lines meet, that's where you shoot. Kills the hog right now, no pain, no fuss — he just falls down dead."

"I can do it, Papa," said the boy.

"Then let's get to work."

Clayborne killed the first hog efficiently and exactly as instructed. The pampered beast keeled over never knowing what hit it. The four men wrangled the three-hundred-pound porker onto a sledge and pulled it from the hog pen nearly a hundred feet to the barn — malodorous hog pens were usually located as far from the house and barn as practical.

"Okay, Tom," said Jim Perry, "I'll dump the boilin' wash pots into the barrel," and proceeded to make good on his word. Meantime, Jim Cooper and Tom and Fred hauled the dead pig alongside the half-buried barrel. When the barrel was about half full, all four men wordlessly heaved the hog off the sledge, aimed it butt-end first at the barrel's mouth, and slid it into the scalding water. Its shoulder and head lolled above the water line in the cold air.

"How long we goin' to keep it soakin'?" asked Jim Cooper.

"Pretty chilly today, and a pretty big hog. Say, half a minute, maybe more," replied Tom. "Right, Papa?"

Jim Perry nodded.

After a short time they hauled the carcass half out of the barrel while Tom leaned over to test the hair. He pulled a handful of hog bristles off and said, "It's too hard yet. A little longer."

They dunked the animal back into the steaming barrel and waited. Out again. Tom tested the hair again. It came off in easy handfuls along with the topmost — and dirtiest — layer of pigskin.

"Now," he said.

They hoisted the beast out of the barrel, turned it end for end and slipped it down into the hot water head first this time. More waiting.

Clayborne asked, "What happens if you leave it in too long, Papa?"

"Cooks the hair right on to the skin, son," he said. "Comes off in big chunks, messes up the skin real bad. It's a poor butcher that scalds a hog too long."

The men hauled the hog out of the barrel and tested the front end. "Just right," said Tom. "Let's git 'er out on the tow sacks."

The scalded hog was laid out on burlap bags. The three men and Clayborne set silently to work pulling hog bristles out of the animal by hand. Fred Blackburn used the scraping knife, laying the blade on the skin, pressing particularly stubborn bristles to the blade with his thumb, and yanking them out. After half an hour of concerted effort, the hog had been cleaned reasonably well.

Now Jim Perry, the oldest and most experienced, took the butcher knife and cut a slit between tendon and bone in both back legs of the hog, down near the cloven hoofs. He placed one end of a singletree into the left leg's slot and the other in the right, bracing the legs apart and providing a convenient handle by which to lift the beast. The block and tackle's hook was slid into the singletree's center ring and the hog hauled up until it hung clear of the ground.

More scalding water was tossed on the hanging hog as a final rinse and any missed hog bristles were pulled out. The animal was rubbed down with tow sacks until its hide veritably gleamed.

"That's a right clean white hog, now," said Tom Perry. He took the butcher knife from his father and began the job of dismantling the creature for storage. He first cut a long slit from top to bottom, belly to throat, and began removing the entrails. The intestines were discarded — Clayborne got the privilege of taking them off a distance to feed the buzzards. Some German folk down in the Hill Country would keep the small intestine, force water through it with a hose or pipe, turn it inside out and make sausage casings. But in the Grand Prairie, the buzzards got the guts.

The hog liver and heart were carefully removed and cleaned and the body cavity rinsed and cleaned. The head was cut off to recover the jowl meat — jowl rhymes with foal as pronounced by these farmers — and some people saved the tongue, but not the Perrys. Jim Cooper took the tongue. But hog ears were saved for souse, the lean meat between the ears was saved for mincemeat, pork snouts were a delicacy. And brains. Don't forget the brains.

The carcass was skinned in sections, the skin and its thick layer of fat chopped into two-inch squares, cooked in a big wash pot to render the lard, and the brown cracklings — the cooked skin — hung up in a flour sack to save for making lye soap to do the wash next year. Sometimes a farm wife would raid the fifteen of so pounds of cracklings from each hog to make crackling bread — corn bread or biscuits, it didn't matter — which was regarded as a savory dish.

The two pork shoulders were prized as were the hams, carefully trimmed of fat to make nice lean meat — the fat saved for lard, of course. The sowbelly was cut into bacon, the ribs cut out separately, the backbone removed, the pig's feet either pickled or cooked with sweet potatoes, the tail used — and the next hog would get the same treatment. Farmers usually tried to have two days of hog killing each year for the advantage of having fresh meat twice before Christmas. Then the big early winter task was done. Some of the meat would keep — salted, usually — until next August.

On February 6, 1925, Clayborne's youngest sister Dorothy was born at home in the new rent house. Now the family was complete: there would be no more children for Tom and Belle. They would rejoice in their four: Clayborne, Hoyt, Nadine and Dorothy.

The school year at Camp Branch came and went, investing new skills in its students and giving Clayborne Perry one last turn of the seasons in the old familiar setting. When the last day of school came in April, 1925, he was ready and planning with his father's approval to go on next year to Duffau school. He considered himself fortunate in that. Most boys being graduated from the little one-room schoolhouse by the creek would go home to be farmers, to live a life of unremitting, grinding physical labor, never to see the inside of a school again, except perhaps to vote. Grandma Perry and Old Grandma felt their prayers were being answered to hear that the boy would stay in school. There was no eighth-grade graduation ceremony at Camp Branch School that last day. The class simply spread dinner at noon and that was it. When he went home, Clayborne knew it was the end of an era for him.

A few days later someone told Old Grandma she could draw a Civil War Pension. In order to qualify, she had only to prove who she was and that her husband had "enlisted and served in the military service of the Confederate States during the war between the States of the United States and that he did not desert the Confederate service." She got her birth certificate out of her old trunk and on the 29th of April wrote her Widow's Application for Confederate Pension. She filled out in detail all the blanks except

"11. Name branch of service in which your husband served, whether infantry, cavalry, artillery, or the navy, or if commissioned as an officer by the President, his rank and line of duty, or if detailed for special service, under the law of conscription, the nature of such service, and time of service."

Old Grandma simply wrote: Don't know.

Her son Jim and a friend from down the road at Iredell, N. B. Ross, witnessed for her. The State of Texas, having passed a pension act in 1913 for Confederate widows, allowed her $8 a month, looked upon at the time as a good pension. She was very proud of it, and made sure everyone in earshot found out about it.

Clayborne helped harvest the grain at home beginning the last week of May, and then hired out with Fouts again to the end of July. When Clayborne was back from harvest and the home crops laid by, Tom Perry told his family that it was time to take an adventurous trip in the Model T to visit Uncle Leonard at his new farm in the Panhandle. It was two hundred miles away, two hundred miles of terrible roads with flat tires lurking around every rutted bend. They caught a few extra chickens, took them to market in Hico, and got the extra money for gasoline.

"Is everything ready? The water jug, extra blankets, the food?" called Belle out the rent house front door.

"Yes, for the tenth time, Belle," said Tom. "Everything's ready and in the car."

"Do we have the spare tire pumped up and the tire patchin' stuff?"

"It's all here."

"Did Clayborne tell my Papa to come feed Pup and the animals and milk the cows?"

"I told him a week ago, Mama," yelled Clayborne from the back seat of the Tin Lizzie. "I reminded him again yesterday. He'll do it." His voice had lost its boyish chime and now rang out in rich baritone authority.

"Come on, Belle, get the girls," said Tom peevishly. "We want to make an early start. Sun's gettin' ready to come up already."

"How come Mama's such a worry-wart?" piped up nine-year-old Hoyt.

"Don't be disrespectful to your mother, Hoyt," advised Clayborne.

"Hoyt only needs one father, Clayborne," said Tom.

"Sorry, Papa."

Belle called again, "Is the blanket for Nadine ready in the back seat?"

Clayborne held it up to the window.

She concluded, "All right, I'll go get her and the baby."

A sleepy toddler came out of the house with Belle. Nadine blinked and shut her eyes again, wobbling on the front porch, hand in her mother's, stepping where the guiding hand led. Belle carried the infant Dorothy while directing Nadine's footsteps to the car. Clayborne opened the back door of the car from inside and lifted the little girl into the vehicle. He sat her down in the middle of the back seat where she curled up like a cat and went immediately back to sleep. Belle sat with baby Dorothy in the front. They were all aboard.

"Hey, Papa, we're goin' West again," said Clayborne.

Tom smiled. "This time we're goin' in style," he said. "And we got a real home to come back to."

They were off. Hoyt and Clayborne peered intently into the mysterious predawn world from opposite back seat side windows. They were fascinated by the new landscapes that emerged and unfolded and revealed themselves with the slowly breaking dawn. Somehow the movement of the car kept in rhythm with the rising sun, with great gnarled oaks overshadowing the road only to give way to sudden blinding glints of orange fire leaving a thousand tiny suns everywhere you looked. The telephone poles beside the road formed a steady beat one after the other, the wires between them falling and rising, falling and rising as they hung from ceramic insulators at the peaks and swooped down to catenary troughs at the bottoms only to return to the peaks in graceful arch over and over again down the long road winding, up and down, up and down, up and down. Passing chords of trees made a counterpoint with rich fields to form the harmony. Happy arpeggios of thought in the watchers' minds became the melody.

It grew into a song, a mythic song in the key of motion, cadenced with new sights at every bend in the road, modulating to new horizons over every little hill, frilled with cadenzas of bird flight here and obligatos of frisking colts in pastures there, all against the ground bass of the Model T's engine chug. They were tasting the first notes of the love song that would soon ravish the heart of America, the anthem of the auto, the opera of the open road, the madrigal of mobility, the *sonata allegro* of speed, rising upward and outward, testing the limits.

The roads were just becoming drivable enough to make music. In 1920, of the nearly three million miles of rural highway in America, only 36,000 were surfaced with anything that could take the pounding of automobile traffic. In 1838 the federal government had begun to give to the states all responsibility for road building, and the states responded by doing next to nothing. But when the automobile came along in droves seventy-plus years later, and every owner was a voter, the muddy ruts of earlier days would no longer do. Car drivers found, as one highway historian said, "U.S. roads were more like those of Siberia than those of France or England." Drivers wanted action quick. By 1919, every state had a highway department and in 1921 the Federal Highway Act put the federal government back in the road building business. As Tom took his family touring through Texas, highway construction was booming at 10,000 miles of new hard-surfaced roads a year.

The road music created the Perrys' day. Into the dawning Western Cross Timbers, through Stephenville, northward over the rough dirt roads, across clattering wood bridges, past tiny morning towns like Morgan Hill and Patio and Santo and Brazos, through open noontime pastures and paved roads and cities bigger than they could remember,

Wichita Falls in the afternoon, and on across ever lower and lower sundown hills, through Vernon to the flat, flat twilight world approaching Childress where you can see twenty miles in every direction with no mott or knoll to wrinkle the straight horizon anywhere and the only windbreak is the Big Dipper. A right turn in the evening shadows at Kirkland, then eight miles north to the night farm of James Leonard Perry, two hundred miles and then some to the final note. The Model T engine was turned off. The day's highway song was done. And not a single flat tire.

Tom and Leonard bear-hugged each other and marveled at how they had certainly grown older and perhaps had grown wiser in the months since last fall. They spent three days, Tom and Leonard, Verna and Belle and all the children, having great fun and sharing all the news of Hico. They talked about the Fred Blackburn family moving back to Dude Flat, and Blackburn children they hadn't seen before. Tom urged his brother to move back home again, to find a better farm near Hico, not out in this open and blowing land even though it sprouted wheat like demons were pushing it up through the ground. Leonard said that he might just do that, the winter had been worse than he expected and the work growing wheat too demanding. If he could sell at a good price and find a suitable farm near home, he'd come back to Hico, he promised.

Three days later Tom's family drove a hundred and fifty miles southwest to McAdoo, Texas, to visit a cousin of Grandpa Jim Perry, Clayborne Perry, the namesake of Tom's son. Young Clayborne had never met this man before, this son of Docton Perry, old Confederate Docton Perry, who had been shot in the mouth at the Battle Above the Clouds in the War Between the States. For a day Uncle Clayborne in McAdoo told them tales of the early days and of his father Docton Perry who seemed to be a strange and unconventional man, uncharacteristic of the Perry clan.

Uncle Clayborne told how Docton travelled from place to place, never staying with his family much, working as little as possible, rummaging from relative to relative, always wearing a large mustache to hide the ragged scar and missing teeth he'd taken from a Yankee bullet. Tom Perry in response told Uncle Clayborne how Great Uncle Docton had even come to stay a while with Jim Perry at Dude Flat a few years earlier, after Tom had got the pneumonia and before he got the pellagra. Young Clayborne smiled, too, remembering how old Great Uncle Docton used to sit in Grandpa Perry's living room and smoke his pipe and not work much. Tom told how old Docton made clothespins, strange and wonderful clothespins he had invented himself, that stayed on the clothes line and held up even the heaviest quilts, and how the clothespins were made on a little apparatus he'd also invented himself, taking telephone wire and bending it somehow with a crank and slipping it onto a couple of pieces of wood to make the finished product. Old Docton would walk around the Dude Flat area selling clothespins for fifteen cents a dozen, making maybe four dollars a month. He was brother-in-law to Old Grandma and Uncle to Jim Perry, and that was good for about a month of freeloading and then Docton was off again.

But Uncle Clayborne told the really peculiar story, the story of how Docton had come by train to the Texas Panhandle in the early 1900s and stopped to visit a grandson at a railroad station. He told the grandson in all seriousness that he was the seventh son of a seventh son and had inherited the power of a mystic and a faith healer, with great influence over the Negro race. After extensive travels trying to gather a following Great Uncle Docton evidently decided that the prophecy business was not a paying concern and had gone off to the Texas old soldiers home in Austin to live out his life and die in mystical peace. Everyone smiled at the story but in part believed it, feeling that a streak of prophecy and grace must run through their reserved and staid family somewhere for them to have endured so many hardships and close calls and still emerge strong and together.

The next day they left the cheerful hospitality of Uncle Clayborne and drove two hundred miles south through the eroded caprock of the Llano Estacado into the heart of West Texas past Abilene to near San Angelo and the little town of Miles. Here they stayed with Uncle Lem B. Elam, widower. It was more than a year now since Cora had died. Lem still grieved over her and felt close to Belle and Tom and the Blackburns, and was glad to see the Perry family. Clayborne renewed the bonds with his cousins J. C. and Charley, and met their sister Foncyne, who was fifteen like Clayborne. She had not come to live with the Blackburns while her mother was dying, but stayed and took care of her mother, taking medically supervised precautions to avoid tuberculosis herself. It worked, for she never contracted the dread disease and lives to this day.

J. C. and Charley took pains to remind Clayborne of his strange behavior back at Grandpa Blackburn's over the lost quarter. Clayborne had come to terms with his misdeed, however, and took their ribbing with stoic resignation. The following day the Perrys headed back for Hico some two hundred miles east. Their total trip came to more than eight hundred miles. They had no flat tires and no mechanical breakdowns and considered themselves fortunate. They were left tired and happy and refreshed in spirit upon their return home. The cotton was almost ready and Clayborne at fifteen first noted that time seemed to be running faster the older he got. The summer was done too soon, too soon.

Starting school in the middle of October rather than the middle of November seemed a little strange to Clayborne, because he could not work the fields to the end of cotton picking season. Small as it was, Duffau School with its 200 students and five teachers and ten grades — most Texas high schools at the time only taught eleven grades — was considered a city school by the local community of some 250 souls, but not by many others. Duffau School superintendent Kate Robinson made no allowance for such rustic matters as picking cotton: you started school in October when you were told. At least the hours were the same as at Camp Branch: 9:00 a.m. to 4:00 p.m.

Duffau School was a sturdy stone building with hailscreens on the windows and two stories of classrooms in a little school yard standing by itself, off away from what used to be the town part of Duffau before the big fire, looking like something out of an Andrew Wyeth painting. On the ground floor, between rooms, there were large wooden doors that could be folded aside to open the teaching space into a vast auditorium. One corner room was equipped with a stage elaborate enough to accommodate backdrops and stage doors and even curtains that really opened and closed. The second floor contained the library and bookroom as well as classrooms. There was only one stairway to the second floor, an outside stairway. By the door of every room stood a fifty-gallon trash drum, each one of them emptied downstairs under the stairway in a collecting bin. No one saw the potential fire hazard and only luck allowed the venerable building to end its days shut down but unscorched many years later.

He set out to make new friends in the ninth grade and to be a good hand with the cotton at home. The way to school was not as easy as to Camp Branch: he now had a walk of three and a half miles to and from class. At home picking cotton, Pup still trailed along the rows behind him although the dog was getting old and arthritic. Clayborne's ninth grade boasted exactly fourteen students and it was not difficult getting to know them all by name. But his fondest school wish was to make the basketball team. When he found his name on the varsity list after tryouts, he was on Cloud Nine. Suiting up in team shirts and shorts definitely boosted his social status at school, but his ambition to dribble his way to fame as an ace forward came to naught: his first year was spent mostly warming benches and playing occasional second string guard during free throws.

After the first month of school, when the cotton was finally gathered in and ginned off and the crop evaluated, Tom one night told Clayborne and Hoyt, "Boys, it's time for another decision."

They gathered around him with their mother at the kitchen table and Pup sitting by the heater. The boys listened: "We made a fair crop this year and got about twenty cents a pound for most of it, early cotton was a little higher, last cotton a little lower. I've talked to the bank and they say it's a good time to buy more land if we're ever going to."

"Our own farm at last?" asked Clayborne. "One we can move to?"

"Prob'ly not yet," said Tom. "Hear me out. We've got maybe three, four hundred dollars in savings. The Harris place right next to our fifty acres down towards Hico is up for sale. It's right about fifty acres, too. If we bought old widow Harris out, that would give us a hundred-acre farm of our own. With no toll to pay, we could make a living on it. But here's the problem. Old widow Harris wants thirteen hundred dollars for it."

Hoyt said in his high voice, "Gee, Papa, if we've only got three hundred, that leaves a thousand over."

"Right, Papa," said Clayborne in ringing baritone. "Is the bank willing to stake us to that much of the total price?"

"That they are, son," said Tom. "We're a good risk now. But that's what I want your advice on. It'll leave us a thousand dollars in debt, and with that kind of debt we can't make a living on a hundred-acre place. It would take two years to pay it off stayin' here in the rent house, farmin' two hundred fifty acres and paying toll to your Grandpa Blackburn. Once we paid off the bank, we could move to our own place, maybe even a little before. Should we go into that much debt?"

"What's happening to land prices, Papa?" asked Clayborne.

"Yeah, Papa," said Hoyt "are they going up?"

"They're goin' up pretty slick."

"Then waiting to buy wouldn't be it," said Clayborne. "Besides, widow Harris won't save her property for us."

"Better do it now, Papa," said Hoyt.

"Yep, better do it now," said Clayborne.

"I think you boys are right, don't you, Belle?"

"They come to the same conclusion we did, Tom," she said smiling. "I'm right proud of how sensible they can be sometimes. Now don't let such praise give you swelled heads, you hear, boys?"

"Yes, Ma'am."

Walking to school in the chill dawn, facing into the northwest wind, was a trial some winter days, but Clayborne found a companion to walk with the last little bit of the way. His name was B. K. Crow, he was a ninth grader, and his father was Brother Ben Crow, pastor of Duffau Methodist Church. Brother Crow preached every Sunday in Duffau and was well known to the Dude Flat community, Baptists who went once a month to hear him preach at Brittain's Chapel on Sunday afternoons when their own pastor was away with another of the circuit's flock. The locals loved this Methodist just like they loved the Baptists. His son B. K., Clayborne's new friend, was one of fourteen children, some twelve of whom now lived at home.

"How are you this fine Monday morning, Clayborne?" B. K. Crow called in the frosty air.

"Colder than a frog," replied Clayborne, his breath freezing around his coat collar and muffler. "How come you're so cheerful?"

"I didn't have to walk three miles from Dude Flat."

"Yeah, but you have to come back to school Saturdays to work janitor."

"The pay's good, fifty cents a day for just cleaning up, and it helps the family. And I still don't have to walk three miles from Dude Flat."

They crunched along the muddy icy road to school, jumping into the grass to avoid being splattered when an occasional car came by.

"How come I didn't see your family in Hico this Saturday?" asked Clayborne.

"Oh, we were there. We prob'ly missed you because we had to drive a different way through town."

"What do you mean?"

"Well, you know we got twelve kids in our family, includin' me, right?"

"Right."

"And we always have to put some of the kids out on the running board, right?"

"Right. Everybody always says, 'Look, there goes the Crow bunch.'"

"Well, last week the Hico City Council passed a new ordinance that says no one can ride on the running boards of a car in Hico any more. Everybody's got to fit inside."

"They did? I didn't hear about it."

"You wouldn't have any reason to with your little family of four kids. They sent us a notice in the mail sayin' they'd fine us if we drove in again with kids hangin' on the running boards. But we started to drive into town as usual and Constable Williams saw us comin'. He ran out in front of us about a block before Main Street, you know, where the little cafe sits over on the left as you come in."

"Yeah," acknowledged Clayborne as they trundled along.

"Well, Constable Williams says" — B. K. imitated his deep voice — "'Brother Crow, you cain't come into Hico no more with all those kids hangin' on the running boards. City Council done passed an ordinance against it. We done sent you a letter about it.'"

Both boys had a chuckle at B. K.'s perfect imitation.

"Well, my Dad gets out of the Model T, points his finger in Constable Williams' face and says, 'My dear friend, can you get my wife and me and these twelve kids all inside and clear the running boards and fenders?' Constable Williams looks at my Dad, looks at the car and all us kids, and scratches his head just like in the Keystone Kops picture shows, and then he says, 'All right, but don't let me catch you drivin' down Main Street, you hear?'"

They roared together at the outcome, Clayborne bent over double with laughter and forgetting the cold and morning road from Dude Flat.

"Clayborne'" said Belle, "how tall are you?"

"Five-foot-ten, Mama. Why?"

"How much do you weigh?"

"A hundred and forty pounds. Why? What's this all about?"

"You're sixteen years old and you've been that size for going on a year. You've reached your growth, son. It's time to put you in a suit of clothes."

Tom and Belle accompanied him to Petty Brothers Mercantile Company store in Hico and instructed the clerk to fit him for a blue serge suit.

" 'Bout time to come out of knee pants, huh, young man?" asked the clerk, sizing him up with a practiced eye.

"Yep," said Clayborne, feeling that he was not only being fitted for a suit. He was going through an important rite of passage, the Texas country equivalent of a Bar Mitzvah. There were no scriptural passages to read, but the duties he felt falling to his lot in the simple act of buying clothes were formidable. Once he had a suit, a real suit with long pants, once he no longer wore only short pants that buttoned at the knee for Sunday, he was certain he would be acknowledged by the greater tribe as a full member, as a real grownup, as an adult, as a *man*. Not a *young* man, as the clerk had just called him, but a *man*. It was a great and mythic image.

Something in him still balked a little at being called a *man*. There was something about that word that was too big, too powerful, required too much of him. Although he wanted the title, tried to act the part, the reality made him inwardly flinch a little. To be a *man* was to lose all protection of being a boy, all claim to irresponsibility, all special pleading. You couldn't yell "Mama!" any more. You had to stand up and take it, whatever it might be. But that wasn't all. When you were a *man*, you were up against other men, like sometimes at harvest, eyeball to eyeball, muscle to muscle, will to will. Clayborne had seen in the rough alleys of Hico enough of the brawling life to know the full force of the adult Texas male, the tomcat violence that lay a millimeter under the skin of many men. That was pretty scary. He dimly sensed that among Texans love and hate, all feelings, in fact, were very near the surface, quick to show, and not scabbed over with false nicety and high manners as in other places. If someone liked you here, they liked you. If someone didn't, you knew it. You made no casual remarks you didn't mean. There was no pretense and wondering. A *man* was the guardian of that tradition. Was he up to it?

He knew, he absolutely knew that the three piece blue serge suit would be his badge of adulthood and the twenty-five dollars it cost the entry fee into manhood. There would be a time while he broke it in, got used to the suit, he imagined, that he would be partially, gradually accepted by the other men. But right away, he knew, he would notice that younger children, especially in Sunday School, deferred to him as a *man*. When the fitting was done and it was announced that the suit would be ready the following week, the clerk gave him a blue knit necktie, his first symbolic gift of power regalia from the tribe of grown men. He was really dressed up now.

The day after picking up the fitted suit at Petty's he wore it to Sunday School. It was a rite of testing: here he was, only a boy yesterday and today he was wearing *long* pants. He felt conspicuous and out of place wearing brand new clothes of any kind, but this, this new blue serge suit really made him feel strange. He gulped hard and went through the usual Sunday School motions, went through his trial by ordeal and nobody bit his head off and nobody challenged his new status. In fact, several people commented on how nice he looked. Perhaps he would live through this manhood stuff.

Shortly after he had broken in the suit, another test of his manly status came upon him: the Ninth Grade Weenie Roast was announced. Now a class weenie roast was an *occasion*, and an occasion meant you had to take a *girl*. It was a date. Somehow, as Clayborne had awakened to the existence of females, he had never really asked around for advice on how to behave on a date. He never asked because he never thought about dates. The whole idea of dates was one he probably would not have invented if it was left entirely to him. But now that he was in a city school, someone — he never knew who — kept arranging these *occasions*. And the first was the class weenie roast. He was about to go out on his first date.

He didn't really know the girls in the ninth grade class very well, they were sort of city kids — well, he was more country than they were, anyway — but he knew Maxie Partain from seeing her at church and from taking cane over to her father's sorghum mill. Maxie was about six years older, but she was a regular fellow — girl — that a guy could talk to without feeling silly. She had gone through ninth grade once, but never went on to finish, and decided to come back and get some more preparation, which was why she was in school and six years older than most of the others. Clayborne had noticed her younger sister Oretta as she was growing up, but she was nearly three years younger than he was and ran with a much younger crowd, just the opposite of Clayborne, who had found himself from about twelve on to be bigger than others his age and running with an older crowd. Maxie would fit in with his bunch better.

So, on the appointed evening, Clayborne talked his father out of the car keys, dressed in ordinary school clothes, counted on the magic of his blue serge man suit hanging up at home, hopped in the Model T and picked up Maxie Partain. There was no awkward silence and no embarrassed hemming and hawing with Maxie. He bade her good evening, admired her school dress, squired her from her front door to the car, even opened the car door for her, and as they drove away chatted easily with her about basketball and the cotton crop this year.

The weenie roast was out in the open not far from the school, in the pasture of one of the ninth grader's father, and just southwest of Duffau Cemetery. They found a bunch of big old tree trunks and branches and boards and built one huge bonfire. Everything was great, the other ninth graders took to Maxie right off, they all sang songs everybody knew, pop tunes from the radio like *Sweet Georgia Brown* and *Don't Bring Lulu* and *Ain't Gonna Rain No More*. Clayborne preferred good old down home country yodeling but he put up with these city kids and their jazzy radio songs easy enough. It was when the lyrics turned to *Gimme a Little Kiss, Will Ya, Huh?* that he realized some of the other couples were definitely boy-girl items, whereas he and Maxie were plain old friends. He suddenly knew that he had no idea how to act on a *date*, but since he had made no major blunders so far, kept up the friendly banter and happy chatter he'd started with. The magic blue serge man suit at home was working.

When the weenies were roasted and the fire died down and it was all over, Clayborne once more opened the car door for his date, drove Maxie home with appropriate conversation, hopped out to open the door for her, kissed her goodnight with a friendly peck, got back in the car and drove away in a cloud of road dust. Buying that magic blue serge suit of manhood must have been just the ticket, he thought. Just having it in the chifferobe at home made him a self-confident, positive and certain success. When he gave his mother a glowing report of the proceedings, she asked in alarm: "You didn't walk her to her door? You just left her standing out there in the road? Oh, Clayborne, when are you going to learn to be a gentleman?"

Who tells you these things? he wondered. *How am I supposed to know?* He was discovering the first of the many age-old tribulations of the adult male: the fact that the universe did not come with a set of operating instructions from the manufacturer. Being confident and positive and certain about how to act was really just a lot of guesswork, he decided. He reckoned he had imposed enough on Maxie Partain and never dated his future sister-in-law again, and did not date anyone any more while at Duffau School. He realized that the purchase of his blue serge suit did not actually have the magic in it he thought it might, and determined that manhood was something to grow into gradually as one's puppy feet shrank.

He did well in Duffau School, very well in his first year. He was always first or second in his class in grade averages. He was admired for his athletic ability and well liked for his level-headed, friendly personality. He had a good time. He ended the school year in early May of 1926 with As and Bs on his report card, looking forward to tenth grade after a busy summer.

In July Clayborne came home from harvest one Friday night and awoke out of a sound sleep somewhere between three and four in the morning.

He did not know why, but sat up a moment, his mind blurred with the slow pumping of his heart and the ebbing force of life in those small hours of the night. Then he looked out his bedroom window and saw the bright skyglow of a fire, a big fire. The tide of consciousness washed the dull shore of his morning brain.

Another fire! It's out south, down toward harvest! I'll bet the cook shack is burning! It's those old coal oil lamps, I'll bet. Poor Tom Roach and Lillie!

He stumbled out of bed to see, stepped to the window. "Oh, no!" he said involuntarily, galvanized awake. Hoyt stirred at his words. "What are you doing up, Clayborne?" the youngster asked.

"Come on, Hoyt," he replied. "Go wake up Papa. The Cooper's house is on fire! We've got to get over and help them!"

Clayborne slipped his overalls on and flew out the door, leaving the front screen flapping and Pup barking wildly. Tom was not far behind. They both ran panting the two hundred yards to the flaming home. Fire had engulfed one complete side and spread to the garage and grain sheds.

"Mrs. Cooper! Jim Cooper! You're safe!" gasped Tom.

"We're out, and we got Jayboy here, but we don't see Daisy and Jewel. They were asleep upstairs, but the fire was worst right at the stairway. We hollered at them but we ain't seen them!" shouted Jim Cooper. His wife was frantic with anxiety.

"Which side of the house do they sleep on?" asked Clayborne.

"North side, up around there, right over the front gallery," pointed Jim Cooper.

"Wind's blowing up pretty good from the south," yelled Tom over the snarl of burning wood. "The cedars next to the house are already burning up, fire's going to be all around the place right quick," said Tom as he and Clayborne ran around the house to the girls' bedroom windows. The intense heat baked their left sides. They rounded the corner just in time to see the two teenage girls clambering down a flower trellis nailed to the front porch eaves.

"Daddy! Mama! Jayboy!" they screamed at the house. "Where are you?" They saw Tom and Clayborne. "Oh, Mr. Perry! Our house is on fire! Where's our Mama and Daddy?"

"They're fine, they're fine, Jewel," comforted Tom, directing them away from the flames and smoke. "You and Daisy will find them and Jayboy right around the upwind side of the house, see there?"

"Oh, Mama, Daddy, Jayboy!" The girls ran to their parents, crying and screaming.

The family was safe. The Cooper place was a total loss.

Just before his sixteenth birthday Clayborne was elected Sunday School superintendent of Prairie Springs Baptist Church. He enjoyed the new responsibility, making sure lesson plans were handed out to all the teachers for the sixty-odd people attending each Sunday, accounting for materials, leading the singing when the regular leader happened to be absent. His deeper involvement with the Baptist Young Peoples Union gave him his first taste of public speaking, getting up on his feet and dealing with an audience. He mastered his stage fright and soon came to enjoy standing before a group and telling them what he knew.

Miss Lois Ballow, another unmarried girl, twenty-three years old, served as principal of Duffau School beginning in October of 1926. She ran the same regimen as before, ten grades, five teachers and two hundred students, give or take. She made sure that her pupils looking toward further schooling got adequate preparation. She was particularly pointed with Clayborne, telling him that if a farm boy wanted to go finish eleventh grade at Hico High School next year, he'd better have a foreign language this year at Duffau School or he wouldn't get into Hico, much less out.

Clayborne got the message, and signed up for his four regular academic subjects plus Spanish. His first day at school in mid-October gave him another little shock: only ten students still remained in his graduating class. The demands of farm labor and lack of motivation had taken its toll, four of his friends now among the walking wounded of the semi-literate masses, never to rise above their origins. It shocked and frightened him a little to see how fragile his hold on education really was, how easily it could be snatched from his grasp as it had been from theirs. He had been a top student in ninth grade and now set out to be valedictorian of his tenth grade class at Duffau School this last year, to be the best. It would help get him into eleventh grade at Hico High, now a more precious goal than ever. He told his close friend B. K. Crow about his resolve.

B. K. told him, "I'm going to give you a run for your money, Clayborne. One of us is going to be valedictorian, and we're both going to work hard for it."

"Are you really going to try to beat me?"

"That's for me to know and you to find out."

A few days after school started Grandma and Grandpa Blackburn moved to a new and smaller farm on the same road into Hico as Tom & Belle's hundred acres, but only about a mile out of town and not far from Jack's Hollow Branch, a stream that emptied into the Bosque in Hico near the cotton gins. They were getting too old to run a big country place any more. The move itself proved to be a source of consternation for Grandpa Charley Blackburn. He had moved to this farm as a child of seven and later bought it from his father. Moving from place to place like a rent farmer just wasn't in his background. So on the great day he simply backed the wagon up to the porch, went in the house, brought out a stack of twelve dinner plates, and just laid them in the wagon.

Jim Cooper, whose burned out house just up the road had now been rebuilt a short way from the old foundations, looked on in amazement as Charley Blackburn randomly stacked this and that, helter skelter in his wagon with no rhyme, no scansion, no sense.

"Ain't nothin' to keep those dishes from breakin', Charley," said Cooper.

"I guess not, now that you mention it, Jim," said Blackburn.

"You don't know a whole lot about movin', do you, Charley?"

"Not a whole lot, Jim."

"I think maybe your wife ought to supervise, Charley."

"I think maybe you're right, Jim."

The next week Clayborne came home from school and called from the front door to his mother, "How's Pup today?"

Belle stood in the kitchen doorway looking glum. "He's still mighty sick, son."

Tom appeared behind her, sorrow on his face. "He's too sick, son. He's too old to fend off what ails him. He's fourteen."

"What are you sayin', Papa?"

"He ain't goin' to make it, Clayborne."

He walked past them without a word, straight to the applebox in the kitchen that had been padded as a sickbed for the old dog a week earlier. He looked down at his little black friend, old and stove up and worn out. Pup turned his head feebly and looked up. The light of recognition glowed briefly in his rheumy eyes. His tail wagged twice and he laid back motionless on the soft rags, exhausted by the effort. His breathing was shallow, getting shallower.

It was true. Clayborne could feel it. Time had done its simple work. The radiance of death glowed all around him. Pup was dying.

"Son . . ." said Belle.

He did not respond.

"Leave him be, Belle," said Tom softly, gently moving her into the living room.

Clayborne sat on the floor next to the applebox bed. He said nothing. He just made a presence, someone there for his friend.

We've laid in the dirt under the little red wagon. We've played in the sun. We've watched the rain from under the cotton wagon. We've gone to Colorado and starved out. We've come a long road back. We've saved you from poison in Oklahoma. We've lived in the old rent house and the new one. We've got our own land. We've hunted 'possums and chased rabbits. We've picked a lot of cotton. I'll always love you.

Pup died before dark. Clayborne silently put the body in a pasteboard box and took it out into the field, well away from the house, away from everybody. He brought the old Number 3 shovel and dug a deep hole, deep enough so the varmints wouldn't dig it up. He put the box in the ground and covered it with dirt.

He looked around at the Texas land and the sky and the fresh dirt.
This is my friend.
He tamped the clean earth with the shovel bottom.
I hope you like it here, Pup.
He lay down on the little mound.

A long time later he got up and went in the house.
That night the owl called.

The spring of 1927 brought with it the senior play, a sentimental dramatization of *The Prince and the Pauper* and Clayborne got a good part. It was a long play in three acts and lasted two hours. The whole senior class performed and had to recruit a couple of juniors to fill the lesser roles. Some rehearsals were scheduled for night by the light of Coleman lanterns in the unelectrified school, and since Clayborne had three and a half miles to walk home afterward, B. K. Crow prevailed upon his mother to invite the boy from Dude Flat on those occasions to stay overnight.

Brother Ben Crow, father of fourteen, was widely known and respected as a man who didn't let any grass grow under his feet. In addition to preaching, he sold insurance, magazines, newspapers, anything salable. He accepted chicken and eggs as payment. In fact he gained a reputation for always carrying a wire and hook to catch his newly acquired chickens. He was known to feed his kiddos well. Sleeping in a room with five other boys in three double beds did not thrill Clayborne, but he would have slept in the barn with the cows for the chance to get one of Mrs. Crow's dinner sacks. He accepted her invitation.

The morning after the first night rehearsal Mrs. Crow packed him a light bread bologna sandwich, a box of vanilla wafers, and a banana. He could hardly wait for dinner time so he could dive into his good food. What a treat! These city folks, Clayborne acknowledged, sure knew how to make a good dinner, not like the plain old country food he was used to, the two biscuits, sausage or ham, a boiled egg, cake and a fruit from the farm. The city food may or may not have helped his performance, but when rehearsals were over and the curtain finally went up, Clayborne was a hit and *The Prince and the Pauper* was boffo in Duffau.

Some time during his last year at Duffau School, Clayborne entered the house to find a shiny new Victrola sitting in the front room. It was a fine hand-cranked spring-wound model with a handsome megaphone-style horn. But the best part was the little stack of ten-inch records Tom had brought home from Hico. Country music. Hillbilly music. The siren call of the cowboy yodel. The sound of geetars and sweet fiddles. The cane-brake cries of "Aw-haw, Jole Blon!" on the descant. It was satisfyin' right down to your shoe leather. Heaven must sound like this. The boys — Clayborne and Hoyt — were enraptured. They would even walk in from plowing in the field for dinner just to play yodeling records until Tom pushed them back to work. Any time a new record showed up on the Victrola they smacked the needle down and waited for the opening refrain. If it had yodeling, they wore it out. They'd yodel to anything, even non-hillbilly standards: *My Blue Heaven* became one of their favorites. They embraced *Oh, Susannah!* and *K-K-K-Katy* and *Yankee Doodle Dandy* and *Alexander's Ragtime Band* and *Beer Barrel Polka*.

Clayborne had gone over to Grandad Perry's on his bicycle occasional evenings to listen to the Crosby radio, but he didn't really like the earphones any more than Old Grandma did. Grandpa Perry liked fiddle music more than yodeling, and there wasn't enough of either on the radio until about 1925, and then he bought some of those fancy loudspeakers for his radio. Grandpa bragged how you could turn the radio on in the front room with those loudspeakers and hear it all the way into the kitchen. And Clayborne showed up a little more often, especially after *National Barn Dance* began coming through from station WLS in Chicago. He couldn't resist the clang of cowbells and the stompin' fiddle rendition of "Hey, Hey, Hey, the hayloft gang is here," and the twangy announcer saying to his fellow hillbillies, "Hello, hello, hello, everybody, everywhere; well, well welcome to your ole Alka Seltzer National Barn Dance."

But his true love was *Grand Ole Opry*, the king of the hillbilly shows from station WSM in Nashville. WSM had a powerful transmitter that reached into thirty states. And the folks on *Grand Ole Opry* were real hillbillies, not drugstore cowboys. They'd come to the station on mules and in wagons to play on Saturday nights and go back home to farm during the week. They'd fiddle and yodel and play songs so old their origins baffled anthropologists: *Greenback Dollar*, *Brown's Ferry Blues*, *Rabbit in the Flea Patch*. They couldn't read music. Every now and then one of them would learn to read a little, but not enough to hurt his playing. They sawed away and plunked by ear, shoutin', whoopin', stompin', whistlin', pounding their dulcimers, whacking their banjos, scraping their washboards, whining in their French harps — harmonicas to the uninitiate — and tooting in their whiskey jugs. It went on from 8:00 p.m. to midnight, Eastern time, and that wasn't near enough for country addicts. How could you help but want more of the unrehearsed tunes of the Gully Jumpers and the Fruit Jar Drinkers, or the fiddle band called the Possum Hunters? The Possum Hunters were mostly farmers, but their leader was a real professional, Dr. Humphrey Bates, physician.

And then there were the local shows, produced in Texas, that tried to out-country Nashville with the Lightcrust Doughboys from Burrus Mills (sponsored by a good-size flour company) and the hillbilly music shows introduced with another good-size flour mill's jingle "It's the best / in the West / It's ahead / of the rest / It's Beuley's Best / . . . And Anchor Feed!" — that last phrase to the lowdown notes of the *Good Evening Friends* "tail" that musicians loved to stick on song endings, G, A, G, B-flat — go try it on a piano if you can't remember it. You've heard the "tail" a million times to the words *Good Evening Friends*, but no telling how many Texas boys have migrated to places where people thought they were crazy for singing the familiar four notes to the words "And Anchor Feed!"

Music also put Clayborne into a moral bind about this time: he would go to a party at some school friend's house and some of the kids would start dancing. The homes were not very close to his community, they might be three or four miles away. But a good Baptist was not supposed to go to dances. Should he stay? Should he leave? He knew his parents would not approve, but he stayed and just watched the dancers from a discreet distance, much as Tom had done those years ago that evening in the park at Wichita Falls. He never told his family about these episodes.

It was much easier to go to a religious singing at some home closer to Dude Flat. A singing was much like a party, but without the dancing and Victrola records. And the songs were all hymns. It was an evening thing most often, sometimes on Sunday afternoons at church.

It had been a good year, the tenth grade. He had worked hard, very hard, and he wanted to be valedictorian so bad he could taste it. It was doubly important because this year the top student would receive a $25.00 scholarship to Tarleton Community College in Stephenville for the next school year. Taking eleventh grade at Tarleton would be even better than Hico High School — if the money was available. But B. K. had been as good as his word, and stayed up there with him at the top of the class. Classmate Marvin Miller told Clayborne near the end of school, "You two are so close in grades they're going to have to count every test to see who's valedictorian." And so they did.

On Monday of graduation week in April, 1927, Superintendent Kay Robinson and Principal Lois Ballow averaged the grades to see who was number one. Tuesday afternoon they announced the final scores: B. K. Crow, 94.8, Clayborne Perry, 94.7. Clayborne was stunned. One lousy fraction of a point. One measly decimal place. There would be no scholarship to Tarleton. He would have to go to Hico. It hurt to lose but B. K. was such a good friend it was impossible not to be happy for him.

B. K. memorized his Valedictorian speech and Clayborne memorized his salutatorian speech. The Friday evening ceremony went off without a hitch, the gathered crowds of proud parents, Tom and Belle beaming, the presentation of diplomas, the class prophecy, the singing of the class song, the class leaders' speeches, valedictorian last. Seeing his friend up there, proudly speaking to the crowd, looking into his preacher papa's eyes, Clayborne was glad, positively glad that B. K. had won the grade contest. When the crowd broke up and began to mill about, Clayborne realized how far he had come. He'd gotten through ten grades, more than his father or his grandfathers or his great grandfathers or any lineal ancestor in living memory. The lost scholarship did not trouble him after thinking about it: Tarleton was an expensive place to go and even in a boom time, what if he couldn't raise the money to finish eleventh grade? B. K. was already worrying about it — he'd figured that it would cost him $300.00 a year to go to Tarleton. The $25.00 scholarship wouldn't even put a dent in it. B. K. had talked to a friend about a job in Waco, and had made up his mind to take it. So the scholarship would go unused and Clayborne would take eleventh grade at Hico.

Or at least he hoped he would.

-10-

THE BLESSINGS OF HARVEST

WITH school out, he signed up again to work harvest with Mr. Fouts, starting the usual time, the first week of June. That taken care of, he still had a few weeks to make arrangements for enrolling in Hico High School. He noticed that very few of his Duffau classmates were planning to go on to eleventh grade: his friend Marvin B. Miller had gone off to California in search of work, others simply went home to farming with no further thought of education. It only added impetus to his determination to get into Hico High.

Three weeks later he had plowed through enough telephone questions and buck passing and contradictory answers about entering Hico High to choke a horse. The confusion all added up to one thing: the Hico Superintendent of Schools, Mr. C. G. Masterson, had to give his approval. And so, on a Saturday afternoon, Clayborne bucked up his courage, took his diploma and walked the eight miles into Hico to get permission. After finding Mesquite Street and walking into a neighborhood of fine sturdy homes, many of them brick, he located the address he was looking for. There stood a fine white-painted frame home with two imposing gables facing the street, a gallery wrapped around the front and side, its seven columns adding dignity, and neatly trimmed low hedges flanking the front steps. Mr. Masterson, Clayborne saw, sat relaxed and reading his newspaper on the front porch swing.

Clayborne felt intimidated by the nice homes and the orderly blocks and neatly bordered lawns, the *town*-ness of the place. He was ready to cut and run. He toyed with the idea of just passing by. No! He'd walked this far, he'd go through with it. With great trepidation the young man walked up Mr. Masterson's sidewalk, front steps and onto the porch.

"Yes, son? What can I do for you?" the superintendent asked, not gruff, but with that deceptive ease often displayed by men who know they have power.

"My name's Clayborne Perry and I live up at Dude Flat just on the other side of Camp Branch school."

"I know the place."

"I got out of Duffau School this year, and I found out I have to ask you. Can I go to school down here?"

"Well, how much work have you had?"

"I finished Duffau School. That's ten grades."

"Did they graduate you?"

"Oh, yes, sir, I graduated. Here's my diploma, right here." He unrolled the fancy vellum sheet. It had become sweaty from his nervous palms.

"Hmm. Looks like you got out of Duffau School all right."

"Yes, sir. We had a big ceremony and all."

"Hmm. I'm sure you did. Well, son, you can't go to Hico High School unless you stay in eleventh grade for two years."

"Two years, Mr. Masterson? Why, sir?" He had a bad feeling about how the conversation was going. Time seemed to him to slow, to crawl agonizingly.

"They should have told you we've got strict foreign language requirements. You'd have to go two years to meet our requirements."

Clayborne was ready to panic. Where had he gone wrong? How had this extra year of language escaped his notice? "Well," he said feebly, "uh, I guess I could go two years, then."

"Look, son. Let me level with you. You country kids don't have it, you simply cannot do the work of a city school."

The country kid swallowed audibly. The words almost stuck in his throat. "I'll work hard. I'm a hard worker."

"Oh, I don't doubt you are. But that's not the point. You simply aren't prepared. You can't cut the mustard in a top-notch school like Hico High. I'm going to have to tell you no."

"But I'll try hard. I'll really try."

"I'm telling you that I've decided not to let you try. We couldn't afford to take you."

"But, Mr. Masterson . . ."

"No, we just can't take you."

He left with "no" for an answer. He was flattened to the ground, lower than a snakebelly. Here was a city school superintendent saying "No!" to a country boy who was pretty shaky to begin with. He went home with a sick feeling in his stomach. He didn't talk much that Sunday, and

Monday he went off to work at harvest. Out among the grain shocks he had plenty of time to think. He had to get into Hico High. Maybe Mr. Masterson didn't realize what a good student he was. He decided to try again. Two Saturdays after his initial rebuff, Clayborne showed up once more, finding Mr. Masterson relaxed and reading his newspaper on the front porch swing.

"You again?" the superintendent queried over his paper.

"Yes, sir, Mr. Masterson. I thought maybe if I'd explain a little more you might change your mind."

"Me? Change my mind? Not likely, son. But if you got something to say, you go ahead and say it."

"Look, sir. Here are my report cards." He produced two years worth of semester grade summaries.

Masterson looked them over carefully. "Hmm. You have a lot of As here, I see. In good subjects, U.S. History. Hmm."

"What do you think, Mr. Masterson? Not bad grades, huh?"

"No, son. Not bad grades. But they came from a country school, don't you understand? There's nothing here to change my mind. They just don't prepare you for city school work. You only went to school five months a year most of your life, then seven months at Duffau. The kids in Hico all went nine months a year, ever since they were six years old. I'll bet you didn't even start to school until you were seven. You'd be so far behind you wouldn't understand what your teachers were talking about. I'm sorry, but the answer is still no."

Down again. "No" again. He went back to harvest, to think and to work and to worry. He tried to think all the way through the problem time and again, but nothing. When he went home weekends, he just did his work, went into town with his family, went to church and didn't say much. In mid-July Tom and Belle became worried about him and when he came home from harvest one Friday night Tom said to him: "Son, put your troubles aside for a day. Tomorrow we're going to the Hico Reunion."

The Hico Reunion was actually a summer carnival verging on a circus. It had been an annual July event for many years; one of the first photographs taken of Clayborne shows him at two years wearing a little duckbill cap stitched with the words "Hico Reunion."

"Hey, the balloon man is back this year!" yelled Hoyt from the back seat of the Model T. "Come on, Papa, drive faster so we can see him up close."

The big tan hot air balloon with its operator suspended in a wicker basket drifted low over the trees half a mile ahead. No rides were for sale: the balloon itself was such a novelty it attracted crowds as a mere exhibition.

Little Nadine hopped up on the front seat and shouted in glee, "Balloon, Papa, Balloon!" Dorothy napped in Belle's arms, oblivious to the hollering.

Only Clayborne was quiet, lost in a brown study relating, no doubt, to getting into Hico High School.

They drove directly under the drifting balloon, and Hoyt said to his Papa, "Hey, he's coming down on Starley's place. Can we drive out and meet him?"

"No, son. We'd like to get stuck out there in that pasture. They got a truck to pick up the balloon fellow, take him back into Hico. He'll go up again several times yet today. You can see him up close when he goes up next from the Reunion grounds, it'll only be another hour or so. You'll want to see him too, won't you Clayborne?"

"What? Oh, sure, Papa."

The Reunion always started on a Thursday at 10:00 a.m. with a parade through Hico, buggies and bicycles decorated with colorful crepe paper woven in their spokes and automobiles festooned with artificial flowers. Horses and farm wagons joined the merry fray, spiffed up the best way available, following the parade route down Main Street, off to the railroad station, across the track, down past the flour mill, across the Bosque River bridge and into Hico City Park.

The peaceful wooded park for a few days became a madhouse, stuffed with ferris wheel and merry-go-round and loop-the-loop rides powered by portable gasoline engines, lined with wrestling and boxing rings where local amateurs could try their luck against travelling strong men, strung with a two-bits-a-throw side show runway replete with fat lady, sword swallower, fire eater, jugglers, snake ladies, hit-the-milk-bottle-a-dime-for-three-balls-winner-gets-a-stuffed-animal stalls and live animal shows featuring a tired elephant and a ratty camel and a few other exotic creatures long inured to the vicissitudes of carny life and grown cynical like their human keepers who they resembled.

Saturday was the culmination of the excitement, last day before the show moved on. The cotton candy whirred onto paper cones, the lemonade flowed by the gallon — all you can drink for a nickel — and the taffy pulling machine gathered its usual youthful crowd of enthralled devotees hypnotized by the shiny metal arms rotating and stretching their burden of stringy candy in crazy loops. The Perry family drove into the melee just after noon that Saturday, planning to stay until ten or so that night. They had put aside several dollars for Reunion and set out to have a stompin' good time. Everyone succeeded except Clayborne. He went through the motions, and smiled in all the right places, but it was obvious that his heart was not in it. He went in circles on the ferris wheel, he went in circles on the merry-go-round, we went in circles on the loop-the-loop, and he went in circles figuring out how to get into Hico

High. He was ready to go home by supper time, but went along with the frivolity for more hours just to please his family. It was fun enough, and it eased his troubled mind a while, but it wasn't like other years when he'd wanted to stay all day all three days. But then other years weren't his last chance to get an education.

He went back to harvest the next Monday and worked and worked, bagging grain now at the thresher, and figuring out how to get into Hico High School. Weeks went by. When he got his final harvest pay envelope the first of August, he went home and brooded some more, wondering what to do. He sat at the kitchen table a lot, and didn't even want to listen to yodeling records with Hoyt. Was there anything, anything he himself had overlooked? Was there anything Mr. Masterson might have overlooked? The superintendent had kept harping on how poorly prepared he was. Why? Why? And why was there an extra year of language suddenly required that would keep him at Hico for two years? One day as he was walking out to the barn to feed the cows it came to him. Maybe Mr. Masterson hadn't realized he'd already had a year of foreign language. Maybe that extra year was the year he'd already taken at Duffau. Of course, that had to be it! And perhaps Mr. Masterson didn't know he had been tenth grade salutatorian. Clayborne didn't like the idea of bragging on himself, but there was no alternative. He'd try one last time. The middle of August he returned to Mr. Masterson's home and found him relaxed and reading his newspaper on the front porch swing.

"You're a persistent cuss, aren't you, son?"

"Yes, sir. And I've thought of something you might have overlooked the times I came before."

"And what's that?"

"Well, sir, you talked about me not being prepared and about needing to stay two years to get my foreign language?"

"That's right, young man. All our students are required to take two years of a foreign language so they can qualify for college. You country kids never seem to think about college. You should have had a year of foreign language in tenth grade, and you don't have it."

"But I do, sir. When I went into tenth grade they told me you had to have a foreign language to get into Hico schools, so I took Spanish. A whole year of it."

"You did?"

"Yes, sir."

"I don't remember seeing it on your report cards."

"It's right here, sir. I got a B both semesters. A strong B."

"Where? Hmm. Oh, I see, under Language. You're right. I thought that meant Language Arts, English. These country schools should write their report cards better so you can understand them. And I guess I should have looked closer. You're right, young man. That is something to think about."

"Sir, that means I have eleven credits total. That means I wouldn't have to stay in Hico High for two years. That makes me eligible to start with Spanish II in Hico High."

"I'll tell you whether you're eligible or not."

"Yes, sir. But another thing. I was the salutatorian in my tenth grade class. I got the second highest marks."

"Out of only ten kids in a country school, don't forget. That only puts you in the top twenty percent — of Duffau students."

"Yes, sir, that's true. But I graduated with a 94.7 average."

"You *were* graduated. *Were graduated* is correct."

"Yes, sir. I was graduated with a 94.7 average. The valedictorian only got one tenth of a point more than me, 94.8. I'm a good student. I've had a year of Spanish already. I am prepared. I can do the work."

"Hmm. And you are persistent." He thought a moment. "Well, son, you come back next Saturday and I'll think it over and let you know. But from experience I've found that you country kids can't do the work."

He left trembling this time. He knew his fate hung in the balance, which way the beam would tilt. That week he could hardly eat. It went by like a dream. He returned the next Saturday for the verdict. Once again he found the consistent Mr. Masterson relaxed and reading his newspaper on the front porch swing. He ascended the stairs of the future, shaking in full fear. He didn't introduce himself or make any prologue, only waited to hear his destiny sealed.

Mr. Masterson put his paper down. He looked the young man seriously in the face.

"Clayborne Perry," he said, "I've decided to let you try."

Elation! "Oh, thank you, Mr. Masterson, thank you!"

"But . . ." the word hung in the air like a palpable Sword of Damocles. "But, if you fail, if you fail I will never let another country kid try in my school. These country schools cannot do the job in five or six months of class what the city schools are doing nine months a year."

"I won't let you down, Mr. Masterson. I promise."

"See to it, or you'll be letting a lot of other country kids down, too. Remember that when you enter Hico High School next month."

When you enter Hico High School next month! Wow-eee! He did it! He had his chance! He left happier than he could recall being for months.

But how was he going to get eight and a half miles from Dude Flat to Hico High every day from the first of September to mid-November? It would be six weeks before his family moved away from Dude Flat to their own farm on the Hico-Duffau road, only three miles from school. The new place would be well within walking distance, at least there was that to look forward to: Tom had reckoned this year's cotton crop would set them up at last, enable them to move onto their own land while still paying off the last year of their bank loan. That would leave only a month and a half of trouble getting to school for Clayborne.

He talked his father into letting him take the family Model T the first few days of school. There simply wasn't any other way to get there. The morning of the first day he parked the car under a big liveoak tree in a stall facing the sidewalk. He still wasn't used to sidewalks, even the *idea* of sidewalks, and he'd been coming into this town all his life. The yellow brick building of Hico High seemed unbelievably imposing, the portals of learning, the gateway to . . . what? A world too complicated for him to understand, too sophisticated to put up with his rustic ways, too subtle for him to catch the nuances? Or a world not too different from the one he'd always known, subject to common sense, yielding to straight thinking, complicated only by the compounding of simples, sophisticated only by the strictures of scientific thought, subtle only in ways a careful student could detect? He was about to find out some of those answers.

The first day of school, he found, always began with an assembly of the entire student body, an orientation session for new students. It always included an inspirational speech from a local official. Today it was to be Judge J. C. Barrow, the current Mayor of Hico. He came to the podium to polite applause and began by extolling the virtues of education in general and Hico High School in particular. Clayborne felt a diffident pride in having made it into this school, at having been permitted to join the ranks of an institution that had a real judge for a first-day speaker. Judge Barrow droned on about the difficulties of getting an education, and how fortunate these gathered students were to be here and have this opportunity and "they'd better by Sam Hill appreciate it." Clayborne looked over the student body and saw bored privilege stamped all over the city kids' faces. They didn't understand what the judge was talking about, how fortunate they were. They took this school for granted. It had always been here, hadn't it? It was their due, they thought. No big deal. They didn't understand, but *he* understood. And then Clayborne heard the words that stuck:

"Young men and young women," Judge Barrow intoned, "I know that many of you are scared, scared of the new environment, scared of the new people, scared of the new school you're in. But let me tell you one thing, and one thing only: no matter what difficulties or obstacles you find in these halls as time goes on, if you will only *try*, try hard, try *real* hard, you will make it through school. And that is my message for you today. You try, and you'll make it. I thank you."

He knew he could try, he knew that much. He could try as hard as anyone. It inspired him, it was a life ring to hang onto when the seas got rough. Right then and there, before assembly was out, he made it his goal for the first few weeks, to try, to try as hard as he could. He tried hard for two days and on the third day he made his first serious blunder.

He had taken the family car again, and had parked it in the same stall, under the big liveoak tree, just as he had the first two days. He had taken his dinner to school in a brown paper sack like the city kids. But the first two days of sitting in the school dining room he found that his country dinner — two biscuits, bacon, a boiled egg with a little salt folded into a newspaper, a fried peach pie and an apple from Grandpa Blackburn's orchard — this hillbilly fare was drawing snickers of contempt from city kids who had brought light bread sandwiches, some with peanut butter and jelly, some with bologna, and storebought cookies and perishable fruit like bananas — things he yearned for but could not afford. It became too much of an embarrassment and he took the easy way out on Wednesday: when the noon bell rang, he simply walked out the front door, went to his car, sat in the front seat and ate his plain dinner alone, away from those prying, laughing, insulting eyes.

After lunch he was abruptly called out of class and to the superintendent's office. There he had to wait in the outer office until Mr. Masterson returned from an errand and called him into the inner sanctum. Clayborne entered and stood trembling, wondering what offense he had committed.

"Young man," began Masterson, "today you have made a terrible mistake. We have truancy regulations forbidding students to leave the school building during school hours except when instructed to by a teacher or other authority. We explained those rules to you on the first day of school in the assembly. You have evidently either forgotten or you're deliberately breaking our rules. Now, I know you country kids aren't used to this kind of city discipline, but you're going to have to follow the rules. So listen to me, and listen good: You are never to eat lunch outside the building again, you hear?"

"Yes, sir. I didn't know. Honest, sir."

"Well, you know now. If you can't be trusted to stay in the dining room during dinner, I'm going to have to assign you to a study hall during noon hour. I want you to eat with the teachers in the study hall for the rest of the year. Is that clear?"

"Yes, sir. It's clear, sir. I really didn't know. I'll do whatever you say. I'll go to the study hall at noon from now on."

"Do so."

He went back to class scared to death. He was seventeen years old and felt like all that about manhood had just abandoned him forever. He felt like a little kid again, not knowing the rules and having to learn the hard way. All his experience, all that education he was supposed to have gotten at Camp Branch and Duffau, where was it now? And all because of his stupid country food. He certainly ate his dinner from then on in the study hall, but he usually picked a seat toward the back of the room so the teachers and other students couldn't see what he was eating. He called up the words of Judge Barrow time and again: "just try hard and you'll get through school . . . try hard, and you'll make it."

It was not easy making friends with the city kids of Hico. They were aloof and put on airs and knew about things that were mysteries to Clayborne: snitching cigarettes from their parents and smoking after school — "got any ciggy-butts, country kid?" — listening to jazzy syncopated Victrola records—"I just love little Ethel Waters numbers like *Oh Daddy* and smooth stuff like *Make Me Know It* by Fess Williams and his Royal Flush Savoy Orchestra, don't you?" — going to a new picture show every week — "last week I saw Janet Gaynor and Charles Farrell in *Seventh Heaven* and this week it was Greta Garbo and John Gilbert in *Flesh and the Devil*" — wearing *fashionable* clothes — "Well, *of course* my mother lets me wear Holeproof Hosiery, just like in the magazines, and in the newest color, *orchid*. . . ."

There were rich kids and there were poor kids, and Clayborne had never known either kind. The rich kids had everything they wanted and the poor kids had nothing — he discovered that even the most wretched of the farm kids at least had something to eat and had other farmers to help out when things got really bad. When you were poor in a city, you had only grocery stores to get food from and neighbors whose names you didn't know. These city kids were so different and surprising and difficult.

There were some kids who didn't go to church at all and even a few who laughed at those who did. There were kids who went to other churches and some kids who went to religious places that weren't even called churches, Catholic kids and Jewish kids and others he knew nothing about, and there always seemed to be that magnetic repulsion, like two south poles pushed together, when he tried to get close to them.

Then he discovered that there were a few other country kids at Hico High, J. D. Patterson, who lived about nine miles south of town, and Teddy Nix, who lived not too far from Duffau, and Austin Giesecke, a German boy from north of Hico. In all there may have been eleven or twelve of them, some in tenth grade, some in eleventh. He wondered if they had all had as tough a time as he had getting around Masterson and into Hico High. He heard from them that a few morning rides were available coming into school, but not many going back home. Clayborne was glad simply to find a way of getting to school. There was no time pressure on getting back home after 4:00 p.m., and he found he could catch an occasional ride from a neighbor driving home. Most afternoons he found himself walking.

The country kids soon noticed that the city boys stuck to their own kind, forming little cliques, and letting it be known that country kids were not welcome in their group. The countryboys found they had no option but to do the same. They stuck together defensively and held their own.

By the end of the second week of school, the football team had managed to turn out only half a dozen not-so-great players, and they all quit in disgust. The coach then put forth a call to all students for basketball tryouts. Anyone was eligible for the basketball team. Candidates would be released from class at 3:15 for practice on the outdoor play field — the hotshot city school boasted no gymnasium. After three days of tryout, Coach J. A. Freeman hand picked his team of ten players from the best candidates. Nine were country kids. Now the hillbillies were in the driver's seat. There were no more rude brush-offs. There was recognition from the teachers and adulation from the girls. Clayborne finally realized his ambition to be an ace forward and dribble his way to school fame. Hico ended up second in the county that year.

English IV was something of a bore. There was a lot of Shakespeare in it, and somehow it all seemed remote and dry, even though at times the words were stirring and the scenes moving. One day the class was studying *Hamlet*, taking parts and acting them out, trying to make sense of Act One, Scene One, wherein Horatio has been called to the midnight parapet by two officers of the watch, Bernardo and Marcellus, to see the wonder of the ghost of Hamlet's father. The country boys had gotten all the parts: Clayborne was Bernardo, Austin Giesecke was Marcellus, Teddy Nix was Horatio and J. D. Patterson was the ghost of Hamlet's father. The teacher, a spinster lady named Charlotte Mingus, urged them to stand up, act like actors, and give dramatic interpretations, not mere flat recitations. The boys fell to it with all the seriousness they could muster in front of their classmates.

Austin: Peace, break thee off; look where it comes again! "This is silly, Miss Mingus, nobody talks this way."

"Just read the part, Austin. It's a very old play, but it's still beautiful. You'll learn to appreciate it."

J. D.: Clump, clump, clump. "Enter Ghost, armed."

"You're not supposed to say that, J. D. It's stage instructions. You don't have any lines."

"How come I'm here if I don't have any lines, Miss Mingus?"

"The ghost isn't ready to speak yet. It just appears. It will only speak to Hamlet. You'll have lines in the next scene. Clayborne, go on."

Clayborne: In the same figure, like the king that's dead. "Does that mean the ghost looks like the dead king?"

"That's what it means. Go on, Austin."

Austin: Thou art a scholar; speak to it, Horatio.

Clayborne: Looks it not like the king? mark it, Horatio. "What's it mean, 'mark it,' Miss Mingus?"

"It means to pay close attention to it. Like you should be doing to the play. Teddy, go on."

Teddy: Most like: — it harrows me with fear and wonder. "Is that a harrow like we pull behind the mules, Miss Mingus?"

"You know what your harrow does to the soil?"

"Yes, Ma'am."

"That's what seeing the ghost does to Horatio."

"Scares him good, huh?"

"Scares him good. Go on, Clayborne."

Clayborne: It would be spoke to.

Austin: Question it, Horatio.

Teddy: What are thou, that usurps't this time of night. "What's that word usurps't?"

"Usurps't. It means to take over, the ghost is taking over the night."

"Oh."

And so they went, fracturing the scene but almost enjoying themselves. It was a single word, half a page later, just before the ghost reenters, that gained wide currency among the country boys.

Teddy: But, soft, behold! lo, where it comes again! "Hey, that's good! Behold! Behold! I like that, Miss Mingus! Behold!"

"Control yourself, Teddy. You've got a dozen more lines to read and class is almost over."

If they got nothing else out of Shakespeare, they got Behold! Every time they saw each other, it was Behold! In the halls, Behold! On the basketball court, Behold! Walking home, Behold! The city kids thought they were all crazy.

One Friday late in September Clayborne could find no ride home when school was out at 4:00 p.m. It was a pleasant enough day and the eight-and-a-half-mile walk was a good hour-and-a-half workout. He opened the front door of the rent house at 5:30 p.m. almost to the minute.

"Clayborne, is that you?" called Belle.

"Yes, Mama. What is it?"

"Come talk to your Papa in the kitchen. The oil pipeline is broken somewhere and they need help!"

He tossed his books on the front room reading table and hurried to the kitchen table where his father was working on the farm ledger.

"What's going on, Papa?"

"A road plow ran into the Magnolia oil line over on Chalk Mountain Road, just about even with where the weaning house used to be. There's oil running all over out there. Mr. Edwards telephoned and asked if you'd be able to come help his foreman. I told him you would. I hope that's okay with you, son."

"Sure it is, Papa. When do they need me?"

"Soon as you can make it in the Model T. Put on your oldest coveralls. It's going to be filthy dirty work. But the pay is going to be just fine. Your mother's got a little something fixed up for you to eat before you run off."

He changed into work clothes, got a bite to eat and drove around Camp Branch school. He could smell the crude oil as he passed over the creek. When he approached the accident site, he was greeted by a geyser of petroleum spouting thirty feet into the air. A dozen or so men stood watching the spectacle, some of them local farmers.

The Magnolia Petroleum Company line foreman called to him as he parked the family automobile off the road: "You Clayborne Perry?"

"Yes, sir," he said, shutting the car door behind him, then shaking hands.

"Good to see you. I'm Hal Raldolph, foreman on this repair job. We're going to need all the help we can get. Can you work the night through if we have to?"

"Yes, sir."

"Good. You don't need to get too close to the puncture while it's still spouting, but we've got a one-by-two-inch hole in that pipe that's got to be fixed as soon as possible."

"I heard the road plow ran into it."

"Yep, they were plowing out the ditch so the road grader can come in and grade the road. The tractor driver didn't know there was an oil line through here — didn't read the warning signs — and I guess he just ran right into it full force. It's a big heavy tractor and it did a good job on our pipeline."

They looked around at the spreading oil in the fading daylight. The flow looked like a wellhead blowout, almost like a river of crude. The thick gooey smelly stuff ran down the roadside, broke through the ditchline several places, oozing over the adjoining pasture and far down into the liveoaks.

"Has it got to Camp Branch yet?" Clayborne asked.

"Yep, it's in the creek. And all over the field and woods west and south. You know this country?"

"I was born in a little house right down there about a hundred yards. It's gone, moved over by where I live now, my uncle's family lives in it. My Grandpa's gate is just beyond this little hill here, up the road maybe half a mile. I guess I know this country all right. How are we goin' to fix the hole in the pipeline?"

"We're goin' to wait until seven o'clock, first. That's when the pump station's goin' to shut down the power. When it does, this here black fountain will stop spraying. Shouldn't be too long now. You don't smoke do you?"

He thought the man was asking for a cigarette. "No, I'm sorry, I don't."

"No need to be sorry. Just wanted to make sure you don't light up. A match in this stuff could give us a lot worse problem than we've already got."

Within a few minutes the pump station had done its job and the spewing oil fizzled to a trickle and then stopped. Randolph gathered his crew and rattled off instructions.

"Hazen, you get the night lights up and running, Carmichael, you're supply man. Make sure everybody has a pick and shovel from the company truck. You and Mitchell file down the shovel blades if they get too dull. There's a lot of limestone rocks in this clay. Garrett, you line out the repair hole, inspect the damage while the men are digging, see what our best fix is. All right, men, grab a shovel and let's see some dirt fly."

The crew filed by the end of the company supply truck in the twilight and took a pick and shovel each. When the portable lamps were up and the scene bathed in yellow light, they started the messy job.

Art Garrett was a repair specialist brought in from Alexander, a little town some forty miles west of the job. He stepped off the boundaries of the hole he wanted to see. "This is what it ought to look like, about fifteen feet long parallel to the pipeline, about six feet wide, maybe eight feet. You four guys will work best one on each corner, you four go two on each side between the corner men. You four shovel the spoil these guys dig up into two piles, one on this side, the other over there. Keep it well away from the excavation. We don't want this thing caving in on us and all this crap running back in."

Clayborne got one of the side shoveler spots. The work was miserable, soft and slippery. The crude had spread over the ground for twenty feet in every direction, soaked in and saturated the dirt at least two feet deep. It was like trying to shovel opaque water in some places and like trying to pick twenty-pound rocks out of a pitch-black fish tank in others. Three hours later they had a hole around the pipe big enough to bury a horse. They stopped and wiped the worst of the guck off their hands and had a sandwich provided by Randolph, who had run into Hico and back for the food.

Randolph asked Garrett over coffee, "What's it look like, Art?"

"Hole's not too bad. Parallel to the grain of the pipe metal, not much danger of propagating a crack around the girth. I think a collar will hold it. We'll have to get pumping in Waco to crank up full pressure, make sure it don't leak. But I think a collar'll hold it."

It was 2:00 a.m. before they wrestled a collar around the punctured pipe section and bolted clamps over the hole. Hazen climbed the pipeline telephone pole, tied his handset in and called the pump station. "Hi, Mack, this here's Jeff. We got a collar on it now. You start up soon's we're off, okay? Then give us incremental increases up to full pressure. We'll call you back if it busts loose. Looks to me like it'll hold, but you never can tell. Okay, start 'er up."

While waiting for the pressure to climb, they had another feed, sandwiches and doughnuts and coffee. By 3:00 a.m. the pressure was up and the collar held — no leaks, no blowouts. The shovel crew went to the spoil pile and threw all the oily dirt back into the hole. The pipeline was restored by 7:00 a.m.

"Hey, Perry, here's your pay," called Hal Randolph. Clayborne walked over to him, wiping the grime off his hands with a tow sack. "Here you go, twelve hours at two-fifty an hour. That sound fair to you?"

Thirty dollars for one night's work! I get three dollars for a day's work at harvest and that's a ten-hour day. Fair? It's a gold mine!

"That'll be fine, Mr. Randolph," said Clayborne.

"I know you're tired, Perry, and I know you'd like to get home and get to bed. But I've got Art Garrett here and I've got to get to the pumping station in Waco right quick. Art lives the other direction over at Alexander, just this side of Dublin. I'll tell you what: if you'll take him home that extra forty miles, I'll put another twelve bucks in the kitty for you. What do you say?"

Twelve dollars for driving forty miles! That's two weeks pay at harvest! I'd have a total of forty-two dollars for one night's work! I've never seen so much money! Yahoo!

"That'll be fine, Mr. Randolph. I'll take him home."

"You can go home first and clean up some. We'll get you some tow sacks to put on your car seat so Garrett won't get your Model T all dirty." Randolph handed a wad of money to Clayborne.

"Thank you kindly, sir." He pocketed his loot and took Mr. Garrett home to Alexander in the morning sun. He whistled all the way back to Dude Flat.

As it turned out, Tom Perry got in on Magnolia Petroleum's largesse, too. He was hired to fix fences and burn off pools of oil in a controlled manner from the fields and woods and ponds along Camp Branch. You could see where Tom Perry was for the next week by looking for the big columns of tar-black smoke. Some of Tom's cows drank the oil and got sick. Magnolia Oil gave him a price for the damages that exceeded his wildest notions of generosity and hired him to go around checking for damage to other farmers' stock.

The Monday after the pipeline repair job Clayborne was feeling great. School was going well enough; Spanish II was not too hard, and solid geometry was actually easy. English IV was a little up in the clouds with all the poetry and plays, but physics was genuinely fun, especially the labs on Tuesdays and Thursdays. But this Monday Coach Freeman called Clayborne aside and said, "Son, I notice that every now and then you drive to school in a Model T Ford. Is that your Dad's?"

"Yes, sir. Why do you ask?"

"Well, the basketball team has a little problem. You know we've got the season coming up on us right now and we're going be visitors every other week. And you know most of the schools we're going to play at are ten, twenty miles off, right?"

"Yes, sir."

"I don't have a car, myself, and none of the other kids are able to talk their Dads into letting them drive the family flivver. If I give you fifty cents a game for taking me and seven players to the other schools every other week, do you think your Dad would let you do it?"

"I don't know, Mr. Freeman. I'll talk to my Papa and let you know. If I drive, then I'd be one of the seven players, wouldn't I?"

"Sure, Perry, you'd be one of the seven players every game we play away."

"And I'd likely get in a lot of play time?"

"Sure thing."

"I think my Papa would like that."

Tom gave in without much of a fuss, happy to know his boy was doing well in sports and getting the opportunity to meet the competition. He worried that Coach Freeman might forget about his promise of fifty cents a trip and urged Clayborne to keep reminding him. Every other week as they pulled out of the Hico High parking lot at 3:15 p.m. with a car full of kids, Clayborne faithfully reminded Coach Freeman of the deal and Coach Freeman faithfully promised to pay up. They went through basketball season, baseball season — Clayborne made pitcher — and track season — Clayborne placed first in the 220 yard dash — and the faithful reminders kept getting faithful promises to pay up. When sports season was done, Tom thought his son had lost fifteen trips worth of faithful promises, but as it turned out, Mr. Masterson himself finally paid the $7.50 due for the year's transportation, and Tom smiled and Clayborne breathed easier and Coach Freeman got off the hook.

Tom Perry made his final cotton crop at the rent house by mid-November and the prices were good. They would be able to follow their plan and move to their own hundred acres this year. When 1927's toll was given to Grandpa Blackburn, they had paid their last rent. They would move to the new house over toward Jack's Hollow Creek during the Thanksgiving holiday.

Thursday morning the menfolk moved some of the lighter items, the linens, the reading table, a few tools. The Honeas had moved out and moved on in the way of all rent farmers, and the farm house seemed empty and lonesome when they brought in the first load.

"Law, it's taken us long enough to be able to stash our own belongings in our own place," said Tom as they deposited the last of the load.

"How long's it been, Papa?" asked Hoyt.

"We'll talk about it over dinner."

The roast turkey and trimmings were waiting for them at noon. Belle had worked for hours fixing up sweet potatoes and corn and turnip greens and cooked tomatoes and okra and a peach cobbler bubbling in the oven, and regular Irish potatoes and so many other good things it was a true groaning board. Nadine, now eight years old, had helped with the dinner and with Dorothy, nearly two, still in the highchair but jabbering away, supervising the work of all within earshot. Hoyt was eleven now, a big help around the house and turning into a regular hand in the fields.

They gathered around the Thanksgiving table, the six of them, and contemplated a feast of the body and of the spirit. It was a special Thanksgiving. They had not grown up with the custom of asking a blessing of the food before meals; Tom remained steadfast in his convictions about public prayer. But today Tom came as close to it as he ever would.

"Well, family," he began, "this is our last day as renters. Tomorrow we're going to be in our own place. We're going to be owners."

Everyone glowed and smiled and little Dorothy clapped her hands in her highchair, the same highchair that Clayborne had used when he was a tot.

"We've got a lot to be thankful for on this Thanksgiving day," Tom said to them. "I've got a lot to be thankful for. For you, Belle, and you, sons and daughters, and for Grandma and Grandpa Perry and Blackburn and Old Grandma, and for just bein' alive. And I've got a place of my own to be thankful for."

"And we have you to be thankful for, Tom," said Belle.

"And us kids have the both of you to be thankful for," said Clayborne.

"We're fortunate, all of us," said Tom. "But don't let's forget the toil and labor we had gettin' to where we've got. Don't let's forget how years ago I had the dream of owning my own land, being my own man, how we moved away out to Colorado takin' up land. The year was 1915. That was, oh, before you were born, Hoyt. You and Nadine and Dorothy don't remember, but Clayborne remembers.

"It was homestead land. It was good land. But there wasn't enough rain to make anything grow. We starved out, we did. Came back to Oklahoma, worked sellin' sody water and ice cream in Cornish, sellin' it in the oil fields and in Ragtown. Hoyt, you were born there. And we couldn't find work to make the money to have our own place.

"So we came back to Texas, worked your Grandpa Perry's land, lived in the old rent house. Nadine, you were born there. Made some good crops, put a little money aside. Worked and slaved for years. Got the pneumonia and almost died, I did. The Lord and Dr. Durham pulled me through. But we made enough money to buy our first place. Moved here to the new rent house, worked your Grandpa Blackburn's land. Dorothy, you were born here. Made some more good crops, put more money aside. Worked and slaved for more years.

"And now it's all come home. We got what we worked for. I don't want you kids ever to forget that. You work long. You work hard. It'll all come home."

He realized how rapt his little audience had become, how caught up in the family history. He saw the looks on their faces, how they had responded to his heartfelt exhortation. He was surprised and a little embarrassed at his own eloquence. It was unlike him to talk so much.

"Well, don't just sit there," he said. "Everyone take out and help yourself now. It's Thanksgiving day." He was sounding more and more like Grandpa Jim Perry.

By the next Monday morning they had everything out of the Blackburn rent house and into their own, all the animals were moved and Clayborne had only three miles to walk to school.

Thursday was always physics laboratory. On a Thursday in early December came the electric jar experiment. Two conductors, a cathode and an anode, were to be placed in a non-conducting liquid and then in a conducting liquid to measure differences in electrical potential between them with a galvanometer. Clayborne's lab partner was Teddy Nix. Today was Teddy's turn to be in charge of the experiment and Clayborne's to be lab assistant. Teddy was to take the measurements, filling the beaker first with distilled water and second with diluted tap water, while Clayborne was to stand on two 4-foot lab stools so he could reach the overhead electrical outlet switch and turn on the 110 volt current at the appropriate time.

The water was correctly transferred to the electrical beaker, but from the incorrect container — it was not non-conducting distilled water, as the first step of the experiment called for, nor was it diluted tap water, as the second step of the experiment called for, but ordinary tap water, in these parts a highly mineralized liquid and an electrical conductor almost as good as copper wire. The metal strip conductors were placed in the liquid and clamped to the electrical jar. The galvanometer was secured in place.

"Okay," said Teddy. "I've got the conductors in the liquid. I've got the galvanometer contact clamped in the liquid between the two conductors. The check sheet says to plug in the 110 volt cord but do not yet turn on the current."

Clayborne installed the electrical cord in the socket. "Got it."

"Okay, the check sheet says review all steps covered so far." He mumbled to himself as he went through his procedure again, step by step. Again, he didn't notice his failure to use distilled water. "Okay, Clayborne," he said. "We're ready to measure no current or a very weak current. Turn on the 110 volts."

Clayborne stood like the Colossus of Rhodes bestride two lab stools, arms raised in salute to science, left hand grasping the electrical cord, right hand on the key switch. He turned the key. The current sped through the wires at the speed of light, give or take a few thousand feet per second. Excited electrons met the metal conductors and leaped across the marvelously conductive water. Within a few milliseconds the conductors had melted and the galvanometer contact had been fried. The tap water was converted to steam and a loud but essentially harmless explosion shattered the peaceful lab.

Students scattered in all directions. All except Clayborne of the lab stools, who was in no position to run. Teddy Nix took care of that. In blind panic he ran between Clayborne's lab stools, knocking the Colossus off his pedestal and off balance. The only way Clayborne could avoid a nasty spill was to grab the departing Teddy by the neck and head and hold on for dear life. Being a pretty hefty old country boy himself, Teddy ran undaunted away with his unexpected passenger. At the east lab wall he stopped and turned around, Clayborne wobbling piggyback atop his beefy shoulders. At the west wall, frightened and incredulous city kids stared back at the spectacle of a destroyed electrical experiment and a country boy Keystone Kops imitation at the other end of the room. Teddy Nix did the only thing possible under the circumstances: he took one step forward with Clayborne on his shoulders, placed his left hand dramatically on his breast, pointed meaningfully to heaven with his right, and with his best Shakespearean delivery pronounced:

"Behold! The damn thing blew up!"

The city kids *knew* they were crazy.

A few days later Grandpa Blackburn had a visitor at his new house near Hico; his brother John came in from Waco in his 1925 Chevy. It was definitely an occasion, and Clayborne walked the two miles between his new home and Grandpa Blackburn's new home to see his Great Uncle John. It was a good family get-together with only one problem: John's Chevy seems to have blown a cylinder head just as he was driving up to

Grandpa Charley Blackburn's place. He needed a ride back to Waco to scout up a new part with which to repair his precious vehicle. It was a point of honor: John's occupation was repairman and his business name was Dr. Fixall. Would Clayborne drive him in Grandpa Charley's 1926 Model T back to Waco? He could stay overnight in John's great big old two-story house, meet John's wife, and see all the best parts of town while chasing down a cylinder head. Of course, said Clayborne. He hadn't seen Waco since he was a tiny kiddo. And so he went to the big city, big enough to make Hico look like a hick town in the boondocks. It impressed him no end and gave him a bigger yardstick by which to measure things local.

Probably the most important thing to Clayborne about Hico High was not Hico High. It was a fortuitous gathering of young country boys under the aegis of a local man who was obsessed with education. His name was Herbert H. Miller and he was the older brother of Clayborne's Duffau schoolmate Marvin Miller. Marvin was long gone to California and not doing too well. Herbert was steadily barraging his errant brother with correspondence urging him to return and go to college at Tarleton, so far without much luck. Fortunately for a number of Erath County country boys, Herbert Miller in December of 1927 turned his missionary zeal to local boys.

Miller convinced ten rural students at Hico High to spend one night a week, only a few hours out of each hundred sixty-eight improving their minds outside the classroom. He was shrewd, and he knew they'd never sit still for an after-class gathering that was just a repeat of their classtime gatherings. So he told them:

"Men, we'll meet outdoors. We'll meet outdoors every Friday night. We'll meet at my uncle's place in the woods. It'll be cold, so we'll have to build a big campfire. We'll get hungry, so we'll have to hunt up our own food. We'll be at the mercy of the elements, so we'll have to strong-arm it. And that's what we'll call ourselves: the Strong Arm Club."

They bought it. They didn't know what they'd bought, but it sounded okay in a offbeat sort of way. What they bought was strange and bizarre and decisive. They bought their futures.

"Members of the Strong Arm Club, come to order," said Herbert Miller by the campfire's blaze.

Teddy Nix, Austin Giesecke, Clayborne Perry, and half a dozen other country kids including Austin's brother Mib sat still and listened.

"The first thing we're going to learn is what order means. We're going to learn Robert's Rules of Order. We're going to learn the proper way of carrying on a meeting."

He drilled them on parliamentary procedure, the election of officers, the presentation of motions to the chair and the fine points of order that simply become fixtures in the well-furnished mind. Once they caught on, the first order of business was a motion to parch some corn because they were all starving. It carried unanimously.

That first night Miller lectured them on the priceless heritage of literature, urged upon them a deep abiding respect for ideas, *ideas*, and insisted that they give heed to their careers, to think ahead, to what their lives would be after eleven grades of school. He held up a battered and well-thumbed copy of Chaucer's *Canterbury Tales*, and asked them:

"Will you be remembered as long as Chaucer? He was just a man. He lived over six hundred years ago. Will you be remembered by anyone six hundred years from now?"

"What difference will it make, Mr. Miller?" asked the Giesecke boy. "We'll all be dead."

"Ah, good question. Chaucer is dead. His body is dust. But his mind, *his mind* lives on in these pages. His mind, in the form of these ideas, will live forever! He has achieved immortality of a very important kind. It's not the kind you find through personal salvation at church, don't get me wrong. But it's important just the same. For Chaucer still influences the lives of good men and will continue to do so for ages to come. You should be men of such good will, with such good and noble ideas that your ideas should live forever, that your minds should become immortal as Chaucer's has. That is a lofty goal."

Mib Giesecke said, "That's too lofty. We don't think great thoughts. We don't know all the fancy words like he did. We don't know how to write those fancy poems and plays."

"Another good point. *The Canterbury Tales* is not poetry as you usually think of it, nor is it a play. It's just what its name says, a collection of tales, stories, that reflect Chaucer's times, the high people and the low, the good deeds and the bad, the sacred and the profane, and we're all full of stories."

"You mean this great Chaucer just wrote stories?" asked Clayborne.

"That's right."

"Ah, they're probably stories of kings and things we'll never have anything to do with!" said Teddy Nix.

"Let's try him," suggested Miller. "Let's see if Chaucer doesn't have a knack for the down to earth. Let's see if he can't tell a tale anyone can understand. Let's read 'The Miller's Tale.'"

He read it aloud to them by the light of the campfire. The country boys were immediately fascinated by Nicholas, a student like themselves, and the old carpenter — they all knew people who were carpenters — who'd married a young wife, Allison, and the merry fooling as the cunning bawdry of Nicholas outsmarted itself in the end. When it was over, they could hardly believe it.

"What do you get out of that story, Strong Arms?" asked Miller.

"I didn't think any great famous person like Chaucer would write so plain," said Teddy Nix. "You know, about this young student going after the wife of the old codger."

"It seemed kind of sinful to me," said Austin Giesecke. "How they fooled the old man."

"It was profane all right," agreed Miller. "And this is a serious moral question in our own lives. Is Chaucer approving profanity? Or does his tale have a moral to it? Did they get away with fooling the old man?" asked Miller.

"Well, yes and no," said Clayborne. "He managed to fool the old fellow sort of, but his plan to get the girl was too clever. It backfired and he ended up with a hot poker whacked across his behind."

"So his sinful plan was punished in the end."

They laughed at the pun.

"So what did you learn from it?"

"Don't get stupid when you get old like the carpenter did," said Giesecke. "Keep your wits about you. Keep your eyes open. Especially if you marry a young wife!" They laughed agreement.

"It tells me not to get so smart that you trip over your own smartness like Nicholas did," ventured Teddy Nix. "And to marry somebody your own age."

"And not to go after somebody else's wife," said Austin.

"Okay, Strong Arms, I think those are good lessons you learned from Chaucer. And I hope you learned that a profane story can teach you some sacred truths. It's about midnight now, and I think you better get home before your folks begin to wonder what you're up to. Is there a motion to adjourn?"

Every Friday night the Strong Arm club met, sometimes in one place, sometimes in another. Sometimes on Little Duffau Creek two or three miles upstream from Prairie Springs Baptist Church. Sometimes on the farm of Herbert Miller's father. Or that of his uncle. They knew where they would meet and they just showed up in the middle of the woods. They'd walk in and clear away a place and build the fire and parch their corn. Regular corn would parch, and swell up a little in the heat of the fire, something like popcorn does, but not turn inside out into fluffy little clouds. They'd wait until they were all there and start. Few of the Strong Arms were tardy or absent. It was a strange compact they had, learning about things that didn't really interest them much. They learned as much here in the woods as in the halls of authority at school.

Miller gradually impressed upon their young minds that there was such a thing as *culture*, and that it was not a mere decoration, and that it was not just a required course in school, and that it reflected the values of the people in important ways, and that it influenced future generations.

When Clayborne came home so late Friday nights, Tom Perry did not really understand what he had been doing, and Clayborne found it difficult to explain why he was staying out past midnight in the woods with a bunch of hillbilly honyocks to improve his mind. It was plain foolishness to Tom. Being out after midnight in and of itself was a bad thing. You couldn't get good results from bad things. He warned his boy to get home at a reasonable hour Friday nights. Clayborne kept coming in after midnight and Tom kept after him to come home earlier, but the father must have sensed the growing character of his son, because he soon made only token complaints, and every now and then he actually asked about the Shakespeare play they happened to be reading or the mock-trial they were carrying on trying to learn something about law.

By February Miller was satisfied that his charges knew where to find the wellsprings of culture and that they understood the basics: that poetry was not rhymes but universal human ideas, that painting was not pictures but symbols of human experience, that music was not tunes but ideas in sound, that art, any kind of art, was the search for meaning, and the trick was getting at all the meanings. And so with this much under their belts, the Strong Arm Club turned to telling tales from their own lives, explaining themselves to each other.

They were urged to dig out things they hadn't thought of for some time, not things of deep significance, just things they didn't ordinarily tell. Miller figured that the twice-told tale probably had some embroidery in it, and he wanted his Strong Arms to be honest with themselves. And so Clayborne one night dug up a recollection from his early childhood, an event from his fourth year, before his family had gone to starve out in Colorado.

In 1914, his father and mother had taken him on the train from Hico into Waco to the Cotton Palace, an elaborate county-fair carnival place, built in celebration of Waco's growth as a shipping center of the cotton industry. He remembered it from the height of a little boy, looking up to distant faces, that it had been after the cotton was picked, that his family had come early in the day, that there must have been five or ten thousand people there, that it had all kinds of shows. He couldn't remember if they had spent the night, because he could remember staying at no hotel, but it seemed to him they had walked through the carnival runways after it was dark out. He remembered bicycle acts, people riding bicycles off towers taller than a windmill into big tanks of water. He remembered musicians dressed up in blackface like Negroes, but he knew that black people were not allowed to bring their families to the Cotton Palace's entertainments. He remembered medicine shows and girlie shows — they had lots of clothes on in those days, the sheriff saw to that — and he remembered hearing singing and banjo picking. It was just an event, and had no further meaning that Clayborne could see.

But Miller knew what he was doing: letting them each see where they had come from, really come from, as a means of forming guideposts to where they were going, really going. Of course, he never told anyone what he was up to. He'd do anything to keep up their interest, hold trials of Strong Arms who'd arrived late, he'd be the judge, one of the boys would be the prosecuting attorney and another the defense attorney. The rest would be the jury. They convicted the offender or freed him as the merits of the case unfolded.

They'd talk about articles in the latest *Scientific American*, about discoveries in physics and chemistry, in biology and geology, by which they learned what sciences exist and what they were about. They'd talk about stories in *National Geographic*, where far-off places were and what was happening there, and what the wide world meant. And Miller never told them what all these meanings were. He left as many questions unanswered as possible. It was all to make them want to go on, to learn more, to thirst, really thirst, for knowledge, for education. By spring his work was done.

There wasn't really much left of the eleventh grade. Spring meant taking business math with his other courses for Clayborne, and a few dates with Naomi White. She'd gone to Camp Branch school, too, and she was just a friend. He'd learned in the locker rooms and in the halls to stay shy of girls: too much interest in that direction led to dropouts and shotgun weddings where everybody pretended to be happy and no one was. He was thinking about what to do after May. He was making good grades at Hico High, ranking well above the middle of the class made up mostly of city kids. Maybe Tarleton. Maybe college.

Mr. Fouts had offered to promote him to thresher operator in another year, the best job at harvest. That was a fine prospect, and staying on as a field hand year around was a stable job. Maybe harvest. Maybe farming.

The kid from Dude Flat talked it over with Mr. Masterson one day in May, 1928. "Well, you already know what I think," the superintendent said. "Country kids just don't have the preparation to go on to college. Oh, yes, you've done okay here at Hico — I've kept a watch on your grades — you're above average, but you're no Einstein. You didn't let me down, but you're no candidate for Harvard or Yale or Baylor over in Waco. You might do okay at Tarleton, but maybe not. Nothing personal, Perry, you're a good kid. But country kids usually drop out of college. Think hard about that before you go spending your folks' money on more schooling. You might start, but will you finish? Spare yourself and your people the time and money. Find a good job somewhere and settle down. Let the city kids go to college."

    At 11:00 a.m. on Sunday, May 20, Hico High School's auditorium rang to the Baccalaureate Service of the Class of 1928. The boys wore white pants and dark jackets and the girls wore white dresses. The local Methodist preacher preached a thirty-minute sermon and religious songs were sung. When it was over, a week of Hico High was left. At school there were only formalities for the seniors during that last week, and the graduation ceremony came quickly. There were no caps and gowns. Again the boys wore white pants and the girls wore white dresses. Eight hundred people showed up to hear Judge Barrow usher the class of '28 out into the cold, cruel world. The eight hundred applauded as the acknowledgements were read, the special awards given out, the usual folderol paraded forth. Then the diplomas were handed out. When his turn came, out of the corner of his eye Clayborne spied his Papa in the crowd, pushing close to see the great event, and his mother weeping and smiling when he shook hands with Mr. Masterson and accepted the rolled up certificate. He'd done it. He'd finished high school. Then the class sang a song they would forget in ten years' time, and never remember its name, but it was the Song of Destiny they sang. When its final tonic chord died away, their lives had been shaped, their foundations completed at Hico High School. It was the end of the beginning. But it was an end, poignant and forever. There was nothing else to do here, nothing at all: that night they all went home and lived the rest of their lives.
    Clayborne felt it, felt it sharply. Here they were again, the perennial human questions: Where to? What next? Why was it so hard to decide? It was plain he was no Einstein. He was just a country kid from Dude Flat that made above average grades. He should do like Superintendent Masterson said, let the city kids go to college. He'd done what his ancestors hadn't, he'd gotten that education, he'd finished high school, he'd answered Old Grandma's prayers. That was enough. Take that job at harvest, be a field hand, be a farmer like his Papa. Why was it so hard to do what was obviously so right?
    He hired on again with Fouts. He enjoyed the sunshine on his back and the wind ruffling his hair and the smell of the earth and the calls of the birds. He worked a week before he figured it out. It was so hard to do what was obviously so right because it was obviously wrong. He was no Einstein, he was himself. He was a country kid, but not *just* a country kid. His grades were a little above average, but that was only *so far*. He had more in him. That's all he knew. His high school diploma was not a

monument to yesterday, but a ticket to tomorrow. There was more in him. His mind had been shaken awake somewhere, he didn't know where, maybe in English IV, maybe in the woods on shaggy Friday nights. But there was more in him now, and that's all that mattered, and his whole life depended on what he did next. The final decision was simple.

Where to?

Tarleton.

What next?

College.

Of course.

-11-

TARLETON

TEXAS was changing in 1928. It was slowly drifting away from its insular pioneer past and joining the mainstream of the United States. It was urbanizing, industrializing, capitalizing. But in the 1920s it was still thirty to fifty years behind the eastern states: Texas cities still retained the flavor of oversize cow towns, Texas industry still labored in its infancy, Texas capital derived from very few sources: petroleum and cattle and cotton, mostly. And the Texas mindset was still distinctively Southern and conservative and suspicious of outside influences. The Charleston and the Mah-Jongg craze, turned-down hose and hip flasks, jazz babies and movie morality — all had little luck trying to wheedle their way into the heart and heartland of Texas. Texas was changing in many ways, but somehow the more it changed the more it remained the same.

Among grass roots Texans — the farmers and cattlemen who dominated the ballot box — questions of melding with the great American stew didn't matter much anyway. True, San Antonio was growing into a cosmopolitan military center, Houston had a few outfits that were actually building factories, and Dallas bankers seemed to think the family farm was an increasingly bad investment, but Texans discounted those local flukes. Some people worried about alien big city culture drifting in on the radio and in the movie houses — but to most Texans show business was just horsefeathers and foofaraw. Rural Texans in the 1920s were little different from their settler forefathers. And those settler forefathers themselves had been little different from their own warrior forefathers, the Yankee-fighters and Indian-fighters and Mexican-fighters. Early nineteenth-century values — seriousness of purpose, shrewd understanding of men's weaknesses, relentless determination to survive and dominate despite any obstacle — none of these had vanished from Texas or had even changed in the early twentieth-century. A contemporary Bostonian or Philadelphian could never have understood the true Texas temper. And Texans were simply not interested in understanding the changes going on in the rest of the nation.

Mainstream America had begun the decade of the 1920s seeking peace and rebirth after the Great War. The era was ending otherwise, raveled out into frivolity and escapism and flaming youth. Getting around Prohibition had become a national pastime. When police shut down a speakeasy, the owner simply opened a new one which was shut down, then another and another ad nauseam — New York's rollicking blonde booze broker Texas Guinan became a legendary feminine exemplar of the art. Then movies became another opiate of the masses. When the first talkie spoke in 1927 with Al Jolson as *The Jazz Singer*, America began listening intently — to the tune of ninety million tickets a week by the early '30s. Movie escapism became a way of life: movie sets became more exotic and movie sex became more erotic and more people paid their two bits at the box office. No doubt about it, mainstream America was changing. Traditional values were dissolving into sour hedonism and romantic cynicism. Novelist F. Scott Fitzgerald advised his countrymen "to find all Gods dead, all wars fought, all faiths in man shaken."

It took Walter Lippmann, a radical highbrow who had been president of the Harvard Socialist Club in 1909, to see the essence of this era of barnstorming daredevils and margin investment and dance marathons. "What most distinguishes the generation who have approached maturity since the debacle of idealism at the end of the War," said Lippmann, "is not their rebellion against the religion and the moral code of their parents, but their disillusionment with their own rebellion. It is common for young men and women to rebel, but that they should rebel sadly and without faith in their rebellion, that they should distrust the new freedom no less than the old certainties — that is something of a novelty."

Prosperity had brought with it ennui. "Disenchanted" became a kitchen word. Good times had brought with them a taking for granted of everything that had always been there and had never been lacking or yearned for. The college girl on the arm of a boy equipped with raccoon coat, ukelele and hip flask delighted in shocking her elders. Anything rowdy or wild was "the cat's meow." And how. Gratification had brought with it the perverse urge to devalue and mock and belittle the old gratifiers — the haven of home, the work ethic, the rock of religion, the plentiful food, the freedom of action itself. Twenty-three skidoo! Go cook a radish.

Despite this seething national ferment, millions of Americans stayed as they had always been. They ignored mobster wars in Chicago and forty thousand Ku Klux Klansmen marching in Washington. They were rural people for the most part — and not just Texas rural people, but those throughout the Bible Belt of H. L. Mencken's coinage — drab and frugal farmers growing cotton and corn and wheat, with no time for big-city nonsense. Besides, the good-time '20s had not brought them any extra cash because farm prices were slipping despite the general prosperity. Farmers couldn't afford big-city nonsense even if they had wanted it, which they didn't. Their God lived, their wars came daily with fickle weather and reluctant soil and their faith in man had always included wide allowances for human frailty. They elected Calvin Coolidge — who studiously spent two hours each workday taking a nap so he could do no mischief — because he told them that government's "greatest duty and opportunity is not to embark on any new ventures." They read their Bibles instead of F. Scott Fitzgerald, never swigged bathtub gin, saw flappers and jazz babies only on an occasional small-town movie-house screen, and were ready to fight for what they believed in if they had to. If these conservative folk had read Lippmann they would have agreed with him, radical or no, but Lippmann, did not write for the *Farm News*. In thousands of small towns throughout America the Roaring Twenties echoed like a noisy mainline freight train on a distant track taking its baggage elsewhere and leaving no imprint on the smooth one-way rails of time. Serene nights and the old dream of ordinary people went forward undisturbed: onward and upward into the murky, malleable future. And devil take the hindmost.

So it was in the wide Texas Grand Prairie of 1928. It was a place of faith and struggling farmers and small towns that didn't care for mainstream America's shenanigans. Grand Prairie citizens didn't mind being ignorant of Wall Street and weren't embarrassed because they couldn't quote from *The Great Gatsby*. Their minds stayed strong with reality and they mistrusted all abstractions and ideologies. They lived in a hard place, but it was a possible place, where a young man like Willie Clayborne Perry could grow up and work for an education and make as much of himself as he was able. And for all that, the Grand Prairie was as much Utopia as you will ever find in this universe.

Clayborne peered ahead. He strode briskly up oak-lined College Street, trying to remember Stephenville's landmarks, wondering if people were watching him through scrim curtains in the tidy frame houses. In the distant late afternoon glow at the end of the street he could just discern the dressed-stone wall and gate pylons he'd come to recognize.

Tarleton, he thought.

A slight smile curled at the edges of his mouth as he walked, registering something between contentment and delight. If busybodies bothered to look, they would have seen his eighteen-year-old features as those of a man grown: wide forehead framed in close-cropped dark hair, straight English nose overshadowing a prominent chin, heavy brows peaked like two roof gables over deepset, intent dark eyes wide spaced — the Perry eyes can be recognized in photographs five generations back, skeptical, quizzical, taking everything in, surprised by no hardship, enduring all, but now glinting in this new generation with the steel of rising intelligence. With a pullover sweater accentuating his beefy country boy's shoulders he looked the part of a magazine illustrator's college athlete.

Clayborne approached the campus corner of College Street and McIlhaney Avenue. Stephenville! — a town only twenty miles from his home near Hico, yet a town four times larger than Hico, a town of nearly six thousand residents. All his farm boy life he'd thought of Hico as a city, and now his sense of scale began to buckle and stretch. He stopped and stared, looking uncertainly back down the long street, past the scattered students behind him, realizing that he'd just walked more than a mile from the room he'd rented on the other side of County Court House Square — and realizing there was still more Stephenville on all sides of his path. You couldn't walk a mile through Hico in any direction without leaving town.

There across brick-paved McIlhaney Avenue lay the college, surrounded by that forbidding wall of native stone. It wasn't that the wall was so high — it was only about four feet in most places. It was the formal stonework, its mortar joints carefully beaded, as if industrial workers had welded the limestone slabs together, that gave it a chilly, aloof feeling. Inside the perimeter dozens of neatly dressed efficient-looking students criss-crossed the manicured lawns. Severe brick buildings gleamed dully in the sundown light. The dean's home straight ahead overshadowed hurrying young men and women with its wide two-story stucco facade, its dormered red tile roof and *porte cochere* on the north to receive visiting dignitaries. Although Clayborne had come to Tarleton several times during the summer while completing his college application, all the people, all the buildings still seemed strange and a little intimidating.

Even the land seemed subtly different — and Tarleton's wall of local stone provided a clue to that difference. Stephenville lay just out of the Grand Prairie on the fringes of the Upper Cross Timbers, just out of the low dark rich clay hills and into the higher hardscrabble limestone formations. Like Hico, Stephenville had been planted by early settlers only a few miles west of the ninety-eighth meridian, west of thirty inches of rain, unreliable rain that came in irregular seven- to eleven-year cycles. But near Hico the deep caliche strata and sodded topsoil held water even where careless farmers had stripped away the protecting grass — and you could make a cotton crop just about any year. On the rocky percolating uplands near Stephenville and beyond to the west the rain fooled you for a few years into thinking you could farm the shallow soil and then forced you into ranching after drought scorched off your cotton three crops in a row.

Nobody really thought about it just yet, but the fact was that Stephenville stood on a nearly invisible ecological border. It had more yuccas and cedars and fewer liveoaks than Hico; its flowering shrubs would have been at home out past Abilene on the dry Llano Estacado — the Staked Plains of the Cap Rock — its animals were more nearly those of the Hill Country to the south, including whitetail deer, and all in all it felt nearly as much like a West Texas town as it did a Grand Prairie town. But Stephenville was only twenty miles from home, and that was a good part of the reason why Clayborne Perry stood here now on the corner of College and McIlhaney hoping to find Tarleton's pre-session pep rally on time.

"Hey, Clayborne! Clayborne Perry! Is that you standing across the street like a dummy?" yelled a familiar voice. Clayborne looked around startled.

"Over here! Inside the gate, you old son of a gun!" came the voice.

Then three young men ambled out of the liveoak shadows in their baggy pants and stood square in the middle of Tarleton's east entrance, each flashing his best eat-a-banana-sideways grin.

"Marvin Miller!" yelled Clayborne. "I can't believe it! And Austin Giesecke! And Teddy Nix!"

He bounded across McIlhaney to join them, unconcerned about the oogahs of oncoming Model Ts and the stares of fellow students strolling by. "Let me shake your hand, fellas! Are you all going to college here?"

Square-jawed Teddy Nix shook his hand and patted him on the back. "You bet! Just like we said we would. And what about you?"

"Of course, I am," grinned Clayborne. "You know how my Old Grandma keeps at me to go to college. I can't let her down! But just look at you!" said Clapborne, circling his old friends admiringly. "Look at us! It's the Strong Arm Club right out of Hico High School!"

"Ya-hoo!," agreed tall muscular Austin Giesecke, "all of us is big ol' Strong Arms."

"Where you goin' just now, Clayborne?" asked Marvin Miller, a smile twinkling in his Nordic blue eyes.

"To the pep meeting. How about you guys?"

"Us too," said Teddy Nix, "soon as we find this lost sheep from Hico named Clayborne Perry."

"Aw," laughed Clayborne, "don't wait for him. He don't amount to a hill of beans! Let's go!"

And off they went, jostling and joking past the Home Economics Building, poking and prodding each other by the Administration Building, shining exuberance into the twilight. Like all healthy young men, they got vitamins from the air and needed no pep rally to inflate their school spirit. Never the less, they followed the crowd into the huge barnlike frame gym, jamming in with some six hundred fellow Tarletonians. The pre-session yell squad — two boys and a girl — stood on the stage dressed in their varsity whites with purple trim and their saddle oxfords, ready for a night of energy and enthusiasm. When the time came, they leaped and waved the audience into silence.

"Listen, gang," the yell captain boomed through his megaphone, "can you believe that we are already beginning another school year here at old Tarleton?"

"Yay!" roared the crowd.

"Stop for a minute and think what Tarleton means to you, to me, to the graduates! There never was a place as grand as Tarleton!"

"Yay!"

Clayborne stood beside his high school chums and took it all in. He was in *college*! Really in *college*! Oh, yes, John Tarleton Agricultural College was no Harvard or Baylor, he knew that. Although it was a four-year institution, the freshmen and sophomores belonged to grades ten and eleven of high school: the college course comprised only two years. But that was two more years of college than most farm kids ever got, and it was reaching for the stars to hope for that.

"We have won three consecutive football championships!" shouted the girl yell leader. "Will we win another one this year?"

"Yay!"

Clayborne recalled what a Tarleton cadet at his rooming house had told him earlier on this clear September day of 1928: his chosen school had been founded here in the modest farming, ranching and rail center of Stephenville in 1898 through a bequest from its namesake, John Tarleton, a local ranching stalwart. For years the little private college sitting on its pancake-flat plateau above the limestone channel of the North Bosque River had struggled and limped along with a single large ornate building, a tiny faculty and a smaller budget, trying to offer four years of college work. Then in 1917 it was rescued and made part of the Texas Agricultural and Mechanical College system, which sheared away its upper division educational offerings. Now it was a junior college with eighty faculty members and a student body of some nine hundred ninety souls.

"The team will do its part," yelled the third leader. The Tarleton Plowboys can beat any team in Texas if we get behind them and fight!"

"Yay!"

The Tarleton of 1928 basked in the reputation of its parent school,

Texas A&M College, but in many ways it was the poor stepchild of a rich institution. A&M President T. O. Walton paid only nominal attention to his Stephenville branch: one year the editors of Tarleton's annual, *The Grassburr*, plaintively noted of him, "Although we are seldom honored by his visits, we are always anxious to have him in our midst." Then there were the instructors. They weren't the cream of the crop: of Tarleton's sixty-five teaching faculty members, exactly one had earned a Ph.D. degree — the head of the Biology Department. Only one held any other type of doctoral degree, a practicing Doctor of Veterinary Medicine who came in to teach animal science classes several times a week. The majority of Tarleton instructors had not earned a master's degree and a dozen, mostly arts teachers, held no degree at all. Tarleton Dean J. Thomas Davis — whose LL.D. from Howard Payne College was honorary, his highest earned degree being a Master of Arts from the University of Texas — had tried since taking office in 1919 to lure more Ph.D.s into Tarleton. It was to no avail, despite his school's connection to mighty Texas A&M. His problem was endemic to smaller state colleges throughout Texas. They could not attract better qualified instructors for a simple reason: state legislators, wary of the farmer majority's hatred of taxes, granted salary funds to "second category" colleges such as Tarleton at a scale little better than high school teachers. Young men and women who had struggled through ten years of college to get their Ph.D.s understandably applied for work at well-endowed "first category" schools such as Texas A&M's central campus near Bryan or the University of Texas at Austin and not at John Tarleton Agricultural College in Stephenville.

"Fellows, get the Tarleton spirit!" screamed the yell captain. "The spirit that has won all these games for us. Learn all the yells. Get the spirit! Come on, now, let's sing the Color Song for the Purple and White!"

"Yay!"

The students brayed through a dozen songs and yells with vim and vigor, but had no illusions about why they themselves were here at Tarleton. Like Clayborne, most of them had worked all summer, saved about four hundred dollars and looked around to see where they could find a year of school for their money. In the eight thousand square miles of the Grand Prairie, there were nearly a dozen other small colleges, but they were all private schools, mostly church-sponsored, with tuition fees of a hundred fifty dollars or more and total costs in the six-hundred-dollar-a-year range. The policy everywhere was cash in advance. Tarleton charged twenty-five dollars a year tuition — twelve and a half per semester, two bucks extra if you wanted to attend all the sports activities and Lyceum numbers — and a parsimonious farm kid who showed up with four hundred dollars in September might even go home in June with some change in his pocket. Most of the boisterous students in this gym were poor farm kids who had selected a poor farm kid's school. And they knew it.

"Get the spirit, talk it up, teach it to the new students, attend pep meetings, and Fight! Fight! Fight! for the grandest school in Texas!"

"Yay!"

Despite its patent weaknesses and shortcomings, Tarleton was not disparaged. The Tarleton spirit was real. Students — and most Texas educators — respected the feisty little college: it had a good library and a growing construction budget just now nourishing a new auditorium. A&M's *president* may not have graced the Tarleton campus much, but its *money* did. Tarleton's instructors may not have been as financially well-favored as the building fund, but they were a game lot who ran tough classes and their laboratory equipment made the private schools look pathetic. The education itself was about as good as you could find in rural Texas. And a two-year diploma from Tarleton would be accepted without question at any four-year state school for those who wanted to go on. In all, Tarleton gave you more than your money's worth. It may not have been the best *possible* education, but a poor farm kid from the Grand Prairie knew Tarleton was the best possible *deal* in education.

"Tarleton first, last and always!"

"Yay!"

The exuberant crowd broke up after the pep meeting and milled around outside the gym in the warm crimson evening. The three-story brick Administration Building was a blue shadow across the lane. The four boys from Hico drifted with the crowd in a knot. A black patch of ashes and charcoal lay in their path as they wandered slowly and aimlessly toward the north side of the gym.

"What's all this?" asked Clayborne. "Looks like something burned down."

"That's what's left of White's boarding house," said Austin Giesecke. "They used to call it the White House like where President Coolidge lives. It burned down about three weeks ago, the day I came up to finish my application. The fire department couldn't save it. Thought they was goin' to lose the gym here too. Vic Seagrest — he lives next door to us now — he was the only one living there when it burned. Told me all about it. Lost everything he owned."

'That's a shame," said Clayborne, pondering the ruins. "I've seen two houses burn up. It's a terrible thing."

The four sidled up to the gym's north wall.

"What classes you goin' to take, Clayborne?" asked Marvin Miller as he leaned against a corner of the wooden building.

"Let's see," mulled Clayborne, chin down and arms crossed. "I signed up for English and college algebra and typing and something else . . ."

"Must have been R.O.T.C." said Teddy Nix, kicking at little rocks.

"No, everybody takes R.O.T.C. That's not what I'm tryin' to think of."

"Hey, Clayborne," said Austin Giesecke, sidetracking his friend's train of thought, "have you got your uniform yet?"

Tarleton operated as a military school: R.O.T.C. classes and uniforms were mandatory for men. Women took no military instruction but wore regulation blue chambrays.

"Oh, yeah, I got my uniform," Clayborne told Austin. "Found a used one that fit. Got a pair of long pants and a pair of tight leg pants to wear with boots, and I got a coat. Cost me fifteen dollars. Even got my boots and necktie and belt — the tie cost a dollar and a half — but I don't have my o.d. shirt yet."

"Wait 'til you see what those shirts cost," howled Marvin Miller.

"Yeah," cried Teddy Nix, "they're ten dollars each!"

"Ouch!" said Clayborne, rolling his eyes heavenward. "There goes my bale of cotton!"

"Did you have your own cotton patch this year?" asked Miller.

"Yep, planted twelve acres of rent land next to our place. Made a bale already. Got almost another bale left. The family's goin' to pick the rest of it for me. Hey, that's what I was tryin' to think of! I knew it had something to do with farming. My other subject is animal husbandry."

"Animal husbandry?" guffawed Marvin Miller. "I thought you wanted to get away from farming!"

"Well, I do," said a testy Clayborne.

"Why'd you take animal husbandry, then?" asked Austin Giesecke.

"I don't know," Clayborne admitted sheepishly. "The fellow at the registration desk said it would be a good elective course. I just took his advice, that's all."

Tarleton, like many state colleges in Texas, provided no student counselling, only a catalogue of course offerings and a list of graduation requirements. Many students stumbled blindly into their first year of college, taking classes they neither needed nor wanted. Some discovered at the end of their second year that no diploma would be forthcoming without summer school to make up vital missed credits.

"You're lucky even if you did get stuck with animal husbandry, Clayborne," said Teddy Nix. "You're able to pay for your school. I made a couple of bales of cotton this summer myself, cleared about a hundred dollars each after paying my Dad rent. But you get to work at harvest with old Fouts and his crew every year."

"What's wrong with that?" Clayborne wanted to know.

"Nothing. But with harvest and your cotton you make enough for a whole year of school. I had to take out a loan from the student memorial fund. Can't afford a decent place to stay, even. Got to live with these honyocks in a couple of little bitty rooms."

"Don't rag Clayborne for makin' enough money!" snorted Marvin Miller. "We all got our problems, Teddy. I'd still be out in California starving if my brother hadn't talked me into coming back to work the farm with him this summer. I come up a little short, myself. And I got to take eleventh grade this year while you guys take college!"

"Shouldn't have quit high school, Marvin," hooted Austin Giesecke. "But anyways, we all got to live with each other."

Marvin Miller said, "Hey, Clayborne, that's something I want to talk to you about. I need a roommate to help with the rent. How about coming in to room with me? Only five dollars a month."

"I already got a place," said Clayborne. "Down past the court house by the river."

"By the river! That's over a mile!" sneered Teddy Nix. "Our place is right across the street, see it right there?" He did a fancy pirouette and pointed extravagantly to a little frame house several hundred feet away. "Behold! The corner house, right on Vanderbilt and Lillian street."

"Yeah," cajoled Miller. "You'll have to rise up extra early to get to school if you stay down by the river. Come on and room with us at Miz Bobo's. She's a nice landlady. She's a widow lady, got a grown boy and girl out working, and two little girls at home to support. She needs the money. And you can jump out of bed and right into the eight o'clock class."

"Well, I don't know," muttered Clayborne. "It really is close to school. I'd like to, but I already stayed at Miz Fant's a couple of nights and I paid her a month ahead."

"Come on," coaxed Austin Giesecke. "She'll give you a refund. Ask her. Come on, all us Strong Arms got to stick together, just like at Hico."

"Yeah, come on," they all entreated.

"How'll I get my trunk up here? My Papa hauled it all the way from Hico in the back seat of the Model T. It must weigh a hundred pounds. And my typewriter, what about it? I got me a good upright Underwood for ten bucks, fixed it, oiled it up good. How'll I get my stuff up here?"

Marvin Miller said, "Miz Bobo's boy works at Henry Ellis Grocery Store. He could pack your trunk up in the delivery car. I'm sure he'd do it to help his Mama get another renter!"

"Yeah, Yeah," they clamored.

Clayborne thought a moment. "Okay, I'll do it. But you got to promise that you won't take somebody else in my place before I can make the switch. It's hard to find a place in Stephenville."

"You got our word, Clayborne," said Miller earnestly.

"We won!" rang the megaphone yell. "The Plowboys did it! We beat Abilene Christian College twelve to six! Let's hear it for the Tarleton Plowboys!"

Pandemonium broke loose in the ranked afternoon bleachers on this overcast last Saturday in September. The jubilation of winning the season's first game filled the cloudy sky. Clayborne screamed over his hoarseness along with his uniformed fellow cadets of B Company. He was glad to be out of the classroom today.

Private Linville McKinney leaned over to holler in his right ear, "I bet you didn't know we'd have to stand up for the whole football game, did you?"

"No, I sure didn't," Clayborne yelled back. "I'm just glad it quit raining this morning so we didn't have to get wet, too."

"What do we do now?" Private George Cardwell shouted into Clayborne's left ear.

"I don't know," cried Clayborne. "Listen to the yell leaders, I guess. Looks like they're through turning backflips."

The rollicking pep leaders snapped out of their frisky back handsprings and waved their audience to grinning silence.

The yell captain's voice surged through the megaphone with triumph: "Our Plowboys have carried Tarleton to another grand victory, gang! They deserve a victor's retreat from the field! Lend a shoulder! Carry them off! I don't want to see a single football player walk off that field, now. You hear, gang?"

A roar of exultation struck the neighboring houses and echoed back.

"Private Perry," boomed Private Cardwell through the din, "that's about the muddiest bunch of ball players I've ever seen. And we got to carry 'em off the field!"

"I'm afraid our uniforms are goin' to end up looking just like those guys down there," said Clayborne. "This is goin' to call for a clean and press for sure. There goes thirty cents for laundry, Private Cardwell."

Clayborne recognized B Company Captain William Elliott signaling his cadets for silence:

"Men, you've heard the call from our yell leaders to carry the team off the field. See to it that we carry off more players than A Company or C Company or the Vidette Company. Regroup at six o'clock at the east gate for shirt-tail parade. Privilege night afterward, call to quarters at ten o'clock instead of eight. Out of uniform tonight only! Dismiss."

Clayborne saw Sergeant Ben Barnes salute and heard him execute the officer's order: "Company, dismissed!"

"What's a shirt-tail parade?" yelled Cardwell as his unit swarmed with the rest of the school down the bleachers and onto the chalked-off football field. "You were here last year, McKinney, what is it?"

"It's a lot of fun, blockhead!" chirped McKinney. "Wait and see!"

Clayborne spotted his B Company compatriot Austin Giesecke and fought through the melee to grab him by the arm. "Hey, Austin, let's go carry off the cleanest guy we can find!"

At the benches near the mobbed fifty-yard line they found only one player not yet riding in glory, Dorsett Risinger, a young man from Sweetwater whom Clayborne had met briefly in English class. Risinger had played guard in the last quarter of the game. Evidently someone from Abilene Christian had introduced him to the turf. His hair was a matted daglock, his features an earthy blackface, his jersey and pants a dun-colored botch. The two cadets faced him in grumpy disgust.

"Think there's any mud out there?" Giesecke asked the football hero.

"No mud on our field," smirked the player. "It never rains in Stephenville."

"You're a mess, Dorsett, but get on up here anyways," said Clayborne, pointing to his shoulders.

"Captain says we can't let you victors do any walkin'. This here's my friend Austin Giesecke and we're going to be your taxicab to the showers."

"Pleased to meet ya, Austin. Call me Rye like everybody else does," said Risinger as the two hefty country boys tossed his mud-compacted form onto their shoulders.

"Hey, Rye, are you the guy Clayborne said was trying to get on the college newspaper?" asked Giesecke, craning his neck as they hauled him off the field amidst the clamor of rejoicing students.

"That's me," said Risinger, waving his arms to the crowd. "I made it, too. Just got word yesterday that I'm the *J-TAC*'s new Assistant Business Manager." The *J-TAC* — acronym for *John Tarleton Agricultural College* — boasted a staff of only ten. It was a distinct honor to be invited into such an elite literary body.

"Congratulations, Rye," offered Clayborne. They marched Risinger up Vanderbilt Street toward the gym as scores of onlookers screamed in adulation.

"Are you going to stay in English?" yelled Clayborne.

"Sure. I need the credit. Besides, all the *J-TAC* writing is off-hours, Monday afternoons. You guys come on and visit us in the office, up in the Admin Building. The *J-TAC* isn't stuck up."

"We'll do it," agreed Clayborne and Austin. They followed the noisy procession to the middle doors of the gym where football players by the dozen had been dethroned and left to their own footwork. The two boys from Hico came to a spontaneous military halt in the throng, tossing their charge to his friends. Risinger landed gracefully and leaped up the wooden steps with his bedraggled beaming teammates, calling back, "Thanks for the ride, guys! Sorry I got you so muddy. See you at the shirt-tail parade."

Austin and Clayborne stood caked with mud, disheveled, watching Risinger disappear into the vast gym. Austin said, "Hey, Clayborne, this game was an official school function, right?"

"Yeah," replied Clayborne, a little puzzled, "it's official. It's listed in the activities we paid our two dollars for. So what?"

"Well, if it's a real honest-to-goodness school activity, and we got all dirty doin' official school business, we ought to get a legal gym shower to clean up for the shirt-tail parade, shouldn't we?"

"You're pretty smart for a country boy," chuckled Clayborne. "It sure would beat heatin' up water for that old Number Three washtub at Miz Bobo's, wouldn't it?"

Austin grinned. "Well, come on then!" he said. "Let's look up Teddy in C Company and Marvin in A Company and get ourselves cleaned up for tonight!"

For five dollars a month, Mary Bobo's rooming house offered no indoor plumbing. The toilet was a wooden two-holer out back and the bathing facilities consisted of a zinc tub and a woodstove for heating water. The four Hico hicks, as friends called them, were becoming expert at finding every available pretext for going across the street to use Tarleton's gym showers and the Administration Building's toilets, which were open twenty-four hours a day, seven days a week. Clayborne had managed to guarantee himself at least one legal shower each week: he'd been accepted for off-hours campus maintenance work at thirty cents an hour, paid by the school's labor fund to help students defray part of their living costs — sometimes sweeping floors, other times chopping weeds or digging flower beds or working Rock Squad, raking the little stones that endlessly pushed their way up through the Texas soil. Clayborne reasoned that his weekly four hours at labor fund toil was exertion enough to work up a sweat and earn a shower. But, alas, labor fund work came only one day a week. The Hico four shrewdly cultivated good friends at the men's dormitory known as The Fort — which had its own bath facilities — and wangled shower invitations as frequently as possible. Then they discovered that physical culture was considered manly and desirable by Tarleton's higher-ups, and began working out in the gym whenever they felt the least bit dirty. So on this football Saturday the four came clean courtesy of Tarleton's sports showers.

With shining evening faces, slicked-down hair and civilian clothes, Teddy Nix, Austin Giesecke, Marvin Miller and Clayborne Perry went in search of the shirt-tail parade. They found it without trying. Rounding the corner of the Administration Building with its triple-arch main entry and its faintly Art-Deco brickwork, they ran into nearly seven hundred fellow Tarletonians who had foregathered at the east gate where College Street entered the campus. Actually, the entrance was more nearly the *north*east gate since Stephenville's street grid had been laid out some thirty degrees cattywampus to the compass, its "north-south" avenues trending almost northwest-southeast and its "east-west" streets pointing

nearly southwest-northeast. But nobody ever paid the slightest attention
to such cartographic niceties, certainly not as the sun went down on the
night of a shirt-tail parade.

Students glanced about looking for suitable partners. Clayborne and
his friends stood near the end of the teeming pack, a good ten minutes of
waiting behind the leaders. A pretty girl turned around and said to
Clayborne, "You're Private Perry in B Company, aren't you?"

Clayborne stammered, "Well, uh, yes . . . I'm Private Perry. How
did you know?" He had not yet become comfortable with the liberated
openness of college girls who introduced themselves. His Hico friends
looked on with unconcealed envy.

"I hope you won't think I'm forward, but I'm Hazel Fenner," said the
girl, shaking his hand. "Sergeant Fenner. I'm the sponsor of the Vidette
Company. You know about company sponsors, don't you?"

The yell captain broke in with his final instructions: "Gang, I suppose
all of you have felt the pressure of having to look your military best these
past two weeks?"

"Yeah!" came the deafening response.

"Well, tonight everything's gonna be jake! We're gonna let our hair
down. You're all decked out in your spiffy civvies, right?"

"Right!"

"Well, gang, everyone follow this military order right now! By the
numbers, pull out your shirt tails! One! Two! Three! Get goofy! Show 'em
we know how to have a good time!"

The cacophony of Yippee and Yahoo matched the little dance everyone
did as they tugged at their shirts. Out popped the shirt-tails and up fled
the roar, "On Ye Tarleton! Let's parade!"

"You ready to parade, chilluns?" screamed the yell leader. "Ok, gang,
scram!"

Off they went. The leaders marched out the gate singing their pep song
at the top of their lungs. At the back of the crowd, Hazel Fenner, her
shirt-tail out like everyone else's, turned back to Clayborne and continued
her conversation.

"Like I said, I'm the Vidette Company sponsor — you know what a
sponsor is . . ."

"Oh, yeah," said Clayborne. "B Company has a sponsor. Leta Lee
Nunn. She's in my typing class. We're all pitching in to buy her a
sergeant's uniform. Fifty cents each. All the R.O.T.C. companies have a
girl to sort of, well, to . . ."

"Represent the company to the student body," completed Hazel
Fenner. "That's right, that's just exactly what we sponsors do. And I do
that for the Videttes. I suppose you know all about the Videttes?"

"Well, sure. That's the drill team company. It goes to all the drill
contests, like the one at the Dallas Fair in February!"

"Right you are," smiled Fenner. "And they go to the Summer Camp just before school, like the one where I threw the watermelon party this year."

"Oh, was that you?" asked Clayborne, impressed. "I read about it in the *J-TAC* last week. You're famous."

She smiled sweetly, and said to him confidentially: "You're going to be famous yourself, Private Perry. The Vidette Captain watches all the other companies on the drill field and picks out the most promising cadets. I suspect you're going to be invited to volunteer for Vidette Company. Don't tell them I said anything to you, it wouldn't be fair. But let's just say I might have overheard Vidette officers who think you know your left foot from your right. Hey! Our turn in the parade is coming up! Come on, let's go, Private Perry!"

Before he could think, the snake dance line had swept him up and Hazel Fenner had placed his hands around her waist and they were stomping and wobbling along College Street toward downtown Stephenville, yelling their heads off. Looking back at his Hico friends he could see that the line had run out of girls and the hindmost were all boys, self-consciously holding the belt-loops of the fellow in front of them, and glowering at Clayborne for getting to hold on to a girl — and such a pretty one at that.

It was a heady experience for a Hico farm boy. Talking to Hazel Fenner meant little to him — it had been all business as far as he was concerned; she was simply working on another recruit for Vidette Company. Let his chums think what they would. But the noisy parade, veering and lurching and zig-zagging through the tolerant nighttime streets, making a howling singing unruly shirt-tail spectacle of themselves, being a real part of the gang — that meant a great deal to him. It was something undreamed of, something that hinted beyond the nonsense. It was more than the fun. It was something that whispered of the wide world outside and brilliant doings in a long future, a sense of belonging like he had never known. In the dusty exhilarated noise of a little town in the Upper Cross Timbers he felt his life surging, opening outward like a fat rosebud. Somehow, it was beautiful and endlessly hopeful.

"Papa, Pet seems all stove up," said Clayborne as he laid an armful of firewood beside the black iron grate.

"You been out in the barn, have you?" said Tom Perry. "She's an old horse, son, almost seventeen years old. She just gets a little stiff in the mornings. But once you get her in harness she's rarin' to go. You hitch her with the other animals and she still wants that lead spot. You should have seen her yesterday when I unhitched her from the cotton wagon. Rolled in the dirt, frolicking like a colt. Yessir, frolicking like a colt."

Clayborne knelt down with his load at the woodbox, arranging the cut slabs. "Papa, I've been thinking about Pet," he said. "I mean remembering things from a long time ago. How she went with us to Colorado when I was just five years old, you remember?"

"I remember."

"How she pulled the wagon in harness with old Jack all those miles to Oklahoma and then back home. How she's pulled the buggy and the wagon into Hico so many times. There's a lot to remember." He paused. "And I went out to see Pup."

Tom had watched out the kitchen window as his son stood over the low mound of a grave next to the cotton patch. It had been two years now without the friendly black mongrel. He knew Clayborne was learning that some lacerations of the soul never heal. He said nothing.

Clayborne got up and selfconsciously said, "I have to write about that sort of stuff for English class. You know, what's happened to you and what does your life amount to and that sort of thing."

"How you doing in college, son? You understand what they're teaching you?"

"Pretty good, Papa. Typing's easy and college algebra is hard. It's too early to tell much, though. I've only been there a month now. Hardly time to take our first test. I'm doing fine so far." He stepped to the drainboard and cranked the water pump to fill a drinking glass. He glugged the glass dry in a single gulp. "But just think of all the miles Pet has pulled us, Papa."

Tom Perry peered over his round glasses at Clayborne, his copy of the *Hico News Review* spread on the kitchen table before him. "Yep, she's pulled us a fur piece, she has." Clayborne turned and noticed that the chronic corneal ulcers on his father's left eye had turned the iris a murky slate gray, and his right eye now seemed to be red and irritated as well.

Clayborne pulled up an old cane bottomed kitchen chair and sat down at the table. "Papa," he said, "I didn't notice in the coal oil light last might, but isn't your right eye getting clouded up?

Tom looked straight at his oldest boy, a pall of resignation over his large country features making him appear older than his forty-five years. "Don't worry yourself none, son. It's just a little inflammation. These spells come and go."

Belle Perry popped in the kitchen door from feeding the chickens and growled at her husband, "Don't you try and fool him none, Tom." She wiped her hands on her apron and took off her sunbonnet, letting her brown hair fall around her shoulders. It was faintly streaked with gray. She was thirty-five years old. "That right eye is troublin' him real bad, son. Those spells come and go, all right. But every time they go that right eye is worse. And your Papa can't hardly see out'n the left one at all any more."

"Papa," said Clayborne, alarmed. "Is that right?"

"Belle, you shouldn't worry the boy none, what with him in college and all that studyin' to do."

"He's a man grown, Tom," snapped Belle. "He sure ought to know what's happenin' to his own father."

"What's happening? What is it, Papa?" asked Clayborne.

"Well, Doctor Curry in Hico says this eye condition's just gonna keep on getting worse. There's nothing he can do about it."

Belle complained, "If Doctor Durham was still alive, *he* could do something about it! He cured you when you took the pneumonia back in 1919."

Tom replied, "He couldn't do nothin' about the peilagra when I took that, remember, Belle? Had to go up to Glen Rose to that Naturopath Millings to get cured. Besides, I've had this left eye all scarred up since, oh, before Clayborne was born. Remember, they wouldn't take me for the Great War on account of it. Doctor Durham — rest in peace — he couldn't do nothin' about it."

"I still miss old Doctor Durham, I sure do," said Belle, shaking her head.

Clayborne asked, "But what do you mean, your eye condition's going to keep on getting worse?"

"I won't be able to see after 'while," said Tom matter-of-factly.

"Your Papa's going blind, Clayborne." said Belle.

Stunned silence.

"Well, then I'll quit college and come help on the farm." He had decided. It was cut and dried. "I'll tell them next Monday."

"Why, the very idea!" said Belle. "Tom, you talk to this boy."

Tom leaned over his newspaper, glaring out of his wounded eyes. "You'll do nothing of the sort, young man. Don't get me wrong, son. It's a fine loving thing to offer. We appreciate it. But college is where you belong. We got Hoyt to help us here. Your brother's not real strong on school like you were. He's happy on the farm. You said in college they have you write about what your life amounts to. Well, I don't know what my life amounts to, but I can tell you one thing: yours is going to amount to more. You're the one of us Perrys that's special, like Old Grandma keeps sayin'. You don't realize how important you are. You're going to be the educated one. You can't quit now. Think of the family, boy, the Perry name. You stay in college or you and me is going to have to go have a talk in the barn."

The image was too much: talks in the barn meant stern gigantic father looming with loosened belt over quaking little boy. Both of them knew that today Tom's slight frame would appear laughable beside Clayborne's muscled bulk in any physical contest — and both of them knew that nothing on earth could make Clayborne raise a finger against his father.

"You win, Papa," smiled Clayborne with affection. "I don't think I could stand another whippin' like that time I pasted all them watermelons when I was twelve." They chuckled at each other as if sharing a conspiratorial secret.

"Good. You mind your ol' Papa and stay in college. Besides, Doc Curry says I got years of good sight left. I can still see good enough to drive the car. I'll show you when we go into town today. I'll be all right."

Hoyt flung open the kitchen door and stomped in with Dorothy and Nadine trailing behind. The two girls ran to hug their oldest brother as Hoyt asked, "You get that wood in, Clayborne?"

"Both woodboxes full," he replied. "Cookstove and heater both. Hey, you little monkies, don't you ever get tired of huggin' me? You're heavy hangin' on me that way."

"He're not monkies," intoned eight-year-old Dorothy. "Our big brother's a monkey!" She dashed off into the front parlor with ten-year-old big sister Nadine, making sure that Clayborne ran close behind in mock pursuit.

"Mama," said Hoyt, "we got all the animals fed and the cream and eggs ready to go. Clayborne's got the wood in. Time to go into Hico. Ready, Papa?"

Tom yelled to the air in general: "Time to leave now! All that's goin' to Hico get in the car!"

The family quickly gathered before the Model T Ford, ready for their customary weekly venture into town. Clayborne looked around, already seeing his home with new eyes even after so short a stint at college. He knew that the modest farm house gleaming in the autumn sunlight among the lanky liveoaks behind them was his parents' pride and joy, the crowning achievement of their lives: their own home on their own land. He realized uneasily how small the house seemed compared to the dean's home at Tarleton. He was getting a glimmer of how meager the Grand Prairie farmer's life really was. And how harsh. How many years his father and mother had struggled and failed and labored some more and saved and ached to finally own this hundred acres! But so what if they'd had to live as rent farmers for years to do it? So what if they'd had to buy it fifty acres at a time, stretching their money year after year, letting their first place out to rent farmers to help pay for the next fifty acres?

Clayborne could see how proud his father was now to live on these two little adjacent chunks of land, land sloping gently eastward to Little Duffau Creek, almost flat, with only the slightest undulation from the gravel farm-to-market road on the north to the county line on the south. Why, the southeast corner stake on the back fifty was not a thousand feet from the very spot where Erath, Bosque and Hamilton counties came together! It was close to Hico, only three miles. His Papa could grow all the cotton he'd need for a living right on this one little place. There was good rent land right next door to the east if he ever needed to make some extra cotton for cash, like Clayborne had needed this year for college.

And the house, Clayborne thought, well, so it had been pushed together from two smaller buildings, one that had been on his Dad's first place, the other on his second. So what? A carpenter friend, Tom Strepey, had moved one building to the other and did a workmanlike job of tacking them together. Now it made a good-sized dwelling for his Papa and Mama, and the four kids — three now that he was off to college most of the time. It had no electricity, but there was running water right in the house, right in the hydrant over the wash basin. Clayborne knew that as far as his father was concerned, it was a fine home and a fine farm, and that was enough for any man. College, he realized, was reinforcing his own feeling that it was not enough. He silently worried whether his feelings were traitorous.

Tom drove them rumbling down the gravel drive past the cotton patch where shrivelled leaves and a few white lint flags in the stems were all that was left of 1928's crop. As he turned left onto the unpaved farmer's market road, Tom commented to the boys in the back seat, "Those cedars are gettin' a pretty good foothold on this cut bank here. Maybe better look to it."

"I'll get 'em on Christmas break, Papa," said Clayborne.

"What's Christmas break?" asked little Dorothy from the front seat.

"That's when I get to come home from college for two weeks at Christmas. It's a holiday. I ought to make up my mind by then what to major in."

"What's 'major in'?" asked Nadine, sitting in the back seat between her two older brothers.

"Your major is what you study most in college. What you major in is what you get your diploma in."

"Oh," replied the youngster, not much enlightened.

Hoyt announced wryly, "I'm majorin' in Ds over at Millerville school."

Clayborne laughed, "Oh, come on, Hoyt. You're doin' better than that!"

"Don't bet on it," the twelve-year-old muttered ruefully.

Belle turned back over the upholstered seat and said, "Clayborne, we got a penny postcard from your Uncle Lem in Miles last week. Your cousin Foncyne is going to college right there with you in Stephenville."

"Foncyne Elam is going to Tarleton? I haven't seen her." Clayborne said.

"Well, I thought maybe you had. She's the same age as you, you know. Seems like maybe you'd have a class with her, or something," smiled his mother.

"There's a lot of kids at Tarleton, Mama."

"I guess so. Well, maybe you can look her up. She lives in the girl's dormitory. Do you know where that is?"

"Sure, Mama, it's a big L-shaped brick building over next to Washington Street, clear the other side of campus from Miz Bobo's. I'll go say hello to her next week."

Tom added. "Speakin' of relatives, son, you ought to go see Bob Bellew when you get a chance. He lives right close to you somewheres, on Neblett Street I think he said."

"That's hardly a couple of blocks away," said Clayborne. "Sure, I'd be glad to go see him. You know, Papa, I hate to say this, but I've only met Mr. Bellew a couple of times and I can't recollect what relation we are to him."

Tom smiled, "Don't feel bad, son. I don't rightly know either. I think he's some shirt-tail cousin or another. He's not on my side of the family. Do you know, Belle?"

"Oh, he's a Blackburn of some kind. I'm not sure, though."

"One of them step-neighbor-in-laws your tribe has layin' out all over the country, I expect," said Tom. "We got a few, too. Like that Uncle Docton of ours in the Old Soldier's Home what thinks he's a prophet."

Tom said, "Well, son, Bob Bellew is one of our inlaws or outlaws or something. It don't make no never mind. He's a good man. Just go see him and tell him you're Tom Perry's boy. He'll treat you right. And Belle, speakin' of your side of the family, we're coming up to your Papa's place here. Want to stop a minute?"

"I see him out raking leaves under the front trees. Just stop a second and let me ask how Mama's feeling."

Hoyt said, "There's Grandma Blackburn in her rocking chair out on the gallery."

The faithful Tin Lizzie chugged to a halt at the little farm house by the road. A stone fireplace on the home's north gable end gave it a countrified log-cabin feel despite its milled shiplap siding and shop-made counterbalanced sash windows. Charley Blackburn looked up from his raking and waved a signal to welcome his daughter's family. The children in the car waved and shouted greetings to him.

Belle leaned out the car's glassless side and called, "Some farmer you are, Papa. Rakin' leaves and takin' care of a lawn."

"It beats plowin' all day, it do," grinned the old man. "Besides, we still farm a little, got our cows and hogs, you know. I'm just as happy your brother Fred's running the old place up at Dude Flat nowadays. Heavy farmin' is a young man's job, ain't it, Tom?"

Tom leaned over the steering wheel to peer past Belle and said, "Younger than me, Papa Blackburn."

"How's Mama doing, Papa?" asked Belle, waving to her mother sixty feet away under the sheltering porch. Laura Blackburn waved back to her daughter, smiling wanly.

"She's feelin' a might puny today, daughter. It's the heart trouble again. Takes all her strength away. She'd come out to say hello otherwise. But after she sits out on the gallery for a while of a morning, she feels better."

"You ought to take her to a doctor, Papa." scolded Belle.

"Well, you know I take her into Hico every week or two for her medicine."

"I mean a heart doctor, Papa. Someplace where they got heart doctors like Waco."

"Doc Curry in Hico is takin' care of that. If she gets any worse, he says he knows a clinic over at Marlin, got the best heart specialists in these parts. But he says it ain't nothing to worry about. We're just gettin' old, that's all."

"Well," said Belle, "you get the best doctorin' for Mama you can. It ain't like you were poorly off, or anything."

Charley Blackburn had in fact done very well as a Grand Prairie farmer, investing his spare cash over the years in commercial real estate. He owned a number of business buildings in Hico including the one his doctor rented. With something around ten thousand dollars in the bank, Charley Blackburn was considered to be very well off indeed.

"I'll do right by your Mama, daughter, I will," grinned her father. "She'll be fine."

"I know you will, Papa. We got to go on into Hico now. Bye for now."

"Thanks for stoppin' by with the grandkids. You have a good time in town now, you hear? So long, kiddos."

The flivver rattled away toward Hico, leaving Charley Blackburn raking his lawn in a cloud of road dust.

As they turned onto Second Street a few minutes later in Hico, Clayborne said. "Papa, would you drop me off at Rainwater's Candy Kitchen before you turn off to the grocery store?"

"Going to get some candy? Have you got a girl?"

"No, Papa. I don't have a girl and I'm not getting any candy. I'm going to walk from there out to the field by Blair Pasture. I saw in the paper they've got airplane rides for two dollars, and I'm goin' to get me one. Saved my labor fund money for it. I'll meet you back in town."

Belle looked alarmed. "You're going up in one of those flimsy things? Is it safe?"

Tom said, "You read stories about those aeroplanes falling all the time. You sure you want to ride in one of 'em?"

"I'm sure it's safe," said Clayborne. "I expect the pilot wants to stay alive as much as I do."

"Hey," yelled Hoyt, "I want to go for a ride, too!"

"Clayborne says it costs two dollars, boy," said Tom. "We ain't got any two dollars for aeroplane rides. Here's Rainwater's, Clayborne." He pulled to a stop alongside parked Chevrolets and Fords near Hico's main downtown intersection.

"Sorry, Hoyt," said Clayborne as he scrambled out of the car. "Take care of Nadine and Dorothy for Mama 'til I get back. You'll get your chance one day."

The airplane ride was both more and less than Clayborne had expected: he got all the pit of the stomach kinesthesia upon takeoff that he dreaded, but once airborne he had none of the hoped-for feeling of liberation, of soaring aloft to the heavens on eagles wings. He found himself crammed into a little wooden cabin with two other passengers, one facing front with the pilot and one facing sideways with him on a bench, and only tiny little round windows to peep out of. It was a technical mechanical dragon he rode, not a poetic Pegasus: he flew with Hephaestus rather than Bellerophon. And he was disappointed to discover that even the infinite vaulted cerulean welkin, the great sky itself, had bumps in it like an ordinary rutted country road. But he bounced with the airpockets against his seat belt in good humor, staring down at the receding earth, spotting familiar landmarks from a strange new vantage point.

Look! There's Grubbs Branch, and the little pond it makes at the edge of town. Woop! The airplane's banking to the right. Hey, you can see Hico High School and the sports field where I used to play, bleachers and all. And now we're right over Jacks Hollow Branch that comes in from Grandpa Blackburn's place. Oh ho! You can even see the roof and front porch of school superintendent Masterson's house on Mesquite Street — I'll bet he's sitting out there reading his newspaper like he always does on Saturday afternoons. I wonder if he's giving some country kid a hard time about getting into Hico High? And here's that new part of town with those wide blocks and not many houses. And the cemetery — poor Auntie Sallie and Cora are down there. Here's the Bosque — water's low this year, lot of sand showing in the bottoms. Woop! That was a big bump... Say, there's the cotton gins and the railroad station, and that's the city park where they have Reunion every year. And out north you can see Papa's farm and Dude Flat and Grandpa Perry's farm, and even out to Rocky and Black Stump Valley where Mr. Fouts lives. And even up to Duffau. You can see everything from up here. It all looks so little. I can pick out Petty's grocery and Driscoll's furniture and the bank and Rainwater's Candy Kitchen and the newspaper office — and there's where Linchie used to have his cafe before Auntie Sallie died. Law, there's not much to this whole country from up here. I lived my whole life down there and it don't look any bigger than a one-cent stamp. The whole blame thing don't amount to a — what had he jokingly said about himself to his friends their first evening together at Tarleton? — *it don't amount to a hill of beans.*

When the plane bounced to a landing in the grassy field above Blair

Pasture, he felt exhilaration and mortification — exhilaration because of the ride, mortification because of what it had shown him about his universe. Some of those new words he was learning in college English seemed to be pointing accusatory fingers at him: provincial, circumscribed, ingenue. Well, everybody had to be from somewhere, he decided. He might have done worse. He might have been born — God forbid — in New York City, or malarial Africa or socialist Russia. The Grand Prairie wasn't so bad. And it was surely pretty to look at, all the grass and trees and the town. Yessir.

After taxiing the plane to a stop, the pilot unstrapped himself, stepped back into the cabin and opened the passenger door. "Well, was it worth the two dollars?" he asked.

"Every penny," said Clayborne.

The next afternoon Clayborne thumbed a ride back to Stephenville's Court House Square and walked the mile to his room next to the Tarleton campus. Marvin Miller was sitting up in his bed reading when Clayborne walked in.

"Howdy, stranger," said Miller. "Have a good time at home?"

"Always do," replied Clayborne. "Chopped some wood, milked the cows, cut some sorghum cane — and I took a ride in an airplane."

"Aw, that's pure-dee applesauce!" asserted Miller. "You're kidding me, right?"

"Nope, really did it."

"You son of a gun! I've never been up in an airplane."

"It was really grand. Went up out of that field across Blair Pasture from the high school, flew all around Hico, stayed up ten minutes or more, paid two dollars for it."

"Well, son of a gun! Could you see my house?"

"Yeah, and Teddy's and Austin's both. And my old place at Dude Flat."

"Wow! That's the berries."

"I'll tell you all about it later. Do we have any Post Toasties left for breakfast tomorrow? We may have to borrow some from the other guys."

"We got half a box, plenty. And the milk truck will stop tomorrow because it's Monday. I had to go over to the ice house for milk this morning. Oh, and I guess I ought to tell you before they get here — some folks from my church are gonna be here in a little while. They'll prob'ly stay an hour or so."

"From your church? All the way from Hico?"

"No, from the Church of Christ here in Stephenville, the one where I been goin' up on Davis Avenue."

"What are they comin' here for?"

"Well, I don't know if you Baptists have this thing, but us Church of Christs have families that adopt visitors like college kids. Not really adopt, like if you're an orphan, they just *kind of* adopt you. You know, come visit you, get to know you, bring you things, make it so you won't feel lonesome away from home."

"Oh," said Clayborne, a little taken aback. "No, I don't think us Baptists do that. We never did it at Prairie Springs church, anyways —but there wouldn't be anybody for them adopt around Hico. I don't know about the Baptists here in Stephenville. But I doubt it."

"Well, this family named Baxter is going to be coming by after 'while. Is that okay with you?"

"Well, sure. You want me to go in the kitchen while they're here?"

"No, you stay. They're nice people. You'll like them. It's too bad there's nothing like that at your church."

"Yeah, that wouldn't be too bad an idea."

"I tell you what . . . "

"What?"

"You know how you're not sure where to go to church here, that you don't know any Baptists?"

"Yeah."

"Well, look. Let's make a deal. I'll go with you to the Baptist Church one Sunday and you come with me to the Church of Christ the next. We'll go back and forth. That way we'll both have somebody we know at church: us!"

"Hey, that's a good idea! No, wait. My folks would have a fit if they thought I was going to a Church of Christ."

"So would mine if they thought I was going to a Baptist church. But didn't you tell me your family goes to the Methodist church when the Baptist preacher doesn't come?"

"Yeah."

"And I'll bet your folks don't mind it too much."

"No, not that I ever heard."

"Well, Church of Christs aren't any more different from Baptists than Methodists are. Why don't you give it a try?"

"Now, look, Marvin, it's okay with me, it's just my folks. They're real strong Baptist. I mean *real* strong. They'd never approve."

"Well, let your conscience be your guide. It's between you and the Lord."

"It's not the Lord that would mind me goin' to your church. But I could sure use a friend going with me to mine. So I'll do it. I'll take you up on your deal. One Sunday to Baptist church, one Sunday to Church of Christ. I just don't think I'll mention it to my parents, that's all."

As the weeks passed, their church agreement worked out well. And as the Baxters visited Marvin Miller with weekly gifts of food and friendship and precious time, Clayborne came to harbor a warm appreciation for the

Church of Christ. And although he remained steadfastly in the Baptist fold, it was a respect he would keep for a lifetime.

"How nice you boys look in your dress uniforms!" said Belle. "And what a beautiful Armistice Day!" Clayborne held the car door open for her in front of Mrs. Mary Bobo's rooming house.

Marvin Miller remarked from the walkway, "Looks like Dean Davis was right. He said in chapel last week that he'd arrange some good weather for us today."

Belle took her seat in the Model T with the rest of her family and looked out the rolled-down window. "Marvin, it's been good seeing you again," she said. "You and Clayborne seem to be doing just fine."

"Thank you, Miz Perry," said the blonde young man. "I'm glad you folks could come by and see our room and all today. Are you going to the ceremony this afternoon?"

Clayborne answered for her: "I don't think so, Marvin. I'm prob'ly just going to take the family around school, show them some classrooms and such."

"Make sure you're back on time, Clayborne," fretted Miller. "Everybody has to be there. You don't want any demerits on your record. And remember everybody stays in dress uniform, all the girls will be in their blue chambrays."

"I'll come back before we have to be at the gym. Papa, do you want to sit with Hoyt and Nadine so I can squire you around the campus?"

"Yep. You better do the drivin'," said Tom, getting in the back seat. "I'd just get lost in all these big buildings."

"See ya this afternoon, Marvin," waved Clayborne as he took his seat behind the steering wheel and started the car.

" 'Bye, Mister and Miz Perry, 'bye Hoyt, 'bye girls," called Miller.

"Well, folks, we're off," said Clayborne, pulling the Tin Lizzie into Vanderbilt street to slowly chug along Tarleton's campus perimeter. "What would you like to see first?"

"I want to see the farm!" exclaimed Hoyt. "Somethin' I can understand!"

"The college farm is outside of town a mile, Hoyt," said his big brother. "We'll save it 'til last."

"What about this chapel Marvin was talking about?" asked Belle. "You never mentioned any chapel to me . . ."

"To the chapel it is," Clayborne smiled. He guided the flivver into the campus through the northwesterly Cain Street entrance. "Chapel's like a class, Mama," he explained. "We have chapel from ten to eleven on Monday, Wednesday and Friday. Everybody goes. See the big old gym here on the right? That's where we have chapel."

"Is it a church service?" his father asked.

"Sort of. Dean Davis usually starts it off with announcements, then we say a prayer, sing some hymns and then a preacher from some church gives us a sermon. Sometimes a businessman comes to talk."

"Is it a Baptist preacher?" Belle wanted to know.

"Sometimes. Sometimes the Methodists send over a preacher or the Lutherans or the Church of Christs. The college invites all different preachers. This is our Administration Building on the left."

"It's three stories high," said little Dorothy in the front seat beside her mother. "And look at all those windows."

"We have classes in there, little sister. The windows make it light. I take algebra and English up there on the second floor."

Hoyt yelled, "Hey, look at the cannon! Do you get to shoot it, Clayborne?"

Belle complained, "You don't have to shout so, Hoyt."

"I think we'll shoot it during maneuvers," said Clayborne. "It's just a decoration for the lawn right now. And that's the Home Economics Building down College Street there. And that big wooden barracks across the street from it is the boys' dormitory. They call it the Fort. And here on the right is the dean's home."

"My, my," said Nadine, "isn't that fancy?"

"That's a mighty big house for one family to live in," said Hoyt. "How many children does he have?"

"None at home," said Clayborne. "They're all grown and out on their own. The dean needs a big house for when they have faculty get-togethers or when the president of Texas A&M comes visiting."

"What's this Conservatory?" asked Tom. "Am I reading that right? Is that what the sign says?"

"That's what it says, Papa. It's the music and art building. That's where I practice with the Boy's Glee Club. I told you about how we went in the Glee Club to give a recital over at the high school in De Leon, didn't I? They took us there on the college bus. But when they took the Videttes to Comanche last week, we had to go in a cattle truck! Can you imagine that? In a cattle truck. We had to get a wagon sheet out and stick it up in front to keep the wind from freezing us."

Belle said, "A little cold won't hurt you, son. You were privileged to get into the Videttes, Clayborne. It's an honor to represent your college like that."

"Oh, you're surely right, Mama," he said.

Hoyt sneered, "Videttes I can see. But Glee Club! Singing! That's sissy stuff. Don't they rag you for bein' a sissy?"

"Well, Hoyt," related Clayborne, "you know Tarleton is an Aggie college and has a lot of great big farm boys goin' here, right?"

"Yeah."

"Well, just about all of 'em in the Glee Club is bigger than me. They're pretty rough ol' boys that just likes to sing. If you called any of 'em a sissy to his face, I think you'd be in a heap of trouble, especially the ones on the football team."

"Is Tarleton any good at football?" asked Hoyt.

"Well, so far this year we've won three and lost three. We were conference champions last year, though. Mama, Papa, over on the left is where they're building the new auditorium. It's gonna be a big one. And this last building on the right with those white columns on the front here is the girls' dormitory. That's where Foncyne stays. I went to see her and let her know where I lived in case she needs anything."

"Is she well?" asked Belle.

"She's just fine, Mama. I talked to her for a while. She takes a lot of Home Ec courses and has a different English class than me, so we never run into each other except after class. And she runs with a different crowd, the ones that have theater parties and all."

"What's a theater party?" asked Nadine.

"It's a girl's club thing. They get together and go to the show with their boy friends and then go somewhere like Holt's Drug Store. They decorate the place up and have cake and ice cream and talk about the show and such."

"Now I'm goin' to drive us out to my animal husbandry class, folks." Clayborne turned east (*north*east, really) on Washington Street and headed for the College Farm, officially Texas A&M College Substation Number Twenty. "I'll show you the big barn and our prize stock and some of the student projects we're working on."

"How do you usually get out there?" asked Tom.

"We walk. It's a couple of miles, but my class starts at one-fifteen, so I've got all of lunch break to make it out there."

"Lunch break," remarked Belle. "They don't call it dinner?"

"Nope, Mama," said the collegiate, "it's all modern talk here. You eat lunch at noon and dinner at night. How about that?"

"Sounds citified," she muttered. "Pure foolishness."

Clayborne asked, "What did you think about this Herbert Hoover getting elected president last week, Papa?"

"Didn't surprise me a bit," said Tom emphatically. "That Alfred Smith didn't stand a chance, like I said all through the campaign."

"Why not, Papa?" asked Clayborne.

"Well, just look at everything he had against him. He's a New York Catholic and he's against prohibition."

Belle chimed in: "I'd never vote for anybody that was against prohibition. Why, there's no more sense than use in that."

"What's a New York Catholic?" Nadine wanted to know.

"Catholics is people what goes to Catholic church," answered Tom.

"They got all those statues of Mary and Jesus. You wouldn't catch me prayin' to no statue."

"Did you vote in the election, Mama?" asked Clayborne.

"Why, of course. I voted every election since women's suffrage passed. It's a patriotic duty. But I leave the politics to your father. Men understand politics."

Tom went on, "Like I say, that Al Smith never had a chance. Ain't never been a Catholic president, never will be. And you heard what they said about Hoover . . ."

"What's that, Dad?"

"It was the Three P's got him elected. He stood for the Three P's: Protestants, Prohibition and Prosperity. I heard it on the radio. The Three P's. That's what did it. And it tells you something that he carried the Texas vote. Can you imagine a Republican carrying Texas by 26,000 votes? Texas has always been a loyal Democrat state. You know how it riles people up when I tell 'em I vote Republican. Republican's been a swear word in Texas since Lincoln freed the slaves. Usually when you say Republican to a Texan, he comes back at you with things like 'Oh, Big Business,' or 'They're not for the little fellow.' But Hoover won in Texas by 26,000 votes. Tells you they'd rather vote Republican than have a New York Catholic what's against prohibition."

"Don't you think Texas may just be getting tired of Democrats, Papa?"

"No siree. This new Senator Tom Connally got elected, and he's a Democrat. And Governor Moody got reelected, and he's a Democrat. All the Democrats won except Alfred E. Smith."

"I guess that's right. Say, I didn't see Ma Ferguson running against Dan Moody, Papa. You think she finally gave up?"

"Oh, I wouldn't count on it. Ol' Ma, she knows Dan Moody is a nice young man. Everybody likes him — he fought the Klan down in Williamson County before he was governor. He's a serious-minded soul and a God-fearing man. He wants to do great things for Texas. He keeps complaining that the governor can't appoint his own administration. Everybody has to be elected. Says it makes the governor powerless. Wants to change the state constitution so's he can appoint his own people to run things. That'll be the day. I think folks are right satisfied with a government that's not too powerful. They just pat ol' Dan Moody on the head and tell him he's a nice boy, and they don't pay any attention at all to what he says."

One Texas historian put Dan Moody's efforts in a nutshell: "Moody was popular and had no trouble in winning two terms. But the legislature and the people ignored his recommendations; Texans liked limited government." It was true. In referendum after referendum, Texans refused to strengthen state government even "to do great things for Texas." It is striking that Texans kept their government so close to the original American concept of 1789 while the rest of the nation adopted more centralized forms.

"But you watch." said Tom Perry. "Folks will get tired of a high-minded governor. Wait and see. Ol' Ma Ferguson is just sittin' with Farmer Jim up on their ranch above Meridian, waiting 'til people decide they'd like some more monkey business. When folks change their minds, she'll be back."

The Hico four walked bundled against the late November chill past the Erath County court house with its gothic three-story limestone gables, its arched red granite windows and high central steeple.

"Think we're in time for the picture show?" asked Austin Giesecke.

"Plenty of time," said Marvin Miller.

They rounded the last corner and stared in shock. A long line trailed away from the box office of the Majestic Theater. The overhead marquee blared incandescently:

IT TALKS!
CULLEN LANDIS
HELENE COSTELLO
IN
THE LIGHTS OF NEW YORK

"Behold!" declaimed Teddy Nix. "The damn crowd got here before us!"

"Look at that!" gasped Clayborne. "I've never seen anything like it. They're backed up past McMahan and Holley's barber shop!"

Marvin Miller sighed, *"Maybe* there's plenty of time."

The four queued up at the end of the line in the cold wind.

"It's because this is the first talkie in Stephenville, that's what," grumbled Giesecke. "Everybody wants to see a talkie. You'd think they were showing *The Jazz Singer* with Al Jolson. I never even heard of this picture before."

"They just wired the Majestic for sound last week," said Nix. "I read it in the *J-TAC*. They tried to get *The Jazz Singer* but it's only showing in big cities. This is supposed to be a gangster picture. It's prob'ly not real good."

"Couldn't be any more boring than that Lyceum number last Wednesday," remarked Giesecke.

"Yeah, with all that old-timey longhair music," said Nix.

"The Schubert Quartet?" said Miller. "It wasn't all that bad. The whole gym was filled up, you know."

"Well, those Lyceum numbers come with our two-dollar activity fee," retorted Nix. "What are people gonna do, just sit at home and do nothing?"

"That Beethoven music is kind of pretty," said Miller. "We're just not used to it."

"I didn't think it was too boring," said Clayborne. "It's not what I'm used to, but that's what you go to college for, to learn new things."

"Say, the Majestic didn't raise their ticket price because it's a talkie, did they?" asked Nix.

"Nope, still twenty-five cents," said Miller. "Says so on the box office, see?"

They managed to get in for the next showing with no trouble. When the house lights dimmed, the customary piano player did not appear at the foot of the stage. But when the screen lit up with the first title, music gushed forth anyway, the scratchy, hissing, tinny syncopated sound of a small studio orchestra trying its best to sound like the New York Philharmonic. *The Lights of New York* was a Vitaphone production, which meant that it used a sound system of wax discs much like ordinary Victrola records of the day, linked to the film projector by an elaborate mechanical system of belts and braces that kept the two more or less in synchronization.

The audience was spellbound, regardless of the paltry sounds that served to remind one of music rather than to reproduce it. Like the silent movies the audience was accustomed to, this film set its mood with a title: "A Story of Main Street and Broadway . . . Main Street — 45 minutes from Broadway — but a thousand miles away." This was obviously going to be another potboiler about the age-old conflict between small-town values and big-city temptations, a theme that was ancient before Sodom was built.

The scene opens upon two small-town barbers, the Good Guys, working in a nondescript hotel that has seen better days; one of them, Eddie, is obviously Our Hero and the other his Good Friend. Fast-talking con men enter, and convince the two innocents that fortune has just smiled upon them: steady workers of good character are needed to staff a new barber shop in glamorous, giddy New York where they can make piles of money catering to the night club crowd. Of course, the big-city barber shop predictably turns out to be just a front for The Bad Guys, bootleggers in this case. And by sheer coincidence, Eddie's fiancee is a dancer in the chorus of a night club right next door to the new barber shop, giving us a good excuse for a number of razzle-dazzle dance routines — this film began life as a series of musical short subjects just before talkies became the rage, and the producers simply patched the gangster story around them to cash in on the new boom. But the audience didn't care how contrived the plot might be: they were enthralled. It talks! Just like the marquee promised.

Nobody noticed the monotonous tone of the voices or how everybody on screen stood stock still in one place during dialogue — sound engineers had not yet learned much about recording technique. The noisy cameras had to be encased in a small stationary *room* on the sound stage, which meant that the fluid artistic camera movements of the silent era were utterly lost. The actors had to bunch up around one single hidden microphone and stay there in camera range. Recording devices weren't very subtle, either, and director Bryan Foy had decreed that his actors E-NUN-CI-ATE very s-l-o-w-l-y and at a constant loudness with no conversational fluctuations so everyone in the last row could understand all the words — a wise precaution considering the crude loudspeaker systems theaters had installed. The languorous plodding speech and stiff immobile scenes counterposed with the world of gangsters, chorus girls, robberies and strangely motionless chases by the cops gave *The Lights of New York* a surreal feeling worthy of Salvador Dali. The audience ate it up.

Our story plods on between dance routines and double crosses: The Bad Guys bump off the owner of the night club next door — to muscle in on his bootlegging racket, of course — and Our Heroine, Eddie's lady love, is falsely accused of doing the wicked deed to her boss. The police are on their way to arrest her. But Eddie has overheard the dastardly plans of The Bad Guys and is the only one who can save his sweetheart. And here we have some of the first classic wooden dialogue of the talkies:

GANG BOSS: The dicks will be here at ten o'clock.

HENCHMAN: Uh-huh.

GANG BOSS: But they *must not find Eddie.*

HENCHMAN: What do you want us to do?

GANG BOSS: I want you to make him disappear.

HENCHMAN: Disappear?

GANG BOSS: Certainly. If they don't find him, it will clinch everything for us. Don't you understand?

HENCHMAN: You mean . . .

GANG BOSS: *Take him for . . . a ride.*

"Take him for a ride" entered popular American speech and made the picture famous. The underworld slang liberally sprinkled through *The Lights of New York*, as intended, fascinated decent folk and gave the movie priceless word of mouth advertising. The film had been shot in under a week for $75,000 and grossed over a million.

Naturally, its final scene had to be a Happy Ending: Eddie escapes from his "ride" but is framed by the Bad Guys and joins Our Heroine in jail. A quirk of fate convinces the police of the truth just in the nick of time. Our Hero and Heroine are released from custody and head back to the Small Town. A surprisingly literate New York cop wishes them well in their life back "where there's trees and flowers and mountains." The End. In Stephenville's Majestic Theater, as in movie houses all across America, when the end title faded out, the audience spontaneously burst into tumultuous applause. It was love at first sound. The talkies had come to stay.

It had been unseasonably cold for a week, but Tuesday night, December 11, 1928, a pugnacious blue norther came snorting and growling down the Great Plains from the Arctic. Temperatures plummeted within minutes to below zero. The iron clouds hammered into Stephenville with frightening power. Clayborne and Marvin Miller sat in their wallpapered room at Mrs. Bobo's rooming house, Miller reading a textbook and Clayborne pounding away at his Underwood typewriter by the 40 watt electric bulb, when the first sleeting wind bawled into town, jolting the walls.

"Holy catfish, Clayborne," yelped Miller. "What was that?"

Clayborne jumped up from the little oak study desk to see what was making such a howling racket and opened the solid paneled door. It blew wide open. Clamoring ice crystals gnashed at the low-roofed front porch and sliced into the bedroom, splashing both boys in the face and scattering their papers. A full gale yammered in the liveoaks outside.

"Shut the confounded door!" bellowed Miller.

"I can't!" croaked Clayborne, struggling against the unexpected blast. "It's havin' a conniption out there!"

The neighborhood's electric lights want dark just as Clayborne drove the door into its jamb. The darkened room seemed to dance: on a utility pole by the house, still shining in the general blackout, a bare electric street lamp in its frilled sheet-metal reflector shook like a weird hobbyhorse, back and forth in the storm, casting prankish shadows over their beds. Clayborne took a match and candle from his desk drawer and gave them some light.

"Better get out your BVDs, Marvin," he said. "And your extra quilt. It's goin' to be a long cold night."

It was a long cold morning that followed. Tarleton's central steam heating plant was simply not up to the demands of prolonged ten-below zero weather. Rime frost decorated the *inside* of classroom windowpanes. Students dithered at their desks, muffled in outerwear, trying clumsily to write with gloved fingers. Morning R.O.T.C. drill classes went on half attended — the usual winter flu had spread alarmingly during the past week and many decided to stay off the drill field in this intense cold, taking no chances. In typing class Clayborne found that his dexterity had vanished: he owned no gloves and his complaining digits refused to answer the call of duty in the frigid classroom.

At two o'clock, afternoon classes were cancelled. The student body was called to chapel at three.

"Hey, look at those girls," yelled Teddy Nix as he walked with his

friends toward the gymnasium. "They've got their short skirts on, sittin'
up in the snow on the wall for those photographers."

"It ain't snow, it's sleet," said Austin Giesecke.

"They're just doing a stunt," said Clayborne. "That's Rye over there
with 'em. He put 'em up to it for the *J-TAC*, I'll bet you sure. We'll be
seeing their pictures in the paper before too long."

Marvin Miller cackled, "If they all don't die of the pneumonia first."

"Get on in the building, you guys," demanded Austin Giesecke.
"Don't just stand there lookin' at girls' legs. It's cold out here!"

"All right, all right," they answered, filing into the big barnlike
structure.

Once inside, Teddy Nix complained, "This gym is too crowded."

"But it's warmer that way from all the bodies smushed together,"
snickered Giesecke.

"You don't think Dean Davis is going to have us pray for warm
weather, do you?" scoffed Marvin Miller.

Clayborne answered, "Well, I don't know what he's going to say,
maybe he's going to let us out early for Christmas break."

"Nah," pooh-poohed Giesecke, "The slave drivers aren't gonna let the
slaves go free, W.C."

"W.C.? Hey, what's this 'W.C.' business, Clayborne?" asked Miller.

"Oh, that's from R.O.T.C.," he explained. "I write my name out as
'Clayborne' on all my R.O.T.C. papers and they just put me down as 'C.
Perry.'"

"They do that with everyone, Clayborne, it's the military way," said
Marvin. "They put me down as 'M. Miller.' They do it with everyone."

"Well, if they won't write out my whole name good and proper, I'm at
least going to have them put down my first initial, too. So I've been
writing 'W. C. Perry' on everything, and Austin just calls me that
because he's in B Company with me."

"But . . . I thought 'Clayborne' *was* your first name," said Miller,
astonished.

"Nope," laughed Clayborne, poking Miller in the arm. "You've
known me for all these years and you didn't know my first name is
'Willie?' Some friend you are!"

"'William?' Really?"

"No, not 'William,' 'Willie,' W-i-l-l-i-e."

"I didn't know, honest. I'm your friend, Clayborne . . . Or 'W. C.', or
whatever you want to be called. I just always heard everybody call you
'Clayborne.' I never gave it any thought it might be your middle name."

"Well, it's nothing to fret about," said Clayborne. "I don't care if
people *call* me 'Clayborne,' I just don't like that R.O.T.C. writing me
down as just plain ol' 'C. Perry.' If they're goin' to letterize me, they'll do
it with 'W. C.' and not just ol' 'C.'"

Dean Davis took the chapel stage, dressed in his black overcoat. The crowd grew silent as he spoke.

"Students, I don't need to tell you how bad the weather has been. And you know that the flu is more prevalent this year than last. I'm certain you have also realized that we cannot keep classroom temperatures at normal in the grip of such sub-zero temperatures. I and our faculty believe it is in the best interests of the entire Tarleton student body for us to advance the beginning of Christmas holidays rather than to try fighting this cold. Our holiday, as you all know, was scheduled to begin the nineteenth, Wednesday a week from today. However, I have informed your commanding officers and all authorities that suspension of duties shall take effect at once. Duties shall resume as scheduled on Wednesday, January second, 1929. We shall simply have to work harder after the holiday to make up for lost time. If anyone encounters difficulty finding a way home, come speak to me in my office. Take care in your homeward travels. I and our faculty wish you and your families a very merry Christmas and a happy New Year. Tarleton will see you again next year. Dismiss."

Clayborne and his friends packed a few belongings, trudged into downtown Stephenville and paid their dollar bus fare to Hico. After a telephone call, Tom brought the Model T into town and hauled his son back home.

The holidays on the farm were not much different from other years except for the hard and persistent cold. But that didn't stop the work. Clayborne cut a lot of wood, talked to his brother Hoyt, fed the cows and horses, played with his sisters, visited with his Grandpa and Grandma Perry and Old Grandma at Dude Flat, stopped by to say hello to his Uncle Leonard Perry and family up at the Elkins place where they now lived just north of Grandpa Perry's. He went out on the road bank in front of the family farm and cut back the cedars that were beginning to clog the fence, as he had promised. And he split some more rails to extend the fence a bit further. He went to church at Prairie Springs Baptist where he had served as Sunday School superintendent since High School. There was a quiet joy at being home for Christmas. He noticed that this year his family seemed to have a little more money for presents. Things, he felt, were slowly getting better.

A few days after Christmas, while the winter lethargy of a huge dinner still wore off, the telephone rang in the kitchen. Tom answered it.

"Hello? Oh, hello, Papa Blackburn. Want to talk to Belle? Not today, huh. Yeah, Clayborne's here. What? Over to Marlin? Is she okay? Good, good. I see. I'll ask him. Oh-Clayborne!"

"What is it, Papa?" the boy called from the front room.

"It's Papa Blackburn. He wants to know if you'll take him for a ride."

Clayborne laughed as he got up and went into the kitchen. "Take him for a ride? He didn't go see that gangster talkie, did he?"

"What, son?"

"Nothing, Papa," said the husky young man, leaning in the doorway. "What kind of ride does Grandpa Blackburn have in mind?"

"He wants you to drive him and Mama Blackburn over to Marlin tomorrow."

Clayborne's face blanched. "To the heart specialists?" he asked. The humor of the "take him for ride" wisecrack turned to foreboding. It left him with a very bad feeling.

"Oh, don't worry," said Tom. "Mama Blackburn hasn't had a heart attack or anything. Doc Curry just thinks she'd improve if she went to the Buie Hospital over in Marlin for a while. She's pretty sick, you know."

"Oh." He did not feel much relieved somehow.

"Well, are you gonna take him? I can't have your Grandpa hang on the phone all day."

"Oh. Oh, sure. I'll take him and Grandma. Tell him I'll do it. What time?"

"What time, Papa Blackburn? Oh, you heard him? Yes, sir. Yes, overnight. Okay, I'll tell him. He'll be there." He hung up the wall-mounted instrument and told his son, "About eight. I'll drop you off at their place and you can drive 'em in their car. It's about a hundred miles over to Marlin, past Waco. Do you know how to get there?"

"Well, I know most of the way to Waco. Marlin's . . . what, southeast of Waco? There's road signs. And I can stop at a filling station and ask if I have to. I'll get 'em there."

"And you'll stay overnight at a hotel in Marlin, come back the next day. They're right pleased you're going to take them, son. Ol' Charley's gettin' too old for that kind of drivin'."

"How old is Grandpa Blackburn, Papa?"

"Charley? He was born 1857 up in Boonville, Missouri. What's that make him? Let's see . . . Seven from eight's one, bring down your one, five from two won't go, borrow one, five from twelve's seven, bring down your seven: he's seventy-one."

"And Grandma?"

"Well I know that one, your mother just mentioned it the other day. She's sixty-five."

The next day, Clayborne drove his maternal grandmother and grandfather to Marlin, Texas. Grandpa Charley sat in the front with the young driver and Grandma Laura took to the back seat so she could lay down if she felt like it. Charley Blackburn kept up his usual line of gab the whole trip, and his ailing wife Laura joined in from time to time, cheerful but a little weak. The Blackburns' 1927 Model T touring car had curtains that could shut out the breeze enough to keep the passengers reasonably comfortable in the bitter late December cold. Clayborne found their vehicle easier to drive than the family Model T and enjoyed the trip. They stopped for a bite to eat at noon in Meridian and arrived at the three-story red brick Buie Hospital in Marlin before supper time.

"Take your time up these front steps, Mama," said Charley.

"Here, let me give you a hand, Grandma Blackburn," said Clayborne.

"Don't fuss with me so much, you two," the wizened old lady smiled. "It just takes me a little time is all. I can walk just fine."

"Maybe you could go let them know we're here, Clayborne," suggested Charley.

The young man bounded up the steps and into the hospital's reception room where he informed the attendant that Mrs. Laura Blackburn had arrived. A wheelchair was waiting for her when she shuffled through the door.

"You sit right in here, Mrs. Blackburn," said the admitting nurse. "We've got your room all ready up on the third floor. You gentlemen come with us up the elevator and we'll get everything taken care of."

Half an hour later Laura Blackburn was sitting up in her bed talking with her husband and grandson; the paperwork was all taken care of and the brief winter sun slipped early over the far Texas horizon.

"We've got to get on over to the hotel across the street, Mama," said Charley. "Got to make sure they're keeping our room for us."

"You comin' back in the mornin'?" Laura asked.

" 'Course we are, right after breakfast. Wouldn't just take off without seein' you first."

"Clayborne, I sure appreciate you takin' me over here. It's too long a drive for your Grandpa Charley any more."

"Aw, Grandma, you know I'd do anything for you."

"You're a good boy, Clayborne."

They left the third floor room and took the elevator to the reception area. A doctor stood talking to the admitting nurse.

"Doctor, I'm Charley Blackburn and this here's my grandson Clayborne Perry. We saw you a little while ago up with my wife on the third floor."

"Oh, yes. I'm Dr. Price. Sorry we didn't have time for formal introductions before."

"How is she, Dr. Price? We didn't want to ask Dr. McMurry in front of her."

"Well, I won't be working directly with her, you know. You'll have to get the details from Dr. McMurry. But I looked at her, and she seems to be resting well. Her fingers are a little blue from poor circulation, I'm sure you've noticed. And her heart condition is serious, no doubt Dr. Curry in Hico told you. There's nothing immediate to worry about, if that's what concerns you. You never really know how each individual heart patient is going to respond to treatment. We'll know more in a few days. But we have excellent facilities here and Dr. McMurry is one of the

best cardiologists in the state. Your wife is in good hands. You can be assured
that she's getting the best treatment medical science can provide."

"Oh, thank you, Dr. Price. Thank you," said Charley Blackburn
gratefully.

They stayed the night at a little two-story frame hotel across the street,
said their goodbyes to Laura Blackburn the next morning and returned to
their homes near Hico. Charley Blackburn seemed in good spirits when
Clayborne left him that afternoon to walk the mile home up the
farm-to-market road.

College resumed as scheduled on Wednesday January 2, 1929. The
year came in as a legacy of the blue norther, beginning with a series of
hard frozen days but no more sleet or persistent sub-zero cold. Tarleton's
central steam heating plant proved adequate to the task of keeping
classrooms livable and everyone dug in to make up the week they'd lost in
December. Everyone including Clayborne spent that first Wednesday
getting used to being in class once again. By the end of Thursday
everyone was back in the groove, slugging away at an education.

Friday morning early, about 7:30, a rat-a-tat knocking on the panelled
door of Mrs. Bobo's rooming house awoke both Clayborne and Marvin
Miller.

"Who could that be?" mumbled Miller under his quilts. "We don't
have class until nine today."

Rat-a-tat.

"Prob'ly Teddy Nix playin' a trick on us again," grumbled Clayborne.
"Prob'ly wants to get even with you for takin' the cream out of his milk
bottle and puttin' water back in. He's prob'ly stole your milk off the
porch and wants you to come chase him. You go answer the door."

Rat-a-tat.

"No, I went chasin' Teddy last time. You get it."

"Oh, all right." Clayborne stumbled out of bed with his hair pointing
in all directions and his nightshirt hanging over his long underwear. He
opened the door.

"Mr. Bellew," he said, surprised. "Come on in, sir. Sorry I took so
long. I thought it was a friend next door hoo-rawin' us."

"That's okay, Clayborne," the heavy-set man said. "Why don't you sit
on back down on your bed. I got some hard news to tell you."

Marvin Miller leaned up on one arm, listening intently. Clayborne sat
with a thump on his bed. "It's not my Papa, is it?" he asked. "He didn't
go blind, did he?"

"No," said Bob Bellew. "It's not your father or mother. It's somethin'
else. I got a call from Charley Blackburn in Hico about half an hour ago.
The doctors called him from the hospital in Marlin yesterday."

"Grandma Blackburn!" moaned Clayborne, dread clamping his throat.

"Yep, it's your Grandma Laura, boy," Bellew said. "Doctors say she passed away in her sleep yesterday early."

"Oh, Lord! But how can that be? They told us there wasn't anything to worry about. Grandpa Blackburn didn't seem worried."

"It was a shock to him, too, boy. Nobody knew. It's just one of those things. They did all they could for her. Her heart was just worse off than anybody could tell. Charley says the funeral's tomorrow. You better git on home now."

Clayborne thought a moment. "I've got to go tell Foncyne first. Foncyne Elam over in the girls' dorm, Mr. Bellew. It's her Grandma, too."

Services were held the next day, Saturday, at Prairie Springs Baptist Church, the little country church between Duffau and Little Duffau Creeks, the church Laura Susan Blackburn had belonged to since she and her husband were married in 1882. Even though she and Charley had talked about transferring their membership to Hico First Baptist Church after they moved away from Dude Flat in 1926, they never got around to it. The procession of cars trailed sadly away from the little rural church and up the long three miles to Duffau cemetery.

Clayborne drove his family in the mournful train of Model Ts.

"Who's going to take care of Grandpa Blackburn, Mama?" he asked.

"Oh, son," sobbed Belle, "His half-brother John's going to move up from San Antonio. Him and Grace and their little adopted boy Johnny are goin' to come live at his place."

"How's Uncle John going to make a living here?" asked Tom from the back seat.

"He told me he'd move his Dr. Fixall business, do what he can with it here," said Belle.

"Goin' to be pretty slim trying to run a repair business in a little bitty town like Hico," remarked Clayborne.

"Why, Hico's not so little bitty," sniffled Belle.

"That's what I used to think, Mama," said her son. "Stephenville's four times bigger. And you should see Waco now. I went through it twice takin poor Grandma to the hospital. It's a big city, must be twenty times bigger than Hico. And Uncle John moved away from Waco so's he could make more money in San Antone. I think it's goin' to be pretty slim."

"Mama," cried Nadine from the back seat. "Tell Clayborne not to talk about makin' a living and all. I don't want to listen. I want my Grandma and she's never comin' back!"

The family and friends buried their love in the terrible cold of a bleak January morning and said their prayers of hope and salvation. Belle's graveside agony transfixed them all, her mother gone, her link with the ages broken, her smothering grief disconsolate. They wept with her. Only one stood there unracked by sobs, only one actually believed the death, only one knew the horror fully and irrevocably: Charley Blackburn looked in pure shock on the sinking coffin, seeing his life, all those years, all that caring, sucked down into the clay soil. That day took the fire out of him. The fire never came back.

The next week at Tarleton, while Clayborne struggled with his grief and fifteen makeup pages of college algebra, a penny postcard came from home. His father wrote that Pet had died of old age and the cold and Hoyt had harnessed the mules to haul her up in the back fifty where the buzzards could clean her up.

He took a long walk around Stephenville away from the college. He hated to lose that old horse. He'd shared so much of his life with her. He had done so much of his work with her. He'd seen her almost every day of his life. Now she was gone like Grandma Blackburn.

At the edge of town he looked out over the desolate winter valley of the Bosque, the river folding and bending down into the Grand Prairie. The great prairie below was like his life, he thought. Time was churning through it like the river flowing, eroding, flooding, drowning, sweeping away all he loved, laying waste the garden of his soul. Was there a dark illimitable ocean where all the rivulets of time emptied? Was there a place where he would ever find all these lost moments again? What an enemy time was, he realized with a jolt. Invisible, untouchable, implacable. Time. It destroyed you piecemeal, strangled you, made you cry in terror. But you couldn't fight back, couldn't hurt it, couldn't take revenge upon it, couldn't even realize what it was.

But, oh, it could fight *you*, hurt *you*, take revenge upon *you*. Dear God, how it could hurt. He stared out alone over the Grand Prairie until the sun went down behind him. He was numb with cold. Then, with gentle surprise, the dusty face of the orbiting moon slid up above the far, far hills. It lighted the icy land with a soft light, and the land shimmered in beauty and hope, hope he was not yet ready for. It was time, relentless time that he watched shimmer up out of the Grand Prairie and despite his pain he knew that the shimmering time was his future rising with the stars.

The school year was over before he really felt better.

-12-

INTO THE WIDE WORLD

CLAYBORNE left his cotton patch in the pre-dawn overcast of September fifth, 1929, and hied himself to the Tarleton campus twenty miles away. There he embarked with ninety-one fellow cadets in a cattle truck that rumbled down newly paved U. S. Highway 377 from Stephenville through Dublin and Comanche, turned south on gravelled Texas Highway 16 through Priddy and Goldthwaite and across the Colorado River. Ninety-two miles out of Stephenville the clattering rattletrap hauled into San Saba, Texas. When the big Ford transport came to a final halt at the wooded San Saba Fair Park Fairgrounds, the cadets piled out into the clearing-off September day and, upon orders, fell into company formation, Companies A, B, C and Vidette.

M. J. Mulcahy, Captain, Infantry, D.O.L., U. S. Army, Tarleton's Head of Military Department, greeted his troops with professional dignity:

"Men, it is my duty and privilege to welcome you to Tarleton's Vidette encampment of 1929 here at San Saba. I will not take a great deal of your time this forenoon. I only wish to remind you that while it is hoped you will enjoy your stay here, this is a working encampment and not a holiday playground. We will maintain military discipline and military courtesy at all times. I expect the utmost of each and every one of you. This year you have an extra responsibility. The Vidette encampment is being held far away from the familiar encampment site of previous years at Stephenville. Your camp officers and I expect you to conduct yourselves in such a manner that you unfailingly bring credit to the Tarleton name among our civilian hosts here in San Saba. You are here to learn. You are here to improve. Keep that in mind and you will find this encampment a source of lifelong inspiration.

"Sergeant Buschman will be your drill instructor for the next ten days. You will receive five and one-half hours of drill and lecture each day in the school of the soldier and the school of the squad. Use your time wisely and bring credit to your company. I have appointed your camp officers as follows: Lieutenant-Colonel James Atlee, camp commander; Major Dorsett Risinger, camp adjutant; First Lieutenant J. W. Frazier, supply officer; Captain Stinson and Lieutenants Scott, Johnson, Tryer and Young, charge of company and platoons. Provisional officer Decker, camp sergeant-major. Give them your military best and we will make this the most successful encampment ever held."

The cadets were then herded across the flat limestone soil into a big barny sheet metal-roofed building that served as livestock judging center during San Saba County's annual fair. Clayborne looked around as he marched into the huge hall; it could have used a coat of paint but was not sufficiently rundown to be regarded as dilapidated. Up the risers and into the bleachers the companies climbed. At the top row, B Company Lieutenant Bert Gresham informed Clayborne's unit that they had arrived at their sleeping quarters. They were to ensconce themselves upon the wooden planks of the bleachers. Down went the duffel, the bedrolls and ditty bags. This would be home until September sixteenth.

"Well," whispered Private Carl Nance, "it's no worse than the barracks back at the Fort."

Brassy military notes sounded outside.

"Hey, there's the bugle," said Private John Cecil Parker. "What call is that?"

"Look at your watch, Parker," laughed Clayborne. "What do you think it is? It's chow call! Come on!"

The stampede had already started down the risers and out into the field. Clayborne and his bunkmates had no trouble finding the chow line: the flowing, surging mob eagerly stormed the outdoor cookery. The process of line formation bore little resemblance to military discipline.

"Hey," said Nance out of the side his mouth as they pushed into line. "Travel usually makes me hungry. But I'm not so sure now."

"What do you mean?" asked Parker.

"Look over there. I thought Sergeant Buschman was supposed to be our drill instructor. Ol' fatty's lording it over the mess tent!"

"Law, he's mess sergeant again!" whispered Parker.

"I hope his food's not as tough as his drill back at Tarleton," said Clayborne.

"Do you think he's going to poison us?" asked Nance.

"No," said Parker under his breath. "But after you taste his cooking you'll wish he had."

"I think I'm gonna upchuck," gasped Nance, dramatically gripping his throat.

"Pretend you like it," advised Clayborne. "If he's as hardnosed here as he is back at school, he'll throw an ax at you if you don't."

They pushed their metal mess kits down the long white picnic table beneath the branchy liveoaks. It lay in the dappled shadows, groaning with heaped biscuits and deep potato salad and massive beans and franks and big white porcelain pitchers of milk. At the end of the serving board, with regulation dinner plates and cups brimming, the three cadets maneuvered to the ranked eating tables where fully half the encampment already sat stuffing their faces.

"Here's the rest of B Company," said Parker, pointing to a long table with his overloaded tin dinner plate, "let's sit here."

They stood to and fed like the rest.

"Haven't seen you all summer, W. C.," said Nance sitting cheerily across the table. "How'd you do with that typing class we were in together last spring?"

"Aha!" said Clayborne between bites of biscuit, "I'm glad you asked me that: I got an A plus!"

"You like your biscuits with baloney, don't you?" mocked Parker on the hard bench, poking his seatmate's ribs. "You didn't make no A plus."

"I sure did," defended Clayborne, guarding with his elbows.

"Well, then, what about algebra?" demanded Nance. "That's a little harder than typing."

"Got a B, I did," smiled Clayborne. "Got a B in R.O.T.C. and animal husbandry, too."

"Yeah? Well what about English? I didn't hear nothin' about English in there," chaffed Nance.

"Got a C," muttered Clayborne through his beans and franks.

"What's that?" taunted Nance. "Can't hear you, W.C. What did you get in English?"

"You heard me perfectly well," hissed Clayborne, looking up and down the table as the rest of B Company eavesdropped intently. "Got a C."

"I think you better back off, Carl," advised John Parker. "I was W. C.'s chapel neighbor all last year. He's a pretty easy-going old boy, but if you keep it up, your grade's gonna be a black 'I' and you won't be able to 'C' anything, get it?"

"Well, let's put Carl on the spot a little, W. C. Nance, what did *you* get in English?" quizzed Parker.

Nance grinned impishly and admitted, "Got me a C in English just like my friend W. C. here."

"Nance, you're not a half bad guy, unless you work at it, you know that?" said Clayborne.

"I try my best," smirked Carl. "Come on, we're all done, let's go back up to those great beds and get some rest before afternoon drill. And tell me more about that Strong Arm Club you started talkin' about. . .when was it? . . last March."

The three left the table together. "Yeah, it was last March," said Clayborne. "We were talkin' about it after one of the Lyceum numbers. You really want to hear more?"

They dumped their scraps into the large central garbage cans, scraping their mess kits. "No joke, we do," said John Parker.

"You're not kiddin' me?"

They sauntered back toward the fair building.

"Honest," begged Carl Nance.

"Okay," said Clayborne. "You know Marvin Miller, my roommate?"

"He's that blue-eyed German-looking fellow that was in A Company last year, right?"

"That's him. Well, his older brother, name of Herbert Miller, is a teacher. He's strong on education, you know, like a missionary preacher almost. He wants everybody in college. And while I was in high school back in Hico he got hold of us ol' country boys — wasn't but eight or ten of us there — and tried to make sure we got interested in education."

"What did he do?" asked Parker, grabbing a grass stalk and sticking it in his mouth. "Give you classes after hours?"

"No, nothin' like that. He made it fun, you know, held our meetings out in the woods on Friday nights 'til all hours. Called us the Strong Arm Club, just to make us feel like somebody. We weren't really too interested, but he just made us want to keep comin' back."

"What did you do?"

"We'd roast corn and hold mock trials, stuff like that. Mr. Miller taught us a little law and how a court works. So if somebody came in late, we'd put him on trial. Mr. Miller would appoint a prosecutor and a defense lawyer. He'd be the judge and the rest of us would be the jury. It was really just a lot of fun and we learned a lot. If it hadn't been for him, me and Marvin and ol' Teddy Nix and Austin Giesecke prob'ly wouldn't be in Tarleton now."

"How so?" asked Carl Nance as they passed beneath the tall stock doors into the judging ring floor.

"Well, we'd never know anything but the farm, not like you city kids."

"Stephenville isn't hardly any city, W. C.," Carl protested.

"Neither is Goldthwaite," said Parker, sucking the grass stem.

"They ain't a farm, either, and you guys lived in town. But, anyways, we all knew how rough it was bein' a farmer. But we never thought much over what we could do about it. And then along came ol' Herbert Miller with his literature and science and law and such. We didn't know what good it was, because we'd never thought about bein' lawyers or anything. But Mr. Miller kept sayin' if you got an education you'd be prepared to really make a contribution to your fellow man and you'd be rewarded accordingly. He says in this country, the sky's the limit. He says success comes in direct proportion to your contribution. It's a principle taught in the Holy Scripture."

"Did he really say that?" asked Parker.

"He really did. He told us to get all the facts and all the wisdom possible. That's the basis of success. I can just hear him tellin' us that. And he said college may not be the only way to get an education, but he couldn't think of anyplace better. We took him at his word. So we all came to Tarleton."

Parker chewed on that idea like he chewed on his shank of grass as they climbed the risers to their piled belongings. "I been going to Tarleton since tenth grade," he said. "You make it sound like heaven, or something. It's just school."

"If it's *just* school, how come you're goin' to it? You know you'll get a lot farther with it than without it, don't you?" said Clayborne, sitting down by his bedroll and stretching out on the hard floor.

"I get the point."

"Anyways, we kept up our Strong Arm meetings some last year during college. We'd go home weekends when there wasn't any ball games or Lyceum numbers and we'd go out to meet Mr. Miller in the sticks up toward Millerville where his grandfolks settled, and he'd start it up again, asking questions, makin' us think, makin' sure we were gonna stick with it. He'd tell us you gotta persist if you're goin' to prevail. He's just about the most unusual guy you can imagine."

"What are you gonna do when you get out of college, W. C.?" asked John Parker, leaning on his duffel bag.

"I don't honestly know. What with all the education and history I'm going to be takin' this next year, I'll have a major in social science when I'm done," said Clayborne. "But, you know, finding a job in social science is one thing they don't seem to be teaching me at college."

"W. C.," said Parker, looking at the ceiling and sucking his well-mangled grass stalk. "What?" said Clayborne.

"Some of Mr. Miller musta rubbed off on you. You're unusual yourself. 'Specially for a farm boy."

The days at Vidette camp spun by like a kaleidoscope, full of military pomp and dogface drill, baseball contests, best drill soldier contests, best Company contests, officer athletic contests and band programs. The list of calls effective at San Saba tells the invariable course of each day:

First call: 5:15 a.m.
Reveille: 5:25 a.m.

Assemble and physical drill (calisthenics): 5:30 a.m.

Breakfast: 6:00 a.m.

Assemble and military drill: 7:00 a.m.

Recall from drill: 10:30 a.m.

Sick call: 11:00 a.m.

Mess call: 12:00 noon

Assemble and military drill: 2:00 p.m.

Recall from drill: 4:30 p.m.

Retreat: 5:50 p.m. (usually attended by local civilian dignitaries)

Mess call: 6:00 p.m.

Tattoo: 9:00 p.m.

Call to quarters: 10:45 p.m.

Taps: 11:00 p.m.

But cadet ingenuity happily combined with San Saba's civic pride to vary the program. There was something new almost every day to weave color and sparkle into the procrustean warp and woof of these routine military calls. The Chamber of Commerce threw two or three little barbecue parties. Various businessmen provided watermelon feasts and ice cream socials. The cadets mostly took care of themselves, however. As the *J-TAC* was to later report in its collegiate prose:

The boys found plenty of amusement while in San Saba. The day's spare time was taken up with playing ball. The band and B Company seemed to hold a special grudge. The boys of B Company, led by "Red" Hester won the series of ball games. The officers played one game, but the least said of that game the better. The evenings were taken up by showing the San Saba girls a good time. The boys were a success at this pastime.

Showing the San Saba girls a good time was not nearly as easy as the *J-TAC* reporter indicated: the local *femmes* were outnumbered three to one by Tarleton's ardent cadets. At an evening social sponsored by the town ladies — a chicken and pie affair — Captain Mulcahy recognized the problem and promptly lined up his ninety-two cadets, ordering every third man to take one step to the rear. The two thirds remaining in the front rank were ordered to resume their seats. The lucky one third in the back rank got the girls, a tidy military solution to a thorny population problem. Clayborne was just as happy to be among the losers: his strict Baptist upbringing meant that he didn't know how to dance and he retained a certain diffidence when it came to girls: he wouldn't really know how to act with a strange girl anyway.

He watched from the sidelines for a while but then wandered back to the camp's stockyard barracks building alone, realizing that his turn at sentry duty came up tonight — the 2:00 a.m. to 4:00 a.m. watch. As he strolled past the men's room preparing to climb the risers, he chanced upon Rye, his friend on the *J-TAC* staff, sitting at the bottom of the bleachers shining his boots.

Clayborne saluted and, mustering up his best military courtesy, said, "Sir! Good evening, Major Risinger, Sir!"

"Aw W.C.," said Risinger. "There's nobody here but you and me. It's Rye, remember?"

"Well I didn't want to take any chances you know," said Clayborne. "Some of you officers are . . ."

"'Martinets' is the word you're looking for, take it from a *J-TAC* staffer!" smiled Risinger. "I know. Like ol' 'Flashlight' Frazier."

"Yeah, goes around making lists all the time, finding things so he can put you on report," said Clayborne.

"That's why they call him 'Flashlight,' did you know? 'Cause he goes around in the daylight with a flashlight looking for demerits."

They chuckled.

"And he sucks up to the higher ranking officers something terrible," added Risinger. "I can't take that guy. Too bad he wasn't a crooked breast."

Cadets commonly applied the derisive term "crooked breast" to the four or five young men who came to Tarleton each year who were physically unable to serve their R.O.T.C. requirement. The phrase had been borrowed from poultrymen: a small percentage of commercial turkeys grew all the breast meat on one side of the keel bone and almost none on the other. Such birds were called "crooked breasts" and sold on the market at a heavy discount. The phrase simply passed into Texas college slang as an appellation for disabled people. Sensitivity to the handicapped had no place in this blunt and harshly demanding world: if you couldn't do a required task, you couldn't. There was nothing more to it.

"What are you doing shining your boots here all alone?" inquired Clayborne.

"Oh," sighed Risinger, "I'm stuck as officer of the day today. Tryer took sick this morning, so I'm pulling his duty for him. I have to call out the men on sentry duty tonight."

"A Major pulling officer of the day?"

"It's a lesson to some of the new Lieutenants. You know how officers are taught this rule 'Rank has its responsibilties, rank has its privileges'?"

"I've heard of it."

"Well, some of these new officers just look for the privileges and forget about the responsiblities. I could have assigned Young to stand for Tryer, but that would have made him officer of the day twice in a row. Or I could have thrown everybody else off schedule. I'm responsible for the selection, so I'm assigning myself to sentry duty. That way the junior officers will see that rank really does have its responsibilities. It'll help keep them from getting uppity. I told Captain Mulcahy about it."

"What'd he say?"

"Said, 'Firmness in discipline is a duty; firmness in self-discipline is a virtue.' He always has a saying like that. I wonder where he gets them?"

"Did you get any chicken and pie tonight?"

"Oh, sure. And potato salad. I was out there at mess like everybody else. At the officer's table. I just came back here when they started that girl stuff."

"Why, Rye," said Clayborne. "I always thought you were a big man with the girls. You're real popular. And you're on the *J-TAC* staff and the football team . . ."

"Yah," said Risinger, "that doesn't mean a thing. I'm all left feet around girls. I mean on dates. I do fine around girls like Estelle and La Vere on the *J-TAC* staff. When we're working. But not on the mushy stuff. Don't be surprised, our football captain is the same way."

"Ol' Earl Rudder? The football hero is shy of girls?"

"Not with a bunch of 'em around, just alone on dates."

"I wouldn't have thought it. He's so confident . . ."

"Oh, he's goin' to be a great military officer some day. And maybe he likes to be thought of as a ladies man. But he's no different than me on dates. I guess we just haven't found the right girl yet, that's all. Who needs dates anyways? Got too much to do. Hey, did you hear that I got promoted from Assistant to full Business Manager for next year?"

"On the *J-TAC*? No! Congratulations, Rye."

"Thanks. Hey, aren't you on sentry duty tonight?"

"Yep. Two o'clock shift. I was just on my way up to take a nap when I saw you here."

"You didn't want to stay out there for the dancin'? You're not so great with the girls, either, huh?"

"Nope, same as you. Haven't found the right one yet, either. Couldn't afford her even if I found her, though."

They laughed.

"You're a good friend, Clayborne. Thanks for stickin' around and talking to me." He looked Clayborne in the eye. "I'll call you at 1:45, Private Perry."

Clayborne smiled. "Good night, Major Risinger!"

Sentry duty was not particularly difficult: two men, starting from opposite sentry posts about three hundred yards apart, marched toward each other, passed in the middle and went to the sentry post of their watch companion. There each made an about-face and marched back. They repeated this simple formula for two hours. A trusty Springfield 30-30 rifle accompanied each on the right shoulder. They had to know the basic peremptory challenge, "Halt, who goes there?" At San Saba it was not required that unidentified intruders be shot. As sentry duty was not difficult, so it was not fascinating.

Clayborne warded off the silent enemy, boredom, for an hour and forty-five minutes. He hoped to end a quiet watch within fifteen minutes. Suddenly the incipient sunrise in the east grew dimmer as a gigantic Grand Prairie thunderhead came skating across the southwestern sky, piled sixty thousand feet high, a cloudy chalice emptying tons of fluid each minute onto the harried Texas soil beneath. Its center passed precisely over the San Saba Fair Park Fairgrounds. Clayborne put on his slicker after being thoroughly drenched and spent the last fifteen minutes of his duty noting that it was actually hard to breathe in the thick pounding cloudburst. After his relief came at four, Clayborne spent an hour cleaning his trusty Springfield instead of sleeping.

For ten days there were inspections for haircut, clean shave, shoes shined, brass polished, uniform clean and press, and weapon care. There were dress parades and retreat ceremonies. The cadets went on night bivouacs out in the woods when it didn't rain and on daytime drill in the stock-judging ring when it did, even though their marching stirred up the frozen music of ancient cow manure. They learned how to stand three rifles bayonet-to-bayonet in a pyramid. A few were privileged to pull the wheeled howitzer around for sham battles. All ran up revetments and down creek banks. They heaved and ho-ed and sweated and strained in combat practice. They listened to lectures on tactics and strategy. They left-right-left-right drilled. Forward, march! They drilled individually. To the rear, march! They drilled in squads. Left flank, march! They drilled in platoons. Countermarch, march! They drilled in companies. Eyes right! They drilled some more. To perdition, march! They ran close order drill for fancy show and extended order drill for combat simulation. Company, halt! They posed among the big oak trees for a *Grassburr* photographer, sharing the limelight with a big German shepherd dog in front of their long lines. They played baseball and stood in chow lines and made small talk with generous hosts from San Saba and a few of them took the town daughters to the picture show or for long walks by the river.

Then it was all over and time to go back to Stephenville for the new school year. The ninety-two cadets — no combat losses — retrieved their duffel bags and bedrolls and ditty bags and piled back into the cattle truck. They peeked between the wooden slats and for the last time gazed at the site of their ordeal. For some reason every one of them hated to leave.

"Hey, look at this," howled Austin Giesecke from his study desk.

"What you got?" asked Marvin Miller, stretched out on his bed in the next room.

"This thing in the *J-TAC*," replied Giesecke. "You and W. C. come in here and let me read it to you."

"You come into our room," yelled Clayborne through the double doors of their downtown apartment.

"No, I'm all set up with my books and everything," complained Giesecke.

"Well, I'm all set up at my own desk," hollered Clayborne around the corner. "We can hear you. Just read it real loud."

"Oh, all right. It's an editorial called 'Forward' and it sounds like pretty-boy Bert Gresham wrote it."

"Bert's my friend," shouted Clayborne through the wall. "He's goin' places in the world. I go up to see him and Rye in the *J-TAC* office every now and then. They don't act so stuck up like officers when they're working on the paper. And besides, just because Bert's all literary doesn't mean he's a sister-girl or anything. He was president of the junior class last year and he's Executive Officer of your own B Company, Austin, and he made the track team, don't forget! What did he write?"

"Listen here to this fancy-pants," Giesecke quoted: "'The tendency of civilization is to move forward. We, living today, surrounded by all luxuries and conveniences, little realize the hardships and trials our forefathers underwent when this country was a wilderness. What would we do without the telephone, the telegraph, the automobile, the radio, or any of a hundred other things that our grandparents never knew? Their mission was to do their bit toward advancing civilization in our nation and their work was nobly done. They fought and suffered that their children and grandchildren might enjoy the harvest of their labors. We take things for granted that they never knew existed.' That's the end of it. Now ain't that somethin'? My folks still live in that wilderness. At home we don't even have electricity! And he says we take things for granted! He is out in left field!"

"It does sound like something Bert would say," admitted Clayborne. "But I think he was writing about city kids."

"You're just sticking up for him because he's a social science major like you," asserted Marvin Miller. "He's a city kid himself, isn't he?"

"No," said Clayborne. "He's from Evant, down in Coryell County. It's not even as big as Hico. But just think about what he said. We take things for granted. Don't you think he's right? Don't you think we should show more appreciation for what we've got?"

"Heck, no!" said Giesecke. "I study all that stuff he's talking about, telephones, radio. That's my major, that's what electrical engineers do. I know how important it is."

"I don't mean us country kids," maintained Clayborne. "We don't have enough to take for granted. I mean all these city kids at Tarleton. Like Jim Atlee."

"The band's drum major?" asked Miller.

Jim and Lou Perry, W.C. Perry's paternal grandparents, 1932

Charlie and Laura Blackburn, W.C. Perry's maternal grandparents, 1907

Tom and Belle Perry, parents of W. C. Perry, 1909.

*W. C. Perry standing with his dog Pup. A cousin,
Otis Perry, rides in the wagon, 1914.*

*The Hico High School graduation class of 1928.
W. C. Perry is standing back row, far right.*

W. C. Perry, cadet at John Tarleton College, 1929.

*W. C. and Oretta Perry on the day of their wedding,
August 22, 1931.*

Five generations of Perrys, 1933. Standing (left to right) *Tom B. Perry, 49; W. C. Perry, 22. Seated* (left to right) *Jim W. Perry, 71; Bobby Perry, 4 months; Elizabeth Glasgow Perry, 94.*

W. C. and Oretta Perry with their son Bobby,

Oretta Perry and daughter Margie,
1945, Meridian, Texas.

W. C. Perry and wife Oretta while at Walnut Springs, 1941.

"That was last year," said Clayborne. "He had to quit when they made him Lieutenant-Colonel of the R.O.T.C. this year. But he's a Houston boy. I think his folks are pretty well off. And he just seems to take everything in stride. Nothin' surprises him. You never hear him sayin' how grand anything is. Isn't that takin' things for granted?"

"Well, maybe so," grumbled Giesecke on the other side of the wall.

"Sure," said Marvin Miller. "I know a lot of guys like that. And some of these Tarleton girls seem to think they're God's gift to mankind. All this modern age is nothing new to them. They've always lived in houses with electric lights, had Frigidaires at home, listened to the radio since they were little bitty kids, go see talkies all the time."

Giesecke laughed, "Have toilet paper in the bathroom instead of corn cobs in the one-holer."

"You got to admit that's easy gettin' used to," smiled Clayborne.

Teddy Nix unlocked the apartment door and walked in. "Hey," he said to nobody in particular, "the lights are all on in the court house across the street. What's the occasion?"

"I think it's that bootlegger trial still goin' on," said Miller as his friend walked by. "It was goin' on earlier today. Where you been so late?"

"Out at the college farm. Workin' on my semester project. Then I stopped off at Miz Fant's to get some supper."

"Was she still serving this late?" asked Clayborne. "It's almost nine."

"No," said Nix as he passed through the empty double doorway and into the room he shared with Austin Giesecke. "I had to make me a ham sandwich in the kitchen. Hello, Austin!"

"Hi, Teddy. You missed a good beef stew by taking Miz Fant's Dining Hall for granted," said Giesecke.

"What?"

"Oh, nothin'," smirked Austin.

"He's just bein' smart-alecky," explained Miller. "We been talkin' about that editorial in the *J-TAC*, Teddy, the one about takin' things for granted."

Teddy plunked himself down on his bed with a thud, dropping his books by his side. "I saw it," he said. "Sounds like W. C.'s buddy Gresham wrote it."

"That's what we thought," said Miller.

"Hey, W. C.," hollered Nix as he took off his shoes, "how much do you pay Miz Fant for food every month?"

"Twelve and a half. Why do you ask?"

"Boyce Irwin told me about it while I was fixing my sandwich. How come the rest of us pay fifteen bucks?"

"That's because I got about ten Tarleton fellows to board with her. Boyce was one of 'em. So I get my meals cheaper. You could do the same thing."

"Not after you smoked out all the takers," nattered Teddy.

"Initiative, Teddy," chuckled Clayborne. "Gotta get out and hustle."

"You're too fast for us, W. C.," said Nix.

Marvin Miller asked, "Was everybody gone out in the hall, Teddy?"

During their second year at Tarleton the Hico boys shared the second floor above Perry's Variety Store — no relation to Clayborne — with two insurance agents, an eye doctor and a chiropractor. The business offices occupied the front of the building facing Stephenville's Court House Square and the student apartment the rear. The apartment was actually two converted office rooms with the French doors between taken off their hinges. It was not a bad deal at five dollars a month per student, but it did mean they had several responsibilities, one of which was keeping the hall light off when not needed.

"Everybody's gone home," said Nix. "I turned the light out."

The boys had left Mrs. Bobo's rooms across from the campus because her own landlord did not like her subletting the place and she found herself forced out of the renting business. Besides, the boys wanted a little bigger and nicer place, but now they had to walk nearly a mile to class.

"W. C.," called Giesecke around the corner. "Are you taking any engineering classes this year?"

"Yeah, one."

"Is it an electrical engineering class? Can you do circuit diagrams?"

"No, I'm taking mechanical engineering. What do you mean by circuit diagrams?"

"Oh, they show voltages at different places in an electrical circuit. I've got a dickens of a problem here. It's called a Wheatstone bridge and the current divides up in four or five different directions. I can't figure out how to find the voltages at all these points in the diagram."

"Don't ask me," said Clayborne.

"Me neither," said Teddy Nix to his roommate. "I'm an ol' agricultural education major and all we take is mechanical engineering like W. C. I can't do that electrical stuff nohow."

"How about you, Marvin?" yelled Giesecke.

"Don't be silly. I'm an ag ed major like Teddy, but I'm only a junior this year. I don't even have any engineering classes yet."

"Then how am I gonna do this problem?"

"How are we gonna do any studying with you botherin' us all the time?" pleaded Miller.

Nix remarked, "What do you mean 'studying,' Marvin? You're always the one that says if I come in and find you studying, to wake you up."

"Hey, Teddy," called Clayborne, "what do you do with a diploma in ag ed? Are you gonna be a school teacher when you finish college?"

"I don't know," Nix called back. "That's what I want to do, but it's hard finding a job. Somebody told me the schools are supposed to start hiring agricultural people, but there's nothing yet. Might be something out by Clairette, but the school board's not making any promises. How about you?"

"I don't know," fretted Clayborne. "I'm gettin' a little worried about it, too. This economics class I'm taking makes me think workin' in a bank might be something to think about. Or maybe I could clerk in a store. But it's all so . . . so mixed up. I keep thinkin' about those questions we used to ask at Strong Arm Club, you know, what good is a college education? I still wonder sometimes. What about you, Austin?"

"I'm going to be an engineer," he snorted. "What do you think I'm majorin' in engineering for?"

"Well where do engineering majors work?"

"The day I get my diploma I'm goin' to march right over to the State Highway Department in Waco and put in my application. I'll bet you I get a job engineering before that first summer's out. But, you know, I've never asked you, Clayborne, where do social science majors work?"

"I wish I knew."

"You can always work at your Uncle Linchie's social science shoe shop down the street," said Marvin.

"Very funny," said Clayborne. "My Uncle Wiley only lets me do little odds and ends, a little sewing and tacking. From what he pays me I don't think he's anxious to have a partner. I think he's got all he can do makin' a living with just himself on the payroll. He's doin' better since he moved from Hico up here last year, but shoe shops don't make a whole lot of money. At least he fixes my shoes for free."

"You guys can shut up, now," said Teddy Nix as he carefully examined his alarm clock. "I'm going to sleep and let you guys burn the midnight oil."

"What are you lookin' at your clock so close for?" asked Austin Giesecke.

"You know why I'm lookin' at it," Nix huffed. "It's to make sure you guys didn't set my alarm up again like you did last week. Gettin' me up at three-thirty in the morning!"

Derisive laughter came from all quarters.

"We just wanted to get even with you for wakin' us up at five-thirty every morning," gurgled Miller.

"You know I got all the way over to Miz Fant's Dining Hall before I realized what time it was, don't you?"

"Oh, we know," cackled Clayborne. "Do you think we could sleep through all the knocking around you did gettin' up? And we couldn't likely sleep when you came back all flustered and mad and hollerin' at us."

Austin Giesecke said, "It was us got the worst of our own trick that time."

"Well, you deserve it, getting me up that way." sputtered Nix, snuggling into his quilt. "Good night!"

"Good night, Teddy," they all mocked sweetly.

Clayborne and Marvin Miller exchanged guilty glances. Austin said to Teddy, "I'm goin' to study with the other guys in their room so I don't keep you up," and tiptoed out, winking and grinning at his two co-conspirators. Miller looked knowingly at Clayborne and Austin, put a finger to his lips for silence and leaned over out of his bed. He snaked a long wire out from under the cheap carpet on the floor next to him. It led directly to Teddy Nix's bed.

They had known exactly when Nix would return and used their time wickedly. The rail and slat beds the boys had brought with them were no marvels of construction: the maple slats holding up the mattress had been cut barely long enough to reach from one side rail to the other. By lining up the slats as far to one side of the supporting bed rail as possible, Clayborne and Austin and Marvin left only a precarious quarter-of-an-inch overlapping the opposite rail. When they looped the evil wire around each slat and trailed it out into the other room, only a strong tug stood between Nix's mattress and disaster. Now they joined hands on the fateful cord. Together, yank!

The slats came sliding off their rail! Down crashed the mattress and its owner! Nix lay dazed on the floor for a moment before he realized what had happened. Then he sat up disheveled on the wreckage of his bed, glaring icily over the bare rails at his tormentors.

With typical aplomb he declaimed: "Behold! The damn bed fell!"

He refused to be ruffled by the gaggle of giggles and slept the rest of the night at floor level on his broken bed.

"'Tis bitter cold, And I am sick at heart.' Where did those lines come from? Who is't that can inform me?" asked Herbert Miller by the bonfire's fitful flame.

"Oh, we know that one, Mr. Miller," said Austin Giesecke, munching his roasted corn. "That's *Hamlet*. We did it back in high school English."

Clayborne asked, "But how's that an appropriate quotation like you said, Mr. Miller? We all know it's bitter cold, it's the end of December. I almost didn't come because with the campfire we're always fried on one side and frozen on the other. But why should you be sick at heart?"

Herbert Miller looked into the hopeful faces of the young men around him, his brother Marvin, Austin Giesecke, Teddy Nix, Clayborne Perry and J. D. Patterson, a Tarleton classmate who had within the past year entered the sanctum of this group.

"Yeah, why?" asked Nix.

"I think you can guess," said Herbert Miller. "You Strong Arms are nearly halfway through your final year together at Tarleton. The club has accomplished its purpose, I think you will all agree. Men, what I have to tell you tonight is not easy to say: Although I shall miss our gatherings, although it makes me sick at heart, this will be our last meeting. I love you guys like I would if you were my own flesh and blood, but it's time for the umbilical cord to be cut and that's that."

"You mean you're *never* going to call another one, Herb?" asked Marvin.

"That's right, little brother."

"Well, what if we call one on our own?" asked Teddy Nix. "Would you come?"

"No."

"Then this really is our last get-together?" asked Clayborne.

"As the Strong Arm Club. What you do on your own is up to you."

"But look how it's helped us, Mr. Miller," began Austin Giesecke.

"Past tense, Austin. *Has* helped. You're ready."

"Ready? Ready for what?" asked J. D. Patterson, not feeling completely at ease since he had not always been a regular Strong Arm member like the others.

"You're ready to be your own self-regulators. There's only one more semester left at Tarleton for you fellows. Except for Marvin, that is, and I'll see to him. The rest of you, your time has come. You're on your own."

Glum silence. They stared into the guttering fire for a long time. They knew he was right.

"Weaned," said Teddy. "I feel like a weaner pig. I know I can fend for myself, but I sure want back at the sow. I never realized how much I depended on the ol' Strong Arm Club."

"Yeah," agreed Austin. "We could talk about *anything* here, just shoot the breeze. Like when the air show came to Stephenville and we tried to imagine what it's like bein' a barnstormer. It's the kind of stuff we never talk out anywhere else."

"You'll learn to make time for those things among yourselves. I sense there's greatness being born. I can add nothing further," said Herbert Miller.

"Well, who'll we talk to when we get feeling low? Like when the Plowboys keep losin' football games?" said Clayborne.

"Cheer each other up," said Herbert Miller.

"We coulda sure used it this year," muttered Marvin Miller, "especially losing the Turkey Day game to Randolph."

"And what'll we do when there's just fun things on our mind?" asked Teddy Nix. "Like when we sang carols around the dean's Christmas tree last year. Remember how us Strong Arms talked a long time around the fire about where Christmas carols came from? You know all that stuff and we don't."

"You know where they keep the encyclopedias in the library," said Herbert Miller dispassionately. "You've learned where to find almost anything. Use what you already know to learn more. And don't forget the fundamental basis for a successful life is found in the Biblical teachings you've grown up with. If you forget those teachings are the foundation, then your educational advantage could be used for evil instead of good."

"Well," said Clayborne, "we'll never forget what you've taught us and what you've done for us, Mr. Miller. You're a great inspiration — and a great friend."

"We really respect you, Mr. Miller," said Austin, a little embarrassed at sounding gushy.

"We'll remember it all. Especially the times we went huntin' for possums at night," said Teddy, trying to lighten things up.

"And when you read us that hotsy-totsy story in the *Canterbury Tales*," said Marvin.

"And when we did Shakespeare's *Julius Caesar*," said Clayborne. "Beware the Ides of March!"

"I'll remember the Ides of December," deadpanned Austin. "I sure shivered enough out here with you crazy guys."

They gradually accepted the fate of the Strong Arm meetings and fell to reminiscing without plan, floating and swimming through the past three years of fraternity and friendship like children in a warm and timeless pool that protected them against the December frost. They paddled and kicked lazily in the evanescent stream of shared consciousness, each bubble they disturbed a diaphanous recollection of delight or sorrow or nothing in particular. It was unsentimental, straightforward and without pain, a simple summing up, the gathering in of a rich trove, snagging and unfolding long polymers of hinged mental images, sorting, inspecting, holding each memory-sheet still for a moment to catch the seeing mind's light, polishing each engraved event like a coin. In the end, their backward looking only made them more aware of where they stood, only brought them forcibly up to present time.

"But you know, Mr. Miller," said Clayborne finally, "we never talked any about the stock market crash. All this about Wall Street worries me. Maybe we could use some Strong Arm advice."

"Ah, yes, Black Wednesday, October twenty-third. Just over two months now. Did you own any stocks that became worthless?"

Clayborne laughed. "The only stock I got is twelve cows, and they're my Papa's. I just milk 'em and feed 'em. But my economics instructor said the crash was more than just stocks and bonds going bad. Professor Ferguson says it's going to affect the whole country for years, it's worse than anybody realizes yet, that a lot of businesses are going to fail. I was thinking about working in a bank, maybe. If businesses fail, banks will fail."

"Do you think he's right?" asked Miller.

"Well, he's an economics professor. I'm sure he knows these things. And cotton prices did go down from eighteen cents last year to sixteen cents this year."

"Prices have been worse," said Austin.

"Wait a minute," said Teddy. "How could stocks and bonds make businesses fail?"

"That's how businesses raise money to run on, by selling stock," interjected Clayborne. "Professor Ferguson explained all that."

"I'm not taking economics. I'm taking ag ed," said Nix.

"Well, it's not too hard to understand. Professor Ferguson says speculators bid stock prices up hoping to buy low and sell high, and they bid prices up beyond what the company's really worth. Then these speculators buy on margin, only pay ten percent to the stock broker and owe him the rest. Like buying on credit. That's what a lot of speculators did the last few years, and then when everybody finally realized they were paying too much for stocks, the bottom fell out of the price and the margin speculators suddenly owed ten times more money than they had. That's why a lot of them blew their brains out."

"Doesn't sound like they had any brains in the first place," remarked Teddy.

Clayborne smiled ironically and said, "Yeah, but there's also a lot of investors who paid in full but bought at the highest prices. They're left holding the bag. After the crash, every dollar they put into a business stock was only worth a dime. Ninety cents on every dollar just vanished. When you add up all the investors in the country, that's a lot of dollars to just vanish from the economy. And think what that means. You can't run businesses if the economy's out of money. So Professor Ferguson may be right."

Marvin Miller argued, "That's crazy, Clayborne. Money is just a way of measuring what something's worth, like a yardstick. Professor Ferguson's idea is like saying you can't build any more houses because you've run out of inches."

"No it ain't," complained Austin. "There's inches everywhere, but money is hard to find."

"You know what Marvin means," grumbled Teddy.

"But what if it's true?" suggested Clayborne. "Here we are getting out of college in a few months, and maybe there won't be any businesses left to get a job at. I've asked around at several banks and some dry goods stores. Nobody's offered me a job yet."

"So that's why you're worried, Clayborne," said Herbert Miller.

"I ain't worried," said Austin. "The Highway Department won't go out of business no matter what."

"And the schools are finally starting to hire a few ag teachers," said

Teddy. "Schools aren't likely to shut down and we'll always need farmers."

"All right, Clayborne," said Herbert Miller, "Nobody has offered you a job yet. It's natural to worry. But I have a feeling about you. I have a feeling that you're going to surpass all of us in due time. I don't know where your future lies, don't get me wrong. But I just have this special feeling about it. You work hard, you get the job done, you have ambition to do better, you're steady as a rock, you've already taken yourself farther than most farm boys, and I think somebody out there will sense all those things in you."

Clayborne asked worriedly, "But, Mr. Miller, what if it's somebody like Mr. Fouts that senses those things and wants me to come work full time with his crew? I'll end my days bein' a field hand and not even get as far as my Papa did, owning his own place. I'm going to college to get ahead, not fall behind."

"You have to know when to say yes and when to say no," Herbert Miller stated quietly. "And that goes for all of you. It's like anything else: what your life amounts to depends on the choices you make. Choices, remember, are made by saying yes or no. And *you* are the one that says yes or no. Napoleon once said the ability to say no is better than the knowledge of Latin."

There was no rejoinder. Their shadows flickered behind them on the bare winter trees of the dormant Grand Prairie. Then Herbert Miller walked away, his steps crackling with finality. The young men stared into the midnight void where he had vanished. They were quiet for a long time.

Teddy Nix stood up in the chill darkness. Looking solemnly down upon his friends gathered around the dying fire, he summed up the summing up: "Behold!" he pronounced, "The damn Strong Arms grew up!" The last meeting of the Strong Arm Club stood adjourned.

Clayborne pondered Herbert Miller's advice for months. It was cold comfort. As winter melted into another Texas Spring and March came around the calendar once more, his worry increased. No offers of employment came his way at Tarleton and he occasionally heard people injecting an unfamiliar word into normal conversations: Depression. Things were definitely growing worse, but strangely worse. The radio talked about economic chaos in the industrial North and East. But in Texas there was almost no industry so there was no industrial unemployment to cause panic as it did elsewhere in America. Millions of Americans went bankrupt because they held newly worthless stocks. But in Texas very few had ever owned corporate securities so there was no financial crisis to afflict the populace as it did elsewhere in America. Prices of everything went tumbling, a deflationary smash resounded everywhere. But in Texas any eight-year-old could remember worse cotton prices and most eighty-year-olds had never lived a single day above what some call the poverty level. By and large, Texans were adapted to living in less than affluence, and economic difficulty did not frighten people as it did elsewhere in America. But nobody in Texas liked the way things were going.

The second of March fell on a Saturday in 1930. Clayborne walked Hico's newly paved downtown sidewalks in the early afternoon, strolling alone from Mr. Rainwater's Candy Kitchen back to the grocery store to meet his parents. He bit into a brown peanut candy with satisfaction. The day was turning into a scorcher and he walked on the shady side of the street, trying to remember the opening of that anonymous sixteenth century verse from *Elizabethan Lyrics* they had studied in Tarleton's English class. How did it go?

> Shine out, fair sun, with all your heat,
> Show all your thousand-colored light!

Well, the sun was listening to the poet today, that was for sure. The Hico gentry accustomed to dispensing their gossip and gems of wisdom while standing on the sidewalks made sure that they too took the shady side of the street.

As Clayborne approached Randall's Grocery, a familiar figure laden with bulging brown kraft paper sacks emerged from its portals: Mr. William C. Fouts, the benefactor who had given him work at harvest since he was a green fourteen-year-old. Clayborne's throat tightened. What if Mr. Fouts was about to offer him a *permanent* job as a field hand? How could he gracefully refuse? He needed the annual summer employment, now more than ever. But how would the good old man react if he rebuffed a generous offer for full-time work? Clayborne put down his dread and deferentially greeted his friend and neighbor.

"Good to see you, Mr. Fouts. Can I help you with those groceries?"

"Oh, Mr. Perry! What a pleasant coincidence to find you here!" said Fouts. "I was just thinking about you the other day. Don't worry about the groceries, this is my car parked right here." He opened the back door of a new Ford Model T touring car and set down his burden on the cloth upholstered seat.

Law, he's been thinking about me. This is it. Clayborne could feel it coming, Fouts was going to offer him a permanent job on his field crew.

"Well, how's Tarleton?" said the older man, standing relaxed on the shady curb.

"The college is doing just fine, sir," said Clayborne, enthusing as much as he could. "Our enrollment this semester was more than a thousand students. First time that's ever happened. We had a Lyceum number last month with Dr. Bruce — he was Tarleton's president when it started up back in 1898. They had less than a hundred students and only four instructors back then. Can you imagine that?"

"That's fine, that's just fine," smiled Fouts. "Glad to hear it. And how's your family?"

"Mama and Papa are just fine. And the kids. They're here in Randall's shopping just like you were. There's our car right down there."

"I must have just missed them. Tell me, young Mr. Perry, are you coming to work for me at harvest this summer? We have that engine operator spot still open for you."

Oh, no, what am I going to do? "Yes, sir, I sure need a summer job." He tried to emphasize that *summer* part without being too obvious about it.

"Good, good, glad to hear it. Now has anyone offered you full-time work yet?"

Here it comes. The choice is mine. I've got to remember that I'm the one that says yes or no. "No, sir, not yet."

"Well, you know our principal at Blackstump Valley School is thinking about going off to seminary in Fort Worth."

What's he talking about? "You mean Reverend Tidwell?"

"Yes, Duncan Tidwell. You know he's never finished seminary and now, after only a year with us, he's seriously thinking about completing his theological studies."

Wait a minute, he's not talking about field work. "I didn't know he was, no, sir. Well, uh . . ."

"I think you might want to look into the situation. You'll be out of college in a few months. You'd make a good teacher for our children and a good principal for our school if he leaves, Mr. Perry. You'd fit right in. We like a man that works hard. If Reverend Tidwell leaves us, we'll have to find a replacement very quickly. Give it some thought, why don't you?"

A teacher? Me? "I certainly will, Mr. Fouts. Thank you for thinking of me. I sure will give it some thought."

"And you might let the other school trustees know if you're interested. Drop a line to Mr. Rucker and Mr. Smith if you can find the time."

Oh, Dear God, a teacher! Do I have what it takes to be a teacher? "Yes, sir. I sure will, sir. Nice talking to you. Good day, sir."

A teacher! He was flattered by Mr. Fouts' confidence in him. But what does it take to be a teacher? He spent a good part of the next week finding out. He haunted Tarleton's administration offices, asking questions, reading state law, exploring his unexpected opportunity. He found that men teachers made a hundred ten dollars a month, more than twice the average worker — a bank teller might make fifty dollars a month and a department store clerk only thirty. He also discovered that a diploma from Tarleton with sixty properly distributed semester hour credits would qualify him for a Texas State Teacher's Certificate. With that certificate, he would be legally entitled to teach in elementary and secondary schools for four years.

There was only one little snag: not having foreseen the possibility of being a teacher, he hadn't taken enough education courses to meet certification requirements. He talked like a Dutch Uncle to the registrar, trying to change courses in mid-stream. No soap. He'd missed the deadline by a week, he was told: it was simply too late to switch his poultry course to an education course.

"And look," said Mr. E. J. Howell, Registrar, "your record shows you've only enrolled in two education courses so far. If you want a certificate that's good for teaching elementary *and* high school — and that's what you really want — you need *four* education courses. You need *two* more. You shouldn't have taken this animal husbandry course I see here during your first year."

"But you're the one that told me to take it, sir." said Clayborne.

"Oh," said Howell. "Well, not to worry, why don't you just take your two education courses in summer school?"

"Summer school?" he asked hopefully. "When does it start?"

"First of June."

"Oh, no! I've got a job on a harvest crew for all of June! I've already promised my boss, and besides, I need the money! Law, how am I going to get those extra courses on time?"

Dean J. Thomas Davis had chanced by the registration desk and stopped to listen. "Private Perry," he said, "I'm so accustomed to students trying to get *out* of taking extra courses I couldn't stand by without helping a man who's trying to get *in*. When does your harvest job wrap up?"

Clayborne was a little taken aback. Until this very moment, the Dean had only been a remote and aloof figure of power and authority to him. "Second week in July, sir. Give or take a few days."

"Then why don't you come to summer school the second session? It starts July fourteenth this year. Ends August twenty-second. You can just make it and get your two education courses. And if you have to be a day or two late because of work, I'll make sure they hold the classes open for you. Sign him up now, Mr. Howell."

With his certification requirements settled, Clayborne crossed his fingers. If only Reverend Duncan Tidwell heeded the call of God and resigned to go finish his seminary work! In preparation for that eventuality, it was time to begin working on the Blackstump Valley school trustees. The first trustee, Mr. Fouts, of course, he could count on. And he knew he could easily count on the second trustee, Mr. Rucker. Clayborne was sure to run into him sometime soon on the sidewalk in Hico. W. B. Rucker would be no trouble to convince — he had sat on the trustee's board of Camp Branch school with his father and had known

Clayborne since he was a baby. His daughter Minnie had been Clayborne's nemesis in third grade at Camp Branch, winning the spelling headmark contest from him to garner a fifteen-cent Horatio Alger book as the victor's spoils. The Ruckers had moved away from Camp Branch to buy a larger farm in Blackstump Valley over the hill and now Minnie's younger siblings Rex and Martha attended school there, three miles or so east of Camp Branch School. Ever the good citizen, Rucker ran for and was elected to the board of trustees at his children's new school.

But the third trustee, Mr. A. C. Smith, was something of an unknown quantity. Clayborne had met him many times at his farm up above Walker Branch: The Fouts crew harvested his grain every year. But he'd never find him on the sidewalks of Hico — it was too far away for the Smiths to do their grocery shopping. No doubt the Smiths went to nearby Iredell on Saturday afternoons. What kind of man was this Smith, and what would he think of a teacher that he'd only known as a harvest field hand? Clayborne decided to write him a letter:

Dear Mr. Smith,

If Reverend Duncan Tidwell elects to go on to the seminary, as Mr. W. C. Fouts has mentioned to me, and does not teach there in Blackstump Valley next year, I am certainly interested in being your teacher for the next year.

I will graduate from Tarleton this year and will have my teaching certificate before school starts in the middle of October.

Sincerely,
W. C. Perry

If that didn't impress him, nothing would. But what if Mr. Smith didn't like being impressed? Clayborne thought of that two days after he had mailed the letter. Oh, well, what could he do? He'd just have to wait and hope for the best.

The spring of 1930 whirled by. Classwork somehow seemed easier. Even the R.O.T.C. sham battles in the fields around Stephenville felt less onerous — it was almost fun trying to take a fortified position from a competing company, firing blanks in his rifle, crawling through the dirt, even though he got more than his share of grassburrs and bruises. Mr. Rucker, as expected, said during a Saturday sidewalk conversation that he'd seriously consider Clayborne's application if Rev. Tidwell resigned. Tarleton won the college conference basketball championship and there was another shirt-tail parade. He even enjoyed the Lyceum number "Rambles through the Rockies" presented by Eben G. Fine, secretary of Colorado's Boulder Chamber of Commerce, and the novelty mental telepathy act of "de gent named De Gen." Clayborne laughed through the

April Fool issue of the *J-TAC* even though Rev. Tidwell had not yet decided whether to leave Blackstump Valley. And when May-Fete came, he could still joy in watching the girls do their streamered pole-dance and the crowning of the May Queen through his growing anxiety.

He was a little disappointed that Tom and Belle did not attend Parents Day at "John's Institute" in early May, but he understood — they really didn't enjoy crowds and they'd seen the John Tarleton campus on other occasions. Senior week came, there was ham and eggs at the lake out of town, farewell pep meetings, recitals, band concerts and privilege nights, but no word of the Tidwell resignation. When school was out and it was time to go home, he promised himself he would not panic. It had been a wonderful school year — *except* . . .

"Hey, W. C.," hollered Austin Giesecke, "have you paid your last five dollars to Mr. Barker downstairs at Perry's?"

"Yeah," Clayborne answered, packing the last items in his trunk, "I paid him last week."

"You pick up your *Grassburr* yet, Teddy?" asked Marvin Miller.

"Got it," he said. "In fact, I got it right here."

"Look on page 199, then," said Miller. "Read this *Extracts From Latest Military Regulations*."

Teddy opened his 1930 Tarleton yearbook and said, "Oh, yeah, that's in the joke section. Let's see what they say. . . Hey! Looky here! It says, 'No soldier from the grade of buck up shall salute any but the following: The Dean of Women; Any Professor of Horseshoeing; Pedestrians in public conveyances . . .'"

"Aw, it don't say that," said Austin. "Lemme see that . . ." He grabbed Nix's annual and read. "Haw! It does! Listen here. You only salute Caretakers of the Horticulture Lab; Socialist Agitators; Hoot Gibson (when uniformed) and Envoys from U.S.S.R. Inc. How about that, Marvin? Think you're going to salute any socialist agitators next year?"

"Maybe with a baseball bat . . ."

"Hey, W. C., you're awful quiet," said Teddy. "You going to the graduation ceremony?"

"I'm not graduatin' 'til I get those two extra education courses in summer school. Wouldn't be much point in going just to watch you two guys get your diplomas, now, would there?"

"I'm not going either," said Marvin Miller. "I'm sure going to miss you all next year. I don't know how I'm goin' to make it without you three."

"You'll be a senior, Marvin," said Teddy Nix. "Room with some stupid freshman that'll think you're smart because he doesn't know any better. But don't you think about quitting college, you hear?"

"I won't," Miller said. "I'm going to be a teacher like you and Clayborne."

"*If* I get to be a teacher," Clayborne muttered.

"Don't get discouraged, W. C.," said Austin. "If that doesn't work out, something else will come up. You're special, you remember that." He stood awkwardly in the middle of the room. "Look," he said, "I'm all ready to go now. It'll prob'ly be a long time before all four of us can get together again, so we ought to say our goodbyes all fit and proper. It's been good rooming with you country hicks the last two years. Shake my hand and wish me luck."

Teddy Nix shook his hand as said, "So long, Austin."

"Austin, I . . ." said Marvin.

"Aw, kid. Don't get mushy on me at the end."

"Get your bohunkus out of here and over to that job at the Highway Department." Miller shook hands with Giesecke and turned away. "And pretend they didn't make a mistake when they hired you right out of college."

"I'm going now, too," said Teddy Nix. "You come see me over at Clairette school, all right you guys? Just ask for the ag teacher."

Clayborne faced his friends in farewell. He dreaded this moment. "Good luck, Austin, Teddy. It's been good," he said. The parting smothered him in grief he dared not show. Between it and the anxiety over his teaching job he thought he would die. "I'll see you guys later." The two disappeared through the door and into the hall. He could hear them stomping down the stairs.

Clayborne stood silent in the bare room with Marvin Miller. "Can you give me a hand with my trunk, Marvin?" he finally asked. "I think my Papa ought to be here with the car by now."

They carried the heavy trunk down the narrow stairway and onto the broad sidewalk facing the court house. Tom Perry sat waiting in the family car at curbside.

"Papa," yelled Clayborne, "will you open the back door?"

Tom obliged and the trunk was duly loaded. Clayborne turned to his friend and said, "You keep at it, Marvin. You'll do just fine your last year here. We'll see each other again. Don't feel down about it."

"I won't. And thanks. Thanks for rooming with me." He could say no more.

Clayborne got in the car and his father drove away. He looked back at Marvin, at Court House Square, at the brick stack of Tarleton's steam plant in the oaky distance, at two years of his life ending. A welter of emotions engulfed him. He did not want to appear over-sensitive or unmanly and all he said was, "It's tough saying goodbye to old friends, Papa. I'll miss college." He watched the scrubby oaks go by at the edge of town. "And it sure is tough to be so unsure about the future."

Tom gazed studiously at the gravel road ahead, sensing his son's discomfort. He remembered times when he had faced his own father, gentle mustachioed Jim Perry, full of roiling emotions of his own that he could not express. "Yep, sure is tough to be so unsure about the future," repeated Tom cryptically.

"Are you raggin' me, Papa? Why are you lookin' so funny?"

"You got a call from Mr. Fouts this morning."

"It's the teaching job! Oh, law, what did he say, Papa? Tell me quick!"

"He says Reverend Tidwell's packed up and gone to Fort Worth. He says the trustees have already talked to several other candidates for the principal's spot. Good candidates. Him and Mr. Rucker and Mr. Smith, they had to think about it a long while, yessir, a long while."

"Well, what, Papa?"

"They figured they needed a grown man that works hard and understands country kids."

"Who'd they pick, Papa?"

"You better go around to their houses this Sunday after church and thank them for even thinkin' about you."

"Is that *all*?"

"Well, they want you bring the contract they sent in the mail. At a hundred and ten dollars a month. They want you to sign it with them. It sure is tough to be so unsure about the future, ain't it?"

His answer was pure joy: "Ya-hoo!"

It had all begun.

Principal W. C. Perry parked his brown two-door Ford sedan up off the road by Blackstump Valley schoolhouse in the early-November chill. The autumn sun still lay low on the horizon over the rolling Grand Prairie. He opened the metal door, unfolded himself to full height beside the car and perused his realm, a daily habit recently acquired. As usual at eight o'clock, he was the first one here. He stood alone, a slim figure dark in his blue flannel suit against the tawny sunrise landscape, schoolmaster of all he surveyed. To the east he saw the stony ground slope gradually away to Walker Branch with its squat willows and green pecans and glinting sycamores and year-long tinkling waters. Bill and Nete Newman's old house poked up slab-sided a quarter of a mile down the road, poor but serviceable. Their boys Raymond, Joe and Coy would be walking up the dusty road to school in under an hour. At the headwaters of Walker Branch the Bowman place showed white against the next low grassy ridge, easier to see than the Smith farmhouse a mile farther south on the same rise where the blinding dayspring sun lofted behind it. Freda Bowman and the Smith boy, W. B., would about now be working their before-school chores. Southward, clumps of little bluestem bunchgrass and Indiangrass pasture waved tall and brittle and yellow on their markless and unobstructed way into the vanishing distance. Down there toward Iredell in the shortgrass pastures of sideoats grama and buffalo-grass dotted with goldeneyes and sunflowers lived Hugh and Rachel Harris. Their five kids, Bill, Annie Maud, Kate and the twins James and Jack, would be starting the two mile walk to Blackstump Valley school in less than half an hour.

Westward, the gullies of Rocky Creek stretched in fading sequence. Past the Odom place and the Hopgood farm and the Dunlaps and Duckworths, clustered liveoaks spread into Mr. Rucker's frizzy cotton fields. His boy Rex and girl Martha would probably be eating their big farm breakfast about now. J. D. McElroy, another student from Rocky, as the creek area was known, milked the family cows at this moment. Beyond the Ruckers' maybe five miles into the flat haze down the old Hico farm-to-market road lay the hundred acres of young Principal Perry's folks, Tom and Belle.

Northwesterly a half mile from school the Fouts place tracked a curl of blue smoke through the cedar-elms and plane trees into the brightening air. Pearl and Marie Fouts would arrive at school within half an hour; Clayborne had seen them getting ready while he helped Mr. Fouts slop the hogs this morning — the Fouts family had urged Clayborne to take his room and board with them at their farm near the school, and, at fifteen dollars a month, he had accepted. He was like a regular member of the family now. Two and a half miles farther off, beyond Bosque County where he stood, down from Erath County ran the little hackberry swale of Camp Branch. On its banks sat the school where he had gone as a child and above it lay the black soil of Dude Flat where he had been born and where Grandad Jim Perry and Grandma Lou Perry and Old Grandma Elizabeth Glasgow Perry certainly stirred this moment on their early chores.

Due north gloomed only Louse Hill and other farmless buttermilky limestone outliers of Chalk Mountain. The low buttes with their ten-acious dark cedars and fraying weatherbashed cliffs pushed not two-hundred feet into the hawk's domain — but, then, any prominence more than a hundred feet above the general rolling prairie came flattered with the name "mountain" in these precincts. Hugging the bottom of these hog plum mountains to the north of the schoolhouse, strung out like seeds on a grass stalk, spread the farms of Walter Harris, then closer in, the unpainted farmhouse of Wick Simpson and then, by the hard bend in the gravel road, the Clyde and Vella Harris place. Cousins of Hugh and Rachel, their ten-year-old daughter Helen just awakened, a sleepy-head today. Much closer in to the north, in past all the farms, right across the road in the coreopsis goldenwaves and dayflowers, Blackstump Valley school's well lay with its wooden cover and hand pump, a tin cup shaking gently in the morning breeze as it hung on a wire from the long handle. A little farther downhill in the ragweed protruded the unlovely spires of two one-holer outhouses, the left one for the boys, the right one for the girls, knotholes in its rough lumber sides carefully patched with tacked-on sheet-metal strips. This, then, was his territory. And as for the remaining students entrusted to his care, Principal Perry counted on perhaps twenty-seven more youngsters from all compass points to creep like snail from their sequestered farms before nine o'clock classtime.

Clayborne looked over the morningtide land a long moment more. He *knew* this farmed and tended place and all its groomed fields and working pastures. He had been born to it, held it from babyhood in his hands and his head and his heart. In the seasoned course of time he had become a man here, and had worked harvest again this year for the seventh summer in a row, had walked and talked and sweated with other men over the sweet grains, labored on every foot of ground as far as he could see in every direction. It was more than home, it was a part of him and he a part of it, his by right of being and belonging here. The place was his to *have*, to have directly and passionately in a way no deed of title could endow. He would never suffer his father's pangs of seeking home in distant places like Colorado where it could never be, for home was not a place to him, nor had it ever been. In college he had realized it sharply one day studying an English assignment in John Milton's 1665 masterpiece *Paradise Lost*. The poet had given to Lucifer, mortal enemy of Clayborne's Baptist faith, the lines that made his inborn knowledge sparkling clear:

> The mind is its own place, and in itself
> Can make a Heaven of Hell, a Hell of Heaven.

How obvious it was now. Milton's message rolled across the centuries to him, affirming the recondite intuition he had carried all along: home is not a place, but a state of mind.

And now he turned to go into the schoolhouse and build a fire in the big old fashioned woodstove with its black iron jacket to take the chill off the two rooms before school started. Blackstump Valley schoolhouse gleamed in the sunup, its whitewashed narrow horizontal siding pierced with long banks of high-sashed windows reflecting the brash and golden dawn. Good to let in healthy light and air. The simple rural school had been built directly atop the highest knoll in the valley, exactly eleven hundred twenty feet above sea level. Most of its forty-two students could look up from home and see the school's faintly church-like gables: an evanescent landmark in this lasting valley. Principal Perry walked up a half-dozen steps to the four front doors at the big front porch, two central doors going into the small cloak rooms, two outer doors opening into the spacious school rooms. After unlocking all four doors, he entered his classroom on the west side of the building, and sat at his teaching desk — in a rural two-teacher school, the principal is one of the teachers, and not simply an administrator as in larger institutions.

He unlocked his desk and opened its top drawer, slipping the day's lesson plan from its folder and laying it out for ready reference. A manila folder in the drawer caught his eye.

My teacher's certificate he thought. Opening the folder he gazed once more upon the impressive piece of paper he had examined so often since it came to him from Austin in late September. It was engraved with fancy scrollwork curlicues like a bond certificate and stated that W. C. Perry had completed sixty semester hours in appropriate courses and was thereby entitled to teach in Texas state secondary schools until 1934. It had been authorized by L. A. Wood, State Superintendent of Public Instruction. Signed, sealed, and delivered.

Now that I've registered it with the Bosque Country court house I better take it home. Law, if I lose this, I lose my job!

It had not yet occurred to him that lost certificates could easily be replaced upon request.

By eight-thirty the big wood stove was throwing off heat to beat the band and the rooms were warming up nicely. Miss Adina Carroll stepped in, precisely on time.

"Ah, the reliable Miss Carroll," said Clayborne. "Good morning to you."

"And a good morning to you, too, Mister Perry. All nice and warm already, I see."

"Yes, Ma'am. Takes about half an hour, forty-five minutes to get it up to snuff."

She slid open a panel of the big central room partition and went to place a stack of papers on her desk. "Mr. Perry, isn't that a different car you came in today?" she asked, leaning around the partition. "Isn't that the third since school started?"

"Oh, well, yes it is," he sputtered, embarrassed. "I'll have to tell you a little story about that. You see, I didn't have a car of my own when school started. You know, just out of college and all."

"I remember how *that* was very well," she smiled as she walked stiffly to the wood stove.

"You know when we had that teacher's meeting over at Meridian just before school started in October?" he asked.

"Yes," Miss Carroll said. "I recall you didn't say much."

"Well, since it was my first time and all, I figured the best way to get through it was by keeping my mouth shut," he grinned.

"Why, Mr. Perry, don't say that. You're always so clearheaded."

"Well, I was clearheaded enough to borrow my Papa's car for those two days. I had to get there somehow. Then when school started the next week I didn't want to hog the family car again, so I borrowed my Grandpa Blackburn's car."

The prim schoolteacher warmed her hands at the heater. "Then the first car I saw here at school was Mr. Blackburn's. I see. And how is that poor dear old man nowadays? I've heard he hasn't been well since his wife passed away — what is it, nearly two years ago now?"

"Has it been that long? I guess it has. Grandpa Charley's not doing too well, Miss Carroll. He just doesn't seem to take any interest in life. My Uncle John and his wife stayed with him, took care of him the last year and a half. But Uncle John couldn't make a go of his repair business out here in the country. They moved back to San Antone a couple of months ago. Grandpa's come to live with my folks now. He really needs somebody to take care of him."

"That's so sad," said Miss Carroll. "Everybody around here just loves him so much."

"Yes, Ma'am. I know."

"Go on with your story. What about the next car?"

"Oh, yes. Well, I didn't want to keep Grandpa's car too long, so I borrowed my Papa's car for a while, the same one I took to Meridian. Then I finally found a good used car over in Waco and went with my Papa and bought it this weekend. That's it out there, a 1929 Model A Ford. Only a year old and twenty-eight thousand miles on it."

"So that's the story of the three cars?"

"That's the story." He sat at his desk in silence for a moment. A question had been eating at him for a week. "May I ask your advice about something, Miss Carroll?" He hesitated to ask, being new to the role of authority and uncertain how close to his vest he should play his cards. But this was vital. He had to know.

"Why, certainly, Mr. Perry. What is it?"

"Have you . . . Can you tell if the kids really think of me as their principal? Me being so young I worry about it sometimes. Some of these older boys have known me since before I went to college. And I'm barely two years older than Rudene Newman."

Miss Carroll smiled. "Makes you uneasy, doesn't it? It did me, too."

"Well," chuckled Clayborne, "I just try to act like I own the place. I went to a school pretty much like this just over at Camp Branch."

"Mine was much the same. And my first experience teaching. I was nineteen when I started teaching last year, Mr. Perry. I just acted like I was taught to at college, to command respect. Like you say, just act like you own the place. I was glad Reverend Tidwell had the top five grades with the older students, but all the children acted just fine. It looks to me like you're handling things just as good as he did last year. I don't see that you have any problem. They know you're the Principal."

"Miss Carroll, I just turned twenty this summer. We're the same age. Is discipline any different teaching the first five grades?"

"It's probably harder in some ways than the last five because the children are so young. Their minds wander. Have you had any disrespect from the older students?"

"No, most of them call me Mr. Perry. There's a few that still call me Clayborne but they seem polite enough. But the thing is, *all* their folks still call me Clayborne. I've worked harvest with most of them, they've known me all my life."

"Parents are one thing, students quite another. You're doing fine as far as I can see, Mr. Perry. You work very well with the children. If there's any problem, it certainly doesn't show."

"Thank you, Miss Carroll. That's reassuring. These are good kids and I want to do the best I can. And let me ask you something else. About their dinners. I see a few of these youngsters coming to school carrying just some biscuits and maybe a little butter or a fried peach pie, not even a hardboiled egg or a slice of ham like I used to bring. Do they always eat so poor?"

"Oh, Mr. Perry, I'm afraid so," Miss Carroll sighed. "I've spoken to a few of the parents here, just trying to drop a hint, you know. Some of them just don't understand nutrition and some — well, they don't have the extra. The meat all goes to the man so he can keep up the heavy work."

Clayborne shook his head. "I've seen one or two of our students fall asleep in the late mornings. I'll bet they didn't have much of a breakfast, either."

"One or two — I think you're right. But most of them seem to be doing just fine."

"If there was only some way to make sure all our kiddos had proper food to eat. . ." said young Principal Perry. "Well, there's not much we can do, but do our best, I guess. Oh, there's one more thing. I don't mean to pry, but about our salary vouchers. . . You taught here last year. Did you ever have to hold onto a voucher or cash it at a discount because the tax money was late?"

"Why, it's not prying at all, Mr. Perry. You certainly have the right to ask about such an important thing as your salary. I've never had the slightest problem with my vouchers, nor did Reverend Tidwell. Blackstump Valley School District Number Seventy is very lucky, too. I know many of my classmates at Howard Payne who now teach in other communities have had nothing but trouble, always having to go to the bank and take a ten percent discount because the farmers hadn't paid their taxes in full."

"Well," said Clayborne, "this is good rich soil around here and the farmers know how to work it proper. But, you know, I just wanted to make sure and all. You're kind to let me know."

"To tell you the truth, Mr. Perry, it's easy working with someone as aboveboard as you. Some people in this profession are so strong about keeping up appearances and so fearful for their authority they never ask questions. And they're usually the people who could use some answers the most. Oh my, I see the Fouts children out the window, Mr. Perry. The students are beginning to arrive."

"Oh, Miss Carroll. Let's be doubly careful making up our absentee list this week. The trustees are worried that flu season is going to start up soon, and they want me to keep them up-to-date on any illness."

"Of course, Mr. Perry."

He grew into the job by stages, playing the part of teacher until it was no longer playing but second nature, behaving as the authority until it was no longer a role and he had *become* the authority. He pursued the time-honored principles of teaching that he knew to work, that he had been taught by as a student at Camp Branch School, that college courses had instructed him to employ: Keep the students busy, let them help one another, work with them closely, play with them in all their games. He explained arithmetic to the slower students and let the bright ones read extra books from the school's meager library. When his trustees took up the state on its offer to pay part of the cost for an encyclopedia — Texas had for several years now been furnishing textbooks to its common schools — he gave all his grades extra time each day to devour the banquet of facts and pictures and slake their thirst for knowledge. He did the simple things, too, taught youngsters how to take a sheet of paper out of their Big 5 tablets — a hundred sheets for a nickel — and fold it to make a drinking cup to take across the road to the water pump and he let the students who brought their own tin cups or slip-ring camping cups keep them in their desks. He never hesitated to paddle an unruly pupil and never had a complaint from a parent whose child he had punished: there were no factions in this community to keep score of who got spanked the most or timid souls afraid to discipline a child by main strength when needed.

He coached all their athletics and really worked on his basketball teams, one for girls, the other for boys. When they were groomed and at their peak of form, he took them for two games at Duffau school. The Duffau boys clobbered his team 16 to 6, but his girls won their game 12 to 8. Principal Perry beamed with victory. He was *very* proud to have his students beat the school where he himself had studied only three years earlier.

Several of his older students showed promise of becoming fine athletes, particularly the two younger Newman boys Joe and Coy. Their older brother Raymond would surely have been another had it not been for a rattlesnake bite in 1927 that never healed properly and had rotted away most of his left heel. But Joe and Coy, Principal Perry found, could raise themselves on the chinning bar fifty times while the next best would give out after twenty. After basketball season, the new principal entered all his student athletes in district track meet. In the Rural School Division Joe

and Coy Newman of Blackstump Valley school came home with five
ribbons between them, for the 110 yard and 220 yard dash, broad jump,
high jump and chinning bar events.

By January, 1931, Clayborne was completely comfortable as a teacher.
He had also paid off his Ford, all three-hundred-ten dollars worth of it. As
the national depression deepened and its effects began to creep into Texas,
he had laid a little money aside and could look forward to a secure future
ahead, assuming that the trustees would re-elect him for the duration of
his teacher's certificate, at least four years of a secure future. Cotton prices
had fallen to 9.46 cents a pound in 1930, but yields remained high and
the large crops softened the blow of falling prices. Even with all the worry
and fret of economic chaos in the land, Christmas at home had been the
best Clayborne could remember. The new year looked bright and hopeful
and fulfilling and a sense of smug self-satisfaction occasionally wafted
over him. He had ventured out into the great world and found success.
He felt ready for anything.

"Anything" appeared on February tenth. It came in the form of a penny
postcard addressed to Mr. Clayborne Perry, Hico, Texas, Route 4. The
printed side held an illustrator's version of a "Sweet Young Thing" in
flowing party dress, hands shyly entwined, moon face demurely averted,
the very picture of appealing propriety. The postcard manufacturer's copy
writer had gratuitously included this saccharin verse: I don't believe /
you'd want me / To say it here in print; / But surely you / will understand /
That this is just a hint?

Clayborne was baffled at first. Who would send him such a piece of
sweetness and light? The handwritten message on the reverse was a bolt
out of the blue:

> Dear Clayborne:
> I am giving a
> "Birthday Party" next
> Saturday night, Feb. 14.
> You are invited. I'll
> send this to your
> home address, because
> I don't know your
> address at Blackstump,
>   Your friend,
>   Oretta Partain

Oretta Partain. He had run with her older brothers during most of his
school years, had been to her home so much her parents couldn't tell he
wasn't one of theirs. He had dated her sister Maxie once or twice while
he was in high school at Duffau. Maxie was six years older than

Clayborne, but Oretta, little Oretta was two or three years younger chronologically, younger than that in attitude and she ran with a much younger crowd. He'd never paid much attention to her when he saw her occasionally in Hico or when his father took the sorghum cane over to her father's mill for pressing. And she was always just another familiar face at Prairie Springs Baptist Church on Sundays. This birthday would be her . . . what? Her eighteenth, he calculated.

He flipped the card over and read the copy-writer's verse once more. ". . . this is just a hint . . ." Hint of what? Was she driving at something? Ah, hint of nothing. Her mother had probably just picked up a bunch of postcards at the mercantile and only noticed the party dress on the little illustrated girl. What the heck, it was only a birthday party and it was on a weekend. He might as well go. He'd have a chance to renew acquaintance with some old friends from around Duffau that he hadn't seen since he started college. It might be fun.

It was fun. He knew most of the twenty-odd young country people who came and he enjoyed socializing with them, especially now that he didn't have to worry about his own status — in high school he'd always harbored a faint uneasiness about parties, wondered if he had overheard correctly those whispers about how poor his family was, how his clothes never quite fit right, how he came off as a country hick more than the others. But now he was someone special. He had a college education and a respectable job and a car and nice clothes and a position of authority and a reliable income. These days, not all that many people even had work. So the party was really, truly fun.

And eighteen-year-old Oretta was a surprise. He had obviously not noticed her much at church lately. She was no longer the skinny kid he remembered from high school at all. In fact, she had grown up to be a rather stunning young woman. Her roundish girl face had lengthened into high-cheekboned, classic chiseled features untypical of the country Texas population. Her rectangular eyes reminded him a little of some movie star he could not remember, Greta Garbo maybe, but without makeup and without the fancy airs. She stood out from the crowd now. He enjoyed talking with her, had a fine time with her friends, bade her good night and went home.

At first he did not realize that the birthday party had been fatal and of full tight bind. The next week in school he could not keep his teacher's mind on class as usual. His normal on-the-ball, right-there concentration kept drifting. It took him a few days to recognize what was wrong with him. Then that night he picked up the telephone at the Fouts place and called the Partain residence over by Duffau. He asked Oretta out on a real date, to have a bottle of sody pop with him. She said yes.

-13-

ORETTA

"OO-EEE! Sis is gonna be mad at me!" smiled Oretta as she hopped in the front seat of Clayborne's Model A.

"Why?" Clayborne asked, looking in puzzlement around the Partain's stony front yard. There, not fifty feet behind Oretta one of her older sisters stormed from around the peak-roofed farmhouse.

"What'd you do to Ila?" Clayborne asked Oretta.

"I'll tell you what she did, young man," said Ila Partain as she stomped up to the driver's side of his car trying to look angry. "She's leavin' me to milk the cow tonight so she can go gaddin' about the countryside with you, that's what." Ila was fifteen years older than Oretta and age lent authority to her complaint.

"We're just gaddin' about to church," Oretta said sweetly as she looked directly at Clayborne. She had a way of making such simple, direct statements sound like cozy little arrangements intended only to bind the two of them together, Clayborne thought. He looked spellbound into her twinkling eyes.

He turned back to disgruntled Ila, saying, "Well, Sis, you know how it is, what with you going with a feller yourself. Aren't you and ol' B. C. Better keepin' company with each other nowadays?"

"His name is Ledbetter, Clayborne!" huffed Ila. "B. C. Ledbetter!"

Oretta teased her sister, "He's so short we just call him B. C. Better, Sis, and besides, I know you think he's Better, you can't fool me!"

"Ohhh!" fumed Ila, half from affection for her baby sister, half from aggravation. "Clayborne, you better drive that little snip off the place before I start peltin' her with rocks or somethin'."

"Yes, Ma'am," he complied. "Don't forget to say hello to B.C. for me." He drove away happily with his sweetheart. "So we're just gadding about to church?" he said to Oretta. "Do you think that made Sis feel any better? You know I said I'd take you for a sody pop after church too."

"Well, I didn't say we weren't goin' for a sody pop. I just said we're going to church, and we are. Anyways, the only thing that'll make her feel any better is for me to milk the cow tonight. Don't you worry about it. She'll get over it, she always does."

Clayborne said, "Ila doesn't worry me. Does your Mama and Papa approve of me coming over so often?" He fought with the car to guide it over the rutted pasture.

"They didn't say anything about it. They know where we're going." She giggled and scrunched closer to him in the car seat.

Clayborne asked, "Have they ever said anything about us? I mean now that I'm seeing you so regular. I wouldn't want to cause any hard feelings?"

"They never say much. I guess they feel all right about it. It makes *me* feel just fine."

He blushed visibly. He had not been raised to be so open about his feelings. This girl was so full of life, so affectionate, she could so easily crack that composure of his, could reach right through his serious facade and make him smile.

"Oh, I almost forgot to tell you the news," said Clayborne. "There was a letter waiting for me when I got back home from harvest yesterday."

"Was it anything important?"

"Yessiree! The board of trustees has reelected me to another year as principal at Blackstump Valley School. Even gave me a little raise. How about that?"

"Oh, that's just wonderful, Clayborne!" She clapped her hands in delight. "I just knew they'd do it. Everybody thinks so much of you and to hear tell, you do so much for the kids over at Blackstump Valley . . ."

Clayborne stopped the car abruptly and jumped out, yelling "Be right back!" He ran to open the gate into a neighboring pasture. The only roads into the Partain place came straight across other farmers' fields, which meant opening and closing several wire fence gates on the way in and out. With the gate hanging open he ran back to the car, jumped in, drove through the gate, stopped the car, jumped out again, closed the gate behind him and jumped in the car again.

He picked up the conversation where he had left off as he drove away, "And I think they really like it that I work with them at harvest. You know, Mr. Fouts didn't come right out and say it, but I could just tell they'd all kind of resent it if I didn't live and work right there among 'em."

"How do you know that?"

"Well, it's kind of somethin' you feel. Like, every now and then somebody — Mr. Smith or Mr. Newman, somebody — they'll let me know how Reverend Tidwell lived off in Iredell, in town, and how he only showed up at school from 9 to 4, and how he never worked harvest at all. They never say a bad word against him, you see. But you can feel it. It's like they're dropping a big hint without getting ugly about it."

"Clayborne, you're so smart," Oretta said beaming. "You really *understand* people."

"Be back in a minute!" he yelled again, stopping the car, leaping out to open, drive through and close another gate. Then they were bouncing once more along the wagon ruts in the Model A.

Oretta said, "You know my brother Forris is going to write away to order himself a car here pretty soon."

"Oh, really? What's ol' Frosty going to get?"

"I don't remember," she mumbled. "Isn't that something? My own brother going to get his first car and I can't even remember what he told me."

Clayborne said, "Oh, it's probably a Model A Ford like this or something close like it. Anything else would cost more than he can afford."

"I think that's what he said. I think. . ."

"Hang on another second."

Another gate, another leap out, leap in, pass through, leap out, leap in.

"Clayborne," Oretta said, seriously this time, laying her hand on his arm. "How's your Papa doing?"

"Not so good, Oretta. He's havin' another spell with his eyes, all red and inflamed. He's losing the sight in his good eye pretty fast. I'm going to drive him to a doctor's up in Fort Worth tomorrow. They've got some kind of expert there, maybe can help."

"But you've already taken him to doctors in Stephenville and Hico and Waco. They couldn't help, and you're missing a lot of work at harvest."

"We've got to try everything. And I've only missed a day or two. He's my Papa, Oretta . . ." That explained it, and they fell silent among the bumps and jolts of the rolling limestone and clay hills.

Prairie Springs Baptist Church filled quickly during Sunday sundown services. For poor farmers the evening rural church provided a multiservice center: bastion of faith, bulletin board for sickbed volunteers, newsroom, lost and found, barter market, gossip box, employment agency, lonely hearts club, courting plaza, and general entertainment operation, particularly the hymn singing, which took merit more from its vigorous piety than its musical mastery.

Tonight Clayborne and Oretta came to the country church not only for spiritual renewal but also as their courting plaza, just as many other couples had: there was scant money in this depressed economy for picture shows and even the blandishment of two nickel sody pops put a savage dent in the average young swain's pocket. So church held sway, far and away the suitor's most popular domicile of modest dalliance. The moment Clayborne's brown Model A pulled into the gravelled parking yard in front of the whitewashed church Oretta's easy and relaxed demeanor shaded into prim and proper decorum. Clayborne approved of her serious public face — she knew how to act and that was important to him.

Not that they didn't have fun: a passel of their vivacious young friends could usually be counted on to enliven before-and-after-church times with vivid impressions of their recent exploits and ample subject matter for good ol' down home talk. But their fun followed a strict code of manners: stern bonds of tradition here demanded no outward show of affection, no holding hands, no putting arms around sweethearts — the shy glance was permitted freely, but even the furtive smile or yearning gesture might draw a frown from more straitlaced neighbors. No sensible young couple could afford such disapproval from the elder community. In consequence, Clayborne and Oretta spent a good part of their evening together apart, talking to the same people separately.

"Clayborne, I've been meaning to congratulate you!" called W. B. Rucker across the crowded church steps. As Clayborne moved toward the summoning voice, waiting hands grabbed Oretta away into a clutch of starched and frilled teenage girls.

Clayborne approached the tall balding school board trustee alone. "Thank you, Mr. Rucker," he said humbly. "I really appreciate the confidence you trustees showed in electing me for another year."

"What? Oh, that!" said Rucker, his modulated voice smoother and more authoritative than his peers. "We all knew you'd get reelected. It's the play I was congratulating you about!"

"The play?"

"Why, sure! That three-act play you had the kids put on right at the end of school, what was the name of it?"

"*Seventeen*," said Clayborne, all smiles. "I'm glad you liked it. The story came from a book."

"Oh, yes," said Mr. Rucker, "no wonder it sounded familiar. It must be Booth Tarkington's novel from a few years ago. Didn't read it myself but I saw the newspaper notices when it first came out." W. B. Rucker was a self-educated man of wide reading and a certain erudition, an uncommon thing among the farmers of the Texas Grand Prairie.

"Yes, sir," said Clayborne, "that's the one, by Booth Tarkington. They made it into a play for schools."

"Well, you did such a good job that even the adults enjoyed it,

Clayborne. We forgot that we were really just looking at the school steps with bedsheets to hide the front doors. Made it worthwhile hauling those benches for the audience up from Rocky church. And borrowin' all those pumpup gasoline lanterns to light up the porch. Now maybe you can let me in on your little stage secret — how did you pull off that part where the kid rips his pantsleg?"

"Oh, you mean when William is getting ready at the mirror trying to look all spiffy for Miss Pratt and everything goes wrong?"

"That's it! Boy, it was perfect! You coulda' heard those pants tear clear down to my place. How'd you do it?"

"Well, we had Raymond Newman — he was playin' William, remember — we had him bring up an old pair of pants to play the part in, one that we could tear up. We made the torn place just like it was a costume. We held it together with a little piece of adhesive tape inside the pantsleg. You couldn't tell it was torn unless you looked real close. Then we had Wynell Hudson behind the backdrop with an old dishrag. When the play gets to that part, Raymond walks behind that desk so you couldn't see. That's the cue he's about to snag his britches. Then Wynell just tears the dishrag a good one, real loud. So Raymond reaches down like he'd really ripped his pants, but he's just openin' up the tear we already put there. Then he comes out from behind the desk and everybody sees the big hole."

"Remarkable!" glowed W. B. Rucker. "That's very clever, it sure is. We sure picked the right principal for Blackstump Valley School. You did a handsome job of puttin' on the graduation ceremony, too. All those attendance awards and honor roll certificates — that was real impressive. And I'd like to thank you for selecting my Martha to play Miss Pratt. It did her a world of good. She hasn't talked about anything else since school let out."

"Well, don't thank me, Mr. Rucker. Martha earned the part. We had tryouts and all. Everybody had a chance. Miss Carroll and I both thought she'd make the best Miss Pratt, that's all."

"I know you're a fair man, Clayborne. Didn't mean to imply otherwise. Just wanted you to know how much it meant to Martha. And the way you teach our kids, keep order in the classroom, play with 'em on the ball field, why, you're a fine, thoughtful teacher. Your Papa must be right proud of you. And how is Tom these days, Clayborne?"

And so it went. Simultaneously, Oretta found herself mobbed with friends from school down at the bottom of the church stairs, down alongside the older women who were absorbed in their own doings. The girls insisted upon knowing *everything* about — well, you know, it's no secret that you and Clayborne are sweet on each other, they twittered.

"Did you have it all planned out, Oretta? Is that why you invited him to your birthday party?" the excited girl asked.

"Law, no, Emmy Jo!" laughed Oretta. "It was my sister Ila's idea to ask Clayborne. I didn't know who to ask, never had a party like that before. Ila said to me 'Why don't you invite Clayborne Perry?' It just seemed natural, so I said all right."

"Oh, come on, Oretta," said her close friend Estel Jones. "You must have had something in mind. Look how quick he asked you for a date — couldn't have been a whole week after the party, even."

"I never in the world thought of going with him, Estel Jones. I've known him all my life. He's run around with Hoot and Forris so much he's just about one of the family. I never even gave it a thought."

"How do you get along with him?" asked Velma Childress. "He's so much older than you."

"He's only two and a half years older."

"Well, you know what I mean. He's so mature, and . . . "

"I know, I know," Oretta fretted. "I know just what you're going to say. I'm young for my age. I'm eighteen and I act sixteen, that's what Mama tells me. But you know I think its because they treat me like the baby of the family all the time."

"How come your Mama and Papa do that, Oretta?" asked Ova Pearl Allen. "You're not the baby, J. D. is. He must be four years younger than you."

"You're right, J. D.'s only fourteen. But he just won't have no part of bein' the baby. He plain won't put up with it. Since I'm the youngest girl, they just sort took me up as the baby. I don't like it, but I guess I'm too easy-goin' to make any fuss."

"So you get treated like the baby," taunted Leola Long. "What does Clayborne think of goin' out with a baby?"

"Well, I think he fell for me right hard, that's what I think."

"You two are so-o-o-o madly in love with each other, aren't you?" snickered Nada Webb.

Oretta nearly lost her composure, but came right back: "You just bet we are."

After the service their bottles of sody pop at the Conner Drug Store in Hico went quickly. But the evening was not without its hitches. One their way home Clayborne's car had a flat tire in one of the pastures near the Partains. It made them much later than he intended, for he had to get up and take his father to Fort Worth to the eye doctor in the morning. It was a quick goodnight.

They had been going together for five months now. They had hit it off right away. Why they did is one of those mysteries of the heart not susceptible of empirical analytics. More than a few of their friends wondered why they ever got together, for the fact is, in some ways their personalities were almost diametrically opposite, and in more ways than simple contrasts in maturity. For one thing, Clayborne had grown up quietly obsessed with getting an education — Grandma Perry and Old Grandma had always been there in the background pushing, sprinkling their conversation with stories of how well some educated person had done in life. To that he added his own inner drive to excel, to overcome his own limitations, to be all that he could be; Oretta had grown up with school as a dutiful address, a place for her to go and learn things for seven months a year — she did well, mind you, above average grades and all, but there were no demanding goads of any kind in her psyche. Her great and indispensible talent, as time would reveal, was as a helper and a rock in time of trouble.

The fact that they got together at all is certainly a matter of origins. We cannot escape our origins, roughhew them as we may. The roots of the Perrys and Partains struck deep into the same reservoir, that great artesian fountainhead of traditional values that watered the landed poor Texas farmer class, nourished its outlook and ethos and fed its *Genius collegii*, its protective binding spirit. Their origins gave Clayborne and Oretta a single place to stand in the world and made them congenial in their wants and goals. They came, after all, but from two clans of one farmer tribe, different enough to get married, same enough to stay married.

And now, near the middle of June, 1931, Clayborne was no longer merely smitten, he grew more and more deeply serious about the Partain girl. He wrote long letters to her — four pages — which was remarkable in itself: the most he usually wrote to anybody was a penny postcard. And he began to write once a week which meant that things were definitely coming to a crisis. But by reading his letters it was impossible to tell. After taking his father to Fort Worth on Monday and helping out around the family farm on Tuesday, Clayborne sat down at home on Wednesday evening and penned the following missive. It is the closest thing he ever wrote to a love letter.

Hico, Texas
June 10, 1931

Dear Oretta,

How are you by now? I hope you are not sleepy. I was just a little sleepy on Monday morning. I went to bed before dark last night, and Grandpa Charley said something about me going to bed so early. Mamma told him she guessed I needed to for I had been up so late for the last three nights. They must have known what time I got in Sunday night. Ha, ha. Who cares? I don't, do you?

I have not started back to cutting grain yet, I guess I will go tomorrow. How is Sis feeling over milking the cow Sunday night? I hope she doesn't feel hurt over the deal. If so maybe she will get all right. Has Forris written for his car yet? I bet he would like to see it.

Do you feel like you could drink another bottle of sody pop? I believe I could drink two by now. Dorothy and Nadine are cutting up so I can't write very good. Dorothy is worrying because she can't find out who I am writing to. I told her it was to J. C. and she said I was a coward to let her see. I would not let her see so she ran off and laughed and said it was to you (Oretta).

I have fixed my flat so it will be OK next time we get ready to go somewhere. Does Sis still think as much of B. C. as she used to?

Well, dear, I guess I had better sign off. I know you can't read this for it is a terrible mess.

> Yours as ever,
> Clayborne

B. By
If you care to answer my letter, you can use this envelope that I am sending.

How prosaic it seems for a love letter. Yet any Texan of the times would understand. The plain talk and commonplaces were merely the content, not the meaning: for a Texas suitor to send his ladylove passionate panegyrics to romance or odes to her various charms would brand him a blowhard and cast doubt upon his propriety if not his sanity. Then, too, Clayborne had read enough Shelley and Keats in college English to know that other men in love had made fools of themselves with flying words and fancy phrases. He understood full well the elegance and immortal artistry of the poet, but he did not trust it, not in such an important thing as love. There were even poets who did not trust poesy in love: had not Edmund Rostand penned these lines in *Cyrano de Bergerac?*

> Love hates that game of words!
> It is a crime to fence with life — I tell you,
> There comes one moment, once — and God help those
> Who pass that moment by! — when Beauty stands
> Looking into the soul with grave, sweet eyes
> That sicken at pretty words!

Many Texas women in that era understood the unvarnished love letters of their men and said, "He ain't no big love maker with words, never was. But he loves me all right, you can bet your boots on that." Clayborne's own offspring would one day look back on his love letters and marvel at their everyday language and at the signature on some of them, the simple initials WCP, but that is getting ahead of our story. The real meaning of his June 10, 1931, letter was the fact that he had written it: *there* was the love of his love letter — the time and effort and care that was its point. And at their mailbox alongside the dusty road by Duffau Creek, Oretta's parents could not help but notice that Clayborne Perry was paying a great deal of attention to their baby daughter.

Dude Flat was much as Clayborne remembered it from childhood. Grandpa Jim Perry's farmhouse still stood next to the best barn in Erath County, albeit the humble residence appeared to be sagging and fading with the years. The root cellar and smokehouse still protected the winter's rations and the windmill and concrete water tank continued their liquid labors. Behind the house among the liveoaks Jim Perry's little blacksmith shed and auto garage still housed their ordinary mechanical miracles.

Jim Perry himself still farmed his acreage although he was 69 years old and his wife Lou still did a woman's work despite her 71 years and Old Grandma Elizabeth Glasgow Perry went on being independent as a hog on ice, alternating between tolerant reserve and cantankerous volubility, mostly as a matter of privilege for having lived 93 years with no sign of slowing down.

"Well, hello there, stranger," said Jim Perry from the cowpen, his eyebrows arched in surprise. "Haven't seen you except in church for a month or more. Thought maybe we wasn't on visiting terms any more."

Clayborne got out of his brown Ford car and tried to look a little sheepish. "It's harvest, Grandpa. I've been off with the Fouts crew again. I understand we're going to come harvest grain for you this year."

"Yep," said the fond old man, beaming at his favorite grandson. "If'n you folks ever get here. Fouts said he'd be here this week, but he didn't show."

Clayborne leaned on the cowpen fence, smiling at his grandfather on the other side. "I know, Grandpa. We just finished the Duckworth place and the Bryants'. We'll prob'ly be here Tuesday."

"What's in the sack, boy?"

"I got some store-bought plums for Old Grandma."

"That was right thoughtful of you. Are they keepin' you too busy to read the paper?"

"Well, can't say as I've been keeping up real good."

"Oh, yes, I understand you're out sparkin' with that Partain kid, which one is it?"

"Oretta, sir."

"That's right. So you haven't seen about how President Hoover keeps saying 'prosperity is right around the corner?'"

"No, sir. But I think it's not right around any of our corners!"

"Just what I was thinkin'. And that's what I was gettin' at. You're going to be old enough to vote next year for president. Has your Pa turned you into a die-hard Republican? Or are you gonna vote Democrat?"

"I don't know Grandpa. Times are pretty rough, but I don't know what a new president could do about it. Papa always says we have higher cotton prices when a Republican's in office, but I keep hearing talk about six-cent cotton this year."

"Right you are, grandson. Right you are. Ain't a lick of truth in that business about Republicans bein' good for cotton prices. Now, you're for the little fellow, ain't yuh?"

"Well, sure, Grandpa. I'd just about have to be, wouldn't I? We're pretty much little fellows."

"Right again. We're the little folks. And Democrats is for the little folks. Don't know who they're goin' to pick for Democrat this election, but take it from your Grandpa, Clayborne. You vote Democrat and you vote for yourself, you hear?"

"I'll keep it in mind, Grandpa. Have you seen Old Grandma?"

"I think she's in the house with Ma. You go see. And don't be so scarce around here. I like seein' you in church and all, but it ain't the same as havin' you right here on the old place like when you was a little tyke."

"I'll get over as much as I can, Grandpa." He waved and walked from the cowpen to the little house where he had spent so many hours as a child. To the west he could see the rent house where his father had nearly died of pneumonia those twelve years ago. He kicked up memories in the dirt with every step to the farmhouse.

Lou Perry opened the screen door under the long front gallery and wiped her hands on her red-and-white checkered apron. "Thought I heard you out here palavering with Pa. How are you, Clayborne? Haven't seen you out here for a spell. And how's my Tommy?"

"I'm doing fine, Grandma. And Papa's gettin' along about as good as you could expect. He can still see a little in the daytime. Gets around all right. How are you doin?"

"Not too bad for an old woman."

"Aw, Grandma, you're gettin' more beautiful every day."

"Pshaw, youngster," she glowed. "You don't even know what you're sayin'."

"Sure I do, Grandma. Got me a girl of my own. I know pretty when I see it. Why, you're gettin' to be as pretty as Oretta."

"You must want somethin', carryin' on so, young man," she grinned. "And I bet it ain't me you want it from. That another sack of store plums?"

"Yep. Just need to talk to Old Grandma a little, that's all."

"Must be somethin' big goin' on if you need a confab with your Old Grandma."

He kept his peace.

"Well," said Lou Perry, still all smiles, "you'll find her down at the Branch spittin' on worms."

"Does she still do that to her bait when she fishes?"

"Yep."

"What's it for? She'd never tell me."

"She won't say. Like always. It's her secret, she says. Ask her when you see her. She's not far. Maybe half a mile. Can't get around any more like ten years ago when she was eighty-three."

He found Elizabeth Perry on the banks of Camp Branch pretending to fish. She sat on the gravel and the bunchgrass enjoying the sun and the silence and her own company.

"Hi, there, Old Grandma!" Clayborne called from a little knoll under the hackberry trees twenty yards distant, hoping not to alarm her.

"No need to holler, young 'un. I heard ye stompin' and a'thrashin' way back there."

"Can I talk to you, Old Grandma?"

"Might just as well. Ain't no fish bitin' today anyways."

He approached her earthy throne and picked a place halfway down the bank on a little limestone ledge where he sat looking up at her.

"Somethin's up," she said without overture. "You ain't come to chew the fat with me since you went off to college near three year ago. And hand me one of them plums in that sack."

He gave her the whole sack and then looked at his fingernails. "Yeah, Old Grandma, somethin's up."

"Well, out with it," she said, picking a sweet juicy plum from the brown paper bag. "I ain't like the rest of your kinfolk, never know what to say, never know when somethin's eatin' their young 'uns."

"That's why it's only you I can talk to, Old Grandma. I've got a problem."

"Are you about to run off and marry that Partain girl?" she demanded.

He flushed crimson. "Well, yes, that's the thing I want to do. You always seem to know what I'm thinkin'."

"What about it, then?"

"Well, getting married is a big step, and I . . ."

"You don't know what to expect. I know. Every young whippersnapper don't know what to expect. No way to tell, either. You just got to go bull your way through. Sometimes it works, sometimes it don't. Nothin' to say about it, though, except this: a woman ain't your property. And husbands what think otherwise is livin' in some dreamworld. My John always treated me with respect, treated me good, worked hard, didn't boss me around. And I always did my part with a free heart young 'un. Just remember that. You may be boss but don't act bossy, you hear?"

"Yes, Old Grandma. But I think I know how to act with Oretta. It's her folks I'm worried about."

"Her folks? What's that got to do with it?"

"Well, should I ask them?"

"To marry their daughter?" she said with contempt. "You ain't marryin' them, you're marryin' their daughter."

"Not so loud, Old Grandma. Nobody knows."

"Don't you worry about that. Nobody's gonna know. But stop and think about this asking business. Asking is for rich folks, young 'un. You ask, and her Pap has to pay for the wedding. The Partains may think they're better off than the Perrys — I seen 'em lookin' down their noses when we take cane over to their sorghum mill, not so much as you'd notice — but they only been in these parts a few years longer than the Perrys, haven't got rich, they don't have enough to pay for any wedding."

"I know they think we're poorer than them," said Clayborne. "They don't mean anything by it. It's just natural for people to feel that way about each other — at least a little. The Partains never *say* anything about it. But, Old Grandma, I've been going over to their place since I was six or seven years old, I've always kind of looked on them as family. I wonder if it's right to just go off without asking. And you know how all those Partains are with each other, takin' on so much, hugging and kissing each other all the time. They got tender feelings. Their feelings would prob'ly be hurt real bad."

"Oh, I know, child. But you keep this in mind. Think what they'd feel like if'n you married their girl-baby and then it didn't work out. It may hurt 'em to lose her, but think how it'd hurt 'em to take her back. You make sure you can keep her forever before you go askin' *anybody* about marryin', her or her folks. Marryin' is for life. Remember, until death do you part!"

He thought about that a long time. Then he said, "But Old Grandma, they're such tender-hearted people. I don't want to hurt them."

"Oh, I know just how you feel. My John thought that way about us Glasgows — we was all huggy and sweet-talkin' with each other. He worried if I could live with his kind, them bein' so sober and not touchy at all. I told him after I married him I was a Perry as much as anybody. Us Perrys, we're not like other folks, boy. You got to have the most serious mind to get ahead. You get all soft on each other and the work never gets done. And in this world, boy, you got to work — *hard*."

"I'm not afraid of hard work, Old Grandma."

"I know. And I'm right proud of you. I don't have no fear of you sloughing off. But you listen here: You're not through with your education yet, you hear? I've asked people that knows. There's more college you can get. And the more you get the better you'll do in this world. All I got to say is your work comes first. And gettin' an education is part of your work. You're our hope, Clayborne. There's greatness in you somewhere. Call it out. That's my advice. Hear me."

"But what about asking the Partains? I still don't know what to do. When I came and talked to you about going to Tarleton you told me I was doing the right thing. That's the kind of advice I'm looking for."

"Yep, I said you were right about going to college. And I told you for one reason, young 'un."

"What's that, Old Grandma?

"You already knew it was right."

"Good goshalmighty, Oretta," yelled Sis in the dark. "That's Clayborne knockin' at the door."

"Hush," warned Oretta from her bed. "You'll wake up Mama and Papa! I'll get up and light a lamp."

"Oretta," came the muffled sound of her father's gruff voice from his bedroom, "that Perry boy is gettin' plumb outrageous, comin' to call in the middle of the night. We've all gone to bed long ago and we don't want no more disturbance like this. You tell him to come earlier or not at all!"

Ila whispered tartly, "Sounds like your Clayborne already woke 'em up."

"Hush, Sis," Oretta replied softly, then out loud, "Yes, Papa." She slipped on her light calico dress. "He has to work late cutting grain with Mr. Fouts clear over by Rocky, you know, Papa. And then he has to drive through all these gates up Duffau Creek. It just takes time. He doesn't mean to be so late, Papa."

The father retorted, "And he should let us know what nights he's gonna be showin' up. It's the middle of the week, for cryin' out loud! Give us some warnin', at least!"

"Yes, Papa. I'll tell him."

"And don't the two of you stay up 'til all hours, you hear?" Willie Partain ordered.

"Yes, Papa. And we'll be real quiet, too."

She flitted from her bedroom across the old board floor and unlatched the front door. There he stood, limned in the light of her coal oil lamp, still dressed in his work clothes from harvest. "Oh, Clayborne," Oretta said, "I'm so glad you could come see me."

"I'm sorry it's so late, it's almost nine and it looks like everybody's gone to bed. I hope I'm not bothering your folks any."

"Oh, no, not at all," she said. "Come on in."

He followed her from the low gallery where old-fashioned vertical siding boards clasped the house snugly, and he walked into the front room, a place as familiar to him as his own, with its stone fireplace at the far end and its floral pattern wallpaper, its rocking chairs and folding bedstead and tall Victrola bedecked with flower-petal megaphone horn and the little library tables sitting around here and there with crocheted coverlets over their bare wood tops. Oretta placed the kerosene lamp on a table and they took seats in adjacent chairs — the room had no divan. They were silent a moment while the creaking house settled again.

"It was real hot today," said Clayborne as quietly as he could. "We were working the Dunlap place."

"Here, too. Why, it was hot enough to fry an egg on the rocks."

"It's still awful close in here. Want to go sit out yonder in my car? It's a lot cooler."

"Okay. Be careful openin' the screen door, you know how it squeaks so bad."

They tiptoed out of the house and into the cool Grand Prairie night. The fossilized light of remote adamantine stars bathed the moonless hills as they walked the crunchy grass to his car. Airglow silhouetted the still dark walnuts and pecans downslope by the creek. The shining prairie of heaven, those glorious orbits all out of reach overhead breathed deeply tonight, transparent now as though you could see through the iron galaxies, see beyond every radiant velocity to the edge of existence where space ravels out into primordial nothingness.

"What did you think of those Fourth of July fireworks in Hico last Saturday?" Clayborne asked as they stepped into the front seat of his Model A.

"That was somethin', really somethin'. Never saw anything like it."

"Are you all settled in here?"

"Yes, Clayborne. What is it?"

"You know I didn't really bring you out here because it was too hot in the house."

"I know."

He would not fence with life in a game of words.

"You know how I feel about you."

"I know."

His moment, his one moment, once, was at hand.

"I've been doing some pretty serious thinking. About the future. About what I want to do with my life."

He would not, God help him, let the moment pass him by.

"I'm going to ask you something, Oretta. It's an important question and you can take your time giving me your answer."

The moment was his. This was it. There was Beauty, looking into his soul with grave, sweet eyes.

"Oretta, will you marry me?"

The love beamed from her face like the endless night sky. She could not speak. A tear started down her cheek. "You know I love you," she said. "Give me some time. Let me think."

"And you know I love you. I'll give you all the time you want."

"You're so good, so patient with me." She hung her head down.

He was quiet for a moment. "Oretta, when you're reaching for your answer, there's something I'd like you to think about."

"What, Clayborne?"

"Just this: I don't have much, but I'll promise you one thing. I'll stick with you. I'll stick with you through thick and thin. As Old Grandma said, 'Marriage is for better or worse, 'til death do ye part.' She quotes it right out of the Good Book."

Four days thinking was enough. That Saturday she said yes.

What happens when the baby of the family wants to get married? Young people in love instinctively grasp how hard it is for parents to let go of their last nestling; they feel in their hearts that any suitor will be put off at best and most likely rejected out of hand if not shot. For the swain to be refused and then go ahead and marry the daughter is to defy parental authority and risk a permanent family breach. No young rural couple wanted that. So Clayborne and Oretta followed the rustic Texas tradition that had grown up to solve the problem of request and rebuff — and expensive weddings the father of the bride couldn't pay for: the couple didn't ask — they eloped.

"What are we going to do, Clayborne?" asked Oretta as they sat in the Model A in front of her house on a warm evening in the waning days of July.

"We have to think about a wedding date," Clayborne answered.

"No, I mean about Mama and Papa. You know they won't let me get married."

"Well, you're plenty old enough to make up your own mind. You're eighteen; you don't need permission in Texas at that age. Everybody has the same problem."

"Shouldn't we ask anyway?"

"Think what would happen. If we say anything to our folks, it'll just kick up a fuss. Look at how all your brothers and sisters did — Lanie ran off with Ethel; Erah and John eloped; Gradus just up and married Lete; and Maxie didn't ask before she married J. D. Your whole family has just gone and gotten married and then told their folks. And I'll bet your Mama and Papa did the same thing themselves. They're expectin' it anyway, you know that. This just makes it easier on everybody."

"I don't know. It makes me nervous."

"Well, it makes me nervous, too."

"Do you think it's right, Clayborne?"

"Marryin' you?"

"No, runnin' off without telling anybody first. Eloping."

"I've thought about it. I've thought about it real hard. All I know is it would be wrong if we *didn't* get married."

"Oh, Clayborne, sometimes you take my breath away. That's a sweet thing to say. It sure would be wrong to our feelings if we didn't get married." She thought about that. "I guess you're right, then. We better decide on a date. When do you think is best?"

"Well, it has to be after harvest is over, and harvest has been late this year. I think we'll be done this week. Could go as late as early August, but I don't think so. And it has to be enough before school starts in October so we can take a week of honeymoon."

"Honeymoon!" said Oretta. "That sounds so wonderful. Honeymoon, honeymoon. It just feels good when you say it. Where will we go . . . on our honeymoon?"

"I don't know. We won't have much money; we'll need all I get from harvest to live on. But we'll think of a place, maybe go visit some kinfolks for a few days."

"But what about your Papa," asked Oretta solicitously. "I mean now that he's blind. Shouldn't we go over and help him out instead of goin' on a honeymoon?"

"He wouldn't want us to do that. We can go over and help out later. We won't be able to make any cotton until September anyway. He can still see a little when it's bright. And Hoyt helps him out now."

"His eyes sure went fast."

"That doctor in Fort Worth said they would."

"Wasn't there anything he could do?"

"Nothing. They don't even know what's causing it. It just makes you feel so helpless. And Papa's such a good man."

"Oh, Clayborne, do we have the right to be so happy with each other when there's so much sadness?"

"Don't ask such a thing, Oretta. Of course we do. The Lord Himself said 'a man shall leave his father and mother, and cleave to his wife.' What we're doing is right. I know it. It's just right. We can't bring back Papa's sight. The Lord understands."

Oretta was silent a long time. Then she said with feeling, "You have a wisdom about you, Clayborne. You're a comfort."

"Don't get all moody, now. We're planning our wedding day. It's a happy time. We've got arrangements to make. Now what all needs to be done?"

"You're right. We got to be practical. One practical thing I been thinking about is what to get married in. Really, I'd like to make a new dress for the wedding, but I can't do it at home. I don't know what to do."

"We'll think of something. And we have to get a marriage license at least three days before the wedding. So the both of us will have to find a reason to go to Stephenville. You be thinking about that."

"And you ought to get a new suit, Clayborne, so you'll look nice."

"And we'll have to have a witness. Who can we get that won't spill the beans?"

"My, Clayborne, I can't think of anybody who wouldn't tell. Not anybody."

"We have to find somebody. We *will* find somebody. But we have plenty of time, three or four weeks, anyway. And we ought to think ahead farther than that, too, Oretta. We ought to think if we want to have any children . . ."

"Do you?"

"Well, we have four kids in our family and you have nine in yours, countin' Lanie and Erah and Gradus and Maxie even though they're off married. I think I'd like to have kids."

"I would, too. I like kids. But . . . how many do you think you'd like to have?"

"I don't know, a couple right off, I guess. You know. . . It would be nice to have a boy and a girl, like everybody wants one of each."

"Just two? I don't know, our big family was pretty happy."

"Well, I mean right off, the first few years. A starting teacher like me doesn't make much for a while, couldn't support more than a couple of kids at first. But then by the time the first two get in school, I think maybe I'd like to have a couple more. We could afford it by then. That's four in all."

"In my family Mama and Papa just had the kids and then worried about supporting them. But I think that sounds perfect, four in all. And I want to do a good job with them, Clayborne. Not baby them so much like I've been. Let them have some responsibility a little at a time, not just hold back and then all of a sudden when you grow up everything hits you at once, do you know what I mean?"

"I know what you mean."

They decided upon Saturday, August 22, 1931, as the big day. And the time went quickly. The Monday before, the details of their weeks of planning began to fall in place.

"Mama, I want to get me a permanent," said Oretta as she walked into the kitchen. "Look at this stringy hair."

"Oretta, permanents cost three dollars," said Margaret Partain patiently as she washed the dinner dishes. "Child, you don't know how hard times are getting. That's a lot of money."

"Oh, Mama, I haven't had me a permanent for a *whole* year, not since before school started in tenth grade." She pitched in drying dishes. "Please? I won't ask you again for a whole 'nother year. Please?"

"Well, I'm not going to pack you into Hico for any permanent. Here, put the skillet on the drain board."

"I don't want a permanent in Hico. Estel says the best beauty parlor around is the Hub Beauty Shop in Stephenville. That's where I want to go, and I'm sure Clayborne would be happy to drive me."

"He'd be happy to drive you anywheres, young 'un." The mother wiped her forehead with a wrist, keeping the soapy hand away from her eyes. "And I want to tell you something. Don't you let him get too close to you now, honey, you hear? He's a nice boy, but he could ruin you good if'n you let him. You know what I mean."

"Oh, now, there's nothin' like that Mama. He's proper strict Baptist like us, you know that. Can I have my permanent? Please Mama?"

"Well . . ."

"Please?"

"What do they want for a permanent at that fancy Stephenville shop of Estel's?"

"Three dollars, Mama, same as anywheres. Oh, come on, Mama. Please?"

"Oh, all right," her mother sighed, "but don't you get into the habit of askin' for expensive things like that, Ruby Oretta Partain. Money's short."

"Oh, thank you, Mama, thank you, thank you!" She hugged her mother and danced around her. "And I promise, I won't ask for expensive things any more. But can I go over to see Maxie this week?"

Her mother hugged her back then held her at arm's length. "What is this? Begging day? 'Mama can I have this, Mama can I do that!' Did your sister ask you over?"

"I told her I was comin' over when she came to see us last Sunday. You heard me tell her yourself. She's expecting me. And I want to show her my new permanent. And truly . . ." she spoke softly, "I miss her, Mama."

"Oh, don't carry on like that. She's been a married woman three years now, baby. You don't understand what that means. She don't have the time to fuss over you like she did before. J. D. wants her to fuss over him now. You'd just be in the way."

"Oh, no, Mama. J. D. likes me. Since his family lost their big poultry business and went to farming, I've helped a lot when I go visiting. I'll help her clean house and milk the cows and slop the hogs and everything. With me there she'll have plenty of time to fuss over ol' J. D."

"You could do the same around here."

"Mama! You know what I mean. I'll be back Saturday evening. It's just a week. I won't be in her way. And Clayborne can take me to her place in Carlton, too. Please, Mama, just this once."

"Oh, get out with you! There's no refusin'. You just make good and sure that your chores are all caught up with before you go off, because Sis is gonna be stuck doin' 'em while you're gone. Don't want to make it worse on her."

"Hoot said he'd help, too, Mama."

"You're 'way ahead of me, aren't you?"

"I'll see you Saturday evening, Mama," said Oretta as she threw the dishtowel on the drain board and dashed out of the kitchen. "I got to go tell Sis and Hoot. And I need to call Clayborne and ask him for a ride."

"That Clayborne Perry could start himself a bus company if you paid for all the haulin' around he does for you," called Margaret Partain out the door.

"Willie," she said quietly, "you heard. Somethin's up."

"Yep," the redheaded farmer answered over his newspaper at the kitchen table, "somethin's up."

"You don't think they'd just go off and do it without sayin' anything to us, do you?"

"I hope not. I like that Perry boy."

Willie Clayborne Perry and Ruby Oretta Partain, being first duly sworn, obtained their marriage license at the Erath County Court House, Stephenville, Texas, at 11:30 a.m. on Tuesday, August 18, 1931. Clayborne slipped the license into an envelope and hid it under the floor mat of his Model A Ford. Their secret was safe. Oretta then got her permanent at the Hub Beauty and Barber Shop down the street while Clayborne got himself a haircut. On the way out of Stephenville he took her for a quick spin around the campus of his old alma mater Tarleton. She was impressed. Then they were on their way to her sister's home some twenty-five miles south.

Carlton is a small town ten miles to the west and south of Hico in Hamilton County, Texas. Maxie Partain had married J. D. Center in 1928, and they had settled in Carlton within the past year to farm after the deepening depression destroyed his father's once-thriving poultry firm. Maxie Center greeted her sister Oretta with joy and said hello to Clayborne on the front porch of her little five-room farm house. Clayborne excused himself, saying he would return to give Oretta a ride home early Saturday morning. So far they had solved the problem of the marriage license. Now to the other details.

After breakfast Wednesday morning, Oretta said to Maxie, "You know, I think I'm goin' to make me a new outfit. I've gone a long time without any nice dress to wear. Would you take me into Hico and help me pick out some good material?"

"Why, honey, I'd be glad to," said Maxie in delight.

They fussed over the material through several stores in Hico, and ended up at G. M. Carlton's dry goods and clothing.

"All the yardage we've seen so far is just not what I'm looking for," said Oretta.

"Well, what is it that you want? I can't even picture it from what you've been saying all day. We better hurry up because I have to get back and fix supper."

"I want something nice, really nice."

"But what? Something real formal?"

"No, not like for a party."

"Frilly and lacy?"

"No, you know me, not that fancy. Something plain but real nice."

"Like you could wear to church?" Maxie blinked suddenly, realizing some of the things that one did in church.

"Yes, like you'd wear to church," said Oretta.

Maxie looked Oretta in the eye. Her kid sister was up to something and she thought she had it figured out. "I'll tell you what, Oretta. I think I know just what you have in mind. I see some navy blue silk crepe right over there. If we followed a basic pattern like I have at home and maybe put a little white collar around the neck, it'd look real good on you. Let's go look."

Oretta and Maxie had walked into Carlton's not half an hour after Clayborne left the store. He had been fitted for a new suit, bought a new dress shirt, a pair of shoes and a hat, all to be ready for pickup first thing Saturday morning.

Thursday and Friday Maxie and Oretta worked at the dinner table, improvising with a basic dress pattern as they had both been taught in home economics classes at Duffau school. After cutting out the basic panels and basting them together, Maxie fit the garment on Oretta, made the necessary adjustments and went to work at her foot-treadle sewing machine. After Friday supper, Maxie had constructed an elegantly simple dress for Oretta and stood back with her husband to admire her own handiwork.

"Now, doesn't that look just fine on her, J. D.?" asked Maxie.

"Sure does," said J. D. "You're a real wizard at that sewing machine, honey."

"Oh, it's perfect!" squealed Oretta, looking in the small hand mirror Maxie held for her. "It's just perfect! I want to wear it tomorrow morning when Clayborne comes to pick me up!"

Somehow that failed to surprise Maxie.

"And Maxie, you've just *got* to come back home for the weekend so you can be there when I show Mama and Papa. Will you let her come, J. D.? Please?"

"Why not?" he said. "I can come pick you up after work Sunday, Maxie. We can be back in time to milk the cows."

Maxie wondered for a moment why her baby sister would want her to come along on their elopement. Then she smiled. Of course. They'd need a witness.

Dawn. Saturday, August 22, 1931. The big day. Clayborne stood on the front porch of his parents' home dressed in his field hand's work clothes. He looked out over the land. The smell of destiny was in the air. The time line of his life was about to pivot on a hinge today and point off in a new direction forever. There was no turning back.

He got in his Model A, drove to Hico, went into the men's department of G. M. Carlton's and changed into his new suit. He had cashed a check for twenty-five dollars at Hico National Bank and put the folding money into his wallet. Now he slipped his loaded wallet into the breast pocket of his new suit. He was all set. He drove to the Center farm to pick up his bride. He knocked on the door. As expected, Oretta was stunning in a brand new dress. Not as expected, Maxie was also stunning in a not so new dress that somehow seemed too appropriate for the occasion. Had Oretta told her? He took no chances and pretended not to notice as he walked into the Centers' living room.

"Well, don't you look nice, Oretta. Going somewhere?"

"I sure am. Going to show Mama and Papa the new dress Maxie made me."

"Did you make that, Maxie?"

"Yessir, I sure did."

"Well, you're some seamstress. That's a real professional job you did there, looks better than store-bought."

"Thank you, sir. And you can give me a ride to the folks place along with Oretta, if you will. I'm goin' to go pay a visit to Mama and Papa for the weekend."

"Leavin' ol' J. D. to batch it for a couple of days, huh?"

"Oh, he's a big boy now. He can take care of himself."

"I expect so," smiled Clayborne. "Well, let's go get a move on."

The ten miles from Carlton to Hico went by rapidly in the Model A. The three sat in a row on the front seat, saying nothing. Clayborne slowed the car as they crossed the Bosque River bridge coming into Hico from the south. A few blocks up the graveled roadway Clayborne pulled the car to a halt across the street from the First Baptist church parsonage. Clayborne slid his vital envelope out from under the floor mat and without a word they all got out of the car, crossed the street, ambled under the big liveoak tree at streetside and then up the curved flagstone walk as if nothing was going on. They paused a moment to look at the neat white house. Its spacious front gallery stood supported by three substantial-looking square wooden columns sheltering a hanging porch swing. A bay-windowed office formed the left end of the gallery, its gable roof pointing to the street. The main portion of the L-shaped home lay comfortably on the flat city land, looking all warm and inviting. They walked up the three steps to the front door and knocked. Maxie didn't say a word.

A short cheerful lady answered the door and beamed, "Oh, Mr. Perry, and here's your party with you I see. Do come in. This is Reverend Thomas and I'm Mrs. Thomas."

The three stepped in and Clayborne did the introductions. "Reverend, Mrs. Thomas, this is Oretta Partain and her married sister Maxie Center."

"So pleased to meet all of you," said the tall distinguished looking minister. "I'm so glad that you selected our church for your ceremony. You brought the marriage license, of course?"

"Right here," he said, holding up the envelope.

"Excellent. Let's get the paperwork out of the way and then we'll attend to the ceremony."

It was like a dream. They stood in the front room of the parsonage, which was arranged like any town family's front room, with not-too-expensive stuffed chairs and a couch, a coffee table, and at the far end a china cabinet on the right and dinner table for six in the middle. At the table Clayborne and Oretta signed their marriage license in the principals' spaces, Mrs. Thomas and Maxie signed in the witness spaces, and Reverend L. P. Thomas signed in the big space at the bottom as officiating clergy. It all went by so fast.

Then Mrs. Thomas with familiar skill herded them to the center of the room, faced them in the proper direction, placed Clayborne and Oretta just so, and stood beside Maxie behind the young couple. Reverend Thomas stepped forward and began, "Dearly Beloved, we are gathered here. . ." It was happening. The minister performed the simple ceremony with dignity and grace, calling upon the couple to make those universal decisions and vows that all Christian couples have made for so many years. It was really happening. They repeated all those well-known words "forsaking all others" and "for better or for worse" and "until death do us part" and all the rest. It was really, truly happening. The small town minister did not ask for a ring: his simple ceremonies omitted that potential for embarrassment, for, like Clayborne, very few young men could afford the price of a plain gold band. "I now pronounce you man and wife." Clayborne kissed his bride. And then, swifter than pulsebeats, it was over. God had bound together. They were one flesh. Civil authorities recognized the contract. They were Mr. and Mrs. Perry. They were married.

When the tension snapped and everybody grinned and laughed, Maxie finally opened her mouth: "You know, I thought that's what you were up to."

After leaving Reverend Thomas two dollars for a job well done, Clayborne drove his wife and sister-in-law immediately to Wiseman's Photography Studio a few blocks away and had their wedding picture taken for close family. But the drive from Hico to the Partain place near Duffau turned into a minor ordeal of its own.

"Maxie, when we get home will you break the ice for us?" asked Oretta.

"You mean tell the folks? You didn't tell Mama? Or Papa?"

"Or Sis, or Hoot or Forris," Oretta said.

"My family doesn't know, either, Maxie," said Clayborne. "Nobody knows but you."

"Oh, boy," said Maxie.

"Don't just say 'Oh, boy,' Maxie," Oretta pleaded. "I'm scared of what Mama and Papa are gonna say."

Clayborne said, "To tell the truth, I'm a little nervous, too."

"They aren't gonna say a thing," smiled Maxie in irony. "I know. It's what they *don't* say that's gonna get you. You're gonna wish you'd told them ahead. You're gonna wish it as long as you live. Believe me."

"That's not much comfort."

When they came to the old farmhouse with its additions and tack-ons, they took a deep breath and jumped into their new life. Maxie walked in with Clayborne and Oretta, all of them realizing how peculiar it looked to be all dressed up on a Saturday afternoon. Willie and Margaret Partain had seen them coming and waited for them, standing in the middle of the living room. Ila slowly took a chair off to one side near the kitchen. Nobody said anything for a moment. Nobody needed to. Then Maxie stepped forward and ventured, "You know what these two kids just did, Mama and Papa? They went off and got married. Clayborne and Oretta just got married."

Willie Partain's face turned beet red, clashing with his coppery orange hair. His lips clamped tight in a thin white line. Margaret Partain's face withered into pain, her eyebrows gathered to a peak in the center of her forehead like a church steeple had been drawn there, hurt written on every line. They said nothing, but the screaming question "Why didn't you tell us?" boomed from their minds. Heartbreak oozed from their pores, the very air grew rigid and stifling with their heartbreak. Nobody said a word for a long time. Everybody just stood there wishing they were somewhere else.

From a corner Ila said, "I figured that's what you two were gonna do. I just figured."

More silence.

"Mama, Papa — Clayborne and me are goin' to go on our honeymoon." said Oretta. "I'll be in my room for a little while." She slipped out of the tableau. Maxie went with her.

Clayborne was left alone facing the stony cold parents of the bride. They didn't even seem like the people he had known for so many years. He felt less like part of their family than before he married their daughter. He was afraid this would happen. He tried desperately to think of something to say. Nothing came. They just stood and looked at each other. He broke out in a sweat.

"I think I better go check on Oretta," he said. As gingerly as he could he walked away from the Partains. He could feel their eyes boring through his back. When he got to Oretta's room he found the two sisters hugging and saying their goodbyes before the honeymoon. Clayborne said, "Excuse me, Maxie. Oretta, get your things together and let's go as soon as we can. I don't think your Papa is very happy about this."

They walked out of the Partain residence within minutes, offering a timid farewell and waving as they went out the door. When the two sat once more in the Model A, Oretta said, "Whew! Are we gonna find the same thing at your house?"

"I hope not. That was tough. I'm afraid we really hurt your folks, Oretta."

Two miles down the road they came to the driveway of Tom Perry and drove up to the white painted farmhouse. Once inside, Clayborne stood Oretta in the front room and called, "Mama, Papa, come on in the front room." He went to the kitchen to bring his father out by the arm — a gesture more than a need: Tom had adjusted quickly to his blindness and managed to get around with little difficulty. They were all in the front room, now, including Hoyt and Dorothy and Nadine.

"Papa, Mama, all you kids, Oretta and me have something to tell you."

"I bet I know," said Nadine.

"Let 'em tell themselves. Don't interrupt," said Hoyt.

"Oretta and me just got married."

They waited for the pall of doom to fall around them. Tom and Belle just stood there for a moment, the younger children watching silently for a cue.

Tom smiled a little smile that he seemed to have picked up in the last few weeks after going blind, a peaceful little smile people would remember years later. "I kind of figured you two were goin' to tie the knot," he said. "So I guess you went and did it."

Belle smiled and said, "I guess you did."

The two excited girls clamored around them, hugging Clayborne's legs and jumping up and down around Oretta. Clayborne told them, "We're goin' to go off on our honeymoon pretty quick, Mama, Papa."

"Where you going, son?" asked Tom.

"Oh, I don't know. I thought maybe over to Uncle Lem's for a few days at Miles. Then maybe up to see Auntie Leona in Breckenridge."

Belle said, "If you're goin' that far you might as well go on over to Fort Worth and see my brother Clyde and his family. We'll let 'em know you're coming.

"And we'll come back to help get the cotton in," said Clayborne.

"No need to do that," said Tom.

"Well, then," said Clayborne, "how about if we come over for some of Mama's good cooking?"

"There's always a place at the table."

And so began the married life of Clayborne and Oretta Perry.

Their honeymoon was as pleasant as their first parental confrontation had been tense. And the silent facedown they had with Willie and Margaret Partain demonstrates something important. It demonstrates a virtue of the taciturn and reticent Texas farmer that outsiders mistakenly think of as inarticulate dullness. It is nothing of the sort. The Partains, faced with a painful reality, did not give in to the pain but faced the reality and kept quiet. City folks would most likely have tried to handle the pain with words, hooting and hollering at each other, blathering in gibblegabble at great length, and all for nothing. To the Partains, the marriage was a fact. Complaining and botheration wouldn't change the facts, but it certainly would erase their dignity. And then there's the other problem: When you say something to a Texan, a Texan assumes you mean it. There's none of this "Oh, I'm sorry, I really didn't mean that." A Texan will accept your apology, but will long wonder why you said it if you didn't mean it. Generations of them grew up believing that hard words make hard feelings. The Partains knew that whatever they said, the memory would never die. Since talk couldn't undo what had been done, they said nothing. So the virtue of laconic Texas farmers is this: They can recognize when talk is futile, which is often, as in the case of drought-killed livestock, flooded roads and kids that show up one day and tell you they're married.

The couple's reception at the Perry farm illustrates the same point but in a different way. The words were spare but accepting. Oretta heard some months afterward from some friends at Prairie Springs Baptist Church that Belle had told them she just hadn't wanted Clayborne to get married. When these friends replied, "But Oretta is such a nice little girl," she said, "It's not who he married; I just didn't want him to get married at all, not yet." It wasn't particularly a stab-you-in-the-back sort of thing, but rather a recognition that saying anything directly to your new daughter-in-law was asking for the fur to fly. Belle Perry would not have considered saying anything to Oretta's face and never did. Tom Perry wouldn't have said it to *anyone's* face and never did — he might have thought it, but he wouldn't have said it. He just wasn't that way. Silence, golden silence, was first among the polite formalities of the rural Texan. Like the honorifics and mechanical formulas of city folk, silence injected a big dollop of lubrication into the moving parts of their society to keep the sand from clashing in the gears too much.

The honeymoon trip lasted a week and took them from Hico to Miles,

Texas, near San Angelo, where they stayed for three days with Uncle Lem Elam and his daughter Foncyne and his two boys J. C. and Charley. From there they went to Breckenridge where they stayed one night with Clayborne's Aunt Leona Collins and her family. Then they drove to Fort Worth where Clyde Blackburn and his family lived and stayed with them a night. The Blackburns had moved from the ancestral Dude Flat farm some years earlier — Clyde had worked in Hico in various retail positions for the Elkins brothers and now operated his own little community grocery store, something like a modern convenience store, on the southeast side of the big city.

It is true that outwardly this honeymoon trip contained nothing fancy, but for Clayborne and Oretta it was the most magical time in their young lives. To them, Tennyson had been right: Marriages are made in Heaven. To any cynics that may have been around, George Bernard Shaw had been right: Marriage is popular because it combines the maximum of temptation with the maximum of opportunity. To the world and time they went back home to, Ralph Waldo Emerson had been right: When a man meets his fitting mate society begins. On the way back from Fort Worth they stopped at Weatherford where Clayborne bought them a ninety-five-pound Black Giant watermelon for sixty cents. It was then he first noticed her habit of saving the heart of the melon for last, eating her slice from the seed line out to the rind and then finishing off the solid succulent core, something his little sisters Nadine and Dorothy would think looked so good they started doing it themselves. The newlyweds returned to Hico on the twenty-ninth of August with most of their twenty-five dollars still in hand.

Clayborne knew they would sooner or later have to live near Blackstump Valley School, but school was still a month and a half away and his father's cotton crop needed picking. He and Oretta drove into Hico on the first of September and looked for a place to rent. They found a little apartment in the home of Alvin and Annie Fewell, a nice place among the liveoaks on the northeast corner of the intersection where Duffau road came in from Tom's farm and met Second Street, the main drag through Hico. They had to share the single bathroom in the house with the Fewells, but the place was only five dollars a month; it was close to shopping in town and only two miles from the Perrys' cotton patch.

The Fewells had an air of congeniality about them, for Clayborne had known their daughter Christine since she graduated a year ahead of him from high school in Hico. Mr. Alvin Fewell had run a successful shoe repair and saddle shop for his Hico clientele for many years — competition from Fewell's was a good part of the reason Clayborne's Uncle Wiley Linch had moved his shoe shop to Stephenville. Christine, the Fewells' only child, lived at home and worked as assistant bookkeeper at Gleason's Milk Plant across from the Katy depot in Hico. She had attended Howard Payne College for a summer, Baylor for a year and North Texas State Teacher's College at Denton for nearly two years. Clayborne and Oretta occasionally took their meals with the Fewells which gave Christine and Clayborne the opportunity to hold interesting supper conversations on the subject of education. Mrs. Annie Fewell in her turn proved to be an accommodating landlady, providing all the young Perrys' furniture, all except for a cookstove — Clayborne went out and bought a coal oil fired iron stove at a local supply outlet. The new couple had a few dishes they'd purchased on their honeymoon, and enough bedlinens to make do. In short, they were all set up. They spent most of September and early October trekking daily to the Tom Perry farm to help get in the crops.

"Hey, Oretta," shouted twelve-year-old Nadine from across the next cotton row, "it's the white part that's supposed to go in the picking sack."

Dorothy tittered her seven-year-old's merriment and Hoyt chortled in a bullfrog voice as they worked along in the black dirt and blistering sun, homemade collecting bags dragging behind them.

"Are you pickin' on Oretta again, little sister?" called Clayborne from far ahead in the middle of the cotton patch.

"We're havin' a good time, Clayborne," pouted Nadine. "You leave us alone, you hear? Just because she's your wife don't mean we can't tease her. She's family now."

Hoyt yelled, "Aw, Clayborne, you know they look up to her like a big sister. A little joshin' won't hurt nothin'."

"It's right true I never was much good at pickin' cotton," said Oretta as she reached into her sack with gloved hands to pick out the stems and leaf trash she'd dropped into it. She peered out from under her bonnet and said to Nadine, "Seems like I get the white part — and the green part and the brown part and half the dirt in creation." Unlike the young Perry girls, Oretta worked all bundled up, gloves, poke bonnet, even a scarf around the neck. She always took care to cover up when she went picking in the fields. Tanned skin was not popular in those days and she was at pains to protect her fair complexion — aside from the fact that she burned easily.

"You're doin' just fine, honey," called Clayborne.

Dorothy stood in her straw hat trying to look imposing like her big brother and in the deepest soprano she could manage mocked, "You're doin' just fine, honey," then squeaked up a storm of giggles.

"Well," said Hoyt to his youngest sister, "she gets as much of the white part in the bag as you, Dorothy."

"That's not fair, Hoyt," Nadine complained. "Oretta's older than Dorothy."

"Oh, my Mama always told me I acted young for my age in school," sighed Oretta. "I guess I'm young for my age in the cotton patch, too."

"Dinnertime!" called Belle from the back porch of the farm house. She stood arms akimbo waiting for some reaction. When her charges were slow to answer, she yelled, "You better come get it 'afore I throw it to the hogs."

"Ya-hoo!" yelled Hoyt as he suddenly made tracks for the dinner table.

Oretta flipped the cotton sack's strap off her shoulder and joined Nadine on the walk to the house. "How come you folks never say anything to your Mama the first time she calls you to dinner?"

Dorothy piped up behind them, "That's easy, Oretta. Hoyt tells us to keep quiet 'cause he likes to hear Mama say she'll throw it to the hogs."

Clayborne came trotting up as they reached the back door. "How's it goin', Oretta?"

"I'm doin' fine. Just like a picnic."

"These girls not giving you too hard a time?"

"They're just havin' fun, Clayborne," she said, trailing into the kitchen behind Dorothy and Nadine. "Gives us somethin' to do while we pick."

"Oretta," said Belle, "you come sit over here in your usual place by Clayborne. Just sit you down."

Tom already sat at the head of the table and Hoyt was ready to dig in, as usual for a teenaged boy with a hollow leg. The rest took seats around the big noon table at accustomed places and the food began to flash from hand to hand. Oretta had by now in mid-October become accustomed to her father-in-law not returning thanks before meals but she could never fathom this family's speed of food intake.

Belle sat down last and joined in. "Clayborne," she asked, "aren't you set to start teachin' next week?"

"Yes, I am, Mama. That's what the meeting was about last week in Meridian."

"Well, are you going to find a place closer to school?"

"We've looked up and down, Mama. There's not a place to be had in Blackstump Valley. We'll just have to stay at the Fewells' in Hico 'til we find something."

"Rain's goin' to start here in another few weeks," said Tom. "You're goin' to have a time gettin' back and forth in that mud."

"I've thought about it, Papa."

"You and Oretta going to stay the night again, son?" asked Belle.

"I don't think so, Mama. I've got my school work to get together."

The meal went quickly, like a streak of lightning, Oretta thought. She watched the food vanish from everyone's plate. Hoyt, it seemed to her, had no more than sat down than he got up again and went back to work leaving an empty plate behind. The others took a little longer, but not much.

"Papa," said Clayborne as he finished his last biscuit, "have the cotton prices got any better yet?"

"Nope," Tom replied between bites of ham. "Still under six cents a pound. All the gins in Hico offering 5.66 cents a pound, Hoyt says. That's the worst I've ever heard of since we first came here."

Belle spoke up: "We're not going to get two hundred dollars for the whole crop this year. This depression is getting pretty bad, Clayborne."

"Law," said Clayborne, getting up to go back to work, "that's terrible. See you in the field, Oretta." He walked out and was gone.

Nadine said, "Mama, do you want me to help with the dishes today?"

"Not today, Nadine," she replied. "Best get that cotton in before the rains come."

Nadine was up and out the door.

Little Dorothy said, "Oretta's gonna be the last finished eating again."

"Leave her be, child. She just eats slow."

"See you in the cotton patch, Oretta," taunted Dorothy as she sprang away from the table and vanished into the outdoor sunlight like a pixie.

Oretta looked at her plate. She was barely started on her meal. Belle was now finished and began picking up the dirty dishes. Tom sat munching on his biscuit and sorghum. Everyone else was gone. At her parental home the whole family remained at table until the last was finished. The young married woman looked up woefully at Belle.

"Don't fret none, Oretta," Belle said. "It's cotton time. Ever'body's in a hurry and nobody stands much on ceremony 'til it's all done. You just go about your eating."

She felt out of place, but there was nothing for it. "Papa Perry," she said timidly.

"What is it, Oretta?"

"Can I help you out to the corn when I'm done?"

"Not today, thank you. When the sun's shining bright I can still see shapes pretty good." Tom still picked corn and shucked it and did many other chores even though he left too many bolls in the cotton to be a good picker any more. "It's just in the house or at night I can't see at all. Even in here I'm getting to where I can find my way around without bumpin' into things as long as nobody moves stuff around. I can see just fine today. Appreciate the offer, though. You're a sweet girl."

School had been in session a week when the first scant fall rains came. The roads got a little slippery, but nothing bad. This country didn't fool Clayborne: He knew it was only a hint of things to come. He redoubled his efforts to find a place nearby. One day in late October a well-known face appeared as he was locking up after school.

"Mr. Perry," said W. C. Fouts from the doorstep, "I agree that we have to do something about getting you a place close by. And I think we've found it. Come with me in my car."

They headed easterly from the schoolhouse in the soggy after-class overcast. The gravel country road looked deceptively solid, just waiting for a good downpour to begin its regular autumnal throes of transmogrification into a long gumbo puddle.

"This deep black dirt is great for farmin', Mr. Perry," said Fouts as he turned left at the intersection just past the Newman place, "but when it rains it's rotten for driving."

Half a mile north Fouts made a right turn into the narrow driveway of the Bowman place. Clayborne saw the familiar white farmhouse with its low roof dormer and brick fireplace chimney facing the road, and the big gabled open porch in the front facing the driveway on the south.

"Here?" asked Clayborne.

"Here," said Fouts.

"Seems to me I asked the Bowmans once about a month ago. They didn't have an extra room."

"They do now. You know Mr. Bowman works for Wick Simpson up the road for a dollar and a half a day and it's pretty tough supporting a wife and two kids on that. I think the idea of some extra rent money may have something to do with this."

The two men got out of Mr. Fouts' nice touring Model A and knocked on the door. Joe Bowman and his wife Mae both stood behind the opened door. "Come on in, we were waitin'."

Mae Bowman walked them across the living room and into the hallway where they faced a set of French doors opening into the dining room.

"Right here," she said, pointing to the dining room. "You can stay right here. We'll take the dinner table out and put it in the kitchen. We can put curtains on the French doors and you'll have a nice little apartment."

"What would you charge me a month for it?"

Mae Bowman looked across the room at her husband, nearly holding her breath. Would it be too much? Would the school principal turn them down? It was pretty high for a single room — two days' wages.

"Three dollars . . ." she trailed off.

"We'll move in tomorrow."

It was nice and it was little. With all their belongings crammed in — now they had four chairs and a round dinette table, a chest of drawers, Clayborne's trunk, Oretta's cedar chest, a bedstead and a coal oil cookstove — they could barely turn around. And of privacy, there was precious little. The French doors could be shut, all right, and the curtains did keep out prying eyes, but living within twenty feet of four other people was not what a young married couple really had in mind. It was what could be had, however, so they made the best of it. But Clayborne kept his eye out for something more to his liking.

The grip of depression tightened around Texas. Disastrous cotton prices in 1931 forced thousands of farmers off the land and into towns and cities where conditions were, if anything, worse. Ross Sterling of Houston sat in the governor's office now — he had defeated Ma Ferguson for the Democratic nomination in 1930, campaigning as a successful businessman who promised a businesslike administration — but he could do nothing to stem the onslaught of economic collapse. Not even President Hoover could do that. Business of all types withered away, farming, mineral production, the infant Texas heavy industry. The only businesslike action Sterling could take was to veto measure after measure after measure passed by the legislature. He had to do it because the state treasury was empty — there was no revenue and no hope of raising any revenue. In most of the state, taxes simply became uncollectible.

Clayborne was lucky. The farmers of Blackstump Valley may have been poor but they knew how to live poor. Their inner values still embraced education and despite slumping farm prices they paid their taxes. People like Wick Simpson up at the foot of the mountains held a lot of land and ran over a hundred head of cattle and had two mule teams to run two plows — that's why he could afford to give work to Joe Bowman. His grain and cotton and livestock didn't bring as much as usual, but he was a prudent man who had known hard times would come again one day and he was ready. He and his neighbors kept money in the school district coffers. So Clayborne had his salary of a hundred fifteen dollars a month, and only about twenty-five dollars in expenses. While most around him could not make ends meet, he actually managed to save most of what he made, stashing it away for more education down the line — and for a family. And he wouldn't mind spending a little extra if he could find a place for two, just him and Oretta.

"It's been right here in front of us all along," said Clayborne one late November day as they drove into Iredell for groceries.

"This old shack?" said Oretta, looking in alarm at the T-shaped farmhouse off the road through the willow brush. "Why, it doesn't look like anybody's lived in it for years."

"Nobody has."

"Well, what in tarnation are you thinkin' about, Clayborne?"

"Look close," he said, slowing to a stop. "The roof looks sound, there's no boards missing in the walls. I came over the other day and went all through it. It's nothing fancy, but we could live in it."

"Law, Clayborne, that tumbledown old thing?" Oretta said. "Why nobody lives on this stretch of road. We wouldn't have any neighbors."

"Sure we would. Look right up there east of the road. That's the Smith place. And Mrs. Morgan lives right up the road toward the school. It would be a place of our own."

"You mean a place of the landlord's."

"You know what I mean. We would have the place to ourselves."

"Well . . ."

"It is absolutely the only place in Blackstump Valley where we can live by ourselves. This is it. It's this or the Bowmans' dining room."

"Could we fix it up?"

"Of course. We could really set up housekeeping. Live like normal people."

"Is it for rent?"

"I don't know. Ol' Tom Laswell owns it. We can stop off at his place while we're in Iredell and ask him. If you're interested, that is."

"Oh, maybe I'm interested. But what about your teaching job? With things getting so bad is it going to last?"

"It'll last as long as there's schools anywhere. And I don't see any of them closing down. The worst that could happen is people wouldn't pay all their taxes and we'd have to take a ten percent discount on my vouchers at the bank. That means we'd be making about a hundred dollars a month instead of a hundred fifteen. We could do just fine on a hundred a month. What do you think?"

She looked wistfully at the ramshackle building. How forlorn and dogeared it looked. But they could be on their own here, live by themselves. By themselves.

"I'm interested."

-14-

BLACKSTUMP VALLEY DAYS

HE land had not really changed much since the Comanche used it. Oh, yes, houses stuck up in Blackstump Valley now, and shallow roads gouged into the flats, and cultivated fields and fences patched its altered surface. But the little wood houses stood aloof from each other, a quarter-mile between the closest, half a mile between most, looking like tree clumps with slab sides more than anything. And the roads merely scratched the soil; all they did was hold down the worst of the weeds for a while, and they turned to mineral soup in the rain. And in the pastures heavy stocks of native plants remained, the bunchgrasses — little bluestem and some big bluestem — and the gramas. Some of the old original buffalograss even lingered on, never very thick in these parts, which the old-timers, third and fourth generation Texans, called "mesquite-grass."

It is true that the plow had begun to show signs of becoming its own gravedigger, not in the big, dramatic way of creating gullies that washed the rock ribs of the land clean and sterile like the farmers had done in the Hill Country down in Hays County and Blanco County, nor in the way of reaping the dustbowl whirlwind now festering farther north in Oklahoma. The Grand Prairie soil never did play out, but remained fertile right up to the day all the farmers died and their children left for town or became ranchers. If there was any money in it, you could still farm the old places today. Simple biology was the problem here, the plain fact of ecological succession. When you disturb a grassland ecosystem that has figured out how to survive the droughts and floods, the wildfires and insects, the diseases and nematodes, the mice and the thousand other pests grass is heir to, you usually get more changes than you bargained for. The bare soil will favor pioneer species, and they will prepare the way for transition species, and they will give out when the subclimax species come, and sooner or later the climax population will arrive, able to reproduce itself indefinitely against all invaders. The first farmers in the Grand Prairie bargained for fertile soil under the grass and they got it. They took the best care of it they knew how. They moved their cotton patches around and let grass cover them in winter and spring and they put out grassfires when they could.

What they didn't realize was that putting out grassfires eliminated the only control nature had devised to keep the pernicious brush in check, and the only reason this place was a grassy prairie and not a scrubby shrub forest was the eternal seasonal fire. But the farmers thought they were being prudent. They had already started putting out grassfires when a German biologist named Ernst Haeckel coined the term "ecology" in 1866 to mean the study of the relationship of organisms to their environment. The Texas Grand Prairie had not read Haeckel either, but its plants followed the natural laws he had discovered. The tender little mesquite trees, the vulnerable shoots of juniper cedar, the soft stems of Spanish oak, these and other brush invaders no longer died in the conflagrations after lightning storms. Slowly they poked above the grasses, greedily eating the sunlight, voraciously drinking the soil water, right there on the best land. The grasses around their swelling trunks began to die because they were weaker and their bodyguard the fire had been put out of work by conscientious farmers who were about to get an unpleasant lesson in the science of ecology, the fact that grass and fire are inseparable, that grasses in nature survive only in a fire ecology. The newly thriving brush grew in clumps at first, then stretched out tentacles of thorny shinnery — brush as high as the shins of a man on horseback — and a few decades later matured into little woodlots of mesquite and juniper cedar and other trees nobody had seen much of before. Later, even the hackberry and postoak expanded from their original boundaries. The republic of grass was about to be swallowed up by the empire of brush.

Even so, the farmers hadn't been very efficient firemen — they would become so — and the process was yet hardly visible in late September, 1932. The red cedars still clutched the crumbling slopes of Chalk Mountain and the juniper cedars still stuck to the roadsides down in the valley. An old Comanche horse warrior of the Penateka or the Quahadis, visitors from the Llano Estacada who sometimes wintered here two centuries ago, if he could still look out on this land of quiet beauty, would recognize all the old landmarks. And in the little schoolhouses called Blackstump Valley and Camp Branch and Garden and Flag Branch there were children growing up with cars and telephone poles and towns and strict rules around them who would have preferred the day of the Comanche. They felt somehow cheated in being born too late to see the wild Texas they read about in school. They yearned to be primitives, to live in the wilderness of yore. They would walk the prairie on summer days and imagine the wilderness back, imagine the scattered houses gone, imagine the curls of smoke on the mesa mountain to be Indian encampments. They liked plowing better than school and they liked hunting better than plowing. They were the first generation of Texans who would find enough civilization around them to want to escape it. They would never resolve the problem of how to live according to the rules of a wilderness that no longer existed, of how to be a primitive in a staid and steady little Texas town on the Grand Prairie. They hid their emotions and stayed inarticulate about it, but they were feeling a theme that would grow as they grew, would one day influence the environmental shape of America. And while they were growing up, Principal W. C. Perry was doing everything he could to help his students cope with the uncertain future, and everything he could to help his wife cope with the uncertainties of expecting their first child.

"Why you surely have fixed this place up, Oretta," said Belle as she took a seat in the front room's only rocking chair.

"Well, we've been here — what — nine months now, Mama Perry," said Oretta. "You'd think we'd have done a little fixing up by now."

"This is fixed up?" asked Hoyt. "Some of those front gallery boards look like you could step right through 'em."

"Mama means compared to when they first moved in," said Nadine huffily.

It was an after-church Sunday dinner at Principal Perry's humble home with his family in attendance. Tom, almost totally blind by now, sat in a straight-backed chair over by the front window and door. He liked to sit where he could see the patches of light in his gathering darkness.

Nadine strolled around the room looking the place over — even though it was at least her fifth visit — while little Dorothy trotted worshipfully in Oretta's tracks, gazing up at the big sister-in-law she idolized and wondering at her bulging midriff that spelled maternity sometime in the next month or so.

"We didn't do a lot of fixing, Mama Perry," said Oretta. "Clayborne went and got some brown building paper for the walls, is all. Must have been back before summer came. I don't think you've been here since we did that."

"No, daughter, we haven't," said Belle.

"You remember from before how it was all just open boards and rafters when we moved in. Well, we just tacked the building paper up like wallboard, up all the walls and the ceiling and it looks just fine. Maybe not too fancy, but it's better than it was."

"Well I think it looks right homey," said Belle.

Clayborne stepped in from the front porch with an armload of firewood for the heater. "You like the way we fixed it up, Mama?"

"I was just telling Oretta, Clayborne. It looks so much better with the paper over the rafters and such."

Hoyt said, "It's not cold enough for a fire, Clayborne."

"Well, it's been cooling off some in the evenings the last day or two. Just in case Mama or Papa get to feeling cool."

"You're a right thoughtful son, Clayborne," said Tom.

"Oh, speakin' of thoughtful, Papa Perry," said Oretta. "Do you know what this son of yours did here just a few weeks ago?"

"I think I'm about to hear."

"He was so worried about Charlene Mingus getting enrolled in college he drove her and her folks all the way over to Tarleton in Stephenville and showed 'em how to do it himself."

"Did you do that?" asked Belle.

"I was just doin' my job, Mama," said Clayborne as he laid out the firewood in a box by the stove. "Makin' sure my kids don't fall by the wayside. You remember how hard it was for me. When you're a country kid at college, it can get pretty confusing. And there's nobody at Tarleton to tell you what courses you need."

Hoyt said, "Did you pay for the gas, too?"

"Well, it's only twelve cents a gallon, you know."

Tom spoke up, "Gas isn't the only thing that's low, is it, Mama? We heard that cotton this year is down to a nickel, even worse than last year. Just hope that Roosevelt fellow doesn't get elected president come November. He sounds just like them socialists up in Oklahoma used to."

"Times are hard, son, that's the gospel truth," said Belle. "You can't imagine it. Why, this depression is getting so bad they're bringing in workers on the road over by the place and paying them a dollar a day just to keep 'em from starving."

"Who's doing that, Mama?" asked Clayborne.

"I don't know. I think it's the state or the county."

"It's the state, I'm pretty sure," said Tom.

"But, son, thank the Lord you're a teacher," said Belle. "Even the men who can bring their own wagons and teams are only getting a dollar and a half for a day's work hauling gravel and fixing the roads."

"It's pretty rough, son," said Tom. "Are you folks gettin' along?"

"We're doing fine, Papa. It only costs us about fifteen dollars a month to live here, groceries and all. We have the cow you gave us for milk, we have the garden and the chickens, and you and the Partains help from your gardens. Then we'll butcher a hog in a couple of months. We're doin' well enough I even got Oretta a wedding ring when we moved in here last January."

Dorothy said, "I remember *that*. It's real gold!"

"Yep," said Clayborne proudly. "Got it in Hico at Conner's Drug Store."

"That was about the time you went down to Blair's and traded in your Model A for that Chevy coupe with the rumble seat, wasn't it?" said Hoyt.

"I can tell you that's when it was, son," said Tom. "In the middle of those dark January days. Clayborne, how do you like that fancy maroon red speedster of yours by now?"

"Can you see the color, Papa?"

"Couldn't back when you got it in all that overcast. Can in the bright sun. I can make it out real good."

"Well, it's a fine car. It's easy to drive. Oretta likes it, anyway."

"How are you gettin' along with her folks by now?"

"All settled down. No hard feelings. I was a little worried about that at first, to tell you the truth. But things are fine. They'd expected it. We go over to see 'em just about as much as we see you. And Oretta just drives over to see her Mama by herself whenever she's of a mind to. She's got the car near as much as I do. Except this last month because of her condition. It's gettin' a little crowded for her behind the steering wheel."

Tom said, "But it's mostly for drivin' you to school, isn't it? To make a living?"

"Oh, Papa," said Nadine, "let's talk about their house. I don't want to hear all that makin' a living talk. Oretta, you even got curtains, I see."

"That we do. But we almost didn't," said Oretta.

"Why not?"

"You tell her, Clayborne. I've got to go get dinner ready." Eight-year-old Dorothy tagged behind her into the kitchen and Belle silently joined them.

Clayborne began, "Well, when we first moved in here, we were just goin' to pay Mr. Laswell rent, you know five dollars a month. Then he came over one day and said to me, 'Mr. Perry, you know I have seventy-five head of cattle running on the place here. I need somebody to feed my cows. I got a lot of hay up here in the field and I need somebody to throw about twenty-five bundles of hay to 'em every other day. Would you do that for the rent?' I told him, 'Why, sure, I'll do that.' So we got the rent for free.

"Well, his livestock just ran loose on the place here. They started comin' right up to the house. We don't have any screens on the doors or windows, and the curtains just blew outside every time a little wind came up. I got home from school one day and there was Oretta, about to have a conniption fit. Those curtains must have looked real good hangin' out the windows like that, because the cows'd just started chewin' the ends right off of 'em. She was yellin' her head off and chasin' 'em with a broom. I finally had to put up a fence around the garden and the house here."

Nadine giggled. "The cows almost ate up your curtains?"

Oretta called from the kitchen, "You wouldn't have laughed if you'd had to chase 'em. Clayborne, can you go down and get some more water?"

"I'll go," volunteered Hoyt.

"Here's the bucket," said Oretta, pushing the zinc container through the kitchen doorway into his hands. "You know where the spring is in the branch, Hoyt?"

"Yeah, down the hill and where that fifty-gallon wooden barrel's stuck in the water around the spring, right?"

"That's right. A couple of buckets, please."

Hoyt started out for the spring where Oretta had dipped so many buckets of water and Clayborne sat down next to his father. "Papa, Hoyt tells me you were out plowing before the crops were laid by. Can you see well enough to plow?"

"Not by myself I couldn't, son. Hoyt gets me started by a fence or somethin' straight that the mules can guide on. I give a 'Giddup' and get 'em goin'. I can keep 'em to a straight line by feel. When they stop and won't answer to a slap of the lines I know I've reached a fence. I just wait for Hoyt to come out and get me started back on the next row and keep on that way."

"Isn't that dangerous, Papa? What would happen if you fell off or something happened?"

"Ol' Sam and Rhody and Sergeant are gentle mules. Never kick or bite or step on you. Haven't had any trouble yet. And it beats sitting around doing nothing. This way I can keep farming a little."

Clayborne told his father, "That's real gumption, workin' when you can hardly see a thing."

"You got to work hard to get ahead, son. You know how us Perrys are. Work up to the day we keel over."

Belle said from the kitchen, "The Blackburns have been that way too, Tom. Even Papa kept up a little before he passed away, God rest him."

"That was a right pitiful thing, Belle," said Tom. "When your Ma died, it took the spirit plumb out of him. He tried so hard to keep interested in life, but it didn't mean a thing to him without her. You could just see he was pinin' away. It wasn't no surprise when he took sick in March and died 'afore April was a week out. Poor Charley Blackburn. Don't you go dyin' on me, now, Belle, you hear?"

"That'll be the day, Tom Perry. I'm goin' to live to be a hundred like Old Grandma Perry."

Hoyt marched in with the first of his buckets full of water.

Clayborne said, "It's too bad ol' Ferman Collins didn't live to be a hundred. What's Auntie Leona doin' since he passed on, Mama?"

"How'd we get on this subject?" whispered Hoyt, handing his burden over to the woman of the kitchen.

Oretta whispered back, "They were recollecting your Grandpa Charley."

Belle went on, "Leona's still living up in Breckenridge, Clayborne, takin' in work as a seamstress. Last penny postcard we got from her she said she's startin' to do custom draperies and painting designs on china and suchlike. Now that was the pitiful thing, her John Ferman Collins just dyin' like that in the prime of life, not even forty years old yet."

"That pneumonia carries away so many, Belle," said Tom. "It near took me away those years ago."

"Lordy, ain't it the truth," Belle said. "And John Ferman was doin' so well, the head salesman at that Ford place. My sisters have all just suffered so terrible. Such dyin'."

Hoyt slunk out of the gloomy talk to retrieve more water.

"You're healthy, aren't you, son?" asked Tom.

"Sure, Papa. Don't worry about me. All I have to worry about is outlivin' this depression. Wages are gettin' pretty low. I worked harvest this summer again and now I'm doing some fall plowing for Mr. Fouts, breakin' stubble and sowing grain for seventy-five cents a day. It's a long day, too. Go to work with the car lights on and go home with the car lights on. But I'll be gettin' twice that much pickin' cotton for some of these folks around here after I've helped get your crop in, Papa. But things are tight."

"Oh, I'm afraid they're goin' to get tighter, too. Did you see Ma Ferguson is running for governor again?"

"Oh, yes, sir. I sure did. It's just like you said back when I was in Tarleton. When people get tired of a serious-minded governor, Ma Ferguson will be back. I remember you sayin' that."

"Well, this Ross Sterling hasn't done a whole lot for the state," said Tom. "But Ma Ferguson is still against prohibition." To Tom and Belle and most of the farm folk of the Grand Prairie this was not merely a political issue but also a matter of the utmost religious gravity. This place was a religious place, a hellfire fundamentalist revivalist place that brooked no quarrel with scripture. There were no dominoes in most of its homes and Tom Perry would never think of allowing a deck of playing cards in his house. "They're the tools of the devil," he would say. And the Devil was not a mere figure of speech to these devout Texans, but a living incarnate unspeakable evil that walked among them as surely as the drought came and night fell. Dancing, of course, was forbidden. And drinking was an abomination not to be tolerated under any circumstances, none. Local farmers would often be heard to say, "The doors of a saloon are a passage straight to hell." Hard liquor was anathema, wine a scourge, even beer with its four percent alcohol could not be countenanced: one farmer from down Hill Country way used to say, "Sneaking a beer past Jesus is like trying to sneak daylight past a rooster." Ma Ferguson may have been a political joke to many Texans but not to these.

Tom said, "There's talk it's going to be repealed next year, even. First thing you know, things'll be a lot worse."

"Prohibition?" asked Clayborne.

"Yep, the wets are making a big push for bringing back liquor."

"Law, can you believe it?" sighed Clayborne.

"But you ought to hear what Ma Ferguson is sayin' on the radio. I mean besides bein' against prohibition. She really pokes at Sterling for being a businessman, says, 'Two years ago you got the best governor money could buy, and this year you can get the best governor patriotism can give you.' Ain't that a laugh after Pa Ferguson took all that money from those beer fellows back in 1917?"

"Well, that's not all, Papa," said Clayborne. "I heard Pa Ferguson says when Ma is governor, he'll be right there pickin' up the chips and bringing in the water for Mama. That's just what he said."

Hoyt walked in and said, "Well, here's some water for Mama. But if it's for Ma Ferguson I'll go throw it back in the branch."

A glorious day, this Thursday. Clayborne looked out across the murmuring September flats of the Fouts place and wiped the sweat from his forehead. The white of shattered limestone fragments, always there in the freshly turned furrows, smeared in the heat waves today into a solid body, like a big clean bedsheet spread over the dark soil, hiding the secret truth of the earth, its invisible black fertility and living nitrogen depth. Only a few mesquites and liveoaks draped their rounded tops over the grass in the swales nearby. Clayborne remembered his long-ago first days behind a rumbling, roiling plow walking with old Pet now dead these two years and the whining insects, the days as a nine-year-old when he entered his novitiate to the black dirt and gave his first labor power to the land. Perhaps it wasn't such a long time ago, thirteen years. And so many of those days had been as shining and pure and incorruptible as this.

He'd spent another day plowing today, and he'd mulled over last weekend's pleasant dinner with his folks, happy that his father had not lost heart with his loss of sight and beginning to be a little apprehensive about next month's end of expectancy — the doctor had told him Oretta was due the last week in October. Fouts' four big mules, unhitched from the tandem plow and standing patiently in front of him, had done a day's work and now it was time to head back for the barn and put on the nosebag.

Instead of walking beside the animals for that mile from the newly plowed field to the house, Clayborne had developed the habit of riding bareback atop the left mule, pulling all the lines up in one hand and driving them just like you'd drive four mules to a plow. He mounted the haw mule this day and rode along the rutted cow path bordering the field the short distance to the outer gate. Halting the mules and jumping down to open the gate, he felt how solid his muscles were, as perfect and pristine as ever, and he reveled in his agility. He rejoiced in his own works, for that was his portion. At his signal, the big lumbering animals walked through the gate and he shut it behind them, twisting the loop of wire over the top of the stick that served as a gatepost. He was back on the haw mule, working the lines, sorting them to make sure they weren't mixed up. The leather was not so worn and smooth up here close to the halters and it felt stiff in his hardened hands.

He never knew exactly what happened. It was probably yellow jackets or maybe a rattlesnake. He had only ridden maybe a hundred yards past the outer gate when something spooked the mules good so they ran away kicking and bucking and screaming like the hounds of hell were after them while Clayborne snatched at the traces trying to get them back under control but the long flexible leather lines got away from him in the wind and tangled around one of his feet before the inside mules crowded leftward when suddenly something grabbed him by the seat of the pants and flung him upward and then hard into the gravel road so he saw only pieces of sky and tasted bitter clay dust all the time they dragged him along by the foot banging the back of his head on the merciless white limestone rocks time after time and tearing the back out of his shirt and plowing his flesh but then he saw only the inside of his eyelids and that one-dimensional space that is unconsciousness.

Later, something in him awoke. It was not the ordinary mind that writes grocery lists and sings hymns in church. It was perhaps that primitive and ancient mind which awakens when deep pain comes, intent only on survival, the tough mind that lifts impossibly heavy objects from loved ones during disasters or pulls its traumatized and broken body from burning buildings to safety. Whatever it was, it awoke in the road and looked around and stood up with the shreds of a shirt hanging from a back gouged with gravel and clotted with clay and blood. This rugged mind somehow realized that the mules had to be gotten back together. A dispassionate, totally objective observer would simply have seen Clayborne Perry walk in among the grazing mules, approach each in turn and starting with the halter, untangle and straighten out all the traces, lay them out behind each mule, gather them together in the proper order and command the wary animals to go. This observer would have seen the young man walk these mules nearly a mile to the inner gate by the Fouts home by the banks of Rocky Creek. The observer would have seen him stand there for fifteen minutes. The basic indomitable mind that had surfaced had by then submerged. Whatever had happened, it seemed like a miracle.

"Will, bring me that box of recipes in here from the front room," called Ethel Fouts from the kitchen.

"Sure thing," answered her husband.

He came out of the little cubbyhole where he did his books into the front room and looked around for his wife's recipe box. The four mules standing out by the gate caught his eye. "Oh, Ethel, Clayborne's finally got back from plowing. It's so late maybe you better put another plate on the table."

"No, Will, you know Oretta's gonna have supper waiting for him."

"Why doesn't he open the gate?"

"What you say, Will?" Ethel Fouts came into the front room to gaze out the window.

"Look, Clayborne's just standing there. He's not opening the gate. Why doesn't he bring the mules in and unharness them?"

"Will," said Ethel, a sudden chill in her voice. "Something's wrong. He's not carrying himself right. Look how he stands. It's not like him. He's usually got his shoulders back and his head up. We better go see."

They ran down the gravel driveway to the gate and unlatched the big swinging barrier. Ethel Fouts ran past the mules and looked into Clayborne's eyes. "Clayborne!" she shouted involuntarily, not recognizing the person staring out of those eyes. He started, and shuffled back and forth a little, almost like a drunk person.

Will Fouts grabbed him by the shoulder. "His shirt's all torn. Look at his back, Mama. He's all bloody."

"Clayborne," said Ethel Fouts, drilling the sound into his head, "Clayborne, what's happened?"

He blinked, looking at his two friends blankly as if he did not recognize them. "I got hurt," he said. "The mules drug me. The mules. The mules drug me."

"Take the mules and unharness them, Will," commanded Ethel. "I'm going to take him to the house and clean up his back and put one of your shirts on him. I'll call Bill Newman to help you drive him home. Something's wrong with him."

The sun hung just above the horizon when Will Fouts and Bill Newman brought Clayborne home. Oretta had wondered why her husband was so late today and when she saw two familiar community members driving the Perrys' sporty Chevrolet coupe up the driveway with Clayborne between them in the front seat, she froze with fear. She fleetingly worried that whatever was about to happen might trigger her labor, might bring on childbirth before her time.

Mr. Fouts stopped the car and got out. "Miz Perry," he called from the driveway, "your husband has been injured. Nothing broken that we can tell, but he's kind of knocked out of his senses."

Bill Newman helped the young man out of his own car and stood him up. Clayborne walked now between the two sturdy farmers, weaving unsteadily as if looking at a rubber world. "The mules drug me. It was the mules. I got hurt. The mules drug me."

"Bring him in," said Oretta, stern-faced and over her first fright. They sat him in a chair in the front room and listened to him trying to tell what had happened.

"The mules. They drug me. I got hurt." He seemed eager to explain what had happened to him, but it was like someone talking in their sleep.

"When did it happen?" Oretta asked.

"Maybe an hour ago," said Fouts. "We saw him just standing at the gate. The best we can make out, something scared the mules and they ran away and drug him in the dirt. They must have scattered, but somehow he got all the mules back together and brought 'em home."

"Has he been going' on like this since it happened?"

"Repeatin' himself and all?" said Fouts. "That's all we've heard from him."

Bill Newman said, "It's like my uncle Hugh. He got thrown by a horse once, talked a lot of nonsense for a whole day. Just kept sayin' the same thing over and over like a stuck record on the Victrola."

"Should he see a doctor?" asked Oretta.

"I should say so," said Fouts. "Can you drive him. . ." Will Fouts stopped in mid-sentence, noting her bulking abdomen, discreetly avoiding a stare. "No, I guess not," he concluded. "Bill and me will take him. Who do you folks see?"

"Dr. Curry. In Hico."

They sat next to their friend in the office of Dr. Richard Curry in Hico. He finished up an extensive examination, holding a pencil before the dazed man's eyes.

"How many pencils do you see, Mr. Perry?"

"One. The mules drug me."

"How many fingers am I holding up?"

"Two."

"Now how many?"

"One. It was the mules. I got hurt."

"Now how many?"

"Three."

"Good," said the doctor, turning to Fouts and Newman. "Well, he's had himself a right good blow to the head, but I don't think we have too bad a problem here. He's probably got a slight concussion, but it doesn't look serious. I'll give him a shot of morphine. He's goin' to have one hell of a headache when he really comes to. And he'll be a little disoriented for a day or two. Tell Miz Perry to keep him at home until he feels well enough to work. Shouldn't be more than a week or so. Does he have a telephone?"

"No," said Fouts.

"Either of you?"

"I do," said Fouts.

"Does he have a car?"

"Yep. We drove him here in it," said Newman.

"Well, you tell Miz Perry if he starts to sweat or has any convulsions to get to your place quick and call me right now, you hear? Oh, wait a minute. She's about due to have that baby, isn't she?"

"She can't drive these days, doc," said Fouts.

Bill Newman said, "We'll look in on him. Don't worry."

"Well, you can take him home now."

He slept until noon the next day. When he awoke he was making sense again. "Oh, law!" he said to the ceiling. "My head! What happened?"

"You got thrown and drug by the mules, Clayborne," said Oretta, sitting by the bed. "You prob'ly got yourself a concussion of the brain. Do you remember anything at all?"

"Mules . . . I remember mules. I was takin' the mules in after plowin'. Somethin' happened. Did I get the mules back okay? Is it night yet?"

"It's Friday noon, Clayborne. You been out since last night. The mules are fine. Mr. Fouts and Bill Newman brought you home."

"Friday noon. I must have hit my head a good one. It hurts like the dickens."

"Doctor says you should stay in bed a day or two."

"Did he come out here?"

"Nope, Mr. Fouts and Bill Newnan took you into Hico. To see Dr. Curry. Don't you remember any of it?"

"Dr. Curry . . . Maybe. I don't know. I think I remember somebody askin' me how many pencils I saw. It's all mixed up."

"Well, he gave you a dose of morphine, but it's likely wore off by now. I imagine so if your head hurts real bad."

"It does, it does."

That evening Bill Newman came by to check in on his friend. "Oretta tells me you got your senses back," said the husky farmer as he hovered solicitously over the bed.

"I guess I was pretty well off my rocker, huh?"

"Sounded like one of them broken Victrola records, you did. Just wanted to talk about mules, the mules drug you, you got hurt, and such like. You feeling better now?"

"I'm feeling fine, except for one grandfather of a headache. I think one of those mules must of kicked me in the head. Or maybe you took a sledgehammer to me. What about it?"

"No, I'd have took it to your foot, get a little free jig out of it."

"Is Mr. Fouts' mules all right?"

"Don't worry about them critters. And say, they caught that cotton and corn thief."

"The one's been stealing the cotton right out of our wagons in the field?"

"And the corn right out of our cribs."

"Well who was it?"

"It was that no good for nothin' Eddie Foster. Wick Simpson caught him redhanded stealing a pig right out of his hogpen. Was gonna ride off with it on a horse, if you can imagine that. Wick held him with a shotgun 'til the sheriff got there. They found a good bit of corn and cotton stashed at his place. I expect he'll spend a year or two up at the penitentiary."

Clayborne smiled. "Well, don't that beat all. Eddie Foster. You know how we figured it was poor folks stealing because of the depression?"

"Yeah," said Newman. "When I'd find a couple of sacks worth of cotton gone from my wagon out by the road I figured it was just somebody between a rock and a hard place."

"Well, that Eddie Foster and his brother Ike have been stealing like that since I was a little kid. I saw 'em once at my Grandpa Blackburn's ten years ago, back in 1922, stealing corn right out of our barn, just shovelin' it in tow sacks. They came on horses then too. Eddie Foster. . . Won't nobody feel sorry for that man when he's behind bars."

The residual headaches had disappeared by the time school started. Principal Perry stood on the broad front porch with Miss Adina Carroll watching his students flock home from their first day at school. The afternoon sun peeked through cotton-fluffy clouds, streaking the shower puddles with gold.

" 'Bye, Mr. Perry," yelled the two Newman boys Joe and Coy in unison. Their pet crow Jim perched on Joe's left shoulder as he fed it corn from his hand.

Miss Carroll asked Principal Perry, "How can you put up with that bird in your classroom? Isn't he a terrible disruption? Goodbye, Irving."

"Ol' Jim?" asked Mr. Perry. "He's no trouble. They keep him on the desk and when he wants to go home he just flies out the window. Goodbye, Emmy Jo."

"But he steals things so bad. Take care, Annie Maud."

"Just little stuff, pencils and such. So long, Helen and James. And remember when they first started bringin' him to school last spring?

Whenever ol' Jim would steal anything, he'd just take it home and the boys would bring it back the next day. They think the world and all of that ol' crow. See you tomorrow, J. D."

"I don't know, I just spent too much time as a girl chasing crows out of the chicken yard. 'Bye, Freda, 'bye Wynell and Ina. They peck eggs and they'll fly off with little bitty chicks. They're just a pest."

"Oh, Jim's not much of a pest. 'Bye, Tom. Well, that's the last of them, Miss Carroll. Another year started off right."

"Yes, indeed, yes, indeed."

"I can tell it started off right," said Principal Perry. "Mr. Rucker had Martha bring me another math problem this morning."

"Is it another one of those solid geometry problems where you have to find the volume of a corn crib or something?"

"It's like that, only this one's his water tank," he said, pulling out the paper with its little diagram and numbers. "Says he has a circular tank under his windmill twelve feet in diameter and five feet high. The water's up to three and a half feet. How many gallons does he have in the tank? Of course, he says it's just so he can figure whether he'll have to pump more water for the next month."

"I'm sure he doesn't know whether he has enough water in the tank after all these years as a farmer," Miss Carroll said sarcastically. "He sure likes to test you out, doesn't he?"

"Oh, yes. But it's sort of a game, you know. He's just real concerned with the education these country kids get. He's a good-hearted soul, and I kind of like doing his problems. Keeps me on my toes."

"And shows him you know what you're doing, too. Well, how does the new school year feel with your pet Marie Fouts gone off to Iredell for eleventh grade?"

"Oh, I'm so proud of her I could bust. And her sister Pearl's gone off to Denton this year. Isn't that grand?"

"At North Texas State Teachers College? Well, I declare. And did that Mingus girl ever get over to Tarleton like she was bragging?"

"Sure did. I drove her and her folks myself. She's all set up with the right courses to be a teacher."

They walked back in the schoolhouse to close it up.

"When's the big day for you and Miz Perry?"

"Oh, not long. Dr. Curry says it'll prob'ly be the end of the month."

"That's just a couple of weeks. My, my. Are you nervous?"

"Me, nervous? Well . . ."

"You're nervous. You can't hide it. All new fathers are that way."

"I guess so."

"You'll soon be used to a house full of squalling and commotion. Oh, and I meant to ask: What was all that commotion I heard through the wall during last period today?"

"All that laughing? That was Spanish class. They're not used to pronouncing Spanish words. You know how kids are. Just got the giggles when they stood up to recite and everybody else joined in."

"Spanish!" said Miss Carroll. "We didn't have that last year."

"I know. I talked it over in private at the teacher's meeting in Meridian with the school superintendent there. He thought it was a good idea. They do it over in their district. I want to teach the courses these kids'll need to enter Iredell High School and graduate in one year so they'll be able to enter college. It was so hard for me when I was a kid and there wasn't a lot of encouragement, either. I'm not just going to sit by and let my kids be scared off from going to college."

"Well, Mr. Perry," said Miss Carroll, putting her hand on his sleeve to make a point. "You don't seem to be having much trouble with students not going on to college. There's Pearl Fouts and Charlene Mingus and Rudene Newman last year."

"I know. But there's Raymond Newman and Bill Harris and W. B. Smith and a lot of other kids that aren't going on — and they could. They could use a good education. What'll they have when they get out of Iredell High School? They're going back to farms with farm prices the lowest they've ever been, they'll never make enough to buy their own places. I feel for 'em, Miss Carroll. They're goin' to have a rough life. Really rough."

"You're a good man, Mr. Perry. But you can't take the burdens of the whole world on your shoulders, broad though they may be."

"I can take some."

Sunrise, the last Sunday in October. The labor pains had begun, far apart and gentle, but very, very definite. This was it.

"Are you sure?" asked Clayborne anxiously.

"Yes, Clayborne," said Oretta, sitting up in bed. "It's just like Dr. Curry said it would be. They start slow and get closer together. It's started."

"Oh, Lordy, what do we do?" asked Clayborne, an edge of anxiety in his voice.

"Relax, first. Go get yourself some breakfast. We don't need to worry much 'til the pains are about twenty minutes apart. That's when the doctor ought to be here."

"Well, how far apart are they now?"

"I think they're still half an hour and more. Go get yourself some breakfast."

"Can I get you some, too?"

"Nope. Doctor Curry said not to eat anything after the pains started. All the pushin' that comes later might make you throw up and choke."

"Oh, Lordy," said Clayborne.

He got up and dressed and made himself some ham and eggs. "It's a right pretty day, Oretta," he called from the kitchen stove. "Sun's shinin' and all. It's a good day for havin' a baby." He wondered vaguely whether that remark sounded as dumb to Oretta as it did to him upon reflection. "Oretta? Oretta!"

He ran into the bedroom with his mouth full of ham and found his wife flat on her back, eyes shut tight and body hunched together in a strong first-stage labor contraction. "Oretta! What's wrong?! Should I get the doctor?" He was on the verge of panic.

She lay a few seconds more in the throes of new life and then it was over. She relaxed on the bed and smiled up at her husband. "Nothing's wrong, just one of the normal pains. That's how it's supposed to be. It'll keep up like that for hours."

"Oh, my."

"But I think you should prob'ly go on up and get Miz Morgan pretty soon. I think sometime about noon you're goin' to have to go get Doctor Curry in Hico."

"Well, do you need anything while I'm pickin' up Miz Morgan, medicine or anything?"

"A little cool water would be nice."

He zipped up the road to Mrs. Zella Morgan's place in his sporty Chevrolet coupe and brought her back to the little wood-floored dwelling he called home. Somehow he felt he'd rather face being kicked and dragged by the mules again than deal with this strange implacable process of birth.

Once in the house, Mrs. Morgan calmly took over. "Hello, there, Miz Perry. Your pains coming closer now?"

"Yes'm."

"They gettin' any harder?"

"Yes'm."

"All right, then. Mr. Perry, you just get yourself back in that car and you go on over to Doctor Curry's in Hico, you hear? Tell him your wife's time has come. I expect he'll be home from church by the time you get there."

Clayborne looked over Zella Morgan's shoulder into the bedroom and the smiling face of his beautiful wife. His whole world looked back at him.

"Don't just stand there like a lump, Mr. Perry," commanded Mrs. Morgan. "You got a job to do. Now, git!"

He gat. He leaped into the driver's seat feeling like cowboy actor Ken Maynard leaping on his horse in the western movie *Phantom Thunderbolt*, one of the few talkies he and Oretta had spent their money seeing this year. He pulled out of the gravel ruts of his driveway and onto the graded road pointing up north to Chalk Mountain. He zoomed past the Morgan place and turned left, stirring up the dust past the Newmans.

"There goes Clayborne, Nete," said Bill Newman to his wife. "Must be Oretta's time."

The little maroon speedster roared past Blackstump Valley School and down the hill, took the sharp left turn and then the sharp right turn that set Clayborne on his westward path.

The Odoms said to each other, "Looks like the schoolteacher. Guess his baby's comin'."

A few seconds later Price Hopgood said, "Dad, there goes Principal Perry in a hurry."

"Birthin' time," said the elder Hopgood.

Down the road he dashed, taking the rightward jog easily.

J. B. Dunlap said, "Look at that Perry drive! I'll bet he's going after the doctor."

Then the father-to-be crossed the eastern branch of Rocky Creek where the Duckworths nodded knowingly to each other and he zoomed over Rocky Creek's western bridge where the Bryants looked out on the streaking car and smiled to themselves.

A few seconds later Mr. Rucker looked out his kitchen window and said to his wife, "How long do you think it will take him to get to Hico tearin' out like that?"

In a small isolated community with little else to do, citizens became interested in each other's lives with an intensity unimaginable to their city-bred brethren. A few were sensitive to it, and in the depression exodus of farmers away from the country a good part of the motive force was not simply economic privation but the driving urge to escape the strictures of constant neighborly inspection and seek the liberating anonymity of the city. But for most, absorption with the lives of others was so complete that the idea of "nosiness" had lost its meaning. Gossip had become simply a way of life, a commonplace to the point that it was the unconscious water that country society swam in, for it was never a fish that discovered water.

After driving through the dust and the attention, it was not twenty minutes later that Clayborne rousted Dr. Curry from a peaceful Sunday dinner and used the telephone to let his mother and mother-in-law know that they were about to become grandparents.

"You go on back home, Mr. Perry," said the white-haired Dr. Curry. "Your wife sounds like she's comin' along just fine. I got to go get my bag. I'll be there after 'while. I know my way. By the bye, how *you* doin'?"

"Scared to death," said Clayborne.

"Good," smiled the old doctor. "It'll keep you out of mischief."

Clayborne beat Dr. Curry back to his place by half an hour. Once at home Clayborne paced and jittered and worried and stood mildly horrified every time a contraction prostrated his young wife. Zella Morgan told him to sit down, which he did, but he managed to pace and jitter and worry even sitting in the chair. Oretta smiled to see his customary calm thus shattered. "Don't you worry none, Clayborne," she said. "Everything's goin' to be just fine. Just fine."

"That's right, Oretta," he said nervously. "Everything's going to be just fine. Dr. Curry will be here in a few minutes. You just stay calm. Don't get excited or anything, you hear?"

She held back the smile and only said, "I sure won't. I'll just lay here and keep my wits about me."

"There's a big ol' Model A roadster going by out there, Mr. Perry," said Zella Morgan.

"Oh, it's Dr. Curry." Clayborne popped up and clomped out of the room. "I'll go bring him in." Out the door he vanished, leaving the echoes of xylophone-toned footsteps on the assorted-length planks of the decaying front porch.

"Do you think he'll live through this?" asked Zella Morgan confidentially to Oretta.

"He'll make it fine."

Once Dr. Curry took over Clayborne felt better.

"You just keep out of my way, young man," Dr. Curry said as he set his bag down on a night table and expanded his gestures to fill the room and dominate it. Your wife's gonna be proper busy here for a while. I won't need you for anything except to hold the birth certificate while I sign it after your baby's come. You just sit here and watch the show. You don't see miracles too often these days. And by the bye, how long you been married to Mrs. Perry?"

"Let's see," said Clayborne. "It's fourteen months now. Why do you ask?"

"Well, most babies take nine months to hatch, but some of these firstborns just show up any old time, you know what I mean? The most amazin' thing. Just checkin'."

Clayborne sat down beside his wife to ponder the doctor's remarks and time passed.

Within the hour, Margaret and Willie Partain appeared, chauffeured by their son-in-law John Guinn. Immediately on their heels Tom and Belle Perry arrived, squired to the birthing by Hoyt. Clayborne came out in the front room to greet them. By now the Partains had come completely to terms with the marriage of their baby daughter and Clayborne enjoyed normal relations with them once more. Civil conversation was no longer a matter of keeping dead silence.

Clayborne said to his father and father-in-law, "I'm glad the baby's coming on a Sunday. At least I don't have to be in school. Would you like to sit in the bedroom?"

"I think us menfolks will just sit out here in the living room," said redheaded Willie Partain, taking the rocking chair. "What do you think, Tom?"

"Oh, I'm happy right here in this straight-back chair, Willie. I been through all this before, done my share of worryin' and bein' scared to death. I'll just sit here this time and let Clayborne do all that. Clayborne?"

"Yes, Papa?"

"I hear you fell off some mules and got your head bashed in."

"Well, yes, sir, I did. I'm okay now, though."

"You remember you were worried I'd fall off my plow? Well, I haven't fell off yet. Maybe you ought to try it with your eyes shut."

"Oh, Papa!"

Everybody laughed.

Oretta called from her childbed, "Are they hoo-rawin' you about fallin' off the mules, Clayborne?"

"It's nothin', Oretta. Papa was just sayin' how he's gonna let me do all the worryin' and bein' scared to death today."

"Now there ye go, Tom," said Willie. "You got a right proper attitude. Let the kids do it. Now if we could just get us a little lemonade, everything would be fine."

Margaret Partain said, "You gents just sit and wait until we've had time to say hello to Oretta and you'll get you your lemonade. Clayborne, you come on back in here with your wife and visit with her. She's workin' hard to bring your new baby into the world."

"Yes, Ma'am."

Belle Perry and Margaret Partain stood on opposite sides of the bed looking down upon the mother-to-be. They didn't need to say much. That feeling was there again: powerful forces of family survival, of generations of toil were at work in this room. The forebears of the Perry line once more prepared to meet their future. Belle Perry sat on one of the chrome dinette chairs on Oretta's right hand and Margaret Partain sat on another on her left hand. Clayborne sat a little in the background, near his wife's head and Dr. Richard Curry went about his doctorly duties preparing his patient for childbirth. Belle thought back to a night twenty-two years ago when she gave birth to her firstborn. Time, she thought. How it runs away from us. Here it turns again. Zella Morgan walked in with hot cups of steaming coffee from the coal-oil fired cookstove. Shades of Granny Marlow, Belle thought, remembering the midwife who helped her through her own ordeal along with Dr. Charles Durham. Both of them were gone now, long dead. And the new life to which both of them devoted their days kept coming on, rolling through the ages, link after link after link in the chain of eternity, and in their own going there was nothing lost, only gathered back to its origins.

"I've got your menfolk set up with lemonade in the front room, Miz Perry. Here's some coffee for Miz Partain and Miz Perry. How'd you like some, Dr. Curry? And you Mr. Perry?"

"Smells good," said the doctor. "I'll take you up on it."

"Me, too," said Clayborne. He sat quietly now, past the fidgets, watching the powerful pangs coming faster and faster, seeing his wife laboring in the birth of their first child with new eyes. The fear was gone from him and the fascination was wearing off. What was left was the bare brute animal physical fact of parturition, new life out of old, literally out of old, the hard muscle strains and the tears in the matrix and the pain, the pushing, the primal force that shoved every child howling into the world, the ogre of time, time to get out, time to breathe for yourself, time to kick the air, time to cut that umbilical, time to live. Time to live. Time was everything. Yes, time to live. Here, child, like it or not, here's the world. Ready or not, time to live. And deep in that brute animal physical act of birth, deep in the despotism of time the eye of God stared out at him. There was religion in it. It was as if God's hand too had reached out, a hard, real hand, not some faint illusion, not some vaporous spirit, but a pulsing, living, real, personal hand, reached out and rebound him to this place, bound him back to his people, tied him with ligaments of new flesh, bound him again and made him more part of it than he had ever been before, blood of his blood, flesh of his flesh. His child was on its way.

"Here's your coffee, Mister Clayborne," said Zella Morgan. "I'll be goin' home now — no need to get up. I can walk up to my place, it's just a short bit. I'll be back tonight after the baby's come." Midwives no longer stayed to help the doctor; Grannies were fading into history, more hired housekeepers than professional baby deliverers. Later on Clayborne and Oretta would give her three and a half yards of material for a dress as a token of thanks.

"Thank you, Miz Morgan," said Oretta through the perspiration and strain. "You come see my baby tonight. You come see my baby."

At about five o'clock in the afternoon of October 30, 1932, the baby was born. Clayborne watched the white and wrinkled little being lifted in Dr. Curry's hands, saw the infant take its first breath, saw its body turn from white to blue to pink in an instant. And he saw that it was a boy. He had a son.

About sundown he went out to milk the cows after receiving the congratulations of his mother and mother-in-law and father and father-in-law. He was glad it was over. He knew Oretta was glad it was over — she'd done all the work, and they didn't call it labor for nothing. He had not been afraid at the last. He was too struck with awe to be afraid. Dr. Curry had been right: you don't see too many miracles these days. And in Texas country style, Oretta gave her plump healthy eight-pound newborn the name Bobby. It was Bobby, not Robert. To Texas country folk a name was a name and not a nickname and that's all there was to it. The boy wasn't named after anybody, Oretta just decided that's what she wanted to name him and so that's what he was named.

The stream of visitors to the humble little house by Walker Branch had grown to a veritable parade by mid-November. The womenfolk and the young girls ooh-ed and aah-ed at little Bobby and the menfolk chucked him under the chin and said what a big boy he was and asked his father what he thought about this Roosevelt fellow that just beat Herbert Hoover in the election for president. Then a neighbor lady brought her little girl to visit. She had whooping cough. Bobby got it.

The first day it just seemed like a case of the sniffles and a little croup and besides colicky babies were not at all unusual. But then the unmistakable deep racking cough came and Clayborne and Oretta were petrified with horror. Little girls almost of school age might shake off whooping cough and suffer only a couple of weeks' discomfort and no complications. Tiny babies with whooping cough commonly died.

Bobby coughed day and night, coughed the profound hollow ringing cough that tore the restoring veil of sleep, slashed the nurturing appetite, wore down the infant endurance to nothing. Clayborne went to school every morning and pretended to be Principal Perry and went through the motions well enough that nobody saw his attention wrapped around that sick baby at home. At night he looked at Oretta and Oretta looked at him as their baby got worse and worse. In a few days the phlegm began to catch in the baby's throat and he choked and gagged and there was nothing to do but for Oretta to pull it out with her fingers. She stayed up with him day and night and day and night for seven ragged, grueling days. A week of constant coughing left Bobby weak and sinking. Clayborne and Oretta were frantic.

They took him into Iredell to see Dr. A. M. Pike. Doctors see enough of the world's miseries to learn how to keep a straight face at most anything, but Dr. Pike nearly gasped when he saw Bobby. He did a quick physical examination and looked seriously at the parents.

"I'm going to be honest with you folks," said Dr. Pike. "It looks like we're going to lose him unless we do something."

"Oh, no!" said Oretta, tears flooding.

"Dr. Pike," said Clayborne with a blanched face, "is there anything you can do for whooping cough once you've got it?"

"Frankly, the book says no. We've had whooping cough vaccines for several years now, but they're supposed to be a preventive. Don't do much after the onset of the disease. But we've got a new one just come out that works different, disrupts the life cycle of the microbe that causes the whooping cough. In theory, it could at least ease up the symptoms. It's never been tried in a case like this, not that I know of anyway. It would be strictly a measure of last resort. But I'd like to try it on this boy, give him a shot of it. With your permission, that is."

"Oh, Dr. Pike," said Oretta, "we'll do anything to save our baby!"

"You have to understand it's just a stab in the dark," said the doctor. "It might not work. You could still lose him."

"We'll lose him sure if we don't," said Clayborne with clenched jaw. "Try it, Dr. Pike. And tell us what we should do for him at home."

"Do you folks pray?"

They prayed. The next day they heard their baby coughing higher in his chest with less of that deathlike booming that has no business coming out of the body of a tiny child. Bobby's eyes had more of their luster and he began to eat a little better. The second day the improvement was definite. By the third day it looked like he was recovering. In a week he was well. Had it been the vaccine? Had the disease simply run its course and a tough baby beaten it with his own biological force? Had their prayers been heard? The boy was healthy from then on.

By March of 1933 Clayborne could put it off no more. He'd gone three summers since Tarleton without adding to his education. His teacher's certificate had been authorized for four years. Its term was running out, and if he intended to remain a teacher it was imperative to qualify himself, for a renewed certificate. He had to go back to college.

There were many places he could have gone. He could have gone over to Howard Payne at Brownwood or out to Sul Ross College at Alpine in the Big Bend country, but he got to balancing out the costs of getting there, living at college with a wife and child and paying tuition and he decided on San Marcos.

Southwest Texas State Teachers College at San Marcos was noted primarily for its splendid Main Building, replete with ornate Rococo pyramidal spires caparisoned in red Spanish tile trimmed with gold paint, triangular Gothic gables combining curved Arabic arches and circular Byzantine porthole windows, imitation Louis XIV chimneys and Romanesque parapets with long horizontal belt courses pierced by arched windows — in all, an exuberant display of architectural indecision. Old Main, as this eclectic gathering of styles is now known, stood atop College Hill, an eleven-acre campus donated by the city of San Marcos after the Twenty-sixth Texas Legislature authorized Southwest Texas State Normal School in 1899. The legislature had been generous enough to provide a $55,000 grant for construction and payment of faculty and Old Main — New Main then — was finished and in business as a Normal School by 1903. All classes met in the Main Building and the students and faculty of sixteen professors and one principal boarded with San Marcos families. In 1923 its name was changed from Normal School to College, but its academic reputation was nothing to shout about.

On March 24, 1911, a vigorous and determined man named Cecil Eugene Evans had been appointed principal of the normal school and spent his entire career trying to make something of his institution. But even by 1921 he could still write to the Texas Council of Teachers College Presidents about accreditation standards for all normal schools in Texas including his beloved San Marcos:

> We know very well that we are not meeting the recognized standards of the Texas Association of Colleges in several respects. Our high school and college work are still lumped together; freshman college courses are not differentiated from junior and senior college courses; heads of departments in many instances do not hold graduate degrees, and in some cases do not even have a bachelor's degree; diluted college courses on a semi-secondary basis are still given in normal colleges in our state.

Evans was a fighter and by 1927, the year a young greenhorn named Lyndon Baines Johnson came to school at San Marcos, the college had been fully accredited. It had been no easy task raising the normal schools out of mediocrity. Evans had often fought with his fellow normal school presidents over deviations from the highest standards attainable. In October of 1917, for example, he carried on a heated correspondence with President W. H. Bruce of North Texas State Normal School in Denton for admitting students from a high school that had lost its classification because it failed to meet state standards:

> In the case of the four students from Iredell High School assigned to your sophomore class without entrance examinations or conditions, the procedure cannot find defense in either graduation from the Iredell High School of 1917 or completion of the tenth grade of 1916, in neither of which years did this high school have classification of the lowest rank by the State Department of Education.

Just as Iredell had gotten its educational house in order since those informal days, so had San Marcos had brought its standards to the point of respectability when Clayborne Perry came to make his choice about further education. That March he drove alone to the registrar's office in Old Main on College Hill in San Marcos, Texas, handed his transcript from Tarleton to Dr. Claude Elliott of the history department and made arrangements to enter the second summer session in mid-July.

The three-act play for Blackstump Valley's graduation, 1933, was a great success, and the school year was deemed another triumph for Principal Perry and teacher Adina Carroll. Everyone looked forward to yet another great session come fall. But things were not going fine in the fields. Harvest did not last long because drought had come and burned off most of the growth: the grain crop was small. Clayborne had saved most of his hundred-twenty-dollar-a-month salary as Principal of Blackstump Valley school, and the shortened harvest season with its shortened paychecks was only a financial hardship and not a disaster. There would still be enough for San Marcos.

The summer showed Clayborne unexpected problems of living in the seclusion of a little house on Walker Branch. To live off all alone while they were newlyweds was one thing, but to live there as a family of three with a tiny baby was quite another. Clayborne found himself working again from before sunup to after sundown, leaving Oretta and Bobby all alone in that little place out away from everybody and everything. The windows had no screens and the doors had no locks and the nearest neighbor was a quarter of a mile away and the next one was half a mile. When Clayborne drove off in the morning, Oretta was left alone, utterly alone, without a car, all by herself with Bobby from dawn 'til dark.

Besides the isolation there were the plain physical problems. Even during a drought year quick hard rains would come pounding the soil for a few minutes and leave Walker Branch and its crystal spring muddy for several days, and that meant the drinking water was muddy and had to be let settle before they could drink it. Then there was college summer session coming up — what to do about the problem of rent? It would not be possible for Clayborne to meet his obligation of feeding Tom Laswell's livestock while at college for six weeks, and it would be equally impossible to pay five dollars a month rent for the Laswell place on top of apartment rent in San Marcos, whatever that might amount to.

The last day of harvest, as Clayborne cleaned up at the Fouts' place before going home, Marie Fouts came out and said to him, "Why don't you bring your family and live in those two upstairs rooms in our house?"

Pearl Fouts, listening from the two-story house doorway called out, "Sure, Mr. Perry, Marie and I are both going off to college up at Denton this fall."

"That's a mighty kind offer, girls," said Clayborne. "But what would your Mama and Papa say about it? Are you sure it wouldn't be imposing?"

"Come on and ask Mama," suggested Pearl. "She's right here."

"You come live with us, Mr. Perry," said Ethel Fouts. "You got no business leaving your wife and child down there on the branch with nobody to visit with all day, every day. You know she gets lonely and scared. Come live with us."

"But what would Mr. Fouts think about another family moving in with him? We have a little baby, you know, and he makes as much racket as any other little baby."

"I wouldn't make the offer if I thought it would impose on my family, Mr. Perry," said Ethel Fouts. "I'm just crazy about little Bobby, and it would be nice to have a youngster like that around — especially now that Marie and Pearl are both going off to college, thanks to your good help."

"It would sure solve my problems," said Clayborne. "But will you talk it over with Mr. Fouts before I say yes? I sure wouldn't want to make any hard feelings."

"Of course, I'll talk it over with him," said Ethel Fouts. "I know just what he's goin' to say. Just like everything else. He'll say 'You do what you want to, it's okay with me.' That's what he'll say, sure as shootin'."

"I sure hope so, Mrs. Fouts," said Clayborne.

"You count on it. You can move your belongings over before college starts and not worry about paying rent until you come back at the end of August. And tell Mrs. Perry we won't expect any big rent, seven dollars or so will be fine."

"That's a mighty attractive offer, Ma'am. You folks are real friends. I'll talk to Oretta about it. I'm sure she'll be delighted."

"Tell her we'll be delighted if she accepts."

The deal was sealed and the Perrys said goodbye to the little house on Walker Branch on Friday, the fifteenth of July, the day before they left for college.

Geographically, San Marcos lies a little more than thirty miles south of the state capitol in Austin and about two miles above the confluence of the Blanco and San Marcos rivers. The town and its campus straddle the exact edge of two worlds, right atop the Balcones Escarpment, a geologic fault line separating the low rolling country of the rich and fertile Blackland Prairie on the east and the buckled limestone misery of the hardscrabble Hill Country on the west. A good number of students attending Southwest Texas State Teachers College came from poor farm families in the Hill Country and to be Hill Country poor was to be poor indeed.

Their land itself was a mere remnant of its original glory of grass, for when early farmers began to put out the wildfires and graze their cattle on its lush body and to plow the soil, they did not have the deep and forgiving Grand Prairie beneath their boots but rather a shallow film of dirt that bore only stunted trees and the hardiest of grasses. The trees were so stunted that nobody among those first·immigrants recognized them. They would say, "Hey, that there little bush looks just like one of them big tall walnut trees back in Missouri," or "Looky there, that's just like a big ol' mulberry bush back in Alabama but it's only a quarter the size." It looked like a walnut because it was a walnut, it looked like a mulberry because it was a mulberry, but growing on the Hill Country's precariously thin soil with roots dug into hard limestone, clutching bare rock six inches below. Because nobody knew how to interpret the signs, early ranchers overgrazed the Hill Country, stripped the grass and then watched their soil and the wealth of their land depart with the rain for the Gulf of Mexico. Of course, it never came back.

And now great patches of the Hill Country's twenty-four thousand square miles are a skeleton of white limestone bones greened up mostly by dark juniper cedars, but there are still secret places where the cedar-elm and plane-tree sycamore and redbud and wild dogwood grace the hard land, and little copses of Spanish oak and wild plum and hackberry mix with ticklegrass in the winter hoarfrost, and riverside paradises of Burr oak, cypress and and wild cherry decorate the Colorado and the Frio and the Pedernales if you know where to look. But of the farmers that came on the heels of the ranchers, well, only the German immigrants ever made much of themselves as farmers and not many of them died rich. Practically all of the pioneer farmers failed, and most of their children failed and many of their grandchildren failed. Their typical homes were little log crackerboxes, usually two crackerboxes built side by side with a roof over the both of them, a sort of breezeway between shacks, the style that's still called a dog-trot house by the locals, probably because that's what legend says the breezeway was used for. People who have seen the struggling farmers of the Grand Prairie and the struggling farmers of the Hill Country know that there's poor and then there's poor.

But the summer sessions at Hill Country San Marcos welcomed the cream of the poor, those ambitious poor from whatever part of Texas who had managed to become teachers and that came here to update their certificates and finish up their degrees. Clayborne fit right in.

The three Perrys found an apartment up on College Hill, two blocks northwest of the school, up on the very highest point of the hill. The mosquitos were terrible there but Mrs. Anderson only charged the Perrys twelve dollars a month rent and it cost a dollar a month for the electricity. Back home, even the Fouts' didn't have electricity. Tuition for the six week summer session was only twelve and a half dollars and the college furnished your textbooks. If you wanted, you could spend an extra dollar for a "blanket tax" and attend all the athletic events and use the sports facilities and attend the cultural shindigs, but in the summer it was hardly worth it. In all, if they lived frugally, the Perry family could make it through summer school for a hundred dollars total.

Total enrollment for the entire summer session 1934 was 2,272, an increase of 619, or thirty-six percent over the summer of 1933. Even the Depression had not quelled the urge for education. Clayborne signed up for two courses at his new school, courses taught by men who could not have been more different, but perhaps it was appropriate to find such variety housed within the miscellaneous architectural styles of Old Main. Educational statistics was the bailiwick of educational professor David F. Votaw, a tidy man in wire-rim glasses who always seemed to wear his suit coat regardless of the heat, a frail man with a perennially pained expression, a man who walked with a cane, perhaps the victim of infantile paralysis in his childhood. Votaw ruled the class by his crisp, stiff efficiency and he taught the rigors of statistics — which stretched and warped the minds of his generally math-poor students with its chi squares and sampling techniques and normal distribution curves — as if it were a holy calling and the charts he chalked on the blackboard had been writ large on stone tablets by the jealous god of polynomials and rectangular coordinates.

American history, on the other hand, happened to be taught in the summer by professor H. M. Greene, who had become nearly as much an institution at Southwest as Old Main itself. He was rugged both physically and mentally, big featured with a square chin and Nordic brow. He regularly trekked the Hill Country to a favorite retreat up at Devil's Backbone where he read and meditated by a little spring in a ravine, and you could always find him storming up the steep sides of College Hill with his nose buried in a book — he read voraciously — passing youngsters half his age at twice their speed. He was as rugged an individualist in academe as you could imagine, absolutely refusing to follow acceptable patterns of professorial behavior and acting as he damn well pleased, in class and out. There is only one reason why he survived in a college in Texas, where the pressures of social conformity are as irresistable as gravity, and that is this: he was that rarest of all men, an original thinker — when he taught, he didn't just *know* his subject, he *was* his subject. He'd received a master's degree from the University of Texas and took a year of his doctorate at the University of Illinois, but quit in 1923 when he discovered that he already knew more than all of his instructors combined. He had already formed his own theory of history and government, and it had not come out of other men's books. This discovery did little to cultivate humility in a soul as big as all outdoors — but some wag commenting on the professor's engaging arrogance maintained that in Greene's own opinion, his humility was second to none. And because he was something of a curmudgeon and heckled the school administrators and liked to put deans and presidents in their places, the students loved him to the point of devotion.

Clayborne had never before met such a man. He was a little surprised when professor Greene came into class the first day wearing a faded khaki shirt and worn trousers, looking more like an out-of-work field hand than a college instructor. There were no two ways about it: Greene was sloppy. His tie was not too tight, his baggy socks didn't match, he didn't get a haircut too often and when he sat down at his big desk in front of the class, he leaned back in his chair and propped his feet on an open drawer. Then he began to teach and none of this mattered a whit.

He closed his eyes and began to speak about American history, not just the dry names and dates Clayborne had been accustomed to, but vibrant *ideas*, unfolding a sparkling clear picture of the democratic process and the forces that make history move. Clayborne had not yet heard of the distinctions between liberal and conservative and thus did not waste time trying to put labels on what professor Greene told the class. It would have been futile anyway: Greene was the kind of liberal that Thomas Jefferson had been, nursing a fierce belief in the protection of individual liberties. He was a radical in the Populist sense of advocating control of the big vested interests and more social and economic programs by the national government. He was a conservative in that he constantly hammered home the responsibilities of the private citizen and the public servant alike. He wanted people to have the privilege of making up their minds for themselves and the responsibility of guarding that privilege from all enemies.

This was a different college experience than Clayborne had anticipated, more stimulating, more sophisticated, opening new vistas of understanding. And it was hard work. But Oretta enjoyed being there even while he was in class or studying, being so close to other people, being right in a town. Bobby was crawling now and babbling and charming the neighbors even in the heat. In fact, he had become everybody's pet. There was no sadness in the days now, even though four months after Bobby had been born the man who delivered him died: Dr. Curry was no more. But now even that was a fading memory and seemed somehow distant from this different place, from San Marcos.

In the late afternoons Clayborne would take them down to swim in the cool and shady San Marcos river where artesian springs bubbled up from deep within the Balcones Fault at a rate of two hundred million gallons a day, the largest springs in Texas. The water came up at a year-round temperature of seventy-two degrees after having been filtered through miles of Hill Country limestone aquifer, creating an idyllic scene of sheltering bluffs and clear flowing springs and serene riverbanks fringed with the big fleshy tropical-looking plants Texans call elephant ears and smelling of green humidity and comfort and deep relaxation.

Bobby loved the water and Oretta loved to listen to her husband as they rested on the riverside grass under the overhanging liveoaks and he told stories of his childhood, she loved to watch that something special in him show through in a brimming sense of life.

"We used to have that old one-wire telephone line back when I lived in the rent house at Dude Flat," he said.

"Same as ours," she said.

"Yep, in fact, I used to call your brothers all the time and have secret talks with Frosty and Hoot," he said.

"Secret? With all those folks on the party line to Duffau?" she said.

"Sure," he said. "We'd have a prearranged code. I'd ring up and Hoot would answer and we'd hear that click-click-click-click as everybody picked up the phones. Then we'd talk for a while about some ordinary thing like homework or what not and everybody would start to hang up, and then we'd hang up, too. Only, we had it agreed that about five minutes later, Hoot would pick up the phone at your place and I'd pick up the phone at my place and neither one of us would have rung up the other and nobody else would be on the line and he'd say, 'Hey, what did you think of that new girl at school today?' and I'd say 'She sure has pretty hair,' and nobody would be the wiser."

"Why, you sneakin' so-and-sos," concluded Oretta, "did you ever talk about me that way?"

"That would be telling, my dear."

And the days passed and the weeks passed and one weekend they decided to visit San Antonio, the big city sixty miles southwest. There they drove through the wooded haven of Brackenridge park and walked through its zoo with some of the earliest barless animal pits that made a try at placing the critters in a more natural setting than the commonplace concrete-and-bars animal prisons that called themselves zoos, and they went into the imposing halls and vaulted ceilings and columned atrium of the Witte Museum, echoing with their footsteps and shushing them into awed silence with ancient artifacts and splendid gowns from the court of the Dowager Empress of China and Woodrow Wilson's big open parade car and an old blind Mexican man who played a harp for pennies among the marble columns, his strange and haunting music like nothing on earth, *brujo* in its seductive power, *temple* in its haughty elegance, his harp strings resonating with the dazzling sun of Veracruz and memories of the farm-and-fisherpeople known as the *jarochos* who invented his style on the peaceful lagoons of the Sotaveno seaboard between the calm Rio Jamapa and the gaping Rio Papaloapan.

When college was nearly out, Clayborne took the sporty Chevy coupe down the street in San Marcos to Dobbins Hudson-Essex Company and traded it in on a brand new 1933 Terraplane four-door sedan. It was an imposing car, black and shiny and befitted a school principal going into the third year of his teaching career.

Within days of trading in the Chevy, Clayborne heard that the Texas State Legislature had passed an act slashing the salaries of school teachers. Finally, even though Governor Ma Ferguson, once elected again, had gone back to her old tricks of pardoning and paroling incarcerated criminals, so it was said, for a cash consideration and performing other amusing shenanigans, she did not veto the hostile legislature's bill to reduce regular appropriations for state government by twenty percent. The depression was just plain getting desperate: County governments were collapsing everywhere from bonded indebtedness and the costs of unemployment relief. Taxes weren't coming in and the money kept going out and the lawmakers finally did something about it, for one thing, they put a ceiling of eighty-five dollars a month on men teachers' salaries and seventy-five dollars a month for women teachers' salaries. There was not the faintest feeling of inequity in setting women's salaries lower than men's: it was correctly presumed that men teachers had a wife and children to support while women teachers either were spinsters who could get by on a little less or were married and providing a second income. And so Clayborne went back to Blackstump Valley School with the college credits to renew his teacher's certificate for four more years only to be cut from a hundred twenty dollars a month to eighty-five.

On the tenth of October fire gutted the house of Tom and Belle Perry, destroying everything. The entire family including Hoyt and Nadine and Dorothy escaped without injury. But they were homeless and had to set up housekeeping in the car shed, the only building left standing that could be closed up. The next week Tom sent Hoyt into Hico to buy a big Army tent in which they would spend the winter as they planned the long and laborious process of rebuilding. They had no fire insurance and would have to start over from scratch. They had lost everything, all their letters over the years, the furniture, the Victrola, everything. At least the livestock had not been hurt, the mules and cows and hogs and the dog and cats. Tom felt as he had felt when they arrived on the benchlands above the Purgatoire River north of Trinchera, Colorado, back in 1915. But he vowed not to let it beat him, even though he was blind and even though the cotton crop looked like it would only bring in 4.66 cents a pound, the lowest he'd ever heard of in his life. He had nearly twenty cows now. He could sell off five or six of them for maybe twenty dollars each. He would manage somehow. He would start over and he would keep on. And that was that.

Clayborne brought Oretta and Bobby to visit his grandparents one sunny day the week after the fire, hoping to cheer them up. They sat in the tent on new kitchen chairs, some that neighbors had given them, others that had been bought after the fire. The sleeping gear was in the garage and the dining table and cookstove were in the tent. The old familiar cane-bottom chairs that had gone so many miles with them were ashes now and that was sad. But the tent gave enough shelter for the meager possessions they had begun to gather again and provided a diffuse all-over light that made even the sadness of ruin seem tolerable. And Bobby, well, Bobby, being the first grandchild got more attention than a child could hope to use and the stolid and prim reserve of Tom and Belle were set aside for the boy. They dandled him on their knee and talked affectionate baby talk to him and hugged him tight and held his hand and did a hundred other fond things they'd never think of doing with an older child, much less a fellow adult.

"I'm going to walk up and down the driveway here with this young 'un," said Tom Perry. "Hoyt, get me out the tent door and point me right

square toward the cotton patch. I can get back and forth from here to
there."

Hoyt obliged his father and when Tom had carried Bobby out the flap,
he went back to nailing the lumber cribwork around the bottom of the
tent.

"Mama, is there anything we can bring you?" asked Clayborne.

"No, son, not a thing," said Belle gratefully. "This is just another one
of those things you got do deal with. We'll be fine."

"Mama Perry, I know I'm not real good with helpin' in the fields, but
I'm goin' to come over and help you get in your cotton with Clayborne
again," said Oretta.

"Oh, Oretta you are a help. Just havin' you around is a help. You keep
the girls happy and jokin' and we need that now, and they look up to you
so."

"And we wouldn't have anybody to hoo-raw if you didn't come this
year," said Hoyt.

"Hoyt," said Clayborne, walking over to where he labored, "is it true
what Papa said about you quitting school after ninth grade?"

"It's true and don't lecture me none about it. I heard all that about how
important education is to making a livin'. I heard how your salary got cut.
And I see all these college graduates in Hico movin' on to big cities
because they can't find work here. And they won't find work anywhere. I
can do fine workin' the farm here. So just don't lecture me, you hear? You
do it your way and let me do it mine."

"Okay, okay," said Clayborne. "I was just askin'."

"Oh, Clayborne!" gasped Oretta, looking out the tent flap, tears
streaming down her face.

Clayborne looked from across the tent in alarm, but only saw the
prostrate blackened remains of the old house out beyond the open flap.
"It's just the house, honey," he said, walking to her. "The family got out
safe. I know it's sad, but don't cry, Mama and Papa will rebuild."

"No, it's not that, Clayborne," Oretta said, love and faith and tragedy
shining from her face. "Look."

There, against the backdrop of the devastated home and the cotton
patch that would hardly pay for itself this year, Tom Perry stood holding
his grandson aloft in the sunlight, looking and looking, looking hard
with his ruined eyes at the happy goo-goo child up at the end of his arms
where the high sun splashed across his little face and traced the tiny
features in bright lines and hard shadows.

"I can see you, today, Bobby," said the frail figure of a man. "I can see
what you look like."

Then he brought the boy back close to his heart and went on carrying
Bobby Perry down the long gravel driveway he'd memorized, humming
to himself.

The Saturday before school started in Blackstump Valley, Miss Adina Carroll submitted her resignation from the post of teacher effective immediately. She had been offered a more attractive position in Glen Rose.

Clayborne was frantic. He had forty students to take care of Monday morning and only himself to do it. He thought and thought — Charlene Mingus was beginning her second year at Tarleton, just as Pearl Fouts was at North Texas. He couldn't call upon them. They were out. What about Rudene Newman? She had finished two years, now! No, she had decided to continue on in college, that's right. It was with a sinking feeling that he drove off to Hico to make arrangements with his father to help get in the cotton this month after school hours.

As he approached Hico, he remembered Christine Fewell. He turned left, went into town and stopped at the familiar frame house on the corner of Second and Mesquite.

He paced up and down the kitchen as Miss Fewell fixed him a cup of coffee.

"She just up and quit!" he raved. "Just like that, Miss Fewell! Two days before school starts!"

"Sure puts you in a pickle, doesn't it?" she said sympathetically.

"Miss Fewell," he said pleadingly, "What am I going to do?"

"Well, I'm sure I don't know, Mr. Perry. Here's your coffee."

He took a sip, then said, "Would you come out there and teach?"

"Me?"

"Sure, you've got more than *three years* of school. You'd be a natural."

"I couldn't teach, Mr. Perry, I never got my certificate, never thought I'd need it. You know I've been keeping the books over at the milk plant."

"They can get another bookkeeper, Miss Fewell. And I can arrange to have you put on as a conditional teacher until we get your certificate from Austin. And that shouldn't take more than a week or two with your qualifications. I'll pay you out of my own pocket if I have to. And that's another thing, you'll make seventy-five dollars a month teaching school, and I know they don't pay bookkeepers more than forty. You can do it."

"You quite take my breath away, Mr. Perry. I don't know . . ."

"Is there anyone who could help you get lesson plans together for the first few weeks? Just until you get the hang of it?"

"Well, I have an auntie who's retired from schoolteaching. I think she'd be willing to help me out on weekends, maybe. But will the trustees agree?"

"Well, I'll just say that Clyde Harris was elected trustee this year."

"Clyde? Why Clyde's known me since I was a baby."

"Well? How about it?"

"I'll be there Monday morning."

By the week before Christmas holidays, Miss Fewell had settled into her new job, bought her own car and roomed with the Clyde Harrisses up past the Bowmans and just before the Wick Simpson place.

"How are you doing by now, teacher Fewell?" asked Principal Perry as he stood on the school porch in the afternoon sun.

"I see you're out here too just before dismissal."

"I gave everybody a study hall this last ten minutes."

"So did I. Great minds run in the same circles, you know. But, to answer you, I'm enjoying teaching more all the time. How do you think I'm doing?"

"Like I told you, you're a natural. You're doing as fine as you please."

"Oh, thank you so much. You're such an encouragement. And what about you? How are you getting along living with the Fouts' this year?"

"Well, it's the nicest place I ever lived in my whole life, and the heater's right downstairs from our room so we're always warm. And it's so close to school, you know, just right down the path there."

"How do you folks get along with the Fouts'?"

"My, oh, my, it's a regular love feast. Mrs. Fouts just idolizes Bobby and Bobby's startin' to talk real good now. He calls her Foutsie and she just loves it. Thinks that's the best thing that's ever happened."

"Oh, that's wonderful! And what about your father? Are they getting rebuilt from being burned out?"

"Yes, slowly. Tom Strepey comes over and helps my brother Hoyt get the new house framed up. They've got most of the walls framed up by now. But it's slow. They won't have it done 'til next summer probably."

"It was really too bad about that, but they're strong people. They sound like they're pulling out of it. Oh, and I meant to ask, I just looked in your classroom the other day when I came to get the chalk box and noticed you don't have a tenth grade class. I thought Blackstump Valley had always gone up to tenth grade."

"It usually does, but I just sent all the tenth graders down to Iredell High School this year. It's better for the kiddos to have two years in the same school, I think. Gives them a better chance to settle down and get good grades so they can get into college."

"But can you just do that?"

"You mean does Iredell School District mind? No. They're glad to have the extra students because the county tax funds transfer with the students. The only thing we have to watch for is to keep at least thirty-six students here at Blackstump Valley so we don't lose our two-teacher classification. But this year we have forty-two, even with the tenth graders going to Iredell, so we're all right. Say, it's time to dismiss."

The dismissal bell was rung and the two teachers once more waved their students home on the broad front porch. Clayborne reached in his vest pocket and then looked around worriedly.

"Have you seen my car keys?" he asked Miss Fewell.

"No, no I haven't. Here, pupils," she called, "some of you stay a minute and help Principal Perry find his car keys."

Immediately a dozen boys and girls began scouring the school inside and out — but no keys. Coy Newman got up from searching under the big porch and ducked as if something had hit him in the head. "I know!" he yelled, and ran home.

In a few minutes he ran back with the principal's keys dangling in his hand. "I knew it!" shouted the Newman boy triumphantly. "Ol' Jim Crow stole your car keys and flew home with 'em. They were right in his box!"

Just before Christmas Clayborne told Oretta that he intended to return to San Marcos the next summer and as many summers as necessary to finish his degree and get a permanent teacher's certificate. He had made the decision. The response was not what he expected.

"Clayborne," said Oretta, looking across their bedroom to where Bobby slept, "you and me has to get some things straight."

"What?"

"I've been thinkin' about things, Clayborne."

"What things?"

"I've been doing some growing up, you know. I'm not just that dumb kid you married a couple of years ago."

"I never thought you were dumb, Oretta. What's this all about?"

"You tell me you're going back to San Marcos this year and next year and so on until you've got your degree. No, don't interrupt, let me finish. That means you're always going to be off working somewhere to make the money it'll take to pay for all that. You aren't home hardly at all as it is. And when you are, you don't show me any affection, you never hug me, or tell me you love me, and you don't have the time to hold Bobby like you ought to, and I just feel so left alone and unloved. You're married to work, not to me!"

Clayborne looked at her in shock. He felt pulled apart. He had never seen this before. His wife, his beloved wife was in pain because he kept the reserve he'd been taught by generations of serious-minded, nearly Puritanical Perrys. His work, his beloved teaching, was another source of his wife's pain, taking his time, taking him away, devouring his hours. Yet he could not change the way he was any more than he could change his height by thinking about it. He didn't know what to say. He looked at her a long time. Oretta saw the hurt in his face, too.

Finally he said, "I do the best I can for you and Bobby, Oretta. I try as hard as I know how. I mean well. If it's not comin' out that way, believe me, I mean well."

Oretta saw what it cost him to say that, could begin to see the unbending rigor of his character, that to him love was not hugging and sweet-talk but taking the best care of his loved ones he knew how. She faintly grasped how far apart her needs were from his. It did nothing to comfort her hurt. But she could see very clearly that he loved her as much as a man could love a woman.

San Marcos that year seemed almost like a vacation. It had been a hard year. Clayborne's Auntie Leona has suffered another terrible loss only two years after her husband had been carried away by pneumonia: her twelve year old son John Ferman, Jr. died of appendicitis. Tom and Belle were still rebuilding from being burned out and had not yet finished their new house. Hoyt had quit school after only nine grades. Farm prices were dipping to total disaster. It seemed like a new County government somewhere in Texas collapsed every day. The three-act comedy put on at the end of the school year by Blackstump Valley school drew only light laughter, as if the audience were too tired and stunned to laugh. All the fuss and change being made by that man in the White House didn't seem to be reaching Texas very fast. Against this chaos, Southwest Texas State Teachers College seemed like a refuge with its orderly classes and the natural beauty of its setting and the ferment of new ideas all around.

They found a place down the hill this year, in the Episcopal parsonage — the preacher lived upstairs and the Perrys lived in a small downstairs apartment. Life settled into its college routine quickly and Clayborne took Oretta and Bobby swimming in the late afternoons. Clayborne became more the person Oretta wanted him to be. It took several weeks for her to realize that Clayborne had not really changed, but simply that when the time was available, he devoted it to Bobby and to her. Yet his Perry reserve was not about to crack. One day she could no longer avoid the realization that this was simply the way he was. Nothing would change him. He loved her and Bobby as deeply as humanly possible. He was simply like a force of nature. She might as well accept him like he was. And so she did.

As tended to happen, life soon changed completely. In early August, a letter arrived for Clayborne. It had been written by Mr. Arthur H. Barsh, one of the new trustees of Blackstump Valley School District Number Seventy. It stated:

Dear Mr. Perry,

The trustees of Blackstump Valley school have entered into discussions with Iredell School District concerning proposed consolidation for the school year 1934-1935.

The two sides have reached agreement in principle, pending your agreement to the arrangements.

Should you agree to this consolidation you are hereby offered the position of principal of Iredell Elementary School, salary to be commensurate with increased responsibility, $135.00 per month.

If you are agreeable to this arrangement, please reply immediately and the trustees will begin consolidation proceedings.

Sincerely,

Arthur H. Barsh

Clayborne notified the trustees immediately of his agreement. At the end of August he took his family back to Blackstump Valley on Cloud Nine.

-15-

IREDELL
ON THE NORTH BOSQUE

FOR some reason, Clayborne Perry's life seems to be tied to the drainage basin of the Bosque River. He was born in its watershed, grew up less than eight miles from its shoals, went to junior college practically on its banks and took teaching jobs progressively farther and farther down its oceanward course to where it empties into the Brazos at Waco. Most of the Bosque, and all of Clayborne Perry's Bosque, is called the North Fork of the Bosque River by mapmakers. They must have had a sense of humor when they counted the East, Middle and South Forks, because the ninety-mile-long North Fork *is* the Bosque for all intents and purposes. The tiny East Fork actually flows into the western half of the river from the north, and the Middle Fork and South Fork put together are not nearly half as long as the North Fork. Perhaps mapmakers have their reasons, but it's hard to see why they just didn't call the North Fork the plain old Bosque River and let it go at that, because that's what everybody in the Grand Prairie did — except, of course, the farmers who lived on the short South Fork and everyone on the Middle Fork, even up to the village of Pancake.

The North Fork of the Bosque arises in two limestone springs some five miles apart in the Cross Timbers region of Erath County, one up toward Washout Mountain near the little town of Huckabay, the other not far from Twin Mountains due north of Lingleville. The streams of the North Fork of the North Bosque and the South Fork of the North Bosque bubble and tumble along their separate cobblestone courses for perhaps ten miles before blending just above Stephenville to become the North Fork of the

477

Bosque River. All these Forks and Norths and Souths are no doubt just another example of the mapmaking profession's obtusity. But the river does not know it has been given such awkward names, and it grows and broadens as it picks up tributaries downstream from Stephenville, first at Indian Creek which runs down from Welcome Valley and then at Alarm Creek and Sims Creek and Liveoak Creek and Green Creek at Clairette. By the time the Bosque flows past the old grain elevator and city park at Hico it has become a respectable river. And with the influx of Honey Creek and Duffau Creek and all the little branches that drain Dude Flat and Blackstump Valley — Little Duffau Creek, Camp Branch, Rocky Creek, Walker Branch, Boyd Branch, Flag Branch — it is a force to be contended with as it glides by the little town of Iredell, Texas.

Nobody really knows how the Bosque got its name. Its meaning is plain enough, though, for "bosque" is Spanish for "woods" or "woodsy" and the cognate "bosky" has come into modern English usage through Middle English dialect. The Bosque is certainly woodsy, rich with pecans and cottonwoods and willows and many other hardwood species that grace its narrow shoreline. Some historians give credit for naming this major tributary of the Brazos to the Spanish Marquis de Aguayo who is supposed to have dubbed the stream for its tree cover in 1719, but others say a French fur trader, one Juan Bosquet, named the river after himself in 1770. The least likely explanation is that the Spanish officer Fernando del Bosque named the river while leading the Bosque-Larios Expedition to Christianize the Indians of southwest Texas in 1675, but he came nowhere near Central Texas and there is little likelihood that he ever saw the river, much less named it. None of this, of course, made the slightest difference to the stricken farmers of the Depression era Grand Prairie.

But the little town of Iredell on the banks of the North Bosque did make a difference to them. Iredell is four or five streets deep from north to south, depending on whether you count the little loop streets right on the riverbank. And Iredell is seven or eight streets wide east to west, depending on whether you count the little loop street east of the school. None of the thirteen gravel streets seem to have had names in the 1930s — nobody can remember any — but since there were fewer than a hundred fifty buildings of any description in town, including businesses, churches, residences and school structures, it would have been hard to get lost.

Iredell had been important to the Perry family, too. It was here, back in 1900, that Clayborne's Grandfather James W. Perry got off the train when coming from Alabama after his family finally starved out on their poor piney woods farm near Heflin. With his wife Lou and their six children, including Clayborne's father Tom, Jim Perry had moved to a relative's little farm just east of town. Aside from the shock of the gigantic mind-soaking horizons here, the uprooted Perrys in many ways felt right at home. At that time the whole countryside around Iredell felt like a small piece of Alabama set down in Texas. Most of the oldtimers had come from the Yellowhammer State 'way back when, and a lot of the newcomers belonged to that same Alabama stock, transplanted from the Cumberland Plateau and the Coastal Plain and the Piedmont hills and the old Black Belt to these gentle Texas hills where things would actually grow and you could get enough ahead to own your own land.

Naturally, Alabama customs came with the immigrants. So most of Iredell's denizens dipped snuff. They dipped snuff to the point that Iredell became known throughout the Grand Prairie as *Snuff City* rather than Iredell, and its citizens were dubbed *Snuff Dippers*. The townsfolk had very little polish, and in fact were rather proud of their humble and earthy condition, so they didn't really mind. In fact, when the literati of Iredell decided to publish a monthly magazine, the title on the masthead said *Iredell* and beneath it stood the subtitle *Snuff City*.

Something like four hundred fifty people called Iredell home in 1934, but its schools combed some six hundred students from around about in the countryside which made the little town the educational center for at least ten miles in every direction. No matter how hard the Depression squeezed these Grand Prairie farmers — and some were flattened like a flea being snapped between two thumbnails — educating their children remained virtually a sacred obligation to be carried out at all costs. And in that terrible Depression year of 1934, educating young people looked like it was becoming a life work for twenty-four-year-old W. C. Perry, Principal of Iredell Elementary School. He resented the name Snuff City when he moved into Iredell, but in time learned to chuckle at it and then to savor its pungent country spice.

"We sure do appreciate you folks letting us rent with you," said Principal Perry.

"Oh, we sure do," seconded Oretta. "Bobby won't be any trouble at all."

"Well, you're right welcome," said Mrs. French, standing next to her husband. "Your boy's such a cute little feller I don't see how we could object. And we're happy to have the new school principal here with us. Are you all moved in now?"

"Yes, Ma'am, that was the last of our stuff," said Clayborne.

"Well, I hope you like it here," said Angus French.

The home of Mr. R. Angus French, owner of Iredell's Magnolia Petroleum Company service station, blended with the short brown grass of late September, an earth-colored flagstone creation of a type becoming more common in Texas. True to its Spanish heritage, the home's exterior of variegated flat rocks showed the skill, even artistry, of careful stonemasons intent on mixing and matching many-hued, many-shaped jigsaw-puzzle elements into a harmonious homey whole. The central peaked gable with its fireplace right in the middle gave the low structure some height while the flanking porches right and left spread it out to hug the groundline, at once a little imposing and a lot cozy. The hard geometric line of the gable's fascia boards gave way to an imaginative and unusual roofline over both the porches: instead of a linear overhanging eave, the stonemasons had stopped the roof slope at the front wall and ran their top flagstone course above the roofline a foot or two, like a short false-front. It was almost as if they had meant to build up higher but, admiring the ragged rock shapes, decided against it in midcourse and left it as it stood, like frozen flagstone flames licking at the sky.

"Mr. Perry," said Mr. French, "have you seen those Roosevelt people coming around to buy up the cows and the cotton?"

"Yes, sir, I sure have. Just yesterday. We were moving our things out of Mr. Fouts' place when they came by. They offered him $12.50 for each cow and $7.50 for each calf. That's a better price than you could get on the open market these days."

"I guess so," said French, not very convinced. "What do they do with 'em once they've bought 'em? I've heard stories that they just shoot 'em."

"That's what they did with Mr. Fouts'."

"Seems like a sorry waste," muttered French.

"Nothin' much else to do. It's been so dry this year they'd have died anyway. All the farmers out in Blackstump Valley just sold off their poorest animals, the ones that weren't goin' to make it."

"Still seems like a waste."

"Well, we asked if we could take one of the calves and butcher it and they said 'fine.' I picked one of the best and showed 'em which one. The government man took out his twenty-two and shot it in the head like you'd kill a hog. They weren't cruel or anything. We dressed it for meat and put it in storage over at the Iredell Ice Plant."

"I don't know," said French, "all this government buyin' just don't seem natural."

"That's what my Papa said when they offered to buy his cotton crop. He told 'em to go away. He'd pick it and sell it at the gin even if it was only bringin' a nickel a pound. Said he couldn't imagine plowin' under good cotton just to make an extra few dollars from the government."

The uneasy attitudes of many Grand Prairie farmers about the Roosevelt administration were beginning to die down by September, 1934. The New Deal's neo-Populist efforts to regulate corporate capitalism had been taken with misgiving at first, but it soon became apparent to Texans across the state that it was not really *corporate* capitalism they thought of when somebody said "free enterprise." As one historian of the times noted, Texans believed strongly in private property and *personal* free enterprise, but personal capitalism and corporate capitalism are two somewhat different things. Texans had no real love for corporate capitalism as it had grown up in the United States between 1862 and 1929; in fact, many Texans blamed the big corporations for the economic debacle that now threatened the nation's very existence. There was not yet much corporate capitalism in Texas — most farmers were only aware of some oil companies and a few construction outfits — and, ironically, the New Deal was soon to become the most powerful force in history to bring the industrial way of life to Texas through dam-building contracts and shipyards and machine tool factories and military installations.

But nobody could see that yet, and now that it was clear that FDR had no intention of doing away with *personal* free enterprise or changing social arrangements in Texas or creating a Soviet of America, the farmers began to find him enormously appealing, particularly when the outside money came pouring in. There were few holdouts like Tom Perry when the cotton man came to pay them top prices for plowing under their crops. Most were like Will Fouts who sold off his weak and dying livestock and kept the best to reproduce his herds — they were grateful for every $12.50 they could get. What they found was that they liked the New Deal but couldn't stand most New Dealers, the eggheads and theorists and highfalutin Easterners from Harvard and Yale, which was nothing new for Texans — they had never liked or trusted such people. What they liked most about the New Deal was that it brought Texans into positions of national power, *real* national power.

John Nance Garner, a basic folk-conservative from that canyon country down by Uvalde and Sabinal and Concan and Rio Frio, was the Vice President of the United States, which made him President of the Senate, where he pushed through most of the New Deal programs for his president. Jesse Jones, a Houston bigshot, chaired the Reconstruction Finance Corporation. In the House of Representatives names like Sam Rayburn evinced growing respect, and Texans chaired the key committees of Agriculture, Interstate Commerce, Judiciary, Public Buildings and Grounds, Rivers and Harbors and — most important — Appropriations. In the Senate, Connally and Sheppard swayed military and foreign affairs with an understated astuteness that out-slicked the slickest Easterners.

And like their constituents back home, these Washington Texans hated totalitarian aggression and resented the fact that the democracies seemed to be doing nothing about it. They hated the Soviet Union and they hated the little mustachioed dictator who had come to power in Germany. If they had had their way, our military forces would have ushered Herr Hitler to his fiery *Gotterdammerung* a few weeks after the Reichstag gave him absolute power in 1933. But most Americans would have considered that impolite and thereby gave the maniac time to set up the greatest conflagration and slaughter in human history. It wasn't so much that Texans liked war, they just weren't as afraid of it as their neighbors.

Despite their inability to convince America to get rid of the Nazis, the Texans still did very well in Washington, wielding their power with skill and purpose. What this all really meant for Texas was a disproportionately large share of New Deal money, more than twenty-five percent above the national average based on population. And the Texans didn't just meat-axe their way into this money, they finessed it away from opponents. Refined and haughty Easterners learned to their everlasting regret that the redneck Congressmen and the Senators in cowman boots and the administrators with big Stetsons, despite their aw-shucks corn-pone image, were not stupid behind closed doors and made suave Eastern big-time operators look like tyros.

"We've come to take your little boy away," boomed the rough voice.

Bobby cried from his mother's lap, " 'Ill! And Foutsie! Mom! Look! 'Ill and Foutsie!" He jumped down and ran out from the front porch on his short little legs to the waiting arms of Ethel Fouts.

"Yes, it's Foutsie!" the woman said, picking him up and hugging him tight.

Oretta grinned as she walked out to the graveled street and stood next to her friends under the liveoak tree. "We wondered if you folks were going to show up this Saturday. We've already got our shopping done and Clayborne's gone off to work."

"Work? On Saturday?" asked Ethel Fouts. "Where does he work on Saturday?"

"Over at Mr. French's Magnolia station. He's worked there the last couple of weeks. You must have passed him when you came into town. He's pickin' up a little extra money doing the service station books for him. It's not much, just enough to pay for the car's gasoline each week."

Will Fouts shook his head and said, "That man's a regular glutton for work."

"Oh, he's all of that," sighed Oretta.

"I can see you've been working, too, Oretta," said Mrs. Fouts. "You've got Bobby all dressed up in a new little outfit. You must keep busy at the sewing machine."

"Oh, it's nothing, Mrs. Fouts. You got to keep your children looking nice."

Mrs. Fouts inquired, "Was the calf good?"

"The one we got from when the Roosevelt men came by?"

"That's the one."

"Oh, you know, we put it in the cold room over at the ice plant," said Oretta. "And the first few days it was wonderful, real good eating. But then, you know, it got moldy and the meat went bad and we had to throw the rest of it out. It was a shame."

"My, that is a shame," said Ethel Fouts.

"Well, Mrs. Perry," said Will Fouts, "that happens, especially in the summer when the ice melts down so quick. But how does Clayborne like being principal of a town school by now? It's been about a month, hasn't it?"

"He's as pleased as punch," she replied. "I go over there with him after school every now and then. He's so proud of the new gym you'd think he built it himself. He keeps tellin' everybody it's the first one in Bosque County. And you know they're using the brand new high school building for the first time this fall. It cost seventeen thousand five hundred dollars, can you imagine?"

"So I heard. We'll have to drive around and look at it on our way out."

"But they got Clayborne and the first seven grades stuck out back in that old-timey two-story rock building."

"They still using that old relic?" asked Mrs. Fouts. "Why it's about to fall down, isn't it?"

"Oh, I think it's still safe," said Oretta. "It's just old-fashioned now. You should hear Clayborne talk about how bad a place it is. He's got some new-fangled ideas about how classrooms ought to be built to make it easier for the students to learn and such. He's been studyin' up on it."

"Well, you'll have to admit he's a special kind of man when it comes to teaching," said Will Fouts. "He has a feel for it. That's why the trustees asked him to come to Blackstump Valley in the first place. But what about here in town? Is it any harder to teach these spoiled town kids?"

"Well I don't know," said Oretta. "Clayborne's come home every two or three days with a tale about how he had to take a paddle to some of the older kids that were rebellious and caused trouble at school. Also he takes a strong position against older kids that abuse the younger ones. They seem to have about the same discipline problems here that they did out in the country. Nothing really serious, these kids have good up-bringing at home."

"Are these town folks against spankin' unruly kids?" asked Will, alarmed.

"No the parents are very supportive, best I can tell. Clayborne hasn't had any complaints from parents. They know the principal isn't going to paddle one of their kids unless he needs it. I think the parents around here understand. That reminds me, what are the parents doin' with the Blackstump Valley school building now that all the kids are comin' here to Iredell?"

"We're keepin' it locked up and in good shape, Mrs. Perry," said Will

Fouts. "If this consolidation doesn't work out, we'll open 'er up again and do like we been doing for years, run it ourselves."

"And how's everybody back in the valley getting along? How's the Newmans?"

"Oh, the Newmans are fine, but their boys are right down in the mouth."

"What's the matter?"

"Oh, somebody that didn't know any better come along the road in their car and saw the Newman's pet crow sitting on the fence and shot him dead."

"Not ol' Jim Crow?"

"Yep, they killed ol' Jim Crow. And it like to killed them boys. They thought the world and all of that ol' bird, you know. Just tore 'em up."

"Oh, no," said Oretta. "I got right fond of that silly crow myself. That's too bad, it's just too bad."

"Yep, it sure is. But how's your husband getting along with these town folks — outside of teaching their kids, I mean?"

"Oh, he's made the change just fine. In fact Mr. Tidwell a couple of blocks over has invited Clayborne to join the Masons here. They have a lodge right down where you come into town."

"Masons, eh?" said Will Fouts. "They must like your man, Mrs. Perry. It isn't just everybody gets invited into the Masons, you know."

"I could tell by the way Clayborne acted, " Oretta said. "He's anxious to join, but it costs quite a bit. He doesn't know if we can raise the money. But he says he's right impressed with the Masons because they profess the belief. . . what did he say?. . .let me think. . .the belief that God is the Great Architect of the Universe. That's just what Clayborne said."

"Oh, I know they're right fine Christian people, Mrs. Perry," said Will Fouts. "And influential in the community, yessir. Your husband will go far as a Mason, mark my words. And speaking of influence, did you see where Ma and Pa Ferguson just up and withdrew from the governor's race?"

"Clayborne said something about that, he sure did," said Oretta.

Ethel Fouts chimed in, "I'll be so glad to see them go I could shout hallelujah! I recollect how Ma and Pa Ferguson were so pleased to see prohibition repealed. I just hope we never bring beer into our county. And I'm not all that sure a woman should be governor."

Oretta asked, "Why did the Fergusons quit, Mr. Fouts? Was one of them sick or something? I can't imagine them just giving up that little cattle business Clayborne talks about — you know, how they sell a cow for five or six hundred dollars to some family that's got a boy in prison and then Ma pardons him."

"I don't rightly know, Mrs. Perry. I expect they just found the goin' too rough with the Depression not gettin' any better, you know. It sure looks like that Jim Allred is going to win since he beat Tom Hunter in the primary. But who can figure politics? I'm just glad to be rid of the Fergusons. Now let me ask you the important question: what time would you like us to bring Bobby back this afternoon?"

"Oh, I know how he loves to visit with you and stay a long time. . ."

"And you know how much we love to have him," said Ethel to Oretta. And then to Bobby: "Are you ready to come see Foutsie? Visit with 'Ill and Foutsie?"

The boy laughed and said gleefully, "Go see 'Ill! Go see Foutsie!"

"That's where you're goin', squirt," smiled Oretta. "Well, how about five-thirty? Can you have him back by then? I know it's a little early, but we're going into Hico tonight to see a Will Rogers picture. . ."

"Oh, really? Which one?" asked Will Fouts. "We might go see it, too, eh, Mother? That Will Rogers is my favorite — except for Shirley Temple."

"It's called *David Harum*. I don't know what it's about. Ever'body says it's just wonderful."

"Well, I know it'll be good if Will Rogers is in it," said Mr. Fouts. "We'll be sure to bring Bobby back before you have to get ready. We wouldn't want to make you folks late to the picture show, now would we, little feller?" He tousled the youngster's hair and Bobby tried to tousle back.

It was not long that fall before Principal Perry settled into his new routine and began to better his lot and that of those around him. He decided that Iredell Elementary could use some school spirit, and calling upon his recollections of Tarleton, he formed his fourth through seventh grades into a pep squad, setting up qualifications and elections for cheer leaders, making sure they had attractive but modest outfits, teaching them yells and taking them to football games. His four elementary grades were larger than Iredell High School's student body and did just as good a job of yelling. Since the playing fields had no lights, all games were played in the daytime and the kids were all home by dark. Principal Perry also organized and coached a girls' basketball team that played surrounding elementary schools just as the boys' basketball team had always done. There was a noticeable improvement in the school's sense of solidarity.

And he managed to come up with $12.50 for each of the first three degrees of the Ancient Free and Accepted Masons. As all beginners, he joined the Blue Lodge and successively learned the secret ritual of the degrees of Entered Apprentice, Fellowcraft and Master Mason. By December, brother W. C. Perry had passed his third degree, Master Mason, and enjoyed the full benefits and privileges of the order. He then worked his way up through the offices of the Iredell Lodge and became Senior Warden in the West, second in command to the Worshipful Master.

The thunderstorm was the first big one in a year and a half. All over the Grand Prairie that dawn in May, 1935, farmers looked up to the glowering sky hungrily, hoping for the salvation of a drenching rain. Spikes of lightning shattered the air everywhere, and fierce patches of rain fell in its wake. It was not the best possible morning for a drive into Waco.

"I can't help it, Oretta," said Clayborne. "Mr. Barsh told me to get over to Baylor today and see if we couldn't find some replacement teachers."

"But it's so ugly out," said Oretta. "You'll get your nice new suit wet. And that road to Waco is so bad."

A nearby crack of lightning wrote an exclamation point to her sentence.

"They've got a lot of it paved, now, honey. Especially that bad curve just beyond Meridian. Don't worry. I'll be all right. It's really important that we get the best teachers we can, you know. We want our kids to get a real education here. Think how you'll feel when Bobby starts in school. And, besides, it'll only seem like a regular work day. I'll be home for supper."

The vast shuddering bass drum of overarching thunder nearly drowned out his words.

Oretta looked out their apartment door to the front porch where slashes of rain slanted in onto the concrete slab. She peered dubiously beyond into the cloud-darkened gravel street. "Well, okay," she said hesitantly. "But you drive careful, now. And at least I can bring Bobby out to the car to say goodbye."

"Look at him," Clayborne said, nodding at his youngster curled up in bed. "He's still asleep. And you'll get soaked."

"I don't know how he can sleep through all this thunder. And I don't mind a little water."

They went out and stood under the shelter of the protecting flagstone porch, watching the pelting rain kick up little clouds of powdery dirt everywhere.

"Look at that," laughed Clayborne. "It's been dry for so long even the rain raises the dust."

"It's just going to all run off," said Oretta. "I've seen it this way before. It won't soak in at all."

"But it'll soak you good if you come out to the car. I'll say goodbye right here. You be good today and take care of Bobby!"

"I will, Clayborne," she smiled wistfully.

Directly over their heads a single bolt of lightning unfolded from one dark cloud to another, slowly, majestically branching and fanning out wider and wider like a complex nerve ending or the great image of some impossible tree in the fiery heavens. Clayborne dashed from the porch toward the driveway and his car.

"Mr. Perry!" called a familiar feminine voice from somewhere in the rain. He stopped dead in his tracks and looked around. There at the archway of the flagstone porch on the other side of the house he saw Mrs. French leaning out into the downpour. He ran and joined her under its shelter.

The aging lady said to him, "I thought I heard you two talking over there!" Then she shouted to the opposite porch, "Hello, Mrs. Perry!"

"Hidy, Miz French," said Oretta, leaning out in the rain to see.

"What can I do for you, Mrs. French?" Clayborne asked.

"It's what I can do for you, Mr. Perry. I forgot to tell you last night. The man up at Mitchell's said for me to let you know that they want you over in groceries this Saturday."

"But I was goin' to work in the bank this weekend."

"That's why he wanted me to tell you. He hasn't been able to get word to you. Charlie Conley put off his vacation so they won't need you in the bank. They need you in groceries because there's a giveaway this weekend and they want you to do it for them."

"I see. Well, thank you for letting me know, Mrs. French. I appreciate it. I got to git, Mrs. French. See you later." He ran out in the rain once more toward his Terraplane.

As he got in his car, he shouted over the metal auto roof, "See you tonight, Oretta."

Since February Clayborne had worked Saturdays at Iredell's Mitchell General Store. He had discovered that you couldn't make a living by teaching alone, not if you wanted to keep up your education and do such things as work with the Masons. T. Mitchell Company offered reasonable pay — a dollar and a half a day plus twenty percent discount on any purchases — and many places to work: they owned half the town, it seemed. Principal Perry found himself selling yardage in the dry goods department for two weekends, posting checks in the bank with a bookkeeping machine the next two, arranging and selling produce in the grocery section the next two, ordering John Deere tractor parts in implements the next two, fitting people with shoes or selling feed or testing all the cream and eggs the next two.

Some Saturdays, Mitchell's would run a promotional giveaway, handing customers a ticket for every dollar's worth of merchandise they purchased and then holding a drawing in the street. The townsfolk seemed to like having Principal Perry working among them, and he became their favorite giveaway master of ceremonies. He'd go up to the center of town, ring the bell, get someone to pick the winning ticket out of a tin can, and then he'd give away a sack of flour one Saturday, a five-dollar bill another Saturday, and occasionally even a ten-dollar bill. Mitchell's worked him on weekends and days off school and had promised him summer work.

He'd need the summer work, for he had relinquished his engine operator job on Will Fouts' harvest crew so he could attend both sessions of summer school at San Marcos, the first of which unfortunately began just as harvest approached its peak. How he fretted to himself and worried over letting that job go after all those years! He'd been with harvest since he was fourteen. It felt like a part of him being torn away when he gave up harvest so he could continue his education. Regardless how easy the transition seemed to others, it was not easy adjusting himself to being a *town* school principal.

He quickly found that principalship in town was much more complex than holding sway over Blackstump Valley School. Out in the country the job had involved little more than teaching. Here at Iredell it was much more than teaching and Principal Perry soon realized that he did not have a firm grasp of what principals were supposed to do — not as firm as he wanted, anyway. There was just too much to do: trying to make sure that his teachers — most of whom simply taught one elementary grade — had one period free each day to grade papers or whatnot, especially in the upper grades, calling in substitutes when regulars fell ill, determining student counts to verify tax allotments, taking classroom responsibilities himself, instructing subjects that his grade-teachers were not prepared for, mathematics in the morning and history in the afternoons. Iredell's school superintendent also called Clayborne over to teach typing at the high school every afternoon — at least the equipment was good, ten sturdy Underwoods with blank keys and metal handshields to keep students from watching their fingers while learning.

All this was a little overwhelming until the new town principal happened to thumb through a catalogue from Abilene Christian College listing its correspondence course entitled simply *The Principal*. Clayborne ordered it and relished the study: he found out exactly what a principal ought to do. By the time he finished the course, he smiled smugly to himself: he'd pretty well figured it out right on his own and his correspondence instruction for the most part merely validated his own intuition. He began to realize that educational administration was truly his calling: he was gifted with an understanding of it.

But this rainy morning there was a highly specific and immediate problem to worry about: finding replacement teachers for those two or three among the seventeen in Iredell schools who had submitted their resignations this spring. And that was the purpose of his trip to Baylor University in Waco.

"Dr. Stretch?" asked the young principal looking wide-eyed into the office, a little intimidated by the sprawling campus and imposing buildings he'd walked past to get here. Baylor was bigger than Tarleton and San Marcos put together — bigger than *two* of them put together.

"Yes, I'm Dr. Stretch. What can I do for you?" asked the pleasant woman.

"I'm W. C. Perry from Iredell Elementary School. Mr. Barsh sent me."

"Oh, yes!" she smiled warmly. "I think we've met before — at teacher meetings in Meridian, haven't we? Do come in. Have a seat. And how is Mr. Barsh these days? I haven't seen him for several months."

"Oh, he's busy as usual," said Principal Perry somewhat circumspectly as he settled into a comfortable office chair beside the desk of Dr. Lorena Stretch.

"Still the promoter, is he?" she grinned, catching his unstated meaning. Obviously this was a sharp lady.

"Yes, Ma'am," said Principal Perry, brightening up. "He's got the new high school building running just fine and has nine buses going off out in the country every day. We must have nearly four hundred elementary students alone this spring. He really keeps things hopping."

"Yes, all those trial consolidations of the rural schools," she mused. "I was surprised when they brought in so many students last fall. I think we'll see a lot more consolidations once we can really see the effects of this new rural aid law and the state's equalization program. I understand you were one of those rural school principals yourself."

"Yes, Ma'am. I came in from Blackstump Valley School. We had about forty-two students."

"How's your consolidation working out?"

"I think all the schools will stick with it. There have been a few problems with the buses breaking down and not stopping at the right places. But like you say, until we find out whether this $17.50 per capita apportionment can really be paid, I don't see how any of those little schools are going to go back to operating on their own. Our teachers are even having to cash their vouchers at the bank for a ten-percent discount because there's not enough tax money for the school district to pay them in full. I think we've seen the last of the little rural schools scattered every few miles."

"In a way, I hope you're right, Mr. Perry. Not that rural schools are necessarily inferior, but I think consolidation has more to offer for everyone, more services in fewer physical facilities. A better value for the tax dollar once everything is sorted out. With the savings you might even be able to replace that ancient castle you're using as an elementary school in Iredell."

He smiled. "Oh, yes, Ma'am. Mr. Barsh has talked some about that. I've got some ideas about new designs for elementary classrooms, blackboard heights and window sizes and these new floor tiles that are coming on the market."

Dr. Stretch made a mental check mark beside the name W. C. Perry for future reference, and said, "That's very interesting, Mr. Perry. I've given some thought to those matters myself. I'd like to pursue the subject with you at greater length. But I'm sure that's not what brings you to Waco in this weather today."

"No, Ma'am, you're right. We've had a few resignations on our teaching staff and Mr. Barsh feels like you'd know just who might fill the bill from your education class here at Baylor. You know, somebody who could fit in with a little community like Iredell, could work hard, could get along with people. Mr. Barsh says you just know who will work out in our kind of school."

"Oh, yes," chuckled Dr. Stretch, "for some reason Mr. Barsh thinks I can read minds. . ."

She probably could. Dr. Lorena Stretch had started out as a country girl herself and had come to her teaching position at Baylor in 1930 with a thorough understanding of the small traditional Texas community. She knew the citizens of the Grand Prairie, she knew her teaching graduates, and she was piercingly astute at matching the two. Principal Perry found he could tell Dr. Stretch that his school wanted a certain kind of person and she wouldn't recommend one she didn't think was exactly right. That first year at Iredell he got only good teachers from Baylor through her counsel. Dr. Stretch usually selected some common girl from a farm family, a girl who understood the commands and taboos, the do's and don't's, someone who would fit into a small hidebound rural town without having to be told all the rules. And of rules there were plenty. Iredell School District had a teacher contract demanding that teachers not drink, that women not smoke, that no teacher would date on week nights, that no teacher would attend a motion picture show on week nights and a number of other highly specific behavioral strictures — a pretty rigid contract. Nor would Iredell schools hire a man and wife teacher team, since it would give two taxpayer incomes to one local family. Married teacher teams had to work in adjacent school systems. In these tough times, no one squawked about the restrictions: they were glad to have any work at all.

In mid-July the Perrys made their third annual pilgrimage to San Marcos. There were no rooms at Mrs. Anderson's this year and they found a place down the hill in the Episcopal parsonage. The preacher lived upstairs and the Perrys lived downstairs. It was a little closer to the grocery store and the rest of downtown, so Oretta didn't mind not being up at the top of the hill. At two-and-a-half, Bobby was toddling around on his own and charming the neighbors.

Shortly before summer they had found new quarters in Iredell as well, moving in late May from the French's two-room apartment to a four-room apartment with a front and back porch. It wasn't far, just two houses down the street to the east in a wood frame house belonging to an elderly widow, Mrs. Ida Weir. And that summer the state legislature did Principal Perry an unwelcome favor: while reenacting the ceiling law for teacher salaries at $85 per month, it set all principals' salaries at no more than $95. Clayborne felt the loss of $40 a month income sharply — it gave him second thoughts about continuing with college, but not very serious ones.

This year he signed up for a teaching methods class taught by Dr. Votaw, and since history was his major, there was another history class with Professor H. M. Greene, the beloved nonconformist. But the lasting history lesson in W. C. Perry's life was hardly recognized as such at the time. It came first in the form of a headline Clayborne noticed in the Southwest Texas State Teachers College student newspaper, *The College Star*, issue of Thursday, August 1, 1935:

Prominent Ex-Student is Named State NYA Head

National Youth Administration to

Aid College, High School

Students

"Oretta," he said, reading at the kitchen table in their parsonage apartment, "listen to this:

Lyndon B. Johnson, graduate of the Southwest Texas Teachers College and well known here, Saturday was appointed Texas director of the National Youth Administration, an agency created to aid youths in obtaining an education. He was named by Aubrey W. Williams, national NYA director.

Johnson, son of Sam Johnson of Johnson City, has been secretary to Congressman M. Kleberg since December, 1931.

The National Youth Administration was inaugurated recently by President Roosevelt to displace the old FERA under which local students have been receiving aid.

Funds from this agency are to be used to help needy high school and college students continue their education. Since twelve percent of a student body is eligible for aid under this Administration, approximately 100 students of this college will be eligible.

Johnson plans to leave Washington within a few days and will open an office in the Littlefield Building in Austin. He will maintain a close working relationship with H. P. Drought of San Antonio, Works Progress Administrator for Texas.

Johnson, who is only 26, is said to be the youngest State NYA director yet appointed.

"Now what do you think about that, Oretta? This Johnson fellow is only a year older than me and he's the state head of the NYA. You see? San Marcos turns out some pretty good graduates."

He thought nothing more about it, but within a few weeks, the Texas country boy who had struggled for an education and made his way into the education field would be introduced to politics by another Texas country boy who would one day make his way into the presidency of the United States.

The story of how Lyndon Baines Johnson was appointed state director of NYA on July 27, 1935, is the story in microcosm of Johnson's entire career, a picture in miniature displaying the phenomenal ambition of the man and the nearly unbelievable loyalty he wrought from those around him.

According to one of Johnson's least sympathetic but most competent biographers, Johnson came to the job not because he particularly wanted to head the NYA in Texas but because he desperately needed a way out of a career dead end. There was nowhere further to go in his Washington job as Congressman Richard Kleberg's secretary — administrative aide in modern federalspeak. Kleberg was not about to step aside even though his aide Johnson burned with ambition to rise above the anonymous ranks of congressional secretaries, to be "somebody," to climb the ladder of political power and become a congressman himself.

At that critical juncture, Johnson was offered a big-salary job as lobbyist for General Electric, which would have meant leaving elective politics forever — anyone identified with "the interests" could never win a Congressional seat in Texas. He was on the verge of accepting, but at the last minute an old friend came to his rescue: Sam Rayburn. Throughout Rayburn's long lonely career as the aloof and incorruptible congressman from Texas, he took only one protege under his wing: Lyndon Johnson. Rayburn, so the whisper goes, at the crucial hour paid a visit to Texas Senator Tom Connally, a man whose voice could influence the selection of the Texas NYA director. It was well known that Rayburn never visited people. Nor had he ever been friendly to Connally. Yet in this case he came into Connally's office and anxiously requested the senator to personally intercede with President Roosevelt to appoint Lyndon Johnson. Nobody had ever seen Sam Rayburn get emotional, at least not anxiously emotional. The astonished Connally agreed but the White House said no. A former union official from Port Arthur, DeWitt Kinard was selected, his appointment as the new director was announced and then he was formally sworn into office as Texas NYA director. What happened next is best described by Pulitzer Prize-winning Johnson biographer Robert A. Caro:

> Sam Rayburn went to the White House. What he said is not known, but the White House announced that a mistake had been made. The NYA director for Texas was not DeWitt Kinard after all, the announcement said. It was Lyndon Johnson.

The story is the archetype of Johnson's life: a seemingly dead-end situation, hope against grasping hope for advancement, utter defeat, then a miraculous snatching of victory from the jaws of defeat. Not many men in history have played this perilous pattern so long and so successfully as LBJ — for one thing, few have reached as high — and a mere handful have pursued a similarly perverse, tortuous dialectical path to the most powerful position on earth. And many of his miracles were the work of friends. LBJ's power to evoke paternal affection from older men — he was a "professional son," some cynics asserted — had worked on Cecil Eugene Evans, president of Southwest Texas State Teachers College, or "Prexy Evans" as he was fondly known. During Johnson's undergraduate years at San Marcos, Prexy Evans created a new position — secretary to the president — especially for the young Lyndon, who, fellow students have said, methodically insinuated himself upward, ever currying favor with Evans from the day he took his first lowly student-aid job as a campus leaf-raker and rock-picker.

Whatever ingratiating methods LBJ used — and there is dispute about that — they worked. Prexy Evans in 1935 held his aspiring alumnus in the highest esteem and warmest fatherly regard. Witness the feeling that Evans displayed in this personal note of congratulation printed in the August 1, 1935, issue of *The College Star:*

> Washington announces the appointment of Lyndon B. Johnson to the position of Director of National Youth Administration for Texas. The appointment carries with it a wonderful opportunity for the promotion of education in Texas, and for government service on high levels. Lyndon enrolled in the College in September, 1926 and graduated in August, 1930. He was Secretary to the President of the College for several years. As a student he had a splendid academic record, was versatile, and took an interest in student activities. He was widely and favorably known among students and among the citizens of San Marcos during his years in College. He taught with marked success in Cotulla and Houston, leaving the latter place to accept the position of Secretary to Congressman R. M. Kleberg, November, 1931, which position he has held until the present time. In congressional circles it is generally conceded that Lyndon B. Johnson is one of the most capable and efficient secretaries in Washington.

> His friends in the college and in Texas join with his Washington friends in giving endorsement to this worthy promotion, and in the confident belief that quality, efficiency, and loyalty of service to the Government will certainly follow.

Some of this effusion must be written off as a campaign speech to make sure that San Marcos got its share of federal NYA money — Evans was above all a good steward to his college — but the unmistakable note of sincerity rings through his mildly pompous words like plucked heartstrings. Evans loved LBJ like a son, and wasn't afraid to show it. Had he any inkling how far his young friend would go?

Perhaps he did, for as soon as he heard of the new NYA appointment, Prexy invited Lyndon to visit the campus regularly from Texas NYA headquarters in the curved-front Littlefield Building on Congress Avenue thirty miles away in Austin: it would add to the prestige of both for them to be seen together. Lyndon made time for Evans, and generously, showing up at least once a week, usually in the early afternoon. Within days of his arrival back in Texas, LBJ drove down to San Marcos wearing his wide-lapelled double-breasted white suit with the handkerchief just so in the breast pocket, his white boots shined, dark tie and white hat with the dark sweatband, its brim straight and not turned down as other men were accustomed to doing. The tall, dapper, imposing young NYA director and the balding, frail-looking academic in his wire-rimmed glasses made quite a study in contrasts as they walked the liveoak studded quadrangle in an afternoon dead-period when and where they would be observed by the greatest number of people — they both appreciated the value of social theatre and knew how to use it.

Prexy and Lyndon would walk and chat and drift to the little pavilion just outside Old Main where several iron-sided benches with wooden slat seats rested under the shade of the heavy liveoaks. They tended to sit on opposite ends of the same bench slightly facing each other, relaxed, easily conversing, comfortably exchanging views. Inevitably, students with an hour between afternoon classes would be attracted and a circle of listeners gathered — and at summer session, the students normally included public school teachers, principals and superintendents, people of community influence. These onlookers thought LBJ was merely being tolerant, that he didn't mind listeners. But the fact is he *wanted* listeners, needed them, for they provided the appearance of a forum and the opportunity to play off Prexy Evans in getting key points about his new NYA job across and reinforcing his image as the astute administrator and the shrewd politician. Lyndon and Prexy could not have done better if they had rehearsed it.

Of course, W. C. Perry happened into the courtyard on LBJ's very first visit to Prexy Evans and later became a regular at the informal but not quite impromptu bull sessions. The wide-ranging, free-form talk about politics was better than any political science class offered within the hallowed halls of San Marcos. Even at that early stage of his career the young LBJ had an aura about him, a will to power that made him seem decades older than his twenty-six years, that gave him a look of authority, and if anything counted in Depression Texas, it was authority. When W. C. Perry first sat next to the bench and looked up at this politico fresh in from Washington he did not see a young country boy only a year older than himself, he saw an authority figure with a kind of maturity seldom seen in Texas — or the world, for that matter. For LBJ, like him or not, was that rarest of rare individuals, rarer even than the original thinker: the original operator. He invented ways of wheeling and dealing and pulled off long shots with a pragmatic audacity and aplomb that still baffles experts in the field.

On that first afternoon, Prexy Evans brought up the subject of teacher salaries and the laws that placed ceilings of $75 per month on women teachers' salaries, $85 on men teachers' and $95 on administrators. This fellow Johnson was in politics — what would he have to say about a subject of such burning interest?

Lyndon B. Johnson shifted on the bench and crossed his legs in a characteristic gesture, revealing his boots just ostentatiously enough to let people know he could afford them, and looked sincerely into Prexy Evans' face, posing for his audience with a practiced skill that made it look perfectly unaffected.

"President Evans," Johnson said, "you remember back when I was in school here at San Marcos, I was so poor I had to beg a place to live."

"I remember it well, Mr. Director," said Evans, giving special emphasis to Johnson's new honorific title, obvious pride glowing from his face.

"You recall I was so poor I had to stay in a car garage on school property. I had no money to pay rent. All I had was makeshift furniture. I had to use the school showers to bathe and shave. It was pretty rough."

He paused for effect and smoothed a pantsleg over a finely tooled boot, subtly coloring his story with the contrast in his condition then and now. What he didn't mention was that his old dwelling place had been *above* a car garage in a two-room apartment, that the school property had been President Evans' own quarters, and that he had been invited to stay there by Alfred "Boody" Johnson — no relation — the football captain who was customarily given the only free accommodations on campus and that living with the most popular student and "Big Man On Campus" gave Lyndon a substantial boost in his social standing at school. But, as many Johnson-watchers have testified, such strategic omissions and embroidery in his "tales from the beginning" were a vital element in building his legend — and the willingness of early associates to go along with Lyndon's version for so long that one day they actually *remembered* it that way is well documented. Lyndon's "splendid academic record" so praised by Prexy Evans, for example, is such a memory of something that never happened: from the day he graduated, LBJ frequently remarked that he had taken 40 courses in college and got 35 As and everybody including Prexy Evans believed it without checking. If you look in the actual records of San Marcos, however, you'll find that he took 56 regular courses and got 8 As — his overall scholastic average was a respectable but not-so-splendid B-.

But now Lyndon Johnson leaned over confidentially and said with conviction, "President Evans, don't turn any qualified students away even if they can't pay for school. Take them in regardless of money."

Evans, ever the good steward, was mildly shocked by this turn in the discussion, especially since his most influential students were listening avidly, ready to take the conversation back home with them all over Texas. Evans diplomatically replied, "Mr. Director, that's a fine noble sentiment. But you're a practical man, too. How are we going to run the school unless we get cash money from students?"

LBJ responded easily: "Our experience tells us that there will be plenty of rich students from big cities like San Antonio to pay enough so the school can stay open. It's a shame to keep students out for lack of money." He looked casually over his audience, sizing up their responses, seeing the frayed shirt collars and worn-out shoes and the old thin-bottomed pants these men were a little ashamed of. Then he went on confidently: "I was completely without money part of my time in school. I was getting along fine in that garage until some faculty told the administration that I was sleeping in the garage without permission. You've got to give youth a hand. And I hope President Roosevelt's new National Youth Administration can help."

Prexy Evans breathed a little easier at the mention of federal help, seeing that the whole conversation was in fact merely a personalized sales pitch to the listening students asking for their endorsement of the NYA. At that, Prexy said to his Lyndon-boy:

"Mr. Director, you're in a position to carry out something I've been dreaming of since this Depression fell upon us so harshly."

"And what is that, President Evans?" asked the director.

"We've had a terrible tragedy among those poor farm boys you're so properly concerned with. They graduate from high school, find their families in such desperate financial straits that they cannot come to college, not simply because they cannot pay tuition, but also because they cannot be spared from the farm to help make ends meet. And once they fall off the path of education, they are off it for good."

"Yes," said LBJ, "that is tragic. And I can see it's beyond your control here in the college to do anything about it. What is it that you've been dreaming about, President Evans?"

"I call it the Freshman College Center concept. I've been thinking about it a long time, a *long* time. It's a way to help students whose families are on relief, those boys and girls who cannot be spared from their farm or ranch duties. There should be centers, Mr. Director, ten or fifteen of them throughout the state, convenient to rural areas, where these farm youngsters could take one or two tuition-free college courses while living and working at home."

LBJ's ears pricked up. He could smell a politically practical plan a mile off and he didn't care where good ideas came from. "Go on, Prexy Evans," he urged.

"Now, a college cannot afford to pay the professors for such a center." Evans paused to let that soak in. "But perhaps the NYA, with its mandate of keeping students in school, *could* afford it, if the idea were worked out properly."

"Centers, you say?" asked Johnson.

"Yes, Mr. Director. And if these centers employed professors who have been laid off and are themselves now on relief, teachers as well as students would be helped."

LBJ now smelled sure political practicality. Strongly. "President Evans, you are an unending source of inspiration," he said. "I'll take up that idea with the national director right away."

"And you, Mr. Director, are an insightful man on the way up," said Evans, smiling. "Where have you set your sights after you've done your job for the NYA?"

"President Evans, I've thought about that, thought what I really intend to do. Let me tell you what I told my Washington friends when I left Congressman Kleberg's staff to head the NYA here in Texas. I told them when I come back to Washington, I'm coming back as a congressman. I want to serve the people of Texas."

The listeners stirred involuntarily. The absolute will of this man peeked out from his homey exterior for just that one second when he'd said, "I'm coming back as a congressman." He hadn't said, "I hope to come back" or "I'd like to come back." He said, "I'm coming back." It was as if he'd found the levers of time and switched all the tracks going into the future so that his eventual election was inevitable. He was going to be elected, and that's all there was to it. The listeners for a brief moment saw a congressman sitting before them. Nothing had ever impressed them like this before.

Young Lyndon went on, "And you know, I'll need good men to help with my campaign. Leaders of tomorrow like you." He looked around and his eyes rested briefly on W. C. Perry. "I'll need leaders of tomorrow like you."

And so it went. Nobody knew during those warm afternoons in 1935 that this astounding young man would make good on his prophecy in less than two years and return to Washington as Congressman Johnson.

Hot afternoon. August fifteenth. A big high ceiling and a roomful of adult students. Professor H. M. Greene teaching history — no, *personifying* history, *embodying* it. Outside, the muted chatter of strolling collegians and the distant cry of — what? At first it sounded like a baby squalling, but then it cut through Professor Greene's resonant voice and became recognizeable: it was a paperboy, and even though the words could not be made out, he was plainly approaching with the traditional sing-song shout "Extra! Extra! Read all about it!"

Clayborne noticed one of his fellow students near the window who was in a position to hear better than the rest. The man stood up suddenly and leaned out into the Texas sunlight, listening as the yelling newsboy came closer. He leaned back in and turned around, his face white. "Oh, no!" he said.

Professor Greene broke off and asked, "Emmett, what is it? What's that paperboy saying?"

The man stammered "Send somebody down to buy a paper, Professor Greene. I don't believe it. It's Will Rogers. He was in a plane crash. With Wiley Post. Up in Alaska. He's dead."

Iredell's superintendent of schools found himself a different job for the fall of 1935. Arthur H. Barsh, the promoter who had built the new high school building, was moving on to greener pastures. His replacement was a tall six-foot-three Iredell native named Jerry Phillips. He was in his forties, a little stoop-shouldered, a hardworking man of few pretensions and a more plodding style than go-getter Barsh. His father ran a business in town, so he hadn't grown up a farmer, but was not much different from the local farmers, and was not offended by people who called his home town Snuff City. He had graduated from San Marcos and took an immediate liking to his elementary school principal.

"Mr. Perry," said Superintendent Phillips, "welcome back to Iredell Elementary. I understand you're working to finish up your degree at San Marcos."

"Yes, sir."

"Come take a little walk with me, will you?"

Principal Perry got up from his desk in the little nook he called his office and followed the lanky man outside the old stone schoolhouse.

Phillips said, "I'm sorry we haven't had time for a get-together sooner. Iredell's school system turned out to be more of a tangle than I bargained for."

"I know how you feel," smiled W. C. Perry as they walked off toward the banks of the North Bosque beside the school grounds. "I've been pretty busy myself. This is the biggest enrollment we've ever had. It caught me by surprise, too. I've got over four hundred and fifty elementary pupils this semester."

"Well, that's what I want to talk to you about. Did you hear that we've got nine rural schools consolidated with us this year?"

"I knew there were more than last year. Nine!"

"Yep, and we've got to stretch those nine school buses a little thinner now. I had to look around to find somebody who'd drive out fifteen miles to Camp Branch and pick up their students. I understand you went to elementary school there."

"Yes, sir, I sure did. Through eighth grade."

"Did you hear about how they came to consolidate with us?"

"I've heard some. My Uncle Wiley Linch moved his shoe store down from Stephenville this summer and said there'd been some talk of consolidating with Hico schools. My Papa told me there was a vote on it, but he didn't really tell me the details. He used to be a trustee out there at Camp Branch, you know, but he lost his sight here a few years ago and doesn't keep up with school matters much any more."

"Sorry to hear that. Well, as for the details, it seems that one of last year's trustees decided he was going to be the leader around Camp Branch. They say he's a real pusher, fellow by the name of J. E. Cooper."

"I know Jim Cooper. Used to be an old neighbor of ours. My Papa and I went and helped when their house caught on fire, oh, back in 1926, nine years ago now."

"Well, it seems it was this old neighbor of yours decided it would be best to consolidate with Hico, tried to convince everybody to go in with Hico. From what I hear he really talked it up. Pretty soon, though, folks must have stopped listening. Hico's a lot closer to Camp Branch than Iredell is, but people started sayin' Hico has high-tax schools, that their own taxes would go up if they went with Hico. They took a vote on it and decided to come fifteen miles away to consolidate with us. Ain't that somethin'?"

"It sure is. It doesn't surprise me too much, though. They probably voted that way just because they don't like anybody pushing an idea too hard. That's just the way they are. Independent folks."

"And I wouldn't be at all surprised if a few of those folks by Camp Branch remembered that you were principal over here. They all speak right highly of you out there, you know."

"Well, I try to get along," said W. C. "By the way, Mr. Phillips, I ought to let you know that the Blackstump Valley trustees have decided to stay consolidated with Iredell. Mr. Fouts tells me you'll be getting a letter here in a few days."

"I'm pleased to hear it. What'll they do with the old school building now?"

"Oh, Mr. Fouts told me they'll wait until next winter when nobody's busy and tear it down then. In a way it's a shame to see these old schoolhouses vanish like they are. There's a lot of memories going with them."

"Progress, Mr. Perry, progress. And speaking of progress, what I really brought you out for is to ask what you think about possibly building a new elementary school over by the street here. . ."

"Would you get the door, honey?" asked Oretta. "If I go the eggs'll burn."

Clayborne went into the front room and opened the apartment door.

Angus French stood in the October Saturday morning sunshine.

"Well, there, Mr. French," said Clayborne. "I haven't seen you around in a week or so. Come on in."

"Thank you Mr. Perry." The tall man stepped in with his hat in his hand.

"Well, have a seat, Mr. French," said Clayborne. "Don't stand on formality."

"I appreciate it, Mr. Perry. I prob'ly ought to ask you how things are goin' at school this year and such, but I won't waste your time. I have a favor to ask and it won't take very long. I know your wife's got breakfast just about ready, and I don't want to be a bother."

"Well, I'll be happy to do any favor I can. What is it?"

"The reason you haven't seen me for a while is my wife. She had to go up to Stephenville to the Terrill Hospital, had a serious operation. Gall bladder."

"Oh, no!" said Clayborne.

Oretta stepped from the kitchen into the front room doorway holding Bobby by the hand. "Is Mrs. French all right?" she asked anxiously.

"She came through the operation just fine, Mrs. Perry. She'll be ready to come home tomorrow. And that's the favor I'd like to ask."

"How can we help?" asked Clayborne.

"The only ambulance we got around here is Mr. Barrows' hearse. Now, my wife's doin' fine, but, you know how it might affect her mind to come home in a hearse."

"Well, of course," said Oretta. "Why, the very idea of comin' home from the hospital in a hearse. And what would people think if they saw it?"

"Well," said Mr. French, looking down at his hat. "I've heard that your Terraplane has a front passenger seat that comes out pretty easy. . ."

"Yes," said Clayborne. "Just pull two bolts and out she comes, clean as a whistle."

"Well, could you maybe put a box or something where the seat goes and prop up some boards longways into the back seat, make a bed sort of a thing? And maybe drive her home in your car?"

The man fairly reeked of reluctance, his sense of self-sufficiency violated, hating to ask a favor, but his love for his wife gave him no alternative.

Clayborne smiled and put him at ease. "Sure we can, Mr. French. And don't you worry about askin'. You gave us a place to stay when we first came lookin' and I'd be right proud to help out. Won't be any problem fixing up a bed in the car. Just tell me what time to show up and we can go up to Stephenville together."

Word of the removable Terraplane front seat evidently got around, because some time later when Mrs. Mae Bowman out in Blackstump

Valley had to have an operation in Stephenville, Principal Perry was once again asked to provide ambulance service and willingly obliged.

The tilted earth moved through its orbit, making the sun-driven seasons turn, and the school year rolled around in the little town of Iredell with football and pep squads and girls' basketball and track and Principal Perry stayed right in there. It was harder to save money now and the extra work at Mitchell's did little to make up for the lost salary taken by last year's legislature. The Perrys tightened their belts and pinched pennies a little harder. Everyone pinched pennies, though, and after all these years of hard times now a sense began to grow that everyone was pulling together somehow, just trying to live through this agonizing, eternal Depression.

Summer school came again in 1936. The three Perrys left their apartment in Iredell and looked around for a place again in San Marcos. The Episcopal parsonage had been more cramped than they liked, and they decided to ask at Mrs. Anderson's up on the hill, mosquitos or no. As fortune would have it, she had a room to rent them, because she had decided to rent out her whole house for the summer to make some extra money. She moved herself out on the back porch where she pinned up curtains for privacy and wrestled out a few necessary belongings. Six or seven families lodged in that big old house of hers, and the Perrys were one of them. Clayborne found that her choice had not entirely suited her, for the back porch caught the sun part of the day and became a sweltering heat trap in the early afternoons. While passing by on the way to class one day, he overheard her talking to herself — a common Texas preoccupation in those days — and complaining about the weather:

"Oh, I get so hot, so hot. I get so tired of this hot weather. Consarn it, I just despise this hot weather. And then when it gets so cold in the winter around here, I hate that too."

Lyndon Johnson did not come to San Marcos so frequently during the summer of 1936, but he showed up often enough to let people know he was still around, and many of his appearances were official NYA inspections. For not only had this remarkable young man put 3,600 out-of-school youths to work building 135 roadside parks across the state, he had also taken President Evans' advice about Freshman College Centers: twenty of them were operating in Texas and NYA directors from other states were looking over the idea to see if they should follow suit.

And another thing: NYA Resident Training Centers had been set up on a number of college campuses including San Marcos. The idea was to provide farm kids with useful skills whether they wanted to stay on the farm or look for a better life in the city. Rural youths were brought to campus for four months of vocational training, learning such things as animal husbandry and how to repair farm machinery while young farm women learned to can food faster and better and other homemaker skills. They lived in school dormitories, got paid twenty-one dollars a month by NYA, and in return for their training they worked on campus projects. San Marcos had several projects for Mr. Director to inspect. For one thing, President Evans had earlier approved the purchase of three old frame houses on College Hill with the intent of turning them into laboratories and classrooms, but there was never enough budget to do the conversion work, and so they just sat there — until NYA. Now husky farm boys dug plumbing trenches through the limestone rock, built retaining walls for landscape projects, built bathrooms (while learning plumbing skills they'd never get on the farm), learned how to read blueprints, do practical math and even how to govern themselves. LBJ had insisted that every campus NYA group elect its own self-governing council and insisted that every college teach NYA students a course of 28 lectures on citizenship covering everything from how to use a knife, fork and napkin properly to how the Constitution protects free speech and individual liberties. And in between his own history and education courses, W. C. Perry watched and listened and learned from a man who was to become one of American history's most consummate politicians.

"Oh, Mr. Perry, you're here! I was so worried I wouldn't find you, what with it still being August and all."

"Well, Marie Fouts!" said Principal Perry. "I'm pleased to see you. I come in here every few days before school starts just to try getting ahead of the rush. I hope you haven't been looking for me too long. What's on your mind?"

"Oh, Mr. Perry, I just got this note from Denton. Look at it!"

"What is it?" he asked, taking the letter. "You got your degree, didn't you?"

"Oh, yes," she said. "I graduated from North Texas all right, but look right there." She pointed to a line of typewritten gloom on the paper. "I'm short one course for my teacher's certificate. One little course! I can't get my teacher's certificate!"

"I see," muttered Principal Perry under his breath as he studied the letter. "Same thing that happened to me at Tarleton." He looked up at the frantic young woman. "Don't they have advisors up there at the Teachers College?"

"No, sir, they don't. What is this going to mean about my teaching job here at Iredell Elementary, Mr. Perry? Can I still teach fourth grade?"

"Well, we've hired you. I recommended you to the board and they've elected you. Pending receipt of your teacher's certificate, of course."

"That means I won't be able to teach this year?"

"Well, nobody can teach without a State certificate. We'd lose our classification if we hired an uncertified teacher."

"Oh, no!" wailed the Fouts girl. "This is terrible. I give up. After four years of college! I just give up."

"Wait a minute, Marie," he said gently. "You know how I am. If there's a way to solve this problem, I'll find it. Just have a seat and let's think a minute."

"Oh, Mr. Perry, one course, *one course!* I could just scream." She collapsed in the hard wooden chair beside his desk.

"Don't scream," he said. "One course. Hmm . . . Let's see, you have a four year degree. You need one course. It's the twentieth of August. It's about three weeks before school starts. It takes a week for your certificate to be processed in Austin. Hmm . . . What subject do you need that course in?"

"Education. Preferably educational methods."

"There's only one way to do it," he said.

"And what's that?"

"A correspondence course. Miss Fouts, let's drive off in my car to Brownwood and stop in at Daniel Baker College. I think they may be able to help us."

"Right now? That's eighty-five miles! You'd do that just for me?"

"Miss Fouts, when school starts in September, I need somebody riding herd on that fourth grade classroom down the hall. You're not the only one between a rock and a hard place here. Let's drive by my house first so I can tell my wife I'll be a little late for supper."

Daniel Baker College was a small private school on the verge of failure — it did not make it thought the Depression, but now, in 1936, it still offered its academic services to the world. Principal Clayborne Perry and Marie Fouts talked to Daniel Baker College's registrar in the early afternoon.

"You see my problem, Mr. Hopkins," said Principal Perry.

"Indeed I do," said Mr. Samuel Hopkins.

"Do you offer education or educational methods courses by correspondence?" asked Marie Fouts.

"Yes, we do. A number of them. All accredited."

"Would you be willing to sign up Miss Fouts here and let her finish the proper course in two weeks if she can? So she'll still have time to apply for her certificate before school starts?"

"There is no time limit on our correspondence courses, Mr. Perry. All she has to do is demonstrate proficiency in the course materials by passing an examination. If she can pass the examination even after only a single week's study, there is no problem."

"Could I administer the examination over at Iredell?"

"Certainly. You are a duly constituted authority."

Marie Fouts pointed to a long list. "How much is this course in your catalogue — Advanced Classroom Method?"

"Fifteen dollars by correspondence. All our correspondence courses are fifteen dollars."

She paid the money, they returned to Iredell, she went home to Blackstump Valley and she studied. She did nothing from morning 'til night for two weeks other than study. On Wednesday, September 4, she came into Iredell and took the test as administered by Principal Perry, which he then mailed to Brownwood. Daniel Baker College paid Principal Perry a dollar for administering the test, graded it, found that Miss Fouts had made a strong B grade, and forwarded the results to Austin. Miss Fouts' teacher's certificate came back before school started and she appeared on opening day at Iredell Elementary to ride herd on the fourth grade in that room down the hall.

Everafter, she told people that it was Mr. W. C. Perry who deserved the credit for making her a teacher. "He encouraged me to get an education. He found a way to save my first job. I'm a teacher because he cared."

When Old Grandma over at Dude Flat heard about it, she said to herself, "I told him. I told him there was greatness in him somewhere. I told him to call it out."

-16-

TRIBULATION AND
TRIUMPH

VEN though Franklin Delano Roosevelt had signed the Rural
Electrification Administration into existence on May 11, 1935,
not much electricity came to the Grand Prairie until November of
1936. Even then REA electricity came in fits and starts, dribs and
drabs, a line here, a hookup there. The problem was politics.

Of course, government had been trying to bring miraculous electricity
to the American farm at least since the Great War back in the 'teens. It
was then that Muscle Shoals dam was built on the Tennessee River in
Alabama harnessing the weight of water and force of turning wheels to
generate the power needed for producing synthetic nitrates — military
explosives. After the war a loud philosophical debate arose over who
should receive the benefits of the $145 million invested by the federal
government in the dam and its explosive factories. There were two
answers: private enterprise in the form of utility companies or the people,
in this case, the backwoods farm people of the Tennessee Valley,
impoverished and hungering for hydroelectric power — only two percent
of them had electricity in their homes or farms. And because there were
two answers there was no answer: bellowing political squabbles
deadlocked the dam — it remained idled and orphaned all during the
Twenties and well into the Thirties.

And all over America the farms remained dark in 1935 after the REA
had been created. Eight hundred thousand farms, mostly in the Eastern
United States, had electricity. Six million did not. While sophisticated
New York debutantes had "coming-out" bashes drenched in liquor and a

505

million lights, Grand Prairie women bent over primitive wood cookstoves, heaved seven-pound irons over their clothes and carried water in from the forks of the branches by the feeble light of a coal oil lamp. This is how one historian saw the problem: Even in towns like Hico and Stephenville and Iredell the bright lights ended at the city limits — utility companies were wary of the huge investments necessary to build lines to farms, of the shaky ability of farmers to pay their monthly electric bills, of the lower and slower profits from rural electrification. Texas Power and Light was one of those wary utilities. Their managers strung lines between towns, but refused to hook up any of the farmhouses along the way that stood more than fifty yards back from their line. That was most farmhouses. TP&L wouldn't even hook up farmhouses if owners had them *moved* to within fifty yards of the line. Nope, might set a precedent. Then who knows where all this rural electrification business would lead?

So the power lines ranged up and down the roads. And in the houses back from those roads farm wives contemplated those power lines running past their houses and not branching off to their rooftops. Every day and every night as the light was going, they contemplated them. Some nights they could see the skyglow of lighted towns just beyond the low hills below the stars. And they occasionally sat down and read *Saturday Evening Post* by lampglow and drooled over the ads for vacuum cleaners and washing machines and lightweight electric irons and felt the pain in their backs and shoulders a little more poignantly. The city women with only their housekeeping chores had it easier to begin with — and they had electricity. The farm women who lived with grinding physical labor had none. They came to resent those power lines and to nurse a smouldering hatred of the power companies. And the farm men too looked at those aloof power lines and wondered how much more milk they could produce if only it would keep longer, if only they had refrigerators. And how many more chicks they could raise if only they had electric incubators. Neither the farm men nor the farm women had the vocabulary to express it, but they felt keenly that they and the cityfolk were living in two different worlds, one a modern, mechanized civilization, the other a peasant-labor preindustrial age.

One enervating political problem facing rural electrification came from the REA's organization as a relief agency, which meant that applicants for government loans to electrify farms had to meet stringent federal relief act requirements. The utility companies approached this catch with great caution. They would have been required to grant farm consumers rates far below profitable levels — profit was not one of the New Deal's favorite things. REA Administrator Morris Cooke dreamed that private utility companies would help electrify rural America if the lure of government loans was held out to them, even if it meant risky investments and lower profits during times that were already hard enough. He was evidently not very good at either arithmetic or psychology because the utility companies, after studying his proposal in an industry-wide committee, told him firmly but politely that they didn't like the strings attached to his federal money and that he should go to the nearest convenient location and fly a kite.

So the Roosevelt administration pragmatically changed tacks. They submitted a bill to Congress in January, 1936, that would convert the REA to an independent agency outside the relief structure and allow farmers to set up their own co-operatives to buy power from federal hydroelectric dams. After much insider wrangling, Congress passed the new REA bill on May 11, 1936, and authorized not only federal loans to farmer co-ops, but also to private utilities for rural electrification and to individual families so they could wire their homes and buy basic electric appliances. Then the electricity began to arrive in the Grand Prairie. But it was still slow in coming.

"Mr. Perry, what a surprise!" said the ebullient man behind the desk. "What brings you over here to Stephenville? And how's the wife and boy?"

"We're all fine, Mr. Tunnell. I heard you'd been promoted from Hico to head the REA here. Congratulations."

"Well. . . thank you. And glad to hear your folks are all fine. But you didn't drive all the way from Iredell just to congratulate me, now did you?"

"No, sir, I didn't. What I'd like is. . . Why I came is. . . I'd like to learn how to wire houses. Do you have someone here that could show me how?"

Tunnell looked up in startlement. "I thought you were principal of the elementary school at Iredell, Mr. Perry."

"I am, sir. It's just that school salaries have been cut back by the legislature pretty hard, and. . ."

"I'd heard that. Now I see. You need some extra work, then?"

"Yes, sir. I've been going to summer school to finish up my degree, you see. That's pretty costly. And there's not a whole lot of extra work right in Iredell. So I thought — what with REA comin' in — maybe I could pick up house-wiring jobs. If I could learn how to do it, that is."

Ed Tunnell smiled and shook his head. "It's a tough job. You've got ambition, I'll say that. But we don't have any formal courses, Mr. Perry. Not even written teaching materials."

"You have crewmen. I could ask questions, maybe follow them around and watch how they do it."

"That's true. You'd have to buy some special tools. . ."

"I understand. I've watched a little right around Iredell. I've seen their insulated pliers and strippers and those wire cutters they call dikes and the other things."

"You've even picked up a little of the jargon, I see. Okay, I'll tell you what. I'm going to let you talk to some of my men, starting with the foreman. Jim Collins is his name. And I'll give you some of our specification sheets. And circuit diagrams. You're going to have to learn how to read wiring diagrams, you know. And you can't take up too much time from my crew."

"Yes, sir. I won't be a bother to anybody."

"And I'll tell you what else. We've got a little farmhouse out south of town where we bring farmers so they can see what electricity'll do for them. I guess ol' Perkins out there wouldn't mind if you took a look through his house to see how it's done."

Ol' Perkins didn't mind. Within a few hours of intensive study, Principal Perry had traced all the wires, looked at the ground rod, noted how the tacks and staples held insulated cable to the ceiling, where a brace and bit and a heavy shoulder poked holes through the walls to let the lights through, how to handle hot lines and the whole thing; he had become a house-wiring electrician. And with this new skill he went home and drove through Blackstump Valley where he knew everybody and offered to wire up their houses whenever the REA lines got there. Just about everyone agreed to his rate of twenty-five cents an hour plus five percent of the materials cost. He made a couple of trips to the Montgomery Ward store up in Fort Worth, finding out what was available by mail order, which switches were best, what the cost per foot was for insulated wire and how the entry boxes and fuses should be connected.

Clayborne Perry discovered to his amusement what a Texas historian would later chuckle at: The same people who fretted and smouldered about not having electricity now began to fear it. When the REA crews finally appeared on the gravel roads to string their power lines up and down Blackstump Valley and Dude Flat, the reality hit them and people began to talk. "It's the same stuff as lightning." "It's dangerous." "I heard tell that if you just touch one of them electric wires it'll knock you clear across the room." "What if my baby touches one of them wires? He'll be killed!" "What about storms? Won't the wires attract lightning?" "What about the cows? If a wire gets blown over, it'll fall on our cows and electrocute them." "And when the REA crew comes to put the wires back up, they'll leave our gates open and we'll lose the rest of our cows!" Some farm women were afraid to touch a light switch, thinking it was like a bare wire and would give them a rude shock. As a whole these country people knew little or nothing about electricity; primal dread was all their minds could call upon. Years later, when a generation of Texas farmers had grown up with electricity, there were still older people who would panic whenever a grandson matter-of-factly approached a broken light switch with a screwdriver — even after turning off the main power switch.

But now in the fall of 1936, uncertain farm families gulped and one at a time let Clayborne Perry into their houses to "bring the lights." It was simple enough for them: when the REA line got to their house, they'd call on Mr. Perry and ask him what to do. He told them what electrical wiring materials to order from Montogomery Ward. Then they waited for the wire and switches and rigamarole to show up in the mail. When it arrived, they spoke to Mr. Perry again on a Saturday in Iredell at Mitchell's grocery store or implement store or the bank or where ever he happened to be working at the time. The school principal took care of the details, working evenings after school and weekends after getting off from Mitchell's.

The details went like so: REA brought their power line from the road to each farmhouse's entry box, but would do nothing inside the house. Most house wiring was a matter of connecting the entry box through fuses to the house circuits, which themselves were formed by running insulated copper conductor across ceilings to light sockets, down the walls of the bare and spartan rooms beside door mullions to switches so the wires would be more or less concealed in the shadows of the awry door trim and occasional branch wires would be strung along floor baseboards for plug-ins. The cost to wire an average Blackstump Valley house turned out to be about twenty dollars in materials, some as much as fifty. The school principal watched with satisfaction as impassive line crews drove through sleepy Iredell on their way to the farther hinterlands toward Chalk Mountain. He figured he'd have work waiting for him all through the winter, following the REA trucks as they slowly spider-webbed the lights across Blackstump Valley.

"Papa!" called Clayborne out the car window from the driver's seat. Tom Perry stopped on his measured unseeing way to the barn and turned to face the direction of the car noise. His dog Smoky barked and pranced, skittering toward the son and then back toward the father as if unable to decide what to do.

"Hello, there, son," Tom yelled. "Did you bring Bobby with you?"

"Yes, sir, it's me and Oretta and Bobby today."

"Well, I hope you'll stay a while," said Tom as he tapped his cane before him. "Haven't seen you folks for quite a spell since you got back from school in August."

Clayborne killed the engine and his family piled out of the car, Tom lifting his cane and stepping toward the noise with that eerie certainty of the blind. Smoky ran circles around him and whined. "Hush up, Smoky. Son, how do you like your new Terraplane by now?" he asked as he stopped just in front of Clayborne.

"Well, it's not hardly new anymore, Papa. We got it last June, remember? But it's just as good as the first one we bought." He grasped his father first by the arm and then shook his hand.

"You don't hardly hear of anybody with Terraplanes around here," said Tom, gripping his boy's hand. "Only place that sells them is Boyton Hudson down in Hamilton where you got this one. Can you get it fixed all right?"

"Oh, sure, Papa, just about any filling station mechanic can work on 'em."

"Now, where's that boy?" asked Tom, tapping around with his cane. "Where are you, grandson?"

Bobby giggled and darted from his mother's skirts to pull his grandfather's pantsleg.

"There you are, you little dickens. I'm a' goin' to git you," Tom grinned, reaching out with his free hand to the boy's shoulders. With deft and sure motions he crooked the cane over his forearm, lifted the four-year-old and held him close in his arms. The youngster pulled at his shirt buttons. "Are you a good boy, little snickelfritz?" Tom beamed.

"I'm a good boy, Grandpa," Bobby said, wriggling in his grandfather's grasp. "But I'm not a snickelfritz! Tee hee hee!"

"Sure you are," teased Tom. "Don't you know a snickelfritz is a good boy?"

"Oh, Papa Perry," said Oretta, "he loves for you to hoo-raw him. He just begs to come see Grandpa Perry all the time."

"See, he's a smart boy. You ought to pay attention to him, bring him over more often. And come on in the house, it's pretty chilly out here. Winter's a' comin'." He bounced the boy in his arms.

"Weren't you goin' out to the barn when we drove up?" asked Oretta.

"What? Oh, no, daughter, I was just goin' for a walk. Gets weary sittin', you know. I just happened to be goin' out that way."

They followed Tom's lead as he marched sightlessly through the late November air to the new house with his grandson in his arms.

Clayborne said, "I see you got all the roofing done now."

"Oh, yes, the whole thing's all finished. We're all rebuilt from the fire. It took long enough. Two years, just about."

Nadine and Dorothy came out the kitchen door to greet them in a flurry of shouts and laughter. Nadine had grown into a pretty young woman at fifteen and twelve-year-old Dorothy was growing like a Texas weed. Belle opened the kitchen door for the mob, squinting in the low morning sun, her forty-three years weighing on her, carving leathery channels in her face, petrifying it into a set look of country resignation. "Come on in, now, you all, I don't want us to heat all out of doors, you hear?" she nagged. The edge of growing cantankerousness sharpened her voice.

"Where's Hoyt?" asked Clayborne, shutting the door behind them.

The two girls tittered and Tom put Bobby down to stand by himself on the kitchen floor.

Belle looked at her son and said, "He did the same as you two, ran off and got married."

"When?" asked Oretta, taken aback.

"Last Saturday," said Belle, not looking terribly happy about it.

"He did?" asked Clayborne in surprise. "Was it that Oxley girl he's been going with?"

"Sure was," said Tom, feeling his way to a seat at the kitchen table. As always, the kitchen table remained the center of home life in this rebuilt house. "Hoyt and Bernice just up and got married at the Baptist parsonage in Hico same as you two. I guess it was about his time. He's twenty now. Come sit on my lap, Bobby." The boy scurried to comply happily.

Oretta said, "Well, Bernice seems like a nice sort of girl. Where did they go on their honeymoon?"

Belle said, "They didn't take much of a trip, just up to Fort Worth for a couple of days."

"What's Hoyt going to do?" asked Clayborne.

"He's found himself a rent farm down by Olin," said Tom, speaking up from the straight-back chair and plain table.

"Down about eight miles south of Hico toward Hamilton?" asked Clayborne.

"That's the place. He's got a pretty good blackland farm off there between Mesquite Creek and the Dry Fork of Honey Creek."

"What's he doin' for farm animals?" asked Oretta.

"We gave him a couple of our mules and a few cows," said Belle. "And he took the wagon and some plows. He'll do all right."

"But what about you, Mama?" asked Clayborne. "Can you and Papa keep up the place here with him gone?"

"Well," said Tom, "we've still got Nadine and Dorothy, don't forget. We'll have to cut back some. We won't grow any more cotton, at least not much. But I can handle the cows just fine. Old Smoky goes out in the pasture to get them for me and I can milk 'em as good as ever. And we got the chickens and the garden for canning, and a little corn and grain for feed. We'll do fine."

"We'll do," said Belle, "but I don't know about that 'fine' part. I can drive the car, and it's a good thing I can. Takin' the eggs and cream and chickens into Hico to sell."

Clayborne asked, "Are you going to get lights when the REA line comes by?"

"What would I want with lights?" asked Tom ironically.

"I mean for Mama," his son replied.

"I don't think we'll be able to afford it," said Belle. "I can get along without lights. Got along without 'em up to now. Can get along without 'em later. And we're goin' to need the money for more important things. We're goin' to have to hire somebody to do the plowing and other heavy work, us women can't do it. And without somebody to turn the mules at the end of the rows Tom can't plow no more."

"Oh, now, Mama," said Tom gently, "we'll make it. Look on the bright side."

She glared at him for a moment, torn between pain and frustration at their condition and admiration for his courage. "Tom, if you could just *see* that bright side you keep talkin' about. . ."

"Son, what have you been doin' for yourself bein' principal this year?" said Tom, averting a confrontation with his wife.

Oretta said, "Tell them about takin' the school to Dallas, Clayborne. That's quite a tale."

"Dallas?" asked Nadine. "Did you take your school to the Dallas fair? Our school didn't get to go."

"You know, Nadine," said Clayborne, "that's what happens at too many country schools, they never get to go on any field trips. I talked to our superintendent about it all last year. This year is the Texas Centennial, our State's a hundred years old, and Mr. Phillips finally agreed to let us take the whole school to the Dallas fair."

"How'd you get there?" asked Dorothy, fascinated.

"Took the train. We all got up must of been two in the morning, got all the kids together across the river from the schoolhouse at the railroad stop. We had five hundred kids get on the four o'clock train, all yawnin' and half asleep. You should've seen those poor little ol' first graders leanin' on their mamas."

"Can you get five hundred kids on the regular train?" asked Tom, dandling Bobby on his knee.

"No, sir," said Clayborne. "We let the Katy know in advance. We had it all paid for and everything. It was just about a special train for us. And we changed trains in Waco to the Texas and Gulf. Got into Dallas about ten in the morning, went out to the fairgrounds."

Nadine asked excitedly, "Did you see the television? What about the television?"

Clayborne smiled and said, "Yes, I saw it. It wasn't much, a little bitty ol' thing about four inches across, the picture was all speckled, you couldn't hardly see what it was about."

"I sure wouldn't want one of them televisions in my house," said Belle.

"Why not, Mama?" asked Dorothy in surprise.

"I wouldn't want anybody to see me when I picked up the telephone. What if I wasn't proper dressed yet? And think what people could do callin' each other up on a television. Why, it'd be sinful."

Clayborne smiled and said, "It doesn't work like a telephone, Mama.

It's more like the radio. You just watch it. It can't see you. It's just like a picture show. But the man at the fair said it'll prob'ly be ten years before you can buy a television."

"Ten years," said Nadine, pondering the future. "Nineteen-forty-six. Think how different the world will be with all the new modern inventions then."

"Well, I don't care," said Belle. "Telephone, television, if they don't work the same how come they call 'em the same? I wouldn't want one of them televisions in my house anyways. Just make you lazy, sittin' and watchin' picture shows all the time. And I wouldn't be too sure they couldn't see you, nosiree, I wouldn't."

"Did you go see Oretta's sister Maxie while you were in Dallas?" asked Tom.

"No, Papa. I didn't have any time. We had a real full day and got the kids on the train back home about eight o'clock at night. We didn't get home until after midnight."

"How's your sister doing after the divorce?" Belle asked Oretta. "Is she getting along?" Belle made no effort to hide her belief that divorce was improper, just plain wrong.

"Oh, she's doing fine, all right," said Oretta. "Once she moved up to Dallas she's started working. We're sure sad she couldn't make it with J.D. But she has a little sewing and dressmaking business at home. She's real talented at it, and a hard worker, too. She keeps real busy."

Tom turned the conversation away from family problems: "Son, what do you think about Roosevelt getting re-elected last week?"

Clayborne stopped the conversation with an admission he knew his father would not care for: "Papa, I sure hate to disappoint you. I know how you feel about President Roosevelt. But I thought it was for the best, so I went and voted for him."

W. C. Perry had been brought up by a conservative Republican father in a rural setting that tended strongly to populist Democrats. Texas since the Civil War had been virtually a one-party State and remained in the 1930s a desert for Republicans and the elysian fields for Democrats. William Randolph Hearst's disenchanted 1935 dictum to his editors that the New Deal henceforth be termed the Raw Deal carried no weight in Texas. Roosevelt's egghead theoreticians nursed quasi-romantic biases in favor of the depressed agricultural regions of America and Texans were well prepared to take any Yankee dollar they could get their hands on. If FDR wanted to give Texas farmers federal money, that was fine with most.

By 1936, Texas industry began to feel the same way. The state Democratic Party in Texas had already come to terms with corporate enterprise and quietly worked with rather than against "the interests" when money and jobs were at stake. Four years of the Roosevelt presidency had shown that the national Democratic Party was moving gradually in the same direction. Despite continuing charges that Roosevelt's closest advisers were pinkos and commies, politically savvy Texans — always astute in separating the rhetoric from the substance — saw that their private enterprise was getting a much-needed infusion of federal dollars and were willing take good care of the golden goose as long as the money kept coming in. And so Texas went overwhelmingly for FDR in his first re-election bid.

Clayborne Perry could hardly avoid this general trend. He took his college seriously and therefore paid close attention to his instructors, especially to history professor H. M. Greene, who, although eclectic and iconoclastic, was on balance a liberal. He believed in letting everybody do as they pleased, which struck most Texans who knew him as anarchistic. But he also believed in government welfare services within a framework of generally limited government, and that was what his former student Lyndon B. Johnson had learned from Prof.Greene. As Clayborne Perry listened to both of them, Greene in the classroom, Johnson under the liveoaks, some of the liberal notions of FDR's welfare state came to influence him.

And so in early 1937 he joined the Democratic Party in Iredell and began attending Democratic Party political meetings up and down the Bosque as the occasion permitted. He found himself drifting away from his upbringing in matters political, found himself willing to accept relief programs, welfare payments, farmer assistance and other doings his father rejected. And as typical in Texas politics, his beliefs were shaped by men he respected more than by abstract ideas or general principles, men such as Bob Poage of Waco who was to become a Washington fixture in the House of Representatives. Principal Perry attended rallies for Congressman Poage and soaked up the speechifying like everyone else: Poage was for the farmer, and Iredell and the whole Grand Prairie was a farming community. If it was good for the farmer, that was good enough: it was only a slogan but anything perceived as helpful to the interests of the common people was accepted without much evaluation — critical analysis was not a habit of Texas farmers. If good for the farmer meant the centralization of government power and the construction of a welfare state, those facts might go undetected for years as long as the immediate financial benefits kept coming in. And the benefits kept coming in. So Principal Perry was happy for the time being and he had a lot of company in the Texas Democratic Party.

"You never been to Gorman, Ma'am?" asked the tanned and rugged man dressed in khaki.

"Not that I recall, Mr. Ross," said Oretta as Clayborne smiled beside her and Bobby peered up with curiosity at the stranger in their front room.

"Well, Ma'am, our construction company is past De Leon, just down Elm Creek from Okra, Texas, straight north from Duster, on the farm road midway between Sipe Springs and Desdemona, right on the Katy line between Rucker and Carbon. Now you know just exactly where Gorman is."

They had a laugh at his tongue-in-cheek geography lesson.

Clayborne explained, "Ross Construction was the low bidder on our new elementary school, Oretta. Mr. Ross here might be interested in renting the apartment while we're in San Marcos this summer."

"Oh, well, then," said Oretta, "let us show you around the place." She walked Bob Ross into the kitchen with Principal Perry and Bobby on their heels.

"We've got four rooms here," said Principal Perry. "It's a nice place, close to the school." They looked into the bedroom and returned to the living room.

"And you'll love Mrs. Weir, she's just so sweet," added Oretta.

"It looks okay," said Ross, sizing up what he saw. "We could use this front room for the construction office. And my family would be comfortable here. Are you sure you have the right to sublet this place?"

"Yes, sir, Mr. Ross," said Principal Perry. "We checked yesterday with Mrs. Weir. She said we could rent it out while I'm at college. No problem there."

"And when will you need it again?"

"Second session's over the last week in August. We'll be gone twelve weeks. That way I can finish up my degree with only six weeks next summer."

"Twelve weeks. That's just about right," said Bob Ross. "Our construction schedule shows us finished the third week in August. I'll take it. When you come back from summer school, you'll have a new school to teach in, Mr. Perry." Oretta vanished into the kitchen to pour the coffee.

"We're really looking forward to it," said Principal Perry. "I've been right close to the planning of this new building since the beginning. Took most of this spring working up the details and the budget."

"You and Jerry Phillips and the other folks did a fine job. Your Request For Bids here at Iredell was as clear and complete as ever I've seen."

"Thank you, sir," beamed Principal Perry. "We put a lot of work into it."

Oretta called, "You all come on and sit here at the kitchen table, now. Your coffee's ready."

They came and sat. Bob Ross's big hands dwarfed the coffee cup and his beefy fingers were unable to slip through the handle. He held the handle pinched between thumb and forefinger.

Ross said, "It's not every school even knows what it wants and some of them come in during construction wanting all sorts of changes made. Just drives the cost through the roof. And that budget of yours is just about to the penny — $20,000 complete including the new and used school furniture."

"We thought about it and figured it for a long time," Principal Perry said. "We knew there'd be seven grades with four hundred students and ten teachers. . ."

"And I see you made sure there was a principal's office big enough so you could turn around in it. We've built some school with principals' offices no bigger than a broom closet. The janitor has more space."

Clayborne laughed. "We all felt that this new building ought to be the highlight of the Iredell school system. And to be honest with you, it was Superintendent Phillips' idea to make the office that big and to put the 'Principal' sign over the door and have my name painted on it."

"You won't regret it. The worst problem you'll find is when they start shoving all their file cabinets in with you because you've got the space. Now let's settle the details about your place here; how much for rent and what day are you goin' to want it back and such."

On the last day of May, 1937, the Perrys loaded their car and made ready to go to San Marcos. The campus of Southwest Texas State Teachers College was for the most part just as they had remembered it, green and restful and content with its traditional buildings, but a new dormitory and laboratory building had come into use, thanks to federal NYA money. The Perrys found their old place at Mrs. Hudgins Anderson's up on the hill and settled into what had by now become their summer routine. By taking four classes this summer — two classes during each of the first and second summer sessions — Clayborne would have only six weeks of work next year to finish his degree. As usual, Clayborne signed up for a history course and an education course.

Afternoon, the first Friday in July. Finished with his lunch, Clayborne stacked his books by the door preparing to leave for history class when Oretta abruptly sank into a kitchen chair with a heavy groan. Clayborne dashed into the kitchen and found his wife gasping and white.

"Clayborne. . ." she said weakly.

Bobby sat at the other end of the table eating a sandwich and looking at his mother.

"It's that stomachache you had this morning, isn't it?" Clayborne said. "It's worse?"

She nodded and said, "It just came on . . . all of a sudden," then leaned forward on the table, deathly pain on her face. Clayborne stood appalled at her suddenly drawn appearance.

"I'm going to get the car," he said calmly, holding down the panic. "I think we need to take you to the hospital. Bobby, come with me. You're going to stay with Mrs. Anderson this afternoon."

They sped across the hot campus streets and the few blocks into town to the emergency entrance of Hays Memorial Hospital, a white stucco building of modest proportions. Attendants took her immediately to examination while Clayborne filled out the papers and then took a seat in the gray visitor's foyer to wait.

He waited for nearly an hour, pacing, sitting, trying to get interested in *National Geographic*, pacing and sitting some more. A white-coated figure came into the foyer and asked, "Mr. Perry?"

"Yes, that's me."

"I'm Dr. Edwards, Benjamin Edwards. Have a seat."

They sat opposite each other, staring across a small coffee table with magazines spread over its top.

"I'm the attending physician for — your wife, is it?"

"Yes, sir, she's my wife."

"Mr. Perry, your wife is in very serious condition. My examination shows a blockage of the lower intestines. It looks like a problem blockage. I don't mean to alarm you needlessly, but we cannot be certain of its exact nature, nor can we do anything about it without major surgery."

Clayborne blanched. Major surgery. He had never encountered such a problem; no one in his family had ever required major surgery. His head spun. Unsteadily, he asked, "What would happen if you don't do the surgery?"

"I'm afraid there's nothing we can do in that case," the doctor said bluntly.

Shock. "You mean she'd die?"

"Without question."

The doctor's words hung on the air like a narcotic, a mind-numbing hypnotic. She would die without question. Without question. Without question. Clayborne felt the urge to vanish welling up in his chest, to be somewhere else, in some other world where his precious wife was not in mortal danger, to avert reality, to confound death. He breathed deeply and cleared his throat.

"When would you want to do the surgery, doctor?" he asked.

"Right away," said Dr. Edwards. "This afternoon. If we wait, there's always a danger of the intestine rupturing and peritonitis setting in. That's not something we should let happen."

"Peritonitis. . . No, no, of course not," said Clayborne in a daze. "What do I need to do?"

"First, we'll require your permission and then you'll have to fill out the proper forms at the desk. I'll have your wife prepped and in the operating room as soon as possible."

"Okay, do it," he said blankly. "You have my permission. Do the surgery. Just save my wife. Just save her."

"We'll give her the best that medical science has to offer. And if you can stand it, I'd like to have you scrub up and observe what we do, Mr. Perry. We may be faced with some decisions you ought to make."

"You mean come into surgery with you?" Dr. Edwards had made a highly unusual request, absolutely forbidden in big-city hospitals and only rarely permitted, much less solicited, in rural medical facilities. To Clayborne the idea was somehow horrifying.

"That's what I mean. We may need you to make some decisions. Important decisions."

"I see. Let me make a phone call. Then tell me what to do."

Clayborne called Mrs. Anderson and told her the situation, asked her to keep Bobby for the night. Then he followed the floor nurse to the hospital's little surgery, donned the paraphernalia of cleanliness and went through the scrub procedure under Dr. Edwards' supervision.

Dr. Edwards then told him, "I'll want you opposite me, Mr. Perry, on the other side of the operating table so you can see clearly when the time comes."

Oretta was duly positioned on the operating table, covered in surgical drapes, already sedated and ready for the anesthetic. The procedure began. Clayborne watched tensely as the anesthetic nurse raised the ether mask over his dear wife's face, while the surgery nurse laid out all the autoclaved surgical instruments on a sterile tray. How cold and businesslike it all looked, how far removed from the everyday of Clayborne's life. The anesthetic nurse nodded.

"We're ready to open," said Dr. Edwards. He palpated the blockage one final time before drawing out his incision plan. "I'm afraid we've got peritonitis in there," he said bluntly.

He drew out the pattern of his planned incision in iodine and began ordering instruments from the nurse. Clayborne swallowed hard as the doctor open the abdominal wall, exposing the life processes inside.

"Look there, Mr. Perry, there's the locked bowel. It's a classic adhesion. One segment of the large instestine is stuck to another where it shouldn't be. It's blocked the passage of material so it's backed up into the small intestines. We got in just in time. I'm going to release this now."

Clayborne looked on as Dr. Edwards manipulated the blockage and released the flow. The rippling surge as the dammed digested matter broke free inside the intestine reminded him of water coursing through a garden hose. The acute problem was solved that easily.

"Now," said Dr. Edwards, "here's the real problem. We've got peritonitis, all right. You see those brownish round spots that look something like bruises up and down the large bowel?"

"I see them," Clayborne said unsteadily.

"If they grow all the way around and encircle the intestine to form a ring around it, that section will die and the bowel will come apart. We can't let that happen. We're going to have to do a lavage, wash the whole cavity here with peroxide, try to get rid of the inflammation."

It was a painstaking and time-consuming procedure. Clayborne watched. And hoped.

Dr. Edwards finished at about 7:30 p.m. He closed the incision and placed a surgical dressing on the wound. "Done," he said. The nurses and an operating room orderly transferred Oretta to a rolling recovery table.

Clayborne looked up at Dr. Edwards, into a face that looked years older than when he had walked in the surgery only a few hours before. A chill shook him.

"How is she, doctor?"

"She'll rest in the recovery room while the ether wears off," Edwards said wearily. The orderly rolled Oretta out.

"But how is she, her condition?"

"It's as I feared. That peritonitis doesn't look good. Things are still pretty inflamed."

Clayborne swallowed hard. The question didn't want to come.

"Will she live?"

Dr. Edwards looked at him with candor. "It's touch and go," he said.

"Can I stay with her?"

"When she's out of the recovery room. Shouldn't be long."

"I want to stay with her."

"You can stay."

"Thank you for doing what you could."

He forgot about supper and went to Oretta's bedside just before nine that evening. He was stunned by her waxen look, by her sunken eyes, by the morphine-induced stupor she now drifted in. He sat beside her and stared at her, watching her breathe, just to make sure. Inhale, exhale. The slow automatic bellows of lungs, up-down, the air gushing in, out, bathing blood cells in oxygen, feeding life. The spark seemed so dim in her, he felt, seemed to flicker. If only there were some way to grasp the intangible spirit, to hold it in the body's confines, to make it yield some secret healing power, to mend the sickness. His hope was a prayer. He could not remember that he ever stopped praying.

It was 2:15 a.m. when he looked up at the nurse come to check Oretta's vital signs.

"How is she?" he asked when the nurse was finished.

"Doing as well as can be expected. She's not going to be running any foot races for the next day or two."

When Dr. Edwards returned at 8:00 a.m., he found Clayborne still sitting beside his wife, haggard and with the stubble of a beard on his face, watching her breathe, just to make sure. Inhale, exhale.

The doctor did a quick examination and said, "Mr. Perry, your wife has come through the night without her temperature spiking, which tells us there's no serious infection. Looks like we cleaned things out properly. She's not out of the woods yet, but if her recovery remains as uneventful for the next day or two she'll be fine."

Clayborne stared blearily at the doctor's news. He tried to smile.

"You'd better go home and get some rest, Mr. Perry," the doctor said. "We don't want to have to treat you, too."

Clayborne slept very little that weekend, trying to care for Bobby's needs and explaining to the boy that his mother would be gone a few days so the doctor could fix her up. He called Oretta's divorced sister Maxie in Dallas and told her the situation, asked her to come help out. Maxie Center arrived in San Marcos the next day and took care of Bobby while Clayborne split his time between the hospital and final examination week at college. Oretta's progress was slow and painful, but on the next Friday, shortly after Clayborne found that he had passed both his first session courses with high grades, the doctor said she was well enough to bring home to Mrs. Anderson's.

Saturday evening Maxie brought Oretta her supper in the bedroom while Clayborne looked over his course material for the second session in the front room.

"You're sure looking better today than when I first came down from Dallas last Sunday," said Maxie.

"I don't know if I feel any better. I can't hardly keep anything down yet. I think I spent half my time at that hospital throwin' up."

"Well, you've kept everything down today," said Maxie. "It must be goin' away."

"Lordy, I hope so," said Oretta, sitting up and taking a bite of toast.

Clayborne came into the bedroom with Bobby. "Hello, Mom," said the boy, standing next to the bed trying to be careful of his mother. "Are you well yet?" He watched her eat.

"Not quite, honey," smiled Oretta. "I sure wish I could hold you, but Mom's got to be careful of her tummy."

"Does it hurt?" asked the boy solicitously.

"It's a little tender, son. It's getting better."

"Does it hurt when you eat?" Bobby wanted to know.

"No, not when I eat. See?" She showed him by taking several bites in a row.

Clayborne asked, "Anything I can get you?"

Maxie said, "Don't you worry none, I'll take care of her. You got studyin' and such to do, got to get that education, you know. Just don't worry none. That's what I'm here for."

"Well," he said, "Bobby and me'll be in the front room if you need us."

When Clayborne had retreated, Maxie said "You're lucky to have a man like that, Oretta, that cares about you so much. I just wish J. D.'d cared a little more about me than about his confounded farm . . ."

"Oh, don't take on, Sis," said Oretta, finishing up her supper. "I know you still feel terrible about the breakup with J. D. I'm sad for you. I'm truly sorry. I wish there was something I could do. Clayborne and I haven't had it perfectly smooth, you know. He's off working alot, you know."

"But when he comes home, he pays attention to you. Here, let me take those dishes."

"He doesn't pay me as much attention as I'd like, but you're right, he's a good man . . ."

"What's the matter, Oretta?" asked Maxie. "You just turned green."

"It's my stomach. I think I'm goin' to throw up. Get me the bedpan, will you? Oh I hate this."

She retched furiously into the bedpan and stayed hunched over for a long time, then fell back on her pillow, moaning, "Oh, no!"

"What?" asked Maxie in alarm. "What is it?"

"My stitches. Look under the dressing. I think my stitches broke."

Maxie swiftly examined the surgical scar that lay open and vulnerable.

"Oh my God! They are broken! Clayborne, come here, quick!"

They rushed her back to Hays Memorial where the surgical team quickly assembled to repair the damage. Again, hours of waiting. Again, Dr. Edwards coming in with a weary aged face.

"We're back to where we were," he said. "We've got some sepsis from the open wound. It's set her back pretty bad."

Again the question didn't want to come. "Will she live?"

Again the answer nobody wanted to hear. "It's touch and go."

They stayed up with her, Clayborne and Maxie, enduring those agonizing hours not sure whether their loved one would live. Sunday passed. Little change. Oretta hovered on the brink. Monday came. Clayborne knew that it would be impossible to begin the second session. He must drop out of school for the summer, leaving twelve more weeks to complete instead of six. Monday afternoon he went into the college registrar's office and informed the clerk of his intentions. Then he went home to Mrs. Anderson's to take care of Bobby and wait for Maxie to return from visiting the hospital so they could trade roles. And again, Oretta fought back slowly from death's reach.

It was another week before Dr. Edwards would release her. Clayborne called Oretta's oldest brother Lanie to drive his car to San Marcos with a bed made in the back seat to carry Oretta home to Iredell. Maxie returned to Dallas with Clayborne's boundless gratitude, and Lanie and Clayborne and Bobby and Oretta began the hundred-fifty-mile journey north on a blistering hot day near the end of July.

Things went reasonably well until they turned off at Waco and passed the little town of Valley Mills. Construction crews worked at building the final new sections of State Highway Six between Valley Mills and Clifton. There the road degenerated to dusty corduroy. The car jolted and swayed endlessly over the unfinished roadbed. Sand came streaming in the open windows, choking and smothering. Hours went by on the miserable road. Oretta became nauseous, seriously nauseous. She began to vomit with alarming force and regularity. They stopped time after time to give her a respite but the heat and stifling dust allowed no rest. The sun went down after their fourth stop but the heat showed no sign of letting up. As they bounced along the new construction in the darkening evening she fell nearly incoherent. Her stitches held, but her breathing grew more shallow and spasmodic by the mile until Clayborne feared she would die of exhaustion.

"Here's Meridian coming up, Lanie," Clayborne said with an edge of fear in his voice. "We've got to stop here and see if we can find a doctor. I'm afraid she's not going to make it."

Five hours of driving it had been when they stopped at Meridian Drug Store about 9:00 p.m. and asked for medical help. Good fortune was with them: it so happened that Dr. Alvin Calhoun, a local physician, was just leaving the drugstore as they walked in. He checked Oretta and gave her a shot of morphine.

"What she needs is rest," said Dr. Calhoun. "If you've got to drive on to Iredell tonight, this is the only way she's going to get any."

She drifted into another stupor but it helped to endure the balance of the trip to Iredell. They arrived about 10:30 p.m. Oretta was completely knocked out. Mrs. Ida Weir greeted Clayborne in surprise, but allowed his family to use her front bedroom at least until the Ross family had time to vacate their apartment. That night after putting Oretta and Bobby to bed he fell harrowed by care into a profound sleep.

When he awoke the next day, it was to a situation he had not faced in years: he was completely out of money. The medical bills and college had drained off their meager savings altogether. Even so, Clayborne called on Dr. A. N. Pike that morning, asking him to take care of Oretta. After the setback her strength was not expeced to return rapidly and a doctor's care was essential. Clayborne had to call upon Mrs. Weir and a neighbor lady to help with Bobby. When he went to tell Mr. Ross about his premature return and the circumstances surrounding it, he got a welcome surprise: the construction boss asked him, "Would you be willing to come to work for me for a while?"

Clayborne replied without hesitation, "Sure. I'd like to help build the new school."

"All right. I can take you on as a helper at first. Thirty cents an hour. Do you have a Social Security card?"

"No."

"You'll have to get one then. I have to pay money into the fund for you and I need your card number to do it. I've got the forms for you to fill out."

Most town school principals would have shunned such a menial job. Working as helper meant heaving kegs of nails and carrying long rafters and lifting bricks at the orders of almost everyone on the site. But Clayborne gave his total effort to the work without complaint or shame: he needed the money and he enjoyed getting his hands dirty in actual construction of the new school over which he would preside in the fall. At the end of his first week, Bob Ross asked him to start work the next Monday as a carpenter at fifty cents an hour — four dollars per day, twenty dollars a week. It was a large amount of money for that time.

Oretta progressed slowly, but the unsettled stomach remained a chronic problem: she could keep no more than half her food down. It was turning into an excruciating recuperation. Clayborne found that Oretta needed more help than Mrs. Weir and the neighbor lady could provide and one Sunday in late August went to his parents and in-laws for reinforcements. Belle agreed to go help but gave him some more unwelcome news.

"Your Grandma Perry and Old Grandma have both come down with a stomach ailment, Clayborne. They've got a nurse come down to stay with 'em from Stephenville. Takes care of them 'round the clock so it must be pretty bad. Maybe you better go over and see them now. They're not gettin' any younger, you know," she told Clayborne. "Your Grandma's seventy-seven and your Old Grandma's ninety-nine this year."

He worried all the way from his parents' house to Dude Flat. There was the old familiar farm house of Jim Perry. As he turned from Chalk Mountain Road into the Perry farm he unconsciously looked to the left, down where the weaning house had been. Where he'd been born. Then to the right, over to the old rent house where his family had lived when they came back from starving out in Colorado. This farm was piled high with memories. When he parked the car beside the little house, he saw his grandfather sitting out in the old rocking chair on the east-facing gallery, watching the afternoon sky.

"Grandpa," he called as he got out of the Terraplane. "I came as soon as I heard. How are they?"

Jim Perry, seventy-five himself and no longer actively farming his place, looked up at his grandson and rubbed his white walrus mustache with a gnarled hand. His perennially arched eyebrows now looked more than quizzical, bathed in pathos. "It's not good, boy. They got some kind of summer stomach ailment, doctor doesn't know what."

"Could they have gotten hold of some bad food?"

"I don't know. Maybe. They cook for themselves and me, you know. It could be some canned something or other that went bad. I don't think so. I didn't get it."

"Is somebody cooking for you since they got sick? I know you can't cook yourself."

"Oh, yes, the Stones over in the weaning house where you lived when you's a little tyke, they're feedin' me, taking care of me. They're good folks, them and their big family."

"Can I go see Grandma and Old Grandma?"

"If you can get by that nurse they sent down from the Terrill Hospital. She put me out here so's I wouldn't be in the way. I'm going to complain when the doctor comes back tomorrow."

"I won't be long, Grandpa."

He opened the screen door and went in the front room. It was sweltering like an asphalt road inside.

"Who are you?" challenged the heavy-set nurse at the bedroom door off to the left of the front room.

"I'm the grandson. Clayborne Perry. I want to see my Grandma and my Great Grandma."

"They're pretty bad off. Don't you bother 'em too much, you hear? And only a minute."

He brushed past the doorkeeper and looked in horror on the two old women in their beds, one on the south side of the room, the other on the north. They lay moaning softly and writhing at a hundredth speed, as if convulsing in ultra-slow motion. He leaned over Grandma Lou Perry and looked her in the face. Her eyes were glazed. She showed no sign of recognizing him.

"Grandma," he said in spite of himself. No response. Grief bundled in his chest. He looked at her a few seconds more and then stepped to the other bed. There lay Old Grandma, Elizabeth Glasgow Perry, within a few months of being a hundred years old, looking up at him, her ancient eyes blazing through the agony.

"Clayborne," she rattled like a dry wind in the yuccas. "You're here."

"I'm here, Old Grandma."

"Good. You sit. Don't talk. Listen." She could speak only in the rhythm of her labored breathing, following the dictates of her lungs, delivering short phrases. Her words were little more than gasps. "I'm so sick. I don't care. If I live. Or die. But you. You remember. Stay in college. *All* of it. Like a doctor. Don't argue. Just do it. For the family. Remember. The dream. Greatness. In you. I'm so tired. I won't last. Go on now."

The room swam with her strong memories from the Old Carolinas and the Westward movement and Georgia and Alabama, pioneering the new lands, of her John long gone, of her family that would live on in this young man. She dreamed. Happy times, happy places. Oh, the sweetness of that America!

Clayborne could barely hold down the powerful emotions as he stumbled out of the bedroom. He took the burly nurse by the elbow and pulled her to the corner of the kitchen out of earshot. He whispered, "Can they make it?"

The nurse turned gruffly away, then looked back at him more softly. She shook her head. "I'm sorry," she whispered.

Grandma Lou Perry died Wednesday, August 25, 1937, and was buried in Duffau Cemetery Thursday, August 26. Old Grandma Elizabeth Glasgow Perry died the next day, Friday, August 27, 1937, and was buried in Duffau Cemetery Saturday, August 28. The Perry reserve cracked at the graveside of Old Grandma, and Clayborne grieved unashamed over the two women who had always been there, who had shaped his life in so many uncounted ways. How he had loved his Grandma. How he had cherished his Old Grandma. And now they were gone. He stood alone, his wife and child at home in Iredell. He tried to grasp the desperate reality of death as he looked over the headstones in this cemetery he'd walked by so many times on his way from Duffau School to Dude Flat. The robins hopping on the lawn did not cheer him. The great sky did not pull on his spirit today. He looked down at the ground, the mounded earth over the graves. His two old loves — lost, all lost, quite lost. When he turned away and went home, the wide world was a poorer, emptier place.

If the Perry reserve cracked when Clayborne wept, it shattered when Jim Perry lost his wife and his mother all in the same week. The old man cried like a baby, utterly devastated. When the initial fountain of grief played itself out, he acted like a man stunned, like he didn't know what he was doing. He kept saying to everybody he met: "The last thing my Lou said was, 'You think I'm dying but I'm in the arms of Jesus.'"

He dreaded going back into the little old house at Dude Flat that had been so friendly, so full of laughter and joking and life. He dreaded going back into that plain little bedroom where his wonderful wife and his sparkling mother had breathed their last. He painfully walked over to the rent house to see the Stones, the people who worked most of his farm, and somewhat childishly begged them to move from the weaning house to his own home. He had been spoiled by his womenfolk, he said. Now they were gone, he said. He could do hardly anything for himself, cook, bring in firewood, he was nearly helpless.

Was he trying to gather close humanity around him as he had enjoyed for so many years with wife and mother? Did he act like a sick animal trying to hide from its sickness, nursing a baseless and illusory hope? He was so pitiful, such a pathetic figure, the Stones could not refuse, although they felt like intruders. They fed him and cared for him and tried to turn him from his grief. But in a week he was a different man. He didn't have much to say now, grew silent and moody, then by turns would talk about his wife and mother, would worry and fret and cry disconsolately. He couldn't get over it. After a while he took to staying with his children for a month or so at a time, first Tom, then Leonard up in Midlothian and then his youngest, Pitchford, who had also moved his family to Midlothian looking always for that greener grass. At least the old man could still drive his car and that gave him an independence that may have saved his poor sweet battered mind.

The new Iredell Elementary School went up over summer vacation and stood ready in its long low one-storey brick modernity when the students came flooding back in mid-September. Principal Perry was proud of his new building, glad to get his students out of the old stone castle a hundred yards away. Now they could learn better with proper light and better desks, and the teachers seemed to have a better attitude in the new school. Counting high school, Iredell had seventeen teachers, the most in Bosque County and the next largest school was Clifton, with sixteen teachers. Iredell had the only gym in the county so the games of basketball could be played inside. Iredell schools again this year had nine school buses hauling about some four hundred students from the country. Teaching, improving young minds, sowing for the future. Principal W. C. Perry felt he had the best job in Texas.

Oretta began to improve very rapidly in October. By the twelfth the vomiting had stopped and did not recur. She was up and around and back to her old self for the most part when November brought the first norther of the winter. The day before New Year, 1938, Clayborne felt the marks that 1937 had left on his life. And he remembered forlornly Old Grandma's last heavy admonition.

Springtime. A clear day in Iredell.

"Mom, look!" shouted five-year-old Bob Perry coming up the walk to the front steps.

Oretta stood in the doorway and looked out in disbelief. "Why'd you get him a *pig?*" she asked her husband as he walked behind the boy who carried a squealing white six-week-old piglet.

"Can't let a dog run loose here in town," said Clayborne. "That's what Bob would really like. But you can keep a pig penned up, and it just wouldn't be proper to pen up a dog."

"Sure, Mom. I can keep him in a pen," said the happy boy.

"Well, where are you going to keep it?"

Clayborne said, "I figured I could go out and take some wood from the old rundown barn in the back and Bob and me could put a little pigpen together. Far enough back so the smell won't be bad."

"Well, don't bring that thing in my house! Take it out and build your pen right now. A pig, Clayborne, a *pig!*" Oretta complained.

"It only cost three dollars. And the boy's ready to learn some responsibility, Oretta," said Clayborne. "It's time he had to take care of somethin'. You recall how you said when we got married that you didn't want our children protected like you were, so everything would hit 'em at once when they get out on their own."

"Well, I didn't mean gettin' Bobby a *pig*," she said.

"It won't be any trouble," Clayborne said.

"No, Mom," said Bob brightly. "It won't be any trouble. I'll take good care of it."

"All right, then, you two. You go around back and be grown up and build that critter a pen. And build it so I don't have to go chasin' 'im back in all the time. Hmmph. A *pig*!"

Clayborne and young Bob took a few scraps of old lumber from the dilapidated barn and built their sturdy pigpen, piling a few boards over one corner to provide shade and a trough for water and feed that extended through the slats so Bob could service it without getting in the pen.

"Well, that ought to give you something to do, son," said Clayborne when they were finished and the piglet nuzzled the ground inside the pen searching for a good place to dig a wallow.

"I'll keep busy at it," the boy promised. "I'll carry water and keep food in the trough. How long can I keep ol' piggy here, Dad?"

"You can keep it until you can't pick it up any more. When you can't handle it any more, that'll tell us you've had it long enough. What do you say?"

"That's great, Dad! Wow! My own pig!"

Before summer Bob had kept his promise and took good care of the pig. They sold it for five dollars and Bob got to keep two.

When the Perrys returned to Southwest Texas State Teachers College at San Marcos the summer of 1938, several things had changed. Lyndon Johnson had seen a newspaper headline February 23, 1937: CONGRESS-MAN JAMES P. BUCHANAN OF BRENHAM DIES. Johnson ran for the vacant Tenth District House seat and on April 10, 1937, was elected to Congress, just as he had vowed to his listeners under the liveoaks. Now in the summer of 1938 he found himself one of eight Texas congressmen running unopposed in the Democratic primary, which meant he would be a shoo-in for reelection in this one-party state. Prexy Cecil Eugene Evans' long relationship with Johnson had already borne fruit in the form of federal NYA grants to the school, and now in a certain sense Johnson became the congressman from Southwest Texas State Teachers College. Within a week of the Perrys' arrival, Prexy Evans got back an opinion from the Attorney General of Texas stating that the board of regents of San Marcos had the authority to request a federal grant for the construction of a building, and Lyndon-boy shortly helped Prexy funnel more big federal dollars into the campus — a building for the Laboratory

School, a place where student teachers could gain actual experience in classroom teaching, the core of teacher training and one of Prexy's long-term dreams. The college's physical plant was already growing apace and enrollment stood at an all-time high. Extension classes expanded rapidly and an enlarged program of senior and graduate classes had begun to turn the college into a university. Principal Perry's last year at San Marcos took place in an entirely different mood than his first.

Twelve weeks at college meant more spare time for the family together and Clayborne took advantage of it. On weekends he and Oretta and Bob trekked off to one recreation spot or another, spelunking through Wonder Cave in the limestone Hill Country, dunking in the Guadalupe River, motoring to San Antonio to Brackenridge Park and Witte Museum, swimming in the giant dogleg flagstone pool at Landa Park in New Braunfels with its artesian spring gushing at the pool head so powerfully that two people could sit bobbing atop its billowing flood and its outflow at the pool's tail spilling over a broad waterfall into the woody margins of the Comal River where little boys hid behind the liquid sheet in a mossy cave. There Bob took to the pure clear water instinctively, learning to duck beneath the surface and watch the comical legs treading water all around him in the crystalline artesian flow and learning how important it was not to inhale. The Texas summer was nature-music and people-poetry, tawny heat and spicy water-chill, heavy humid green smells of the earth and jungle growth vines hanging from the oaks along the rivers, rides in the car on the fast paved highway south and lying in the college grass hoping the chiggers wouldn't bite, watching the red moon rise and shopping in the grocery store for good things to eat, studying on a hard-slat campus bench and going to a picture show once in a while, particularly when Shirley Temple in *Little Miss Broadway* played at the Palace downtown and the theater advertised "Free China to the Ladies!" When the Palace switched programs to *The Texans* starring Randolph Scott and Joan Bennett, they read the newspaper ads that said

Adolph Zukor presents. . .

Brave men, Heroic women

Fighting shoulder to shoulder

Fighting to create a vast new empire from the wilderness!

They thought about seeing it but decided to save their money and go swimming in the San Marcos river at the springs. How easy it was to submerge in the Texas summer's peace and joy.

Before it had started it was over. On August 19, *The College Star* ran the headline:

Lyndon Johnson Will Deliver Radio Address at Commencement

Evans to Confer Degrees to over 200 Graduates

21 Are Candidates For Post Graduate Degrees

The body copy read:

The Hon. Lyndon B. Johnson, congressman from this district and a graduate of Southwest Texas State Teachers College, will deliver the address, which will be broadcast over the radio, at the summer Commencement exercizes to be held at Riverside on Wednesday, August 24.

President C.E. Evans will confer over 200 Bachelor's and possibly 21 Master's degrees to this summer's graduates.

Two hundred four seniors have made application for Bachelor of Arts and Bachelor of Science degrees. The twenty-one Master's candidates will provide the largest group to be graduated from the school since the graduate school opened here during the summer of 1936.

The College Band under the direction of R. A. Tampke will play a concert of six pieces to begin the commencement program. The invocation will be by Dean H. E. Speck, after which Dr. Evans will confer the degrees.

The Baccalaureate sermon will be preached Sunday night, August 21, at 7:30 at Riverside on the Island, by Rev. E. W. McLaurin, D.D. of the Presbyterian Seminary, Austin. Rev. Carroll Cloyd will give the invocation. Rev. T. H. Pollard the scripture reading, and Rev. Frank L. Meadow the benediction. The Choral Club of the College, with H. Grady Harlan as director, will sing.

A list of the candidates will be printed elsewhere in the Star.

Under the "P" listings of degree candidates appeared the name W. C. Perry. When Wednesday came and the outdoor Riverside pavilion was jammed with caps and gowns and proud relatives and the sun's last glow washed the dome of night and the scene was reminiscent of the brush arbors of revival, Congressman Johnson gave his inspirational speech and President Evans gave out the degrees.

Clayborne came marching down the stage to his family holding a Bachelor of Science in history with minors in social studies and mathematics, which entitled him to a permanent state teacher's certificate. As he walked down from that era in his life he pondered, oblivious to the crowd. It had been eight years since he left Tarleton and ten years since he started college, a long time to work toward an undergraduate degree. But now he had it, he had his degree, his permanent teacher's certificate. He did it. He was done. Now he could go home. As he walked down the long ramp he felt drained, sapped of the power to learn any more. He was accomplished and done with being a student. He had worked so long and so hard for his degree he gave no thought to further education that night.

But driving home to Iredell the *Star* headline niggled at him. *21 Are Candidates For Post Graduate Degrees.* The thought crept in *What about a post graduate degree?* He brushed it aside. It was not a serious thought. But it would not stay away. The old feeling came back, the feeling he'd had after high school. There was more in him. He felt it. Maybe he wasn't done. But that wasn't possible, it wasn't part of his plans. And then he heard Old Grandma — dear sweet cussed loving Old Grandma, God rest her — just as if she was there in the car with him. Why had she given him such a charge? *Stay in college.*

He argued with her: *But it's so hard, Old Grandma.*

Don't talk. Listen.

But Old Grandma. . .

She wouldn't be still, even though months dead. *Stay in college. For the family. Just do it.*

It was useless to resist. The sob in his throat came out merely like a sigh.

Oretta looked over to him and asked, "Are you all right, Clayborne?"

"Sure," he said. "I'm fine. Just a little tired."

"Well, you're done with college now. You can relax a little."

Bob sat in the back seat, looking out the window watching the Texas land go by.

When they turned off toward Iredell at Waco, Clayborne asked, "Oretta, what would you think if I was to take a course or two over at Baylor?"

-17-

STORM CLOUDS

ICKEY Rooney ended up as the top box-office star of 1939, toppling the four-year ascendancy of Shirley Temple, who fell to fifth place, a victim of normal growth hormones. But adorable little Shirley had presided in moppet majesty over the celluloid dream factory for much of the Depression '30s, doing her best to bring joy and forgetfulness to millions of burdened Americans. The movies of the 1930s were not intended to be works of art. The art had gone out of movies as the nation had sunk into misery. If art is the search for meaning, not many wanted to find the meaning of this dark time — entertainment and escapism ruled in the cinema of the day, and that was enough. Hollywood gave America entertainment in spades and America in return gave Hollywood its weekend quarters and Saturday matinee dimes — 85 million times a week.

Depression era picture shows became devoutly escapist, and since 1934 had been squeaky clean as well. That was the year the nation's Roman Catholic bishops had banded together to form the National League of Decency and bade Hollywood bow to an extensive laundry list of demands: no more long kisses, no more stories about adultery, no more criminals triumphing over the law, no more double beds on screen, not even so much as a bare baby bottom. No longer could Mae West ask her beaux "Why don't you come up and see me?" or W.C. Fields crack some of his more earthy ad-libbed jokes.

The push for public decency even affected David O. Selznik's Civil War extravaganza *Gone With The Wind*. This classic film had been years in the making, had an incredible budget for the time, and brought together one of the most felicitous combinations of talent in film history. Not only had Selznik discovered in Vivien Leigh the perfect Scarlett O'Hara and in Clark Gable the perfect Rhett Butler, but also in Margaret Mitchell the perfectly literate author whose novel could be readily transferred to the screen. Mitchell had originally titled her 1,037-page novel *Tomorrow Is Another Day*, but her publisher complained that too many books had "tomorrow" in their titles so she turned to Ernest Dowson's poem, *Non Sum Qualis Eram Bonae sub Regno Cynarae* and the line, "I have forgot much, Cynara! Gone with the wind!" The title was perfect, the novel was perfect and the movie was perfect. But when on December 15, 1939, the film climaxed its Atlanta premiere with Rhett Butler's exit line, "Frankly, my dear, I don't give a damn," a public battle raged to have the word "damn" expunged from the script — it was profanity, and that was that. The Texans in the Grand Prairie who went to see it, and that was most of them, were not very concerned with either the word or the flap over the word — they had cussed and discussed matters in piquant language themselves from time to time and they liked Mr. Selznik's picture, cussing and all. Butler's disgusted departure remained intact to become legendary, but it was the only profanity in any American film released during the Depression. The movie moguls straitened their laces and toed the line.

Hollywood's flirtation with strict morality was not a matter of principle, it was a matter of money, and *Gone With The Wind* out-moneyed them all, even with Rhett Butler's moment of backsliding. The hard-drinking, fast-living, loose-mouthed flapper of the Roaring Twenties had vanished with the boom-times. No longer did the scornful, mocking world of a snide Sinclair Lewis grab an audience. No longer did the snob heaping derision upon Middle America sell tickets. The dire spectacle of a nation in economic shambles had brought with it not only the need for escape, but also the popular urge to restore the basic sober proprieties to their once-central place in American values. The League of Decency, time showed, had not created the new atmosphere, it had simply reflected the public mood. Hollywood's actual morality may have ended at the box-office tally and the daily-gross sheet, but producers knew that their tally reflected the public will and they gave the public what it wanted.

And America wanted Mickey Rooney in the *Andy Hardy* series. And Spencer Tracy in *Captains Courageous*. And Judy Garland in *The Wizard of Oz*. And Jimmy Stewart in *Mr. Smith Goes to Washington*. And John Wayne in *Stagecoach*. And Gary Cooper in *The Plainsman*. And Shirley Temple in just about anything. The nation needed heroes and it got them. Even the bad guys developed a certain style: Humphrey Bogart's tough guy and Bela Lugosi's *Dracula* personified evil rather than glorifying it. The screwball comedy — Claudette Colbert and Clark Gable in *It Happened One Night* — hit the public funnybone alongside the classic slapstick of the Marx Brothers. Special effects became a movie star with the outsize mechanical gorilla of *King Kong*. And animation came of age with Walt Disney's *Snow White and the Seven Dwarfs*.

Film critics such as John Gould Fletcher panned American movies for "the emotional monotony, the naive morality, the sham luxury, the haphazard etiquette, the sentimental and the acrobatic that are so common in the United States," but voices of his ilk were drowned out in the clatter of tons of money that ordinary citizens plunked down for "fluffy white operettas" starring Jeanette McDonald and Nelson Eddy — dubbed by cynics "The Iron Butterfly" and "The Singing Capon" — and for twinkletoes musicals starring Fred Astaire and Ginger Rogers. The report on Fred Astaire's first screen test had said: "Can't act. Slightly bald. Can dance a little." After his first movie, *The Gay Divorcee*, RKO insured his legs for a million dollars. America knew what it wanted. The critics didn't.

While the average man, woman and child thus endured the years of penury with frequent doses of movie magic, America's horn of plenty remained clogged. As the decade of the 'Thirties drew to a close, the Depression was not getting a whole lot better. The frantic search for economic salvation brought with it strange and disquieting tremors to ruffle what composure the weary nation had been able to muster. An intense middle-aged man named Fritz Kuhn had become president of something called the German-American Bund and led off meetings in New Jersey with right arm outstretched, saying "The Nazi salute is the coming salute for the whole United States." National Socialism, Kuhn said, would save America. On the wall behind him hung the American flag and the Nazi swastika flag, flanking a portrait of George Washington. With a straight face he told his audience, "Washington was the first Fascist."

In Hollywood and New York, bubbly intellectuals soaked up the new Soviet line called the Popular Front. Moscow had realized that Hitler would one day attack the Russian Motherland and issued orders to stop calling capitalists nasty names and form the widest possible alliances to protect the birthplace of actually existing socialism. Their new sales pitch said that Communism's share-the-wealth concept would save America. Innocent Americans fell for such slogans as "Communism is Twentieth Century Americanism," and didn't even wonder why Communists who a few years earlier had plotted an armed revolution against the United States were suddenly waving American flags and trying to look homespun and respectable.

Front groups with outlandish names such as The American League Against War and Fascism were welcomed to Washington by Interior

Secretary Harold Ickes. The Hollywood Anti-Nazi League raised piles of cash for its Communist leaders with the avid help of the Screen Writers' Guild. Many stars held fund-raising parties in their own homes, supposedly helping General Francisco Franco fight the Nazis, ignorant of being Red dupes. Simply detesting the enemy — the Nazis — was enough, and nobody in the United States bothered to find out what the Communists were saying in their own nest. If anyone had read the Moscow proceedings of the Communist International — the Comintern — for 1938, they would have known that leader Georgi Dimitrov told a plenary meeting that "One sympathizer is worth more than a dozen militant Communists. A writer of reputation is worth more than 500 poor devils who don't know any better than to get themselves beaten up by the police."

Then came the reckoning. On August 23, 1939, Party Secretary Stalin toasted Hitler's good health after the U.S.S.R. signed the Nazi-Soviet peace pact: "I know how much the German nation owes to its Fuehrer." Even the most dedicated American Popular Front activists couldn't swallow that piece of double-think. American Communist Party membership fell off drastically. As one historian remarked, "thousands of Americans who had been pursuing good causes under a Red banner awoke to the realization that they'd been had."

If the Texans of the Grand Prairie even heard of these goings-on, they paid little attention. Intellectuals and ideology were of little use to them. They understood Nazism much more directly. They uneasily sensed the growing danger radiating from the Third Reich in Berlin. Hitler had the disquieting habit of taking whatever he wanted when he wanted it, coldly and efficiently and finally. In 1938 Hitler had annexed Austria. In March 1939, Hitler's forces occupied all of Czechoslovakia. In April, 1939, Benito Mussolini sent his troops to seize Albania and shortly afterward signed an alliance treaty with Hitler. In September, 1939, Germany invaded Poland. Instinctively Texans knew Hitler was their enemy, more clearly and more fiercely than any other segment of Americans, as both *Fortune* and Gallup polls showed. They hoped and prayed to stay out of war but were ruled by their ingrained habit of dealing summarily with enemies, a belligerance sharpened in the Mexican War and the Civil War and the Great War. Had it been up to these Texans, President Roosevelt's policy of cautious interventionism would have been escalated into outright hostilities with Germany, instanter. Texas historian T.A. Fehrenbach has called the attitude of Texans in 1939 "barbarian awareness of true danger" but took pains to point out that "barbarian awareness of true danger can be an asset to any society, as well as a barbarian willingness to believe that straight action, not interminable moral confusion, is sometimes required." Texans put the trouble in Europe out of their minds day to day, but it was always there, niggling, prodding, disturbing, hovering, impending. In their deepest hearts they knew it would come to a fight.

"Grandpa, will you return thanks?" Tom asked his father.

All at the Sunday dinner table bowed their heads in reverent humility as seventy-seven-year-old patriarch Jim Perry sat at the head of the table and said grace.

"Our heavenly Father, we ask Thy blessing on this food Thou hast so graciously given us, that it may strengthen our bodies to Thy service. And bring Thy special blessing we ask to all the families gathered here on this Thy Sabbath that they may do Thy will in obedience and in health. Bless Tom and Belle and their girls Nadine and Dorothy. Bless Clayborne and Oretta and young Bob and little baby Margie. Bless Hoyt and Bernice and little Sherry. And, Lord, we ask that You bless and keep all those we love that have been gathered to Thy bosom. With steadfast faith in Thy eternal salvation and Thy promise for the Resurrection, in Jesus' name we pray. Amen."

"Amen" echoed the fervent voices around the table and around Tom and Belle's big kitchen where the young people stood waiting for their turn to eat. Texas custom held that when too many came for Sunday dinner to be served at one sitting, the elders ate first and the youngsters had to "take an old cold 'tater and wait," as a country singer once put it.

Tom Perry, long blind and growing gradually enfeebled, smiled a big smile this Sunday noon and said, "Everyone take out and help yourself now. And, Grandpa" — everyone called Jim Perry Grandpa these days, even his own son — "thank you for that beautiful blessing. We appreciate you remembering us."

Voices stirred around the room, mingled with the clinks and clanks of moving serving bowls and utensils — "Yes, indeed." "It sure was beautiful." "You're so thoughtful to remember us all." "We love you Grandpa."

"Well," said the old man, "it's only proper and fitting, you know. I'm sure Tom would do the same if he thought it was right to pray in front of people."

"You know how I feel about that, Grandpa," Tom chided over the noise of dishing up food.

Belle broke in, "Oretta, how are you doing with that new young one? She's about five weeks old today, isn't she?"

Nadine and Dorothy stood by the cookstove and cooed across the room at the newest Perry.

Oretta clasped the tiny infant daughter as her husband dished out Sunday dinner for her. "Oh, we're getting to know little Margie right well," Oretta said.

Clayborne grinned, "Especially in the middle of the night."

Bob, just turned seven years old, piped up from where he stood by the dish cabinet: "I help Mom with Margie, too, when I'm home from school. I go get the clean diapers and I can even hold her without dropping her. Betcha' I didn't cry like that when I was a baby, though."

Everybody smiled as the brimming bowls of chicken and potato salad passed around the table. Grandpa Jim Perry rotated a chicken drumstick in front of his teeth like it was corn on the cob, smirked wryly and remarked to Bob, "No, you didn't cry like that, boy — you had a pair of lungs on you could be heard clear into the next county."

"Aw, Grandpa," giggled the boy, pulling his chin down into his Sunday shirt and leaning back against the wall.

Hoyt chewed his biscuit and asked, "What do you think of having a girl this time, Clayborne?"

"Just what we ordered — we always wanted one of each, you know."

Hoyt's wife Bernice paused between bites of squash and chimed in, "I thought Oretta said you wanted two of each."

Oretta grinned, "That's right, but we always figured on gettin' 'em one at a time like most folks."

The grownups at the table chuckled as they ate.

Clayborne asked his brother, "What's it like raising a girl, Hoyt? Sherry's about a year and a half, isn't she?" Little Sherry sat babbling and eating happily in a high chair next to her mother.

"Yep, she's a July baby last year, you remember. Well, raising a girl's no different from raising a boy, far as I can see."

Bernice said, "How would you know? We've only got Sherry."

"We've watched Bob grow up, Bernice," said Hoyt, holding a big glass of milk and glancing at the boy on the far side of the room. "It's just the same with boys or girls, feed 'em, change their diapers, put clothes on 'em, make sure they learn to behave, send 'em off to school when the time comes."

"Oh, Hoyt, there's a big difference and you know it!" exclaimed Bernice. "You men. Girls need attention and affection."

Oretta asked between bites of okra, "You mean boys don't? Wait'll you have one of your own!"

"Girls," insisted Bernice, "are different, they need more mothering, they like to have somebody to lean on. I don't think they're so independent."

"Nadine and me are independent," retorted fifteen-year-old Dorothy. "Aren't we, Mama?"

Belle said, "When it comes to chore time you two sure are."

"Mama!" said Nadine. "We do our chores. We know you and Papa need us."

"She's just funnin' you, daughter," soothed Tom. "You know how we appreciate you stayin' with us now that you're all done with high school. And you know how I told you we missed you when you came back after going off to work for Mitchell's dry goods in Iredell last year."

Jim Perry said "You better appreciate her quick, too, son. I've seen how she takes to that Land boy, what's his name?"

"Henry," said Nadine, a little huffily. "Henry Land. He's got a good job with a chemical company down in Texas City on the Gulf. Comes to see me once a month, sometimes more. Drives all that way just to see me. He's going to have enough saved up to buy a house in another year. I'm twenty years old, Grandpa. Henry is a nice young man and it's time I started thinkin' about settling down."

"You see," said Grandpa Perry.

"Grandpa," said Clayborne, slathering a biscuit with sorghum, "how are you getting along now that Hoyt and Bernice are living with you at the farm?"

"They ain't livin' with me," Jim Perry answered. "They're out there at Dude Flat by themselves. I've been stayin' here with your Papa and Mama the last week or two."

"I thought. . ." began Clayborne.

Hoyt broke in, explaining, "Bernice and me and Sherry are all moved in and working Grandpa's place, Clayborne." Hoyt then sat back from his cleaned plate. "Grandpa's not there because he just decided he'd like to keep moving around like he has since . . . you know, since Grandma and Old Grandma passed on."

Jim Perry bowed his head a little at these words, slumped his shoulders, spoke softly to himself. "Oh, Lou, oh, Mama, how I miss the two of you! Oh, Lord, it sure is a vail of tears You put us in here. . ." He began to sob. The youngsters stood around the room silently embarrassed for him, felt his anguish, felt pity for him.

Belle reached over the dish of tomatoes and patted him on the hand, murmuring, "There, there, don't take on so. It's the Lord's will, Grandpa Perry, everything's for the best. Here, wipe your eyes with my napkin. I haven't used it."

"Oh, thank you, daughter," moaned the old man. "I just plumb come apart when I think of them, you know. Don't mind me. Go on with your talkin'." He dabbed his eyes and nose.

"I'm sorry Grandpa," said Hoyt. "I didn't mean to remind you. It's just that. . ."

"I know. You can't hardly tell your brother what you're doing without bringin' it up, that's natural. It's no fault of yours. Just don't pay no mind to me. I'll be all right. You go on, tell him what you're doin'."

Hoyt felt caught in a double bind — "damned if he do, damned if he don't," as his neighbors would say. He went on uneasily, "Bernice and me and Sherry are all settled over at Dude Flat, Clayborne, living in

Grandpa's house there, like I said. We're taking care of the place, running some cattle on it, keeping the buildings up. I don't expect to try making any cotton with the prices so low. Grandpa comes and goes as he pleases, spends a few weeks with Pitchford up at Midlothian, then stays a while with Leonard, then with Julia and her husband down below Iredell there. Now he's stayin' a bit here with Papa and Mama. You're right independent, aren't you Grandpa?"

"What's that? Oh, yes, yes, I am. I can still drive my old Ford and I come and go as I please, just like Hoyt says."

"I'm glad to hear it, Grandad," said Clayborne, feeling sorry for his aging grandfather, trying to recall the respect and admiration he had felt for this man since boyhood. Sweet dear old Grandpa Perry! How time had come to ravage the proud farmer, how bittersweet the lees of his life!

"And how about you, Clayborne," asked Hoyt. "How are you and the family doing since you got your new house?"

"Just fine," answered his brother. "We're comfortable."

Oretta said, "Why, that little seven-room rock house is the nicest place we've ever lived, Clayborne. We're more than just comfortable, let me tell you. Why, it's *real* nice. It's just a block or two from where we rented with Miz Weir, right near the Iredell stores."

"Clayborne told me the house cost $750 when you bought it," smiled Hoyt.

"That's alot of money, yes sir, alot of money."

Tom Perry pushed back in his chair and said, "It sure sounds like just before the Great War, it does. It was a mistake ever to let Germany have an army again. They're just plain a warlike people, they are. President Wilson tried to keep us out of that war in Europe back then but he couldn't do it. That was supposed to be the war to end all wars. Hah! Now, just a month ago that Hitler went and destroyed Poland. President Roosevelt is tryin' to keep us out of this war in Europe. And I'll tell you, it won't work this time, either. We'll have to go over there and save Europe again, you mark my words."

Belle said, "All right, you men, if you're going to start all that war talk again, you've had enough time at the table. Get on up and let the kids eat."

As the grownups vacated the table for the second shift, young Bob came up to his grandmother and said, "Grandma, at school they taught us how to tell people what our parents' names were in case we get lost."

"That's nice, Bob," said Belle.

"Dad's name is Mr. W.C. Perry, and he's the principal of the school," announced the boy proudly. "and my Mom's name is Mrs. Oretta Perry. And I know Grandpa's name: It's Mr. Tom Perry. But, Grandma, what's your name?"

The grownups hovered around to hear the exchange. Texas culture had for long nourished an almost mystical respect for a person's given name; not only were children never to address their elders on a first-name basis, but also even adults avoided first names except among the closest of friends. Many lifelong acquaintances knew each other only as *Mister* So-and-so or *Miz* Such-and-such. Husbands and wives commonly referred to their spouses as "He" and "She" rather than use their given names in polite conversation, even at the beginning of a conversation when the listener had no rational way of knowing who "He" or "She" might be, but listeners knew — "*He* came home late last night," or "*She's* visiting over at her mother's." A first name was like a magic amulet to these people, not to be used by the uninitiate. The moral force of this rule was palpable: even an innocent boy bringing up the subject released a thick cloud of perceptible tenseness in the room.

Belle smiled broadly and chanted the old rhyme, "What's my name? Puddin' and tane. Ask me again and I'll tell you the same."

"Puddin' and tane?" asked Bob, baffled.

Everybody laughed.

"Puddin' and tane! It's just a saying, Bobby," smiled Belle, laying her hands on both his shoulders. "Grownups used to say that to me when I was a little girl and asked their name. It's just a tease to let youngsters know they have to respect their elders. But here's the truth: if someone asks you what your Grandma's name is, you tell them her name is Mrs. Belle Perry."

"Mrs. Bell Perry, Grandma? Like the bell that rings in the church?"

"No, boy, it's spelled different. Have you learned to spell any yet?"

"I can spell real good, Grandma, o-n-e, one; k-i-t-t-y, kitty; M-i-s-s-i-s-s-i-p-p-i, Mississippi." Mississippi, the perennial playground favorite, was inevitable in the spelling repertoire of any first-grader.

"Well, my name is spelled B-e-l-l-e. It means a pretty lady."

"I think you're a real pretty lady, Grandma."

"You've got yourself a smart boy, son," smiled Belle at Clayborne. "He'll go far. But right now he better go far to a seat at the table."

Friday afternoon, November 10, 1939. "Clayborne!" cried Oretta. "I'm sick!"

"What's the matter?" Clayborne rushed from the kitchen to the living room chair where Oretta sat tending baby Margie. Oretta hunched over trying not to crush the six-week-old girl as the spasm passed. Young Bob came in the room and stood immobilized with alarm. After nearly a full minute of agony Oretta straightened up a little, enough to look up at her husband.

"It's my innards again," she said weakly, her face white with pain and fear. "It came on all of a sudden."

"Maybe it was just a gas pain," suggested Clayborne.

"I don't think so," she said weakly. Suddenly another bolt of visceral affliction doubled her over. Clayborne took crying Margie and held her close while laying his free hand on his wife's shoulder.

"Bob," he said calmly to his son across the room, "maybe you better go over next door and tell Mrs. Bradley your mother's sick. Ask if she can come sit a while so I can go get Dr. Pike."

"Okay, Dad," said the boy looking worriedly at his mother. "I'll run. Right now, Dad." He scooted out the back door and was gone.

"Oh, Clayborne," moaned Oretta, still doubled over in torment. "It's bad."

"Let's see if we can get you to the bedroom so you can lie down," he said with the baby howling in his ear.

"Not yet," she gasped. "Wait." The gnawing in her bowels subsided momentarily and she sat back in the chair. "Okay," she said. "Now."

Holding Clayborne's arm and relying upon his strength, she managed to hoist herself from the chair and step unsteadily to the bedroom. She thumped on the bed like a thing inanimate, drained by the hurt. Clayborne helped her get her feet onto the bed while juggling little Margie who somehow sensed the problem and cried all the louder.

The back door opened and shut. "Are you in the bedroom?" came the strident voice of the neighbor lady, Mrs. Mae Bradley. Margie paused between squalls, her attention drawn to the sound.

"Come on in," called Clayborne. "She's resting on the bed now."

Mrs. Bradley stopped at the door and surveyed the scene, Bob peeking around her skirts. "Why, you're white as a sheet, Mrs. Perry," she said. "Mr. Perry you give me that baby and get on around to Dr. Pike's house. Your wife looks like she can use some doctorin'."

Clayborne complied, instructing Bob, "You stay here son. I'm going to walk around the block and get Dr. Pike. If your mother needs anything, you get it for her, you hear?"

"Yes, Dad. I'll do it quick, too."

The good doctor came with Clayborne immediately from his home a block away. Dr. A. N. Pike looked at the situation and thought he knew what the problem was. But before making a final decision he gave Oretta a mild laxative medication and told Clayborne to come tell him later if it worked. It did not.

By bedtime the whole neighborhood had become aware of Oretta's disorder, and you could feel the human concern and the prayers settling like an angel's breath over the little rock house on the nameless north-south street in the little Grand Prairie town. Dr. Pike came twice in the middle of the night. Mrs. Bradley stayed up with Oretta for hours. By dawn there was no doubt.

"Mr. Perry," said Dr. Pike as the Saturday sun rose over the rim of east

Texas, "your wife has a locked bowel. Same problem she had when you were down at San Marcos. I think you'd better take her up to Terrill Hospital in Stephenville. Right away. I'll telephone ahead. Both the Dr. Terrills will be expecting you. I image Dr. Vance Terrill will do the admitting and Dr. Jim Terrill will do the operation. You get going."

Clayborne prepared the Terraplane for Oretta as he had for others in days past, removing the front passenger seat, placing a box in its place, laying planks for a bed and wrapping the planks in bedding. While Clayborne placed a pillow on the makeshift ambulance bed, Ralph and Mae Bradley — Ralph worked with Clayborne as the agriculture teacher for the Iredell school system — walked up from their house on the lot facing the back of the Perrys' and offered to take care of Bob while Oretta was in the hospital.

"Our Billy is just a year older than your Bob, W. C. " said Mr. Bradley. "They play together all the time anyways, and Mae says we might as well have him stay with us while you take care of this."

"I'm obliged to you," said Clayborne, deeply touched.

"No, W. C., we're obliged to you. For all the things you do to make Iredell better. This is the least we can do in return."

Mrs. Hyacinth Sadler, one of Principal Perry's teachers at Iredell Elementary, came up the street. She volunteered to accompany Clayborne and Oretta to Stephenville and take care of little Margie on the way. Oretta's sister Ila, for years a Stephenville resident, had agreed over the phone to take care of the baby for as long as Oretta was sick.

Before turning to get in the car and drive away, Clayborne faced his son who looked back anxiously. "Bob, you be good at Mrs. Bradley's. Mind her and don't make a mess. And help her around the house."

"Yes, sir, I will." The boy stood wavering in front of his father, in front of the car, glancing through the window at his mother laid out on the hard narrow bed inside and at Mrs. Sadler sitting next to her on the back seat holding his little sister Margie. Bob was old enough now to realize that when people went into the hospital they didn't always come back out. "Dad," he said with all the Perry reserve he could recruit, "is Mom going to be all right?"

Clayborne looked into the anguished young eyes. Something in him reached out to his son, spiritually bonding them, soothing the tumult in the boy's soul. "Your mother will be just fine son. She may need an operation, but remember that she got well in San Marcos. You say a prayer for her."

"I will, Dad. I already said a lot of them."

The Terraplane cruised over the alternately paved and graveled road to Stephenville. Modern highways had begun their slow reach into the heartland of the Grand Prairie, making travel a little easier and smoothing some of the bumps for suffering Oretta. Even so, it was more than an hour's drive before the tall stack of Tarleton's heating plant appeared on the near horizon of the Cross Timbers and they pulled up to the emergency entrance of Terrill Hospital in Stephenville.

Oretta was admitted, diagnosed with an intestinal adhesion and prepped for surgery in little over an hour. While Dr. Vance Terrill took care of Oretta, Clayborne drove Mrs. Sadler and baby Margie to Ila Ledbetter's home some two miles across town. Oretta's oldest sister Ila had married her "B. C. 'Better,'" as people used to tease her, not long after Oretta and Clayborne had eloped. But no one teased her any more: B. C. had gone to the Veterans Hospital in San Antonio one early December day in 1937 to apply for disability compensation from his service in the Great War and a week later died of a massive heart attack. Now Ila lived the lonely life of a widow lady, supported by the military compensation that had ironically been granted after B. C.'s death.

"You just leave little Margie with me, Clayborne," she said at the front door of her modest Stephenville home. "Come to Auntie Ila, baby. There, now. Oh, she's so sweet." She crooned to the bright-eyed child, then looked up. "You get back to that hospital, Clayborne. Let me know as soon as there's something to tell. And if you need anything later, come on over, dinner or whatever. Now go on."

Back to the hospital and Mrs. Sadler. As they strode to the admission desk Mrs. Sadler told Clayborne, "You've got things to attend to. I'll have my husband come pick me up, Principal Perry."

"Mrs. Sadler, I don't know how to thank you, you've been such a help."

"Just stay with Mrs. Perry and don't bother, you hear? We'll be praying for you."

The admission nurse said, "Mr. Perry, Dr. Terrill said you were to go up to surgery as soon as you got back."

Climbing the stairs Clayborne had a sense of deja vu, his precious wife in mortal danger once again, the hospital sights of institutional pale green walls, the hospital smells of ether and antiseptic, the pounding fear.

"Mr. Perry," said the surgery nurse outside the swinging doors, "there's a gown and mask for you inside. Dr. Terrill wants you to attend."

Again he donned the surgical garb, again he sat in a chair across the room from the surgical table, again listened to the crisp orders for sterile instruments, clamps, again heard the doctor tell him of his discovery: blocked intestines. Again the hours of manipulation and drainage of the dammed organs, of lavage and repair, hours that seemed like days.

Then, at last, "We caught it early this time, Mr. Perry," said Dr. Jim Terrill from his position beside the patient. "There's some damage, all right, mostly heavy inflammation, but there's no peritonitis and no necrotic tissue like you had down in San Marcos."

"Thank the Lord," gulped Clayborne involuntarily.

"But I'm worried that we had this recurrence, Mr. Perry. Your wife can't stand another one of these episodes. With your permission I want to try a new procedure. I'm obligated to inform you that it is experimental and not medically proven, but the clinical test results are promising."

"What is it, doctor?"

"Before we close, I'd like to do a peritoneal lavage with a new compound extracted from the afterbirth of a calf. We'll bathe the intestine with a pint of the fluid. In tests it has prevented these adhesions from recurring. Medical science is searching for a more effective compound, but there's nothing yet available except this."

He held up a container of clear fluid.

"Can it do any harm?" asked Clayborne.

"No," said the doctor. "The worst that could happen is that it would simply be absorbed and eliminated without proving effective. It has no side effects that have been observed in hospital tests."

"Yes, use it. Do what you can."

Half an hour later, when Oretta had been finally released from surgery and wheeled into the recovery ward, Dr. Terrill took Clayborne aside. As he removed his mask and surgical gown, the doctor spoke confidentially. "How many children do you and Mrs. Perry have?"

"Two, doctor, a boy seven and a girl six weeks. Why?" He dreaded the answer.

"That's good. One of each. The inflammation we found seems to have involved the female organs, Mr. Perry. I don't know how extensive the damage is. But I think you should be advised that your wife may not be able to have more children."

"Are you sure?"

"You can wait and see. Perhaps the damage will repair itself. But I don't think so. The important thing is that we caught the blockage before peritonitis set in. Your wife is going to recover, Mr. Perry. She'll live, and that's what matters now."

Clayborne took up residence once again at Oretta's bedside. He watched her slowly, groggily come out from under the ether, mumbling incoherent phrases at first, then gradually growing lucid as the tide of consciousness washed clean the drugged and muddied shores of thought.

"Clayborne," she said as though speaking through a mouth full of cotton. "Is it over?"

"It's over," he said, clasping her hand. "They got it in time. You're going to be fine." He looked at her with love and relief and thankfulness to his Maker. "You're going to be fine."

The next two days remained a foggy time for Clayborne, sitting with his pale and weakened wife, driving to Ila's to give her the news and call the relatives, visiting with baby Margie, grabbing a bite here and there, at Ila's, at the little hamburger stand near the center of town where he ate a nickel burger and a fried pie and drank a coke as he had back in Tarleton days. Tarleton days! How remote and ancient they seemed! How alien and callow the new crop of students seemed that surrounded him at the little eatery. Was he once like that, green and contingent, prospecting in the formless future? Time and change, time and change, they were one and the same.

Then he sat again by Oretta's bedside, chatting, comforting, keeping company. The ward nurse brought in a little cot as evening drew into night, and he slept there next to his wife Saturday and Sunday.

Very early Monday morning he told Oretta, "I have to go back to Iredell for a while."

"Oh, Clayborne, how long?"

"Don't worry, I'll be back this afternoon. I have to teach typing and algebra classes, but I'll be back before you know it. You rest. You rest."

He drove the forty miles and arrived at school in time for his first class. If everyone on the school staff had not already heard of his wife's ordeal, no one could have felt anything wrong. Principal Perry was cordial and helpful as usual, taught his obligatory classes as usual, went to his office and handled the paper work as usual, and in the late morning looked up to see his son standing at his office door.

"Well, young man," said Principal Perry, "I see from the attendance slips that you got to school on time today."

"Yes, sir. I got here early. I wasn't sure you'd be here." The youngster stood waiting silently, the question shouting in his mind.

"Your mother is fine, Bob. She had an operation yesterday and the doctor fixed the problem. He even gave her a medicine that will keep her from getting sick again."

Bob's face burst with joy and he nearly yelled "Yahoo!" But he remembered where he was and merely smiled broadly and asked, "When can Mom come home?"

"Doctor says it'll take about a week in the hospital to make sure everything stays right. I imagine it'll be next Saturday or Sunday."

"That's a long time."

"Not as long as last time, remember?"

"I sort of remember."

The next Sunday they brought her home. A neighbor lady, Mrs. McAdden, accompanied Clayborne to Stephenville to help with baby Margie on the return drive. Another neighbor, Mrs. Plummer, came to cook and take care of the baby at home while Oretta finished recuperating. When the ordeal of pain and the days of worry for his wife ended, Clayborne had not missed a day at school.

Early evening. Clear yellow sunset skies over the Rocky Creek hills northwest of Iredell. Shadows on the knuckles of limestone showing through the brown dirt, liveoak silhouettes.

"All right, why don't you folks come right on in, now," hooted Mr. H. H. Ramage at the wide-open double French doors of his sprawling flagstone ranch house. His two dozen guests on the terraced patio looked up at him from their after-dinner conversations. "I know it's almost the middle of May," he went on, "but it still gets a little nippy outside of an evening here in the hills above town. We can listen to the radio inside, or play dominoes, or talk religion and politics."

Muffled laughter bounced through the clatter of chairs and shoes on the stone patio pavement. Oretta and Clayborne pushed away from the huge dinner table, Oretta holding the eight-month-old Margie and Clayborne ushering Bob into the crowd. Their foursome joined the party that now slowly filed past their host into the comfortable and ample living room.

In front of her, Oretta heard the wife of Iredell school superintendent Jerry Phillips say, "That was a wonderful brisket you and Mrs. Ramage served tonight." Oretta hastened to add, "And those pickles, Mr. Ramage, sakes alive, they're the best we've ever had."

Mr. Ramage smiled, "Thank you, Mrs. Phillips, and Mrs. Perry, my wife will be happy to give you the recipe. And that little Margie's just the best baby you could want. She didn't raise a fuss once at dinner. And Bob, you're a very well-behaved young man."

As the women-folk and children passed ahead into the house, Clayborne stepped aside with superintendent Phillips and host Ramage. "We sure do appreciate you having all of us over this Friday evening, Mr. Ramage," Clayborne said.

"Well, you know how much we like to have a few neighbors and school people visit with us, Mr. Perry. Keeps us in touch, you know."

Superintendent Phillips said, "Did you know that Mr. Perry is now Senior Warden in the West in our Iredell Lodge, Mr. Ramage?"

"I saw the notice in the Masonic Newsletter that you'll be installed at our next meeting, Mr. Perry. My congratulations. That puts you second in command of the Lodge, now, doesn't it?"

"Yes, sir, next to the Worshipful Master," Clayborne said with quiet pride.

"Now, something else, Mr. Perry," said Ramage. "What's this Superintendent Phillips tells me about you thinking of going over to Walnut Springs to be Superintendent of Schools?"

"Well," said Clayborne uneasily, "the position is open and I *have* been with the Iredell system for six years now, and the school board over there has made me an attractive offer. . ."

"Principal Perry is being modest, Mr. Ramage," said Superintendent Phillips. "I kid him about Snuff City not being good enough for him any more, but the truth is those folks over at Walnut Springs are just about stumbling over themselves trying to get him to shape their schools up. I've encouraged him to accept the position. It's the next logical step up in an educator's career."

"That's fine, Superintendent Phillips," said Ramage. "It will be a great loss to our community, but I like to see ambitious people, Mr. Perry. That's what makes the world go 'round, good solid ambition. And Walnut Springs is a fine little town."

The dinner party now settled into the homey western-style ranch house living room. Card tables quickly attracted domino players. Little clutches of conversationalists found their own chatty inglenooks amid the leather furniture. Stand-abouts clustered around the shoulders they liked best to look over.

The Ramage home had grown into a center of local Texas society carefully cultivated by the prominent ranching couple. An invitation to the Ramage place might mean the establishment of contacts that could make or break a career in the professions; it was essential to anyone interested in making a local political name for himself. But the Ramage events themselves had none of the sweaty-palmed anxiety of a mid-Western smoker or the snotty viciousness masquerading as wit of an East Coast cocktail party — it was all downhome and low key: the more real power a Texan had in those days the more downhome he tended to act.

The radio had captured its usual circle of devotees who surrounded the elegant console box with the lighted dials. They stood or sat in almost theatrical poses, seeing with their ears, listening eyes sharply focused on the scenery of their minds. NBC's Red Network antennae in New York and Los Angeles radiated the popular 7:00 to 7:30 p.m. show "Amos 'n' Andy," a comedy in black-voice loaded with stereotyped Negro personalities, each portrayed by a white man: Freeman Gosden played "Amos" to Charles Correll's "Andy." Tonight the routine featured two other characters, the meek "Lightnin' " and big-man-about-Harlem "Kingfish."

Kingfish: Now, Lightnin', de reason I come is to ast yo' to pay some o' yo' dues dat yo' is back in. De record show dat yo' ain't paid but thirty-five cents in de last two years, an' dat's a disgrace to de lodge dat's puttectin' yo' like it is.

Lightnin': Yessah. Well, I is behind wid ev'rything'. My coffin money's even back now. Insurance man come oveh dis mornin' lookin' fo' ten cents — I had to duck de man — I think dat's done lapsed on me.

Superintendent Phillips looked up from his dominoes and said to his partner Clayborne, "That Amos 'n' Andy always has a laugh in it. Makes you feel good about those Negro folks."

Clayborne said, "I like Fibber McGee and Molly better. Everything falls out of his closet. And The Lone Ranger program. Always a good story. You better pay attention to your dominoes or I'm goin' to beat you this time."

"Oh, I'm paying attention. Did you hear about the dams on the Paluxy getting washed out?"

"I know what you're doing, trying to get me distracted here," grinned Clayborne. "I heard about those dams. The trouble was they built 'em back during the dry years, 1926 and in there. Just used rocks and concrete, wasn't much to them. Now with all this rain and runoff they just can't hold the water back. They'll all be washed out before long." He fleetingly remembered Grandpa Jim Perry's wooden bridge over little Camp Branch and how proud the old man had been to see it weather one flood after another, but he said nothing.

"The Paluxy dams *are* all washed out now. That was the last one went out last week."

"That right?"

Superintendent Phillips' wife, looking over her husband's shoulder, asked Oretta, "Well, how is that little girl coming along?"

Oretta hugged the baby and said, "Oh, she's just such a sweet little girl. I don't know how we got along without her."

"You know, it was a surprise to me when she arrived, Mrs. Perry. I hadn't known you were expecting. But I guess I hadn't seen you all summer."

Clayborne said, "You know, Mrs. Phillips, there was another lady in Iredell mentioned that same thing one Saturday morning when we went to the grocery store in the car. We'd just got out with the baby and — who was it? Mrs. Sadler? I forget. But we got out with the baby and she said 'I didn't know you'd been expecting, Mrs. Perry.' And old Mose Dawson was sitting by and he spoke up, said, 'Oh, I noticed for several months Mrs. Perry hasn't got out of the car when she came into town of a Saturday.' So you're the second person that's said that, Mrs. Phillips."

No one mentioned Oretta's bout of illness in the Stephenville hospital; it was assumed in polite company that if anyone wanted to talk about medical problems they would bring them up themselves. So conversation lapsed and attention drifted back to dominoes and Amos 'n' Andy.

Kingfish: Wait a minute heah, don't fo'git dat dis lodge is givin' yo' puttection.

Lightnin': Well, I just ain't got no dues. If yo' would lend me some money, I would pay the lodge.

Kingfish: Whut yo' mean, *me* lend yo' some money? I is flat as a pancake. I got about fifteen cents, an' I gotta got a dollar by tonight somewhere. We goin' to have compn'y fo' supper. De butcher done tighten up on me. I gotta git a couple o' po'k chops in dat house some way. Yo' can't ast de people comin' to supper to eat gravy *all* de time. . .

Lightnin': Yessah.

Kingfish: Can't you go to some friend?

Lightnin': I ain't got no money friends — all my friends is sympathy friends — dey listens an' feels sorry fo' me, but den dey's gone.

Kingfish: Dis is some sorry mess yo' leaves me in, Lightnin'. I got a good mind to. . .

Announcer: We interrupt this broadcast to bring you a news bulletin from the Red Network Newsroom.

Newsreader: "The British Broadcasting Company in London announced only minutes ago that reports are filtering in from intelligence sources in France that today, May 10, 1940, thousands of unidentified paratroops have landed in Belgium and cut off communications to the outside world. Unconfirmed reports indicate that airborne invaders have also isolated Luxembourg and the Netherlands. Military observers believe the invaders to be German Blitzkrieg commandos of Hitler's war machine. British authorities fear the invading forces will use their new strategic position to outflank the Maginot Line and invade France. The situation is grave indeed, says. . ."

"Turn that thing off!" shrieked a woman in a voice a little too shrill.

The radio went dead. Iron silence shouted in the room. Everyone, the domino players, the stand-abouts and the conversationalists, looked at the radio crowd, now stiff and self-conscious.

A timid woman's voice half-whispered, "You don't think it's another fake news program like that man-from-Mars thing last Halloween, do you?"

A gentle male voice said, "I'm afraid that wasn't Orson Welles this time, Mrs. Wirtz."

"Belgium," said Mr. Ramage, standing in the middle of his living room.

"And maybe Luxembourg and the Netherlands," said Jerry Phillips. Clayborne said, "The Germans just took Denmark last month."

"And Norway. They're still fighting in Norway," said Dr. Pike.

Ramage said, almost as if in a reverie, "They've got all Europe now, all except for France. You can see it coming." Then he shook his head. "Well, my friends, we are safe here in America. Let's see if we can carry on with our party. I'm sorry our evening has been shaken up with all this war stuff, but just think to yourselves that today's not the day when we'll have to do something about Mister Hitler. I expect it'll come, but not today. Now who was it that was telling me about going to the New York World's Fair last year? I want to hear that story again about Elsie the Cow in the Borden Exhibit, you remember, about the squad of Western Union boys who came on her birthday to deliver that singing telegram, "Mooey Birthday to You."

"Psst. C'mere!" whispered Billy Bradley from around the back of his father's car.

"What, Billy?" asked Bob Perry from where he sat lost in daydreams on his back porch steps.

"My Dad didn't take the car to school today! Let's get some cigarettes!"

"Hey, okay!" he called back in a hoarse imitation of a whisper. Bob sauntered casually across the backyard shared by the two homes trying to look nonchalant.

"Here, come around this side so my Mama can't see us," rasped Billy as he gingerly opened the car's right front door. Bob obeyed, crouching conspiratorially in broad daylight.

Billy slid across the upholstered bench set to the driver's door and felt around in the fabric door pocket.

"Are there any Lucky Strikes?" whispered Bob.

"Yeah. But only one pack and it's not open. My Dad'll know if I open it. Wait. Here's his Prince Albert can and some papers. You stand out there and act natural while I roll a couple."

Billy expertly rolled two long fat Prince Albert cigarettes, then said to Bob, "Let's git." He slid noiselessly back over the seat and out the passenger door, swinging it shut with elaborate caution. Both boys leaned their shoulders into the shut door to latch it silently. That done, they strolled toward Bob's house.

"How come we never get *your* Dad's cigarettes, Bob?"

"Billy, my Dad doesn't smoke!" muttered the boy.

"Oh, yeah. I keep forgettin'. Well, every other grownup I know smokes. Your Dad is kind of weird."

"No he's not, he just doesn't like to smoke. He says cigarettes are bad for your health."

"Well, my Dad smokes cigarettes and a pipe, too. He likes to smoke. All men like it. 'Cept your Dad."

They leaned against the stone back wall of Bob's house and Billy popped two home-made cigarettes up from this closed fist. Bob took his and Billy lit them both up. They took deep puffs but did not inhale, letting the smoke pour out of their mouths in oh-so-adult gestures. They felt really grown up.

In the middle of a deep manly puff, Oretta happened around the back of the house and caught them in the act. "You boys should be ashamed! Look at you, standing there smoking like old men. Don't you know what that smoke is doing to your lungs?"

Billy looked at Mrs. Perry bug-eyed with embarrassment at being caught, not knowing whether he should just hold on to his cigarette or try to hide it. "No, Ma'am," he said weakly, "what's it doing?"

"Why cigarettes coat your lungs with all kinds of terrible stuff! They stunt your growth and make you short-winded."

"Is that right, Mrs. Perry?" asked Billy.

"Yes, siree, that's right, young man. And think about being a football player. You can never be an athlete if you smoke, didn't you know that, Bob?"

"No, Mom, I didn't know that," Bob said apologetically.

"Well, now, the both of you know it now. And what do you think you ought to do about it?"

The two boys looked at each other guiltily.

"Gee, Mom," Bob stammered, "I . . . I guess we ought to quit smoking these things." He looked disgustedly at the cylindrical shape in his hand. It had gone out while they were being reprimanded.

"Yes, Ma'am, Mrs. Perry," said Billy, "We just ought to get rid of these things completely. Right now. Here." He ceremoniously unwrapped his extinguished cigarette and let the shredded tobacco fall and drift in the wind. Bob followed suit. They both wadded up their remaining cigarette papers and swore off smoking forever.

"Good," said Oretta. "I'm proud of you boys. You did the right thing."

That afternoon when his father had been home for an hour or so, Billy found an open pack of Lucky Strikes in the family car. Once again he called to Bob from his back porch steps: "Psst! C'mere!"

"What, Billy?"

"I got some of Dad's Lucky Strikes. Let's go back behind the chicken house and have a smoke."

"Okay, let's go."

They leaned against the wood back wall of the chicken house and Billy popped two ready-roll Lucky Strikes up from his front pocket. Bob took his and Billy lit them both up. They took deep puffs but did not inhale, letting the smoke pour out of their mouths in oh-so-adult gestures. They held their cigarettes in the manly poses they had seen in magazine advertisements and felt quite grown up.

This time they did not get caught.

"Mister Miller!" shouted Superintendent Perry from the coach's bench. "Have you been there in the first row all this time? I didn't expect to see you at our first football game. Come on over here." He waved a topcoated arm in the chill late afternoon air.

"Well, Mister Perry," said Marvin Miller as he slid under the front rail of Iredell High School's bleachers and sauntered to the sidelines, "I couldn't let you down after you got me that great job at Walnut Springs." He sat on the cold bench.

"Walnut Springs Elementary needed a good principal and you had the qualifications. The fact that the new superintendent and the new grammar school principal were roommates in college had nothing to do with it. You know Coach Hartford, don't you?" Clayborne introduced Miller to the man sitting at his other side.

A roar from the crowd jerked their attention to the muddy football field. Iredell High scored another touchdown.

Coach Hartford shook his head and muttered, "Sorry, Superintendent Perry."

"Your troops aren't doing so good, W.C.," said Marvin to his boss.

"No, I'm afraid not. I wanted to win this game so bad I could taste it, too. My first time out as the new superintendent of Walnut Springs! I thought I was going to go back to my old stomping grounds here at Iredell and enjoy a nice victory."

"Well," Coach Hartford said, "Iredell High is a little bigger school than Walnut Springs High, you know."

"Oh, I'm not going to use that as an excuse. I'll take it on the chin."

"Did you bring your family?" asked Miller.

"Yes, Oretta's with Margie and Bob up there next to the band."

"Oh, right, I see them. I was surprised how big Bob was when he showed up for second grade."

"He's seven years old now, be eight later this month."

"I heard something on the radio this afternoon, W.C. The Roper Poll says Roosevelt is going to win his third term."

"I heard about it."

"You think he'll win?"

"Nobody's tried for a third term in a hundred-forty-four years now. But I don't see how anybody can beat him. If ol' Cactus Jack Garner couldn't beat him last time this Wendell Willkie sure can't this time. Hartford, your boy Tate needs a little more practice passing. That's his third incomplete this quarter. And there's not much of this quarter left."

"Yes, sir."

Miller went on. "The Republicans are going to try making an issue out of the draft bill they just passed last week. Those America Firsters are real upset. They don't like the idea of a peacetime draft."

"Some peacetime. Have you been listening to Edward R. Murrow on the radio, Marvin?"

"You mean those programs where he always starts out 'This . . . is London,' and you can hear the bombs and the sirens in the background?"

"He's been doin' that since August when Hitler started bombing London. I don't think we're just going to stand by forever and let Hitler get away with it, do you?"

"Prob'ly not."

"That Hitler's already got France, and Dr. Pike was telling me when we moved from Iredell that France had the most modern army of any democracy there was. I don't mind the draft. If we don't get busy doing something, we might find ourselves caught with our pants down."

"Looks like your team just got caught with theirs down, W.C."

Iredell High's defensive backs intercepted one of Walnut Springs passes and charged down the middle of the field with great speed and power, leaving behind a trail of stiff-armed would-be tacklers all the way to the goalpost. Iredell easily made the extra point. Pandemonium in the bleachers. No time on the clock. Iredell 21, Walnut Springs 7.

"Coach Hartford," said Superintendent Perry, "I'll leave you to console the boys. Tell them I'm proud of their fighting spirit and I'm counting on them to win the next one."

"Yes, sir."

"Come on, Marvin, and say hello to my family."

The two men fought their way up the bleachers against the flow of the dispersing crowd. School band members in their colorful uniforms passed every which way, bearing clarinets and flutes, trombones and euphoniums, saxophones and snare drums, polished metal flashing in the late afternoon sun. Oretta's eyes lighted up when she saw the two men approaching. She held year-old Margie and stood up. Bob stood with her.

"Hello, there, Mister Miller," Oretta said, all smiles. "I didn't see you in the crowd. Did you bring your family?"

"Oh, no, Mrs. Perry," said Miller. "With the mob of kids I've got we can hardly get them into the car. Hello, little Margie. Hello, Bob."

Clayborne said, "Bob, shake hands with Principal Miller."

Bob obeyed and said, "Hello, sir. I see you in the hall looking into the classroom every day!"

"That you do, young man. Just checking up to make sure all the boys and girls are minding the teacher."

"Oh, we mind real good!" said the boy.

"Mrs. Perry, have you and the family had time to get settled into your new home since the school year started?"

"Oh yes, Mr. Miller," she grinned, "we moved to Walnut Springs back in July, just after Clayborne signed his new contract."

Clayborne added, "We hired a man to move all our stuff on a truck for seven dollars in the real hot weather. I've had my Masonic Lodge membership transferred, and all. We've been settled in for right on three months now."

"I wish I could say that," smiled Miller sardonically.

The crowd around them thinned out and they stepped down the bleachers.

"I understand you barely managed to find a place in town before school started," said Oretta.

"That's right. We're not far from you folks. You're just a couple of blocks up from the Baptist Church, aren't you?"

"Yep," said Clayborne, stepping down the last step to the ground and helping his wife with Margie.

"But we've been so busy getting the house in order," said Miller, "we haven't had time to socialize any. Otherwise we'd have had you folks over before now."

They all stood at the base of the now-empty bleachers. Clayborne looked back at the scoreboard as they began the walk to the parking lot. "Twenty-one to seven. Well, there goes my big victory."

"Oh, don't fret yourself," said Oretta. "There'll be other football games."

"Marvin, do you need a ride back to Walnut Springs?" asked Clayborne.

"No, I came in the old Ford. Parked next to a fancy new two-tone green Plymouth. It was a four-door sport sedan, really caught my eye."

"That's our new car, Mr. Miller," said Bob.

"Is that so?"

"Yes, sir, Dad just bought it this month. It's a 1941 car and it's still only 1940! How about that?"

"Oh, that sounds wonderful," grinned Miller. "And it sounds like you really enjoy your new life in Walnut Springs, young man."

"I do!" cried the boy as they approached their parked cars. "Sort of, anyway. I've got a bicycle now, a Hawthorne! Mom says I can ride it back here to Iredell to see my friends. I miss Iredell, Mr. Miller. Things aren't the same in Walnut Springs. . ."

"Why, it must be ten miles back here to Iredell," said Miller.

Clayborne said, "A little over ten."

"And I've got a dog, too, Mr. Miller! His name is Hunter. And I've got a bird, too! His name is Canary. We keep him in the house in a cage so he won't fly away."

"Well, you've really got yourself a fine new home."

"Yes, sir, Mr. Miller."

Marvin and Clayborne both had their car keys out and stood by their vehicles. The last few departing cars still poured out of the parking lot.

"Have they got you on a busy schedule superintending, W.C.?" asked Miller. "I hardly see you with me in the elementary building and you stuck away over next door in the high school."

"Oh, pretty busy. We've got a full house of students this year, but everything started up nice and smooth. The usual administrative chores. And I still have to teach two classes, plane geometry upstairs on the second floor and typing right across the hall from my office. It's in a spot where I can take telephone calls and such without too much bother."

"Well, we'd better be getting on home instead of standing here in an empty parking lot, Superintendent Perry," said Miller.

"You're right, Principal Miller. I'll try to set some time aside so we can actually get together and go over old times."

"And tell stories about Tarleton."

"And the Strong Arm Club."

"Right. Good night, you folks."

"Good night," said Oretta and Bob in unison.

The four Perrys sailed home in their fancy new car, out through Iredell where they had lived for five years, north across the Bosque River bridge, eastward on graveled State Road 927, across the Katy Railroad tracks, northeasterly past Dinner Hill and the low Texas mountains that form the western rampart of Corn Gap, and so into Walnut Springs.

During the early 1920s Walnut Springs had been the glory of Bosque County, the largest town, with nearly two thousand residents, and all because of the railroad. The busy Katy shops with their huge overhaul equipment and track maintenance machinery nestled along the banks of Steele Creek, right across from the downtown commercial center. Four passenger trains a day stopped at Walnut Springs and dozens of freights rumbled through from dawn to dawn. Engineers and mechanics and foremen and brakemen and conductors stationed here brought their better money and their higher skills and their more cosmopolitan experience to the Grand Prairie, and filled the houses in this town that was nine streets wide, east to west, and six streets deep, north to south, not counting the four-street-by-five-street grid south of the creek, up on the hill where the schools had been built.

In its heyday Walnut Springs boasted a city band that played concerts in Katy Park, a car dealership that gave you the best deals in the county, nice schools with a good solid tax base, and a fine bank with deposits unthinkable for a farmer-dominated Grand Prairie town like Snuff City down the line. The city fathers, in a gesture of uncountrified grandiosity, even gave their streets *names*, so the five major north-south streets became First, Second, Third, Fourth and Fifth, and the three central east-west streets were named Denmark, Sweden and Norway — but only on paper: they never got around to putting up signs and nobody in town knew any of the streets even *had* names.

But then the railroad boom years began to peter out and the Katy branch that ran through Walnut Springs went sour. About 1928 the executives of the line decided to move their big shops to Waco and some three hundred Walnut Springs families moved with them. Their cherished good homes remained unsold, unrented and untended. Once they settled themselves in Waco and word got around, these homeowners sacrificed their old places to predatory brokers and house-movers for three or four hundred dollars, some of the more astute holding out for as much as seven hundred. The distress-sale houses were sent on rollers to empty lots all over Central Texas and for years it was a commonplace to scorn any hifalutin new farmhouse by calling it "one of them Walnut Springs bargains."

And so the town quite literally fell apart. When the houses slipped away behind mule teams, the car dealership shut down, the city band, like Milton's dancing nymphs and shepherds, played no more, the fine bank failed and closed its doors one day and the school found its tax money lost with the bank closure. Depositors eventually got back five cents on the dollar. The four or five hundred people who stayed behind suffered through the disaster and tried to keep up what social standards they could, but it was a losing battle. The forces of permanence so bountifully scattered across the Grand Prairie were not with them: most were transplants from the anonymous city, most had lost their Biblical commitment to neighborly unity if they ever had it, most had little if any education. While the local farmers had plentiful lack of education themselves, it did not eat away their moral substance as it did the town dwellers of Walnut Springs. A Saturday in Iredell might find farmers lounging on the sidewalks and spitting snuff in the streets. A Saturday in Walnut Springs might find a fistfight or two and drunken locals reeling. Uneducated farmers felt it was progress when the school district insisted that all children attend Iredell schools. Uneducated townsfolk felt hateful suspicion and resentment when the school district insisted that all children attend Walnut Springs schools. But by 1939 the city fathers had stabilized the town's decline, and the school board even dreamed of boosting the quality of their school system. They searched for talent, tried a new superintendent and then found W.C. Perry. They wasted no time in hiring him.

Now on this October evening in 1940, the Perry family pulled into the driveway of their Walnut Springs frame house on Sweden Street (they, like all the other town residents, didn't know the street had a name) and got out of the car contemplating their loss of the first football game of the season to Iredell.

"Here, Hunter!" called Bob. "C'mon, Hunter old boy!"

The dog burst from the shadows wagging its tail and leaping off the ground in joy. Hunter was the type of dog described in those days as a "Heinz dog," after the famous canned-food company's sales slogan, "57 Varieties." Clayborne walked ahead to open the door for Oretta and Margie, with Hunter running circles around everyone. When Clayborne opened the door and turned on the electric lights, Hunter stopped in his tracks and growled deep in his throat, his hackles standing up like fretful porcupine quills.

"What's wrong with that dog?" snapped Oretta.

Bob pushed his way to Hunter's side. "What's the matter, boy?"

The youngster froze. "Look over there, Dad!"

A large king snake lay half-coiled on the living roam rug, directly under . . . the bird cage!

"How did that snake get in here?" asked Oretta, then gasped, "Oh, Clayborne! The bird cage is all messed up. And it's empty! Canary's gone!"

"Oh, no, Dad," said Bob. "Look at the snake's gullet. There's a bulging place that's just the size of Canary! The snake ate poor little Canary!"

"Well, I'll be switched if he didn't," said Clayborne, striding to the broom closet and coming back armed with a shovel. "Get out of the way, folks." He quickly slid the shovel under the torpid digesting snake and scooped it out the front door. A few well-placed licks and the reptile was dead. The family gathered around the remains of friend and foe combined. They eyed the pathetic bulge in the snake's upper midriff.

"Poor little Canary!" said Bob, with tears in his eyes.

"Poor little Canary!" said Oretta, holding Margie tight.

"Poor little Canary!" said Clayborne, shaking his head.

Winter. A little before 9:00 a.m. Bob waddled toward his second grade class heavily bundled against the arctic wind that combed the gray morning land. He looked like a beaver walking the ditchline southward through town along Farm Road 144 to school, all brown in his coat, a scarf encircling his face, a toboggan hat pulled down over his ears. His mother had protected him well, but he wistfully mused that he should have gotten up and ridden to school at 7:30 with his father — Clayborne did not believe in being too gentle with the boy and usually let him walk to school, which was three-quarters of a mile from home.

If only it were still summer! Bob yearned for summer's warmth this chill day even as he recoiled from a July memory, one of his first after moving to Walnut Springs. His mother had taken him fishing that bright sunny day to the little nameless pond just north of town not far from the new electric power transmission corridor. As he and his mother had drowsed on the banks with their fishing lines in the peaceful water, the offhand conversation of three boys on the other side of the pond — probably fifth or sixth graders — came drifting across the thirty feet of rippling surface and hit Bob like a slap in the face. His ears were assulted by liberal doses of "hell" and "damn" and coarser words of Anglo-Saxon origin. The gross boys obviously knew they were being overheard. His ears burning, Bob stole a sidelong look at his mother, his sweet, shy, almost bashful young mother who had not uttered a curse word in all her twenty-six years. Oretta studiously ignored the foul words. Bob gulped. The swearing had startled him at first, but now fright gripped him, fright at the boldness of these boys who would use bad language right here in front of his mother. What kind of unruly, aggressive people lived in this town? What would he face in the days to come?

Even now, as he crunched along the schoolward road with the high summer sun only a months-old memory, he had not yet come to terms with living in Walnut Springs. He felt that many of the people here somehow seemed mean. He had heard of men fistfighting in the streets. He had seen men drunk. And yet he had to admit that the place possessed a few redeeming virtues. Last August when he had walked the four blocks from home to the main drag and got turned around, hadn't those two teacher-ladies in the drug store been good to him? When he couldn't find his way home, hadn't the two old-maid women named Gertie and Birdie Crow helped him? All he'd had to do was tell them he was lost and ask if they knew where W. C. Perry lived. And hadn't they even taken him home in their 1932 Model A Ford?

And what about the people in the churches? They were certainly the nicer kind of people he'd been used to all his life. His father had made a habit in Walnut Springs of taking the family to each of its churches, their own First Baptist Church, the Church of Christ and the Methodist Church, an expression of his friendly desire to be one of the townspeople in every way he could be. And even when the church people would argue about doctrinal differences — the Methodists with their Baptism by sprinkling and the Baptists by immersion; the Baptists with "Once saved, always saved," and the Methodists with the tenet that failure to live in scriptural paths could un-save the converted — even in these arguments, hadn't they always respected his father's smiling refusal to get caught up in any ill feelings?

Bob mused as he came to the long straight stretch of road where he normally crossed over to the west side and trudged up the hill to the school. Today, lost in reverie, the protective scarf blocking his view both ways in any event, he stepped into the thoroughfare without looking.

The screech of tires on cold pavement scared him witless. He jumped and looked up in time to see a 1938 Ford front grill lurch to a stop bare inches away from him. The driver's door flew open and a tall lady leaped out. She ran to him, frantically calling, "Are you all right? Son, you scared me to death. You almost got run over just now!"

Bob tried to smile at her but could only stand there woodenly as the adrenalin surged through his veins. He recognized the agitated lady as Mrs. Edge. And she recognized him.

"Good heavens, it's Bobby Perry. Thank the Lord I didn't hit you. Are you all right?"

"Well, it's a little cold today," the boy said shakily.

"Is that all you've got to say? Come on, get in the car with Jane Ann and me. We'll give you a ride up to school."

"Thank you, Ma'am."

The boy piled into the front seat with his books and plunked himself next to Jane Ann.

"Hi, Bobby," said the pretty girl.

"Hi," he answered, shyly admiring this pupil leader of the second grade rhythm band.

"You didn't get hurt, did you?"

Mrs. Edge interjected, "I don't think he did, did you, Bob?" as she resumed her seat behind the wheel.

"Unh-uh."

"Cold out there, isn't it?" said Jane Ann.

"Sure is," Bob replied and fell quiet as they took off.

A vague worry about this classmate gnawed at him. Jane Ann Storey, he knew, was Mrs. Edge's niece and lived with her in Walnut Springs because her parents were divorced and lived apart somewhere up north. He tried to imagine living apart from his parents and felt waves of dread. What kind of people could get divorced and not keep their child? How sorry he felt for poor Jane Ann.

"Here you are, children," said Mrs. Edge as they pulled up in front of the faintly decaying Walnut Springs school buildings. "Bobby, you tell your daddy I'm sorry about almost hitting you. And you remember to look both ways before crossing the road now."

"Yes, Ma'am," said the boy, jumping out the door with Jane Ann close on his heels. "I think I'll just tell him you gave me a ride 'cause it was cold."

Mrs. Edge smiled understandingly as the boy slammed the car door and ran with Jane Ann for the school entry. The two waved goodbye and went in. Bob glanced into his father's office on his way to class, expecting no special welcome. Clayborne seldom spoke to his son in school: he wanted to show no favoritism. But this morning Superintendent Perry looked up from his desk and said through his open door, "Well, I see you didn't freeze in the cold today, Bob. Study hard now, you hear?"

"Yes, sir," the boy replied and vanished down the hallway.

He never told his father of the incident.

"Dr. Stretch, I really want to thank you for coming out and giving the commencement speech last Friday night," said Clayborne as he stood in the professor's Baylor office.

The woman beamed back at him from behind her heavy desk, "I was proud to do it. I've given a lot of them out in that country, you know. I was born in Meridian and I'm no stranger to Walnut Springs."

"Oh, yes, Dr. Stretch, I know. But this one was special for me, what with it being the first time I've presided over a graduation as school superintendent."

"Yes. Well, I'm sure it won't be your last. Have a seat and we'll go over your program. But let me be the first to congratulate you and welcome you to Baylor. I'm sure you're aware that your application has been accepted and you are an official candidate for a master's degree in administrative education. My own signature as head of the Education Department is on your acceptance. I've expected to see you here for many years. And now here you are. So let's get down to why you're here."

Clayborne sat beside the desk and looked at his program folder with his advisor.

Dr. Lorena Stretch solemnly intoned, "You're planning on completing your classwork in summer sessions only, am I right?"

"Yes, Ma'am. I don't see any way to take classes during the regular school year."

"I've heard there may be Monday evening classes during the 1941-'42 academic year, but it's not firm yet. So let's plan on summers only."

"Okay."

"Let's see, thirty-six semester hours of class work are required for a master's, you know. How are we going to work this out? Are you going to be able to take both sessions during the summer?" she asked.

"Yes, ma'am, I sure will."

She muttered to herself a few seconds, then announced, "Well, it looks like you can finish in three years. But are you going to have the time to study? You have a special problem as superintendent that you wouldn't as a principal."

"You mean because I have to work in the office during summers?"

"Right. Have you settled on anything with the school board yet?"

"Nothing final. They don't mind me going to school, in fact they like the idea. But I think they'd like me to take all my classes in the morning so I could get back and do a full day's work on into the evenings."

"That may be a problem, but I should have expected it. Let's see, your first lineup will include, hmm, advanced classroom technique, history, and . . . oh, this is all just basic master's material. I'm sure we can find morning classes for you in all four courses."

"Well, good," Clayborne sighed.

"It might not be so good. Take a look at this: your first class will begin at 7:00 a.m., you'll go straight through with a new class each hour and you'll be finished at 11:00 a.m. How far is it to Walnut Springs?"

"Sixty-five miles."

"And how long to drive that?"

"It took me an hour and a half today."

"Then it looks like you're going to be getting up about 4:00 a.m. five days a week for the next three summers."

"And getting to bed about 11:00 p.m., if I judge my superintendent workload rightly."

"Can you do it?"

"I'll do it. We're getting ready to move into a little house owned by Mr. J.W. Gosdin — you remember him — right next to the school. I'll be able to walk to the office any time day or night. I'll do it."

Dr. Stretch, a very formal woman who never called Clayborne by his first name, said, "Okay, Superintendent Perry. But that's only your class work. You'll have to select a specialty for your thesis. A master's thesis is not like an undergraduate honors thesis where you simply research work that others have done and then comment on it. There's some of that — you'll need the Baylor library to do some of your thesis research, but there must be an element of original research as well, something original in the field of your choice. Have you given that any thought?"

"Yes, Ma'am, I have. I've been reading about the new lunchroom programs they're trying in the bigger cities. I think I'd like to put my thesis emphasis on lunchroom programs."

"Lunchroom programs . . . Not much has been done in that field. You're not going to find much literature on the subject."

"I saw a government report on the Harris County program there in Houston. It had some references in it. Somebody must have written something about it."

"I'll tell you what, Mr. Perry, give me some time to think over this lunchroom idea. I need to check the literature to see if there's enough for you to work with before I approve it. And let's both think about the practical aspect of your thesis: what are you going to do that will constitute original research?"

"Well, I've given that a little thought, too. I think it would be best if we could begin a lunchroom program at Walnut Springs. It would help the kids and give me a solid base to study from. I could see the problems for myself. My thesis could actually mean something, it could help others get started."

"Just like that?"

"What do you mean?"

"How do you intend to get this lunchroom program started?"

"Oh, I couldn't do it, Dr. Stretch. I mean the school board and the WPA program. We don't have the available money in the school budget to do it by ourselves; they'd have to join the federal lunchroom program."

"There's no such thing in all of Bosque County right now, Superintendent Perry. What makes you think Walnut Springs is such a seat of willingness to try something new?"

"I don't know, Dr. Stretch. Maybe it's the fact that they've been fighting a downhill slide for so long. Maybe it's the fact that they fell from a higher place when the Depression hit, what with all that railroad money they'd been used to. But I just have the feeling that they'd like to do something to help the community. We've got poor kids that come to school with no lunch at all. The school board knows that. Everyone on the board has been reading about the city schools and their lunchroom programs. It isn't as if it's a completely unknown idea. I just think they might get the bee in their bonnet this summer to apply for the federal lunchroom program."

"With a little help from their superintendent?"

"Could be."

And so the summer went. Up in the morning at 4:00 a.m., drive sixty-five miles to Waco, grab some breakfast, be in the main building on the Baylor campus by 7:00 a.m. to take four classes, rush to the parking lot at 11:00 a.m., drive sixty-five miles to Walnut Springs, grab some lunch, be in the office by 1:00 p.m., work on school business until 5:00 or 6:00 p.m., go home to the little rent house across the street from the school, eat supper, study and type class reports until 11:00 p.m., go to bed, up in the morning at 4:00 p.m. and so on around the days. But this satisfied the school board and all was well.

One early afternoon in July, master's candidate Perry happened to meet his old friend Marvin Miller coming out of the store that Walnut Springs used as a bank. They stopped to chat on the main street's sidewalk. Low stone buildings lined the avenue: the post office, a dry goods store, Adams' grocery store, a drug store, a lumber yard.

"Well, Superintendent Perry, where have you been?" asked Miller a little nervously.

"I just drove in from Waco. Taking some summer classes at Baylor."

"What a coincidence. I just drove in from Waco, too." He shuffled his feet a little.

"Oh? You're not taking some classes there, too, are you?"

"No, no I'm not." Miller straightened up and looked his old friend directly in the face. "Look, W.C., I don't know quite how to say this, but, ah, I'm going into the bank to, ah, well, to cash a check. My last check. I've found it very difficult to support a large family on a teacher's salary."

Clayborne did not like the sound of that "last check" remark.

"Marvin, I know how hard it's been for you," he said. "And we haven't had the time to get together like I thought we would. But how will cashing that check help?"

Marvin Miller looked at the ground. "It's been more than hard, W.C.," he said. "It's been impossible. I went to Waco today looking for a job, something that pays more. I'm cashing this check to move to Waco."

Clayborne had a sinking feeling. "Wait, Marvin, before you do that let me talk to the school board. I can't let an old Tarleton friend down. You've done an outstanding job here as principal and I'm sure they . . ."

"I know, W.C. They've already offered me as much of a raise as any principal can get under the law, $10 a month more than my starting pay.

That will only put me thirty dollars a month behind instead of forty. And the Tarleton thing, getting together to reminisce — I'm glad we didn't have the time, to tell you the truth. I've gone up to Stephenville looking for work. Everything's different now. You can't go back, W.C., not even in a friendly conversation. It's gone. Those years are gone. They were fun while they were happening, but that was then. I've spent too much time looking back as it is. No, W.C., I've already taken a position with Montgomery Ward in Waco."

"With Montgomery Ward? Doing what?" Clayborne had that feeling again of the vagrant wind ransacking his soul, an ineffable sadness that choked the breath out of him.

"Selling furniture, W.C."

"You didn't go to Tarleton to learn to sell furniture, Marvin."

"I didn't go there to learn to starve, either. They'll pay me $250.00 a month, W.C. That's as much as you make. Maybe more."

"But it's not teaching . . . "

"It's earning a living."

"Marvin, I need you here. You know how hard it is to find men after they passed that draft law last year and all the men are going into the Army buildup. What'll Walnut Springs do for a principal?"

"That's another thing, W.C. If war comes, and it sure looks like it will, every man will be drafted. We'll all be in the Army. I have to try to catch up while I can, put a little something aside, even. You know how hard our folks said it was during the Great War. This thing that's coming, it looks worse, W.C., worse than anything anybody's ever seen before. We might not come back. None of us. You'll find a replacement for me here. Don't worry. And I'll keep in touch. I promise."

"You're going then?"

"I'm going."

He went. And as it turned out, Marvin Miller had been right about some things at least. When the summer of 1941 was over and Clayborne had earned his first semester hours toward his master's degree and Walnut Springs schools opened in September, another principal had been hired, a stranger.

And, wonder of wonders, Walnut Springs did start the first federally subsidized school lunch program in Bosque County. The school obtained WPA labor to run the lunchroom. Iredell schools hadn't had a cafeteria; the children just sat and ate a sack lunch with each other, perhaps with a little thermos of cold milk from home. Walnut Springs had been the same way at first, but now there was a lunchroom, and a lunchroom program. The school got a little federal flour and some corn meal and some turkeys, and some money — and they got on the federal milk program. They served daily a half-pint of milk to each student, at a federal subsidy of two cents per half-pint. They served a good lunch for seven cents a day or thirty-five cents a week for a meal ticket. If the student's family was officially within the poverty level, the meal ticket was five cents a day or two bits a week. For those a certain degree below the poverty line, the meal ticket came free, but the fact was never mentioned. A hush-hush veil of protective secrecy covered the free lunch families — and in some cases that free lunch was the only hot meal the child ate, period. As the months went on, Superintendent Perry found himself spending a lot of time escorting visitors from other school systems through his lunchroom program, demonstrating methods, explaining administration.

Despite his not inconsiderable duties during the regular school year at Walnut Springs, Clayborne was delighted to find that classes would be offered at Baylor on Monday night from 6:00 p.m. to 9:00 p.m. He arranged to continue his master's study one night a week, leaving home for Waco, sixty-five miles away, at 4:30 p.m. and returning at 10:30 p.m. His autumn days grew to be almost as laborious as his summer days had been. And the Grand Prairie months of 1941 waned into clear and cold December.

One Sunday afternoon Clayborne and nine-year old Bob busied themselves washing the family car, their sporty two-tone green Plymouth four-door sedan, in front of the wood-frame rent house across from the Walnut Springs school complex. They had the radio on and heard a special news item begin. It was 2:20 p.m., Eastern time. Unknown to the millions of listeners all over the land, White House Press Secretary Steve Early had just gotten the press services together on a multi-party call to release the facts that were broadcast that afternoon in Walnut Springs, Texas. The facts froze in the minds of those Americans forever. Millions would be able to tell you for decades exactly what they were doing when they first heard about it. Something completely expected and completely unexpected had happened.

A thirty-two-ship Japanese fleet had steamed in two parallel columns from the Kurile Islands by the northern route under radio silence to a point north of the Hawaiian Islands and upon receipt of the radio signal, "Climb Mt. Niitaka," released their 353 carrier planes in three waves that bombed Pearl Harbor on the Island of Oahu, destroying eight American battleships, three light cruisers, one-hundred-eighty-eight planes and killing 2,400 men. The Japanese lost 29 aircraft, five midget submarines and one fleet submarine. Aside from these losses, the Japanese suffered no casualties; although they had expected to lose a third of their fleet, it had not even been detected. The surprise attack on Pearl Harbor had been pulled off with consummate skill and precision. The American Pacific Fleet was destroyed and Japan owned the Pacific. The emperor's plans for a "Greater East Asia Co-Prosperity Sphere" — a Japanese Empire — were set. He and his military now expected to fight a limited war and, once they had won the territory they wanted, to defend it until the United States and Great Britain were worn out and willing to negotiate a peace. Their surprise attack had worked perfectly.

Yet on January 24, 1940, not two years earlier, Secretary of the Navy Frank Knox had written to Secretary of War Henry Stimson that "Hostilities would be initiated by a surprise attack on Pearl Harbor." In April, 1941, the Pacific Fleet commander himself, Rear Admiral Husband E. Kimmel, had told his staff: "Declaration of war might be preceded by a surprise attack on Pearl Harbor." Late in 1940 the U.S. Signal Corps had cracked Japan's code "Purple," giving nine high U.S. officials dubbed "Ultras" the ability to read the most secret instructions of Tokyo to its diplomats in Washington — President Roosevelt was one of those "Ultras." They knew a sneak attack was coming. They had known for days. The "Ultras" had all seen years worth of briefings that told them Pearl Harbor was the likely target. But when the time actually came, they put Panama and other logical points of attack on full alert but not Pearl Harbor.

And now, on this sunny Texas afternoon, while events 12,000 miles away were about to turn the world into 1,364 days of conflagration, the Perrys listened in dumbstruck awe as an impersonal radio announcer dug the foundations from under their lives. Two-hundred miles south in San Antonio, a brigadier general answered the phone and said, "Yes? When? I'll be right down." His wife Mamie asked Dwight Eisenhower when he would be coming back from headquarters and he said he didn't know. The next morning, fifteen-hundred miles east, Franklin Delano Roosevelt called his secretary Grace Tully into his study for some dictation. Her notebook shows this entry: Yesterday comma December seven comma nineteen forty-one dash a date which will live in infamy dash

-18-

THE WAR IN
WALNUT SPRINGS

COME on in, Superintendent Perry. It's bitter freezing out there."

"Thank you sir," said a heavily bundled Clayborne as he shuffled into the Walnut Springs School lobby. A frigid tide of February night air sloshed at his back.

"Let me take your coat," said Mr. A. F. Fair of the school board. "And go right on in to the conference room. Everybody's here already except Theo Rundell. The road to his ranch is prob'ly bad tonight."

"Whoosh," said Clayborne, wiping crystal frost from his forehead and surrendering his heavy topcoat, "Any colder out there and I'd be stiff as the government freeze on everything."

Clayborne entered the meeting room. School board President Gus Morrison smiled at him from the end of the long table. "Have a seat Superintendent Perry. Tonight we're going to talk about that government freeze."

"Is that coffee over there?" asked Clayborne.

Board member J.E. Brock said, "I'll get you a cup."

Clayborne took his accustomed place at the opposite end of the table from President Morrison, quietly saying his hellos to Jim Caddell, C.T. Hilliard, and Wendell Brister, the local undertaker. Six of the seven-man school board sat in place for their second wartime meeting, the first to consider serious wartime actions. Brock placed a steaming cup of coffee at Clayborne's elbow just as the final board member, rancher Theo Rundell, stomped in from the cold.

"Wowee," coughed Rundell, "It's colder than a frog out there."

"Well, come on in and have a sit-down," called Gus Morrison.

"Did you hear on the radio?" asked Rundell.

"What?" several asked in unison.

"The Japs got Singapore today."

"Singapore? Where's that?" asked Caddell.

"Somewhere out in the Pacific, I think," said Rundell. "Other side of the Phillipines."

"Looks bad," said Brister.

"Everything looks bad these days, folks," said President Morrison. "But we got to get this meeting going anyways. You all ready?" He looked around the table. "I declare the meeting open. First item of business: Superintendent Perry, how would you like to go to California?"

Clayborne sat upright in his chair, surprised. He held the hot coffee cup in both hands, half smiling, not knowing whether to take his boss and neighbor seriously.

"Well, I hadn't planned on it," he replied. "I don't think I'd like it."

"We'll pay your way. We want you to go, W.C." continued Morrison. "We just got word from the American Association of School Administrators that the annual convention this year is going to be a big part of the war effort."

"What are you talkin' about, Gus?" asked board member Hilliard. "I haven't heard anything about that."

"Just got word today, C.T. It says right here that the seventy-second annual convention is going to teach all school superintendents in the country how to administer this new government rationing program."

President Morrison let that sink in a moment.

"W.C.," he went on, "we want you to go out to San Francisco for the AASA Convention because you're going to be running the rationing program around here."

"I am?"

"You are. You remember the Wage and Price Board's Directive Number One last month?"

"I remember," said Clayborne. "They told the Office of Price Administration that everything's going to be rationed as soon as the government can get it set up."

"Well, I've got the convention notice right here and from what it says, superintendents are going to be running the ration program."

"But what if I get drafted?"

"You can go talk to the draft board about it. They might take you, but I think you're going to stay right here. I've got it on good authority that the Army's only taking school personnel up to the rank of principal. We'll lose all of the men teachers we've got left and we'll probably lose our principal. But superintendents are going to be essential home front manpower according to the scuttlebutt I hear. The school board might get drafted, too, except for Theo — they're not takin' farmers, either — but you, Superintendent Perry, you're just about sure going to stay right here. You're going to run the schools and the ration program by yourself for the duration of the war. Oh, and they're likely to leave you the agriculture teacher, too. He'll be helping farmers raise more food."

"The rationing program. . ." muttered Clayborne. "Sounds like a lot of red tape. Does it say what it's going to be like?" asked Clayborne.

"I hoped it would be better than this freeze on everything," said Morrison. "But let me read you something that came in the mail with this convention notice. I think it tells us real good what to expect. Rationing is going to be a mess of little books and stamps with points for everything you buy."

Morrison pulled out a booklet imprinted with the bold-face title *War Ration Book 4*. "Let me read you what this here thing says."

Gus Morrison peered over his glasses and read aloud:

"All RED and BLUE stamps in War Ration Book 4 are WORTH 10 POINTS EACH. RED and BLUE TOKENS are WORTH 1 POINT EACH. RED and BLUE TOKENS are used to make CHANGE for RED and BLUE stamps only when purchase is made. IMPORTANT! POINT VALUES of BROWN and GREEN STAMPS are NOT changed."

Morrison looked around the meeting table. "Any of you got the slightest idea what in tarnation that all means?"

Everybody shook their heads, baffled.

"That's what rationing's going to be like. And that's why we need you to go out to San Francisco, W.C. They're going to ration everything, gas, tires, you name it. There's going to be little books and stamps for every damn thing you can think of. Now stop and consider what that could mean to the people here in Walnut Springs. If they don't understand how to use rationing, they could lose goods they're entitled to. And I have a feeling there's not going to be much they're entitled to in the first place. Now, we don't want any more than our fair share for Walnut Springs, but this rationing looks like it's going to be so complicated we better have somebody running it that knows how it works. We need you to go learn how to run it for us."

"When is this convention?" asked Clayborne.

"Starts the twenty-third. That's a little over a week from now. I know you're worried about your night classes at Baylor. You'd miss two Mondays."

"I'm not worried about that. I can let my professor know and make it up later. I'm thinking about how long I'll have to be away from my family."

"Ten days, two weeks, something like that. And how is that family of yours, anyway? Does young Bob still protect that little Margie like a broody hen?"

"Oh, yes, I'll say so. He just takes such care of her."

"Well, I hate to ask you to go off from them for a couple of weeks, but our women folks will try to help your wife out if she needs it. *We* need you to go to California. What do you say?"

"If you need me to do it, of course, I'll go. How long's it take to get out there on the train?"

"Three days, W.C. I checked with the Katy. You'll have to take that little doodlebug passenger train they got runnin' through here now. It's the only thing they'll let civilians on any more. You'll change trains in Cisco and go to Los Angeles through El Paso. You'll change trains again in Los Angeles for San Francisco. Come back the same way."

Clayborne said, "Well, I'm not going to be like that woman congressman that voted against declaring war, what was her name?"

"Jeanette Rankin, that no-good-for-nothin' pacifist," grumbled A.F. Fair. "She said she didn't believe the Japs had bombed Pearl Harbor. Can you imagine? Then the pictures started coming in. . ."

"Well, I'm not like that. You can count on me. I'll go."

"Mr. Jackson, how many school superintendents do you expect they've got on this train?" asked Clayborne over the interminable clatter of steel wheels measuring steel rails.

"Must be fifty, anyhow," frowned his seatmate, a thin, frail looking man from San Angelo. "You and me are the only ones from Central Texas. The rest I've talked to come from Oklahoma and West Texas. And New Mexico and Arizona."

The two of them sat facing each other next to the window, had sat that way since noon, sometimes talking, sometimes lapsing into reverie, their conversation surging and ebbing without pattern. They gazed out at a mauve sunset fading over the Pacific Ocean. Clayborne felt the brief rush of memories from a long-ago train ride, a childhood ride through dry prairie not much different in color from these sere brown coastal hills, a ride that had ended in the ordeal at Trinchera, Colorado. But his memories dissolved against the California splendor of surf crashing on rocks bigger than any he had ever seen.

"Have you ever seen the ocean like this?" he asked Mr. Jackson.

"The Pacific? No, just the Gulf down at Galveston. And the Atlantic over where my folks live in North Carolina."

"The waves are so big here," said Clayborne. "You can see them coming in 'way out there. Look how they line up in those long rows, one after the other. Down at the Gulf they don't hardly have waves at all. At Galveston you can wade right out a hundred yards."

The conversation lulled and the sway of the train rocked them into contemplation. Ancient sea stacks kept sentry watch along the battered shore. Spindrift foamed in bubbly froth on sandy embayments scalloped between headland cliffs.

"Did you get enough sleep last night?" asked Jackson.

"Not really," said Clayborne. "That little hotel they put us in was kind of a fleabag. Noisy. We got in so late and then the traffic noise started up so early. . . I never heard such a noisy city as Los Angeles."

"Yeah, me too," said Jackson. "And I wish they had a train that started for San Francisco earlier. I don't know why we had to wait 'til noon."

"Ah, it's this war scheduling for everything."

"That means another late night tonight."

"Yep, we won't get into the station until midnight or after."

Again their talk ebbed like the waves they watched and the noises of the railcar gave the illusion of surf sound to the images inaudible below.

"They're going to have fifteen thousand school superintendents in San Francisco, did you hear?" said Jackson.

"I saw it in the Los Angeles *Times* this morning."

Quiet again.

Then Jackson said dreamily, "That is quite a sight out there, all right, the daylight fading over all that huge ocean."

"Sorry, gentlemen," said the conductor, leaning over them to lower the heavy fabric window shade. "I'm going to have to take your view away for the rest of the night."

"What's that all about?" asked Clayborne, suddenly aware of the coach's run-down interior again.

"Our aisle lights are about to go on. We can't let them be seen from the water."

"What do you mean?" asked Mr. Jackson, a worried look on his face.

"We don't know who or what is out there looking this way. It's a new War Department order to all trains. No lights visible at night."

"The Japs. . ." gasped Jackson. "But how could bombers get all the way from Japan?"

"Wouldn't have to be bombers, sir. Remember Pearl Harbor. They came in with little fighter planes from aircraft carriers. This is officially a war zone we're running through, you know. Wouldn't want to make an easy target, now, would we?"

"Target? Oh, my God!" gasped Jackson as the conductor made his way further down the aisle pulling shut window shades and explaining the situation.

"Makes you feel real safe, doesn't it?" said Clayborne wryly.

"It's so hard to get used to," said Jackson. "War. It all seems so unreal. War is what happens somewhere else. But then something like this thing with the window shades comes along. It makes you realize that it is real. And how serious is it. And everybody keeps saying they've put things off 'for the duration.' I hate those words. 'For the duration.' Not like back at Christmas time. It didn't seem so bad at first."

"I know what you mean," said Clayborne. "But those Japanese seem desperate. They'd do anything. I even heard they're attacking those islands up in Alaska Territory. The Aleutians. Desperate."

They rode rocking in the dimly lit rail coach for another two hundred miles, not talking much, worrying and wondering and waiting, half-hearing faraway explosions with every change of pitch in the rail noise over bridges and road crossings. It was after midnight when the train finally hissed into San Francisco Station. The superintendents' bus ride to the St. Francis Hotel seemed interminable and registration felt like it took forever. Clayborne trudged through the process half in a stupor of exhaustion. His room was adequate but sleep came fitfully. He arose in the foggy dawn with his sleep not properly out and made his tired way to breakfast. In the lobby the headline of the San Francisco *Chronicle* Final Morning Edition shook him awake like a punch in the gut. In four-inch letters it screamed:

SUB SHELLS CALIFORNIA!

War Strikes California

Big Raider Fires on Oil Refinery 8 Miles North of Santa Barbara

He bought a copy and read it as countless others in the hotel lobby read it, drifting in a group like zombies to the breakfast room, attention welded to the front page. It read:

Axis shells fell for the first time on California soil last night. A big enemy submarine, presumably Japanese, surfaced half a mile from shore in the Santa Barbara channel, and hurled some 15 shells from its deck gun in an attack on an oil refinery near the town of Goleta, eight miles north of Santa Barbara.

Dear God! thought Clayborne. *Our train ran right by Santa Barbara!*

There were no fires, no damage, no casualties, in this, the first and long expected attack on the United States mainland in this war. The shelling appeared to be directed at the Bankline Oil Company refineries and derricks on the edge of the Ellwood oil field, one of America's big petroleum producing centers 350 miles south of San Francisco.

The 11th Naval District in an official announcement early today released an account of the shelling by F. W. Borden, superintendent of the Bankline refinery: "At 7:10 p.m. (PWT) one large submarine came to the surface about one mile offshore and fired approximately 15 shells from a deck gun," Borden reported in the Navy statement. "One direct hit was registered on a well, causing minor damage to the pumping unit and the derrick. There were several close misses on a crude oil storage tank and a gasoline plant. Apparently no damage was caused by these shells," Borden said. "A complete survey of the ground has not yet been made and there may be superficial damage. Whatever other damage is discovered will not be extensive."

The audacious attack occurred at about 7:15 just as President Roosevelt was delivering his radio address from Washington. It appeared probable in some quarters that the submarine commander deliberately timed his attack to coincide with Mr. Roosevelt's speech.

Clayborne sat in the St. Francis restaurant stunned by the overwhelming sense of reality.

War. War right here on American soil. They're firing at America.

He felt a new outrage welling up to displace the fear of bombing, an untapped spring of patriotism that surprised him a little by its intensity. They were shelling American soil. That was simply intolerable. Absolutely, unthinkably intolerable. The Japanese would regret it. They would be destroyed for it.

Clayborne read on to an account of President Roosevelt's fireside chat of the previous evening. The headline said, "U.S. Warned to Expect Further Setbacks Before Tide Turns. Thousands of U.S. Troops Already in Southwest Pacific." The president had called for three high purposes for all Americans on the home front as a means of combating Axis attempts to divide and conquer: 1. No work stoppages because of labor-management disputes until the war is won; 2. No special privileges or special gains for any group or occupation; 3. Cheerful sacrifices for the war effort. But on the combat front we must expect further setbacks before the tide turns.

Before the tide turns. But what if it doesn't turn? How will it all come out?

The talk was all of the Santa Barbara shelling as hundreds of conventioneers ambled the foggy city blocks from their hotels to the Civic Center's columned entrance. Fifteen thousand school superintendents milled in the lobby and spilled into the auditorium. When the orderly mob finally settled into their first general session, the welcome was not what they expected.

A Civilian Defense officer sternly addressed the gathering: "Ladies and gentlemen, you are hereby instructed upon the authority of the United States government to remain in your hotels when not in this convention facility. In view of the perilous circumstances surrounding last night's attack on the Goleta oil field, bomb shelters have been prepared throughout the city. In the event of enemy attack, you will proceed immediately to the nearest shelter and follow all orders of your air raid wardens who can be identified by prominent armbands identical to the one I am wearing. Long wailing sirens will be sounded as soon as an enemy threat is detected and a long steady siren will signal all clear. You are urged to give your full cooperation to this effort. Thank you."

The silence of fear strangled the audience. Not a sound from fifteen thousand.

Dr. Alexander J. Stoddard, superintendent of schools of Philadelphia, then came to the podium to give the keynote address in the same solemn tone:

"My fellow educators, what we here now and those back home do or fail to do this very day and in the strategic days that lie ahead may determine the course of mankind forever.

"Our schools must become an integral part of the war effort. Vast changes must be made. We have seen that the enemy is prepared to bring war to our very shores. We have seen the march of dictatorship push our troops in the Phillipines into the last ditch of Bataan. We have seen the Japanese Empire spread its tentacles to Bali, to Singapore, throughout the Pacific, even to the Aleutian Islands of Attu and Kiska. We must resist this dictatorship with our full will and strong arm. And our schools must become a sinew in that strong arm.

"We will be called upon to administer many wartime programs on the home front. We will be called upon for strong leadership. We will be called upon for sacrifice and unstinting labor. And we must be ready to answer that call with a will and a power that will rise to smash the Axis and frustrate the evil ambitions of the emperor in Tokyo."

In session after session that first day, scattered in hotel meeting rooms and the Civic Center, patriotic rhetoric gave way to the details of wartime school administration, ideas were discussed, programs outlined, and changes stressed. That first evening, John Lund, senior specialist in education of school administrators, United States Office of Education, addressed a general session. He told them:

"Any picture of what is involved for education in wartime, to be understandable, must be projected against the strategic background of the total national effort. The war and the peace must be won together. The line between war and peace is not going to be sharply and nicely drawn. We are not going to be at war one day and at peace the next.

"The will with which we fight, the knowledge with which we fight, the purpose for which we fight and the spirit in which we fight will determine the kind of a peace that we win.

"Now, will and knowledge and purpose and spirit are not produced in factories. They are the products of that process of growth that goes on in every human individual. The schools are the soil in which that growth takes place. When you go back home, as school superintendents you will have to promote individual gardens to be cultivated by all citizens, Victory gardens, for there will be a shortage of food. When you go back home, those of you in rural schools will have to provide training and facilities for farmers to repair their own farm equipment, for there will be a shortage of both mechanics and materiel. When you go back home, those of you in city schools will have to build a shop in your school where small-machinery businesses can bring their equipment to repair it, for there will be shortages of spare parts. When you go back home, all of you will have to promote programs for older people to contribute their time to the war effort, because there will be a shortage of manpower. When you go back home, you must be prepared to use the same school buses, the same automobiles, the same tires, everything you have now, for the duration of the war, even if that means years.

"We must fight the dictators and all their forces, not only with greater force, but with ideas and faith. The schools and colleges of America are in the midst of a conversion process every bit as significant and vital as the conversion of the factories in America. I wonder if we realize fully that all of this business of expansion and acceleration that occupies so much of our time and attention is not going to stop when the war is won. The planning job for education extends far into the future. We must plan for full teaching of the democratic concept, both as an inspiration for full effort to defeat dictatorship and as a full guide for the peace that is to follow."

The rest blurred into hectic action, crowded conference rooms, impossible seminar schedules in half a dozen hotels, discussions and arguments and ideas and plans, unremarkable restaurant food, evenings with elaborately staged government entertainment little short of war propaganda — and paradoxical nights of loneliness crammed with too much togetherness left over from the day for good sleep. Three days later it was over and the trains took them all back home.

The trains took them back home different people. They now fully grasped the terrifying danger of the war. They had been told of the massacre of dozens of allied tankers and freighters by Nazi U-boats lying off New York and Miami, how hardly a day went by that some oil-soaked survivor did not stagger up on the Florida beaches, how the entire Pacific Coast was now officially a combat zone that might at any moment become a battlefield, how Japanese ships continually reconnoitered San Francisco and Los Angeles and Seattle, testing, probing American defenses, passing messages to Japanese agents on shore. The educators went back home different people. They went back home soldiers without guns.

"I'm sorry, Mr. Caddell," said Clayborne, looking around the abject man to the long line of Walnut Springs citizens standing in his school hallway waiting to hear the fate of their auto travel. "I'm going to have to give you an A card for your car." He inly cringed because this man sat in judgment over him on the school board. But there was nothing for it.

Jim Caddell spoke up, trying to sound brave but knowing in advance he was defeated: "That's only three gallons a week, Mr. Perry. I won't be able to keep track of my properties, keep them in shape, you know."

"I know it's not much, Mr. Caddell," Clayborne replied sympathetically. "But that's what the ration guide says, and that's what we have to stick with. If you had a truck or a farm tractor, we might be able to give you a ten-gallon card."

"Mr. Perry, you know that everything's off the market now. I couldn't get a truck anywheres even if I wanted one. Heck fire, you can't even get a car anywheres. Or tires, for that matter. Not 'for the duration.' The duration! Hmmph . . . How long is this 'duration' going to last?"

"For the duration, Mr. Caddell. But, if any of your properties are being used for vital defense purposes, we might be able to give you a five-gallon sticker."

"They're just houses, Mr. Perry. Ain't likely the gov'ment is going to want them for ammunition factories or storage depots or anything. They're just houses."

"I'm sorry, Mr. Caddell, like I say. But as it is, all I can do is give you an A card. Now can you give me the registration number of your car so we can get you enrolled?"

As Mr. Caddell pulled out the wrinkled and stained form that was his automobile registration, he spoke up: "Mr. Perry, you know what this gas rationing thing is?"

"What, Mr. Caddell?"

"It's a snafu, that's what it is."

"Snafu? What's that?"

"Haven't you heard?" chuckled Caddell. "Why, you don't keep track of all this new Army lingo the boys are makin' up. Now, I can't repeat what it *really* stands for . . ." He paused. "But use your imagination a little. Snafu stands for Situation Normal, All Fouled Up."

Clayborne chuckled at the idea, although not particularly pleased with the implied expletive. "Yes, I guess it is a snafu," he admitted as he filled out the gasoline ration form.

"You mark my words, though, Mr. Perry. It'll get worse. Next it'll be a Tarfu."

"And that means?"

"Things Are Really Fouled Up. And then it'll turn into the worst of all, a Fubar."

"Which is?"

"Fouled Up Beyond All Recognition."

Clayborne laughed. "Mr. Caddell, I don't know where you pick up that kind of thing, but I do know this."

"What?"

"You're all signed up for an A card and there's a mob of folks waiting behind you for theirs."

All day every Saturday for two months the people of Walnut Springs and its surrounding territory stood in line, got the bad news and went home a little sadder, a little madder, a little more frustrated. Large farmers went home with separate ten-gallon-a-week allotment cards for their farm equipment. School and government officials required to travel on defense business went home with five-gallon-a-week cards, and everybody else — everybody else — went home with three-gallon-a-week cards.

The A sticker on car windows soon loomed as a humiliating badge of insignificance, a constant reminder of personal triviality, a cursed blotch telling the world that one was a mere knicknack of the war. To a nation totally unaccustomed to any kind of wartime sacrifice, gas rationing came as an utter shock. However, within weeks Yankee ingenuity recuperated enough to begin wheedling and begging and paying those who didn't need any gasoline. A thriving black market in gas cards grew up. Gas-chiseling became a way of life for an unscrupulous few — but as time went on most citizens began to feel guilty at all the billboards along federal highways asking in huge letters "Is This Trip Really Necessary?" and made do with the patriotic three gallons a week.

And then in May, 1942, came food rationing. It was a bureaucratic nightmare.

"Are you going to have to sit at that food registration table all day again today?" asked Oretta as she finished up the breakfast dishes at the west-facing kitchen window. The dark lingered outside beneath branching liveoaks and pecans. The morning glory blossoms had already opened, their heavy sweetness cloying the air.

"I'm afraid so, every Saturday for a while now, like with the gas rationing," answered Clayborne as he held little Margie and chucked her under the chin. The two-year-old giggled and buried her face in his beefy shoulder. "Oh," he called to Oretta, "and I've got to go out to Rocky Church tomorrow afternoon with the ag teacher to help give out the seeds for their Victory gardens."

"I hope you won't have to do too much gaddin' about for all this Victory garden business. It uses up so much gasoline."

"No, I won't. We're being real careful about gasoline. You know how we cut back all our football games so we only play teams close by. No, we'll be staying right close to home for the duration, it looks like."

"I'm so glad we're just right across from the school so you can walk, Clayborne. Are you going to be home for dinner this noon?"

"I'll be home."

"Dad," asked ten-year-old Bob, "is it true that we won't have enough to eat any more?"

"Who told you that?" asked his father.

"John Dunlop at school. We know about the food rationing. It'll be like gas rationing and you won't get enough."

"No, Bob, it's not quite the same," his father reassured. "It's just a way to make sure we don't waste food and that some people don't start hoarding food."

"What's hoarding?" the boy wanted to know.

"That's when people get scared there won't be enough and they go out and buy up a whole lot of food all at once. That's hoarding, buying up more than you need for everyday. But if everybody did that, lots of people wouldn't get anything at all because the greedy people would have taken it first."

"Oh," said young Bob, trying to understand the alien idea. "But that's against what our church teaches, being greedy like that and not loving your neighbor."

"Well, son, not everybody goes by the teachings of the Holy Scripture, you know. And even good people have their frailties, too. So that's why I've got to work with this food rationing, to make sure everybody gets their fair share."

"Gee, that's nice, Dad. Are you sure there'll be enough?"

"There'll be enough. We won't go hungry. But there won't be enough to waste and there won't be enough to hoard."

"Dad, do you own the school?"

"What?"

"Billy Jones told me in the hall that his dad says you own the school. Do you?"

Clayborne laughed. "No, son, I'm the Superintendent of Schools. That just means I make sure everything runs right, that we have enough teachers, that we don't have discipline problems. I don't own the school, the local school district does."

"Oh," said Bob, not quite sure what the local school district was.

"Clayborne," said Oretta, walking into the front room drying her hands on a dishtowel. "You were going to show me how that food rationing list works."

"Oh, I forgot," he said, quickly rummaging in his satchel for the long government publication. "Did you hear what Bob just said? Billy Jones says his daddy thinks I own the school. It's too bad more people don't understand how their own government works."

"I don't think people here in Walnut Springs are very much like the people back in Iredell, do you?" she said.

"Where is that thing?" he muttered. "I'm going to have to explain it all day. I hope it's not lost. Oh, here." He pulled out a long folded document and turned it over. "Here," he said, "this little box right here explains the whole thing." He pointed to a section of print:

WARTIME SHOPPING GUIDE

Item	Weight	Point Value
Porterhouse Steak	1 lb.	12
Hamburger	1 lb.	7
Loin Lamb Chops	1 lb.	9
Ham	1 lb.	7
Butter	1 lb.	16
Margarine	1 lb.	4
Canned Sardines	1 lb.	12
Canned Milk	1 lb.	1
American Cheddar Cheese	1 lb.	8
Dried Beef Slices	1 lb.	16
Peaches	16 oz. can	18
Carrots	16 oz. can	6
Pineapple Juice	46 oz. can	22
Baby Foods	4 1/2 oz. jar	1
Frozen Fruit Juices	6 oz. can	1
Tomato Catsup	14 oz. bottle	15

"Okay, now look at this stamp book," said Clayborne. "These stamps each have a point value like on the chart, see? This kind of stamp has a picture of wheat on it, so you can use it to buy flour or bread and that sort of thing. And this kind of stamp has a picture of vegetables coming out of that horn of plenty, see? You use it to buy corn and potatoes and all your vegetables. They'll have stamps for meat and milk, too. Every kind of food will have point values like on this chart. Every month we'll be issued more ration stamps based on how many people to feed in our family. So we'll end up with a certain number of points for each kind of food for the family for a month. You can buy food until you run out of points."

"You mean you don't have to pay cash for the food?" asked Oretta.

"No, that's not what I mean, you still have to pay cash for the food. You have to have stamps, too. The prices won't change, they're all OPA Ceiling Prices, and they'll stay the same on each kind of food. But when you give the grocer the cash, you have to give him the same number of stamps as the point values of the food you buy. All the ration stamps do is tell you how much food you're allowed to buy. When you run out of points each month, that's it. No matter how much money you have, you can't buy more food. They just won't sell it to you without these point stamps."

"You mean I'll have to take both stamps and money to the store?" Oretta asked.

"That's right."

"I don't mean to sound unpatriotic, but, oh, Lord, I thought I had a hard enough time shopping as it is! Stamps and cash . . . "

"I know. But pity the poor grocer, Oretta. He has to figure out the right number of points and mark it on every can of food he sells. And meat and vegetables and everything else. And he has to paste the stamps everybody gives him on gummed sheets and give them to his wholesaler so he can replenish his stocks. The grocer won't be able to buy groceries without stamps any more than you will. And the wholesaler then has to turn in his stamps at the bank to get credit to buy more food."

"This is enough to drive me crazy!" complained Oretta.

"I know," said Clayborne. "You're not the only one. We're all in this together. Well, I better get across to school and start driving everybody else crazy."

"Oh, are you going to class at Baylor next Monday night?"

"Yes, why?"

"Can you stop by a notions store in Waco and see if they have some new sewing machine needles? Nobody's got them around here, and I'm down to my last one."

"I guess so. I'll take off a few minutes early to make sure. This new 35 mile an hour speed limit really drags out that trip into Waco, though. I hope I can get there before they close."

"Don't forget you have to drive the school bus after school this week."

"Don't worry, I've got Mr. Gosdin driving on Monday afternoons when I have class at Baylor."

"It's sure not how it was before all the men were drafted, is it?"

"It's sure not."

Autumn. Walnut Springs began to close up early that afternoon: a school football game would be starting in half an hour. Businesses shut their doors, housewives interrupted their domestic chores, workers abandoned their tasks for a football game in this time and place. Inter-school football was not just a pastime here, but a *sport*, a community event of substance, a very serious matter for the school and townspeople alike. And this glorious warm azure day seemed made for them.

At the edge of the civic athletic field next to the business section of town, agriculture teacher W. H. Heartsill stood collecting from the people now beginning to filter in from all around — dimes and quarters dropped in his canning jar, clinkety-clink, the admission fee paid by all youngsters and adults who would see the great contest. The school's own playfield up the hill across Steele Creek lay empty by the closed school buildings, never used for interscholastic sports events.

"Hello there, Mr. Adams, Mr. Paulson," greeted the ag teacher. "Glad you came out to see the Hornets beat Cranfills Gap."

The two businessmen nodded and give him their quarters. "Wouldn't miss it, Mr. Heartsill," said Adams.

The flow of spectators soon increased to a veritable throng. The money jar jingled merrily. There were no bleachers for patrons to sit on or lights for night games, but Walnut folks didn't care: it was their town, their athletic field, their team. The game was everything. Before long all but stragglers had crowded into the spectator zone.

With ten minutes left before game-time, Mr. Heartsill approached Superintendent Perry, holding up the money jar for him to see. "I haven't counted it yet, W. C., but I think we took in about twenty-five dollars. Doesn't look like as much as last game."

Clayborne seemed distracted, his attention on the upcoming game. "It'll be enough," he said. "It'll cover the expenses, fifteen dollars for gas for the visiting team's drivers like usual. Oh, I promised to pay Mr. Parker $2.50 for calling the game."

"Parker's going to call the whole game by himself?" asked Heartsill.

"We just can't find referees since the draft started. We're lucky to get Mr. Parker."

"There won't be much left over to put in the athletic budget, W. C."

"I sure wish this war left us more than the $164 we got for football this year. You just can't spread $164 over uniforms and footballs and the like."

Tableau: the chalk-lined football field lay ready in the Grand Prairie afternoon, encircled by spectators who crowded and bulged around the sidelines. The visiting team from Cranfills Gap gathered around their coach on the far side of the field next to their bench. The Walnut Springs team stood by their bench looking at Superintendent Perry — the coach. Clayborne had taken over high school sports duties when military service took Walnut's regular coach.

"It's almost time for the kickoff," Coach Perry muttered to the ag teacher. "I can't figure out why Moffett's not here."

W. H. Heartsill turned and looked at the Walnut Springs team standing looking back at him. "Tarnation!," he said. "Moffett Cook's *not* here. And I only count twelve players, W. C. Looks like that leaves you without your best back — and only one substitute."

"That's what I'm worried about," the coach said nervously. "Only twelve players if Moffett doesn't get here soon."

"Hi, Dad," said Bob as he walked up to the sidelines. "Hi, Mr. Heartsill."

"Hello there, Bob," said the ag teacher. "Too bad you're not old enough to turn out for football yet. Looks like your Dad needs some help today."

"Yes sir, Mr. Heartsill. You mean because Moffett's not here yet," said the boy. "I sure wish I could play. I will some day."

No time left. Coach Perry strode purposefully to the Walnut Springs sideline and called the team toward him. They stood together waiting for the coin toss. Still no Moffett — and he was the only back Walnut Springs could count on to really make things happen when he got hold of the football. Coach Perry looked across the field to the Cranfills Gap players taking last minute instructions from their coach.

Heartsill sidled up to Clayborne and said under his breath, "The Gap boys look bigger and tougher than last year."

"So I see."

The Gap won the coin toss and chose to receive the kickoff. Walnut chose the wind. Walnut's team captain jogged back to his coach and the team gathered around for their last minute instructions.

"Men," Coach Perry said, "still no word from Moffett. I just can't understand why he's not here, but we can't wait any longer. It's 2:30 and the ref is signaling for us. I know you can all see that Cranfills Gap has bigger players than last year. They will test us. We're going to find out what we're made of."

The Coach looked each man in the eye. The air tingled with emotion. "I expect you to out-hit, out-hustle and out-think 'em for forty-eight minutes. I expect a victory. I expect you to win! Understand?"

He stood silent for a long moment, his electric will swelling their courage. Then he said, "Get 'em!"

Eleven players swarmed onto the playing field for the kickoff. Coach Perry looked down at his lone substitute, Joe Bill Buswold. The young man weighed exactly one hundred pounds on the school scales and his football jersey draped generously over his slight frame, the number 67 almost illegible in the large folds.

The coach said solemnly, "We will be tested today," and then sat down with him on the bench.

The kickoff! Up into the clear Texas air, arching over and down! Cranfills Gap received the ball deep in their own territory and began a long sustained drive toward their goal. Three downs went by.

Mr. Heartsill came and sat next to Clayborne. "The Gap's pretty tough," he said. "That's three first downs in a row."

"W. H.," said Clayborne in frustration, "you're the ag teacher. Moffett's in one of your classes. Do you have any idea why he's not here?"

"He's prob'ly planting oats with the tractor at home, W. C. You have to figure how Miz Cook's situation is since her husband died. It's just her and those four kids — and it's only Clifford and Moffett that's big enough to be much help."

Clayborne listened distractedly, his eyes and attention molded to the players, watching Cranfills Gap determinedly driving downfield. Heartsill, watching every play, then said: "The Cook farm must be two hundred acres, W. C. Work just comes first. Aw, look at that — the Gap made another first down. The Cook boy is out of school nearly a day a week. He wasn't at school all day today. To tell you the truth, I doubt if he's going to show up."

Clayborne was not pleased with the prospect. He watched the quarter dwindle away as Cranfills Gap pushed closer and closer and then across the goal line for the first score. They easily made the extra point. The first quarter ended with the Gap ahead 7 to 0.

The second quarter had just gotten underway and started to look like a repeat of the first quarter. Suddenly Clayborne heard a breathless but familiar voice approaching from behind him.

"Mr. Perry, I'm here! I'm sorry I'm late, but Mama just wouldn't let me come 'til I finished sowing the oats in the south field. I'm sorry."

"Moffett!" said Clayborne, rising and turning toward the familiar voice. "Come on over here."

The big high school junior lumbered up to his coach looking apologetic. Clayborne spoke to him earnestly. "Moffett, I need you in there. This is going to be one long afternoon if we can't turn things around." Both looked out on the field where Cranfills Gap seemed to be moving in for another touchdown.

"How much time left before the half?" asked Moffett.

The coach said, "Probably seven or eight minutes." He looked at Moffett standing there dressed in work clothes. "Why didn't you get suited up?"

"The janitor had already locked the gym, Mr. Perry. I couldn't get in."

Clayborne thought quickly. There really wasn't time to unlock the gym for Moffett. "What are we going to do?" Clayborne muttered to himself. He looked at Joe Bill and he looked at Moffett. He had an idea.

He said, "Moffett, I see at least you brought your cleats."

"Yes, sir?"

"You and Joe Bill go down behind those willow trees by Steele Creek and change clothes with each other. And you hurry back. I need Moffett in the game and now!"

The young men disappeared unnoticed and within five or six minutes reappeared at the bench. Moffett Cook stood in Joe Bill Buswold's uniform with the number 67 spread across a muscular chest and Joe Bill Buswold stood in Moffett Cook's street clothes.

"Moffett, get in there and replace Paulson," ordered Clayborne.

The Walnut Springs Hornets' star offensive and defensive back entered the game just minutes before halftime and barely staved off a second Cranfills Gap touchdown. The Walnut Springs team spent the halftime interval regrouping while Coach Perry tried to figure out how to turn things around. When the time was out, the team trotted back on the field with new energy and determination for the second half.

Cranfills Gap kicked to the Hornets who moved the ball back to their own thirty-five yard line. The Gap hit and they probed, but they could not keep Moffett Cook from making huge chunks of yardage play after play. When they had the ball they could not keep Moffett Cook from demolishing their carriers. He was all over the field. They tried everything. Nothing worked. When the final whistle shrilled, it was Walnut Springs 13, Cranfills Gap 7. The Walnut cheerleaders went wild and fans thronged onto the field paying homage to their heroes.

When the players returned to the bench amid the crush of enthusiastic students and fans, Clayborne grabbed a sweaty Moffett and vigorously embraced him. "Glad you could make it, Cook," he confided. "I may forgive you for being late." Then the superintendent-cum-coach turned and motioned Joe Bill to follow him. Clayborne put his arm around the boy as they went to meet the Cranfills Gap coach in midfield. The opposing coach stood there looking at the gangly boy in oversize khaki trousers and shirt for a moment and then at Clayborne. He said: "Perry, I thought we had you. Then you sent Buswold in. That did it. But tell me, how come he wears a lineman's number?"

Perry just said, "Did he have on a lineman's number?" smiling and shrugging his shoulders.

The Cranfills Gap coach set his jaw sardonically. "Whatever. I'm mighty glad you held him out most of the first half—but why did you do it?"

Coach Perry grinned and said nothing. The three began drifting toward the Gap bus.

"I guess you have your reasons," sighed the Gap coach. "Well, that Buswold's a heck of a football player, that's all I can say."

Clayborne looked down at the oddly-outfitted boy encircled by his left arm and answered, "Yeah, I owe Buswold a big favor for today."

They turned away leaving the Cranfills Gap coach shaking his head. As they walked off the field, Joe Bill looked up at his coach and said, "Mr. Perry, I'm anxious to see the writeup on this game in the *Waco News Tribune*. I know Moffett Cook is the real hero. But when you call in the results, don't forget 67's name is Buswold, will you? Joe Bill B-U-S-W-O-L-D."

Clayborne laughed. The memory of this day remained bright and clear for decades.

In the days that came after, when he finished Walnut Springs High School, Moffett renounced his right to military exemption as a farmer as his older brother Clifford before him. They believed it their patriotic duty to serve regardless of personal or family sacrifice. Clifford had enlisted in the Navy, assigned to duty in Europe. The next year Moffett did the same, also assigned to European duty. Within months of Moffett's enlistment, the red-rimmed service flag hanging in Mrs. Cook's kitchen window no longer showed a blue star representing a man in the service, but bore a gold star, indicating a man killed in action.

A few weeks later, the emblem held two gold stars. The community's shock and pain never went away.

"Good to see you again, Clayborne," said Hoyt. "You all come on in and say hello to Mama and Papa."

Oretta and the children entered Tom and Belle's farm house, tromping happily into the living room full of greetings and hugs.

"Is that you, Bobby?" called Tom from his chair by the window.

"Yes, sir, it's me, Grandpa," Bob answered.

The aging man smiled faintly and said, "Come sit on my lap, young 'un, and let me feel your ol' hard head."

It had become a ritual. Tom with his sightless eyes all gray — no sign of the iris or pupil remained, filmed over with an unknown disease — always begged the arriving boy to come let him run his hands through his hair, to see his grandson through his fingers. Today as always the boy happily obliged as little Margie and Oretta settled down in the farmhouse living room.

But Clayborne stayed aside with his brother Hoyt a moment.

"How is Papa?" Clayborne asked quietly.

"Oh, he's so-so. He's getting pretty feeble now, but I think it comes from being blind more than anything, you know, not enough exercise and all. He can still pick a little corn and clean up in the barn."

"He doesn't try to plow with the mules any more?"

"No, I've got his mules at the place over by Robinson now. Papa doesn't plow, or much of anything. He just sits around mostly. Look how he's hardly even feeling Bob's head today. He's getting pretty feeble, like I say."

"He's only fifty-nine, Hoyt. And Grandpa Jim is eighty this year. I don't like it."

"It's the blindness, Clayborne. Nothin' we can do about it. We best get on into the living room."

Belle got up from her chair and came to greet her oldest son. "Oh, Clayborne, how glad we are to see you. It's been so long. You look so good and the children are getting so big. And go say hello to your Papa."

Clayborne walked with deliberate foot clomping to Tom's chair. Bob got up from his grandfather's lap as his father approached. Clayborne looked down at the slight body and the radiance of mind that was his father. He bent over and said "Hello, Papa. How are you doing?"

"I'm gettin' on, son. I'm gettin' on. Glad you came."

Clayborne stood there a moment considering his father, falling into a brown study, feeling that Tom had shrunk, withered, begun to dry up. Look there, those sinewy arms and strapping back of his plowing days grew weak now, unused, nearly useless. Pitiless time. Look there, that ambitious mind and indomitable will of his planning days faltered now, cut off from the light by afflicted eyes, the awareness guttering like a torch tormented by too strong a wind. The winter night of pitiless time. All too clearly Clayborne saw it. The storm of time would soon extinguish this lampglow altogether.

Oh, Papa! It shouldn't come to this. Not you. Not after all your work.

"I'm glad we could get here, Papa," Clayborne said cheerily. "What with all this gas rationing we don't get much of anywhere these days."

Clayborne then went and sat in the family circle, watching Bob and Margie playing with Hoyt and Bernice's four-year-old daughter Sherry.

"Well, Hoyt," Clayborne said, "how's farming over by Robinson?"

"It's good, Clayborne. The soil's a lot better than Grandad Perry's place — Grandpa's rented the Dude Flat farm out to the Andersons, did you hear? It's still being worked — but the roads are good at our new place, and it's only about eight miles south of the market in Waco. We're doing mostly tractor farming nowadays. It's a pretty big operation, lots of acreage. I'm ashamed to say it, but we're making enough money to live on because of this war."

"And the Army didn't get you, thank the Lord," said Belle. "Not to be unpatriotic or anything."

Bernice spoke up, "They've been pretty good about leaving the better farmers at home, Mama Perry. They haven't taken anybody around us except some of those hobby farmers that barely raise enough to feed themselves, and those were mostly city folks that moved out in the country not long before the war."

Oretta said, "You had to come a long way from Robinson today."

"We've got a ten-gallon card," explained Hoyt. "What with my tractor and my truck and the size of the crops we grow, we pretty much insisted on it. They didn't argue much at the school when we signed up. The superintendent didn't know us very well then, but he does now. So every now and then we have enough extra gas to come to Hico."

"And I buy gas for him on our card," said Belle. "I know I shouldn't. We siphon it out with the hose. But we don't need much for what little driving we do now."

Bob chimed in, "It doesn't cost any gas when I come on the doodlebug."

Belle smiled at the boy and said, "It doesn't cost your daddy's ration card, it doesn't. You're such a big boy, coming to see us all by yourself on the train from Walnut Springs."

Bernice asked Oretta, "Do you let him ride the train by himself?"

"Well, sure we do. He insists on it. He gets off at the Hico station and walks out here from town. It's not that far and he loves to visit grandma and grandpa so."

"Sometimes a farmer picks me up on the road and I get a ride," offered Bob.

"Well, we love to have him," said Belle. "He keeps us from getting lonesome."

"Oh, don't talk about lonesome," said Oretta. "Every time we come over here now I miss Nadine and Dorothy, Mama Perry. How are you getting on without them?"

"Oh, we hardly even notice any more. It's been nearly two years now, Oretta. They've both been married since before the war started."

"Has it been that long?" asked Bernice.

"That long," answered Belle primly.

"It doesn't seem like it. Is Nadine's husband still working down in that defense plant at Texas City?" asked Oretta. "Or did he get drafted?"

"Henry Land?" said Belle. "Oh, he's still working there at that Union Carbide plant, working as a tinner, I think it is, isn't it, Clayborne? They won't draft him."

"What about Homer Wilson, Mama?" asked Clayborne. "We haven't heard from Dorothy in a while either."

"I think he's being called up, son. I don't know what Dorothy's going to do with her husband in the service. She just idolizes that Homer Wilson. And this war is so uncertain. We see windows with those little gold star flags, you know, the ones they give you when . . ."

"We know, Mama," said Clayborne. "We've got some in Walnut Springs."

"I just hope he comes back." Belle said. "Alive," she added.

The adults in the room stirred uneasily. All except Tom.

Hoyt said, "And you, Clayborne, what have you been up to while we've been farming at Robinson? How do you like being superintendent at Walnut Springs?"

"Fine, Hoyt. Fine." Clayborne recalled, "We moved from that place near the church and the stores and all. Now we're renting a place the other side of Steele Creek, right across from the Walnut Springs School."

Young Bob said, "It doesn't have an inside bathroom like the place right in town had. But it's got a toilet out back with room for two people at a time!"

Oretta smiled at her boy and said, "We've made arrangements with Mr. Gosdin — he's the man we rent from — to put in a regular bathroom for us, you know, with a commode, and a bathtub and a little wash basin."

"Well," said Clayborne, "the place is just about like most people's houses in Walnut Springs. It's all right. And the school work has been mostly administering the gas and food rationing, to tell you the truth. There's no money to do much with the schools. But we've still got our lunchroom program."

"You mentioned that last time, too." said Hoyt.

"I guess I did. We've had that lunchroom program two years now. Well, we go out and try to get people to grow Victory gardens, you know, W.H. Heartsill and me — he's the ag teacher — and we meet in churches or rural schools. I guess we've organized ten or fifteen garden clubs around Walnut Springs. We just tell them how to grow easy things like beans, how to plant food in their flower beds and such. The government gives us $20 worth of seeds for each little community so we end up giving each family maybe two or three dollars worth."

"Some school superintendent job! Maybe I made the right decision being a farmer," smiled Hoyt.

"Oh, I know it doesn't sound interesting, but the people are fine folks. I enjoy being around them. But you have a point — we don't have any men teachers left at all, except the ag teacher and me."

"Who's doing the teaching, then?" Hoyt asked.

"Well, it's women teachers, of course. But some are going into the Women's Army Corps and a lot of them are going to those high-paying factory jobs in Houston and Dallas, so we're getting short of women, too. Now we're even having a hard time getting women teachers with degrees. The state is letting us hire women with two or three years of college and no degree because we can't find anybody else. And did I tell you, they drafted all our school bus drivers. I have to go out and find farmers or men who were too old so we'll have somebody to drive those buses. And the buses are getting pretty run-down, but they tell us they'll have to last for the duration."

"Same with my farm equipment," said Hoyt. "I sent Bernice into Waco for some truck transmission parts last month and the dealer told her we'd have to make them ourselves in the machine shop. They're out of transmission parts for the duration."

"They're out of everything for the duration," said Oretta. "Clayborne had a dickens of a time even finding sewing machine needles in Waco."

Bernice said, "And try to find hair pins or eyeglasses. I sure don't like this war. It's worse than the Depression."

"We've got enough money to live on now, honey," said Hoyt. "Don't forget that."

"But there's nothing to buy with it," Bernice said.

Clayborne began to feel anxious about his father's silence and seeming remoteness from the conversation. He didn't like the way Tom just stared sightlessly to infinity. He didn't like the way his father sat still, not moving his head in agreement or disagreement, isolated in the coffin of his smothering blindness. Clayborne decided to bring up one his father's pet subjects to lure him into the talk.

"Say, Papa, have you heard how the war's going? We lost Bataan and Corregidor here a couple of months ago. General Wainwright had to surrender. Doesn't look so good. What do you think they should have done?"

Silence.

Hoyt understood his brother's intent, and added, "The Japs got General Chennault's Flying Tigers, too. They've shut down the Burma Road flying over 'The Hump' up there in the Himalayas. General Stillwell's had to retreat into India. What did they do wrong?"

Silence.

Clayborne ached with pity for his father. Now, young Bob looked intently at Tom Perry, realizing that all was not well with his grandfather.

Clayborne tried once more: "There's a little good war news, too, Papa. Jimmy Doolittle led a B-25 raid on Tokyo. Bombed 'em good. We must have used an aircraft carrier to get the planes close enough to Tokyo, because when some reporter asked President Roosevelt what base they used, he just laughed and told them 'Shangri-La!' How about that, Papa?"

"Shangri-La," said Tom Perry, suddenly relaxing. "Shangri-La. That's the name. I heard a story about Shangri-La on the radio. It came on the Lux Radio Theater, it did. I remember listening to it with Mama just a while ago. Don't you remember, Belle?"

"I remember," she said, fighting back a sob.

Tom went on, his face beginning to light up. "I remember that story about Shangri-La. I sure do. It had Ronald Coleman in it. When it came on, it was almost like I could see again, all those wind sounds and the airplane sounds and all. It made me think of such things, oh, such things! All about this fellow that crashes up in them real high mountains in Asia. He gets rescued by some strange people that take him to Shangri-La. Then he finds this Shangri-La is a magic place where nobody ever gets old. He falls in love with this woman who lives there. He wants her to go back with him to civilization. She can't leave because the only thing that keeps her from dying is the magic of Shangri-La. But she loves him so much she goes with him anyway. And in just a few minutes time catches up with her and she's two hundred years old. You should have heard it."

Tom's dead eyes glistened as some inner sight blazed outward through their wreckage for a moment. Then he said, "That's what's happened to me. Time caught up with me all of a sudden. I've cheated it all my life. But now it's got me. One thing about that program I can't recollect. What did they call that Shangri-La story, son?"

"*Lost Horizon*, Papa," said Clayborne. "It's a novel by James Hilton."

"Lost Horizon," repeated Tom Perry, entranced. "What words! Who can think up such words? Lost Horizon. It almost makes you see the edge of the world, it does. Lost Horizon. Oh dear, that's *my* horizon."

"We never seem to do anything right," said W.H. Heartsill as he piled a stack of reports on Clayborne's desk.

"What are you talking about, W.H.?" asked Clayborne, leaning back in his office chair.

"That battle at Midway, W.C. Just the other day."

"Where we sunk those four Jap aircraft carriers? What's wrong with that?"

"We lost the Yorktown, that's what. Don't you feel bad about that?"

"Of course I do. But that's not too bad a score, four aircraft carriers to one. And Elmer Davis on the radio said it was a real victory for us. Jap ships don't outnumber ours so badly any more. Lordy, I hope he's right."

"It's not just that. I just wish we'd start fighting back, is all. Don't you just want to smash the Japs good sometimes?"

"All the time, W.H. And the Germans, too. Every American does."

"Well, we hear about all this war production we're supposed to be turning out. And don't get me wrong, I believe every word of it. But where is it going? Why don't we attack? And how come the Japs can come onto our own territory, into the Aleutians, and capture Attu and Kiska? They're not just fighting over those islands any more, W.C., the Japs captured them yesterday! In our own Alaska Territory! It just makes me so damn mad I could go out and enlist right now!"

Clayborne sat up in alarm. "Hold it right there! Don't you dare enlist," he said. "Who would run the ag program and the farm repair shop? Think of everybody that needs you around here. I can't do any more than hold the line with this gas and food rationing mess. Don't forget our soldiers have to eat, too, you know. If the government thought you could do any better with a gun in your hand they'd have drafted you six months ago. I think the heat is getting to you, W.H."

"Ah, I'm sorry, W.C. You're probably right. This is the hottest June I can remember for years. The summer of '42 will likely make some kind of record."

"Well, don't you go talking about enlisting any more, you hear?"

"You probably feel frustrated, too, sometimes, don't you, W.C.?"

Clayborne leaned both arms on his desk and said wearily, "Between having to drive 35 miles an hour to Baylor every morning in this heat and getting my lunchroom thesis written up and trying to find teachers for next year that can spell and then running this gas and food rationing mess, yeah, every now and then I think that when the war is over I'll just check in at some sanitorium and go crazy for a while. But until then, I'll just do what I have to and leave the war to the generals. And if they're not doing such a perfect job, I went over my books this afternoon and found out there's a family on a big farm up north that should have got a ten gallon card and I gave them a five gallon card. Now I've got to go set things right with them, and I'm not sure whether they can make up for the lost gasoline or not because the regulations don't say anything about that kind of a. . . . What's the matter, W. H.?"

"Is that your wife running across the school yard, W.C.?"

Clayborne twirled around in his swivel chair and looked out the window. "It sure is. Looks like there's a problem. I better go meet her."

He jumped up and hurried down the hall, then out the side door. "What is it?" he called across the field.

"Margie!" Oretta screamed. "Her leg's broken!"

Clayborne intercepted Oretta in mid-stride and grabbed her shoulders. "What happened?" he asked in shock.

"Run," said Oretta. "Quick."

They ran together the hundred yards between the school building and their wooden frame rent house. Clayborne could hear the shrieks of pain and fear from his little two-and-a-half-year-old daughter.

"Around back," shouted Oretta, loping breathlessly. They rounded the white-painted house and saw Bob standing over little Margie and holding his bicycle up as if it were some evil weapon like a knife or a gun. The little girl screamed and tried to grip her left leg. The limb bent in places where a human leg should not bend.

"Margie's hurt, Dad! I did it! I hurt her! It was an accident," Bob cried, beside himself with worry and fear. "I was giving her a ride on the bar and her foot got caught in the wheel spokes. I lost my balance and the bike fell on her. She's hurt, Dad. She's hurt real bad. Her leg's broken and I did it! Can't you get a doctor for her? Oh, poor Margie, my poor Margie!"

The boy stood like a guilty thing, not knowing whether he had fallen utterly from grace, not knowing whether the offer of his loving touch to comfort his injured sister would be welcome any more, stewing in perplexity, that special agony of the unintentional culprit. He had always been so protective of her, guarded her so jealously, saw to her welfare so solicitously. But now! Oh, but now!

Clayborne bent over his panicky little girl, touched her face tenderly, and sized up the break. "It's bad," he told Oretta. "I can't tell, but it looks like both bones are broken between the knee and the ankle. You start the car and I'll lay her down in the back seat, Oretta. You can ride with her in the back on the way to Dr. Holt's in Meridian. Bob, you stay with the next door neighbors, you hear? We'll be back as soon as we get things taken care of. Don't you fret any, now, you hear? It was an accident and you're not to blame."

Then Clayborne was off, bearing his crying girl to the car. Oretta got in back with Margie and Clayborne took the wheel. They tore off for Meridian, some nine miles to the south.

Bob stood there forlornly beside his bicycle, burning with guilt and regret, watching all that he loved racing away for medical help. He felt utterly alone as he watched his family disappear in the distance.

When they arrived at the professional offices of Dr. R.D. Holt, the doctor was not in his office. His partner was gone, too. There was no one in Meridian to help them. They were told to go on to Clifton, eleven miles southeast on Highway 6 toward Waco. At the Clifton Clinic they found Dr. Seth L. Witcher in attendance, who expertly palpated the injury, diagnosed the break points, set the leg and applied the plaster cast, all the while soothing the little girl, easing her hurt body and hurt mind. Soon she could manage a wan smile, and indicated she was ready to go home with her new appurtenance. The plaster cast looked almost as big as she did.

Within a week Bob had begun to come to terms with the event, and Margie was gamely dragging her bum leg around behind her in its cast, never thinking to blame Bob for the accident. In two weeks she was walking with expertise, hardly hampered by the burdensome appliance. In six weeks the cast was cut off at the doctor's office and she was free and mended and under the broody-hen protection of her big brother.

The year 1943 came into Walnut Springs on the crest of a blue norther reviving ancient memories of cold in the Texas land. As far as the public was concerned, the war was still uncertain. The only thing completely obvious to everyone was that the Axis did not have the strength to defeat the Allies decisively any time soon. Americans did not relax, but they knew they would not all be speaking German in the immediate future. Allied leaders knew by now that Hitler could not win his war at all. Hitler's Germany was showing the first signs that its two-front war was simply unsustainable. On the second of November in 1942, the British began the decisive battle of Alamein, to sweep Rommel's Afrika Korps away, followed by English-American landings in Morocco and Algeria six days later. The German Volga-Caucasus offensive withered against stiff Soviet resistance. The generals knew then that Hitler not only couldn't win, but also that he couldn't force a stalemate. It was only a matter of time, bloody time, before his utter defeat.

Nor did the American public worry about imminently having to learn Japanese. The Japanese navy's master-spirit, Admiral Yamamoto, had been assassinated by American fighter planes as he conducted a tour of Solomon Island defenses during April, 1942. President Roosevelt had personally approved the order, and had been able to do so only because of American technical superiority in breaking Japanese codes. Kazuki Kamejama, head of Japan's Cable Section, refused to believe that Americans could rapidly break his super-complex codes, and when Admiral Yamamoto began his fatal tour, asserted, "The new code only went into effect two weeks ago and cannot be broken." In fact, American code specialists had broken it by dawn the day after it went into effect.

Admiral Halsey knew exactly where Yamamoto would be and exactly when. Shooting him down proved to be a routine combat mission. In June, 1942, the Japanese suffered the catastrophic defeat at Midway, outsmarted by American code-breakers and a convenient cloud cover that hid American fighter planes until it was too late. By mid-November, 1942, Japan was having a hard time fending off the first American assaults on their island strongholds in the Pacific: the Japanese airport on Guadalcanal was under full attack and in the fighting the Imperial navy had lost two battleships, a heavy cruiser, three destroyers and eleven transports. Even so, the Americans had paid a terrible price for their progress, and Guadalcanal was not yet secured: the aircraft carriers *Hornet* and *Wasp* were sunk, along with four Allied cruisers. The USS *Enterprise* was the only American carrier active in the Pacific. But within days the Soviets had launched their counteroffensive at Stalingrad and the German-Japanese Axis began their inevitable slide into oblivion. President Roosevelt even stated publicly — and he was fanatically cautious never to sound over-optimistic — "It would seem that the turning point in this war has at last been reached." The tide was turning. Against the Axis. For the Allies.

The early sense of unreality about the war had completely vanished now, and the suppressed panic that had followed on its heels was gone, too. The year 1943 found in America only a grim determination, a grim determination to hold on, to build up, to construct overwhelming technical superiority, to fight back, to win the war absolutely and unconditionally. But holding on to such terrible determination for too long blunts the sensibilities and invites boredom, which ran plentifully through the Grand Prairie of 1943: everyone had dug in for the duration and the thrill was gone. The war effort on the home front, that grand source of patriotic enthusiasm back when the war began, now seemed reduced to trivia: civilian defense wardens watched for enemy planes that never came, housewives counted out endless reams of rationing stamps, everyone put up with shortages of sugar and coffee, and the diehards saved old toothpaste tubes and cans of cooking fat for ammunition.

True, the factories down at Texas City and Houston kept up morale by counting every gun and tank and ship fitting and airplane part they turned out, and they turned them out in what was shortly to become a prodigious, unbelievably vast stream. Every factory day was a fight against deadlines and quotas. But for everybody else, the only battles to be fought were against tedium, the only combat was with disgust. Citizens seized upon anything to do. The government's scrap paper drive prompted such an enthusiastic response that receiving stations lay drowned in old magazines and newspapers and Washington had to call it off.

In spite of it all, in spite of the foreign threat and the internal humdrum, Walnut Springs was intact. Aside from the fact that not many young men could be found 'round about, life had not really changed much at all. Gosdin's still sold its groceries, Simpson's still vended its hardware, Adam's Grocery still offered good cuts of meat if you had the ration stamps to go along with your cash, Hickock's still had lumber for sale, and malted milks still rotated furiously in Oaks' Drug Store soda fountain. Children still ran through summertime lawn sprinklers and teenage girls had pajama parties to make the grownups tut-tut at this flighty generation. The bandstand in Katy park was no longer the town's pride and joy as it had been before the railroad pulled out and left Walnut Springs in decline, but the lovely old grove of pecan trees thriving in the park on the banks of Steele Creek still bowered picnic tables and benches that remained the favorite haunts of local families. The Victory gardens did better than anybody had expected: Sunday Walnut Springs farmers produced at least a third of all the vegetables consumed in town — and the same thing happened everywhere in America. The schools in Walnut Springs continued teaching reading and writing and 'rithmetic and also fixed tractors and plows and helped local farmers to hundreds of government publications telling them how to farm better. Clayborne found time between going to night school at Baylor and running the schools in the daytime and overseeing the rationing program in odd hours to advance to second in command of the Walnut Springs Masonic Lodge. The war in Walnut Springs went forward.

Clayborne had no way of knowing it, but the future hid beckoning ten miles or so down the road at Meridian in a controversy over dancing. The trouble had arisen between Meridian Superintendent of Schools Hensley and his students: Hensley was a devoutly religious man adamantly opposed to dancing in any circumstances. His students wanted to jitterbug and cut a rug in the school gym. Mr. Hensley refused to even consider it and the boys and girls thus went down by the river of an evening to swing and sway to portable hand-cranked Victrolas playing Jimmy Dorsey and Glenn Miller platters. Mr. Hensley got wind of it and demanded the students be punished. The parents split over the issue, but most saw nothing wrong in dancing and felt that a properly supervised and chaperoned school dance now and then might be a good thing. The Meridian Board of Education split over the issue, and the teachers split over it, too. Total impasse. The friction wore on and began to affect school life. Grades suffered. Teacher morale suffered. Parent support suffered. School board unity suffered. And finally, Meridian school district's accreditation was threatened. Deputy State Superintendent of Education of District No. 15, W. C. Perkins, was called to Meridian High School twice in early 1943 to help resolve the smouldering struggle between Superintendent Hensley's supporters and opponents. Nothing budged.

On May 20, 1943, the Meridian Board of Education president sent a letter to State Superintendent of Public Education Dr. J. W. O'Bannion in Austin:

Deputy Perkins has been advised of the developing friction between the Board of Education and the Superintendent, and between the Superintendent and faculty. There is no doubt in the mind of Deputy Perkins that this friction has reached the point of interfering with the usual school program and even the point of making it impossible for the school to maintain general required standards.

It is evident that a certain amount of friction has existed in the school for several years. The fact that the present incumbent is the third superintendent in five years would make the situation appear questionable. The lack of rightly placed authority in the hands of the superintendent, possibly the lack of judiciously executed authority on the part of the superintendent, and the lack of solid support of the executive officer by the Board all enter into creating the problem.

In view of the above facts, and in view also of the fairmindedness of both the Board and the Superintendent, and their expressed desire to work out this unhealthy situation, I recommend that the school be given a warning and sufficient time to correct this embarrassing condition. It is recommended that the Deputy give special attention to this school during the coming school term of 1943-1944.

While this controversy flared a few miles away, Clayborne presided over another successful graduation at Walnut Springs schools and went on to summer school again at Baylor. He realized that this was the last term of his master's degree program, and with some alarm remembered that the thesis he had been working on since spring was due on August first. The research work on "Management and Operation of a School Lunch Room Program," as he decided to title it, was nearly done. He had mailed dozens of questionnaires to other schools to document the varieties of lunch room program management techniques and their effectiveness, and most of the responses had come back. He had raided the literature on the subject, what there was of it in 1943, and had cited and critiqued every relevant authority and publication. Now he began to tabulate the questionnaire data and formulate his thesis, working day and night, spending hours in the Baylor library, driving to school at 35 miles per hour and driving home at 35 miles per hour in the growing June heat.

One June day Clayborne found himself invited to a job interview on the Baylor campus by a representative of Conaway Teachers College in Conaway, Arkansas. His master's degree would qualify him as a college instructor, he was told, but when salary was discussed, the numbers were nearly the same as he was making at Walnut Springs. Clayborne declined the offer politely.

Then in July, Baylor president and former Texas governor Pat Neff called Clayborne into his office and asked if he would like to take over the management of the Baylor Book Store. His master's degree, he was told, would qualify him as a book store manager, but when salary was discussed, the numbers again were nearly the same as he was making at Walnut Springs. Again, Clayborne declined the offer politely. And he began to wonder just how much a master's degree was really worth, anyhow.

Clayborne's superintendent's salary was simply too low. He found it necessary to work at odd jobs around Walnut Springs during the summer months. The summer of '43 brought Gene Palmer to the town's little railroad station with several freightcar loads of surplus government wheat for sale. Farmers from all over came to the subsidized grain, filling their own tow sacks they had brought from home. Clayborne worked for Mr. Palmer every afternoon for several hours, helping farmers bag their grain, weighing each sale and collecting for it. Young Bob, now eleven years old, tagged along with his Dad and helped farmers sack up grain, not for regular pay, but for tips from the customers. One customer named G.B. Jones came frequently from down the road at Meridian, bringing two grandsons about Bob's age who talked and joked with him and helped the time pass happy away. Bob was thrilled with his financial success that summer, making good money, 35 cents, sometimes as much as 50 cents a day. But Clayborne was not thrilled with his financial success that summer, for when the boxcars were empty and the Katy switch engine hauled them away, Palmer didn't pay up. It was a very unusual situation in the Grand Prairie, for most people there had high ethics and were as good as their word. It was the only time in all Clayborne's years that someone who had promised to pay him failed to live up to the agreement.

But the sting did not linger: Clayborne was busy with his master's thesis and beat his submission deadline by two weeks. On July 20 he presented the written thesis to his graduation committee, presided over by Dr. Lorena Stretch. By the first week of August he had made the required corrections — he had become a high speed typist over the years and whacked out the original and four carbon copies of his 96 page study in short order — and now stood ready to defend his thesis in his final oral examinations.

Graduate students all dread the ordeal of defending their thesis. You prepare as well as you can, you check the accuracy of your facts as well as you can, you try to overcome the intimidating fact that the friendly professors who have advised you over the past years are now going to subject you to close questioning that borders on the exquisite agonies of the Spanish Inquisition; and when the day comes, you just do your best. Clayborne entered the Baylor examination room one day in the second week of August and came out some hours later with a slip of paper that said he had passed with flying colors and would be permitted to graduate.

And so, on Wednesday evening, August 18, 1943, Clayborne drove with his family to Waco Hall where he received his master's degree in administrative education from University President Pat Neff. In his rented black cap and gown, coming last after all the undergraduates, he reached another milestone in his education.

As he strode across the stage and took his degree in hand, his sole regret was that his father was not here to experience, if not see, his achievement. But Tom Perry had been diagnosed with Bright's disease, glomerulonephritis, a degenerative process affecting the kidney's capillaries. Its cause was unknown. There was no cure. There was little treatment beyond bed rest and limiting the intake of water. Clayborne's hour of triumph was dimmed by what he knew must follow for his father.

Tuesday, August 22, 1943, four days after receiving his master's degree, Clayborne found himself in the fields of Theo Rundell picking cotton some miles south of Walnut Springs. Field hands were so scarce that all able-bodied men in the wartime community helped bring in the cotton crop. Clayborne had promised, despite the crush of paperwork on his desk, to pick a full sack of cotton for one farmer every day after work. It was really nothing unusual. Even the schools had come to provide cotton-picking brigades. The second or third week of school in September had now become a wartime holiday: older students were bused to the cotton fields to pick all day for a week. To the kids it was a lark, riding the school bus as it pulled off the road into one farm after another, eating sack lunches in the fields, weighing up their bags on old-fashioned scales, making fun of the ancient horse-drawn wagons still in use on some of the less developed farms, admiring the tractors and trucks that pulled modern cotton trailers on more mechanized modern farms. Clayborne had taken his students picking last year; he would do it again this year. The extra money was always welcome to the pickers and to the farmer the extra help was essential.

Clayborne enjoyed the weight of the rough ducking sack pulling over his strong shoulders this Tuesday afternoon; it reminded him of his childhood, of his young and hopeful father dragging a young sleeping boy on his collecting bag through the rows, of his boyhood days when he helped his father pick in the Perry fields at Dude Flat. It also reminded him of the dreadful days when he had picked alone, fortified with Old Grandma's yellow cake and homey advice, expecting every evening to come in to the rent house and find his father dead of pneumonia. And it reminded him of his father lying now in bed at his farm near Hico, kidneys slowly failing, time piling up in heaps on his slight body, time clotting until its sands could run no more.

He could not get his father out of his mind. Yes, he was a father himself now, with a wonderful wife and a fine boy and girl, the people he owed his closest ties. But, oh, poor Papa. There would be no miraculous recovery this time. How would he ever bear the loss? He tried to prepare himself, to take the idea philosophically: so many young men in Walnut Springs had died in action. Why, just the other day Mr. Adams who ran Adams Grocery Store had gotten a letter at the post office telling him his son, a pilot, had been shot down and killed. But it did not work. Philosophy did not help. Oh, poor Papa. His heart could not bear the idea.

It was late in the evening, sundown, when Clayborne weighed in his picking sack and drove home from the cotton patch in the family car. As he pulled up to his modest white frame house, he saw a 1941 Plymouth parked in the gravel street in front. He pulled past the car into his driveway, peering hard in the failing light to see who sat in the vehicle. He parked his car alongside the house and saw Oretta standing on the front porch. Bob and Margie could be heard playing in the back yard in the softly falling dusk.

He walked to Oretta's side and asked, "Who is that?"

"Oh, I'm so embarrassed, Clayborne. They caught me running around barefoot when they drove up and there was nothing I could do."

"It's not against the law. Who caught you running around barefoot?"

"They asked if they could talk to my *father!* Do I look that young? They thought I was your *daughter!*"

"Who thought you were my daughter?"

"You better go talk to them. I think it's important."

"Talk to who, for pity's sake, Oretta?"

"Go talk to them."

He stepped out over the dry and brittle summer grass of his lawn to the gravel street and the waiting Plymouth. He strained fruitlessly to see through the windshield's reflected sunset as he walked to the open driver's window.

"Mr. Perry?"

"Yes, sir. What can I do for you?"

"I'm Sam Lawson and this is Dr. Holt. You and I have seen each other at regional school meetings, and I think you know Dr. Holt."

Clayborne knew C. T. Lawson, the man everybody called Sam, as the president of the Meridian Board of Education. He also knew that Dr. Russell D. Holt sat as a member of that board.

"Well, sure, I know him," Clayborne said, "we go to Dr. Holt. What brings you folks up from Meridian? Won't you come on into the house for a cup of coffee?"

"Mr. Perry, we need to talk to you a few minutes." said Lawson. "We won't take long. There's no need for us to come in. You can get in the back if you'd like."

"Okay, fine." He was not quite sure what was going on, but got in the car and sat in the center of its back seat while both men turned to face him over the crown of the front seat.

Mr. Lawson said, "I hear that you just got your master's degree from Baylor."

"Yes, sir. As a matter of fact, I did. In administrative education."

Dr. Holt said, "I understand you're doing a pretty good job as superintendent of Walnut Springs school district."

"Well, the school board thinks things are going pretty smooth."

C. T. Lawson said, "Let us come right to the point, Mr. Perry. We'd like to offer you the job of Superintendent of Schools for Meridian. You'd have a larger school district to oversee and we're prepared to offer you an attractive salary."

Clayborne was speechless.

"I know you'd probably like some time to think about it," said Dr. Holt.

"Yes, I would," said Clayborne, completely taken by surprise.

"And I'm sure you'll want to talk over the details with your family, and with your school board members," said Lawson. "Here's what we're talking about in terms of salary." Lawson handed Clayborne a small piece of notepaper with the number $325 on it. That was considerably higher than his present income of $285, forty dollars a month higher, and much better than all previous offers. Now he knew what a Master's Degree was really worth: $325 a month and a challenging job.

"There's not much time until school starts again, only about three weeks," said Lawson. "Mr. Perry, we need you to run our schools. We have fine people in Meridian. We have a fine town. Could you discuss it with the Walnut Springs board soon? To see if they they'll give you leave?"

"Well, today is Tuesday" said Clayborne. "I'll talk to them tomorrow if I can. Thursday, for sure. I think I can let you know by Thursday. Is that soon enough?"

"Thursday will be fine," said Dr. Holt.

"Thursday will be fine," said C. T. Lawson.

Clayborne spent the rest of the evening struggling with himself. He knew that the two former superintendents at Meridian had been fired after serving only two years each, and he had no idea why they had been dismissed. He also knew that taking on the assignment of a larger school district such as Meridian was the next logical step in his career.

Wednesday he spent talking in turn with the members of the Walnut Springs school board and they all agreed to let him go. But Gus Morrison spoke the magic words: "W. C., you've been the best man we've ever had and you'll be hard to replace. But we'd be ungrateful to hold you back from an opportunity like going down to Meridian. We'll arrange to find a new superintendent somehow if you'll agree to work half a day here for a month or so while our new man learns the ropes. You go ahead and tell Mr. Lawson and Dr. Holt that you'll take their job. We'll work out the details later."

On September first, 1943, the Perry family pulled up stakes and moved down the Bosque River a little farther toward Waco to Meridian. They bought the house of former Superintendent Hensley at 404 North Main Street. Board of Education President Lawson sent a colored employee named Louis Crawford to do the moving at Mr. Lawson's personal expense. The Perrys had done their part for the war in Walnut Springs.

-19-

BATTLE NEAR AND FAR

hated to leave Walnut Springs, Oretta," said Clayborne over his morning coffee. "They were so good to us."

In spite of himself he looked out the dining room window and thought about this substantial new dwelling on Meridian's Main Street, relishing the feel of it all: a stucco abode with a *floor furnace* — a real Cadillac of a home — the pecan trees in his yard, the neat rows of houses on the tree-lined thoroughfare only two blocks from downtown, the more affluent community, the very *size* of his new hometown.

"Oh, I was sad, too," Oretta replied. "I'll miss all those folks, the Adamses and the Morrisons and the Heartsills and everybody. But it was getting time to move on Clayborne. You've finished your master's degree now, and that ought to count for something."

"You know what, Oretta? This new job means that we'll be out of debt soon. After all those years of struggling, I think we're going to be comfortable now. Remember that letter from Pioneer Savings and Loan yesterday?"

"Yes, what about it?"

"It was the approval for our note on the house here. They'll take the $900 we got for the house at Iredell as down payment. . ."

"I'll miss having that house there," said Oretta wistfully.

"We weren't doing anything with it, just renting it out, you know. I don't think we'd ever have any reason to live there again, do you?"

"No, but it's just the idea of having our own house somewhere."

"Well, *this* is our own house now. And the payments are going to be $43.50 a month, including principal and interest, five percent interest."

"Can we afford that?"

"We sure can. That forty-dollar increase in salary just about took care of our whole house payment. And we got about five hundred dollars for the furniture that Superintendent Hensley included with the house."

"Do you have any idea why he let all his good furniture go with the house?"

"Just what he told me. He said he was getting a furnished house when he moved away — after resigning here."

"After getting fired, you mean. Does that worry you, Clayborne? They seem to go through school superintendents pretty fast here in Meridian."

"It's too soon to worry, Oretta. I'm so busy trying to run both school systems I don't have time to worry — work 'til noon in Walnut Springs, then the rest of the day here in Meridian. Just getting the new school year off and running smoothly is hard enough. But it's been a couple of weeks now and everything seems fine so far. I sure hope we find a new man for Walnut Springs pretty soon. This is a rough schedule."

"Don't work yourself sick, now."

"I won't. But I feel like working hard, Oretta. Mr. Lawson and the board here have given us a big chance, you know. I think about that all the time. I'm thirty-three years old now, thirty-three years old, Oretta. I feel like it's time I really *did* something for the people who've helped us, really *did* something."

"Don't you fret about that, Clayborne Perry. I know you. You're just plain good for people. You just be your natural self and everything will come out fine. You'll see."

"Well, I'm not taking any chances. Tonight I'm going to go visit some more of the businessmen here in town, introduce myself, get to know them, see how they're doing with their gas rationing and such. I think I'll drop by Sheppard's Drug Store and Benson's Food Market and Brantley's Barber Shop and maybe see Eddie Paulson at his insurance company, and. . ."

Oretta laughed out loud. "You see?" she smiled. "You see? Just be your natural self. Now, you'd better get on up to Walnut Springs this morning before you're late."

He found Gus Morrison waiting for him in his office at Walnut Springs school.

"Good morning, Superintendent Perry," he said, beaming. "Things are looking up. The war's going better, did you hear? Italy surrendered. Hitler's lost a lot of his muscle."

"Heard it on the radio. Everybody's breathing a little easier now."

"And you can breathe easier pretty soon. I think we've found our man."

"Let me guess: you talked W. W. Williams into taking the job. Right?"

"Right you are."

"He's a fine educated man, Mr. Morrison. Mighty fine. I've been thinking about him for the last week or so myself. He's a good mature man, sir, maybe fifty years old. And he's unemployed just now. When can he start?"

"Well, we're talking to him about that right now. He'll have to write Austin and make sure his credentials are in order, but that won't be any trouble. He ought to be ready about the first of October, just another week or two."

"Well, I certainly hope you have a good year here in Walnut Springs, I sure do. You folks have been mighty good to me. I'll take care of showing Mr. Williams around, let him know where all our files are, make sure he's ready to take command."

"We'll do our part to groom him up, too. Don't you worry. You know, Superintendent Perry, our first football game of the year is coming right up this week. We're playing Meridian, you know?"

"Oh, yes, I knew. Everybody keeps asking me since I'm superintendent of both school systems which team I'm going to root for."

"Well?"

"You know, it's hard to decide after being here for so long and everybody treating me so fine. But I've moved my Masonic Lodge membership and everything. I'm going to be living in Meridian now, so I think it's only fair if I root for them."

"I knew it, W. C. I'd do the same. Now I'll let you get on with your half-day here so you can get down there to Meridian and make sure your team is ready for us. You better hope they've got some big ol' farm boys, you sure better!"

That languid Texas September afternoon the sun slanted into Clayborne's first floor office window in the old Meridian Junior College Building, a 1909-vintage gothic stone fantasia of turrets and parapets now housing the town's high school. Classes met on only two of its three ample stories; the remarkable old edifice had been allowed to run down so that neglect left its upper floor to the cobwebs and mice. Superintendent Perry gazed out into the sunlight over the tree-dotted campus to the grammar school, pausing briefly in his long day to muse on nothing in particular, getting ready to close up shop. A delegation of youngsters and adults appeared outside his door.

"Superintendent Perry?" asked a woman tentatively, seeming unsure whether she and her associates should walk in.

"Yes? What can I do for you?"

"I'm Mrs. Gates and this is my girl Peggy. These are some students and parents. Could we talk to you for a minute?"

"Of course," said Clayborne. "Come on in, all of you."

A dozen people filed into his small office, identifying themselves as they entered. A husky, good looking young man introduced himself as Joe Montgomery.

"Isn't your daddy sheriff here?" Clayborne asked.

"Yes, sir."

"And aren't you the captain of the football team?"

"Yes, sir."

The group crowded his office space. Clayborne did not let his surprise show when the grammar school principal, Mrs. Clara Richards, came in quietly at the tag end. He knew Mrs. Richards as a forceful woman of some means who had once served in the elective office of county superintendent — and her father was Mr. Angus French, the same Mr. French from whom he had rented his family's first apartment in Iredell. Mrs. Richards' presence in this group reminded Clayborne how green and fragile his hold on authority was here in Meridian. He turned to face the students, the football team captain in particular: "Joe, I hope you fellows win this first game against Walnut Springs. I'm for you, you know that."

"Thank you, sir," the young man said uncertainly.

Clayborne told everyone, "I'm just sorry there's not enough chairs so you folks can have a seat."

Mrs. Gates replied, "We'll stand, if you don't mind. This won't take long."

"Well, what's on your mind?"

"Superintendent Perry," began Mrs. Gates, the obvious leader of the delegation, "we'd like to ask you about a touchy subject." She spoke nervously and her tone set Clayborne a little on edge. He was taken completely by surprise at her next words: "It's about a school sock hop."

"A sock hop? You mean a dance?" he asked. *What kind of touchy subject is a dance?*

Peggy Gates, a vivacious and sparkling young woman, spoke up: "Sir, some of us here in the senior class would like to ask permission so we can hold a dance in the school gym. We'd play some Glenn Miller records and Jimmy Dorsey numbers, just the usual things." She stood waiting for a reaction, as if she were a little gun-shy. Everyone in the room, students, parents and teachers alike, watched their new superintendent apprehensively.

Clayborne sat on the edge of his desk, looking back at them, sensing their discomfort, feeling puzzled and uncomfortable himself. He asked, "Well, have you spoken to our acting high school principal?"

"It's not that, sir," said young Joe Montgomery. "Mrs. Adkins has no objection, but. . ." His voice trailed off.

Peggy's mother said, "We've had some trouble in the past, sir.

Superintendent Hensley never allowed the students to use the gym for a dance."

"Couldn't he get chaperones?" asked Clayborne, his puzzlement deepening.

"He objected to dancing, sir," said Mrs. Gates. "He's very religious. Church of Christ, I think. They don't countenance dancing at all. There was some trouble about it."

A short woman broke in, "Mr. Perry, I'm Mrs. Bill Curtis. My husband runs the Meridian Ice and Cold Storage Company, you know, the turkey dressing plant. Let's be frank with him, Mrs. Gates. Mr. Perry, last year when my Bobby was a senior, his class held their own dances down by Lake Meridian. They did some of this jitterbug stuff, you know, the boogie-woogie and such. They sang some of those silly songs like "Der Fuehrer says Ve iss der Master Race." Just harmless fun. Mr. Hensley wanted to punish them for it. We fought with him for two years about dancing. We don't see anything wrong with a properly held school dance. The kids in this town have to have something to do. But he simply wouldn't hear of it. That's why he got fired."

Clayborne tried not to let his astonishment show. "Over school dances?" he asked as evenly as he could.

Mrs. Gates said, "I didn't think the school board would tell you when they brought you in, sir. But you need to know about it. It was terrible. It was like those sniper battles with the Japs you hear about on the radio. Everybody got to bickering. It affected everything, teachers, pupils, everything, Mr. Perry. It didn't matter what the high school principal or the teachers or the pupils thought. That's why we came to talk to you in private."

"I see," said Clayborne, now standing and pacing with his hands clasped behind his back. He thought rapidly for a long tense moment as he paced. *Dancing! Mr. Hensley was fired over dancing!* So this was the policy briar patch that he had half suspected. *Nobody told me about this.* He knew what havoc it could wreak if he mishandled these people. *This kind of quibbling could go on for years if I don't put a stop to it.* He knew how tenuous his grasp on the school was after only a few days on the job. *I can't let the students and parents just take over running the school. But I can't just ignore them, either.* He knew he had to be firm yet flexible. But how?

"Chaperoned dances have been held in school gyms around Texas for years," he said, looking squarely at his little audience. "To be honest with you folks, I didn't know dancing was such an issue in the Meridian schools. So I'm going to do this: I'll take it up with the Board of Education and we'll get a decision for you. If they turn it down, you'll take it fair and square and not make a fuss. If they approve, *and* if you can find legitimate sponsors *and* responsible chaperones *and* set reasonable hours, I'll let you hold your sock-hop. Is that fair?"

"Fair?" asked Mrs. Gates, "that's wonderful, Mr. Perry!"

The little office buzzed with excitement. Principal Richards, who had stayed in the background, smiled openly. Mrs. Curtis said, "You're a very reasonable man."

"Now, don't think this means we're going to have any loose discipline around here," said the superintendent sternly as his visitors turned to leave. They stopped to look at him.

"I expect nothing but the best effort from our students, and from our teachers and from our parents. Mrs. Gates, we could use somebody with your energy on the PTA. I'd be pleased if you'd volunteer. Mrs. Curtis, even though your boy is out of school now, you might consider leading our War Bond drive this year. Mrs. Richards, would you make a note to remind these ladies in the next few weeks that we'd appreciate their good help? And Joe, don't forget, I expect a victory Friday night, you hear?"

"Yes, sir," the boy said, all grins. "Yes, sir, Superintendent Perry!"

The school board duly approved properly sponsored school dances by a vote of 7 to 0. The first sock hop at Meridian High School in many years came off two weeks later without a hitch. Student enthusiasm ran high and the new superintendent had passed his first policy crisis with great community credit and thanks. Two weeks afterward another dance was held in the school gymnasium, but the crowd was smaller and the enthusiasm less intense. Another dance followed in another two weeks and the crowd that showed up hardly deserved the name. The pressure for school dances had been relieved and the demand dwindled accordingly. The issue was settled.

One day not long after the dancing delegation's visit, as Clayborne rummaged through the school files in a continuing effort to familiarize himself with the ins and outs of his new job, he spotted a copy of a letter that he hadn't seen before. It was dated May 20, 1943. He took it out and examined it. He sat down at his desk and read in disbelief. Here was the letter of warning that Meridian schools would be officially placed on probationary status by the State Department of Public Education. Attached was a list of scholastic deficiencies and community conflict situations that demanded remedy. Meridian schools, the attachment soberly announced, would lose their state accreditation if timely corrections were not forthcoming. Shock. Then realization. He didn't bother to wonder why the school board had given him no idea how low the system at Meridian had sunk. He realized very pragmatically how much he was on the spot to pull his schools up out of the mire. He told nobody about his discovery, not members of the school board, not even Oretta. He decided silently and simply to correct the situation by himself, once and for all.

Sunday, October 10, 1943, Clayborne drove to his parents' home near

Hico and brought his sightless father to the little Meridian hospital run by Dr. Holt. The kidney attacks were getting worse and Tom had grown frail and feeble. By Wednesday the treatment had produced no improvement. Clayborne stopped by the hospital after work that evening.

The doctor was blunt: "Mr. Perry, there's nothing for it. Your father's urine still shows too much infection. There's nothing we can do. His song's about sung. You don't need to say anything, but I think you've probably run out of money anyway — don't tell me you're not paying for him, because I know you are. You take your daddy home, sir, and let him die in peace."

It was bad for the next few days. Neighbors came in, sat up with Tom all night, helped Belle take care of him. He drifted steadily downward. Clayborne and his family visited nearly every day. During the afternoon of Wednesday the 20th, the crisis came. Tom cried out in his blindness and pain. The heedless Texas sun shone down on his little farm. After some hours of agony, Thomas Bunyon Perry died. With simple sorrow the helping neighbors prepared his body as the sliding orange disk of the sun silhouetted liveoaks out the farmhouse door. They dressed him in his blue serge suit and laid him out on a little cot in the bedroom. The undertaker from Hico quickly came with an ambulance and took his body to the funeral home where it was laid in a wooden casket with a gray velvet outer cover. According to the custom of the times the body was returned immediately to the Perry farm house in the ebbing light.

Clayborne and Oretta and Bob and Margie travelled the paved road from Meridian to Hico that evening after work at dusk as they had in the suffering days before, not knowing of the afternoon's fateful event. When they arrived, Belle said, "Clayborne, your Papa's dead." They went and viewed Tom in his casket in the parlor. It was after dark when the family went in one by one to pay him their last respects. Young Bob watched at the parlor door as his father went in, stood a moment looking into the casket and then kneeled beside the bier.

Clayborne stared down at the lifeless face. He felt the awesome power of death hovering about. He was not afraid. He simply looked. And looked. Somehow death had smoothed the trouble lines deposited by the years on that worn face. Peace rested upon Tom's countenance. It was almost as if the time-storm that killed him had itself been vanquished now, as if time had here been defeated by eternity.

I loved you so much. I couldn't stand seeing you die.

Bob peered into the chilly room and saw only the outward signs, his father down on one knee leaning over his dead grandfather and looking, looking on that dear face. Clayborne loosed his voiceless grief, not wailing or crying out, but in simple dignity leaning lovingly over Tom where he looked and looked and breathed and breathed with long deep sighs time and time again.

Go to your rest, my wonderful Papa.

The funeral service began at three the next afternoon in Hico First Baptist Church. Half an hour later the burial party drove to Hico cemetery on the hill east above town. Tom's brothers Leonard and Pitchford came with their families from Midlothian and brought their father Jim Perry. Tom's sister Julia Russell came with her husband Arthur. Oretta's parents, the Partains came. Oretta's younger brother J. D. helped dig the grave, as did John Guinn, Oretta's sister Erah's husband, along with several neighbor men. Hoyt and his family came. Clayborne and his family came. Some teachers from Iredell and Meridian came. Belle stood alone. The little band filled the cemetery and the scrub prairie around it with their memories of the gentle, striving, questing, strong, tenacious, doomed man in the casket. They felt his spirit near.

All bent with sadness waiting for the diggers to finish the grave. The men ran into a hard ledge of limestone about five feet into the earth. Their picks and shovels could not cut the rock, could not break through, as if the tools were reluctant to let them say this goodbye, to permit a final farewell to this good man today. The burial party had waited nearly an hour when Clayborne and Belle made the decision to cease more work and lay the coffin to rest a foot shallower than custom held. And so Tom was laid in the ground and the pastor of Hico's First Baptist Church said the words over the grave. Heavy grief floated to heaven. Hoyt sorrowed most openly. Clayborne gazed in silence at the wooden casket. Nadine and Dorothy stood in silence. Tears were flowing openly and unashamedly. Papa was gone.

Dear God, thank You for our Papa.

The autumn sun that day struck the sailing wings of a golden eagle hunting from nesting crags north in Chalk Mountain, casting its shadow in downward rays of benediction across the wide Grand Prairie.

Belle Perry stayed by herself on the farm a while, then sold it and bought a house on Avenue B in Hico.

The radio announcer asked, "Is the sweatheart you married the husband you expected him to be? Has the war created new problems for you in your marriage?"

In clipped radio diction and stentorian yet smarmy tones, he went on, "To answer these and other personal problems brought in by your friends and neighbors, Arrid presents John J. Anthony, founder of the famed Marital Relations Institute, in a brand new program of daily sessions of kindly and helpful advice. Just as Mr. Anthony by examples in this studio is helping thousands of men and women solve their personal problems,

Arrid, too, is helping thousands to solve the personal problem of underarm perspiration. . ."

"Hi, Mom," called Bob at the back door. "Can me and LB here have a snack?"

Oretta stacked the dishes on her kitchen sink's drain board and turned to look at her son standing in the rear entryway. "Of course you can," she said over the sound of the radio. "Come on in."

She wiped her hands and turned the radio off as the two jacketed boys trooped in. Margie tottered in sleepily from her bedroom at the sound of her brother's voice. She clutched a rag doll under her arm.

"Now, who is this young man LB?" Oretta asked about the country waif in roughscuff garments.

Bob proudly declaimed, "This is my friend Bobby Pounds, Mom. He lives down by the Purina Feed store."

"Where's that?" she asked.

"You know, Mom, over by Mr. Lawson's feed store and the gin."

Oretta recognized the southeast part of town; it was not prime residential property.

"Well, hello, Bobby Pounds," she said. "Pleased to meet you. And this is Bob's sister Margie."

"Hello, Mrs. Perry," said the open-faced lad. "Hello, Margie."

"Hi," said the four-year-old, giggling and burying her face in the doll's midriff.

"Don't mind her," said Bob. "She's just bashful."

"How come Bob calls you 'LB,' Bobby?" Oretta asked.

Bob answered for his friend: "Aw, Mom, that's easy. 'LB' stands for *pounds*. Him and his mother and brother moved here just before we did. We're both new kids in town."

"Well, you new kids come on in and have some milk and some peanut butter on bread. And look there out in the driveway, Bob, your dad's coming home early today."

"Dad! Wait'll you meet my dad, Bobby!"

In a few seconds Clayborne stepped in the back door, said hello to Margie and glanced at the young visitor. "Hello, there, Bobby. How are you today?"

The boy was a little intimidated, but smiled and said, "I'm fine, Mr. Perry."

"Do you already know Bobby, Dad?" asked Bob.

"I see him in your class at the grammar school now and again. How do you like Meridian by now, Bobby?"

"Just fine."

Oretta said, "You're home early, Clayborne."

"I had to go to the draft board this afternoon."

The love between them could be felt in the air, but there was no kiss or outward sign of affection as husband and wife greeted each other. The customary Texas reserve had, if anything, stiffened during the war. But Margie came over and hugged one of her father's legs.

Oretta said to Clayborne, "Come on in the kitchen and tell me all about it while I make a sandwich for these two starving boys. Margie, you come along, too."

Bob yelled, "LB and me are goin' out to look at my chicken coop, Mom!"

"Can I go out, too, Mom?" asked Margie.

"No, you leave them alone. Bob, I'll call you when your eats are ready." The back door slammed and its screen door flapped in the boys' wake.

"Why does Bob call him LB?" asked Clayborne.

"Stands for pounds," Oretta said knowingly. "Clayborne, what did the draft board say?"

"They were real nice. Said it'd be best for the community if I stayed here and ran a good school. I guess that leaves just me and Lester Smith. Looks like the superintendent and ag teacher are going to be the only men on staff, just like at Walnut. Well, except for Joe Cureton."

"Who's that?" she asked, getting the bread out of the metal breadbox. "Margie, do you want some peanut butter on bread?"

"Yes, Mom."

"Joe Cureton's the new football coach. Just a young fellow, only graduated high school himself last spring. Army turned him down for the draft. We just pay him a little something, not regular salary. His daddy's a lawyer with his office down near the court house."

"So the draft board isn't going to call you up?"

"Guess not, not yet, anyway. That could all change, though, you know."

"I know. Who is that boy Bob brought home?" She scooped peanut butter out of a jar and spread it gingerly on three slices of bread.

"Bobby? Oh, he's about the poorest kid in school, him and his younger brother Billy. They've got no daddy and their mother works housemaid for Mrs. Odle."

"The Odle that runs the dry goods store?" She poured three glasses of milk while Margie fidgeted on the chair.

"Yep. Mr. Markman that owns the Purina feed store told me he rents them a little ol' bitty one-room house for five dollars a month, has a tin roof, no bathroom, not painted. You know, Oretta, that's the kind of folks that need help most and are likely to get it least. And you give him plenty of peanut butter there. That Bobby is a pretty bright kid, but something must have gone wrong — he's in Bob's class, but he's a year older, must have failed a grade somewhere."

Oretta set three plates and three glasses of milk on the breakfast nook table and opened the back door. "Bob! Snack's ready. And you be good to Margie, let her sit with the two of you, you hear?"

"Yes, Ma'am." The boys scampered to their places and Margie crawled up the side of her chair.

Oretta stood nose to nose with Clayborne and tapped him on the lapel, saying, "Don't forget we're going to have supper again at the Lawson's tonight and you've got a lodge meeting tomorrow night."

"Oh, that's right. I almost forgot!"

"Are we going to Mr. Lawson's, too?" asked Bob.

"You and Margie are going, too," said his mother.

The Lawsons had taken a liking to the Perrys. It was their second dinner invitation in as many months. Again that winter evening, Margie enjoyed the fancy high chair she got to sit in; young Bob wondered why the Lawsons waited so late to have supper; and Oretta noticed how differently the Lawsons ate, how generous they were to serve finer cuts of meat, how savory the sauces, how sophisticated the desserts Mrs. Lawson prepared — in all, impressive and a little mystifying, the closest thing to gourmet cooking she'd ever experienced.

Clayborne had observed for several months now that his hosts spoke impeccably correct English and that their lilting Texas speech sounded modulated and refined, but still Texas. In the middle of the evening meal, while he was telling the Lawsons one of his favorite family stories, Clayborne realized that it was not Texas that education and position had smoothed out of their voices, but *country*. These were not country people. But they seemed to enjoy country people.

Clayborne went on with his story. "Grandpa Charley Blackburn's second child was named Bethel," he said with a twinkle. "She married this country boy named Charlie Slaughter — he was one of nine children. Now this Charlie Slaughter was a good accomplished horse racer from what I've been told. Before I was born, I guess it must about been some time around 1900, he used to go up north to St. Louis and Kansas City to race horses every year. He'd usually come home with a purse of at least five hundred dollars. In those days that was just a huge sum of money, and ol' Charlie usually bought a store building in Hico after each successful race. You could buy a store building for five hundred dollars then. He'd rent out the stores for five dollars a month and had a nice income."

Sam Lawson said over the fine china table setting, "Mr. Perry, you told us your Grandpa was a strong Christian man. What did he think of his daughter marrying a horse racer, a gambler?"

Clayborne smiled, "Well, Charlie Slaughter's kind of horseracing seemed to be okay, because I can't recall any member of the family thinking Uncle Charlie's money was bad."

"I see," grinned Sam Lawson. "That's quite a family. Where did you all live?"

"Up by Camp Branch. But the real name of Camp Branch was Dude Flat."

"Dude Flat?" asked Mrs. Floy Lawson. "I can't place it."

"Oh," said Clayborne with mock-surprise, "I thought everybody knew where Dude Flat is. Let me tell you so you'll remember for sure. Dude Flat is bound by Brittain Chapel on the west, Rocky on the south, Blackstump Valley on the east, and Louse Hill on the north."

"You're hoo-rawing me, Mr. Perry," Mrs. Lawson laughed. "I never heard of any of those places."

"Well, just to the north and west of Dude Flat was Duffau."

"Duffau I've heard of."

"Yes, and you'd think Duffau would have heard of me, because I went to school first at Dude Flat, then at Duffau and finally at Hico high school. But I never really knew where I was from because the Duffau people called me the Perry boy from Hico and the Hico people called me the Perry boy from Duffau, so I guess I was really from Dude Flat, Texas."

"Mrs. Perry," said Mrs. Lawson, "your husband tells better stories than the radio."

Oretta blushed and looked at her brimming plate. She was still the slow eater.

Sam Lawson said, "I agree, my dear. But, tell me, Mr. Perry — and I don't mean to talk shop at supper — how's the school system coming along?"

"Just fine. Smooth. Right now I'm thinking about recommending to the board that you hire Lee Erickson as the girls' basketball coach." Clayborne prepared to take another bite of veal cutlet. "Can you tell me anything about him?"

"Well, I know he's never gone to college," said Lawson. "He's working for Bill Curtis down at the turkey dressing plant right now. He seems to be bright enough and a diligent worker, a strong man."

"Good," said Clayborne, "glad to hear he's strong, because he's going to have to work as the school janitor, too."

Sam Lawson smiled wryly. "They call them school engineers nowadays."

"Oh, yes," Clayborne smiled back. "School engineers."

"I think Lee will do a good job. I'm sure the board will approve him. And have you visited the colored school yet, Mr. Perry?"

"Yes, sir," Clayborne said. "I've been over there several times to see how Mrs. Crawford's doing. She could use some new textbooks and it's a . . . Well, they have an adequate little one-room building."

"You can be candid with me, Mr. Perry. I know the building is run down. Do you know how we acquired the colored school, Mr. Perry?"

"No, sir, I don't."

"It was originally an outbuilding of Meridian Junior College. It came with the sixty-acre campus when the school board bought the college out after it closed in 1927."

Mrs. Lawson asked, "Really, dear? I didn't know that."

"Yes, indeed. When the junior college failed for lack of students the school board paid, what was it, four thousand, six thousand dollars, something like that, and bought the whole kit and kaboodle. Including the grammar school, which was built in 1912, and the gym and what we now use as the high school, which was built in 1908."

Clayborne said, "Why that's two years before I was born. That building's thirty-five years old."

"And you're in much better shape than our school buildings, Mr. Perry. We've let things run down. The colored school has run down faster than the other buildings, I'm afraid. In our fair state it is the coloreds' unfortunate lot to get their schooling in separate but equal facilities as the law provides. I imagine one could make a case that the colored school receives a share of our annual budget equal to their numbers, but . . ." He paused, recognizing he was treading on a taboo subject. "How many students does Mrs. Crawford have this year?"

"She has twenty-five in her class, Mr. Lawson, counting all eight grades. But I do wonder about something."

"What's that, Mr. Perry?"

"Where do the colored students go after eighth grade? I don't know of any colored high school in Bosque County."

"Ah, yes. That's because there is none. The eighth grade is the end of their educational road. Unfortunate."

"That is too bad."

"Mr. Perry, did colored people live where you grew up at Dude Flat?"

"No, sir. And there wasn't a colored person in Hico or Duffau or Iredell or anywhere."

"I see. Yet you don't seem bothered being around colored people. In fact you seem to have a certain feeling for them."

"You seem to get along fine with them yourself."

"Oh, yes. Always have. Since I was a boy. I have many friends and customers over behind the school in Niggertown." — so every black ghetto in small-town Texas was called in those days — "And you know I've got a colored man running my gin and feed store."

"Yes, sir, I remember Louis Crawford. He's the man that helped get us moved from Walnut Springs. He was very friendly and helpful. Is he any relation to Mrs. Crawford at the colored school?"

"Indeed he is. His brother Jim is Mary Crawford's husband. Jim's a cook at the Coffee Shop cafe downtown. And that reminds me of something ironic, Mr. Perry. You don't usually think of it, but a man came in the feed store this summer from New York, a Yankee. He asked why he saw colored people getting their food from the cafe on a plate at the back door. I told him it was the law. They couldn't come in and eat inside. But it made me think, Mr. Perry. Jim Crawford can work in the kitchen but he can't sit down at the counter. It just makes you think."

Sam Lawson mused with squinted eyes for a moment as if oblivious to the room and the forbidden subject. Clayborne sat uneasily. If he read his host correctly, Lawson was suggesting that state law might be unjust, an idea to be pondered. Then Sam's mood shifted. He smiled at his guests and said, "Bob, how do you like living in Meridian by now?"

"Oh, I like it fine, said the boy. "It's got the biggest school I've ever seen. There's the Capitol Theatre not two blocks from our house. There's four grocery stores and two drug stores and a doctor and Dad says there's even a dentist. It's got more streets to ride my bike on than Walnut Springs and Iredell put together. And the sign at the city limits says Population 1016. That's more than a *thousand* people! And the people are really nice. They have nicer houses, too. I think Meridian's keen!"

"You're a thoughtful, observant young man, Bob. You'll go far," said Sam Lawson.

Bob glowed in the compliment, noticing that his father seldom made such remarks to him. But he enjoyed this adult taking him seriously.

Mrs. Lawson brought in the evening's dessert.

"This is a Jell-O recipe that a good friend in Waco gave me," she announced. "It's blended with just the best wine sauce you ever tasted."

Bob watched his parents, knowing they had no use for alcohol. But neither his father nor mother made any comment. They ate their desserts as proper guests should.

As Clayborne ate his wined jello, he mulled over his son's feeling about the larger town, the more affluent community. Now he sensed clearly in himself the boy's attraction for this better life, yet he felt fiercely the iron bands of loyalty to his origins. Meridian had given him something by which to measure his origins, and that he found disturbing. Here he recently got his first inkling of what "cultured" might mean. Here he recently saw polite table manners of such refinement — settings with two forks — that it made him self-conscious. Here he recently found smooth speech and daily dignity and people who reeked of leadership and authority — and money. Here he recently saw finer furniture and beautiful possessions, not just in solitary homes scattered about, but in many households, an affluence broader and deeper than he had ever dreamed. None of this existed in his country past.

And that was what struck him so hard. This world of a higher social class had existed all along, he realized, not thirty miles from where he was born, right here in this town on a hill above the Bosque River, and he had been only dimly aware of it. And he now suspected that in the larger towns such as Waco the differences were even more pronounced. And Dallas and San Antonio and Houston must be truly unbelievable. His fellow country folk were for the most part totally unaware of it. Totally unaware, shamefully ignorant. But how could they know about this sophistication, this affluence, this scope? Their life, their labor, their being was absorbed day by day into the land, into the farm, into the soil, the soil endlessly demanding, scantily rewarding. He had lived it himself. He had escaped a lifetime at it only narrowly, and as much by lucky chance as by design.

This wide lovely Grand Prairie was a Trap, Clayborne thought, a beautiful, tempting Trap baited with cotton and grain and livestock and land you could own and ravishing summers and a tightly knit community of fellow country people. But how many of his students, he grimly mused, had ended their rural education with high school or grammar school or even less? And for what? To work on the land, to live the country life, to see your womenfolk grow old before their time, to give everything you had to that dirt, trying to make it produce something useful, as his father had. It wasn't the Grand Prairie itself, but rather the *country* that was a Trap, he concluded.

Maybe it was a Trap, but, oh, the country was a paradise too in its own way, the love, the closeness of wide-spaced neighbors, the pride of independence, the wise innocence, the toughness of wresting a living from the wholesome earth, the sense of knowing things directly, how the seasons turned and the crops struggled and the animals increased, the sense of community and the sense of place. Yet Clayborne had no special feeling for the place itself, but only for its role as a background for the human adventure. Yes, it was a paradise, but perhaps there came a time for everyone to escape from paradise, whether the idea sounded sacrilegious or not. Perhaps there was not an escape time. Not for everyone. He had escaped in a way. But he knew that the country's roots, the roots of paradise, would always remain in him. Perhaps the most he could ever achieve was to move at ease in both worlds, the town and the country. Perhaps that's what he should strive for. It was worth thinking about.

Clayborne finished his wined jello, left his spoon in the serving glass and said to Mrs. Lawson, "Ah! That was right nice."

One night at midnight the year of 1943 blended silently into 1944 and the mild winter lingered. Clayborne had in his four months at Meridian learned who ran things and who didn't. He did his best to enlist support for the school system from both those who ran things and those who didn't. He joined the community, became part of its daily life. He volunteered for tasks on the Board of Deacons of the local First Baptist Church. He began working his way through the chairs of Meridian's Masonic Lodge in the brick building at the corner of Erath and Morgan streets downtown.

Meridian's streets had names like those in Walnut Spring, but unlike the smaller town, Meridian had signs up so everybody knew what they were. Like most other towns in the Grand Prairie, Meridian had been laid out in a grid cocked off due north so its streets ran parallel to the skewed county lines. Main Street, the in-town portion of State Road 144, trended from northwest to southeast, with only two streets to westward before the hill dipped off into the Bosque River. Main was flanked on the west by Erath and on the east by Bosque Street, and in the heart of town Main crossed Morgan, the southwest-northeast trending arterial. Morgan was flanked on the north by Hamilton and on the south by River Street. The county court house lay on the square downtown between Morgan and River where Bateman Street crossed them.

The schools had been planted on the old junior college campus, a part of town to the northeast with its own street grid where the grammar school fronted Second Street (northwest to southeast) between A Street and C Street (southwest to northeast). The colored school lay to the northeast of the white schools on F Street right on the edge of Niggertown, an enclave encompassed by H Street northward and F Street southward, and by C Street westward and State Road 174 eastward. Downtown, Morgan Street extended southwest over the Bosque River bridge and became State Road 22 to Cranfills Gap (13 miles) and Hamilton (32 miles). A half mile southwest of the town square, State Road 22 intersected State Road 6 to Hico westward (23 miles) and Waco eastward (45 miles). The cloverleaf intersection of these two paved roads had become known simply as The Circle, and now a few commercial outliers of Meridian were beginning to spring up there to take advantage of the traffic, including the Circle Cafe. As in many Grand Prairie towns, everyone was absolutely certain that the streets ran due north and south and east and west, which gave them peculiar ideas about where things were located, ideas that often baffled outsiders unfortunate enough to ask them for directions.

Meridian seemed to bring out the best in Clayborne. He matured a personal style all his own now, his manner sharpened and solidified into a distinctive trademark. Everybody recognized his smiling, easy-going, friendly exterior and came to know the muscular determination that lay beneath. His astute handling of the school dance issue had won him wide community liking and his methodical insistence on classroom excellence had won him wide community respect. When faced with unpleasant choices, he made the tough decisions quickly without flinching. In January, rather than continue offering a class in physics without a qualified teacher, he chose to eliminate the course altogether. When dealing with discipline on the sports field, he let things alone until the students strayed beyond a certain point, then brought them back in no uncertain terms. Once when he found it necessary to expel a high school student for disrupting classes, he was quietly, absolutely adamant, and the school board stood behind him, so that despite parental pleas and threats the boy stayed expelled. And even in his relations with the school board he soon showed his personal power of leadership; he let them know that he was loyal to their goals but more and more found his own ways and means without consulting them. When he could get the job done with smiling soft-voiced requests to his subordinates, he did. When the job demanded that he boss people around, he did. And the job was always accomplished.

On February 10, State School Supervisor W. C. Perkins forwarded his report to Austin:

Last year this school was warned because of the unsettled condition throughout the system. Sufficient evidence is now available that a satisfactory school is in progress to warrant a request that the Department remove this condition. The Board of Education, Superintendent and faculty seem to be cooperating in every way to build a good school program and the Deputy has no doubt that such will be accomplished in time. A capable Superintendent has been selected and control of the school placed in his hands. Good results are noticeable.

The curriculum is satisfactory and meets the need of the community. Some courses will likely have to be dropped next year, as there will not be not enough student demand for them. The policy of offering some courses every other year will take care of this problem.

Instruction in the Meridian school is average, and some very good papers and notebooks were examined. English, both written and usage, needs careful attention throughout the school. Each teacher should grade on English the same as subject matter. The school must become English conscious.

The school is commended for its effort in the salvage program, its bond and stamp sales, its Red Cross work, and the infantile paralysis campaign. The war films are used each week and increased interest is manifested in them. It is recommended that the Texas School of the Air be used when adequate radio equipment permits.

The State Department of Education appreciates the effort of this community and its school officials in bringing this school up to required standards.

Signed: W. C. Perkins

By May, Meridian schools were officially removed from probation. Clayborne took profound pleasure in being able to announce the fact to the public.

"Clayborne, come look at this," said Oretta one day in June as she stood by the back window at 404 North Main Street.

"Just a minute. I'm figuring out the ration stamps we can get for the school lunch program," said her husband from his paperwork-plastered desk.

"That lunchroom program is going to be there when school starts again, but this is going to be over pretty quick. Come look."

Clayborne reluctantly got up and clumped to the window. "What is it?" he grumped, looking outside.

"I think Mr. Nevin is giving Bob a lesson in business. Listen."

Out in Bob's backyard chicken coop, A. C. Nevin casually sauntered around the inside perimeter with the youngster, his hands in his pockets, nodding his head at the boy occasionally but most of the time watching hens and chicks as they managed to stay out from under foot. The natural-born horse-trader had been talking about the entrepreneurial life to the boy, inquiring now and then about buying some chicks. Bob listened to him intently:

"You know," Nevin said, "I think I'd like some of these little banty chickens. They lay cute little bitty eggs. What'll you sell me some of these banty chicks for?"

The boy walked around with the farmer, calculating in his head. "Well, let's see," he said, "I think I can sell you this bunch here for about ten cents each. This hen has a dozen chicks." Bob knew he could make a tidy profit by selling at ten cents each.

Nevin kept walking around the chicken yard, Bob by his side. "Did you build this chicken house by yourself, Bob?" he asked.

"Yes, sir. My Dad bought the lumber and nails and I did all the work myself. Well, most of it. It's six by eight. Keeps the varmints out."

"Mmm," said the man noncommitally. "Did you hear about the big invasion at Normandy the other day? Looks like the Allies have ol' Hitler on the run."

"I heard about it on the radio, sir. It came on in the middle of one of my programs. Jack Armstrong was just about to catch this Nazi spy" — Nazi of course, prounounced "Naeh-zee" rather than "Not-see" in Texan — "when the bulletin man broke in and told about the Normandy war. I wish he'd waited 'til the program was over."

"War news is very important, son."

"That's what my Dad says, too."

"I guess you'd rather sell chickens, though, eh?"

"Yes, sir."

"Ten cents each, eh, boy?"

"Yes, sir."

"That's good. I like the price. But they're kind of young yet, don't you think? What would you charge me to feed 'em, take care of 'em until they're big enough to take away from their mother?"

Bob kept a straight face but inwardly broke into a sweat. He did not know how to calculate the cost of feed over time. He realized that his sale could be ruined by hesitation, so he confidently said, "I'll do it for a penny a day for the whole batch." That sounded like enough.

"And you'll keep them in the pen, not let them fly all over the neighborhood when they get bigger?"

"Yes, sir, I'll do it. How long do you want me to keep them for you?"

"I'd say about three more weeks, wouldn't you?"

"Three weeks. Yes, sir."

"Is it a deal, then?"

"It's a deal."

Clayborne said to Oretta as he walked back to the overflowing desk, "I think you got me up to watch Bob get skinned."

Oretta said wryly. "I think I did."

Three weeks later Nevin settled up with the boy. Bob was obligated to run around the chicken coop and catch the dozen banties. Nevin took them with a smile.

When the farmer drove away, Clayborne stepped into the back yard and asked Bob, "How'd you come out on that deal with Mr. Nevin?"

The boy looked sourly after the vanishing Ford pickup truck taking his banty chickens away. "Not too good, Dad. I lost money feeding those birds for three weeks. If he'd just taken them with him the day we made the deal. . ."

"He makes his living buying and selling, son. Cows, horses, sheep, chickens, you name it. He's a shrewd negotiator. Did you learn anything from him?"

"I sure did. When he starts talking about everything except the deal, he's thinking up a way for you to spend money and him not to."

"Are you sure you've got everything, Bob?" his mother asked in the midmorning Texas sun.

"Oh, quit pestering him," said Clayborne with a grin. "He's got everything. It's just a train ride to Texas City." The resting locomotive chuffed in readiness as passengers boarded the few grimy cars at the little station on Highway 22 just east of town.

"I want to go on the train," complained Margie.

"You can't go this time, squirt," said the almost-twelve-year-old as he stood on the platform with his little suitcase. "I'm fine, Mom. I've got my clothes and I've got 'Deen's address and I've got the nice sack lunch you fixed me."

"Do you have your train ticket?"

"Yes, Mom, I've got my train ticket."

"And your money?"

"The five-dollar bill is right here." He waved it proudly.

"And don't forget to call us after you get there. Do you remember our telephone number?"

"Mom!" squeaked the youngster, "Of course I remember my own phone number! It's Meridian 152!"

"I know our phone number, too, Mom," crowed four-year-old Margie. "It's 152."

"For pity's sake, Oretta," said Clayborne. "How can he call us if Nadine doesn't have a phone?"

"Well," said the broody mother, "He can call from somewhere else, a pay phone. I just want to make sure he's got everything he needs. I wouldn't be so easy about it, Clayborne. Remember just last week you got sunstroke yourself because you didn't bring a hat to pick cotton in."

"Oh, now, that was nothing," said Clayborne a little sheepishly, "maybe just some indigestion."

"It was sunstroke and you know it, Mister Perry. You can't be too careful. Now, Bob," she said, "you know where to get off the train?"

"Yes, Ma'am, in Hitchcock after we go through Houston. It's the stop closest to Texas City."

"Okay, and like your father says, remember your Aunt Nadine and Uncle Henry don't have a phone in Texas City, so you'll have to save some of your money for a pay phone call home. Don't spend it all on the train."

"Yes, Ma'am. I think I'd better get on now. They might leave without me."

"Go ahead, son," said Clayborne. "Be sure and tell Nadine and Henry hello for us. And tell them to write more often."

"Do you think I'll be able to see any fireworks, Dad?"

"Your train won't get to Hitchcock until about 9:30, so I imagine if you watch out the car window on the Houston side, you might see some. They're supposed to have a big display down there every Fourth of July. But with the war and all I don't know how big it'll be."

"Okay, Dad, I'll watch close anyway."

The boy packed his suitcase up the steps and into the coach car. He reappeared momentarily inside the car, framed by a soot-stained window.

"Oh, Clayborne," said Oretta, "I hope Nadine got your two-penny post card in all this Fourth of July mail."

"I don't see why they wouldn't. I mailed it two days ago. I'm sure they know he's coming."

The conductor at the end car cried, "All aboard!"

"Bye-bye, Bobby!" yelled Margie at the boy's grin showing through the smudged window. The train jerked forward and pulled slowly out of the small-town station, taking the cindery image of Bob with it.

"Goodbye!" shouted Oretta.

"So long," called Clayborne.

Bob settled in for his long train ride, the longest he'd ever taken. With his sack lunch open and a sandwich for munching he eyed the men in uniform seated here and there among the civilians and then tried to see through the bleary window. He could make out the low rolling hills of Central Texas flashing under the high sun, the limestone rock sizzling white, the air too almost white in the heat, the bunchgrass brown already in early July, the liveoaks looking scrubby gray in their clustering groves. He rolled and swayed with the train down the track alongside cattle behind barbed wire fences, young steers flicking flies with automatic tails. Farther off from the clackety rhythm of the train horses in beige-green meadows rolled around on their backs kicking up dun-colored dustclouds. Black-eyed-susans dotted the cutbanks along the track like a million tiny suns. Summer once more in its infinite rounds gripped the great land like a lover, lazy-by days, lolly-gagging nights, rapturous heat and simmering stonefaces cut here and there by chill streams gurgling up from secret artesian fissures tapping oceans locked in the rock vault of the earth. Somewhere in the car a war ballad crooned *When the lights go on again all over the world* making the war seem even more remote and unreal in this vastly peaceful Texas landscape. Bob never tired of watching it all go by.

In late afternoon the train pulled into midtown Houston under the viaduct where derelicts carved squatter caves in the high sandstone banks of Buffalo Bayou and the seamy city edge gave way to the skyscrapers of the center. The tall Renaissance birthday cake that was the Gulf Building and the twenty-story Greek temple of the Esperson Building loomed over everything. Bob looked with awe at the high structures peeking through the slits between nearby warehouses and store-backs. The layover in Houston was two hours, but Bob enjoyed some more of the sandwiches, fruit, and cake that his mother had provided, along with more of the soda water for sale by the hawker who walked through the aisles even while the train waited for its next departure.

Night had begun to fall by the time the train rolled out of Houston. Soon the dark flat coastal plain showed only as a line of lights here and there indicating suburbs and towns on the way to Texas City. Bob watched back toward Houston for a long time but did not see any fireworks. At 9:30 the train stopped in Hitchcock and Bob got off with his little suitcase.

Hitchcock, Texas, he saw in the night, was nothing but a depot; no line of lights stretched off in any direction. No one stood on the station platform to meet him. A lone man got the mail from the train, but left quickly with his locked canvas bag. The train pulled away into the shadows leaving Bob alone in the dark with the dingy glow of two bare bulbs in the warm still Gulf Coast air. Bob sat and waited for his Aunt Nadine and Uncle Henry Land. The tideflat keen of ocean salted the cicada-lulled sky, a smell that seemed to the boy ancient and enormous, and only added to his sense of loneliness. An occasional automobile appeared out of the blackness and streaked by, vanishing down the road beside the little station. He waited an hour. No one came.

Bob squelched his fear and decided that something had gone wrong so 'Deen and Henry would not be coming. He couldn't call because they had no phone. There was nothing for it but to get there on his own, he decided. But he had no idea where they lived, only some numbers on a piece of paper, and no one to ask what those numbers meant. Bob sat for another quarter-hour. Then out of the summer gloom a lone man strolled by along the roadside. Why was he abroad so late? Never mind. Bob hesitantly approached the stranger and asked directions to Texas City.

The nocturnal pedestrian stopped, gazing impassively at the boy. "It's seven miles that way, down Highway 6 toward Galveston for three miles to the Y, then take the east fork and go four miles." He walked on without inquiring why the youngster was out at this hour. Baffling.

Seven miles was too far to walk at nearly 11:00 p.m., Bob thought, so he stood beside the road and stuck out his thumb at the infrequent passing cars. The second driver must have thought it strange to see an eleven-and-a-half-year-old boy hitchhiking this late at night and he stopped to give him a ride.

"Where you goin', boy?" he asked as he opened the passenger door to let Bob in.

"Texas City," the boy said evenly, hiding his fright.

"Get in." Bob scrambled nervously into the front seat with his suitcase and slammed the door behind him.

"I'm goin' to Houston," said the overalled driver, evidently a mechanic. "I can take you as far as the Y. You can hitch a ride to Texas City from there. It ain't far, three, four miles."

"Mister, I'll pay you if you'll drive me to Texas City. I've got money."

"You ain't got enough money to make me late for work."

"You work in the middle of the night?"

"Yeah. At Reid Roller Bit. In Houston. That's where I live. I was just visitin' my brother tonight in Alta Loma. Ain't you never heard of graveyard shift?"

"No."

"You must live out in the sticks, kid. Doesn't anybody work in a factory where you come from?"

"No. We don't have factories in Meridian."

"Meridian? Where's that?"

"Up by Waco."

"You *do* live out in the sticks."

"Can't you please drive me into Texas City?"

"Nope. Sorry, kid. I gotta get to work. I got a family to support, you know. You shouldn't be running around at this time of night anyway."

"My aunt and uncle were supposed to pick me up. They prob'ly didn't get the penny post card on time."

"Too bad, kid. Can't help you. Somebody'll give you a ride. I did. Here's the Y comin' up. Texas City's over that way. See the lights?"

"Yes, sir."

"That's Texas City. You can't miss it. You can thumb a ride right over there by the grass." He pulled the car to a halt. "So long now." The boy got out with his suitcase and stood on the crushed oystershell road shoulder looking forlornly at the driver. "Thanks for the ride, sir."

"Good luck, kid," the stranger said as he drove off into the night. There was not even a bare bulb now to light his fearful path. Bob stood in the intersection not knowing what to do. Texas City still lay several miles off, he could see its cracking towers in the refinery glow. No moon overhead, only the symbolic stars writing their crystal message on the sky to remind him of his size and importance. No cars came. After a few minutes of jittery indecision Bob started down the right side of the road to Texas City.

After perhaps two miles and several hours of frightened desolate walking with no cars to thumb down, Bob stopped with a jolt of terror. Voices! Wild, wheeling voices! A strangled baritone. And a metallic soprano. But he could see nobody around him. Were they ghosts? If so, he decided after listening a moment more, they must be very nasty ghosts, for their tongues had a tang that included the crudest of vulgarisms. He walked a littler further down the road and witnessed a dim spectacle as bizarre as a Witches Sabbath. A carousing man and woman wretchedly drunk staggered obscenely around a 1937 Chevrolet stuck far off the road in a ditch. The two screamed invective at the machine, kicking it, wobbling around it in a whisky haze, beating it with their fists and calling it unseemly names, some that were new to the boy. Then they saw him.

"Hey, sonny," slurred the harridan, "c'mere, will yah?"

"What? Whozzat?" mouthed the drunkard, turning to look. "Hey, it's a kid. Hey, kid, can yah help us git this car started? Yah know anything about cars?"

Bob walked over to the woozy inebriata — they reminded him slightly of certain Walnut Springs distillery denizens — and saw that their car had evidently been badly burned at some time in the past.

"Does your car work, mister?" he asked.

"Hey, Harry, he's got a suitcase," mumbled the brassy woman as she leaned sloppily on a fender. "Where yah goin' with a suitcase, kid?"

"I'm going to see my aunt and uncle in Texas City. They didn't pick me up at the train station so I'm looking for a ride."

Weaving Harry tried to walk toward Bob but stumbled and barely caught himself by grabbing the blotched car's doorpost. "We'll give yah a ride if you'll help us get this damn car started, kid."

"Yeah, don't worry, kid," hiccupped the slattern woman, "we'll give yah a ride. Just as soon as we get this crummy car started."

Bob drew closer and got a sudden whiff of boozy halitosis from the two. He felt not a little fear over these sterling specimens. "Does your car work?" he asked again.

"Of course it works," stared blotto Harry. "How the hell do you think we got out here in the damn middle of nowhere? Right, Mabel?"

"Yeah, you dumb-bunny," added coarse Mabel. "It just won't start now, it's in the ditch, that's all."

Bob decided he was in over his head and simply walked back to the road.

"Hey, where you goin', kid?" yelled vile Harry, trying to stand alone. "Look at that, Mabel, he's just walking off."

Bob kept going, a step at a time, hoping they could not run after him.

"Hey, where you goin', you little creep? We're goin' to give you a ride!" shouted tawdry Mabel.

The boy went on fearfully, as if in a nightmare, slowly drawing away footstep by footstep.

"Come back here, kid! Help us git this damn thing started," cried loutish Harry.

Their voices grew fainter as Bob went on, not looking back.

"Come back here, you. . ." screamed Mabel.

"How d'ya like that, Mabel? He just walked away. It's this car, this lousy rotten car you made me buy." Harry kicked the vehicle and the sound vanished in the starry night.

A car finally came by from the right direction and Bob thumbed it down.

"What are you doing out at two in the morning, youngster?" asked the man.

Bob told the driver his story as they rolled away to Texas City. The driver turned out to be a refinery engineer who offered to let him off in front of his workplace. The man was apologetic for not having the time to help him find his relatives. "You'll be safe in front of the refinery, son. Just wait and somebody will be sure to help you." The man let Bob off in front of the Texaco Oil refinery and drove into the plant.

Thousands of lights filled the refinery night. The roadside was bright as day. Bob felt better, safer. He sat on his suitcase for an hour, waiting for daylight. About 3:00 a m. a car drove out of the refinery and the driver stopped stock still beside the boy. He rolled down his passenger window and yelled, "Boy, what are you doing out at this hour? Do your folks know where you are?"

"I'm trying to get to my aunt's house. I came on the train from Meridian but they didn't pick me up at the station so I hitched a couple of rides. Do you know where Evans Street is, sir?"

Bob gave the man his precious piece of paper with Nadine's address.

"I don't know this town too well, son. Only been here a couple of months. Don't know where this address is. But I know who does. Come on. Get in. I'll take you to the police station. I know where that is."

The man let him off at the police station where he told his story yet again. The two police officers on duty were kindly and solicitous. After hearing him out, a tall, slim officer asked, "Would you like us to call a taxicab for you?"

The cabbie dropped him off at 3:30 a.m. and asked for 75 cents. Bob paid the man, waved him off, and walked up to the front door of his Aunt 'Deen's home. The little frame house couldn't have been any larger than six or seven hundred square feet. Bob sat his suitcase down, knocked on the door and waited in the caressingly warm humid night. Muffled sounds came from somewhere inside and clomping footsteps approached. Nadine Land opened the door. The sounds of an electric oscillating fan came from the heat of another room. The boy could see cockroaches skittering across the kitchen floor in the yellow light behind his aunt.

Nadine looked down and said, "Bobby! What on earth are you doing here? Did you run away from home?" She hugged the boy to her without waiting for his answer.

"I didn't run away, 'Deen," Bob said. "I just came to visit. But nobody picked me up at the train station in Hitchcock. Didn't you get Dad's post card?"

Nadine looked the boy in the face. "Poor Bobby!" she said. "We didn't get any post card. Nobody told us you were coming. We'd have come to pick you up for sure, honey. But I'm so glad you're here. Come on in and let's try to be quiet so we don't wake up baby Kenneth."

"How old is he now?"

"A little over nine months. Now tell me all about how you got here. . ."

The next few days were a carefree climax to the boy's long night's journey into the strange wide world. Henry and 'Deen — he didn't call them "aunt" or "uncle" — took him wading in the bathtub-warm Gulf. He liked to look at the sea horizon, that razor-sharp straightedge on the drafting board of God. How huge the Gulf was, what strange emotions it

aroused. The play of the wind and the waves echoed the music of Debussy
in his mind although he had never heard *La Mer*. 'Deen treated him to red
snapper fried in flour rather than cornmeal — "That sure is good, 'Deen."
They showed him Texas City for three days and then put him on the train
back home. Although he had dutifully called his parents from a pay phone
during his visit, he did not tell them of his great adventure until he got
back home.

Meridian schools started as usual in September of 1944. Three weeks
later the war had swung into a critical phase. The Soviets had taken
Rumania, Finland, and Bulgaria and the British and Americans had
entrenched a secondary invasion in Southern France. The casualties were
enormous but Hitler's forces slowly crumbled. Many gold stars hung in
Grand Prairie windows. The war now touched every life. Every night
every radio in Central Texas tuned to the news in Europe and in the Pacific
where the fate of the world was being determined in gunfire and bomb
blasts and bloodshed. The Meridian School Board felt it would be in
everyone's best interests to dismiss school for a week and encourage
students to help the local farmers pick their cotton. Virtually every
available able-bodied man had by now gone to the war. Farmers joined
with the women who sang the lament of Tin Pan Alley's hit tune *They're
Either Too Young Or Too Old*. It was impossible to get farm help.

"I'm going to take this bus load up north to the Wilson's place,
Lester," said Clayborne.

Lester Smith said, "I'm set to take this bunch south and east, W. C.
I'm going out to the end of Farm Road 1991, three or four places out there
need hands. Joe Cureton's going with me. The whole football team is
coming along. Your boy coming with you?"

"Oh, yes. Him and Bobby Pounds have a little competition going to
see who can pick the most. How many students you have?"

"Twenty-six. Got three girls in this bus."

"Me, too. The Gates girl got 'em to volunteer. Well, we'll see you back
here around, what? Five-thirty?"

"I imagine so. I don't know if I like picking cotton or teaching school
best. The only trouble I have in the fields is keeping the kids from
chunkin' cotton bolls at each other."

"Well, good luck. Come back with all twenty-six."

The superintendent and the agriculture teacher mounted their
respective bus-driver seats and prayed that the elderly 48-passenger
vehicles would not break down again today. Clayborne called back to his
riders, "Did the water barrel get put on the bus?"

"Yes, sir, Mr. Perry!" shouted a dozen voices. "We wouldn't forget
that!"

"Well, are you ready for another day picking cotton?"

"Yay!"

"Here we go." *I hope.*

The engine revved up and the rickety bus pulled out of the gravel school yard without complaint. They were off. The three girls convinced everyone to sing the Meridian Yellow Jackets fight song and the early morning bus rolled out of town amidst joyous noise.

Once in the white-mantled fields with his ersatz farm hands disgorged from the parked yellow bus, Clayborne took up his usual place at the cotton wagon, manning the weighing scales, handing out picking sacks, supervising the unskilled students, hauling water buckets down the long rows to the thirsty, recording each picker's tally for later payment and picking a little cotton himself.

The late September sun drew upward in the morning sky and the green smells of the nearby Bosque River mingled with the dust from the rows. As Clayborne progressed from bush to bush picking what he could between tasks, his son would from time to time work by his side. But the father never gave any sign of favoritism, no special greeting, no different treatment, no kinder words. The boy knew he was expected to make no trouble and to do everything right, no missed school days, no volunteer effort turned down, no sagging grades. Bob looked at his father this morning across a brown and white row and felt a fleeting stab of anguish at the spartan treatment that was his lot.

Wartime crept forth day by autumn day. Allied forces cleared France and Belgium of German troops by late October, and the first norther of the season swept into Texas in early November. The boys and girls of Meridian High still wanted sock hops every Friday but only a few attended and the dances for 1944-45 were rescheduled every other Friday. The Christmas program at school came off nicely and the holidays proved cheery. When school resumed in January, 1945, Clayborne found himself driving the school bus daily, along with ag teacher Lester Smith. The war across the seas took more and more men, even those turned down by the draft in earlier years. The Soviets had entered Czechoslovakia and East Prussia now. Hitler rolled back in retreat. Hirohito rolled back in retreat. Yet the battles afar grew in fierceness even as Allied victory became inevitable and every battle cost men. Men to drive buses on the home front were nowhere to be found.

The battles near took the form of little holding actions to keep the rattletrap buses going another day, to keep the textbooks readable another month, to keep the community going another year. In February Clayborne felt he had won a small victory by hiring Mrs. Annie Freeman to coach the girls' basketball team, even though he still had to keep his interscholastic game schedule to a minimum and play only teams close to home to save precious gasoline for the military. In March General Bradley and Marshall Montgomery stopped quibbling with each other long enough to cross the Rhine and in April Western forces met the Soviet Armies at Torgau in Saxony.

On April 12 the only four-term president in American history died suddenly of a cerebral hemorrhage. The body of Franklin Delano Roosevelt was borne in a train from Warms Springs, Georgia, to the Capitol where a mourning nation saw him laid in state. Popular radio announcer Arthur Godfrey broke down and wept openly on the air while broadcasting the funeral procession. The president was buried on the family estate at Hyde Park. He missed by only a month seeing Germany collapse.

Then one fair day in May as America tried to recover from its grief under the untested leadership of President Harry S. Truman, the war in Europe stopped. The German war machine lay in ruins. The Thousand Year Reich fell short. Hitler was dead and Germany's unconditional surrender ratified in Berlin.

"What 'cha doin'?" asked the slurping boy in the Perry's back yard.

"Hi, Pounds," said Bob Perry. "I'm buildin' a rabbit pen. Where'd you get the sucker?"

"Got it at Benson's. It's chocolate. What's the rabbit pen for?"

"What do you mean, what's it for? Rabbits, that's what for."

"You gonna raise rabbits instead of chickens, huh?"

"Yep. Dr. Holt down at the hospital says he'll buy 'em from me."

"What's he want rabbits for?"

"He needs 'em for rabbit tests. To tell if ladies are goin' to have a baby."

"How does a rabbit know if a lady's goin' to have a baby?"

"The rabbits don't know. Dr. Holt gives 'em a shot with the lady's blood or something. He explained it to me. If the lady's going to have a baby, it does something to the rabbit, makes some organ swell up. Dr. Holt kills 'em and cuts 'em open so he can see. Then he tells the lady."

"Oh."

Bob expertly nailed 1x6 decking boards onto the hutch frame.

"Can I do that?" asked Bobby, sucking his sucker.

"Nope. It's too hard. You don't know how. I've been nailing 12-penny brights into boards since I was six years old."

"No, you weren't."

"Yes, I was. I remember pounding nails into the old lady's house that we lived in at Iredell. Used to do it for fun. One time I drove a nail clear through the wall, right behind the ice box. Mrs. Weir wasn't too happy about it."

"Well, I used to nail things too."

"No, you didn't."

"Yes I did." Bobby sucked his sucker some more. Then he said, "War's over."

"No it's not."

"Said so on the radio. Heard when I bought my penny sucker at Bensons."

"Just in Germany. My Dad says they're still fighting with Japan."

"Is that so?"

"Yeah, that's so."

"I want to nail some."

"Nope."

"C'mon, let me nail some."

"Nope."

"I won't hurt your la-de-da rabbit pen. I'll give you the rest of my sucker."

"Really?"

"Really."

"Well, okay. It's a deal. Here's the hammer. Lemee see your sucker. Hey, there's not much left."

Bobby took the hammer and said, "I won't nail much."

"I don't know, this is a bad deal."

"It's a deal. You said so. Don't be an Indian giver." The racial slur was so ingrained it slid off the boy's tongue without jogging the slightest mental image of an American Indian or of giving and taking back.

Bob sucked the dwindling chocolate lollipop and kept a hawk eye on what his friend was doing to his rabbit hutch.

Bobby asked, "What's that black stuff rolled up over there?"

"Tar paper. My Dad bought it for the roof. To keep the rain off the rabbits."

"Oh."

"I don't think I want the rest of this sucker. I'm gonna nail up the rest of the boards myself." He set the candy on a clear yellow pine board.

"I ain't through nailin'." said Bobby.

"Come on, gimme back my hammer."

"Rassle you for it."

And so it went.

Japan was not yet defeated but by now no one doubted the inevitable. Europe lay in starving shambles and Japan was next on the list, and that was that. The outlook was by no means sparkling, but it had brightened perceptibly since Germany had been destroyed. Many G.I.s from the European Theatre were reassigned to the Pacific Theatre, but a trickle of men actually began coming home from the war. As springtime came to Texas in riotous wildflower color, Clayborne was able to hire Mr. Claude Everett, a returning war veteran, as high school principal, who took over coaching of all male sports as well.

"Mr. Everett, I'd like you to meet our home economics teacher, Mrs. Launa Morrow," said Clayborne. "This is our new principal Mr. Everett, Mrs. Morrow!"

"I'm so pleased to meet you," said the home ec teacher. "It's so nice to see another man back at the school."

"Thank you. It's great to be back, I can assure you. Looks like you have a busy program here. What is this?"

"Oh, you don't know about our Canning Center, then," said Mrs. Morrow. "Superintendent Perry, let me show Mr. Everett around."

"You go ahead. I've got to talk to Lester Smith about some farm tools we've been asked to fix."

Clayborne strode off purposefully to the far end of the long room as Mrs. Morrow took the new principal by the arm on a guided tour.

"Now, Mr. Everett," she began, "The Meridian school is an official federal canning center for the farm folk around about, did you know that?"

"No, Ma'am, I didn't."

"Well, the government set up this program, gave us a little money and a few WPA workers. Farm wives come in here and use our school facilities under my supervision and can up anything they want. And our agriculture teacher Mr. Smith also supervises when he's not busy repairing farm tools. We have all sorts of handy things here. Like over there. That's Methiel Sneed working our mechanical sheller getting in her early beans. And there's Mr. Grimm's wife and Gussie Koerth, they drive in together. They both live out northwest of town about three, four miles, have big gardens. It's too early for most things, but you just wait until July."

"You'll still have this when school's out?"

"Oh, yes, it's a regular federal program for the farm wives, like I say."

"What do they think of doing their canning with a lot of other women?"

"I think that's what they like best about it, Mr. Everett. Gives them some company. Somebody to talk to." She whispered, "And gossip with."

Clayborne reappeared and said, "Getting the tour?"

"Oh, yes, Mr. Perry," said Principal Everett. "Mrs. Morrow's an excellent guide. This is quite a program."

"We're proud of it," said Clayborne. "Mrs. Morrow, let me steal the principal here for a while. And thank you besides for showing him around."

"Oh, think nothing of it. I've got to get back to my ladies anyway. So glad to have met you, Mr. Everett."

Clayborne said, "Come on down here, Mr. Everett, and I'll show you our farm mechanic program. I think you'll really like it."

They ambled alongside the clean canning tables and out to another high-ceilinged room. Chain hoists dangled with tractor engines. Welding equipment crackled in use. There Clayborne spent the rest of the morning regaling his new principal with stories of farm emergencies handled and farm equipment repaired and the war effort forwarded.

At the end of May Clayborne presided over his second Meridian graduation ceremony and saw another 28 students receive their diplomas. The senior class officers had come to him earlier, however, and said they wanted something special, something after graduation for a real send-off.

Clayborne took the request to Sam Lawson. The president of the education board replied, "Mr. Perry, you know this war is going to be over one of these days. Things are looking up pretty good. I'd like a little celebration myself. I think we can afford to provide these kids a little extra excitement. What do you say?"

And so, a few days after their caps and gowns went back to the Waco rental store, the graduated seniors took off with Sam Lawson and Clayborne in a five-car caravan to Fort Worth for a razzle-dazzle day trip. They went to the zoo, they went to the livestock yard, they went to the park. They laughed and they romped and they gawked at the tall buildings and they behaved like teenagers loose in the park. As a fitting climax to the big day, C. T. Lawson, the exalted president of the school board, took everyone to a fine steak house about 5:00 p.m. for a big one-dollar steak dinner. The day was a smashing success. It was the best graduation present they could have wanted.

In mid-July the watermelons came in. Clayborne saw Bob moping around the house one bright Saturday noon and said, "You've done all your chores, fed the rabbits and all. Why don't you go downtown and see if you can't find something to do? Mr. Nevin's usually somewhere around the courthouse square. Maybe you can cook up another deal with him."

Bob smiled. "I think I will, Dad. And I haven't forgotten about the banty chicks, either."

Bob had learned something of the horse-trading business from A. C. Nevin, or at least the sheep-trading business. The young entrepreneur had bought a sheep here and a goat there and sold them in hopes of turning a profit. So far his ventures had not earned spectacular returns, and depended in large part on feed subsidies from his father. But he was beginning to sell a few rabbits regularly and hope sprung eternal in his breast.

Today he found Mr. Nevin sitting on a bench staring across the busy shopping-day street. Saturday was a big day, a regular social event in small-town Texas. Farm families from all around came in to do the weekly shopping as it had been done for decades, only now in pre-war Chevrolets and some Ford pickup trucks and other automotive conveyances somewhat the worse for war-wear. "Hello, Mr. Nevin. What you looking at?"

"Oh, Hello, Bob. Glad to see you. Come sit. Watch over there."

"Where?"

"See that young man standing next to his pickup truck? That one backed into the curb in front of the courthouse? With all the melons?"

"Yes, sir. I know him. That's W. E. Boyd from Iredell. He's some kind of distant cousin of my Dad's."

"Well, he's been there all morning trying to sell that truckload of watermelons. They're good big plump ones from around that Iredell sandy soil, too. He's not havin' much luck. And he's gettin' antsy for some reason. Just watch."

They watched. The young salesman hawked his wares. "Ten cents each!" Then in a few minutes, "Five cents each." A few minutes more, about 2:00 p.m., "any price, you name the price."

"Now's the time," said Nevin. "He's prob'ly got a big date tonight and he's just itching to get back to Iredell. I'll tell you what you do. Let's buy these watermelons from ol' W. E. ourselves. We'll pay him five dollars for the load. I'll provide the capital and you sell 'em and we'll split the profit. What do you say?"

"Are you goin' to start talking about the war news now?"

"Nope. You caught on to that one. Just a straight deal. What do you say?"

"It's a deal."

A. C. Nevin bought the watermelons, probably fifty of them, from W. E. Boyd for five dollars and they all helped unload and stack the green fruit on the courthouse sidewalk. The melons seemed to range between twenty-five and forty pounds each. Somehow they seemed to look more appealing sitting there on the curb than they had in the truck bed.

Young Boyd eagerly took Mr. Nevin's five dollars and skedaddled down Morgan Street on his hurried way back to Iredell.

"I tell you what, Bob," said Nevin, standing in the street. "Set one of those big melons here in this parking place where ol' W. E.'s pickup was, will you?"

"Out in the street?"

"Sure. So nobody can park there. That way all the cars driving by can see our melons up here on the curb. If some car parks here how can anybody tell what you've got?"

"Okay."

And so Bob picked a big beautiful ripe watermelon from the stack and carefully placed it smack in the middle of the parking space.

"There," said Nevin. "Now you can get to making money."

"What should I sell 'em for?"

"As much as you can get."

"What do you think? Two bits for the little ones?"

"And thirty cents for the big ones. See you later."

"So long, Mr. Nevin."

Bob stood there for a few minutes hawking his wares as ol' W. E. had, but doing much better at it. He had sold half a dozen melons when an old man in a two-tone green Buick came up to the parking space.

"Hi, Mr. Wentz," called Bob. He knew Mr. Wentz's daughter who worked for the post office.

"Hey, boy, move that watermelon out of the street there," piped Wentz irritably from the driver's seat.

"No, sir, I can't move it. Mr. Nevin told me to put it there, and we're going to leave it there so people can see our big stack of watermelons so I'll be able to sell 'em."

Without a word old man Wentz just drove right into the parking space on top of the watermelon and squashed it good. Bob looked on in disbelief. He pursed his lips as the feeble man doddered out of his car, looked down at him and went on his cantankerous way. Bob started to yell an imprecation, but thought better of it. How would it look calling a feeble old man names, anyway? He recalled his father once telling him that it takes both brains and courage to keep your mouth shut in a tight situation. Bob turned silently back to his melons, the shape of true manhood growing within him.

As things have a way of turning out, Mr. Wentz's car didn't make much difference anyway. Bob sold all the melons that afternoon and walked away with nearly twelve dollars in his pocket. He split the profit with Mr. Nevin and walked home proudly to tell his father about his first big business deal. Clayborne was pleased and obviously approved of his dealing with grown men. The boy liked to be taken seriously by adults, considered himself a serious person, but he noticed that his father never bragged on him, and that somehow left an empty place in him. The boy didn't know that such was the growing trademark his father was leaving in the Central Texas life of 1945: to make much over others but not over himself or his own.

On August 6 that summer, a 1943 prediction of the leading Japanese physicist, Yoshio Nishina, was found to be mistaken. He and his government had built five cyclotrons in search of fission weapons, but concluded that not even the U.S. economy could produce an atomic bomb in the foreseeable future. They realized their miscalculation when Ground Zero at Hiroshima vaporized in righteous plutonium vengeance.

Immediately after this awkward discovery, the Japanese government called Nishina to Tokyo and asked whether the Hiroshima bomb had been a genuine nuclear blast and if so, could he duplicate it in six months. Japanese Prime Minister Admiral Suzuki and the two chiefs of staff were in no mood to give up. B-29-san, they said, probably had only one such monstrous weapon in his bomb bays anyway.

On August 9 that summer, the Japanese government's estimate of the U.S. nuclear stockpile was found to be mistaken. They realized their miscalculation when Ground Zero at Nagasaki vaporized in more righteous plutonium vengeance. On September 2 that summer, the Japanese surrender was formally signed on the deck of the American battleship *Missouri* in Tokyo Bay. The long battles near and far that had begun with Hitler's remilitarization of the Rhine in 1935 and the capture of Ethiopia for Italy in 1936 and the sneak attack on Pearl Harbor in 1941 now ended. The First Nuclear War was over.

-20-

AFTER VICTORY

O H, listen to this, Clayborne," whispered Oretta. "What a beautiful prayer!"

The Perry family could barely hear over the sounds of the train. The radio program filtered from somewhere in the Santa Fe passenger car amid static and rail clatter and conversation but the words somehow rang clear.

Lord God of trajectory and blast
Whose terrible sword has laid open the serpent
So it withers in the sun for the just to see,
Sheathe now the swift avenging blade with the names
    of nations writ on it,
And assist in the preparation of the ploughshare.

There was more, they thought, but proud music came up and swallowed the words. Then an announcer said:

"The Columbia Broadcasting System is pleased to have brought you this presentation of its award-winning radio drama Petition After Victory, first broadcast in May, 1945. Today's re-broadcast commemorates the first full year of peace in Europe. This program was written by Norman Corwin and brought to you by Sal Hepatica, America's outstanding saline laxative that so many physicians recommend. Stay tuned for the CBS news with Edward R. Murrow. . ."

"Wasn't that just wonderful?" said Oretta, stroking sleeping Margie's curls. The six-year-old girl shifted uncomfortably on the train seat, recovering from a nasty spill in the aisle earlier in the day.

"Those were fine words," said Clayborne, "mighty fine."

"Dad," asked Bob, a maturing thirteen, "how come there's so many soldiers on the train?"

"Maybe they've all been stationed someplace."

"But Dad, the war was over back when school started, right?"

"Yes, that's right."

"That was nine months ago, Dad. If there's no war, how come there's so many soldiers?"

Clayborne gazed around the coach car. Glare of setting sun splashed through long rows of unwashed windows onto a knurled khaki wall of soldiers standing in the aisle swaying in time to the rackety-rack of the track. They jammed the car, blocking the aisle, laughing with each other, kibitzing with friends trying to play cards, standing reading old magazines, sitting alone and staring at nothing, catnapping, leaning over seats telling raucous stories, none of them about the war.

"I don't really know why there's so many, Bob," said Clayborne. "Why don't we find out?" He leaned across the aisle and spoke with contagious dignity to a man in uniform. How like his father, Bob thought.

"Excuse me, there, sir. I'm W. C. Perry, and I wonder if you can tell me why there's so many servicemen on this train?"

The bored war veteran who could not have been a day over 21 turned to Clayborne's words, startled into enthusiasm. "Why, yes, sir, I sure can. It's kind of you to ask. My name's Jerroll Stringer, Mr. Perry. Why we're all here is we just got discharged from Fort Sam Houston, down in San Antonio, you know."

"Well, congratulations! Is Fort Sam still the big Army post it was during the war?" asked Clayborne.

"It's the big mustering-out point these days, that's for sure. I think there's a few guys on this train got released at Fort Hood down by Killeen, too. But the whole Army's running a big demobilization program everywhere this month."

"You're all going home up north, then?" asked Clayborne.

"Yes, sir, that we are."

"Where's home for you?"

"Cedar Rapids, Iowa, sir."

"Is that right? Well, we're all going to Fort Wayne, Indiana. I'm the school superintendent for Meridian, Texas, and I'm taking my family to Fort Wayne to pick up our new school bus at the factory. We're going to drive it back home."

"Is this your family?"

"Yes, sir, it is. This is my wife Oretta, and my son Bob, and my girl Margie asleep there."

"Why, she looks just like Joyce."

"What?"

"Your girl. I've been watching her and her brother playing, she looks just like my kid sister Joyce." He sighed. "But I'll bet Joyce has grown up. I haven't seen her in years. Oh, it'll be great to be back home!"

Oretta asked, "What's the first thing you're going to do, Mr. Stringer?"

"Sleep for a month, Ma'am. And not get up for anything but some of Mom's good ol' home cooking. And maybe read. I hear *The Egg and I* is a good book. And the guys say *Forever Amber* sounds interesting."

"A little spicy, from what I hear," put in Oretta disapprovingly.

"After the last few years I could use a little spice, Ma'am. Those paperback books we got to read on the front were pretty dull."

Oretta smiled and said, "I guess so. What then?"

"Look for work, Ma'am. Or maybe go to college on that new G.I. Bill of Rights. Or just join the 52-20 Club."

"What's that?" asked Bob, admiring the cleancut military man.

"Every discharged serviceman gets 52 weeks of unemployment pay at $20 a week, son. 52-20. Something from Uncle Sam to tide you over while you get settled down. It'll help pay for some new civvies. We've got a month to get out of uniform after we get back home."

"You mean you can't keep your uniform?" asked Bob.

"Oh, we can keep it. Just can't wear it after a month. I sure won't miss it, I tell *you*! And what have you been doing during the war, young man?"

"Me?" said Bob. "Nothin'. Going to school. I'll be in the ninth grade next September. That's a freshman in high school. I'm looking forward to going out for football. Last year I got to practice with the high school team."

"Really?" asked the soldier. "You played football in the eighth grade? The schools must have changed during the war."

"Well, our high school didn't have enough players, sir," said Bob as his father looked on. "The coach just let me suit up and stand around markin' a spot. On defense, usually. I didn't do much, really. But everybody in Meridian came out Fridays to see the game. We had a real good team. And I helped in the War Bond drives, I bought Liberty Stamps. What did you do in the war?"

A strange, smiling mask drew over the soldier's face. He said in a voice subtly changed yet unchanged, "Same as you. I didn't do much. Just stood around and marked a spot."

"Oh, I'll bet you did a lot," the boy said. "Look at all those ribbons you got. And what's that black eagle on your sleeve for?"

"That? That's just my Division's insignia, the 86th, they called us the Black Hawks."

"Did you fight the Japs?" Bob asked eagerly.

"Well, I served Occupation duty in Japan a while. Fighting was over by then. Just sat at a desk and filled out papers. Fought in Europe before that."

"Did you shoot a lot of Germans?"

"Shot *at* a lot of 'em. It was pretty messy. You couldn't really see if you'd hit anybody or not."

"Did you go to Berlin and see Hitler?"

Stringer smiled. "No, son," he said, "just a couple of places you prob'ly never heard of. Little town named Ingolstadt, another place called Dachau." The smiling mask drew tighter, hiding the memories of what he had seen in Dachau, things that human eyes were never meant to see.

"Are you going back to a girl at home?" asked Oretta.

"Well, I think so, Mrs. Perry. Her name's Marlene. She's kept on writing me. But you know how it is in a war. People change. I'll see when I get home. I haven't got a "Dear John" letter from her, anyway."

A soldier stirred sleepily next to Stringer. "Don't let ol' Jerroll fool you, Ma'am," he said leaning forward. "That girl is crazy about him. He talked to her long distance this last month 'til he ran out of quarters. My name's Babcock, folks, Fred Babcock, from Chicago. Did I hear your name right, you're the Perrys?" He got half out of his seat to lean over Stringer and shake hands with Clayborne.

"Yes, sir, we're the Perrys," Clayborne said.

"Guess I was catchin' forty winks when you started talkin' to Jerroll. What's the world been doin' since the war was over, Mr. Perry? I got stuck at Fort Sam guarding POWs for six months until they sent 'em all back to Germany. Jerroll got put in a demobilization cadre briefing all the disabled men about adjusting to civilian life. No in-town passes for either of us. Can you get cars yet?"

"Were you in the same unit as Mr. Stringer?" asked Clayborne.

"Oh, no, I was in the 42nd Division most of the time. But headquarters just jumbled us all up when we came back, we got men from everywhere at Fort Sam. I served Occupation duty in Germany a while. Our unit was at Dachau where Jerroll was, but he got wounded and then sent to Japan. I didn't even meet him 'til we got assigned to the same barracks at Fort Sam. Isn't that something? But what about cars, sir?"

"Well," said Clayborne, "there's a few cars on the market, more coming all the time. You hear lots of stories how cars are so scarce dealers go to old women who don't drive much and pay them sky-high prices for good used cars. I managed to get a new 1946 Plymouth last November; traded in my old worn-out 1941 Plymouth."

"What's a new Plymouth going for these days, sir?"

"Well, I paid $1,600 to the car dealer where I live in Meridian. Mr. Lomax gave me a thousand for my old one and turned around and sold it to a fellow named Jay Kerlee out south of town; I imagine he made a little something on it. And I only paid $640 for it in 1941. But I heard that new cars were going on the black market for $2,100, can you imagine?"

"If you loved cars like my Dad does, Mr. Perry, you could imagine," said Babcock. "He's part-owner in a meat-packing plant and cars were his hobby before the war, just like he was a kid. Did you have to wait long for your new Plymouth?"

"Didn't wait at all. Mr. Lomax was able to get two at the same time. Sam Lawson — he's the president of our school board — he got the first one. I showed up next, so the car was mine. But I had to go up to Ft. Worth to pick it up, they didn't deliver it."

On they talked, chatting the evening happily away, soon with half a dozen other men in uniform. Margie awoke and caught their eye, her smile winning trinkets and little war souvenirs from men throughout the car, men reminded of their own daughters and sisters. When the coach lights dimmed around ten o'clock the conversation abated slowly like the fullness of a floodtide ebbing in surges as everyone talked on now and then while trying to find a comfortable position for the night in this vehicle without sleeping accommodations. It was then that the Perrys got their shock. Jerroll Stringer reached down and laboriously unstrapped his artificial leg in preparation for sleep. More than half the men in the car similarly took off various prostheses in token of grievous personal sacrifice. Artificial limbs appeared everywhere, a macabre display made all the more gripping for its matter-of-factness. The jolt of horror showed on the Perrys' faces. Oretta held her breath but could not keep the first tear of pity from brimming over.

Stringer said gently across the aisle, "Don't cry for us, Mrs. Perry, we came back alive. I just happened to be marking the wrong spot when a jeep hit a land mine at Dachau. I lost a leg, but the driver — his number was up."

Clayborne gulped, deeply moved. "And you stayed in and went to Japan after *that*?"

"Oh, I could have come back home. But I'd look like a quitter, Mr. Perry. And they needed clerks after Japan surrendered."

Oretta fought for control but choked on a sob. "I can't help it, Mr. Stringer. You all gave so much. And you're so young."

"Weep for the boys that came back in a box, Ma'am. Or the guys we left overseas. We just did what we had to do. Don't worry about us. We'll get along."

Clayborne spoke with all his heart: "That's a great and patriotic thing to say, Mr. Stringer."

And so it went. Two days and a night they rode the train with veterans whose bodies showed wounds but whose souls did not. One by one the discharged soldiers left the coach car and then, in the low hills and hardwoods of northeastern Indiana, a few miles from Ohio, the conductor called "Fort Wayne!"

"Here's the keys, Mr. Perry. She's all yours, paperwork and everything. Ain't she a beaut?" The final assembly supervisor dangled the school bus keys before the Perry family as they stood in the waving Midwest heat of the factory drive-out lot.

"It's a sight for sore eyes, Mr. Cheney," grinned Clayborne. "I haven't seen a new school bus anywhere for five years."

Bob circled the bus in a saunter, playing inspector-in-chief.

"And this is a real tough bus here, Mr. Perry, like I'm sure your boy can see" said Cheney. "A new Chevvy chassis with our 48-passenger Wayne body — it's a new design from one end to the other. It'll take all the punishment school kids and chugholes can give it. Just make sure you break 'er in gradual, don't hot rod it for the first thousand miles — I'm sure I don't need to tell you that, sir."

"It's not going to get cranky on me, is it?"

"No, sir, Mr. Perry. You take care of it, it'll take care of you."

"Oh, my husband will take good care of it, you can count on that," said Oretta.

"Can I ride in the front seat behind you, Dad?" asked Margie.

"Yes, you ride next to your mother in the front seat, and Bob, I want you to sit in the very back seat for a while, I want a little peace and quiet while I'm driving in this strange city. Mr. Cheney, how do we get back to Texas?"

Cheney smiled, "You want to see the sights, or just go straight?"

"Let's see a few sights."

"Then you go right to the center of town to Lafayette Street a little north of the City Hall and there's old Fort Wayne. It got kind of run-down during the war, but it's a real interesting place, historical museum and such. Then go north to State Boulevard and turn left on Goshen Avenue, go past Franke Park — that's a nice place — to U.S. Highway 24 and turn left. About thirty miles out you get to Huntington, turn south on State 37. It takes you to Indianapolis. You keep goin' in that general direction three or four days and you can't miss Texas."

By the time they got out of town in Meridian's new school bus, Clayborne looked down the asphalt strip and spotted veterans far ahead with their duffel beside them, Army, Navy, Army Air Forces, Marines, Seabees, all branches, all with their thumbs out, all heading home in the massive demobilization.

"Oretta," said Clayborne, "look at the servicemen along this road up there."

"I wonder why they're hitchhiking? And so many of them!" she answered.

"Well, you know how poor transportation is nowadays. Remember how crowded the train was and how late it always ran."

Clayborne slowed the bus.

"Oretta," he said, "we've got 45 extra seats in this bus. I think we ought to pickup every serviceman we see."

"Do you think it's safe? I mean. . ." She looked protectively at Bob back at the far end of the bus and Margie next to her.

"They wouldn't hurt us," he said. "Think of what they've been through. Some of them are crippled, like those men on the train. And remember the second commandment, 'love thy neighbor as thyself.' I think we owe it to them."

He stopped the bus at the first group of servicemen.

Clayborne's quick determination to live his beliefs had by now become characteristic of the man. His obedience to the Biblical precept to love his neighbor had grown more and more ingrained as his stature and responsibilities had increased. And, in the folkways of his upbringing, like thousands of other rural American faithful, he had come to think of the precept simply as he called it today, the second commandment. The name led many to assume that it was the second commandment of the Decalogue given to Moses at Mount Sinai in Chapter 20 of Exodus, despite its actual origin in the words of Jesus written in Matthew and Mark of the New Testament. In the King James translation of 1611 — the only Bible these people knew — Chapter 22 of Matthew tells the story thus: Jesus had just finished dealing with a number of Sadducee priests, answering their objections to the doctrine of resurrection with stunning authority —

But when the Pharisees had heard that he had put the Sadducees to silence, they were gathered together.

Then one of them, which was a lawyer, asked him a question, tempting him, and saying,

Master, which is the great commandment in the law?

And Jesus said unto him, Thou shalt love the Lord thy God with all thy heart, and with all thy soul, and with all thy mind.

This is the first and great commandment.

And the second is like unto it, Thou shalt love thy neighbor as thyself. (verss 34-39)

Although this Christian idea does not appear at all in the Judaic Holy Scriptures — the Old Testament — nor even in the synoptic gospel of Luke, and only in paraphrase in the Gospel according to Saint John, it was without question *the* single most powerful Biblical admonition and guide to behavior in the Texas Grand Prairie, an absolute truth not to be questioned.

Rural Texas of this era cannot be understood without grasping two religious facts: the power this second commandment held for the people, and the simplicity of country faith that lived its beliefs without picayunish quibbling over chapter and verse. Whether it was the second commandment given by God to Moses as a covenant on the sacred ground of Mount Sinai or the second commandment stated by Jesus in answer to a scheming lawyer in the streets of Jerusalem didn't matter. It was in the Bible and that's all there was to it.

"You folks mind riding in a school bus?" Clayborne hollered down to the clutch of servicemen standing by the steaming noontide roadway.

"No, sir!" half a dozen grinning men in uniform called back.

"Well, we're bound for a school in Texas by way of Kentucky, Tennessee and Mississippi, so if you're going our way you're welcome to come with us."

The men piled gratefully on board, expressing their thanks effusively as they found brand new seats in the brand new vehicle. Clayborne looked back on them in satisfaction and drove off. The gleaming school bus sailed smoothly down the country road, seats filled half with men, half with duffel, windows open to let the July wind burble through and cool their prickled faces, stopping at some Indiana crossroads to pick up more veterans and at others to let them off. Clayborne took it slow, letting the skein of miles shilly-shally at leisure beneath the new tires, enjoying the hot green summer day and the warm friendly talk of the servicemen.

A garrulous Navy mechanic sat in the right front seat across from Clayborne, explaining, "No, sir, Navy food's not as bad as Army chow, but I never hope to look another C ration in the face. No, sir, I'm gonna eat proper Tennessee homecooked, I'm gonna sleep in a proper Tennessee bed and I'm gonna go to a proper Tennessee church. No more of them green scrambled eggs, no more of them bunks and hammocks and no more of them military chapels. How's the churches in Texas? Are you a churchgoer, Mr. Perry?"

Clayborne smiled. "As a matter of fact I am, I've been a Baptist deacon since back in 1935 when we lived in Iredell — that's a little town close to where we live now in Meridian."

Margie ran up and down the aisle flirting and laughing with the servicemen. Oretta called, "You be careful, now, Margie. Remember your spill on the train."

The Navy man said, "She's sure the cute one, Missus. Now, Mr. Perry, I'm Baptist, too. Not a deacon, though. Expect I will be after a while back in Murfreesboro. How was it keeping the churches up during the war? Pretty slim?"

"It sure was," said Clayborne. "The Meridian deacons had been planning on a new church back when the war started. Weren't able to do anything for five years. Now that things are finally settled our volunteers just finished tearing down the old church building so we can build the new one."

The Navy man said, "That means you've got no building at all. What are you goin' to do for a church 'til the new one's done?"

"We're renting the auditorium in the old three-story grammar school from the board of education. We can use it Sundays and Wednesday nights when it doesn't interfere with class. It's working out just fine."

Oretta said with quiet pride from across the bus aisle, "Clayborne was elected by the Deacon Board to be chairman of the church building committee. He's been working on getting this new church built since the war was over."

"That right?" said the Navy mechanic, well aware what that meant in a small town where social life focused around church membership. "How do you go about building a new church, Mr. Perry?"

"Well, the members have to vote on it first. Our congregation's about 400 strong, really fine people. They voted this April to go ahead with the new building. Then you have to raise the money for it. We had a good church drive, pledges, rummage sales, socials, things like that, all total we raised about $20,000."

"That's a lot of money." said Navy.

"We figure it's going to take $35,000 before we finish. We have a local man named Burney Warren who's the contractor on the brick and concrete work, and we hired a carpenter named Sim Baxter to frame the building — he's in charge of construction, I'm in charge of purchasing and management of the building site. We all work together. But building materials are scarce and prices are going up so fast you don't dare hesitate once you start. We've had our problems, but Paster McBeth, Cecil McBeth, he stands behind me, and the Deacon Board stands behind me. The board's got good men on it, our town doctor and one of our car dealers, and such. . ."

Oretta said, "Don't forget about the fire chief. And Mr. Grimm does something for the government, doesn't he?"

"Oh, yes," Clayborne said to the Navy mechanic, "Cotton Dorman's the town fire chief and Gus Grimm's a soil conservation man with the federal government. Like I say, all our Deacon Board members are good men."

Navy said, "You know, Mr. Perry, talkin' to you makes the last four years all seem more worthwhile somehow. You prove something to me, yes, sir, you sure do. . ." He leaned back, not explaining himself, tipped his sailor hat over his eyes and pretended to sleep.

At sundown the bus droned into the gravel lot of a roadside tourist court near Louisville (pronounced LOO-uh-vul) in Kentucky. Clayborne turned around in his driver's seat and told his riders, "We're stopping for the night, folks. The sign back there said you can get a nice room here for four or five dollars. They sell breakfast for thirty-five cents. We'll be back here about eight in the morning and you're all welcome to ride with us some more if you want."

Some men anxious to get home thumbed with duffel bag over shoulder into the warm Kentucky night and were gone. Others stood ready to board when the Perry family appeared next day in the slanting sun of morning. For three days and three nights they passed marklessly through the states, reading the Burma Shave signs aloud and picking up and letting off veterans and soaking in old America: Kentucky and Tennessee where Navy got off at Clarksville, then through Mississippi towns, Tupelo and Columbus and Meridian. It was close to Alabama, Clayborne thought, where his people had come from, where Old Grandma had moved from after marrying John Bunyon Perry in South Carolina. He had not thought about Old Grandma for months, it seemed. But now he could feel her living soul whisper to him again of education, of pushing forward, of getting up that ladder, of learning all there was to know, education, education, and more education. Every time they passed a school or a little college he felt a twinge. Why wouldn't she leave him alone? He had his master's degree, didn't he? He was an educated and respected community leader now, wasn't he? That was enough, wasn't it?

The flat Gulf coastal plain sloped those days away through Jackson and Vicksburg where the Second World War was over but the Civil War was not, and on into Louisiana in resin smells of loblolly and slash pine and little open-air sawmills and curious shanties where black people and poor whites lived squalid by the roadside, huts framed from pine poles and covered only with large battered sheet-metal billboard signs advertising soft drinks, bent to form walls and roof, a poverty-gaudy style of hovel architecture known to the locals only as a "Coca-Cola shack," inelegant but adequate for brute shelter.

On the fourth and last day of the trip, after they had crossed through Monroe and Shreveport from Louisiana into the glaring Texas sun and now rode not far from Dallas, Bob and Margie visited with a soldier bound for Denton. The young veteran asked the children: "Are you two anxious to get home now that you're gettin' close?"

"Nope," said Margie.

"Not me," said Bob. "Are you?"

"Sure," said the young corporal. "I've been away a long time. Don't you like home?"

"Sure, we like home, don't we Margie?"

"Yep," she piped sweetly, prim in a gingham dress her mother had made. "I've got a playhouse at home down in the cellar that's all my own. I've got my dolls in my doll beds and *nobody* can come in without *my* permission. 'Cept Mom and Dad, of course. But not my friends and not

Bobby. But I like to ride and go sightseeing, too. 'Specially in a school bus."

"Are you in school yet?"

"Nope," said Margie. "I'm almost seven but my birthday comes on the first of October, so I couldn't start school last year. But I'll be in first grade when school starts again."

"I thought you looked big for somebody not in school yet. Bob, what do you do at home?" asked the serviceman.

"In the summer?" said Bob. "I play with our little chihuahua dog Midget. I ride my bike around. I mow yards and do jobs for my Dad. And I work to make money for the auction sales."

"Auction sales? What do you buy?"

"Sheep. And goats. I keep 'em a while, feed 'em up, then sell 'em at the auction sales."

"Do you keep the goats at home?"

"Yep, we have a big back yard. Got a rabbit pen there, too."

"You raise rabbits?"

"Yep, last year I had almost seventy at one time. Slaughtered 'em myself, hit 'em in the back of the head with a little old pipe, hung 'em up, skinned 'em, cut out the entrails, washed 'em. Sold 'em to people. There's a lot of good meat on a rabbit."

"Did you eat them?"

Bob looked away. "Nope."

"Why not?"

"Well, rabbits are . . . Well, they're like a dog or a cat. You know, like a pet."

"I know what you mean. I used to raise rabbits, too, before the war. Never ate 'em either."

"You didn't?"

"Nope. I knew those rabbits. I couldn't eat 'em. It would be like eating your friends."

"Yeah," said Bob, gazing out the window at the hot Texas landscape now, turned away from the conversation to daydreaming of other subjects, other times. "It would."

"Come on in, Superintendent Perry," said Dr. Lorena Stretch brightly. "How are you?"

"I'm doing fine, Dr. Stretch. And yourself?"

"Fine, too. And the family?"

"Everybody's fine."

"Have a seat. And tell me what this mysterious question is that you need to ask me."

Clayborne had lost track of how many times he had taken a seat thus in Dr. Stretch's office at Baylor. He looked at her and said, "A lot of water's gone under the bridge since I first walked in here looking for advice."

"That it has, Mr. Perry. Tempus fugit."

"Time flies," said Clayborne.

"I see you remember your Latin."

"A little. Dr. Stretch, we've had men returning home from the war for quite a while now. We'll be able to run a normal school this fall."

"It's the same everywhere, Mr. Perry."

"And I've spent the two weeks since we got back from Fort Wayne trying to find materials so we can repair the old grammar school building. You know, even with rationing gone you still can't find much, and the quality is so poor you feel like you're wasting your money."

"That's too bad."

"After the board of education saw how I'm doing with the new First Baptist Church, they want me to look into building a new elementary school next year. They want it to have an auditorium and a modern cafeteria."

"That's wonderful. But you're beating around the bush. I know you too well, Mr. Perry, you must have a really important question to ask this time."

Clayborne smiled at his old counselor who was now his old friend.

"You're right. I need some serious advice. I've been thinking about what to do. I want to continue in public school administration, but I don't want to just stay put. I want to go to the top of the ladder. I might want to move someplace else where the requirements are stricter. With all the men come back from the war — and they're different, Dr. Stretch, they've seen things, they've been places, things are changing — there's going to be competition like never before. If I had a doctor's degree, I'd stand head and shoulders above those who don't. How do I get one?"

"Ump," said Dr. Stretch, a little taken aback. "That *is* a question."

"What's the answer?"

"Well, you know that Baylor doesn't offer a doctoral program — yet. We're going to one of these days. It's in the works, but it has to go through the board of trustees and the administration and so on. It's not approved yet."

"When?"

"I don't know. Probably a year. Next summer, most likely."

"A year? A year's a long time."

"You could go to the University of Texas down in Austin. . ."

"No, I've thought about that, it's too far away. I'd have to move, find another job, it's too complicated. I want to go to Baylor. A year for sure, no more?"

"I think so."

"Summer of 1947?"

"A pretty good bet."

"Then I'll wait. I want to go to Baylor."

"If you want to go to Baylor for a doctorate, you'll *have* to wait. But I'll tell you this: if you give me your word that you will wait and go to Baylor, I'll volunteer right this minute to be your advisor. As head of the education department I can make sure you get the help you need. Your word?"

"Done."

"All right, Mr. Perry, here's how it will go. You could get a Doctor of Philosophy or a Doctor of Education. A Ph.D. will require one more class in a foreign language than an Ed.D."

"Which would you recommend?"

"I'll tell you honestly, Mr. Perry, if you're going to stay in public education the Ed.D. is the degree to get; it's respected more highly in those circles than the Ph.D. A Ph.D. would be better if you planned on going into academia."

"I'm thinking about public schools."

"Then the Ed.D. it is. Have you been thinking about any particular specialty?"

"Yes, Dr. Stretch, I have. The newspapers and magazines are talking about a war-baby boom, the birth rate is going up to beat the band. That'll mean the need for more schools for the next twenty years. And then their children will need more schools. It's the wave of the future. Planning and administration of new school construction is what I'd like to specialize in."

"That may give us some problems, Mr. Perry. I'm not sure we'll have courses in everything you'll need. But we'll manage somehow. The Ed.D. program I've suggested to President Neff requires 66 semester hours of class work. That's two years going full time, and I know you'll be going something under one-third time, like you did on your master's degree. Are you ready to work on a doctor's degree for six or seven years, until — what would that be? — until 1953?"

Clayborne sat back unsmiling. "Until 1953!" he said to himself. "And it's 1946 now! My, that sounds like a long time."

"It *is* a long time. And that's only the class work, Mr. Perry. A doctor's degree requires a dissertation as well. A doctoral dissertation is nothing like your master's thesis. The requirements for a doctorate are much more strict. You will have to perform genuine research that adds significantly to mankind's store of knowledge. Your dissertation must be accurate and it must be valuable. It will enter the literature of education and be cited by others for years to come. It may take as much as another three years to finish. You may have to work until 1956 to get a doctor's degree. Are you game?"

"Nineteen-fifty-six. . ." Clayborne laid his chin on his clasped hands and thought. Was that Old Grandma prodding him on in the recesses of his mind? "Ten years. . ." he muttered. Then he straightened up in the chair and said, "In ten years it will be 1956 whether I work on my doctor's degree or not, won't it?"

"Yes," smiled Dr. Stretch, "it will."

"If I don't, I'll be Mr. Perry, and if I do, I'll be Dr. Perry, won't I?"

"Yes," said Dr. Stretch, "you will."

"Dr. Perry," he mused for a long second. "Dr. Perry. I like the sound of that. I guess I'm game. You let me know when I can start classes, will you?"

"I certainly will. And I'll try to hurry the doctoral program approval through our Baylor administration — so you can start classes next summer for sure!"

As the war had formally ended in September of 1945 so the duration finally ended in September of 1946. There was no proclamation or official declaration to put those hated words "for the duration" to rest, for they were simply forgotten in the skyrocket takeoff of the American post-war economy. After a year of retrenchment and regrouping, after all the surviving men had been home long enough to sleep off the war like some hideous drunken binge and decide in the sober light of peace what they wanted to do next, about the time schools started again all over the country, American business and industry began charting the greatest economic boom ever seen on the face of the earth.

The war technology that had once turned out Norden bombsights and radar and aircraft engines by the thousand now turned full force to remaking the peacetime nation in refrigerators and automobiles and automatic clothes washers by the million. The country hung on the brink, ready to explode in a starburst of civil affluence unprecedented in its breadth and depth in human history. It was to be the best of all possible worlds for a few gleaming moments. There still remained enough Depression privation for everyone to pull together and people still remembered well enough why the war had been fought for patriotism to remain in fashion this year. It was the dawn of a new hopeful age of peace rising in the remnant glow of an old vanquished age of war. This time nobody was stupid enough to believe it had been the war to end all wars, so the plowshare factories still made a few swords, particularly the atomic ones, just to stay on the safe side.

Taken all in all, it was an authentic new beginning, a yeasty ferment of top-speed industrialization in the matrix of patient agrarian culture, of the growth of cities and the living wage and the ample table and the ambitious struggle for true wealth, of new events like the rise of the

service sector's doctors and teachers and insurance salesmen and account-
ants on the shoulders of loggers and foundrymen and steel mill workers
and road engineers. For a while America was destined to shine as a joyous
radiant beacon in the night of a destroyed world. They were to be
wonderful years.

"Oretta, this is the first time school has started like it ought to since
1941," said Clayborne happily over the dinner table.

"What do you mean?"

"It took me a week to realize it. We've got plenty of *men* to go around."
He counted on his fingers for effect: "We have Claude Everett for
principal in the high school *and* Mr. Evans for principal in the grammar
school. *And* We've got Lee Erickson to coach the girls basketball team,
and three other men working as teachers."

Oretta said, "And I see you even got a man to take over the young
people at church — now that you're Sunday School Superintendent."

"Yes," said Clayborne, "That Billy Warren is a fine man. Oh, did I tell
you he and Lola are moving into Mrs. Jones's garage apartment up the
street?"

"No! Is that right?" smiled Oretta. "It'll be nice to have 'em so close."

"I like Mr. Warren," said Bob.

"That's good, son," said Clayborne. "He's doing a fine job working for
his Dad on the new church building."

"His Dad?" asked Bob.

"Mr. Burney Warren, son. You know him. That's Billy Warren's Dad.
They're in the contracting business together now."

Oretta said, "There's so many new things going on in this town! I
heard that Bobby and Faye Curtis bought the picture show. They're
remodeling it right now. Going to call it the Capitol Theatre."

"And Bobby Pounds will still be able to work for 'em," interjected
Bob. "Isn't that good?"

"It sure is, son. I'm real glad," said Clayborne. "You know, we had a
teacher's meeting today and I reminded one of our new teachers that these
poorer kids like Bobby need to be encouraged. The better-off kids have
plenty opportunity, but the poor ones, well, they need a little extra help
— it's the only way they'll make it. Seems like that's a new idea to some of
these younger teachers."

Oretta said, "You keep it up, Clayborne, it's the right thing to do. Oh,
and did you hear that Red Nichols's boy Ed is starting up a new car place.?"

"He's going to sell Willys Jeeps," said Clayborne.

"Is that like Army jeeps, Dad?" asked Margie.

"Pretty much like them, only for ranchers and deer hunters and such."

Bob said, "Dad, I heard that Mr. Nichols had to kill some people
getting away from the Germans. And he rode back to France on a
motorcycle! Has he told you about it?"

"No, son. He just shuns you off if you ask. It was his Dad, Mr. Red Nichols, that told me about the Germans. Ed doesn't talk much about the war. None of the servicemen do. I think they just want to forget about it."

"Well, I don't blame them," said Oretta, "I don't like war talk, either. Bob, how do you like school now that you're a freshman?"

"I haven't been a freshman long enough to know, Mom. The lunch room has better food this year, and that's good . . ."

"Rationing's over," said Clayborne. "We can buy what we can afford."

Oretta said, "I'm sure glad we don't have to fool around with all those stamps any more. But steak has gone up to fifty cents a pound. I was worried what would happen when they took those ceiling prices off. If meat keeps going up, I've half a mind to try what my Papa used to do, take a shotgun and go down by the river and shoot me a squirrel, fix up squirrel and dumplings."

Clayborne smiled, "I remember your Papa doing that. He'd feed a table of twelve on squirrel and dumplings. As I recollect there was always more dumplings than squirrel."

"Oh, Dad, that big tall new boy you brought in to class, remember Bennett Moser?" — pronounced Moz*her*, just as groceries was pronounced gro*sher*ies. "Yes, son, what about him?"

"He's a lot of fun, Dad. You know how we play chase at recess? Well, ol' Bennett's pretty tough to tackle. And he tells these strange stories about all the places his family's been. He even brought his guitar to school and sang yesterday at lunch. But, Dad, some of the kids make fun of him behind his back."

"Oh?" said Clayborne noncommittally.

"Well, he's kind of a hillbilly, y'know. And he's seventeen — that's as old as the seniors, Dad. Why is he still just a freshman?"

"His family moves around, son. He hasn't been able to stay in one place and take care of his studies like most kids. I wouldn't call any attention to his age now."

"We don't, Dad. He's real good to us thirteen-year-olds."

Bob sat thoughtfully for a moment. "Dad, why does Bennett's family move around so much?"

"They cut posts on the cedar mountains for a living, son. It's the kind of work that you just stay long enough to cut out of posts in one place and then move on to the next good cutting spot. I don't imagine they make much from it."

"Dad, do you think Bennett was serious about the Shredded Ralston?"

"What do you mean?" asked Clayborne.

"Bennett says his Dad buys their family Shredded Ralston for dinner, puts a whole box in a dish pan in the middle of the table, puts sugar and skim milk on it, and the seven kids and everybody just digs in with a spoon."

"Why Shredded Ralston? Why not Post Toasties or something?"

"Bennett says it's because his Dad listens to his programs with him sometimes when it rains and he can't work. Says he likes Tom Mix. He got it from the Tom Mix song."

"The Tom Mix song?"

"Yeah, Dad, Tom sings it on the radio at the end of every program. The announcer comes on and it goes like this:"

Bob did a perfect imitation of the ingratiating voice of the announcer and the cowboy singer's jingle set to the tune of *When It's Roundup Time in Texas*.

ANNOUNCER: Say, here's how to make breakfast as exciting as a circus and a three-day rodeo rolled into one:

TOM MIX: Shred-ded Ralston for your breakfast
  Starts the day off shinin' bright,
  Gives you lots of cowboy energy
  With the flavor that's just right,
  It's delicious and nutritious,
  Bit size n' ready-to-eat,
  Take a tip from Tom
  Go and tell your Mom
  Shredded Ralston can't be beat."

Oretta said, "Don't sing at the table, son."

"I'm sorry, Mom. I was just trying to tell Dad why Mr. Moser feeds his family Shredded Ralston. He says if Tom Mix says it's nutritious, it's good enough for him."

"Don't you spread that story around school, Bob, you hear?" cautioned Clayborne. "If Bennett wants to tell it, let him. But don't you repeat it. Their family has a hard enough time as it is."

"Yes, Dad."

"So you're doing all right at school, then?" Clayborne asked his boy.

"Well, I kinda miss going down to the river every day and staying inside isn't really much fun."

"You got to be quite the outdoorsman this summer," said his father with circumspect satisfaction, "running all over with Bobby Pounds. But now that school's started, you know I expect you to keep your grades up whether it's fun or not."

"Yes, sir, Dad."

"I'm making *good* grades, Dad," said Margie proudly. "Mrs. Ennis gave me a gold star on my spelling today."

Next afternoon at school Bob and his friend Bobby Pounds joined in a basketball game in the huge old school gym — nothing official, just eight or ten boys playing for fun. Bob was determined to make a good showing in sports this year, to do more than just mark a spot. He had been on the varsity football team, although he was on the second team and saw almost no action in the games. Sports were the focus of community life in

Meridian, the sure path to recognition and achievement. The boys put everything they had into the basketball play today. A keen competition suddenly blossomed between the two, and, as can happen in such impromptu contests, one of Bobby Pounds' passes went wide of the mark and Bob missed it.

"You threw that out of bounds !" shouted Bob, angrily marching up to his friend.

"Aw, you're blind as a bat, Perry! That was in by a mile. You just can't catch for sour apples." Pounds stood his ground, matching Bob's bellicose gestures. They stood eyeball to eyeball. The others broke into grins and closed in, egging them on: "Get 'im, Pounds. Don't let Perry push you around." "Come on, Perry, show 'im what's good for him."

"Listen, Pounds," said Bob, "you threw wild. It's your fault."

"You're just a no-good basketball player, Perry!"

"If you could throw the ball straight, I would have caught it, Pounds!"

"Dammit, I still say you're no good, and I ain't goin' to pick you on my team next time!"

"Oh, yeah?"

"Yeah!"

The fists started windmilling fast. Most blows glanced off hard muscles but a few landed good and square. Bob took a dead right to the jaw and came back with a quick right to Pounds' left eye. Pounds landed a few more. Perry landed a few more.

Principal Everett came out of the coach's room at the first sound of disturbance, storming up to the flailing teenagers and shouting, "All right! Knock it off, you two!" He separated them quickly, using all the authority he had learned in the military. "Pounds, you made your point. Perry, I expected better of you. Both of you go sit in the bleachers. Any more of this stuff and I'm going to get my paddle out."

After school as Bob walked down B Street toward home, rubbing his aching jaw and realizing that he had come out the loser, Bobby Joe came running up from behind. Bob instinctively whirled, ready for anything. Then he saw the smile.

"Hey, Bob, let's go out to the highway and hitch a ride to Phauney's place. He's got some baby chicks to look at," said Pounds.

Bob looked at his fourteen-year-old friend in surprise. "No hard feelings? Then how come you ran up on me so fast?" he asked.

"Hard feelings?" Pounds asked, genuinely puzzled. "Oh, the sluggin' match! You think I'd stop likin' you just 'cause of a few friendly slugs? And I ran up so fast so's I could catch up to you. I had to finish sweeping the classrooms for Mr. Graves."

"You're not mad any more?"

"Mad? Me? Why, I'm real insulted that you'd think so," grinned Pounds.

Bob relaxed. He cherished this friendship that fighting could not erase. He said, "Why are you sweeping classrooms in the grammar school for Mr. Graves? *He*'s the janitor."

"He's just bein' nice to me, gives me ten cents a day. Ol' Mr. Graves — he says to call him Dick but I call him Mr. Graves anyhow — he pays me out of his own money, the school don't give him any extra for me helpin'. I think he just likes me, he don't have any kids of his own, never got married. I don't mind the sweepin' and it gives me fifty cents a week, you know. Now, what about goin' to see those chickens?"

"All right, how about a snack at my place first and then let's go see Phauney's chicks. And let's see if we can find ol' Bennett Moser to go with us."

"It's a deal."

That night at the dinner table Bob could not chew hard food but said nothing of his plight. His father looked at him for a long while and then said, "I understand that Bobby Pounds got the best of you this afternoon."

"Who told you, sir?"

"I know these things."

"I guess he did."

For several days Clayborne watched his boy chewing gingerly at meals, favoring soft foods, wincing with pain. The jaw hurt so badly that Bob thought it was probably broken, but he said nothing to anyone about it, particularly not his father.

Seniors at Meridian in 1946 enjoyed hazing freshmen. By the time school had progressed three weeks, Bob and many of his classmates had borne half a dozen humiliating senior paddlings, had polished several dozen pairs of senior shoes before school, had done several hundred pushups at senior insistence and had said thousands of "yes, sirs" to beardless seniors bent on intimidating their underclassmen. The seniors on the football team seemed to particularly enjoy tormenting freshmen. Bob wondered occasionally why his father permitted this kind of behavior on campus, but never said anything about it.

Wednesday, October second, the day after Margie turned seven years old, Bob stood outside the great stone high school edifice after lunch with his friends Bennett Moser and Bobby Pounds along with a few other freshmen. The captain of the football team walked up with his clique of sycophants, just back from getting their lunch at a downtown cafe. The captain was a proud young man with a streak of the ruffian. His team's first game of the season had been against Whitney, a little school that had lost the less-than-spectacular scrimmage and splashed glory over Meridian's football captain. However, today the football captain was still trying to live down Meridian's second game, which he had lost last week 40 to 0 to Clifton. Bob was just as glad he had stayed on the sidelines during that game. Venom glinted in the team captain's eye as he ambled up to the little group of freshmen and addressed Bob's friend Bennett Moser.

Bennett Moser was fairly tall, almost six feet, and the same age as the seniors, but a little on the skinny side, rawboned and as countrified as they come. He truly longed to do well in school, perhaps felt his scholastic inadequacies more keenly than others, and had tolerated the seniors' hazing better than most. The team captain, dressed in slacks and western cut dress shirt, contemplated Moser who stood there in his work jeans and hickory shirt and high topped brogans. Then the senior spoke: "What's your name, frosh?"

"Bennett Moser, R. C. You know me."

"Bennett Moser, *what?*"

The freshman sighed and gave in: "Bennett Moser, *sir.*"

"That's better. And what kind of jackass are you, Bennett Moser?"

Bennett bit his tongue.

The team captain stepped closer to Moser and repeated, "What kind of jackass are you, Bennett Jackass Moser?"

"What did you say, R. C.?" asked Moser as evenly as he could manage.

"I said 'What kind of jackass are you?' And call me 'sir.' Now answer me, jackass!" The team captain pushed Moser back with a haughty gesture.

A bully-buddy called, "Show 'im who's boss, R. C."

"What are you talking to me that way for?" asked Bennett calmly.

More pushes from the team captain. The freshmen kept their mouths shut and their eyes open. Bennett allowed himself to be pushed back until he thudded against the dressed stone school wall.

"That's enough, R. C." he said quietly, staring steadily into the team captain's eyes.

"That's not enough for a jackass!" yelled the team captain as he pushed Moser hard into the stone once more.

Bennett Moser stood stock still and drew himself up to his full height. Quicker than sight his fists lashed out, bouncing the football captain's head twice, once left, once right. The startled captain tried to lunge forward but found himself suddenly flying backward, Moser's head in his belly and the ground rushing up to knock the air clean out of him. He was flat on his back on the Texas dirt with Moser sitting on his chest. The ingominious fall left the captain paralyzed with humiliation. He could not even cry out in pain.

Moser asked firmly, "Are you through callin' me a jackass, big Mr. Captain toughass?"

The glazed eyes of the football captain tried desperately to signal surrender, for he could find no voice in his throat, his lungs refused to work.

Moser got up off the boy's chest. R.C. started to breathe again. But he made no move. The domineering football captain lay domineered, the intimidator intimidated. Fear oozed from his pores. Moser turned to the other seniors who looked on stupefied. The lanky freshman's fists were still clenched. What a great opportunity for a line out of a cowboy movie — "Next?" or "Anybody else want a dose of the same?" But Bennett Moser was not the articulate type and let his actions do the talking. He turned to his freshmen friends who walked wordlessly into the school building with their new hero.

That night at dinner Bob waited for his opportunity.

"I got a letter from the real estate agent today," said Clayborne to Oretta. "The sale went through. Grandpa Jim Perry's farm at Dude Flat is sold."

"Oh, Clayborne," said Oretta, "that's where you grew up . . ."

"And where I was born. It went to some folks name of Hamilton. My, I sure hate to see that place leave the family. But Grandpa is just about an invalid now, living there in Iredell with Aunt Julia and Arthur. He needs the money more than the land. He'll never farm it again."

"Did they get much for it?"

"Enough. Nine thousand. I had the agent put it in the First National Bank of Hico so Grandpa's expenses can be paid from it."

"Well, I'm sure it'll help him and the Russells. Arthur and Julia have been so good to your Grandpa."

Silence at the table as everyone went on eating. It seemed like a bad time for Bob to talk about school problems. He let the moment go by.

Then his mother said, "Clayborne, I hear that your college friend from Tarleton has bought one of those outdoor theatres in Waco."

"Marvin Miller? I'd heard he was thinking about it. Drive-Ins, they call them. I guess he's just become a regular businessman. I don't expect we'll see him teaching ever again."

"I suppose not," said Oretta.

Bob saw his chance. He got up his nerve and asked his father. "Dad, why don't you do something to make those seniors leave us freshmen alone?"

Clayborne looked at his son as he chewed on a bite of pork chop. He saw his son's struggle to get the message across yet to stay within bounds of proper respect. How to explain that putting the foot of authority down too hard risked genuine rebellion as Meridian had once had over school dances?

"Dad," said Bob, "really, these seniors aren't playing. They hurt people."

"Son, from what I saw out my office window at noon today, seems like I ought to do something to protect the seniors from the freshmen. What do you think?"

In a week or two, by late October, Clayborne had reached a significant milestone as a Mason: he had worked his way through the chairs and became Worshipful Master of the Meridian Masonic Lodge — and he had completed the York route and went to Waco to be installed in the Kareem Temple as a Noble of the Mystic Shrine. Some fifteen qualified Masons went that day in cars from Meridian, Bill Warren, the young man Clayborne had appointed Sunday School teacher in the First Baptist Church, and Bill's father Burney, and the lumber yard manager Garland Davis, and the wool and mohair bonded warehouseman Jack Kirby, and the agriculture teacher Lester Smith, and Guy Briley of the auto supply store, and several others Clayborne was not as close to, and together they became Shriners, going through the ceremonial, receiving the obligations, taking instruction in the meaning of the shrine. It took nearly a whole day, finishing about 4:00 p.m. When he came out Clayborne was entitled to wear the Shriner fez and take part in all the celebrations and parades and charity work.

As winter came on and the holiday season came and went and 1947 appeared on all the new calendars, Clayborne kept up his steady routine, supervising the construction of the new church as it went apace, and at school, making sure teachers and students got where they were supposed to go and do what they were supposed to do. He still taught a class in geometry, keeping his oar in the nuts and bolts of education along with his lofty administrative duties. And he regularly wandered through the study halls and around the campus.

"Mr. Perry," called Donna Cameron.

"Yes," he responded across the study hall, "what can I do for you?" He ambled over and took a seat next to his across-the-street neighbor.

"I'm having trouble with this history class, Mr. Perry," she said in a low voice to avoid disturbing the two dozen others in the room.

"What's the problem? Is your asthma bothering you today?"

"No, it's not that."

"Is the work too hard?"

"No, I can do the work. Being a freshman in high school is harder than it was in grammar school, but that's not it. It's just that history is so boring and so useless. These people we're studying about have all been dead for years and I just don't see what possible good it can do me to learn about them."

"I see," said Clayborne. "Is your teacher trying to make it interesting?"

"Oh, he thinks it's super-interesting talking about the Greeks and Romans. But I don't. Why do we have to learn this?"

"Well, now, Donna," said Clayborne, "We do some things in school to develop good habits. History teaches us the habit of thinking about our past so we can avoid making the same mistakes in the future. Like we get into the habit of brushing our teeth in the morning, the reason we do some other things is like an exercise, to develop good thinking and study habits. You might not find all of it very interesting, but history teaches you the habit of thinking about the past before you act."

"I never thought of it that way, Mr. Perry," said the teenager.

"Glad to be of help. I expect you'll have similar questions next year in my geometry class. A lot of students can't understand why they have to study that."

By March it became evident that the First Baptist Church construction fund was in trouble. The $20,000 raised by the congregation was dwindling rapidly in the course of normal construction and it still looked like $35,000 would be required for completion. In early May it happened: the church fund ran out of money. The $20,000 they had raised was spent to the penny. Dr. Holt, as chairman of the church finance committee, accompanied Clayborne to the First National Bank of Waco and, amid cajolery and a little friendly arm-twisting, made arrangements to borrow $15,000 to finish things up, pledging additional church funds that now began to appear each Sunday in full collection plates. By now the form of the new church had fully materialized — the imposing roof and walls were framed and covered, some of the brickwork was up and visitors could see the large auditorium, the banquet hall and some twenty Sunday School classrooms taking shape. All it needed now was finishing and the bank loan made that a living certainty. With Clayborne supervising as usual, the construction went on. And amid the flurry of construction duties Clayborne received a terse note in the mail:

Program approved. Doctoral degree now available at Baylor. You can start in June. See me for course approvals. — L. Stretch, Ph.D.

"Hello, Mr. Perry, Hello, Bob."

"Well, hello there, Bobby Pounds!" smiled Clayborne. "What are you doing here in the square so early Saturday morning?"

"I was talking to Mr. Curtis at the Capitol theatre, Mr. Perry. How was the senior trip, sir?"

"We had a good time in Austin and San Antonio. We went on the school bus and stayed three whole days!"

"That's neat."

Clayborne said to the youngster, "We'll be doing it every year, Bobby. The seniors got to see all the sights and ate frogs legs and took pictures of everything. We visited the State Capitol and the Alamo. But you'll get to see for yourself. You'll be going with us when you graduate, too, you know."

"I don't think so, Mr. Perry."

"What do you mean?" said the superintendent. "What's the matter? You look like the sun didn't come up today."

"I'm moving away."

"Moving away?" said Bob. "You can't! When?"

"Next week. My Mama got a good job in Brownwood."

"Brownwood! That's over a hundred miles!"

"I know."

"I'll come see you . . . I'll . . . "

"It's all right."

Clayborne extended his hand to the Pounds boy. Bobby grasped the hand hesitantly. "Bobby," said Clayborne solemnly. "I wish you all the best. You're a fine young man. I've enjoyed having you at school. You'll do fine in Brownwood."

"Yes, sir."

Bob looked at his friend. Clayborne said nothing, remembering how he once looked that way at childhood friends never seen again, how he once spoke the mortal fear his son now voiced.

"Are you really moving away?"

"Yep."

Once more the family rode a train northward out of Texas, leaving Dallas at five in the afternoon, arriving in Chicago at eight the next morning, ending up over in Detroit by two that afternoon. They picked up a brand new Plymouth at the Chrysler plant and drove on through the days first to Montreal and then Quebec, marveling at the francophones and the old buildings, coming back into Maine and through New Hampshire and Vermont, through New York and New Jersey and Pennsylvania and on into Washington, D. C. Further down the long road they would see the cities of Atlanta and Tallahassee, and drive through the Alabama of their ancestors. But while they lingered in the marble city of Washington, absorbing their heritage through their eyes, Clayborne asked his family, "What would you think of taking a regular vacation after I finish my session at Baylor this summer?"

"Yay!" cried Margie and Bob together as they drove down the Mall past the Lincoln Memorial.

"Where would we go?" asked Oretta.

"I've been thinking about that. Seeing all this history here in Washington clinches it. We ought to go out and see where my folks tried to be pioneers in Colorado. We ought to go back to Trinchera."

"Wow!" said Bob. "And see the dugout houses?"

"If they're still there. That was over thirty years ago, you know. Look here, we're going to go right by the Washington Monument. Look out the window!"

"Oh, Clayborne," said Oretta. "You've told us about Trinchera so many times I feel like I've been there already. I'd love to see it in person finally."

"Can we see Ol' Donkey, Dad?" asked Margie.

Clayborne smiled. "I don't know about *my* Ol' Donkey, but I'm sure we'll see *somebody's* ol' donkey along the way."

"Dad?" said Bob.

"What is it, son?"

"Thank you for what you said to Bobby Pounds."

In mid-June Clayborne began getting up at 5:00 a.m. and driving forty-five miles to Waco for the first classwork on his doctoral degree. Five days a week he carried a full load of four courses from 7:00 a.m. to 11:00 a.m., drove home by noon, ate lunch and went to work at the school office from 1:00 p.m. to dark, had supper and studied until bedtime at 10:00 p.m. He studied educational administration and statistics and the planning and construction of school buildings. During Clayborne's crowded, swirling six weeks at Baylor, Bob got his driver's license at age fourteen — the youngster took the family's second car, an old 1937 two-door, six cylinder, 60 horsepower Ford, took it to the Bosque County courthouse on the square in Meridian where the state driver's license bureau operated an office one day a week. And Bobby Curtis built another picture show in Meridian, across from the courthouse and called it the new Capitol Theater. They kept the old one open on the weekends only and named it the Bosque Theater. And Clayborne still supervised the construction of the First Baptist Church. He also decided to get in on the building boom himself: he and Oretta formed a partnership with Dr. Holt and bought three old rundown houses in Meridian with the idea of fixing them up and selling them later to make a little extra money and giving Bob something to do to keep him busy in the summer.

In late July they went looking for their roots, retracing the doomed footsteps of those Perry and Blackburn and Dozier visionaries who went out to Colorado looking for a new American life, taking up land by Trinchera. They did not suffer the shrewd bite of winter wind in a cattle car nor the sooty exhaustion of a long passenger train ride: Clayborne and his beautiful wife and his handsome young son and his sweet little girl dovoured the miles in a plush upholstered new Plymouth equipped with Floating Power and all the latest advances in automotive engineering.

They drove through the fine day disregarding the miles. When night came they did not peer fearfully through wooden slats at a skyful of galactic fire burning down on a desert plain of timeless silence and ancient grass and solitude and space, they stopped at a tourist court and slept in comfortable beds. Because they wanted to, they wound around through Lubbock instead of turning north to Amarillo, and went to Seagraves, Texas, eight or ten miles from the New Mexico border. There they stopped overnight at the home of Jerry Phillips, former superintendent of Iredell schools, their neighbor of many years who now pursued his career out here in the Permian Basin country with the pink dust and the rangeland and the lesser prairie chickens and the cotton and the invading sand shinnery oak two feet high and ten miles wide.

They drove the next day to Santa Fe and the next to Eagle Nest Lake and then to Trinidad where the streets were still paved with splendid red brick that looked to Clayborne only a little more rounded and the old Opera House falling to disrepair and the Victorian Rococo Bloom house and the Greek Revival Baca house both now historical museums and the streetcars a thing of the past, evaporated in the blazon of time. The Jerryville coal seams hadn't played out, really, but the old coal-fired locomotives were giving way to diesel engines nowadays and then, too, people were turning more and more to commercial airlines to get from place to place and the words of a long-gone Trinidad miner talking to Tom Perry echoed in Clayborne's memory — "The coal business will never go bad, not as long as there's trains, and that'll be forever." They visited Pike's Peak up the winding road with the endless cliff on one side, the gravel road which seemed so narrow that two cars could not pass and Margie felt that her Dad was the bravest man in the world because she was absolutely terrified and he seemed so cool and confident.

The next day they drove to Trinchera on a road that hadn't been there thirty-two years before but the railroad station sign still said TRINCHERE in illiterate unconcern and the gravel path north to the old homesteads had been graded. They stooped north now, eager in anticipation, all of them. The flat plain of scanty grass appalled them in the summer sun. No crops could grow here, it was plain to see. A house could be found on occasion, and a few head of livestock punctuated the featureless waste here and there: not many. Five miles north of Trinchera they lost the trace.

Fences guarded the land now, posts and barbed wire wandering in dress parade over the blank battlefields of ants and mice and winter snowstorms, and Clayborne could not find his way. He drove to the nearest house, a little frame farm house, and knocked on the door. It opened.

"Are you lost?" asked a short lady in a long calico dress with an apron tied around it.

"Yes, Ma'am. I'm W. C. Perry from Meridian, Texas, and my Papa and my uncles used to live somewhere around here back in 1915. But I don't know the way. Would you know where to direct us?"

"Perry?" the woman asked. "Was your daddy's name Leonard Perry?"

"No, Ma'am, he was my uncle. My daddy was Tom Perry."

"I haven't thought of Leonard Perry in a long time, a long time."

"You knew him then?"

"I was ten years old. Him and his wife and his little kids used to stay near here summers. I'd go visit them on their homestead, the Newcombes own it now. I'd see them going into town in their wagons. Leonard Perry would stop and tell funny stories. Lived here maybe five summers. Worked in the winter up at Pueblo in the coal mines. Is he still alive?"

"Yes, he has a farm near Midlothian, Texas. He's doing fine. Can you tell me how to get to where they lived?"

"Wouldn't do you any good."

"Why not?"

"There's no road and a lot of fences."

"Can you get there in a car?"

"You can, but you don't have the key to the gates and I do. Why don't I just come with you? I'll *show* you where to go."

"I'd be much obliged, I sure would. I hope you don't mind riding with my family, Miz. . ."

"Baker, Effie Baker. My friends just call me Effie."

They drove away north again after the round of introductions and Effie Baker navigated from the back seat with the children peering ahead at her directions.

"Okay, you bear a little right at this rise, no right here, right here, that's it. It's been a long time since I been out here, years and years. And let's see, the hill over on this side lines up with that hill over there. . ."

Everyone was baffled by her notion of "hills": everything around them was flatter than an amateur yodeler. She could see hills where the merest suggestion of a bulge showed on the horizon and directed herself accordingly. They went on following her inspired directions for several miles it seemed.

Then Effie Baker said, "Stop here."

Clayborne stopped the Plymouth and everybody got out.

Effie said, "The dugouts are right here."

"Where?" said Bob, straining in every direction to see.

"Where?" said Margie in disappointment.

"Where?" said Oretta skeptically.

"Right here," said Effie pointing to a shallow grassy crater.

"This can't be right " Clayborne said. "The dugouts were four, five feet deep. These holes are just a couple of feet deep."

"Wind brings the dust, fills 'em in, rounds 'em off, brings the seed.

You're looking at thirty years of dust, Mister. This is the place, all right. Your uncle Leonard Perry lived right here. There's two more dugouts, come on, I'll show you."

She paced away due south, first to one crater nearly identical to the first and then due east to another, the Perry family drawn along in her slipstream.

"I guess this is right," said Clayborne at the third dent in the dirt. "They're in the right places one to the other. This would have been where the Blackburns lived." He looked around at this strange empty place trying to convince himself it had been his home once.

The desolation was shattering.

"I can't imagine *living* here," said Oretta, thunderstruck.

Clayborne looked more intently now, staring hard at the cancelled prairie, trying to match the present reality with the virtual images in his memory but finding no fit.

"It must be the right place," said Clayborne unsure of his own words. "Then our tent must have been just due north from here, and the spring where we used to get water right straight east."

"Don't know about no spring," said Effie. "But they always had water. Must have been some around here someplace."

"I know where it is," said Clayborne. "Come on, I'll drive us over there."

They all ran back to the car and piled in. They flattened a mile's worth of grass and fetched up at the brink of Rail-O Canyon's nameless subcanyon where lay the clear water of the past.

"This is it," said Clayborne, jubilant at last. Now he believed it without reservation. "There's the trail down to the spring!"

They clambered down the old familiar path still carved unchanged in the cliffside. And as he knew, in the bed of this subcanyon stream rose a series of five substantial springs, bubbling up cool and pure from the rocks, strung on the creek like big blue beads. Down they went into the living chasm and in due time set foot on the bottom.

There it was! The first spring! It still overflowed the magic life of the earth out onto the rocks, serene and stone-embraced, exactly as it had flowed thirty years ago. For a dizzy moment Clayborne was a boy again, five and a half years old, a syrup bucket full of water in his hands pulling his young shoulders down, his uncle's laugh crackling behind him at some joke he had told, his father's step crunching in front of him, his father living again, living, alive and strong and full of hope. . .

He turned away from the image and said to his son, "We hauled water up out of here, oh, I don't know how many times."

"It must have been a hard life, Dad," said Bob, eyeing the steep trail back up.

"Not so hard," said Clayborne, loving what lived in his memory, "Not so hard."

Once he got back up on the bench land out of the canyon, it began to come back to him, Clayborne thought. The places, the shapes of flat on flat on flat regained their foothold in his mind, the far sharp unflat ridges to the south especially. Then he noticed. Oretta and Bob and Margie, his loved ones, saw the past here, immersed themselves in it with fascination, but he did not. This place was not the past, it was the present. The real past had vanished in some direction he couldn't find again, like it was playing a trick on him. Oh, the place was right, the past had *happened* here, right here, among these visible objects, but the place, even though he had stayed hundreds of miles away from it all these years, had somehow kept pace with him day by day, following him up to present time like a shadow follows your footsteps, always in the present, always in the present, while the past had stolen around some corner in the mind of God. He might just as well have been created this very instant with the illusion that there had been a long past. He could not show his family the tent, or old Pet, or his dog Pup, or the makeshift chicken coop, or the Mexicans who lived down in the canyon.

You could never *really* go home again, he realized stoically. You could never *really* find your roots again because your roots are in the past that vanishes once it's played. There is no past *out there*, outside your skin, not even back there in the corkscrew orbit of the earth around the sun around the galaxy where Trinchera used to be thirty-two years and sixty billion miles ago. The past was only inside, in your memories, the batteries that store up time. There it was again. Time, perplexing time! What is it? Is it an artifact of the mind? What does it mean? He had felt this way before, felt it when people died, when Pup had died, when changes came. It was such a helpless feeling. Change, that's all time did. Time changes everything. Yes, he had felt this way before, but he was old enough now to sense a new truth: There's that in you which time cannot change. Spirit? Soul? Something. Perhaps he could not master time, but perhaps time could not master him either. And now he decided there was nothing for it but to face the changes of time with dignity.

They dropped Effie Baker off at her farm house amid profuse thanks. Clayborne walked the friendly farm lady to her door, thanking her again. When he got back into the Plymouth, Oretta slid over to him on the bench seat and he put his arm around her as they drove back to the little town of Trinchera. Margie and Bob kept that simple image of two rare affections, an image of a loving mother and father, an image that never left them.

They stopped at Doherty Mercantile Company and inquired after Joe and Eddie Doherty who had known the Perrys and Blackburns and

Doziers. Oretta and Bob and Margie gathered around. A very elderly gentlemen told Clayborne that he was Eddie Doherty. Joe had passed away some years ago, he said. Yes, he vaguely recollected the settlers up on the Picketwire that starved out. Their names were Perry, you say? Oh.

Clayborne talked old times with Eddie Doherty and felt at peace with himself. When he ran out of conversation he and his family went across the street to the tiny post office of Trinchera, Colorado, a little wooden shack with shaky old doors. Nobody there remembered any Perrys. They chatted a while and bought some postcards and then got back in the comfortable new Plymouth and drove home to Meridian, arriving the next evening.

Life in Meridian had hardly skipped a beat when they got back home. Clayborne took up the administrative work of the Meridian Independent School District. They went visiting on weekends, to Hico to visit Clayborne's mother, who always had a garden growing next to the house, to Iredell to visit Clayborne's Aunt Julia and her husband Arthur and sick, disheartened old Grandpa Jim, and to Robinson to visit Hoyt and his family on their farm. In the days of August heat Bob worked odd hours repairing the houses his parents had bought with Dr. Holt. He missed Bobby Pounds. But he began to talk to the Theirkins brothers Herman and Sherman and they made plans together to enter the September junior bulldogging contest in Waco, plans that began to consume him. Faster than heat lightning the summer ended and school started again.

Being a sophomore in high school did not impress Bob much, yet he put his usual dutiful effort into classwork, but always thinking ahead to the bulldogging contest. What if he won? He'd get himself a fine heifer to keep and groom for a year, a heifer he must return to the show in 1948 when his animal would stand for judging.

"Dad, can I take a job at Mr. Lomax's filling station?"

"Well, Bob, I thought you already had work with Dr. Holt at the hospital. Did you play out on that?"

"No, sir. I'm still doing cleanup at the hospital, two hours every morning, just like usual. I'd work after school for Mr. Lomax."

"Will you have time enough left over for your studies?"

"Yes sir, Dad."

"Why don't you ask Mr. Lomax if you can work for a few Saturdays and see if you can handle both jobs?"

"Okay, Dad."

"You're really set on winning one of those heifers, aren't you?"

"I got picked for the bulldogging team in my ag class, Dad. Me and Sherman Theirkins are going to the Stock Show for Meridian High School. I've got a good chance, Dad, a good chance. Gotta pay for the feed somehow . . ."

The big night arrived in hubub and cattle smells at the McLennan County Stock Show rodeo scramble. It was not the vast coliseum in Houston, to be sure, it was just a little building over by the Baylor campus in Waco that couldn't hold more than three-thousand or so spectators, but it seemed like the whole world was watching to the sixteen young high school bulldogging entrants. The arena itself was official rodeo size, a big, glaring, exposed area just laying there ready to humiliate you for the smallest slip-up.

Clayborne and Oretta and Margie sat together in the jammed rows of wooden seats encircling the arena, ready to cheer on their intrepid youngster. The announcer called the event over the echoing public address system, imperious and commanding: the bulldogging scramble with eight heifers picked from the cream of local herds, to be downed and haltered by sixteen entrants from Central Texas high school agriculture programs. Every boy has a fifty-fifty chance of going home with a beautiful little one-year project or a pocketful of regrets. And the gates are open!

Eight calves burst into the arena in wild confusion, shadowed by sixteen darting swarming teenage cowboys running, tripping, colliding, grabbing that head, bowling it down, slipping and sitting in dismay as they lost their animal and the heifers hoofed it off every which way, all to the frenzied yells of friends and parents in the stands — Get 'im, Bill; Get 'im, Bob; Get 'im J. B.; Get 'im Cecil; Get 'im Sherman, and so up to the ringing rafters. Bob ran first after this calf and then after that and then after the other, seeing them grabbed and stopped one by one by one until — impossible! All eight calves had been grabbed, half of them down already, some even haltered and won. No more calves to catch! Defeat! How could this happen? Bob stared at the seven other empty-handed cowboys who stared back at him, daunted and distraught. Suddenly a calf pulled loose from its captor and the chase was on again. A lucky break. Bob galvanized into flashing action and veritably leaped on the calf, grabbed it hard and held to it like a Junebug on a duck, stubborn and ferocious. He pulled its head and body down in a single motion, splat, flat on the arena floor. In half a second the noose flew over the heifer's head and it was his calf! Victory!

His family was elated. To Margie he was a hero nine feet tall. He had won a fifty dollar calf — which was an expensive critter in those days — and a great year-long ag project. When the Perrys could relax enough to look around the arena, they saw that Sherman Theirkins had downed a calf, too. Meridian had two winners tonight. They took the beasts home where they would care for them for the next year. The animals were washed, groomed and curried like tender babies. Clayborne bought a Jersey cow so Bob's heifer could nurse and gain weight fast. Bob hand-milked two quarts of milk each morning for the family before the young heifer calf got her share. Clayborne knew it was better for his son to be working on calves and sheep and rabbits than some of the other things he could have possibly become interested in. Bob's beast was pampered, fed royally and tended to like a visiting dignitary for the next year.

Those autumn evenings saw Clayborne driving faithfully to class at Baylor, slogging in the darkness after that distant doctor's degree. And every spare moment saw him supervising the last stages of his church construction tasks. Meridian's First Baptist Church stood all but complete, its dignified red brick walls now a seamless garment, cloaked and protected by a finely-wrought slate roof, its spacious welcoming white-columned entry capped by a high steeple spire, the earthly finger pointing aloft to God. Only the sidewalks and a few interior fixtures remained to be done. And one day in early October even they were finished.

Late in the month more than five hundred of the faithful turned out for the evening dedication and open house. The Meridian First Baptist Church was now open for God's business. The congregation entered reverently and bowed in prayer as Pastor McBeth consecrated the new sanctuary. They marched joyously as he led the way into the great banquet hall of shared fellowship. Tours of the classrooms and choir dressing room had been arranged. Friends and visitors thronged the new building, overflowing the large hall, waiting to hear the opening message from their church leaders. Mr. J. T. Lomax, deacon, prominent merchant, civic leader, took the microphone and addressed the crowd.

"We've all looked forward to this great day for more than a year and a half. We've all worked hard to make this dream come true for the Lord. People from all around are already beginning to say that Meridian has the finest Baptist church building in Bosque county. But one man has worked harder than the rest of us to make this dream come true for the Lord, and you all know who I mean. Come on up here, school superintendent W. C. Perry! And you, too, Mrs. Perry! Don't be shy!"

Applause arose, appreciative, thunderous, loving. The unsuspecting couple were shocked into immobility for a moment. Then they walked in dignity up to the hall podium and stood beside their friend and mentor before the audience. J. T. Lomax continued:

"There's no way we could possibly pay this man for all the dedicated effort he's put in to make this event tonight possible. And there's no way we could pay back this lady for all the hours we've taken her husband away from hearth and home. But as a token of our undying gratitude, the members of Meridian First Baptist Church hereby present you both with this certificate, which is good for a hundred-fifty gallons of gasoline just in case you want to get away for a while from all your construction duties. And Mrs. Perry, next week you will find installed in your home a brand new Bendix washing machine."

Applause, grateful, cherishing sounds from expressive human hands — it filled the great hall and it filled the great hearts. There were more gifts and more applause, but it all blended into an overwhelming feeling of love from the congregation, a warm and vibrant glow that lingered into the weeks through Christmas and warded off the cold of New Years, 1948.

"Clayborne, this is Julia."

"We must have a bad connection, Aunt Julia."

"It's not the telephone, Clayborne. I just can't speak properly yet."

"You sound like you've been crying."

"I have. Grandpa died a while ago."

"Oh, no."

"Come see us, Clayborne. Bring your family. Grandpa will be in his casket back here at home by the time you get here. Arthur's taking care of it."

"We'll be there soon. I'll call everybody."

"God bless you, Clayborne."

The funeral of James W. Perry was held the next day, January 17, 1948, at Iredell Baptist Church. Leonard and Pitchford, the surviving sons, came from their Midlothian farms.

"He was so sick and feeble, sister," said Leonard, "laying in bed like that these past two years. You Russells were so good to take him in."

"He wasn't any trouble."

"It just took everything out of him when Mama died," said Pitchford, the youngest. "He outlived her by eleven years, but his heart just went right in that grave with her back in 1937."

"Clayborne," said Leonard, "will you be administrator of Papa's will? You've been handling his financial affairs and you know how to do it."

"I'll get Grandpa's affairs all settled up," said Clayborne. "And I'll get the proper materials to the heirs."

They took Jim Perry's mortal remains to Duffau cemetery and laid him to rest in the winter freeze beside his beloved Lou. He had been born in 1862 during the Civil War, and died at the age of eighty-six in a time of peace.

He was the last frail link from that Perry immigrant past which had shuffled and bumbled westward from Alabama, from Georgia before that, from the Carolinas before that, from Virginia before that and England before that, to come here to make a new life in Texas. And now that last link was broken.

Beyond the mowed and oak-shaded cemetery, out beyond the yucca flats to the harder limestone caps, a little wren was seen foraging by the prickly pears.

-21-

UPBUILDING

THE time of victory proved to every American that democracy and clean living would always triumph in the end. But the time of peace that came after victory was not so certain. It soon became evident that America's world leadership did not carry with it guarantees of liberty and justice for all: the Soviet Union brazenly tore up its wartime agreements with the Allies and viciously enslaved all of Eastern Europe. Soviet armies did not demobilize. Soviet leaders did not turn to thoughts of peace. Communism was clearly marching to the old tune of Marx and Lenin toward world conquest. The only thing standing in its way was America's monopoly of the atomic bomb.

It seemed bulwark enough in early 1948. Texans had lost little sleep over Winston Churchill's May 5, 1946, speech at Fulton during his U. S. visit describing the "Iron Curtain" dropped by the Soviets to insulate themselves from the West physically and ideologically, nor over Bernard Baruch's speech of April 16, 1947, at Columbia, South Carolina, dubbing this the era of the "Cold War." When Texans worried about communism they seemed to worry more about President Truman's efforts at eliminating the poll tax and federalizing offshore oil lands than Moscow's thirty tank divisions weighed against America's one, or the three Soviet combat airplanes to our one or the four Red Army troops to our one, a lesson that lay germinating in the cold Korean soil of the future. But now those magic years of work, that compass heading of the future, that golden age of prosperity and optimism rolled like a touch from the hand of God through the Texas Grand Prairie.

"You can't be looking for a car, Mr. Perry," said Ed Nichols. "You always buy Plymouths."

"Just looking at your fine new Willys Jeeps," smiled Clayborne. "They looked so good from outside I had to come in and take a closer peek."

"Uh-oh," said Nichols, "Who's selling who here? Why do I have the feeling that Meridian's schools need something from me again?"

"You just know me too well, Ed," said Clayborne.

"Have a seat, W. C. And tell me what really brings you out on a cold February night. And please accept my condolences — I heard that your grandaddy passed away last month."

"Thank you, Ed. We miss him a lot. But you know, he'd lived a good long life and he told us time and again that he was ready."

"He was a good man. Now, to you, sir. What's on your mind?"

"Here's why I'm really here, Ed: You know that the school board has put a bond issue on the ballot for March so we can build a new elementary school."

"Yes, I know all about that. I've seen it in the paper. It's a hundred-thousand dollars, isn't it?"

"A hundred thousand."

"What do you need ol' Ed for, W. C.?" asked the young man.

"Well, ol' Ed, I need you to talk up the bonds to the *Meridian Tribune* when Mr. Dunlap interviews you tomorrow. Remember, Meridian can be the best place to live in all of Texas."

"Wait a minute. How do you know the *Tribune*'s going to interview me tomorrow? No, let me guess. The school superintendent asked 'em to, right?"

"Pretty good guess. Will you do it?"

"Oh, of course I will, W. C. You know how much I believe in schools. This town won't be complete until we've got good modern schools to replace those worn-out relics we're using now. I'll help."

"I really appreciate it."

"In fact, I might ask some friends and see if we can't get together and buy an ad in the *Tribune*, you know, one of those quarter-page deals that says 'We're for school bonds' or whatever, and lists the names of all the businesses below."

"Say, that's a good idea. Let's see, who can you call that might help out on an ad . . . Wendell Brister said his funeral home would support the school bonds. And Garland Davis, too."

"Ol' Garland over at Spencer Lumber? Glad to hear it."

"And of course Meridian Hardware and the Implement Company . . ."

"I know we can get them to chip in something for an ad. Sam Lawson owns 'em both. It'd look pretty funny if the president of the education board didn't support the school bonds."

"And J. T. Lomax said his Chrysler-Plymouth agency would help out."

"Never tell me about the competition, W. C. Have you talked to the drug stores yet? Sheppard and Turner?"

"No."

"I'll talk to them in the morning. How about Briley's Auto Supply? And ol' 'Snapper' Benson at the Food Market?"

"Briley and Benson both. They're on the school board too. And I've talked to Clyde Morgan at the Morgan-Alexander Service Station. He'll back us. And Olin Brantley at the Barber Shop."

"How about Jack Kirby at the warehouse?"

"I'm ashamed to say it, but I'd forgot all about him. And I just went into the Shrine with him four months ago."

"Will Bill Curtis at the turkey-dressing plant help?"

"Don't know. He plays his cards pretty close to the vest. Can't even tell if he likes me or not."

"I know what you mean. I'll ask him anyway. How about Harris-Spreen Home Furnishings? And Meridian Lumber Company? And John Robertson's Humble Station?"

"I've talked to John. He's a Mason at the Lodge. He'll help."

"What about Burford Hall over at his cafe?"

"Haven't talked to him."

"I think I'll buy me a cup of coffee from Burford tomorrow. And I think we can get you a pretty good ad in the paper the day or two before elections. But don't you think, Superintendent Perry, that it's about time you started going through the chairs in the Chamber of Commerce? Just so you can buttonhole all these fellows yourself, of course."

"You know, I've been thinking that very thing."

The campaign for schools became the winter event in Meridian for early 1948. School officials and supporters quietly but firmly pushed for passage of the bond issue, collaring votes where ever they could be found. For weeks conversations dwelt upon little else. The new elementary school had become a symbol of community pride, even community survival into the future, a goal that seemed essential if Meridian were to actually become that best place to live in all of Texas. By early March, when the election was held and the results duly announced, the job had been done: only seven voted against the bond issue versus two hundred sixty-eight for. The town was jubilant. The school officials were overjoyed. It would happen. The vintage grammar school would be torn down and a new modern facility build in its place.

Immediately the education board began design selection and soon contracted with the firm of Wilson & Patterson, architects and engineers, of Fort Worth. Clayborne devoted the better part of his working days now to advising and pushing and coordinating design plans with staff architect Jay Dunlap, a native of Meridian who had been assigned to manage the project for his firm. Dunlap knew the town intimately and made friends quickly; he and Clayborne and the education board grew in to a tight team, rushing the plans as March blended into April and April blended into May, hoping to begin construction the first of June.

Clayborne joyed in the excitement of watching the design concept take shape on blank sheets of drafting vellum, seeing cerebral ideas appear one after another as concrete but two-dimensional realities under the magic hands of the master draftsman, making changes here and improvements there, cross-checking specification sheets, approving exterior elevations and construction details from floor coverings and toilet seats to blackboard heights and window placements. It was the future unrolling on a drafting board. The plans were finished and bids went out to general contractors all over Central Texas.

Postwar inflation stood ready to deal them a body blow to the pocketbook: the lowest bid to build the new school was $125,000, $25,000 over estimate. The school board was dumbfounded but did not panic. There was no possibility of going back to the citizens and asking them to pony up another $25,000. The interest rate on the bonds they would have to offer, they also learned, increased with the amount of bond money actually sold, a sliding scale from two-and-a-half percent for the first bonds issued to four percent for the last, a disincentive to overspending. At a special two-man education board meeting in early June Sam Lawson talked turkey across the conference table to Clayborne.

"You know we're in a pickle here, W. C."

"Yes, sir, we sure are."

"You know we've got to build a new elementary school and the lowest bid's a mile too high."

"Yes, sir, it sure is."

"I've been thinking, W. C. You worked with Jerry Phillips before he moved out to West Texas, didn't you, back when he was school superintendent at Iredell?"

"Yes, sir."

"Didn't you tell me once that you helped him when they built the new school there?"

"Yes, sir."

"And you managed the construction of the new church — and I'll tell you, we've had word from all over what an excellent building it is. I heard about you driving all over the state to find low-cost building materials for it. And I know that what you built for $35,000 would normally go for closer to $80,000. You're the master of the know-how, W.C., you know where everything is."

"I've tried my best."

"Now, I'm goin' to say something you may not want to hear. I know you and your family just got finished driving our second new school bus down from Indiana, and I hate to say this, but I think that's going to be your only vacation this year. It's only logical that we save ourselves some money and appoint you as general manager of Meridian elementary school construction for the next six months."

Clayborne sat silently, looking at Sam Lawson.

Lawson went on: "You wouldn't have time for a regular vacation this summer, but you'd be able to go to Baylor in the mornings like last year."

"I see."

"W. C., we can turn over most of your administrative duties to Principal Everett when school starts again. You know enough about building to let all the school construction contracts yourself, don't you?"

"Yes sir, I do."

"And you can build that school for under a hundred-thousand dollars, couldn't you?"

"Yes sir, and buy all the furniture, too."

"You keep telling me this can be the best place to live in all of Texas. What do you say? Will you do it?"

"Yes, sir, I will."

"Good. I thank you. And, incidentally, here's your report card from the state schools supervisor." He handed a letter across the table to Clayborne.

"Well, aren't you going to read it?"

Clayborne took the letter and opened it. He read the official annual supervisor's report to L. A. Woods, State Superintendent, State Department of Education, Austin, Texas:

> The superintendent, trustees and community are to be congratulated upon having voted a tax increase and one hundred thousand dollar bond issue to replace old, worn-out buildings and equipment. The building program should include needed improvements and changes in the high school building.
>
> Since the high school enrollment in slightly above the probable lower limit likely to be set by the accrediting committee, Meridian should make every effort to add any adjoining territory available now.
>
> The school's general program is good. The school spirit is excellent and a very fine spirit of cooperation was evident on the part of both teachers and pupils. The school's leadership in sponsoring community activities is commendable.
>
> — R. R. Kay
> Deputy State Supt. Dist. 11

Sam Lawson said to him, "You realize that we're now in the full graces of the State, don't you? All question of us being on probation is finally removed. You get a lot of the credit, W. C. What do you think?"

"I can see two things coming."

"What?"

"It's going to a be a busy summer because I've already promised Congressman Johnson to be his Bosque County Senate campaign chairman."

"You did? Lyndon Johnson? Why'd you do that? I thought you were a Republican."

"It was my Papa that was the Republican. I guess I've always been for the little guy and the Democrats are supposed to be for the little guy. I've gone to all the Democrat rallies for years, Sam."

"Now that you mention it, I guess you have. But why Lyndon Johnson? He's got a reputation for being slick as a snake belly, you know. You remember there was some kind of stink over Mansfield Dam down by Austin, Johnson pulling strings or something. Big money behind that boy. And there's going to be one hellacious fight in Texas over getting Truman reelected —Governor Jester doesn't like him a bit. And the international picture's getting muddy, too, what with Jan Masaryk killed and Czechoslovakia turning communist."

"Well, I don' know about that part, but I met ol' Lyndon Johnson years ago while I was going to college at San Marcos. That's where he went to school himself, and he'd come back and hold these discussions with Prexy Evans outside Old Main. He was a schoolteacher for awhile, too. I'd thought he'd forgotten all about me, but sure enough, just a week ago his campaign people called me up and said the congressman had personally asked if I'd be his Bosque County chairman. Can you beat that?"

"I'd take it as a compliment, W. C. But remember, politicians always have long memories when they want a favor. Now, we'll help you out somehow so you can do your politickin' and work on the school both — how about inviting Johnson to give a speech at the high school when he's up this way? We'll think of something. But you said you could see two things coming, W. C. What's the other one?"

"We're going to have to build a new high school one of these days, too, Sam."

Far away the Soviets began their blockade of West Berlin in a futile attempt to drive out the Allies and the war of wills between East and West gathered steam with the fourteen-month Berlin Airlift.

In June the building began. Clayborne approached it with equal amounts of confidence and qualm. First he got together privately with Burney Warren and hammered out a contracting agreement for the concrete and masonry work, $3.50 an hour for bricklayers and they'd search out every possible method of saving a dollar. Clayborne drove around town offering seventy-five cents an hour for laborers and a dollar and a half for carpenters and got plenty of response from local farmers and some from Niggertown. The first thing they did was tear down the old grammar school building to salvage the lumber that would be used to build the new elementary school. Day by day Clayborne went to classes at Baylor in the mornings and then donned his khaki work clothes to supervise construction work in the afternoons.

Two of the oldest school buses, both already replaced, were now stripped of their coach bodies and converted to flatbed trucks in the high school machine shop. Laborers drove the trucks some days to Waco for cement and on others down to the Bosque riverbed for gravel. Bob Perry found summer employment at seventy-five cents an hour too good to pass by.

"You kinda little to be workin' laborer, ain't you, Bob Perry?"asked Harvey Lee Davenpport as he shoveled river-run gravel into one of the school's flatbed trucks.

"I'm fifteen, Mr. Davenport," said Bob as he shoveled gravel into the other. "Be sixteen in October." He had never worked with a black man before.

The black man said, "Well,you just don't slow me down none, you hear? I got a wife and two kids to feed. And you call me Harvey, you hear?" He shoveled vigorously.

"I can keep up with you."

"Ain't no contest, now. I can drive off soon's I've got a load and leave you in the dust if I want. But you seem like a nice boy, Bobby. Your daddy's boss of this job, huh?"

"I work as hard as anybody."

"No, that ain't my meanin'. I see you workin' hard. Just you're under the gun with your daddy standin' over you all the time. Gotta prove it, don't you, boy?"

None of Bob's friends had ever put this fact quite so plainly.

"Yeah, I guess you're right."

"Sure I'm right. Seen it in the Army. Lot of them boys in the colored unit had to prove it. Only it was colored folks provin' to white folks then, but now you got boy folks provin' to daddy folks." Harvey laughed.

"What did you do in the Army?"

"What ever the sergeant said do, boy, whatever the sergeant said."

"I mean did you see any action."

"I was stationed in Cal-i-for-nia for the duration, boy, in Los An-ge-les." He drew out the words in style. "That's where they got Hol-ly-wood, you know. After dark they had all kinds of action, I tell you!" Harvey laughed again.

"What about combat?"

"Not with the enemy, boy, but plenty on the home front."

"Oh, Mr. Davenport."

"Harvey! And don't go takin' me serious, Bob Perry. I come back home to my Gladys honest and true. I'm just givin' you the per-son-al-ity treatment. You got to have per-son-al-ity, that's all. That's what gets you places in this world, boy. Besides, it livens up the work, makes it go faster."

"It doesn't take any personality to shovel gravel."

"And it won't get you places, either. You ever hear of any movie star shovelin' gravel?"

"No, but I see the both of us shoveling gravel. And we've just about got the trucks loaded down to flatten the tires, look!"

"I see those tires. An' you see me drivin' off home every day in a new Ford car, too."

"Is that your car, that Ford?"

"It sure is. Got me a back check from the Army. A little over a thousand dollars! Went and bought me a good car, a good car. Now I expect we ought to drive this here gravel back up to the school. What do you think?"

"Wow!"said Bob. "A thousand dollars!"

"You see, you're thinkin' per-son-al-ity already!"

Through the sumptuous Texas summer the new elementary school took shape, the solid refection of the flat images on drafting vellum that were the plane reflection of dimensionless cerebral ideas in living minds. Clayborne finished another summer session at Baylor, a year closer to that doctoral degree. There was time for a picnic now and then at Lake Meridian where the bream fishing was the best in Bosque County, and they tried to make all the rodeos they could, and Clayborne and Oretta decided to take up square dancing for fun. Midget continued being his tiny lovable bug-eyed-dog self. And Oretta advanced in her Order of the Eastern Star work and at home mastered some of the fancier recipes for company-come-to-supper. They were full, lucid, glowing days, but too soon slid into that irretrievable past.

Meridian's 1948-49 academic year began in mid-September as usual. But this year it was near chaos. The first seven grades had no place to go — the old grammar school had vanished, razed to the ground, and the fine new elementary school was just being framed over the plumbing and utilities. So school officials dusted out the third floor of the castle-like high school and stashed the bulk of the elementary grades there, but what to do with the two or three classrooms that were left over? In a fair-trade turnabout, the Meridian Independent School District made an arrangement with the First Baptist Church to rent Sunday School class rooms during the week when it would not disturb sacred services and finally school was ready to begin — the church, after all, lay only two blocks down A Street from the school campus.

Some weeks before school started Oretta had gotten word that her father was deathly ill and began a long series of daily visits to the old home farm north of Hico to help care for the elderly man. At first Margie accompanied her mother but when school started she could only go on weekends— but soon Margie's enthusiasm for the Saturday trips waned.

"Mom, we've gone over to Grandpa's a million times. Let me stay here this Saturday. I can fix supper for Dad and Bob like you do on school days, and I can clean up the house and such."

Oretta smiled. "And you can ride Doylene's horse and play football in the street with the big boys if you stay home, too, can't you?"

"Oh, Mom, there's nothing for me to do over at Hico with all those old folks. I'll come tomorrow and help with Grandpa. Okay?"

"Okay. But you do like you said and keep the house clean and put on supper like usual. I've got tonight's food in the refrigerator. Just do like always and warm it on the stove and make the iced tea."

"I'll do it, Mom!"

Margie was better than her word: when evening came she decided to make some cornbread for her Dad and brother to go with Mom's pre-cooked supper. She remembered everything except the baking powder. When supper arrived on the table and Margie and her brother and her father sat to eat, only Clayborne took a slice of the poor-looking cornbread after the blessing. Bob and Margie watched their father eat his meal uncomplainingly, wretched cornbread and all.

After supper Bob whispered to his sister, "What did you do to the cornbread?"

Margie whispered back, eyes misty, "I forgot the baking powder. And it tasted terrible. I took a bite to see. Bobby, Dad ate that awful stuff just so he wouldn't hurt my feelings. He's so sweet."

"Yeah, I know. But don't forget the baking powder next time, okay?"

Hiram Woosley, Jr., became a name to conjure with that year. He'd been elected captain of the football team and a few weeks later president of the junior class. And since Bob in his junior year found himself on the football team, doing better now, turning into a fairly good player, Hiram Woosley became a part of his life.

"You want to go with me on a delivery to Fort Worth, Bob?" Hiram called from his front porch.

"What? Right now?" asked Bob as he strolled home from a Saturday morning's work on the new elementary school.

"Yeah, right now. There's no school tomorrow. I got this truckload of cattle in the back that's got to be in the stockyards by six o'clock. I just stopped off bringin' em from Phauney Calvery's place while I get me some dinner. We'll be back from Fort Worth about midnight. You want to go or not?"

"Yeah, I'd like to go. But I gotta ask my Dad. He's back at the school supervising."

"Well, I'm gonna get the GMC fired up. I'll drive the rig by the school and see what your Dad says."

Bob raced back to school and breathlessly explained the situation to his father. There was something about Clayborne on the work site that made him seem larger than life, a raw power that you could feel in the air but could not see with your eyes. His smiling countenance and friendly gesture was unchanged, his encouraging remark and warm fellowship no different. But there was the *feeling*, the feeling that left no question who was boss, none whatever. Bob made his case and said, "Please, Dad, can I go?"

"Do you have some change with you so you can get some supper?" Clayborne asked.

"Yes, sir. I have a whole dollar."

"That Woosley boy is a fine young man. I expect you can go if you want to. I'll tell your mother you'll be home late."

"Thanks, Dad! Here comes Hiram with the truck. See you tonight!"

They took the long and wending farm roads to Fort Worth, Hiram maneuvering expertly through the limestone hills and small towns along the way.

"Do you do this all the time?" Bob asked.

"Drive the truck for my Dad? A lot. That's how my family makes a living, you know, trucking things around for people. But not always. Summers I mostly work Dad's combine, out harvesting grain."

"That's why I never see you. My Dad used to work at harvest around here when he was a teenager."

"Was your Dad ever a teenager?" grinned Hiram.

Bob laughed. "Hard to imagine, isn't it?"

"He's stricter than my Dad, and that's *strict*. Is he hard on you?"

"No, I don't think so," said Bob. "I have to work and all, but he doesn't make me buy my own clothes or anything like some kids. I guess you'd say he's tough okay, but he's real good to me and my sister. We know he cares about us, that's for sure. How about your Dad? How does he treat you?"

"Oh, he's pretty strict on getting the work done and all. But I hear him tellin' customers about me making straight As at school."

"Do you make straight As?"

"Yep, sure do."

"That's great, Hiram. Especially with all your other work."

"Hey, Bob, you wanna double date next Sunday night? There's an Ava Gardner movie at the Capitol. Why don't you ask Maria Houston? I think she kinda likes you."

"Sunday night? I might just do that. Who'd you take?"

"Oh, Patsy Warren, prob'ly. I've dated her a couple of times. Hey, did you hear about the two guys drivin' along?"

"I think I'm about to."

"Well, the guy that's drivin' says, 'Hey, man, I'm gonna turn right. Is anything comin' behind us in the right lane?' The second guy says, 'It's okay, man, just a dog.' So the guy turns right and suddenly they have this big wreck. When the smoke clears the first guy climbs out of the mess and says, 'Hey, man, I thought there was just a dog in the right lane.' The second guy says, 'Yeah, man, it was a Greyhound.' Get it?"

They drove on into the jocose afternoon, discussing Phauney Calvery's cattle and pigs, the virtues of GMC shortbed trucks as opposed to semitrailers, why Hiram's father was bald-headed, the chances of Meridian winning the district championship in football this year and the steady progress of the new elementary school.

"Mr. Perry?"

"Oh, hello, there, Mr. Roberts!" said Clayborne at his front door. "Come on in. Oretta, it's Mr. Roberts from the Jones Baking Company."

"I have a little something for you here, Mr. Perry. Are your children home?"

"Margie's doing her homework. Bob's around somewhere."

"Maybe you should call Margie."

"I'm here, Dad, I heard. Hello, Mr. Roberts."

Oretta came into the front room right after Margie. "Oh, hello, there. Is it time already?"

"Yes, Ma'am, eight weeks has gone by. And here's your little fellow."

He opened an overcoat pocket to reveal a tiny brown bug-eyed chihuahua puppy.

"In return for breeding your Midget to my black female," said Roberts gratefully. "I got the black pup that I wanted and here's a brown one for you folks, looks just like his daddy. I'm sure glad you brought Midget out to the bread truck to show me that morning last summer."

They ooohed and aaahed over the tiny chihuahua pup that shivered in Roberts' hands. Midget pranced into the room, all wiggly at the smell of the new pup. Margie took it protectively and said, "Oh, don't be scared little baby, I'll take care of you. Looky here, Midget, a new friend for us! It's your little boy! Oh, he's so cute!"

"Oh, Clayborne," said Oretta, "he *is* cute!"

Bob walked in from the back yard. "What's this?" he asked.

"It's the new puppy Mr. Roberts promised us. It's Midget's little boy dog."

Clayborne looked fondly at the hairless creature and said, "He looks just like a junior-sized Midget!"

Margie looked up and said, "That's it, Dad. We'll call him Midget Junior. Hello, Junior. How are you, Junior?"

Mr. Roberts said, "Well, Bob, did you take your heifer to the Waco Stock Show yet?"

"Yes, sir! I won second place, reserve champion, too! Sold 'er for five-hundred-fifty dollars. Sherman Theirkins won grand champion! The top two places went to Meridian this year, how about that?"

"That right? That's great, Bob! Congratulations! That's really great. You sure deserve a prize for all the work you put in on that animal. I saw you out there many a time, washing 'er, brushing 'er all up pretty and everything. Good for you!"

"I sure hated to part with that calf. I hope I sold her to somebody that would breed her and not just slaughter her."

Clayborne said, "Well, they paid you more than beef animals are going for. A fed-out steer only brings about thirty-five cents a pound and you got near twice that. I expect whoever paid that much will breed her."

"I sure hope so," said Bob. "And thanks, Mr. Roberts, for bringing us the puppy."

"Well, congratulations again, Bob," said Roberts. "I think my job's done here." He smiled upon the tiny dog as Margie bent down to put its nose to Midget's. "Looks like you folks have yourselves a new family member."

Bob noticed that his Dad had not bragged on him to Mr. Roberts for winning reserve champion, and realized once again that his own accomplishments would have to speak for themselves, that his father's sense of fairness to the community would never allow the slightest nepotism to creep in. He had to prove it.

In the turn of the season Oretta's father died. For a time the family turned in upon itself as they grieved over William Daniel Partain and the memories of him flooded back.

Lyndon Baines Johnson's helicopter landed in the harvested maize field next to Meridian's old stone High School in early October. A sizable crowd waited for him in the bleachers of the football field, some hundred-fifty yards away. A staff aide jumped out of the far side helicopter door and ran through the maize stubble around the whirly-bird's nose to open the candidate's path. Johnson's steely-eyed-squint flashed quickly in the sunlight as he paused in the aircraft door to size up the crowd and set an invisible stop-watch running in his mind.

The local delegation waited on the school side of the fence, just outside the whup-whup of the rotor blades. Clayborne stood in an even rank with Sam Lawson and Sherrill Benson, wondering if the Senate hopeful would be able to tell which was his "old buddy from San Marcos days." Johnson stepped to the maize field's barbed-wire fence, mashed it down with one hand, straddled it and swung over with down-home expertise just like a farmer, then unerringly strode straight up to Clayborne and shook his hand. "W. C. Perry, I'm so pleased to see you again. Brings back the good old days in front of Old Main. And this must be Mr. Lawson." Johnson pumped Sam Lawson's hand an exact number of times and Clayborne quickly made the last introduction: "And this is Mr. Benson, our school board secretary." Clayborne briefly wondered if some aide had identified him for Johnson from a dossier in the helicopter.

Johnson smilingly kept them on schedule: "Looks like you folks brought out a real good crowd, I'm much obliged," and marched toward the bleachers with his flying aides and local cadre trying to keep up.

Lyndon Johnson attracted much attention in 1948 for campaigning in a helicopter, but less attention for carefully lining up advance men to bring out crowds and microphones, perhaps the first Texas politician to do so. He could talk to sixty thousand voters a week while his opponent for the Senate seat, former Texas governor Coke Stevenson, piddled around the state in an old Plymouth not even rigged with a loudspeaker, sliding into towns, chatting mostly with old friends and pressing the flesh at a few courthouses and gas stations.

At Meridian Johnson stuck to the arch-verities of rural Texas life: in his aw-shucks drawl that outpaced a machine gun, he was for farm-to-market roads, rural electrification, river development, and aide to the aged. In rapid-fire order he attacked "Calculatin' Coke" Stevenson for making a "secret deal" with a "labor leader racketeer" to oppose the Taft-Hartley Act and thus win the endorsement of the Texas State Federation of Labor, which had no friends in the rural Grand Prairie; he pointed out that President Truman regarded Good Ol' Lyndon as the legitimate Democratic Senate candidate for Texas; he promised control of tidelands oil to the states rather than the government; he pointed out how well he had served his district as a congressman for all these years, and now won't you take the next logical step and send me to the Senate where I can work for the whole State of Texas?

LBJ was back in his helicopter in less than fifteen minutes, waving goodbye like an angel ascending to heaven and leaving everyone with the impression he'd graced the eyes and ears of Meridian voters for more than an hour.

"But Mrs. Perry, Margie has seriously swollen glands in her neck. She's very sick."

Oretta spoke slowly over the telephone:"Now, Mrs. Durham, you're not the first teacher that's been fooled by Margie's neck glands. She did this twice last year. Dr. Holt has assured us several times that Margie simply has very sensitive lymph nodes in her neck.It doesn't mean she's sick at all. She just has slight allergies. Did you take her temperature?"

Silence on the other end of the line. "Well, no, Mrs. Perry. She seemed to be feeling so bad I just sent her home."

"She does that with every new teacher she gets. Now, Mrs. Durham, I took her temperature and it's 98.6 degrees, just like it ought to be. I think my little Margie is pulling our leg again today. I'm sending her back to school, and you please take her back in class, will you?"

"Well . . ."

"If you have any questions, ask Mr. Perry, will you? He'll give you all the reassurance you'll need."

"Hey, Jimmy, let's go down to the hospital."

"What's the matter, somebody sick?"asked Jimmy Hanna, son of Wylie Hanna, who lived across the street from the school.

"No, nothing like that,"answered Bob. "Bill and Lola Warren just had a baby! Everybody says you gotta go down and see Billy and Lola's big boy. Wanna go see him?"

"A big baby?"

"Yeah, Mrs. Cameron said he weighed eight pounds."

"Is that a lot?"

"I guess so. They said so. Wanna go?"

"Yeah, let's go see him," said Jimmy.

"Hey, Bob,"yelled Jimmy Hanna into the breeze, "have you seen those neat Cushman motor scooters that Reuben Lumpkin's selling?"

"Oh, boy, have I!" wailed Bob. "I want a Cushman so bad I can *taste* it! Rueben let me drive one out to the Circle last week."

"That red one?"

"Yeah, the red one! I asked my Dad if he'd get it for me. I pleaded! I *begged!* I did everything but cry for it. He wouldn't even talk about it. Just said no."

"Yeah, mine, too. Dads just don't understand modern inventions."

"I told my Dad it's safe. But he wouldn't listen a bit. Boy, I'd like one of those things!"

At the hospital the two boys walked up to the reception desk. Bob asked, "Mrs. Evans, where do they keep the babies?"

Jane Evans looked up and smiled, "The nursery is down the main hall, second hall to the left, Bobby. There's a window you can look through but you can't go in."

"How can we tell which one's Mr. Warren's?"

"You can ask Mr. Warren. He's down there visiting right this minute."

The boys scrambled down the hall in orderly disorder, trying to be quiet. They met Bill Warren on his way out.

"Hi, Mr. Warren."

"Hello, Bob. Hello, Jimmy. Did you come to see my new boy?"

"Yes, sir. Which one is he?"

"Last one on the left when you get to the window, the one with the black hair. Name's on the bassinet."

"See you, Mr. Warren." The boys disappeared toward the nursery, but Bill lingered just around the corridor to overhear their conversation.

"Hey, Jimmy, that's him."

"That one there?"

"Yeah, see it says 'Boy Warren'. Are they just goin' to call him 'Boy' like in the Tarzan movies?"

"I don't think so, Bob. They prob'ly just haven't named him yet. He doesn't look very big to me. How about you?"

"Nope. Doesn't look very big to me, either. He's not much bigger than Midget."

"You brought me all the way down here to see this little tiny baby?"

"I'm sorry, Jimmy. Everybody said he was big. You just can't trust old people these days I guess."

The new Elementary School was finished just before Christmas of 1948. The floor tiles were put down during a powerful norther and the cold mastic failed to set properly: the tiles did not stick. At the first thaw in January 1949 new tiles were set and they stuck. Thus, after seven months of construction Meridian had its new building.

Grades one through eight were moved in as swiftly as possible. The first morning in the building all eyes were agog at the modern fluorescent light fixtures and modern windows and the big auditorium and the shiny cafeteria. Clayborne had his own office moved from the old stone high school to the new space designed for him by the architects. It felt good and new and comfortable and *proud* in the new edifice.

When time came to decide on the date for a proper dedication and open house ceremony, the school board meeting in the new building calculated that Clayborne had built their new facility for $90,000, including new furniture, leaving $10,000 of authorized unneeded funds.

"W. C.,"said Board Secretary Snapper Benson, "Do you realize you built this place for $5.65 a square foot?"

"Is that right? I hadn't done any figuring."

A. C. Nivin said,"You're not just a school administrator, W. C., you're a shrewd businessman in disguise. You know that most schools these days are running ten dollars a square foot?"

Clayborne said,"I've been studying construction costs in my doctor's degree classes at Baylor. Eight dollars is the average we're dealing with. Our figures must be out of date, because I don't remember them being ten dollars."

"I got those figures from the new school they just finished in Temple. And that's not including furniture,"said Guy Briley. "You just pulled off an economic miracle, professor." Briley did not realize it, but he started the community calling its doctoral candidate "professor" as a nickname at once honorific and familiar.

H. J. Seidel said across the meeting table,"And I hear nothing but good things from the parents, W.C. They like the building because their kids like it. Your work on this new elementary school has sure made a lot of people happy."

"Thank you, H. J."

"And the publicity is outstanding," said John Hanna. "We've had notice of the quality and cost of our new school even in the Waco paper."

"The fact that the taxes won't go up is what pleases most folks, W. C.," said Dr. Holt.

Sam Lawson said, "We'd like to honor you at our dedication ceremony, W. C. I know you don't care for all the talk. Anything you'd like me to do in particular?"

"Yes,"said Clayborne. "Wait until you can say we've just finished the new high school this town needs. Then I'll feel like we've really done something."

"You better get up, Bob," said Clayborne. "You're going to be late."

"Dad, it's cold and I'm tired — I really got in late last night. Can't I sleep in just this once?"

"No, you can go to school." Flat. Stern.

The boy looked bleary-eyed from under his pillow. "Dad," he said in a sleepy voice, "I don't get it. Hiram Woosley skips class once or twice every week. You don't seem to worry about him missing school. Why can't I come in late or miss a day once in a while?"

The room filled with emotion just short of anger, with overtones of indignation. Clayborne stood at Bob's bedroom door and chose his words carefully. "Son, there's two differences between you and Hiram Woosley. Number one, Hiram has to work to help support his family. And number two, Hiram makes straight A's. The last time I noticed, you didn't qualify on either account. When you do, let me know and we'll discuss the subject."

Clayborne walked down the hall and out of the house.

Bob did not skip class that day.

Or any other.

"Well, there's another class graduated, professor," said Sam Lawson. "Would you and Oretta like to come over for some coffee later?"

Clayborne could hardly hear in the happy racket of dispersing seniors and family. "Did you say coffee later?" he shouted across the head table on the stage. Lawson nodded and Clayborne nodded back, calling, "After we've closed up here. I've got to go mix now."

Superintendent Perry stepped down the side stairs into the thronged auditorium, shaking hands and patting graduates on the back.

"Oh, Mr. Perry, you did it again!" said Mrs. Rabb. "It was just a lovely graduation ceremony. And my Bert looked so proud when you handed him his diploma. I just bawled."

"Thank you, Ma'am. Bert's been a fine student. He has a great future ahead of him."

"Hey, prof, when is the senior trip to San Antonio this year?"

"Starts this Saturday at seven in the morning, Mr. Topham. Is Marie coming with us?"

"Oh, yes, she'll be there. I just wanted to make sure when to have her packed and ready. Oh, and congratulations on being elected Vice President of the Chamber of Commerce!"

"Thank you!"

"Dad, Dad!"

"What is it, son? Hello, Maria."

"Hello, Mr. Perry," said Bob's date for the evening.

"I just saw Mr. Benson, Dad. He offered me a job in his grocery store this summer. I said yes. Is it okay if I don't go to Detroit with you and Mom to get the new car this summer?"

"You're old enough to begin shiftin' for yourself, Bob. You'll be a senior next year. We'll miss you on the trip,, but I'm sure you'll be fine. I'll talk to your mother about it. She and I are going over to the Lawsons after I close up here. Have a good time tonight and don't stay out too late."

"Bye, Mr. Perry," said Maria. The couple turned toward the backdoors where the crowd drifted away.

"Here comes Mom now," said Bob over his shoulder, pointing to the aisle at the far end of the stage.

Oretta walked up to her husband, calling across the auditorium to the youngsters, "Hi, Maria! Bob, Mr. Benson tells me you're working at his place this summer. Not going with us to Detroit, then?"

"No, Ma'am. I just told Dad. He said it's okay."

"Well, have a good time at the dance down at the library. Don't be too late."

"No, Ma'am, we won't."

Oretta looked in her husband's eyes. "Another year, Clayborne, then he'll be gone, too. All these boys and girls going off to work and college. Time goes so fast."

"And I miss seeing Ed Nichols down in that front row. I just hope things work out with that new subdivision he's building by Waco."

"He's putting in a new Spiegelville up above where the old one's being flooded out by the new dam, isn't he?" she asked.

"Yes, he is. It's a big project. Quite a change from selling Jeeps."

"Mr. Perry, could Lyle and Pepper and me have a word with you — in private?" Doyle Weatherford stood before him, a foreman at the local Ice and Cold Storage Company — the turkey dressing plant, Meridian's sole large industry.

"Well, sure, Mr. Weatherford," said Clayborne. "Oretta, we've been asked over to the Lawsons' later — would you go get things set with Floy?"

Oretta took the hint.

"Now, gentlemen, what can I do for you?"

"Mr. Perry," asked Weatherford intensely, looking around to see there was no one to overhear. "Is it true what we heard?"

"Is what true, Mr. Weatherford?"

"Don't play games with us," said a surly Lyle Skinner, owner of an auto repair service. "It is true about the niggers?"

"Yeah," intruded Pepper Lang, an official with a local utility, "what about the niggers? Did you let 'em in here last night?"

Weatherford hissed, "There's a lot more than just us upset about this, Mr. Perry. A *lot* more. Did you let the nigger school have their graduation in here last night?"

"I sure did, gentlemen." He stood still, gauging their tempers.

Lang shifted, suppressing the anger that seethed in his veins. "Now what the hell did you go and do a fool thing like that for? This is a *white* school."

"Mr. Lang, the colored school asked me if they could use the new auditorium for their graduation exercises. I saw no reason to refuse."

"You saw no reason to refuse?!" sputtered Skinner. "What do you mean you saw no reason to refuse?"

"The colored folks wanted to use it Thursday and the whites had it for Friday. There was no conflict."

"Damn it, Perry," seethed Lang, "there *is* a conflict. They're *niggers!* This is a *white* school. I don't think you better let this happen again next year."

Clayborne scanned them one at a time, eye to eye. "Gentlemen, obviously you feel that I didn't have proper authority to let the colored school use this auditorium. So I will submit your concerns to the full school board. I'm sure you agree that they have the authority, don't you?"

The three men stood blocked, stymied.

"Don't you, gentlemen?" repeated Clayborne.

"I know what you're doing, Perry. That Sam Lawson is a nigger-lover. But you be careful, I'm warning you," gritted Weatherford.

"I'll be very careful, Mr. Weatherford. I appreciate your warning. Thank you for your courtesy and concern. Goodnight, gentlemen."

On July 11, 1949, Governor Beauford Jester died of a heart attack and was replaced by Lieutenant Governor Allan Shivers, a tall, dark man of substantial talent. The Shivers administration was to have considerable impact on Clayborne's life in an indirect manner: Shivers was a political pragmatist who skilfully thwarted the special interests that insisted on saving $3 to $5 million in taxes by not buying any new textbooks — a political pragmatist who also convinced a special legislative session to increase the Texas cigarette tax so the state could increase appropriations for the eleemosynary institutions, school salaries, retirement benefits, farm-to-market roads, and old-age pensions.

As Bob had done the year before, so in 1949 Margie confessed and was baptized at Meridian First Baptist Church. The religious faith and moral force of her family carried on in another soul.

After some time of pleading Margie got her piano lessons, but shortly found they had unexpected drawbacks. Margie talked for weeks about the mean piano teacher who one day grabbed her hands and cut off her fingernails because she wouldn't cut them short enough by herself. There were dancing lessons, too, through these years, tap and ballet and acrobatic. The dance class, of course, had to show its talents and by the time she entered fifth grade some time later, Margie got to travel to all the big towns in the Grand Prairie to perform, Stephenville, and Waxahatchie and Dublin. Because she reached her growth spurt at an earlier age than her classmates and towered over most of the other girls, she always got the boy parts in her dance routines. If it was Hansel and Gretel, she was always Hansel; if it was Romeo and Juliet, she was always Romeo. Oretta made her costumes and volunteered to make some for a few of the other girls as well — and continued to make all of Margie's personal clothes.

The summer of 1949 shuttled through the cosmic warp and woof as Texas summers always had, faster than other times of year, more alluring to the senses with its languid days and baking nights, its swimming holes and fishing lakes and patios calling the Texas weary to rest and recreation. Even so, Bob went every day to work at Benson's Food Market from 7:00 a.m. to 6:00 p.m., driving delivery truck, sweeping floors, stocking shelves, trashing used shipping containers, anything that needed doing. He found that Mr. Benson — everybody called him Snapper — owned a little farm outside town where he raised Appaloosas, the spirited gray horses with the spotted rumps that had been bred by the Yakima Indians in faraway Washington State's arid Columbia Basin hills, the ones they called Horse Heaven Hills. He also found that Snapper Benson had a sharp sense of humor that eased the tedium and sped the parting days. Bob particularly enjoyed driving Mr. Benson's Jeep on deliveries when he brought it in from the farm. Then in a twink, before you could say "come and go," another Texas summer became history.

Clayborne began his first complete school year with the new elementary school building and trudged once more the back-and-forth to the old castle-like high school in the daytime and the Monday evening back-and-forth to the doctoral classrooms of Baylor as he had every summer day, creeping up on that far degree, climbing the ladder slowly, slowly. In the glad disarray of school startup, he greeted seniors passing in the hall, saying "Hello, Bert; hello Landon; hello Hiram; hello Bob;" and realized, really realized, that his son was a senior. He felt quietly proud of the boy who insisted on working at Benson's Food Market after school each day and who had made the football team again this year. The Meridian High Yellow Jackets had a good team and held high hopes of winning the district championship.

Seniors, Bob found, were still special people on campus, but he was fascinated to discover that hazing of all kinds had vanished. He thought with satisfaction that his father had answered his pained freshman question by patient action, making known through leadership that bullying and intimidation were not to be countenanced by civilized people. And Clayborne knew it too: he had set the tone, smiled approval and frowned with the brow of scorn; he had hired new teachers and fired old ones with cause; he had set all policy and the school board had backed him every time. Gradually, gradually, he had acquired utter authority and control. Now things ran his way. And his way was to help his town grow up, morally, spiritually, physically.

The senior class had just assembled that third morning of school, all twenty-one of them, in the huge three-sectioned auditorium-like room on the second floor of the old stone high school that had once been a college. In the eastern third of the room sat the sophomores and freshmen, in the center the juniors and on the west side the seniors, tolerating the roll check by home room teachers and waiting for any announcements.

Bob saw his father come in walking up the stairs slowly. Behind him the school secretary, Maribel Dunlap, walked with a new student. The three entered the room and all eyes went to the approaching new girl: five-foot-two, dark blond hair, slender, not an ounce of fat on her, the right age to be a senior. Then they saw the braces on her legs and the spasms that turned her head to one side and opened her mouth at unpredictable intervals and the arm that tended to swing over her shoulder when she walked. They had never seen the devastation of cerebral palsy before, nor the shining courage that looked back at them out of those beautiful brown eyes in that sweet pale olive face.

"Class," said Clayborne, "This is our new senior, Mary Ann Dinius. She comes to us from Breckenridge, Texas. She now lives here in Meridian. She's a straight A student. Patsy Owen, will you show her where her classes are this first day."

That's all he said. Mrs. Dunlap showed Mary Ann to the senior seating section and Clayborne left the room silently, leaving behind the clear understanding that if anyone so much as whispered about the new girl's disabilities they would have him to deal with.

Mary Ann struggled across the floor, barely able to walk, perspiration beading on her forehead from the exertion of coming up the stairs. Silence soaked up the students' feelings; they were appalled and jolted and full of pity and uncertainty how to react.

Donna Cameron, a senior now, got up and said to Mary Ann, "Come, you sit next to me."

And so Mary Ann Dinius came into the life of Meridian High School.

The handicapped were not exposed in polite society in those days. The public school in Breckenridge had rejected Mary Ann, ostensibly because the school stairs were "not safe for her," but in fact because she upset other students who were unprepared to open their hearts and minds to her. Mary Ann's parents were sufficiently affluent to send her to Meridian where Clayborne insisted she be accepted. Mary Ann stayed with the Krugers, a brave family that ran a little private school for handicapped children in their home. The Krugers had a handicapped daughter of their own and had determined to provide educational help for others while doing their best for their own.

Bob had always delivered groceries in Mr. Benson's Jeep to the Krugers and, both at school and at her dwelling place, gradually got to know the difference between Mary Ann and her cerebral palsy. Mary Ann had a terrible time talking, could hardly speak in more than a whisper, but if you listened carefully you got her message, which was more often than not a witty and fun-loving remark or a friendly comment designed to put the listener at ease. Mary Ann had an old typewriter that she used for much of her communication — some people were simply unable to decipher her speech. Sometimes she would leave a message for Bob on the Kruger's kitchen counter telling him to come into the little home's "classroom" and chat with her among the children with Down syndrome and polio and cerebral palsy. The third week in September Bob began noticing that Donna Cameron was there visiting Mary Ann almost every time he delivered groceries.

Donna Cameron had her own problems: severe asthma racked her nights so frequently that she came in late to school several days a week looking haggard and exhausted. But she had her own reservoirs of inner strength. She attended all the school dances and even tried out for football cheerleader — when the winners were announced they were: Mary Lou Munden, Wayne Mize and Donna Cameron.

"You're late again, Donna," said Clayborne from his first-period geometry class chalkboard.

"I'm sorry, Mr. Perry," the Cameron girl said, staggering along the back wall half-asleep. "It was the asthma again last night."

"Well, I'll give you the easiest question from our lesson on weights and measures: which is heavier, Donna, a pound of lead or a pound of feathers?"

"It's a pound of feathers, Mr. Perry," she muttered as she made her way up the row.

Clayborne laughed and said, "I thought you were still asleep."

"Oh, Mr. Perry, you always play a joke on me when I'm late." She took her seat at a front row desk. "I just took the bait without thinking. I know they're both measured in the . . . "

"It's avoirdupois." whispered Mary Ann Dinius from the seat next to her.

"The avoirdupois system, Mr. Perry."

On September 23, 1949, a White House news release announced that the Soviet Union had exploded an atomic bomb. Dr. Harold C. Urey, Nobel Prize-winning chemist said "There is only one thing worse than one nation having the atomic bomb — that's two nations having it." Fear crept into the everyday fabric of American life now, fear that dimmed the glorious days after victory, fear of Communism, fear of war, fear of nuclear extermination. The potent optimism of America did not shine so brightly in the world. America found itself faced with a powerful alien ideology — historical materialism and the inverted Hegelian dialectic and the doctrines of class struggle and the dictatorship of the proletariat — reaching out from Moscow with nuclear tentacles, and did not know how to cope with it other than sheer resistance.

"Mr. Lawson, I think the school board should be aware that one of our text books has drawn some unfavorable attention in Houston," said Clayborne to the trustee's meeting.

"Well, what is it, W. C.?" asked H. J. Seidel.

"Yes, what do you mean?" inquired A. C. Nivin.

"It's Magruder's *American Government.* There's a new quarterly newsletter called the *Editorial Reviewer* put out by the Texas Daughters of the American Revolution that says it's not patriotic."

"Not patriotic?" said Dr. Holt. "We've used that Magruder text since 1937. What does the DAR know about education?"

"Well, there may be a problem," warned Clayborne.

"What kind of problem?" asked Sam Lawson.

"There's a section on government controls increasing as society becomes more complex. You know, things like the Food and Drug Administration and the Atomic Energy Commission."

"Well, I can see not liking government interference in State's Rights and such, but what's unpatriotic about that?" asked John Hanna.

"Professor Magruder wrote this at the end of the section on government controls. Let me read it to you: 'the country is capitalistic with strong Socialistic and even Communistic trends.' That's the problem."

"My God, our government textbook says *that?*" asked Sam Lawson.

"Yes, sir. But I've contacted Austin and they say that Professor Magruder has changed that paragraph because he now says those trends are actually welfare-capitalism, things like federal power projects and old-age pensions. The next printing won't mention Communism."

"Well, then what's the problem, W.C.?"

"The Houston school board has voted to reject the Magruder text and teach without one. There might be pressure. . ."

"I see," said Sam Lawson. "You're sure the next printing will change that about Socialism and Communism?"

"Yes, sir."

"Then to hell with the pressure, "said Lawson. "Magruder's the best government text we've ever had. We've used it for twelve years and never heard about that sentence before. I expect we can forgive Magruder just one lapse. Let your teachers know not to teach out of that part until we buy new texts."

"We never have anyhow, Mr. Lawson," said Clayborne. "It's in the last chapter and we've always used a workbook at the end of our course instead."

In early November Bob found a note on his home-room desk. It said in familiar typed letters: "Dear Bob, I would be very pleased if you would attend the Sadie Hawkins Day dance as my date." It had been signed in a tortured but recognizable scrawl: Mary Ann Dinius.

He fought with himself for two days without saying anything to a soul. He avoided Mary Ann. He was so accustomed to the athletic grace of his fellow sportsmen, to the beautiful vigor of the active girls in his class . . .

On the morning of the third day Bob said at the breakfast table, "Dad, Mary Ann Dinius invited me to the Sadie Hawkins dance."

Clayborne said nothing, just listened as he ate his oatmeal. Margie looked at her father almost as intently as Bob. Oretta ate her toast without apparent attention to the remark.

Bob gazed helplessly at his father, hoping for a comment. None came.

"Dad," he said, "I can't decide if I should go with her. It would be . . ." he stumbled and choked on the word ". . . *embarrassing* to go with her. But I don't want to hurt her feelings. I don't know what to do."

Clayborne listened to his son wrestle with himself. But he said nothing.

"Dad, what should I do?"

Clayborne finished his oatmeal and blotted his lips with the napkin. He looked at Bob and said, "I don't expect it's a question of *knowing* what you should do. I expect it's a question of having the courage to *do* what you should do."

He left Bob at the breakfast table pondering.

Oretta called after her husband, "Don't forget you're being installed as President of the Chamber of Commerce today."

"Thank you," he called back as he left for work, "I won't forget."

That morning Bob sought out Mary Ann and said yes, positively and forcefully yes, he would be glad to be her date to the Sadie Hawkins dance. The girl smiled her delight. As Bob walked away he felt his self-respect soaring. He had done what was right simply because it was right: to have said no would have been weak and cheap.

When the time came for the dance, Mary Ann showed up in the Krugers' 1939 two-door Chevy coupe, Mrs. Kruger driving, and squired Bob to the Sadie Hawkins shindig. Since there was no question of Mary Ann being able to dance, Bob took her to the punchbowl and sat with her in polite conversation. Within a few minutes half a dozen boys surrounded them, talking to Mary Ann, kidding her about her Sadie Hawkins country dress and asking what she thought about the substitute English teacher that had been inflicted upon them. Bob began to feel left out when Mildred Wilson asked him to dance.

"Do you mind?" he asked Mary Ann.

She looked over the shoulder of "Pee Vee" Standford who was in the midst of telling her a shaggy dog story, and waved him off.

Every popular girl came and asked Bob to dance that night; every popular boy spent time talking and having a good time with Mary Ann. Everyone had a good time. No one told Bob what a good sport he was. No one acted as if anything special had happened at all. Bob had simply come to the dance with a popular girl as usual. Mary Ann had been a delightful person as usual.

Finis.

On October first, 1949, the Communists under Mao Tze-Tung announced a central peoples government in China.

When Christmas night came around, some Meridian boys went out to The Circle to celebrate the holidays with some great fireworks by the highway. They set up their sacks full of fun in the parking lot of Billy Curtis's two-year old Circle Theater and began to blast away with cherry bombs and sparklers and rockets and roman candles. In the laughter and commotion too many flaming missiles from too many roman candles landed on the theater roof. The theater burned to the ground along with the Circle Food Market next to it. The New Year of 1950 came in more somberly than most.

While the second half of the 1949-50 school year got under way, on January 27, 1950, Klaus Fuchs, a British physicist who had worked on the A-bomb at Los Alamos, confessed that from 1942 to 1949 be had fed atomic secrets to the Soviet Union. Four days later President Truman issued a terse statement:

"I have directed the Atomic Energy Commission to continue its work on all forms of atomic weapons, including the so-called hydrogen, or super bomb."

Within two weeks Albert Einstein had voiced a concern that would never go away: "Radioactive poisoning of the atmosphere and hence annihilation of any life on earth has been brought within the range of technical possibilities . . . In the end, there beckons more and more clearly general annihilation."

As fear grew in America the old optimism and eternal innocence faded a little bit more.

In early Spring, Clayborne happily announced that Meridian High School's girl's basketball team coached by Lee Erickson had won the district championship and would go on to State playoffs in Waco. There they won but a single game, but managed to do better than last fall's Hornet football teams, which didn't even reach the 500 mark.

Superintendent Perry had to look on his scheduling calendar before approving the 1950 Junior-Senior Banquet theme, "Moonlight and Roses": the new cafeteria was in constant demand as the banquet center for the entire community including the farmers round about. When he saw there was no conflict, he let the decorating committee set up trelises all over the new elementary school cafeteria and entwine them with roses, hundreds of real roses. The committee mothers took special pains to see that their children had the most beautful experience they could manage. The big event proved that some of the old American innocence still survived: the juniors and seniors who strutted and lounged easily by informal day turned shy and quiet and just good friends by formal night. There the seniors took their vote: Mary Lou Munden came out as Most Beautiful; Donna Cameron was judged Best All Around; Mary Ann Dinius was voted Most Popular.

And at the April Board of Trustees meeting the question of letting the colored school use the new elementary school auditorium for their graduation ceremonies came up and the blacks gained permission by a unanimous vote. Clayborne stared down the cluster of bigots who dared not protest openly now, feeling only contempt for the hate that spattered around him. He knew what was right and he had done it.

For several years now Clayborne had secretly hoped to stretch time, to hold off that day when his son would finish public school and leave home. But now in 1950, as he found himself planning that annual senior class trip to Austin and San Antonio, there appeared the name Bob Perry on his class manifest. And sure enough, Bob went with them this time, enjoying his *ave atque vale* with the other twenty-one seniors. When the night of graduation ceremony came around, Clayborne knew better but found himself a little startled when he handed a diploma to the boy he'd watched being born in that little old run-down house in Blackstump Valley, that boy he'd lived with in Iredell all those years ago, that he'd watched grow up in Walnut Springs and become a young man in Meridian. He felt too full and too empty at the same time and simply shook hands with the new graduate and called the next name.

And then it was breakfast the day after graduation. Oretta asked, "Have you got everything you're going to need, son?"

"I'm all packed, Mom."

"You're all set with Lester Smith to get to Huntsville?" asked Clayborne.

"All set, Dad. Mr. Smith should be here in a minute. He has our apartment rented and we're all enrolled in Sam Houston University for the summer."

"You three boys will get along, won't you?" asked Oretta.

"I've known Dan Wells and H. A. Standifer for four years, Mom," said Bob. "And Mr. Smith will be living near us, you know."

"I know," said Oretta.

"I just worry. You've never been off for so long before. I'm going to miss you."

"Aw, Mom, don't cry."

Margie said with eleven-year-old brashness, "I'm not going to cry. I'm glad you're leaving, 'cause now I can have all the dessert I want without having to share with you, brother!"

"Margie!" said Oretta.

"Let squirt say what she wants, Mom. I don't mind."

"Well, son," said Clayborne, "you do all right at Sam Houston and you'll have a little head start at Baylor this fall."

"In the fall we'll be going to school together, Dad," smiled Bob.

"That's right, we sure will. We sure will."

Silence.

Bob asked, "You're going alone to pick up the new car this year, Dad?"

"Yes, I've got a Superintendents Association meeting in Chicago first, and then Mr. Appleby and I will fly over to Detroit and drive home together. Won't be a regular vacation drive at all."

"It was sure fun when all of us went to pick up the cars together, Dad," Bob said.

"It sure was," Clayborne agreed.

Silence. Then a honking car horn.

"There's Mr. Smith now," said Bob, getting up and going to the front door. He hugged his mother and sister and his father and hauled his old tin suitcase out to the waiting car. And he was gone.

Somehow the days went slower that summer. After the meeting in Chicago and the drive back from Detroit and the resumption of five days a week at Baylor, Clayborne found himself taking Margie fishing to Lake Meridian and promising to hook her worms for her so she'd go with him. Margie found herself tagging along with Mom and Dad to the summer rodeos in Waco and Fort Worth and even to the Houston Fat Stock show where Roy Rogers and Dale Evans were featured and Oretta made her a Dale Evans cowgirl suit with a hat and boots and everything and she went along with them to the Square Dancing Convention in Fort Worth where they stayed in the biggest hotel Margie had ever seen and her friend Doylene Hennessee went with her. It was fun enough.

And Margie tagged along with Mom and Dad to picnics and she went to movies on the weekend where she sold tickets and popcorn to get in free and she felt the empty place at the table and silently cried to herself that no one tried to take the last dessert from her and nobody took her along with the big boys and poked and joked and laughed with her and it hit her and everybody else in the family how quiet things were around the house and they spoke his name whenever they could because that was a comfort.

If she really started feeling down or bored, Margie picked up the telephone and talked to the operator because the operator knew where everybody was that day and knew all the latest gossip and sometimes all Margie's friends would get on the phone at the same time and have a a big gabfest because they were all on a party line.

On June 25, a cable from the United States Embassy in Seoul came over the wire: North Korean forces invaded Republic of Korea territory at several places this morning.

A massive invasion from communist North Korea rolled into South Korea, and within a month Red troops had occupied most of the peninsula. On July 1, President Truman ordered American GIs to the battlefield, and Major Gen. William F. Dean landed in Pusan with an advance battalion of the 24th Infantry. For the second time in five years, the United States was at war. The shock to the American public took months to subside.

On August 16, Clayborne celebrated his fortieth birthday. Life begins at 40, his friends told him. The future seemed bright enough, but even though the full load of classes at Baylor kept him scurrying and school and family kept him busy otherwise, it was still hard getting used to that bedroom without his son in it and that empty chair at meals and that presence that was so hard to forget. Nothing much else happened that summer and it took a long time for it not to happen. When September came again in the scheme of years, the busyness of school was a relief, actually. Bob had come home long enough to pack again before taking off for Baylor where he lived in room 329 in Kokernot Hall. He was gone again. But everybody knew what to expect this time and life went on.

The Meridian parents this fall, Clayborne noted gratefully, began to talk about building a new high school. Several school officials began to feel out the sense of the community about the idea, then to push lightly, investigating the possibilities, cautiously, since it had only been three years since they had asked the citizens to assess themselves for a $100,000 school bond issue. A few articles ran in the *Meridian Tribune* without the slightest squawk of disapproval coming back. By the end of the year, the school board got up enough gumption to vote 7 to 0 in favor of placing a $60,000 bond issue on the February, 1951, ballot, bonds to pay for a new high school to be built on the same basis as the elementary school, which everybody still called the new elementary school. And again, a new school building became the winter's talk.

Then the headline of the *Meridian Tribune*, February 23, 1951, informed the populace:

MERIDIAN DISTRICT TO VOTE ON NEW HIGH SCHOOL BONDS SATURDAY
Board Presents Plan for Erection of Modern New Nine-Room Structure Here

An attractive perspective rendering of the new building by Fort Worth architects Wilson & Patterson accompanied the text. The *Tribune* printed a message from the Meridian School Board on page one, urging citizens to approve the new school bonds:

The present Meridian High School is outdated, and in bad state of repair. The Board feels that we should offer our children the best educational opportunities we can, within the means of the district . . .

The Board feels that this work should be done now, in spite of the international situation. In fact we believe that the present crisis makes it imperative that we go ahead with a building program as soon as possible. We will need very little critical materials. As to high prices and costs of materials at present, experts generally agree that prices will very likely rise even higher, and don't anticipate lower costs anytime within the near future.

That Saturday Proposition No. 1 asked the citizens: Shall the Board of Trustees of Meridian Independent School District be authorized to issue bonds in the amount of $60,000 to mature serially from 1952 through 1986 for school building purposes; and shall there be annually levied and collected on all taxable property in the District for the current year and annually thereafter while said bonds are outstanding, a tax sufficient to pay the current interest on said bonds and to pay the principal as same becomes due?

Thirteen of the citizens answered "no;" two hundred seventy-one answered "yes," The board had its bonds. Now the drafting pencils could mark the blank sheets of vellum, the survey crews hang their plumb-bobs, the shovelers dig their dirt and load their gravel, the cement mixers whirl their pours, the carpenters drive their nails and square their corners and all perform their labor in a workmanlike manner according to specifications. And Clayborne could realize his dream of a new high school to match the new elementary school, building, working, striving toward that best place to live, toward that ideal community.

A few days later as Clayborne grabbed a quick bite to eat in a Waco cafe before evening class at Baylor an old acquaintence spotted him at the counter.

"Prof! Is that you? Well, I declare, W.C.! Haven't seen you in a coon's age."

Clayborne turned and shook hands with the man, giving his chin a quick wipe with the paper napkin. "Dan Feeley!"he said. "We've missed you at Chamber of Commerce meetings since you moved to Waco."

"I know you must be gettin' ready for night school at Baylor, so I won't hold you up long," said Feeley. "You go ahead and eat, now. Are you still president of the Chamber?"

"No, that's over, I'm past president now. How's your locker plant going — and how do you like living in Waco?"

"Locker plant's fine, Waco's fine. Nice town, all my neighbors are friendly and good folks. How's the family?"

"The wife's doing fine, she's gone up to Junior Matron now in the Eastern Star."

"Good for her."

"And the daughter's a pretty good forward on the girls' basketball team. And Bob's doing well in his second year at Baylor."

"Say, that reminds me, I think maybe you ought to talk to one of my neighbors here in Waco, fellow name of Johnny Carrigan."

"Where've I heard that name before?"

"He played professional baseball and broke the outfielding record playing semi-pro — sixteen put-outs in one game. And baseball's what you Meridian folks ought to talk to him about."

"Why's that?"

"He wants to start up a summer baseball camp for kids, call in big league coaches, invite boys from all over the country. He's thinking about putting it in Waco, wants to associate with a high school, but he can't find anybody that's interested. Meridian schools seemed pretty civic minded. Maybe you two could work something out."

Clayborne saw the possibilities. That best place to live could get better. He said, "Why don't you have your Mr. Carrigan get in touch with Sam Lawson or myself and have him come talk to the board one day soon? It's worth a try."

"I thought you'd say that."

Into the rhythm of days came Johnny Carrigan, determined, alive with enthusiasm for his idea, persuasive. He came to Meridian wrapped in confidential discussions with the school board, talking, agreeing, disagreeing, bargaining, compromising, agreeing. After a time he was asked to make his presentation to the assembled Meridian Chamber of Commerce.

He told them his vision: "This is what I've offered to your Meridian School Board: A baseball camp, a summer camp that'll bring kids in from everywhere, all the forty-eight states, lots of foreign countries, here to Texas, here to the Big State Baseball Camp — that's what we'll call it. We'll give them the best coaching they can get, professional coaching by men who've been in the big leagues. I've already got Firpo Marberry set to head the coaching staff — he played with the Detroit Tigers. Joe Lucco has agreed to be an instructor — he's scout for the Cleveland Indians.

"All we need is a ball field and living quarters for ninety kids at a time

— three session of three weeks each, ninety kids in each session: no more than that because we want to give personal attention to every kid that shows up. You people here in Meridian are building a new high school — that old stone building's pretty well shot as a school, I agree, but I've looked at it, and it's structurally sound. If the woodwork was all refinished and some bunks were brought in, it would make a great dormitory for ninety kids. You've got space on the school grounds right in back of the old high school where a first-class ball field could be built, grandstands for two thousand, professional class dugouts and all. You've got a fine cafeteria in your elementary school, plenty big enough to handle ninety hungry ballplayers.

"I'll incorporate the business side and serve as camp director so the school district and the community have no liability problems. It'll cost each kid $115 for a three-week camp, $25 down and $90 on arrival. We'll have a scholarship program for poor kids. We'll split the gross every summer right down the middle, fifty-fifty. Big State Baseball School, Inc., will pay my coaching and instruction staff and handle all the enrollment paperwork. The school district will feed and house the kids and build a suitable ballfield. Any profits from the school's half of the fees can go to your general athletic fund," said Carrigan. "I figure it'll cost $15,000 initial outlay to set everything up. That's a lot of money. But it's for the kids. The school board has approved the idea in principle. But we need your help to get the community behind it and help us raise the money. Well, gentlemen, what do you say?"

Roy Avirett of the insurance company said, "Mr. Carrigan, I agree that it would be a fine addition to our school and our community. Some of our own athletes would benefit from it greatly, I'm sure. But $15,000 is a lot of money and we just voted a big $60,000 public bond issue a month or two ago."

Clayborne said, "We had no trouble selling those bonds, either, remember, Mr. Avirett? What if we offered interest free bonds to everybody in town? There's over a thousand people living here. That's only fifteen dollars each for a facility that would bring national attention to Meridian."

Jack Kirby of the bonded warehouse said, "You're right, prof. That sounds pretty good to me. I think we could probably sell $15,000 worth of bonds for a camp like that. Let's give it a try, gentlemen, what do you say? Shall we put it to a vote?"

They did. It passed. Johnny Carrigan organized the Big State Baseball School and the Chamber of Commerce pushed the bond drive, selling school district bonds to Meridian citizenry in denominations from $25 to $50 to $100 to $300 and a few at discreetly undisclosed higher sums. The school board had large notebooks of bonds printed up, official, scrollworked, real-live non-interest-bearing bonds. When a taker signed on the dotted line, the seller tore his bond out of the notebook on the perforated edge and gave the buyer proof of a worthwhile investment in his community — or at least a nice piece of wallpaper if things didn't work out financially. They raised the the $15,000 in short order.

In April as high school construction plans matured, Clalyborne's administrative duties again were spread among others and he became a general contractor. Again he teamed with the architects from the very inception. Again he donned his khakis and started work on a school building. Again he hammered out a suitable arrangement with Warren and Son for concrete, brick and plaster work. Again he found common laborers and skilled carpenters to shovel the dirt and gravel and to frame and sheathe the new structure. He had a telephone installed on a braced two-by-four in the smack middle of the building site to stay handy — and in communication and control. Again a work site saw his friendly smile and shared his fellowship and felt his commanding presence. And once again it was a joy.

"Where do we dig this trench, Prof.?"

"Right along that chalkline, Cletis."

The days fell into rhythm now, six hours on the site, two in the school office, upbuilding, upbuilding.

"Who signs for this load of electrical equipment, W. C.?"

"I do, Jim."

The pulse of the days brought meetings at church, and even there the talk tugged back to the construction site, upbuilding, upbuilding.

"I got this sewer line laid, Mr. Perry. Water supply'll be in next week. Say, you going to Detroit to get a new car again this year?"

"Yep, taking the wife and daughter, too, be gone about a week soon as school's out."

"What color's this one gonna be?"

"White."

"Faan-cee!"

The metrical beat of the days brought lodge meetings at the Masonic hall, where the talk of course ran only to the new high school going up, up, upbuilding.

"How many truckloads of gravel today, Mr. Perry?"

"Two will do it, Harvey."

"Your boy going to work here this summer?"

"Soon as the school year's done at Baylor."

The scansion of the days brought times with the family, teaching twelve-year-old Margie to drive in the long driveway of the house on Main Street and in the dirt streets at the edge of town where there wasn't too much she could injure. It made Oretta a nervous wreck, but Clayborne seemed to think the girl could handle the old Ford whether she tended to whack the hedge by the house or not. But even at home the subject always turned to the new high school, up, up, upbuilding.

"Here's the first load of brick from Acme in Waco even if we're not ready for it, Professor. Say, you going to summer school at Baylor this year?"

"Sure am, Roy."

"How long is that doctor's degree goin' to take?"

"Another year, I expect."

Dawn to dawn over the Grand Prairie in the elegant periodicity of nature he felt the power of growth, the high school growing, the community growing, his education growing, the country growing despite the war in Korea and the dimming of general optimism. None of that seemed to matter here. Here it was different. Outward, expanding, upbuilding, pressing forward, forward, forward into that unknown future, that better place, always that better place.

"How do you keep track of all this construction work goin' on, W. C.?"

"I just do it."

"You know, W. C., I bet you'd do as well in business as you do in education."

"Thank you, Emmett."

In early June, after Bob came home from college for summer work and the rest of the family returned from Detroit in their fine new white Plymouth and Clayborne began drudging the steady morning grind at Baylor sixty miles away, Reed & Son of Meridian finished its $16 million contract work on Whitney Dam some fifteen miles northeast of town. The elder Reed lived on a fine cattle ranch six miles into the nearby southwestern hills, still in the Meridian School District. He had heard that Clayborne was looking for a good deal on low-cost framing lumber and offered to sell the school all the dam's concrete- form timbers and scaffolding — for fifty dollars. Clayborne went to look at it and found enough suitable material to build the entire high school plus bleachers to seat 600 for the football field and grandstands to cover and seat 500 for the baseball field to boot. There was only one hitch: it had to be hauled away within three days.

While Clayborne pondered the transportation problem, Bob drove the school's flatbed truck down to the Bosque riverbed and found an old friend.

"Hey, hotshot college boy, look at you getting out of that old truck! Why, you' a grown man!"

"Harvey Davenport! It's good to see you again!"

They shook hands vigorously and affectionately clapped each other on the shoulders. "You're not going to tell me I'm a little small for the job this time, eh?"

"You can shovel gravel with me all you want." Harvey Davenport beamed at the young man. "Come on over here by my truck where the gravel's all one size. The diggin's good," he said in a fatherly-brotherly voice. "Look at you. My, oh, my! You got so big! How you doing at that ol' Baylor school?"

"I'm doing fine, living in the dorm, and studying hard."

"Yeah, you' the right age for gettin' drafted, too. You better watch out for that ol' Korean War, it' gonna get you like the Second World War got me."

"The draft is already after me, Harvey. But if you're in college they'll let you finish before they take you — if you keep your grades up."

"You gonna go in?"

"When I'm through at Baylor, yeah, I expect so. Oh, the military service won't be that bad, do you think? But what about you? What have you been up to all this time?"

"You' so serious! I can't get over it. And me, I'm still the same. Doin' as well as you could expect. Pickin' up work where I can. My Gladys gets on me for drinking too much."

"I heard. The men on the job said you got in a fight with ol' Red Mathews."

"They told you that? What do they know?"

"Did you?"

"He's a mean one when he gets that whiskey in him, Bob Perry.You watch out for that ol' Red. He come swingin' at me one night in the town square. He broke his right arm when he hit me in the jaw. I broke his arm. Am I tough or am I tough? That Dr. Holt had to sew up my cheek. Nice fella. Told me I ought to quit drinkin' and fightin' so much, though."

"You still drink rot gut?"

"Just on the weekends, boy. Just to let off steam. Weekdays you got to save up your strength for work."

"Do you work steady?"

"Whenever they's somethin' to do. Like now. Not much to do around here, tough. Most colored folks went to the big city after the war. They got jobs for colored folks in the city, not like here in a quiet little town. But I like this quiet little town. Not so much hate, you know."

"Is is hard being a Negro, Harvey?"

"No, boy, but it's hard bein' a nigger. In the big city, you' just a nigger. People spit on you. Put you down. Don't let you execute. Here in Meridian we got maybe a few white folks feel that way. But Mr. Lawson, and your Daddy, some of the others, you stand up when they go by, boy."

"What do you mean?"

"They treat everybody the same, black folks, white folks. Let the black folks use the white school for graduation. They stand up for what's right, don't just watch out for their own, so you stand up for them."

"It's nice of you to say so."

"Not just nice, Bob Perry. True. Like your Daddy, he's a big man in this town, but he make' you work hard as anybody. Maybe even harder. You might not like it, boy, but it's right."

Bob said nothing on that subject. "How's your good wife and family?" he asked.

"Just fine. Did you hear we got another little boy since you went off to college?"

"No! Congratulations! What's his name?"

"You might be surprised. I thought a long time about what to name him, thought back on those days we shoveled gravel before, you know, when you had to prove it, remember? How you had to prove it all the while you was in high school here, but you just grit your teeth an' keep goin.' I want my boy to be like that. I name' him Bobby, after you."

"Really, Harvey? Did you really? Bobby Davenport. I just hope you're never sorry for it. Harvey, you're a great friend, you make me proud."

"Hey, what's that comin'?" said Harvey in alarm.

A car careened around the river road, roaring down into the gravel bed. In a blur the Chevy sedan lurched beside them and abruptly stopped.

"Mr. Kirby!" said Bob in amazement.

"Both of you, come quick!" Kirby shouted.

Harvey bent over into the car window and gripped Kirby's arm. "What's the matter, Mister Kirby? Is somebody hurt?"

"Is anything wrong?" asked Bob, peering into the car. "Is it my Dad?"

"Nothing's wrong," said Kirby, "but it's your Dad all right. He's found enough lumber to build the whole high school. Get that gravel out of the trucks. We've got three days to haul a mountain of wood from Whitney Dam!"

"Whitney Dam? Three days?" asked Harvey. "What's the deal?"

"Government contract. Ol' man Reed just finished the dam. He made a deal with the Professor, all the forms and scaffolds for fifty bucks. But now we got to get all that wood off the site quick because the government contract says it's got to be clean three days from now. We don't have a minute to waste! Every truck in Meridian is going to be working day and night. When we're done we'll have more lumber than you can dream of. Come on, pile that gravel off and get going to Whitney Dam!"

Day and night. Every available man helped, going to the dam, dismantling forms, loading boards and beams on trucks old and new, driving twenty loads the first day, twenty loads the second and seventeen loads the third, fifty-seven loads in all, trucked and unloaded and piled in disarray on the high school construction site waiting to be sorted and cleaned and stacked, enough to build the new school and then some.

The following day Clayborne found another treasure trove: the Katy Railroad had just built a $3 million high bridge across Lake Whitney now backing up behind Whitney Dam. The contractor agreed to give the school all the gravel it needed, just for the shoveling and hauling.

The first framed classroom walls took shape above the high school foundations on June 17. And that day the *Meridian Tribune* ran a front page story headlined:

Baseball School Opens, Boasts World-Wide Enrollment

Youngsters from Holland, Venezuela, Canada, Hawaii and the West Indies joined boys from nearly every one of the forty-eight states at Johnny Carrigan's Big State Baseball School, said the story. Two baseball fields complete with modern concrete dugouts and outfield board fences had been finished and put in top shape for the opening, acclaimed as one of the best ball parks in the smaller cities of America. The old stone high school had been completely refurbished, the walls and woodwork refinished and 104 beds made ready for the class, the staff and visitors. The senior boys had their own clubhouse with showers and lockers of their own and the junior boys used the school gymnasium's facilities.

The Meridian Chamber of Commerce had wheeled and dealed with the Atchison, Topeka and Santa Fe Railroad to bend its firm policy of never stopping at Meridian. It may have been one of the largest towns on the Grand Prairie, but Meridian was just too small for the Santa Fe to provide with passenger service. Yes, there was a station east of town there a mile from the school, but it was mostly to handle freight on the little siding. But now, for the beginning and ending of each session, the railroad moguls agreed to discharge and pick up boys for the Big State Baseball School — just baseball kids, mind you, and only during session changes, mind you — but the camp had rail service practically door to door to any point in America.

"Here's today's groceries, Miz Greenwade," called Oretta as she and Margie stepped into the elementary school dining area.

Head cook Lillie Greenwade peeked around the cafeteria kitchen door and smiled her big housewifely smile. "I'll get my cooks to help bring them in," she said.

Mrs. Bass — homemaking teacher at the High School and dietician for the baseball camp — called to Oretta from the kitchen, "That's one mob of groceries you've been getting every day."

"Ninety kids is a lot of kids to feed," said Oretta. "Along with all the coaches and such. Oh, Mrs. Greenwade, I hope I got the right brand of flour for your biscuits this time. Margie, you go help the cooks get the groceries in."

"Yes, Mom. But don't forget you said you'd take me to the roller rink this evening. Butch Thompson's taking me for a Coke afterward, okay?"

"I didn't forget and you tell that Butch to get you home by nine."

"Are you and Dad coming skating tonight?"

"Not tonight, we've got to take the boys up to Mr. Reed's. We'll be back home before you get there, though. Now get on in there and help with the groceries, you hear?"

"Yes, Mom."

"Miz Greenwade, can you take care of things here? I'm going on into the office to answer the phone until Clayborne gets back from Baylor."

"Sure can, Miz Perry. You go right ahead. Everything's under control here."

"I sure don't know how you do it, cooking for the junior boys and then the Senior boys, and with five children of your own."

"I've got a good staff and my children are mostly grown, Miz Perry. But that family was good practice for baseball cooking, I tell you."

"Oh, Miz Greenwade, don't forget we've got a group of visitors from San Antonio this afternoon at two."

"Another bunch?"

"This baseball camp has just put Meridian on the map, Miz Greenwade. I've never seen so many strangers in town."

"Well, we'll have the kitchen spic and span when those visitors visit."

"And there's no supper tonight, we've got that old-fashioned barbecue for the boys up at the Reed ranch. Oh, and no supper tomorrow night, we're taking everybody to the rodeo at Cleburne."

"Yes, Ma'am, Miz Perry. I got it marked on my calendar."

It was like that all summer, busy dizzy summer, crowded with living, jammed with life and growth and upbuilding. The Big State Baseball School sessions came and went one by one, leaving a trail of lifelong memories in two hundred seventy young minds and serene accomplishment in the community round about. When the last days of August dawned over Meridian's low rounded hills and the last boy had gone home to Saskatchewan or New York City or Aruba, the astonished school board discovered they had made enough from their half of the take to pay back every penny of their non-interest-bearing bonds. In a single session of the baseball camp their obligation had liquidated itself. They wrote checks for a total of $15,000 and paid off their bonds less than six months after issuing them. When Clayborne handed a $300 check to J. T. Lomax Motors, the owner told him, "Professor, I can't take that check. I can't take that check, I want to give it to the school." But it was all paid back anyway, to the last measure.

And now it was done. The high school stood low and wide and handsome, framed, sheathed, bricked, plastered, windowed, floored, painted, fixtured and finished on the fifth of September, still in the heat of summer, ten days before the start of school. Work still remained on the football field bleachers and the lights for both baseball and football fields. When the school board's treasurer totted up the construction costs,

Clayborne had spent $56,000 of the $60,000 bond issue. They voted to spend the remaining $4,000 on furniture, and as the students poured back to class to occupy the town's two new buildings, the still-gleaming elementary school and the brand spanking high school, the board realized that Meridian Independent School District had saved about $20,000 by using their superintendent rather than a general contractor.

Everyone in town felt it: the sense of work finished, of mission accomplished, of the action-time and growing-time fulfilled. And they sneaked and whispered among themselves and in the late fall the whole town secretly thronged to the new high school to celebrate the fact of its completion and to surprise the man who had ramrodded its construction. As the Perry family was waylaid safely aside to avoid suspicion, the people came streaming to school. Sparkling hallways and spotless classrooms rang with the approving sounds of the crowd. The phenomenal cost savings achieved by Clayborne's construction crew hung in graphic dollars and cents on a huge poster on the main bulletin board for all to see.

In the cafeteria they gathered at 8:00 p.m. to honor the man of the schools. At the head table sat the Board of Trustees: C.T. Lawson, President; Sherrill Benson, Secretary; Dr. R.D. Holt; H.J. Seidel; A.C. Nivin; John Hanna; Guy Briley. And then the conspirators hustled the unsuspecting star of the show into the hall, W.C. Perry, Superintendent, and his wife Oretta. Sam Lawson stood and grinned into the microphone, "Ladies and gentlemen of Meridan, we've done it! We surprised 'em!"

Spontaneous overwhelming applause greeted the astonished Perrys. It was just like the church ovation, Clayborne thought.

Sam Lawson said, "Sit down, Mr. and Mrs. Perry, and all you folks. Well, Professor, we managed to get you to this surprise banquet on time, and from the looks on your faces we kept the secret pretty well, too. I know how you dislike this speech-making, so I'm goin' to be brief. Friends and neighbors, back when we finished the new elementary school three years ago, I asked Superintendent Perry what I should do to publicly honor him. At that time he said I should wait until we can tell Meridian that their new *high school* was finished so he could feel like he had really accomplished something. Tonight, ladies and gentlemen, I can make that announcement. So, Professor, you'll just have to sit still for it and let us honor you.

"We're all privileged to be able to open the doors of our new Meridian High School building to the general public. For all of us this is a night to be proud. It is a night of achievement. It is a night of gratitude. We are proud of the fact that our Meridian school plant is now completed and equal to the very best in Texas!"

Loud applause.

"Achievement in the fact that so many of *us*, our community, We the People, gave our time and our effort to make this symbol of Meridian's spirit a reality. And gratitude in that we all owe so much to those who devoted the last six months of their lives to the construction itself, to their ingenuity in finding resources where none seemed to exist, to their ability to find endurance when the effort seemed too much, to their willingness to find time when most of the rest of us had none. To all you volunteers and members of the Board of Trustees, we owe our sincere thanks."

Roaring applause as the trustees stood while Clayborne and Oretta looked on from the end of the table, adding their applause to the din.

"And to their wives who gave so many hours of family time to help with the details, to bring food and water to the site, to run for spare parts when equipment failed and a thousand other things — and Oretta Perry, you know I'm including you for all you did with the Big State Baseball camp, too."

More roaring applause.

"Now you know we're not able to give you a boost in salary, Superintendent Perry, but we can do this. H. J., show Mrs. Perry the new Roper cook stove we got for her."

The audience clapped heartily, all contributors to the gift fund.

Oretta's eyes went wide.

"And A. C., show them the new dinette set, too."

Clayborne and Oretta both just smiled and shook their heads.

"And it wouldn't be complete without this certificate for a thousand miles worth of gasoline and the school board's approval for ten days off work so you can use it."

Sam Lawson had to wait for the enthusiastic applause to die down. Clayborne felt like he was reliving the First Baptist Church awards for sure.

"And finally, I want to make my own personal tribute to this remarkable man. You know, there are times when I feel like the motto of our town newspaper, the *Meridian Tribune,* applies to one special man. It says: *Devoted to the Upbuilding of Meridian.* If this town had to pick one man as *the* Upbuilder, as Mister Meridian himself, I think the vote would be unanimous. He's a big part of the reason this is the best place to live in all of Texas. He's the reason why we're all here tonight. Ladies and gentlemen, I give you Superintendent W. C. Perry. . ."

Out in the warm September dusk above the gathered town, above the tumult of the Texans' gratitude and love spilling out on the grass with the windowglow, over the liveoaks and limestone hills in the amethyst glow of lingering twilight, old starshine bathed the luminescent land and fulfillment washed the Grand Prairie. The years of community striving added up to something down there in those new buildings in the little town of Meridian tonight. The upbuilding had reached its goal. The place and its people stood at a pinnacle, a season of ripeness and harvest. And the earth turned a little more to slowly reveal the ruddy face of the horizon-brimming moon, and the pivot of accomplished time turned with the earth tonight, slightly, moving in the hand of God so no one down there noticed. But now the compass of the future pointed away somewhere else, waiting for a living soul to notice it and follow.

-22-

GRAND PRAIRIE FAREWELL

DRIVING the long road to Waco no longer required much attention; endless repetition had rendered it automatic.

In June of 1952 Clayborne had company on the way to Baylor every day: twelve-year-old Margie went along to attend North Waco Junior High School. Her October first birth date had kept her from entering first grade until she was nearly seven years old. Clayborne had been adamant about not bending the rules for his own daughter. If no other six-year-olds with a birth date after September 15 got into school, Margie would not. That meant she had always been the oldest in her class, a year behind her own age group.

At junior high age it began to make a difference to Margie; she desperately wanted to fit in her own age group, to go to class with all the friends she had come to associate with in the years at Meridian. Her teachers felt she should be double promoted, skipped a grade. To Clayborne, there was only one proper way for her to skip a grade: by not skipping it all. He sought and obtained permission for his daughter to complete the entire seventh grade during the three month of summer, paying North Waco Junior High the out-of-district tuition, and taking her to school there every day, the same schedule he followed during this last summer of his doctoral classwork at Baylor. And so they spent two-and-a-half hours each weekday together in the new Plymouth.

"I didn't know you listened to cowboy music on the radio, Dad," said the youngster on an afternoon trip back home.

"I like music," her father replied over the strains of Hank Williams.

Country music as miles went by.

"Dad, are you sorry that Midget died?"

"Yes, honey. He just got old and he got glaucoma and the operation on his eyes just weakened him more so he caught pneumonia. I'm real sorry about it. But we still have Junior."

Long silence with background of country music.

"Is there something on your mind, Daddy?"

"Yes, honey. But nothing to worry about, just something about Baylor."

"Are you flunking?"

Clayborne laughed in spite of himself. "No, honey, I'm making good grades. It's an administrative question. If anything comes of it, I'll tell you all about it."

"Okay, Dad."

After supper that evening Clayborne took Oretta aside and said, "Honey, today Dr. Stretch told me I should go by Dr. White's office before going home."

"The president of Baylor? What did he want?"

"You're not going to believe this: he asked me if I'd like to come to work at Baylor as Dean of Men starting the first of September. Actually, he said I could start anytime after July first."

Oretta was taken utterly aback. "What did you tell him?" she asked.

"Why, I told him I'd have to talk to you before I gave him an answer."

"Did you ask about the salary?"

"Yes. It's in the range of five hundred a month to start."

"You're already making five hundred sixty-five here."

"I know. It would mean a drop of sixty-five dollars a month. That's not a very good deal."

"What's happened to the Dean of Men?"

"I think Dean Wright wants to finish up his doctorate somewhere."

"It's quite an honor to be invited to work at Baylor, Clayborne."

"I know. What do you think?"

"I don't know. Meridian has been so good to us. It's a growing town. They're just putting in the swimming pool up by the school. And the money could be a problem. But, you know, you have to do what you think is right. What do you think?"

"I don't see any reason to leave. I think we ought to stay here."

"When will you tell President White?"

"Tomorrow."

"We talked about the presidential nominations in civics today, Dad."

"That's nice."

"We talked about General Eisenhower and Governor Stevenson. Who are you going to vote for?"

"It's only the middle of July. I might change my mind. But General Eisenhower, probably."

"I thought so."

"Really? What made you think so?"

"Governor Stevenson says that education is soft, and I didn't think you'd vote for anybody that says bad things about education."

"Education is soft? What did Governor Stevenson say?"

"Here's what I copied off the board today. Governor Stevenson said, The softness which has crept into our educational system is a reflection of something much broader, of a national complacency. . . 'What's complacency, Dad?"

"That's when you're self-satisfied and you don't think about the problems you have to solve. When your mind gets lazy."

"'. . . of a national complacency. We have lacked, I fear, the deep inner conviction that education in its broadest sense unlocks the door of our future, and that it gives us the tools without which "the pursuit of happiness" becomes a hollow chasing after triviality, a mindless boredom relieved only by the stimulus of sensationalism or quenched with a tranquilizer pill.' Do you know what that means, Dad?"

"Yes, honey. No wonder they call him an egghead. He's just using big words to say that we have to be educated to make the best of ourselves."

"Why didn't he say so, Dad?"

"That's a good question. Did they have you write down anything that General Eisenhower said?"

"Yes, Dad, it's right here. He said "I want nothing more from the presidency than that Americans say "He has been fair. He has been by friend."'I can understand that, Dad."

"Who do you think is going to win the Republican nomination?"

"I think General Eisenhower."

"And what about president?"

"General Eisenhower, too."

"Me, too."

Long silence with country music background.

"Are you working hard at Baylor, Dad?"

"Yes, Margie. I just started the second session of this summer's classwork. This is just about the last of it. Dr. Stretch is helping me design my dissertation."

"Is that the long paper you told me about before?"

"Yes, it is. I'll have to start on it pretty soon now, and Dr. Stretch finally approved my subject and title."

"What's it called?"

"*Planning and Construction of School Buildings.*"

"You know a lot about that. You built two of them."

Long silence.

"Daddy, is something on your mind again?"

"Yes, Margie."

"Is it the same thing again?"

"Yes, honey."

That evening Clayborne took Oretta aside and told her, "I was working with Dr. Stretch again today putting together my list of dissertation requirements. My advisor's going to be Dr. Ralph Schmidt."

"Is he some expert in schools?"

"He sure is. I'm really lucky to get him for a degree advisor. Dr. Stretch is going to get us together pretty soon. And she told me to go see Dr. White again."

"What was it this time?"

"Same thing. He told me the job is open right now. He told me he'd like me to consider becoming their new Dean of Men."

"Same salary offer?"

"Same salary offer. But he told me about their retirement plan. Baylor pays for theirs and I pay for the one here in Meridian. Baylor has a better retirement plan by far."

"You won't retire for another twenty-five or thirty years."

"I know. What do you think?"

"Same as last time. It's an honor, but it's up to you. What do you think?"

"I think we ought to stay right here."

August 11, 1952.

"Daddy, I think I'm getting As in everything."

"That's good."

"I'm going to go into eighth grade next month for sure! That's so great! Are you getting As in everything?"

"As and maybe a B plus. The grades don't worry me, it's my dissertation.

"Is it hard to do, Daddy?"

"Yes, it is."

Long silence.

"Daddy, is something on your mind?"

"Yes, honey."

"Same thing again?"

"Same thing."

That evening before supper when he took Oretta aside Clayborne was distinctly agitated.

Oretta spoke first: "They asked you again."

"Yes."

"You look worried."

"Oretta, they offered me five-fifty a month this time. Dr. Gooch came in with Dr. White — the president and executive vice-president both. They said they were desperate. They need me. They even said there would be other benefits to make up the fifteen-dollar-a-month loss, maybe an automobile expense allowance. And the Baylor retirement program."

"That's getting pretty good, Clayborne. You look like you're sorely tempted."

"I am. Only it's not the money or the benefits. Well, it *is*, but that's not all. Oretta, I've been working on my dissertation for nearly a month now and I've spent just about *every minute* in the Baylor library. I have to document every statement I write. I have to find chemistry journals for facts about the paint on schoolroom walls and psychology journals for facts about how much light children need to read by. Oretta, I can't even write a *sentence* in my dissertation without a big library like that."

"Dear Lord!" The meaning of the situation soaked in. "Clayborne, you can't commute to a library forever. Unless you take that job you might not be able to finish your doctor's degree."

"Not in a reasonable time. That's what it adds up to."

"I think you'd better talk to Sam Lawson."

"I think I'd better."

Ten minutes later he was on Lawson's front porch.

"W. C., I had a feeling we'd be having this talk one day," said President C. T. Lawson, Jr., of the Board of Trustees.

Clayborne looked at his shoes. "I know what it must seem like after everything Meridian has done for me."

"What it seems like is that talent gets the rewards. You didn't betray any trust. You proved your ability and the offer came to you unbidden."

"That's the very truth, Sam. I didn't go looking for it."

"Then the answer is plain. We have to look out for ourselves first. You take that job at Baylor. Meridian will do all right."

"I want to ask the other board members, too."

"Let's get in your car and see them right now. I'll go with you."

They talked to them all and got the same response from each: I wish you'd stay on with us, but there's no doubt Baylor would be better for you in the long run.

The next morning Clayborne walked out to the car when he heard Mrs. Jean Cameron call across the street: "Yoo-hoo, Professor Perry. What's this I hear about you leaving us for Baylor?"

"It's true, Miz Cameron. I'm just on my way to tell them I'll take their job."

"Oh, now, Professor Perry, I'll have you know that's not a job you're going to, it's a *position*."

Clayborne mused on that as he got in the car. "Yes, Mrs. Cameron, I think you're right." He grinned mischievously from the driver's seat, "And the position they have in mind is probably nose to the grindstone."

Margie stood in the living room watching her father drive away. She could hardly believe the news. "Mama," she wailed, "after going to summer school just so I can be in the same class as all my friends I'm about to *lose* all my friends." She wept melodramatically: "My life is ruined!"

Oretta hugged her girl and patted her, saying, "Oh, no it's not. We'll all miss Meridian. But there's a big future waiting out there. Waco's just another step toward it."

Midmorning Clayborne walked into Baylor President W. R. White's office and said, "I've talked it over with my wife and the school board. I accept your offer. I'll be your Dean of Men. Give me a few days to get things settled."

Then he looked up his son on campus and told him of the change.

"Congratulations, Dad, it doesn't surprise me a bit. You deserve it," Bob said, books under arm. "I'm glad for you, really glad."

Later that day the Meridian Independent School District gave Clayborne his official release from duty.

"One thing we ask, though, W. C."

"What's that, Sam?"

"Help us find your replacement."

"I think I have. Have you ever heard of W.B. Parks over at Moshiem? He's a young superintendent of a little eight-teacher school there about seven miles south of Valley Mills. I've known him four or five years, gone to association meetings with him. He's a solid administrator looking for a challenge. And he's smart: he's trained up an assistant that can step right into his shoes. His principal is ready to take up where he leaves off."

And so it went the next day. Like Swiss clockwork, the Meridian school board interviewed Mr. W. B. Parks and offered him the job. He accepted on condition that his own school board hire his high school principal to replace him. The Moshiem, Texas, school board promoted their principal to superintendent and the Meridian, Texas, school board hired W. B. Parks. All in one day.

Now it could be released. The headline of the *Baylor Lariat* for August 13 read:

W. C. PERRY APPOINTED NEW DEAN OF MEN TO REPLACE DEAN WRIGHT
Capable Administrator, Superintendent of Meridian Schools Will Take Over Sept. 1

The body copy announced:

W. C. Perry, former superintendent of schools at Meridian, has been appointed dean of men at Baylor university, according to Dr. W. R. White, president. He will assume the position on September 1, and will replace Dean F. E. Wright, who has requested release so that he may complete work on the doctorate at Peabody Teachers College.

Every day Clayborne trundled back and forth between Meridian and Waco. First he rented the wonderful cream-colored stucco house full of so many memories to the new superintendent of Meridian schools. Second he drove with Oretta and Margie up and down the streets of Waco, neighborhood by neighborhood looking for a house. At the western edge of town a fine, a home in a dignified new neighborhood instantly caught their eye. The FOR SALE sign had a SOLD sign plastered across it. After a few minutes of discussion with the owner they had reached an agreement: the tentative buyer had not placed any earnest money yet, and, worse, had to go through a real estate agent — and the owner had to pay the fee. If the Perrys could work without an agent, the owner would sell to them instead. Clayborne gave the man a $500 earnest money check then and there. They had their house at 3912 Austin Avenue.

On his forth-second birthday, August 16, 1952, Clayborne unlocked his office in the Baylor administration building for the first time. Summer school was over, he thought, for this year and forever. The two course credits he lacked could be obtained at his discretion. Now he worked here. At Baylor University. Half-days, at least.

Back and forth he went, moving furniture when possible, working half a day at Baylor trying to figure out what a Dean of Men did for a living, half a day at Meridian helping Superintendent Parks figure out what the Meridian school superintendent did for a living. At Baylor former Dean Wright showed up for an hour to show Clayborne where the files were kept. At Meridian Clayborne spent half of the next three weeks explaining the situation to W.B. Parks.

One day as Clayborne got into his car preparing to go back to Waco, Bill Curtis, owner of Meridian Ice and Cold Storage Company —the turkey-dressing plant — came up to him and said, "Mr. Perry, I understand that you're thinking about leaving Meridian and going to Baylor."

"Yes, sir, that's right." Clayborne had always wondered how he stood with this poker-faced businessman and it looked like he was about to find out.

"If you will change your mind and not leave, I'll personally solicit five thousand dollars to supplement your salary, a thousand dollars a year if you'll stay another five years."

Clayborne didn't know what to say. After an awkward pause he spoke, "Mr. Curtis, I certainly appreciate you for thinking so highly of me. But I'm afraid my resignation has already been accepted here. They've hired another man. A good man. And I'm already working part-time at Baylor."

"I'm sorry to hear that, Mr. Perry. I've always admired your work here. You'll be missed."

The town of Meridian threw a going-away party for the Perrys. It was a time to find out who his friends were. When you walk up to the people you've worked with for nine years and say "I quit," it's a time you're saying "I don't want anything else from you people; it's all over." You're open and vulnerable to whatever you've brought with you to this point. There were some, the Doyle Weatherfords and Pepper Langs of the Grand Prairie, who didn't show up for one reason or another, mostly because they resented something he had done, a disciplinary action, a rejection of bigotry, something. There were those who disliked, perhaps, like the Lyle Skinners, even hated him for something or another. He found the rest of the community dewey-eyed and shuffling its feet and blowing its nose as they tried to say good-bye to him. The relationship he had severed, it hit him, was more like a marriage than anything else.

> When the *Meridian Tribune* wrote it up, they said:
> Mr. Perry has received full cooperation of the members of the Board of Trustees and the citizens of Meridian Independent School District and his achievements, too numerous to mention, which he promoted and supervised, will stand as a monument for his tireless work while with us and he will always be remembered as one of our most loved and useful citizens.
> All regret the loss of this estimable family, and wish for each of them, continued success, health and happiness.

Then the whirl was done. He read the clipping in a comfortable chair in the new home he'd settled into in Waco, the home on the edge of town at 3912 Austin Avenue. He felt the loss that the newspaper writer described, too, but he wasn't sure about the regret. He had certainly made the biggest change in his whole life, and that alone carried a sort of fright that gave one second thoughts, but regret? Probably not. Just a certain sadness at friends left behind.

He was not one to look back, but he looked back anyway. From where he sat he looked back *to* the Grand Prairie. Here he was living in Waco, Waco that was not part of the Grand Prairie, not geologically, not geographically: it was where the Grand Prairie ended, properly part of the Eastern Cross Timbers or the Black Waxy Prairie, depending on just where in Waco you happened to be standing. The Bosque River no longer flowed near his door as it had all his life: a few miles away it emptied its Grand Prairie waters into the Brazos, the *Rio Brazos del Dio* of the Spaniards, the River of the Arms of God. And his employer was now the largest Baptist university in the world, situated beside the River of the Arms of God.

When the school year began at Baylor, it became quite evident why the university needed a strong new Dean of Men. Day after day Clayborne saw undeniable proof that discipline here had slid from decorum to hi-jinx to fracas to outright rebellion. Baylor needed him, all right, just like Dr. White had said. And as in his first days at Meridian, nobody had said why. Then one night he got an emergency call. Baylor students had set fire to a wooden street bridge on campus, a police captain snarled into his ear over the telephone. Come immediately. Students were interfering with firemen and police trying to control the blaze. Baylor was desperate, all right, just like Dr. White had said. Now he knew why.

He got there as soon as he could. It was like Saturday night in hell: the flaming bridge, the rowdy students, the frustrated firemen and the angry police. *This is impossible!* In the midnight shadows thrown by the guttering flames against an unruly crowd Clayborne asked himself:

Dear Lord, why do I take on such burdens?

But as soon as he asked he knew the answer.

It was the answer that had ruled his whole life.

It shone like a steady beacon in the darkness.

Why? The goal was a simple one, really:

To set things right.

SELECTED BIBLIOGRAPHY

No footnotes accompany the text of this biographical novel to avoid interrupting the narrative. However, virtually every paragraph has been documented in multiple dimensions: economic conditions, contemporary machinery, Texas dialects, medical problems, world events, literary allusions. A complete bibliography for this book would be another book. This abbreviated list should serve as a guide to anyone interested in pursuing the subject further.

Agricultural Statistics, 1936 Government Printing Office, Washington, D.C. 1936 pp. 75, 76.

Atwood, E. Bagby *The Regional Vocabulary of Texas* University of Texas Press Austin 1962.

Barr, Alwyn *Black Texans: A History of Negroes in Texas, 1528-1971* Jenkins Publishing Company The Pemberton Press Austin, Texas 1971.

Barrett, Miriam *Closing of C&S Railroad Station At Trinchera Marks Formal Passing of Era Already Fading Into History* in *Chronicle-News* Trinidad, Colorado May 25, 1966.

Bassett, John Spencer *The Relation Between the Virginia Planter and the London Merchant* American Historical Association 1901 Annual Report.

Baylor University *Lariat* (student newspaper) 1940-1952 Waco, Texas.

Beveridge, W.I.B. *Influenza: The Last Great Plague: An Unfinished Story of Discovery* Prodist New York 1977.

Boddie, William *Southside Virginia Families* Vol. II "Perry of Isle of Wight and North and South Carolina" pp. 338-343 Genealogical Publishing Company Baltimore 1956.

Bones, Jim, Jr. and Graves, John *Texas Heartland: A Hill Country Year* Texas A & M University Press College Station 1975.

Brown Group, Inc. *Brown Group: The First Hundred Years* (internal corporate history of Buster Brown shoe manufacturer) Brown Group, Inc. 8400 Maryland Avenue St. Louis, Missouri 63105 1978.

Burbank, Garin. *When Farmers Voted Red: The Gospel of Socialism in the Oklahoma Countryside, 1910–1924.* Westport, Connecticut: Greenwood Press, 1976.

Caro, Robert A. *The Years of Lyndon Johnson: The Path to Power.* New York: Random House, 1981.

Carroll, H. Bailey. *Masonic Influence on Education in the Republic of Texas.* Waco, 1960.

Carroll, H. Bailey. *Texas County Histories: A Bibliography.* Austin, Texas: The Texas State Historical Association, 1943.

Carter, James David. *Masonry in Texas: Background, History, and Influence to 1846.* Waco, 1958.

Catton, Bruce, *Centennial History of the Civil War.* 3 vols. Doubleday, 1961-65.

Corporation Commission of the State of Oklahoma. *Eighth and Ninth Annual Reports For the Years Ending June 30, 1915, and June 30, 1916.* Oklahoma City, 1916.

Corwin, Linda Whigham. "Stratigraphy of the Fredericksburg Group North of the Colorado River, Texas." *Baylor Geological Studies,* Baylor University Bulletin No. 40, Waco, Texas, 1982.

Cottrell, Fred W. *The Railroader.* Palo Alto, California: Stanford University Press, 1940.

Crosby, Alfred. W. *Epidemic and Peace, 1918.* Westport, Connecticut: Greenwood Press, 1976.

Dale, Edward Everett. *The Cross Timbers: Memories of a North Texas Boyhood* Austin: University of Texas Press, 1966.

Dallas Morning News. Texas Almanac, 1958-1959. Dallas, Texas, 1958.

Davis, Edward Everett. *The White Scourge.* San Antonio, Texas: Naylor, 1940.

Donegan, Jane B. *Women & Men Midwives: Medicine, Morality, and Misogyny in Early America.* Westport, Connecticut: Greenwood Press, 1978.

Donnan, Elizabeth. "Eighteenth-Century English Merchants: Micajah Perry." *Journal of Economic and Business History* Vol IV (November 1931), No. 1: 70-98.

Dunning, John. *Tune In Yesterday: The Ultimate Encyclopedia of Old-Time Radio, 1925-1976.* Englewood Cliffs, N.J.: Prentice-Hall, Inc.

Eby, F. *The Development of Education in Texas*

Edwards, Mike W. "The Virginians." in *National Geographic,* November 1974.

Elliott, L.R. ed. *Centennial Story of Texas Baptists.* Dallas, 1936.

Evans, C.E. *The Story of Texas Schools.* Austin, 1955.

Ferguson, Walter Keene. *Geology and Politics in Texas, 1845-1909.* Austin: University of Texas Press, 1969.

Ford, Worthington Chauncey, contributor. "Some Letters of William Beverley." *William and Mary College Quarterly* III (April 1895), No. 4.: 223 ff.

Franks, Kenny A. *The Oklahoma Petroleum Industry.* Norman: University of Oklahoma Press, 1980.

Frantz, Joe B. *Texas, A Bicentennial History.* New York: W.W. Norton & Company, 1976.

Gibson, Arell Morgan. *Oklahoma: A History of Five Centuries.* 2nd ed. Norman: University of Oklahoma Press, 1981.

Gould, Lewis L. *Progressives and Prohibitionists: Texas Democrats in the Wilson Era.* Austin: University of Texas Press, 1973.

Guildhall Manuscript 2480, Vol. 2. *Monumental Inscriptions and Armorial Bearings in the Churches Within the City of London* Arthur John Jewers p. 617, note 5. Guildhall Library, London.

Guildhall Manuscript 3074, 1877-78. *Memorial Inscriptions from Various London Churches.* Dr. John Howard. Guildhall Library, London.

Guildhall Manuscript 4517/1. Register of burials 1717-52. Guildhall Library, London.

Henderson, Alice Corbin. *Brothers of Light: The Penitentes of the Southwest.* Harcourt, Brace and Company, 1937; rpt. Santa Fe, New Mexico: William Gannon 1977.

Hirleman, Nancy Colvin. *Historical Map of Las Animas County, Colorado.* Box 12, La Veta, Colorado 81055, 1982.

Hume, Ivor Noel. "First Look at a Lost Virginia Settlement." *National Geographic,* June 1979.

Johnson, Elmer H. "The Natural Regions of Texas" *The University of Texas Bulletin* no. 3113, 1931.

Johnson, Paul. *Modern Times: The World from the Twenties to the Eighties* New York: Harper & Row, 1983.

Johnson, William Perry, compiler. *1740 Tax List of Perquimans County, North Carolina.* Perquimans County Court Minutes and Inventories of Estates, 1738-1761, File No. 77.003, pp. 55-57. State Department of Archives and History Raleigh, North Carolina.

Kennedy, Mary Ann. "C.P. Newcombe, Pioneer Ranchman of Trinchera Area Looks Back on Early Days East End of County." in *Chronicle-News,* Trinidad, Colorado, August 23, 1945.

Lillywhite, Bryant. *London Coffeehouses.* London: George Allen and Unwin, 1963.

Litoff, Judy Barrett. *American Midwives: 1860 to the Present*. Westport, Connecticut: Greenwood Press 1978.

McCorvey, T.C. *Alabama Historical Sketches*. Virginia, 1961.

Molyneaux, Peter. "Economic Nationalism and Problems of the South." *Arnold Foundation Studies in Public Affairs* (Southern Methodist University) II (Fall, 1933), No. 2.

Morgan, Anne Hodges and Strickland, Rennard, editors *Oklahoma Memories*. Norman: University of Oklahoma Press, 1981.

Morris, John W., Goins, Charles R., and McReynolds, Edwin C. *Historical Atlas of Oklahoma*. 2nd ed. Norman: University of Oklahoma Press, 1976.

Myres, S.D., Jr. "Texas: Nationalist or Internationalist." *Arnold Foundation Studies in Public Affairs* (Southern Methodist University) (Summer, 1935), No. 1.

National Archives. *Federal Land Records, Alabama*. Washington D.C.

Newcomb, W.W., Jr. *The Indians of Texas*. Austin: University of Texas Press, 1961.

Ogilby, John and Morgan, William. *A Large and Accurate Map of the City of London, 1677*. Reprinted by Harry Margary in association with Guildhall Library London. Introductory note by Ralph Hyde. Lympne Castle, Kent 1976.

Osborn, June E., editor. *History, Science, and Politics: Influenza in America 1918-1976*. New York: Prodist, 1977.

Owen, Mark Thomas. "The Paluxy Sand in North-Central Texas." *Baylor Geological Studies*, (Baylor University) Bulletin No. 36 1979.

Pool, Oran Jo. "Old Hico on Honey Creek" *Southwestern Historical Quarterly*, LXVII, (April, 1964) No. 4: 485-490.

Perry, Max. *The Descendants of Perry-Peterson Families*. Midland, Texas, 1977.

Reed, Saint Clair G. *A History of the Texas Railroads and of Transportation Conditions under Spain and Mexico and The Republic and The State*. Houston: St. Clair Publishing Company, 3702 Mt. Vernon Street 1941.

Richardson, Rupert N., Wallace, Ernest, Anderson, Adrian N. *Texas, the Lone Star State*. 4th ed. Englewood Cliffs, New Jersey: Prentice-Hall, 1981.

Royal Commission on Historical Manuscripts (National Register of Archives) *Documents of Micajah Perry, File T* (bills of lading, receipts, letters) Quality House, Quality Court, Chancery Lane, London.

Saint Katharine Cree Church. *Vestry Minutes*. 26th March 1695, 86 Leadenhall Street, London.

Shirk, George H. *Oklahoma Place Names.* 2nd ed. Norman: University of Oklahoma Press, 1974.

Simonds, Frederick W. *The Geography of Texas.* Boston, 1914.

Six Gun Heroes: Viewer's Guide. ETV Endowment of South Carolina. Columbia, South Carolina, n.d.

Southwest Texas State Teachers College. *The College Star* (student newspaper). 1930-1940. San Marcos, Texas.

Spivey, Towana, editor. *A Historical Guide to Wagon Hardware & Blacksmith Supplies.* Museum of the Great Plains, Lawton, Oklahoma, 1979. (Edited reprint of portions of hardware catalogue of George Worthington Company, Cleveland, Ohio, 1909).

Stinnett, Tom. *Early Days in Hamilton County.* Vol. XIII, Frontier Times Austin: Western Publications 1936, pp. 450-453.

Strobel, Jerry, editor. *Grand Ole Opry.* Vol. 7, *WSM Picture-History Book* 2nd ed. Nashville: WSM, Inc., 1982.

Tarleton Agricultural College. *J-TAC* (student newspaper). 1920-1930. Stephenville, Texas.

Texas Historic Crops Statistics 1866-1975. Texas Crop and Livestock Reporting Service. Austin, 1976, pp. 13, 14, 17.

Time-Life Books, editors. *This Fabulous Century.* Vol. II and III. New York, 1969.

Treolar, William Purdie. *A Lord Mayor's Diary 1906-07.* London, 1920, pp. 229-259.

United States Census. *Population enumerations from 1790 to 1910 Thirteenth Census of the United States: 1910 Population* (Hico City, Texas). Supervisor's District 11, Enumeration District 68, Sheets 1A through 15A. National Archives, Washington D.C.

United States General Land Office. Homestead Patent Number 754678, James Leonard Perry, 1921 in Las Animas County, Colorado, Patent Deed Records Book 268 p. 71, Trinidad, Colorado.

United States Geological Survey. *Trinchera Cave, Colorado, Quadrangle* (Map). Colorado—Las Animas County 7.5 Minute Series (Topographic). See Sections 5 and 6, Township 33 South, Range 59 West, Sixth Principal Meridian for Perry homestead sites. Denver, 1971.

United States Department of Labor. *Descriptions of Occupations: Railroad Transportation.* Washington, D.C.: Government Printing Office, 1918.

United States Military Service and Pension Records Confederate Pension Application of Elizabeth Glasgow Perry (Old Grandma) National Archives Washington D.C.

Utley, Francis Lee, Bloom, Lynn Z., and Kinney, Arthur F, editors. *Bear, Man, and God: Seven Approaches to William Faulkner's "The Bear"*, New York: Random House, 1964.

Walker, Alexander. *The Shattered Silents: How the Talkies Came to Stay.* New York: William Morrow and Company, 1979.

Walker, James Lafayette and Lumpkin, C.P. *History of the Waco Baptist Association of Texas.* Waco, Texas: Byrne-Hill Printing House 1897.

Webb, Walter P., editor in chief. *The Handbook of Texas.* 3 vols. Austin: Texas State Historical Association, 1952-1976.

Wiegle, Marta. *Brothers of Light, Brothers of Blood: The Penitentes of the Southwest.* Albuquerque: University of New Mexico Press, 1976.

Wertz, Richard W. and Dorothy C. *Lying-In: A History of Childbirth in America* New York: The Free Press (Macmillan), 1977.

Wiley, B.I. *Embattled Confederates: an Illustrated History of Southerners at War.* Harper, 1964

William and Mary College Quarterly, "Unpublished Letters at Fullham." IX (April 1901), No. 4.

———————————"Abstracts from Records of Richmond County, Virginia" XVII (October 1908), No. 2: 78.

———————————"Micajah Perry" and "Will of Micajah Perry" XVII (October 1908), No. 2: 264-267.

———————————"Thomas Lane" XXX: 104-105.

Winslow, Ellen Goode. *History of Perquimans County.* Baltimore: Regional Publishing Company, 1974, pp. 1-27.

Wright, Louis B. *Cultural Life of the American Colonies, 1607-1763.* Harper 1963.

———————————*Letters of Robert Carver, 1720-1727: The Commercial Interests of a Virginia Gentleman.* San Marino, California: The Huntington Library, 1940.

Zlatkovich, Charles P. *Texas Railroads: A Record of Construction and Abandonment.* Austin: Bureau of Business Research, University of Texas at Austin and Texas State Historical Association, 1981.